Praise for *Anonymous Rex*
A *People* Beach Book of the Week

"Vincent Rubio has a washed-up Los Angeles detective agency, lousy credit, and a dead partner—on top of his addiction to basil and hard time keeping his tail tucked away in his latex human suit. Witty, fast-paced detective work makes for a good mystery, but the story's sly, seamlessly conceived dinosaur underworld contains all the elements of a cult classic. A."
　　　　　　　　　　　　　　　　　　　　　　　　　—Entertainment Weekly

"Debut novelist Eric Garcia pulls off this parallel dino world to a T (rex). [His] descriptions are delicious . . . inventive and imaginative. He cleverly avoids what could have been a one-joke book with charm, sly humor, and a terrific narrative pace."　　　　　　　　　　　　　　　　　*—USA Today*

"Audacious and imaginative. You might not believe any of this thirty seconds after you close the covers, but while it's going on you're going to be dazzled by Garcia's energy and chutzpah."　　　　　　*—Publishers Weekly*

"Garcia plays it almost completely straight, respecting all noir traditions, and comes up with lovely touches."　　　　　　　　　*—Chicago Tribune*

"Vincent Rubio . . . is so likeable, the story handled with such deftness, that it actually, incredibly, works. Spider Robinson meets Sam Spade. The writing is sardonic and strong in the hard-boiled tradition and laced with jokes about the history humans think they know: Oliver Cromwell was a brontosaur, and 'Capone and Eliot Ness were just two diplodoci with a grudge to settle.'"　　　　　　　　　　　　*—The Richmond Times Dispatch*

"Garcia's tough-guy deadpan is perfect for navigating his outrageous lost world, and the easy, familiar tone is probably what makes the premise so simple to swallow."　　　　　　　　　　　　　*—The Miami Herald*

continued . . .

"A quirky farce. *Anonymous Rex* is solid proof that Garcia is one of those rare authors who can combine good writing chops with colorful, if somewhat warped, characters and story lines."

—*The News and Observer* (Raleigh, NC)

"Not only a delight to detective story fanciers, but to all lovers of imaginative fiction . . . truly funny." —*The Sunday Star-Ledger*

"Clever . . . well written." —*Cleveland Times*

"Fast, funny, and smoothly written." —*Seattle Times*

Casual Rex

"May be the most entertaining book out this year . . . dripping with tongue-in-jaw wit, snappy action, funny lines, and plot twists. It's obvious Garcia had fun with *Casual Rex*. Readers will, too." —*The Columbus Dispatch*

"Every bit as delightfully strange, richly imagined, and just plain funny [as his debut]." —*Seattle Times*

"A prequel that's as daringly, darkly loopy as *Anonymous Rex*." —*Kirkus Reviews*

"Garcia's manic energy and chutzpah are infectious, and it's good to see Vincent Rubio back on the case." —*The Miami Herald*

continued . . .

"You could call *Casual Rex* dino-mite."   —*Gotham Magazine*

"A funny book. I can't remember an author pulling off a more difficult premise, unless it's T. Jefferson Parker."   —*Los Angeles Times*

"[Eric Garcia's] *X-Files* take on the classic detective tale will appeal to both mystery and SF readers. Here's a series with dino-sized legs."
                           —*Publishers Weekly*

"Hugely entertaining . . . Seamless, wonderfully clever world-building, a little dino-depravity, and an abundance of tongue-in-cheek humor to keep things rolling along."   —*Booklist*

Hot and Sweaty Rex

"Crisp, clever, and, at times, terribly naughty."   —*Columbus Dispatch*

"Garcia has enormous fun spoofing both classic detective novels and *The Sopranos* . . . [a] marvelously detailed, kooky world."   —*Booklist*

"Irresistible . . . outrageous. You can't stop smiling, even through scenes of murder and torture. Brilliant . . . Funny, poignant, dramatic, satiric, brutal, and tender, the dinosaur world is a marvelous place to visit."
                           —*Publishers Weekly*

"Crisply written and . . . sure to keep everyone entertained and chuckling aloud."   —*Wilkes-Barre Times Leader*

"Clever and most enjoyable."   —*The Kansas City Star*

"A striking fantasy."   —*Library Journal*

ANONYMOUS REX

ERIC GARCIA

CASUAL REX

ACE BOOKS, NEW YORK

THE BERKLEY PUBLISHING GROUP
Published by the Penguin Group
Penguin Group (USA) Inc.
375 Hudson Street, New York, New York 10014, USA
Penguin Group (Canada), 10 Alcorn Avenue, Toronto, Ontario M4V 3B2, Canada
(a division of Pearson Penguin Canada Inc.)
Penguin Books Ltd., 80 Strand, London WC2R 0RL, England
Penguin Group Ireland, 25 St. Stephen's Green, Dublin 2, Ireland (a division of Penguin Books Ltd.)
Penguin Group (Australia), 250 Camberwell Road, Camberwell, Victoria 3124, Australia
(a division of Pearson Australia Group Pty. Ltd.)
Penguin Books India Pvt. Ltd., 11 Community Centre, Panchsheel Park, New Delhi—110 017, India
Penguin Group (NZ), Cnr. Airborne and Rosedale Roads, Albany, Auckland 1310, New Zealand
(a division of Pearson New Zealand Ltd.)
Penguin Books (South Africa) (Pty.) Ltd., 24 Sturdee Avenue, Rosebank, Johannesburg 2196, South Africa

Penguin Books Ltd., Registered Offices: 80 Strand, London WC2R 0RL, England

This is a work of fiction. Names, characters, places, and incidents either are the product of the author's imagination or are used fictitiously, and any resemblance to actual persons, living or dead, business establishments, events, or locales is entirely coincidental. While on several occasions actual, living persons are referred to by name and identified as dinosaurs, the author leaves it entirely up to the reader to decide whether these persons are, indeed, dinosaurs.

PRINTING HISTORY
Ace trade paperback one-volume edition / December 2004
Anonymous Rex: originally published by Villard books / 2000
Casual Rex: originally published by Villard books / 2001

Library of Congress Cataloging-in-Publication Data

Garcia, Eric.
    [Anonymous Rex]
    Anonymous Rex ; Casual Rex / Eric Garcia.
        p. cm.
    ISBN 0-441-01275-2
    1. Rubio, Vincient (Fictitious character)—Fiction. 2. Private investigators—Fiction. 3. Dinsaurs—Fiction. I. Garcia, Eric. Casual Rex. II. Title: Casual Rex. III. Title.

PS3557.A665A82 2004
813'.54—dc22

                                                                                    2004052577

PRINTED IN THE UNITED STATES OF AMERICA

10 9 8 7 6 5 4 3 2 1

Contents

For my beautiful daughter, Bailey Jordan,
who snuggles up close to me
and whispers all the really good lines

"Two leaves of basil. Folded, not torn."

—RUBIO, VINCENT RUBIO

mprovisation is the modus operandi when you work with Ernie Watson.

"You doin' okay, kid?" he asks me, and all I can do is mumble back a reply—shag piling pressing up and into my mouth, my nostrils—as I'm momentarily assaulted by the stench of six thousand pairs of shoes and one incontinent household pet. "Stay down—I almost got the damn thing."

As an insistent burglar alarm whines away in the background, Ernie fumbles with the system's plastic keypad, doing his best to shut the contraption up, or at least send it to a better place. Ten seconds have passed, and in twenty more we're as good as bait for the neighborhood security patrol. Fortunately, they don't carry weapons. At least I think they don't carry weapons.

"The code," I say. "Put it in already."

"I did—"

"You didn't. It's still beeping."

"I did. And it's wrong. The code's wrong."

A leap to my feet—Bruno Maglis today, clearly the inappropriate attire when one is breaking and entering, but at eight A.M. this morning I expected a non-felonious workday—and I'm beside my partner in a beat, punching in the code over his protestations. Ernie's a crack PI, but it doesn't change the fact that his eyesight's slowly dropping off the low end of the scale—last time, he insisted to the ophthalmologist that the reading chart was mocking him, by God—and most likely he's simply hitting the wrong numbers.

There: 6-2-7-1-4-9-2. Just like it said in the Rolodex on the new hubby's desk. We found the code scrawled down as a phone number listed for a Mr. Alvin Alarming, and you can bet the farm it took the stellar mind of a T-Rex to come up with that brain-twister. I take my time and carefully depress the numbers on the keypad in their proper sequence.

The beeping continues. Twenty seconds down. This ain't good.

"Hey," I say, "the code's wrong."

Ernie fixes me with a cold, familiar stare. I grin. "Damn," Ernie mutters, "he musta changed it."

"Maybe *she* changed it—"

"No." Simple, monosyllabic. I don't argue.

Fifteen seconds. My gaze slides toward the doorway we came through, then out to the driveway and the suburban streets beyond. No security patrol so far, but that doesn't preclude an imminent arrival. The time has come to beat a hasty retreat, exit stage left, mission aborted. I was getting hungry, anyhow.

But before I can grab Ernie by the lapel of his blue bowling shirt and haul him out of the building and down to Pink's for a chili dog with extra onions, he's somehow managed to tear off the face of the keypad, exposing the simplistic guts of this seemingly complex security system. Wires spill out like loose spaghetti, electricity snapping through the open gaps, and Ernie shoots a queasy glance in my direction. "Get down, kid," he says. "And stay there."

No argument here. Over a decade of snoop work with the guy, I've learned that when Ernie gets that pained, cramped look—that *I've-just-licked-a-human* grimace—it's time to listen up and listen hard. I drop to the floor.

An array of stunted claws flash out from Ernie's suddenly exposed paw, latex human fingers flapping loosely off the wrist. A flick of the forearm, a sweep through the air, and those four sharp razors slice their way up and through the assortment of high-tech wizardry bolted to the wall. Sparks fly, showering Ernie in a wash of miniature fireworks, but he stands his ground and holds tough despite the burn marks spreading across the surface of his polysuit.

The alarm, if anything, grows louder.

Moving with some real urgency now, Ernie grasps a severed wire in each hand and twists the two exposed ends around each other into a single sparkling braid.

Light. Hissing. A small explosion, perhaps.

And silence. The distinct smell of sulfur hangs in the air. Wires and buttons and lights and computer chips lie in a small mountain of rubble on the foyer carpeting, and I have to stamp out the smoldering mess with the bottoms of my designer shoes in order to prevent a small fire. The things I do for this job . . .

But Ernie is triumphant, arms aloft, the latex fingers on his left hand clutching the exposed claws of his right, jumping up and down like the winning pugilist after an early-round knockout. There's glee in that little dance, in that smile spreading across his face. I know that smile. There's no getting past that smile. That's pure Ernie.

"Nice job," I say. "You gonna fix that before we go?"

Ernie shrugs. "Don't know how."

"So there goes the covert entry."

"Yep. There it goes."

"You got a kick outta that, didn't you?" I ask.

A short laugh, almost a choke, as Ernie turns his head, avoids making eye contact. "I sure as hell ain't sad, kid."

We move farther into the house.

Tight hallways and small, sectioned rooms are the norm in this wood-paneled home, a restored throwback to the cobblestone-wall and modular-furniture days of the late seventies. The rooms practically pulse with disco backbeat. A vaulted ceiling rises above the main living area, in which a Steinway grand piano lies dormant, a thin layer of dust having settled across the keys.

"She still play?" I ask.

"How the hell should I know?"

"I thought maybe you—"

"No."

Rows of framed photographs hang side by side in the main hallway, some of them old, most of them recent, all of them dinos in disguise. In the back of one group shot—a family reunion, I gather, from the striking clan resemblance—I believe I can make out a familiar guised face, a familiar squat body. No time to check, as Ernie's already through the hall and into a bedroom.

"What are we looking for?" I ask. Ernie's on his knees by the side of a California King Craftmatic adjustable bed, hurriedly rummaging through a battered oak nightstand. Books and old receipts fly onto the floor as my partner digs through the drawer with an intensity bordering on frenzy. This is not a careful archaeological expedition, to say the least.

No answer. I tap Ernie on the shoulder, and he barely flinches. "What are we—"

"I'll know it when I see it," he says.

I sit on the edge of the bed, and it nearly sinks to the floor under my meager weight. I don't even hear the creak of springs, as they must have given up the long, hard battle some time ago. This must be the side that the new husband sleeps on; T-Rexes, frame notwithstanding, are not known to be light snoozers.

Ernie has successfully transferred the entire contents of the night-stand's upper drawer to the floor, and as he starts in on the lower one with the same troubled deliberation, I realize I'm going to be in for a long evening. Once my partner gets his mind set on something, there's little short of a cannonball or a side of mutton that can stop him.

"I'll go stand guard," I offer.

"For what?"

"In case they come back."

"They're at the opera."

"Maybe they'll leave after the third quarter," I say, and Ernie waves a hand in my general direction. I take this as my cue to leave, destination already in mind. A squadron of little demons resting inside my belly are clamoring for their evening feast, scratching at the lining of my stomach with their pitchforks, and I can't deny the monsters for much longer. The kitchen, therefore, is the first stop.

Clean. Sparkling. And well appointed. I am a particular fan of the Sub-Zero fridge: easy to open, and, thanks to its excellent layout, easy to raid. Being careful not to disturb the other contents, I pluck a leftover leg of lamb from the bottom shelf, snag a bottle of hot mustard, and make my way to the kitchen table. The demons intensify their poking and prodding, and my stomach growls in protest.

A munch, maybe two, and then it's no more time for food as a pair of lights swing across the peach curtains that line the front windows of the house. Headlights, I'm sure of it, accompanied by the unmistakable purr of an import automobile.

"Ernie!" I call out, achieving new dino land speeds as I race down the hall. "We've got a problem—"

But he's engrossed in the same project as before, this time rummaging through an old bureau set against the far wall. In the few minutes since I'd left him, a miniature tornado must have localized itself in this bedroom: the floor is covered with knickknacks and loose sheets of paper, strewn about in every direction. "I think I'm onto it," Ernie says, oblivious of the F5-size mess he has created.

"Not anymore, you're not onto it," I tell him. "They're here."

"I know," he says wistfully. "I smelled her two minutes ago."

Even though the inhabitants of that car must have been ten blocks away two minutes ago, I have no cause to doubt Ernie's schnoz in cases such as this. Still, we have to vamoose. I grab Ernie by the shoulder, but he shrugs my hand away and continues digging.

I can hear two pairs of feet clomping up the front walkway, and now I, too, can smell them—one scent strong, musky, thick, and cloying, a bargain-basement cologne; the other is full of lilac and warm oatmeal.

And now the key is turning, opening the lock in the front door, and it won't be long before the rightful owners of this house walk into their foyer and step directly into a homeowner's nightmare represented by a pile of charred plastic and silicon that used to be their primary means of defense against intruders great and small.

"Ernie, we can't wait around—"

Front door creaking, opening, a matter of milliseconds—

"—for you to sniff this thing out, whatever it is—"

"Found it," says Ernie, his voice even, almost melancholy. I try to take a gander at the small, yellowed piece of paper in his hands, but he's already out the sliding glass door, leaving me to wade through the bedroom wreckage. I'm barely onto the patio when I hear the chorus of gasps and angry voices emanating from the foyer, but by then I'm at full tilt and rising fast. Past the pool, into the yard, over the fence in a single jump (with a little more effort than it used to take, I must admit), and hauling my carcass through the neighbor's backyard, Ernie a good ten yards ahead.

We're in my beloved Lincoln two minutes later, panting hard and catching our breath as we keep an eye out for anyone who may have seen or followed us. But the only movements in the shadows are your basic suburban staples—basketball nets swaying in the breeze, lawn flamingos falling off their rusted metallic legs, neighborhood cats prowling their turf, cruising for a good time—so it seems that for the moment, at least, we have escaped unnoticed.

The stomach succubi are displeased with my recent unexpected exercise, and are threatening to return the little lamb I was able to shove into my mouth to the land from whence it came. I swallow hard, trying to maintain some degree of professionalism. The last thing I need is to spend the rest of the evening cleaning up the Lincoln's front seat.

Ernie's engrossed in reading the sheet of paper he pilfered from the house, and after a time I ask him, "You wanna show me what you got?"

He folds the paper once, twice, then stuffs it into his front shirt pocket. "Let's get outta here."

"Best plan I heard all day." I turn the key and the good old American engine rumbles to life, breaking the stillness of the night. As I flick on the lights, Ernie reaches over and flicks them off again.

"I kinda need those."

"Go down her street," Ernie tells me.

I shake my head. "That ain't smart, Ern." I pointedly turn the lights back on again. "We got lucky once. We'd be asking for trouble—"

"Keep the lights off, no danger. C'mon, kid. For me."

I'd argue—really, I'd be more than happy to—but I can predict my own defeat ahead of time. So in order to save myself a few hours, I wall off the argumentative part of my brain behind some strong mental brickwork, flick off the lights, and drive down the street.

The front door is open, every light in the house in full-on blaze position. The exterior halogens have popped to life as well, and the home glows with nuclear intensity. I take my time coasting through the shadows, barely touching the accelerator.

Snippets of sound from inside—"the jewelry . . . did they get the . . . where are your rings . . . check the safe . . ."—accompanied by a side order of rancorous scents. The block is slowly filling with the smell of chestnuts roasting on an open fire, but for dinos that aroma means fear and anger as opposed to Jack Frost nipping at your nose.

The lady of the house, perhaps sensing our presence, perhaps simply in need of a break from the difficulty of accepting a home invasion, steps out of her doorway and onto the front porch, staring off into the night. Does she see us? Possibly. Does she recognize us? Unlikely.

It's been some time since she's had her guise professionally aged—I can tell even from this distance that the wrinkle set usually required for the early fifties hasn't yet been sewn into her face—and as a whole, she looks similar to the last time I saw her, more than three years ago. Short blond hair puffed into a tight little ball against her head, a collection of mid-range jewelry adorning her small, thin wrists. Eyes covered in blue shadow, lips more pink than red, and the traces of good nature turning up the corners of her mouth even amid all this danger and disappointment.

"She's still got that smell about her, don't she?" Ernie says, and his wistful tone pulls me into a similar reverie. A soft pat on my partner's back, and this time he doesn't move my hand away. We issue a collective sigh.

"A real sweetheart," I say.

"You don't gotta rub it in."

"Rub what in?" I ask. "You said she had a great smell, I said she was a sweetheart. Am I wrong?"

Ernie scratches his chin, massaging the stubble he so carefully applies once a week. He'd thought about getting that facial hair kit from Nanjutsu, the one in which the hairs actually grow *through* the skin at a predetermined rate, but decided that the beard replacement packs (at least one every two weeks) weren't worth the cost. "No, you ain't wrong, kid," he says. "She's a sweetheart all right."

In a single move, Ernie reaches into his pocket, extracts the slip of paper he took from the house, and tosses it into my lap. I open it slowly, the old, worn pages crackling beneath my fingers, and hold it beneath the small light from the LED clock display.

A marriage license. Louise and Ernie's marriage license, to be specific, and I fold it up as reverently as possible and hand it back to my partner, who is still unable to take his eyes off his ex-wife standing in the doorway of what used to be their house.

There's a moment when I think she's looking right at us, a moment when I think her eyes and Ernie's eyes make some connection, when I think I can hear her saying *It's okay, I understand,* but then she turns, walks back inside, and closes the door. The front lights are extinguished moments later.

"Drive on home, kid," Ernie says to me. "Don't stop for gas."

When Ernie says "home," he means our office, the corner suite on the third floor of a building in Westwood that has neither adequate water pressure nor a proper mail-delivery system. Half of the time I find myself plucking envelopes out of the mud beneath our outdoor mailbox, and when I return to the office I'm barely able to wash the grime off my hands thanks to a six-drop-per-minute water flow.

The sign out front reads WATSON AND RUBIO, INVESTIGATIONS, and although I've never put up a fight about the order of the names—never cared one way or the other about it, in fact—Ernie nevertheless offers to flip-flop status with me at the end of every year.

"This is your big chance, kid," he always jokes with me. "Rubio and Watson's got a helluva nice ring to it."

Not interested.

On this night, the mailbox has been properly filled, and though there are at least ten envelopes and a package lying in the dirt below, I can't find any down there addressed to us. Mr. Toggle in 215 is going to have quite the fit, on the other hand, and though he's a human, that man can roar like a Stegosaur with a hangnail.

Elevator's broken again, so it's the stairs for us. Two flights, both short, but Ernie's starting to pant. Pack a day of the long ones will do that, and I can't understand why he doesn't quit; it sure as hell ain't the nicotine keeping him there.

The door to our office is ajar, a thin band of light streaming into the darkened hallway. Thin, tinny music escapes from within, some big band bopping away on our subpar, tweeter-impaired stereo. Ernie and I approach cautiously, sticking to the shadows, backs pressed against the rough exposed concrete walls.

"Thought I told you to close the door," Ernie whispers.

"And I told you to turn off the lights," I whisper back. If I had a gun, I'd be reaching for it. As it is, the fingers of my left hand are fumbling with the glove on my right, ready to whip out the claws should push come to slice.

Edging closer to the door, Ernie motions for me to flank him on the

other side. I hold up three fingers, then two, then one. Time to grind the
teeth.

A well-placed kick sends the door flying back on its hinges, and like two
hyperactive feds busting in on a raid, we leap into the open doorway, claws
at the rough and ready.

"Hiya, fellas. What took you?"

There's a pudgy-faced midget sitting on my desk, dangling his squat legs
in the air, kicking his feet to the beat of the music, leafing through the papers scattered across my desktop, and running a stubby index finger below
the words as he reads. He's got manicured nails and a tailored suit and decidedly black hair. Greasy black hair. Dripping, greasy, black hair. As the
door bangs loudly against the side wall, the little guy shoots us a grin that is
supposed to look ashamed, but doesn't quite make the grade.

I slam the door closed behind me and storm my way up to the minuscule marauder. "You can't do this, Minsky—"

"What?" he asks. "What'd I do? What's the problem?"

Ernie flashes out with his claws, waving them past Minsky's angelic expression. "You were about five seconds from meeting your ancestors, that's
the problem."

"What, you were gonna kill me?"

"The moment ain't passed yet."

"Hey—hey—wait—I didn't break in," says Minsky. "How can I break in
when I own the building?"

I have no urge to get into a discussion over landlord-tenant rights at this
point in the evening, so I cock an eyebrow at Ernie—one of our little "back
off" signals when interrogating witnesses—and he slowly steps away, retracting his claws. Minsky smiles.

"How's it going?" he asks. "Business good?"

"Whaddaya want?" I say. Formalities and chatter with this fellow have
been known to eclipse entire weekends, and I have sleep to catch up on.

"Can't a landlord check in on his favorite tenants?"

"No." A firm grasp beneath each armpit and I lift the undersized
Hadrosaur up and off my desk, depositing him on the ground. Now his head
reaches no higher than my waist, which makes me a little more comfortable
with his presence. It's odd to see such stunted growth in a dinosaur nowadays,
but forty-five years ago, back when Minsky was growing up, a lot of us neg-

lected the dino side of nutrition. Fast-food burgers and tacos may nourish a human child, but it takes a little more than that to raise a healthy Hadrosaur.

"You guys have the rent?" he asks.

"Rent ain't due for another two weeks," Ernie says. "I got it all in my calendar." He puts a firm hand behind Minsky's back and begins ushering our landlord toward the door. "You be sure to come back and see us then. Better yet, I'll drop the payment in your box, and you don't have to come near the joint at all, okay?" I open the door as Ernie grasps Minsky by the seat of his pants and prepares to toss him into the hallway.

"Wait, wait," he squeals. "I've got a question—I've got a case—"

"Sorry," Ernie says, "business hours are over."

But Minsky's squirming in Ernie's grasp, flopping like a fish on the hook, trying futilely to push his way back into the room— picture a Peewee League linebacker trying to get by the Miami Dolphins' entire offensive line—and I can see that Ernie's doing his best not to break up laughing.

"What the hell," I say. "Let him in."

Ernie reverses the direction of his throw, and Minsky stumbles back into our office. With precise, deliberate motions, he straightens out the paisley tie that doesn't quite match his otherwise well-tailored suit, reassembles his dignity, and struts confidently back toward the desk. At this moment, the thought hits me that Minsky's guises, custom-made as they must be for his extraordinarily small frame, must cost a fortune. Are we overpaying in rent? Is the dental business that profitable?

"I've got this mistress," Minsky begins, and Ernie and I sigh as one. I push back from the desk and stand up.

"Goodnight, Minsky," I say, fully preparing to take up where Ernie left off, flexing those muscles that might be best for midget-tossing.

"It's different this time," he says.

"It's always different. Hell, it's never different," I say, my volume climbing, rising along with my ire. "You get yourself in some hot seat with a floozy and want us to bail you out with the missus."

"No, please, you don't understand. . . . Her name's Star, and she's an Allosaur. I found her up on Sunset. She's fantastic."

"Teenage runaway?" I ask.

"Not exactly. Well . . . she's nineteen. So, technically, yes, she's a teenager, but she's not a runaway per se. She's more like an entrepreneur."

Ernie's picking his fingernails with a letter opener, but he looks up at this. "A hooker."

Pain slides across Minsky's face as if Ernie had slapped him a good one. "Never! What—why would you say that?"

"You said you found her up on Sunset Boulevard, she's not 'exactly' a runaway, and she's an entrepreneur. Do the math, Minsky."

"I'll have you know that Star is not a prostitute, thank you. She sells maps."

"Maps?" I ask.

"To the stars' homes."

It takes some time before Ernie and I are able to stop laughing.

"I'm glad you find her profession amusing," Minsky says once our hysterics have dwindled to the occasional chuckle. "But she makes a good living, and she's smart, and she's kind, and she's the sweetest girl I know."

"Fine," I say, cutting short the love sonnet. "So if she's so sweet and you're so damned happy, why come to us?"

Minsky lowers his head, his voice somehow dropping past the midget register, lowering a full tone. "I think she's stealing nitrous from me."

"Sweet girl."

"And ether."

"Real sweet girl."

"And maybe some prescription pads, I'm not sure."

Minsky may be one of the premier dino dentists in Los Angeles, and he may have the corner on the filed-down-tooth and human-molar market, but he's got a lot to learn when it comes to women. This is the fourth mistress we've heard about in the last two years, and I am quite sure that there were many more who floated by without getting a mention. Then again, maybe I'm the one who's got a lot to learn; Minsky's certainly fulfilling his reproductive duty a heck of a lot more often than I am.

Still, they always seem to screw him over.

"Whaddaya want us to do?" I ask.

"Find her."

"You don't know where she is?"

"Not . . . not exactly."

"Maybe this *is* the ideal relationship," I chuckle.

"And I want you to find out if she's stealing from me."

"And if she is?"

"Confront her. Or stop her. Get the stuff back."

"Why don't you just ask her?" says Ernie. "Ain't that what relationships are based on? Trust and honesty and all that crap?"

Minsky shrugs, a toss of his teensy shoulders. Is he shorter than he was a minute ago? "I'm afraid if I ask her, if I tell her to stop . . . she'll leave me. Or . . ."

"Or she'll tell Charlene about you two." Charlene is the wife. The jealous wife. The jealous wife six times his size.

Minsky nods. "Yes." He's growing smaller by the second. Any moment now, I expect him to shrivel into a pea and wink out of existence.

Ernie and I glance at each other, allowing our eyes to lock for no more than half a second. It's all we need nowadays, a momentary chance to read the other's thoughts on the matter, and then the issue is settled before the client even realizes that the question has been asked.

"We'll do it." I sigh, and Minsky looks up, beaming with gratitude.

"Really?"

"Give us a week or so," Ernie says.

"How much?" asks Minsky, reaching back for his billfold.

Another glance between me and Ernie, and I say, "Three months' rent."

"Done," says Minsky.

"And two free visits," Ernie adds. "I gotta get a new M-series set of caps for my lower left. Maybe a new bridge, too."

Suddenly, Minsky's hopping off the couch, waddling up to my desk. Without a hitch, he leaps on top, kicks a few papers out of his way, and stands over Ernie, who obediently opens his mouth for the doctor's small, skilled hands. Minsky purrs over the worn set of false teeth he finds within.

"I can fix you up with the new Impresario brand," he says. "Real sweet set of choppers, George Hamilton model. No problem." Suddenly, Minsky turns his attention toward me and shuffles across my desk, kicking up even more paper as he moves in for the kill.

I back off. "Thanks, but . . . no thanks, I'm fine."

"Come, Vincent—oral cleanliness is next to godliness," he says, stubby arms reaching out for my clenched jaw.

"And I'm a dental atheist. Back off, little man."

Minsky shrugs and hops down off the desk. "I appreciate this, fellas."

"We're gonna need info," says Ernie.

I scribble down some necessities on the back of an envelope and hand them to Minsky. "Full name, date of birth, where she's from, maybe some pictures."

"X-rated?" he asks.

"G is fine."

And with that, Minsky is gone. I set to cleaning up my desk, picking up the papers that have dropped to the floor, and Ernie takes off his coat and hangs it on a brass hook set into the back of the door.

"You believe that guy?" Ernie asks me.

"Poor son of a bitch."

"Every six months he's in here with another sob story about one of his dames."

"Some guys . . ." I begin. "Some guys . . . they don't know how to handle themselves. They don't know where the line starts and where it ends."

"I'll tell you what it is," Ernie says. "He thinks his answer is in women. Minsky thinks that Minsky isn't Minsky unless he's with a woman."

"Can't live that way."

"A guy can stand alone," insists my partner. "A guy *should* stand alone."

"You're right, Ern. You're right."

We clean up the rest of the office in silence, and say our goodnights. I freshen up in the small bathroom down the hall, and when I return—my face still wet, water dripping down the false bridge of my latex nose, small puddles forming on the floor—I find Ernie curled up on the couch, shoes off, a rough wool blanket pulled tightly beneath his chin, a small throw pillow clenched between his arms, and a light snore buzzing out from behind his thick lips.

I drive home alone.

'm in the office late the next morning, thanks to a Hemp for Humanity rally in front of the monolithic Federal Building, which towers over Wilshire Boulevard down near UCLA. Traffic was backed up for a mile in all directions, which isn't so odd for Los Angeles, but because the air conditioning in my car isn't up to snuff, I had to keep the windows rolled down for fresh air, and the incessant folk music and strong scent of extralegal substances blasting out from the rally quickly threw me into a particularly foul mood.

Ernie's not in; the blanket has been folded up and put away, I see, and the couch has been fluffed and primped back to proper buoyancy. It's been at least six months that Ernie's been sleeping in the office, and I don't bother him about it anymore. If the crumpled ambiance of his new bachelor pad in Hollywood doesn't allow him to get in a good night's sleep, who am I to tell the guy any different?

A note on my desk, large but neat letters drawn across an entire sheet of yellow legal paper. DENTIST APPOINTMENT reads the letter, and I don't think he went to Minsky's for that checkup they discussed. More likely, he's checking out our client's office, maybe his home, maybe the love nest where Minsky and his teenaged Allosaur shacked up. Take him at least an hour, maybe more. This should give me time to straighten out the burgeoning pile of paperwork that's threatening to throw off a seismic tremor and completely bury my desk beneath an avalanche of demand letters and eyewitness accounts.

A knock at the partially open door, and I turn to see a familiar face—

recently familiar, in fact—peeking in from the hallway. "Is . . . is Ernie here?"

Warm oatmeal and lilac flood the room, and instinct takes over as my mind stages a temporary strike. I find myself shaking my head, sitting my rump down on the edge of the desk. My arms fold across my chest of their own accord. "He's out."

"Oh. It's good to see you, Vincent." She steps inside, knockoff Chanel handbag slung across one shoulder. Wrinkles still missing where wrinkles should be.

"It's good to see you, too, Louise." We trade strained grins. "How's the new husband? Terrence, right?"

"Terrell."

"Sorry. Terrell. He's well?"

"Under the circumstances, yes. He's got some respiratory problems."

"T-Rexes often do."

"Yes," she says. "We do."

Silence for a moment, as I try to figure out if we're breaking any specific code of conduct, veering off on any moral tangent, simply by being in the same room together without Ernie present.

Louise speaks first. "We're not—I mean, you're not . . ."

"Mad at you?"

"Mad at me. Yes. You're not—"

"No. No, of course not." I grin, in order to prove my sincerity. At least, I hope it comes across as sincerity.

"Thank you. I'd understand if you wanted to . . ."

"I don't. It's between you and . . . I mean, you divorced Ernie, not me. I'm not involved."

Louise seems to accept this, and takes my lack of ire as a cue to step farther into the office. I extend a hand toward the couch and she takes a seat. A moment later, she wiggles her bottom, reaching under her rump as if to scratch in a decidedly unfeminine fashion. Her hand comes up with a dark night mask.

"This looks like Ernie's," she says.

"Looks like it."

"Does he—is this where he's sleeping?"

"Once or twice a month," I lie. "On late nights."

This could go on forever. Louise could sit on that couch and I could perch on the edge of my desk and we could talk about Ernie—rather, we could *not* talk about Ernie—for days, exercising whatever part of our brains that specialize in strained cocktail-party chatter, but I have a quick breakfast and the aforementioned paperwork to get to, so I come out with the standard question that always gets the clients moving in or out of the door in a real hurry:

"What can I do for you, Louise?"

A steady stream of tears rolls out of the corner of her left eye, welling in the joint formed between natural scaled skin and latex polysuit. If I didn't know Louise as well as I do—eight, nine years now—I'd think that she was crying, upset perhaps at her reason for coming to see me, perhaps at the situation between her and Ernie. But Louise is just one of those unfortunate dinosaurs for whom the lachrymal glands are still overproductive, even after millions of years of evolution worked this kink out of the rest of our systems. This is nothing more than the near-literal representation of crocodile tears, and I've handed the woman enough handkerchiefs over the years to know that this isn't sadness; it's just salt water.

"Excuse me," she says, dabbing at the corner of her eye with a tissue. "I leak sometimes."

"I know. Do you want to wait for Ernie to come back? He should be here—"

"No," she says abruptly. "I'd prefer if we spoke, just you and me. At first. Then maybe you could pass it on to Ernie, okay?"

I nod and take a seat behind my desk, attempting to straighten the papers back into some semblance of a pile. "Start from the beginning, Louise. That's my best advice."

A deep breath, shoulders rising quickly, then gently falling back into place, and she's ready to lay it out. "Last night, someone broke into our house."

And don't I know it. It takes a special effort, drill-sergeant tactics, to convince my facial muscles to retain their neutral placement.

"I'm so sorry," I say, tone remaining perfectly even. "Did they steal anything?"

Louise shakes her head. "Not that I know of. They destroyed our alarm system, ransacked the bedroom, made a terrible mess of the kitchen." Actually, I thought I'd left the kitchen rather tidy, despite the leg of lamb abandoned on the breakfast table, but I've always had a slightly more lax standard of neatness than my peers.

"So you weren't home."

"Thank God, no. I can't imagine what those monsters would have done."

"The world is full of them," I say, nodding with what I hope comes across as mellow resignation. "Did you call the police?"

"Of course," she says, and my heart takes a small jump backward. "But they couldn't find anything of use. They were dinos, we think, and apparently guises don't leave good prints."

"I see. So how can we be of help? You want us to take a look, try to grab some smells, see if we can find out who did it?"

"Oh, I think we know who did it," she says, and suddenly I'm thinking it wouldn't be the worst idea to keep a defibrillator here in the office. Was this the whole purpose of her visit—to face me one-on-one and confront me with my misdeeds? I usually have no qualms about breaking or entering or "borrowing" or any number of assorted illegal activities Ernie puts me up to, but it's the betrayal of whatever friendship Louise and I have going that puts me on edge.

"How do you know?" I ask, involuntarily pushing my chair back from the desk. "If the police found nothing . . ."

Louise is somber, locking her gaze with mine. "I know because . . . I know."

I hold that look, refusing to flinch away. Play this out till the end. "Then why don't you tell me?" I suggest, hoping she'll do exactly the opposite, that she'll get up and walk out of the office. "Tell me who broke into your house."

"The Progressives," says Louise, and my circulatory system pulls out of the pit stop and races back into action.

"The Progressives?"

"They're a . . . a religion. A cult, I guess."

"I don't follow you. What kind of cult?"

"I don't know. They're all dinosaurs, I know that. A dino cult."

"And why would they break into your house?"

"To get money, maybe?"

"But they didn't take any money."

"Because I don't keep any in the house. That's probably why they wrecked it."

"Why would they break into *your* house, Louise? Why not my house, or Ernie's house?"

"Because I know them. Rather, they know me. Rupert is one of them. He's a Progressive."

"Your brother?"

Louise nods. "For about two years now. I didn't tell anyone when he was getting into it, partially because it scared me, but . . . Honestly, I was hoping that it was a passing thing."

"A phase."

"A phase, yes. He's had enough of them. Remember the hang gliding?"

I can't help but chuckle, and I'm glad to see that Louise joins in. "Of course I remember it," I say. "And the bungee jumping and the trips to India and the Peace Corps and the spelunking. Rupert's a good soul, but a little lost."

"And then a couple of years ago he started selling whatever he had left—his bike, his share of Mom's house. He'd ask me for money, and wouldn't tell me how he was spending it. And now he thinks he's found himself," Louise says. "He says he's found Progress."

"What's that mean?"

"I have no idea. I wish I did." Louise delves into that magical purse of hers—how anything other than a single tube of lipstick could fit in that small compartment I'll never know—and comes up with a folded sheet of paper. "I got this letter two weeks ago, and I've been beside myself since." She hands it over, and I unfold it and take a gander.

In a strong, heavy-handed script, the letter reads:

Dear Sister,

When, in the course of our shared events, it becomes necessary for one portion of the family of Raal to assume among the creatures of the earth a position different from that which they have recently occupied, but one to which the laws of the ancestors and of the ancestors' ancestors entitle them, a decent respect for the opinions of dinokind requires that they should declare the causes that impel them to such a course.

I hold these truths to be self-evident: that I am like no other creature on this planet; that I have a natural beauty inherent within all the family of Raal; that I have a moral and genetic obligation to the ancestors; that I have the capacity to understand myself as myself.

The time will come, in a few short weeks, to retrieve our heritage from the fossil pits of time. I have found Progress, and Progress has found me. My blood is becoming pure as I accept the wisdom and ways of Raal and our forefathers. Until you too accept yourself as a product of the product of the ancestors, I will not see you again. I love you.

Your brother, Granaagh

"Granaagh?" I ask.

"I don't understand it either. The ancestors, that part about the genetic obligation, this Raal character, retrieving their heritage—it's all beyond me. When I got the letter, I was so worried. It had been months since I'd heard from him, but this . . ." She's starting to cry again, but this time it's actual tears streaming out of those big brown eyes. I'm torn between staying at my desk and joining her on the couch. I remain in place.

"The last two weeks, all I've been doing is looking for him. I've been everywhere. Phone calls, letters, faxes . . . No one knows where he is, even his old friends down at the mission where he used to volunteer. They got letters like mine."

"And the cops?"

"I told the police," she says, "but they say they can't do anything. Religion is . . . religion. They can't touch these places unless they break the law, and Rupert's in his twenties, old enough to make his own decisions."

"I'm very sorry about your brother," I say. "He's a good kid. Mixed up, but a good kid. Anything I can do to help . . ." It's a cursory offer, nothing more, but my mouth has this annoying tendency to speak before it's conferred with the brain.

"I want you to find him," says Louise. "I want you to find him and get him to come home."

"Whoa, whoa, wait up," I say.

"You said you'd help—"

"Sure, but . . . Slow this down a second. Let's even say I can find him, right? That letter doesn't sound like he's the most rational guy in the world right now. Who's to say he'll go with me?"

There's a telltale pause—long enough to make it seem like she's thinking the question over, short enough so that I know she's already thought it through way before she stepped into my office, that this was the real reason she came to see me today.

"Then I want you to kidnap him."

In the two seconds it takes for me to formulate a proper, polite way to say that there is no way on earth I'm going to commit what amounts to a major felony in order to remove a full-fledged adult from a situation he has presumably chosen for himself, that there is no possibility of Ernie and me taking on a case that, if the right charges were pressed by the wrong people, could land us jail time and a hefty fine, that I can't even begin to think about the circumstances under which a kidnaping, even in a situation as odd as this, could possibly be justified, Ernie opens up the door to our office and charges inside.

"She cleaned Minsky out real good," he announces as he lumbers toward his desk, not bothering to glance over at the couch. He drops a file folder on the seat of his chair and proceeds to rifle through it.

I clear my throat. "Ernie—"

"She got the ether, all right, and some nitrous, and some prescription pads, but I searched the doc's office, and I checked with his secretaries for a listing of what's usually in the storage cabinets—"

"Ernie—" I try to interrupt. Futile. I look at Louise—she looks back—we both look to my partner, who's still got his back turned.

"—and they gave me a whole list of things. And guess what? The crazy bitch took a whole bunch of dental drills and scrapers, too. That's freaking insane, right? I mean, what's she gonna do with fifteen metal scrapers?"

"Hey, Ernie—"

"Wait a sec, Vincent, you gotta see this list. You won't believe—"

"Hello, Ernie." Louise this time. Soft, kind, deliberate.

Ernie clams up and slowly turns on his heel. I can almost make out the knot forming in his throat; wrinkles appear in the manila folder as his hand clenches, knuckles widening.

"Louise."

"You smell well," she says, and I'm worried that I'm going to have to sit around for a replay of our earlier conversation.

Ernie nods at Louise's compliment, doesn't return it. "How's Terrence?" he asks.

"Terrell," Louise and I say as one, and I'm blasted by a vicious look from Ernie. I back off and let them take the conversation down whatever path it needs to go.

"He still doing construction work?"

"He's a contractor," Louise says defensively.

Ernie looks to me. "You two have a lunch date?"

I knew it would come down to accusations eventually; the earlier feelings of guilt well up. "No, Ern—she came by to ask—"

"I need something investigated," says Louise, rescuing me. Now Ernie can hear his ex-wife out, listen to each word carefully and patiently, then toss the idea on the skids, and we can get back to looking into the Minsky affair.

Ernie moves out from behind his desk, each step slow, conscious. "Whatever we can do to help." From here, I can see his nostrils flaring— he's trying to get a whiff of her, catch the aroma that he loves so dearly.

"Rupert's joined a cult," she says plainly. "I want you to find him, and, if he won't come home with you, I want you to kidnap him."

No hesitation from Ernie. "Certainly."

Certainly? *Certainly?* I must be throwing off pheromones at an unnatural level now—some dinos can smell themselves, but I've never been able to—because Ernie holds up a hand in my direction, a clear signal that I should clam up and calm down.

"Louise, Ernie and I really need to talk this over," I say. "But if you come back tomorrow—"

"No need," Ernie interrupts, moving closer to his ex-wife. They're only a few feet apart now, and each is clearly into smelling the other. "We can take the case."

"Thank you," says Louise. "I gave Vincent all the details."

"Good. We'll see what we can do—"

I hop forward and wedge myself between these two conspirators. "Now wait just a second," I say, but Ernie sidesteps me and opens the office door.

"—and give you a call once we have something concrete."

More tears coming out of Louise's right eye again, and this time I can't be sure if they're chemically or emotionally produced. "I can't thank you enough," she says. "Whatever it costs—"

"No charge," says Ernie, and now it takes all the strength I can muster to keep my eyes from blasting out of my head like a cartoon character who's accidentally ingested half a ton of chili powder. I grab a hold of the side of the door, if only to keep myself from shooting into the stratosphere.

Louise issues Ernie a peck on the cheek, a polite "Bye, Vincent" to me, and then she's out the door and down the hall, and Ernie's back behind his desk. When the red haze of rancor has faded from before my eyes and my blood pressure has returned to triple digits, I find Ernie sitting calmly at his desk, highlighting the dental inventory sheet he brought back from Minsky's.

"This is a *partnership*," I begin, keeping myself at a moderate pace so that I might choose each and every word with caution and clarity. "If you do not understand the concept of *partnership*, perhaps I could explain it to you. Shall we get a dictionary?"

Ernie looks up from his work. The whites of his eyes—the only dino part I can see of him right now, as the brown contacts he's wearing cover up the natural blazing green of his Carnotaur irises—are choked with red veins wiggling and squiggling in every direction like a first-grader's art project. Even through the thickness of his latex mask, his cheeks look sunken and hollow, and his entire body refuses to remain in a perfectly upright position; his shoulders slump, pointing down to the floor.

"For Louise" is all he says, and it's enough to stop the final dribbles of steam from pouring out of my ears. "For Louise." *For Louise* should be Ernie's motto, etched into his forehead like a pair of monogrammed Mickey Mouse ears, and though I cannot fully empathize with my partner, I can understand the power of those words, if only because I've never had a Louise to do anything for.

"We're talking felony here," I point out. "Kidnapping's a step beyond anything you've tried before."

"We might not even find him, Vincent."

"And if we do, then what?"

Ernie shrugs. "Then we tell him that his sister loves him and misses him and we want to help. Rupert might come along willingly."

"And the odds on that?"

"There's lots of definitions of 'willingly,'" Ernie says, some sparkle returning to that defeated body. "And there's lots of ways to make fellows think they're willing. Look, I don't want to break the law any more than you—"

"Hah!"

"—so first we try to talk sense into him. If that doesn't work, you and I drop back and discuss what's next." Ernie's eyes are wide open now, part of his tried-and-true trust-me-I'm-honest face.

"So, we discuss, a serious discussion—like, a *discussion* discussion—you and me, before we get into the heavy stuff? Promise?"

Ernie nods. "Promise."

I hold out my hand, and we shake on it. A mere formality, but my partner and I don't have to make deals like this very often, so it seems right to mark it with such a canonical gesture.

I walk back to my desk, feeling victorious that I was able to pressure Ernie for once, that I was able to force him into a binding agreement. Then I replay the scene in my mind, piece by piece, and quickly come to realize exactly which way the ball bounced. "I just got talked into this, didn't I?"

"Like a tourist in a trinket shop," says Ernie, and returns to his highlighting.

3

There are any number of ways to approach Hollywood Boulevard, but for pure shock value, the key is to strike at the heart of the beast, right where the cheese factor is highest: the intersection of Hollywood and Highland Avenue. That's Limburger Central, baby, with a side of extra stink. You cruise on up the street, passing Santa Monica and Sunset, all-for-a-dollar stores slowly replacing the discount movie-prop and video-editing services, and by the time you hit the Boulevard, you're a prime-time player in a full-fledged Warhol/Escher urban nightmare. There are the usual tourist hot spots, of course, but it's the locals who make the original sin city worth the pricey parking lot fees.

Things have changed, I'll let that much slide—it's not the eighties anymore, when Mohawks were to Hollywood Boulevard what crew cuts are to the Marines, but the hairstyles are still plentiful, large, and kaleidoscopic. Many of the denizens of the area have found new, impressive ways to express their self-loathing, primarily by locating body parts to pierce that were previously unknown to medical science. The hate-the-world sneer, so popular only five short years ago, has recently been replaced by the I've-seen-it-all smirk, which is less visually disconcerting, but still troubling nonetheless. And the clothing is still a hoot; though ripped jeans have been usurped by ripped leather, the end result is the same: ragged clothing, soiled flesh, and a brown-tinged aura that acts as a bumper sticker—DON'T BOTHER ME, I'M DANGEROUS. Heck of a town.

Dinos, as a rule, do not frequent this part of the city; we find it difficult enough to live our double lives without having to disenfranchise ourselves from the rest of the world by choice. Still, there are exceptions, and I've smelled a few of our kind among the runaways and hustlers lining the gold-sprinkled streets. This, by the way, is not a colorful description—a number of years ago, the Hollywood Chamber of Commerce actually voted to embed flecks of gold plating into the asphalt of the Boulevard itself, so that the city streets could truly be said to be paved with gold. Delusional, to be certain, but that's why I love coming up here.

"I hate coming up here," Ernie says to me in the car. It's round about three in the afternoon, and we've just finished up doing some preliminary investigation on Star, aka Christine Josephson, Minsky's little fruit tart. She's sweet, all right—the kind of sweet that'll rot you from the inside out. Three lockups in juvie, two arrests as an adult, no small cookies when you're only nineteen.

"We're in, and then we're out," I say. "All I wanna do is talk to Jules, and we're done. If anyone has a handle on this Progressives thing, she will."

"She creeps me out."

"She creeps everyone out. Bite your tongue and try not to kiss her."

Dingy golden stars pass by underfoot, each engraved with the name of a so-called celebrity. Some are famous, some slightly less so, some have been plucked from the *Encyclopedia Obscuria*, but they've all paid to get there. The sordid secret about the Walk of Fame is that there's no particular distinction in having one of these hunks of bronze, apart from the honor of knowing that your studio paid ten grand to the city of Hollywood. That's all it takes—a picture of Salmon P. Chase on a little green bill and you, too, can be pissed on by some of the most erudite bums in the universe.

We pass by Danny Kaye (Ornithomimus) and Bob Hope (Compy—actually, the only one I've ever laughed *with* rather than *at*), and a host of other dino-cum-celebrities, and eventually arrive at the famous Hollywood Wax Museum, where twenty-four hours a day you can witness the spectacle of wax slowly melting under ultraviolet light. It's not as exciting as it sounds.

I pay the husky female attendant my eight dollars—"Highway robbery," mumbles Ernie—and as the woman turns around to give us our tickets, I take a deep whiff near the back of her neck. I'm rewarded with the musky odor of fermented yeast and peanut shells. This chick's a walking baseball game, but at least now I know she's a dino.

"Is Jules in today?" I ask, spinning around to make my scent glands readily available to her.

"I don't wanna smell ya," she barks. "I gotta smell the crap walking down this street all day long, I don't need any more."

"Just tell us if Jules is here," says Ernie.

"Yeah, it's here today." A push of a small button beneath her console and the front door to the museum buzzes open. "It's in the back."

"I know where to go," I say and lead Ernie into the darkness.

We pass through the chamber of terror—this is where it all gets a little spooky, mind you—and once we're over the shock of how similar the Michael Jackson sculpture has become to LaToya's over the years, we enter the actual Hall of Horrors, replete with larger-than-life figures of Franken-stein, the Wolfman, and more than a few real-life serial killers.

We make our way to the back of the museum, passing a few tourists along the way—mammals, all of them—until we reach the pièce de résis-tance, a diorama with attendant wax sculptures depicting the fighting med-ical men of the 4077th, the lovable team from $M*A*S*H$. Not content with having extended the Korean War three times longer than necessary, Hawkeye, Radar, and the rest of that wacky crew now invade reality every day via six thousand pounds of wax and a couple of shaky-looking plastic army tents.

"Last I saw her, she'd moved the workstation back here," I say, leading Ernie past a partially melted B. J. Hunnicut and toward one of the small tent facades. A quick series of knocks on the "false" door on the front of the tent, and after a few moments, a muted scuffling emanates from the other side.

"Turn around," comes a raspy voice, shot through with sultry overtones.

"It's me, Jules. It's Vincent."

"Then you know the rules, lover. Turn around."

A small compartment slides open near the door's peephole, and I will-ingly place the back of my neck against the wire mesh, presenting my scent glands for inspection. A strong inhale from behind the screen, a moment's whiff of delight, and a second later the lock turns.

As the door opens, I notice that some form of unnatural human perfume is at work in this place, nearly overpowering Jules's natural lemon chiffon aroma. She must be slathering on the Obsession again, a filthy mammalian habit she can't seem to break. We walk through the door to find Jules strutting back toward her workshop, wiggling that tight guised-up rear as she goes. She's sporting a pair of form-fitting black jeans this afternoon, along with a sleeveless blouse that's got all but two buttons undone. Long, curly black hair hangs down to that small waist of hers, and the legs stretch in all the right directions. For a human female, Jules is a knockout.

Too bad she's a Velociraptor, and bad over again that she's male.

"Close the door, fellas," purrs my favorite dino drag queen. "So sweet to see you."

"I'm gonna be sick," Ernie mumbles to me, and I fix him with a hard glare. It's not rare for dinosaurs to be homosexual, but the spectacle of a male dino wearing the guise of a human female is just too much double deception for most of our kind to take. There's persecution and there's persecution, but ostracism knows no bounds for a dino who's crossed genders. As a result, Jules spends most of her time in this cramped, musty back room, practicing her special brand of guise reconstruction away from the public eye.

Moving quickly after our host, we head down a short corridor and soon enter the workshop. Great multicolored balls of wax line the wooden floor of this simple, spartan studio; the concrete walls are bare of decoration, and an intricate shelving system hangs down from above, bolted into the ceiling via strong iron clasps. Within these drawers and cabinets and compartments are the tools of Jules's trade—scalpels, syringes, putty knives, and mallets—along with a few samples of her work so that she might give customers a chance to see in advance what they'll look like once their requested procedure is complete. Photographs line the walls, intricate close-up work detailing the before-and-after nature of her profession.

"You come for your lips, Vincent doll?" Jules asks me as she takes her place behind that wide oak table. "Mmm, we could fatten those up a bit, make 'em smooth and kissable."

I smile and say, "Not why we're here, Jules."

"Of course it's not why you're here, but a little help every now and again doesn't hurt a man, does it? Us ladies aren't the only ones who need the nipping and the tucking. Ten-minute procedure, tops." She beckons me closer, and, always amused at her little antics, I obediently step toward her open hands. A slight tug at the top lip of my mask as she brings up a long, red fingernail, tracing it along the fleshy underside. "One cut down the main line, then I implant, say, twenty cc's of wax, re-sew, even it out, and suddenly you're a dreamboat."

"Forget the lip job. We need some information," Ernie blurts out.

Jules falls back behind the desk, landing hard on her simple wooden stool. Her eyes meet mine—dazed, a little hurt.

"It's not that we don't think you're a great plastic surgeon," I explain. "We think you're the best. But we've got an appointment. Soon. We just don't have the time."

"I *am* good," she pouts.

"I know you are."

She turns to Ernie, eyelids blinking, flashing at strobe-light speeds, bottom lip puffing out, turning it all on. "And you, big boy?"

Ernie looks to me, and I pointedly look away. No help here; Ernie's never been the most tolerant of fellows, and though he's certainly an old dog, there's a few new tricks he's gotta learn.

"Fine." He sighs. "You're good. You're the best. Can we get on with this?"

All smiles now, Jules reaches out and pinches Ernie's cheek. "We sure can, lover."

"Have you ever heard of the Progressives?" I ask.

A wad of phlegm slaps onto the concrete floor, and it's a stunned moment before I realize that Jules is the culprit. "Why would you want to know?" she mutters.

"Guess you've heard of 'em," Ernie says. "What can you tell us?"

"Only secondhand information, darling. I hear what I hear from my friends on the street, but my friends on the street aren't always the most reliable queens in the world."

"What could make them reliable?" I ask.

"A little bit of basil, a little sniff of snapdragon," singsongs Jules, smiling all the way. "Unfortunately, the drag business isn't what it was five years ago. Did you know they're shutting down the Shangri-La next Saturday? It's becoming a coffee shop, of all the horrible things. Times are tight for my little friends, the poor dears."

"They're good, they'll find work."

"They're the best, but the best doesn't work for free, darling."

She's avoiding the issue; this is what Jules does when she's uncomfortable with the conversation at hand. But two twenty-dollar bills are soon making their way from Ernie's wallet to the oak table, and when I give him a little nudge, he adds one more to the pile. Jules scoops up the money, folds the bills in half, and tucks them inside her shirt, presumably into some bra we are unable to see.

"You don't want to deal with them," she begins. "They've screwed up a lot of good dinos."

"That's why we're looking. Go on."

She sighs, but the lady knows she's got to talk once the money's been put away. "Started up about thirty years ago by some nutcase vacuum salesman," she begins, formalities having been dispensed with. "Built it up out of the back room of his little store up in Pasadena, but over the years they got more and more converts. Business folk. Finance folk. Entertainment folk. Anyone with money, or access to money, anyone looking for a way outta their regular life. From what I hear, they've got their tendrils all through the city by now."

"What's this guy's name?"

"Don't remember. Doesn't make a difference anyway, honey, 'cause he's dead. Caught some bug and bit the big one 'bout ten years back."

"Bummer. Coulda been a good start."

"You wanna start somewhere, sugar, go sign up. The Progressives have a storefront down by Hollywood and Vine," she says. "My friends tell me they've got quite the operation going out of there."

I shake my head. "Can't be. Been by that corner a dozen times and I've never seen it."

"And if you tell people that this isn't a wax museum," says Jules, "if you tell 'em that it's just a front for black-market guise surgery, how fast do you think they'll call the loony bin on your sweet behind?"

"Go on."

"It's a tourist crap shop on the outside. Three T-shirts for ten dollars, plastic Hollywood signs, fake California license plates with your name on it. They're all over the Boulevard, but this one's got a little something extra where something shouldn't be."

Ernie can't hold back. "Bet you know that real well."

Jules doesn't mind the crack. She blows him a wet kiss, tongue waggling through the air like a panting dog. "Your friend is catty today, Vincent," she says to me. "I like that in a man."

I let it go—no need to wring the tension rod even tighter—and say, "Let's pretend we're interested in talking to one of these Progressives. Say we're interested in finding out more about the group. We walk into the tourist shop and . . . what? Is there a code word?"

"You've been in this business too long, Vincent. No code word. In fact, you don't even have to walk inside. Those cats are always on the prowl, waiting outside the shop, smelling the air for dinos walking by. They catch a whiff of one, they invite you inside the store, and that's when the fun begins."

"Fun, eh?"

"It helps if you look lost."

"Maybe we should buy a map."

"*Spiritually* lost. Emotionally lost. Pretend you've just lost your job and your house kind of lost. Pretend your dog ran away kind of lost. Pretend your wife's left you kind of lost."

At this, Ernie spins and stomps back toward the door. "Come on, Vincent. We've got what we came for—"

"Ernie, wait—she—she didn't—"

"Forget it," he growls. "I'm done with this shit. Let's go."

"I'll meet you outside," I call after him. I hope he's heard me, as he's already through the door, into the museum, and winding his way past Hot Lips and Frank on his way toward the exit.

"Did I say something wrong?" asks Jules.

"Not so you'd know it. His wife . . . He's grumpy right now. Don't mind him."

"I won't. So . . . how's it going, sweetie? Got any hot punches on your dance ticket?"

I shake my head. "No one like you, Jules. Listen, I spoke with your father, like you asked me to."

"Oh." Her hands begin to fiddle with the instruments by her side. She absentmindedly rolls a ball of wax around the table, gaze averted from mine, as if by not looking she can shield herself from the truth. "And?"

"And . . . it's the same as it was."

"He won't see me," she says, trying to keep the warble out of her voice.

"No. He won't."

Jules issues a game little shrug, tossing her hair back across one shoulder. "Well, it's his loss, right?"

"Exactly. His loss." I'm not good at this comfort thing. I should probably put out my hand for her to take. I should probably put an arm around her shoulder. I should at least convey my apologies for not being able to convince her severely opinionated father that his only son is not a freak of nature, that he's just doing what he feels is right in a world where not only do the sexes masquerade as one another, but the species can't even keep their tails on straight. But as it is, I just stand there mutely, waiting for Jules to let me out of the awkward situation.

"Go on, Vincent," she says quietly. "Go join your cult."

ur destination is about six blocks down from the wax museum, and in a driving town, that's practically a marathon. Only time you'll find most Angelenos walking that far is when their car runs out of fuel six blocks from a gas station. And even then, the resourceful ones find a way to have a few gallons delivered to the side of the road.

Schwab's Drugstore is gone. Brown Derby? Vanished. Diners and celebrity hot spots and places to see and be seen? Vamoosed. Not quite the entertainment crossroads it once was, the corner of Hollywood and Vine now boasts four fine establishments: a liquor store, an empty lot, a gas station, and High on Hollywood, the tourist trap Jules told us about.

"You didn't have to be so mean to the gal," I complain as we make our way past yet another SPACE FOR LEASE sign.

"Yeah, and she—he—whatever—didn't have to bring up Louise leaving me."

"She didn't even know about Louise. She was just giving an example."

"Oh." He clams up.

"See, not so high and mighty now, are you?"

"Don't push me, kid."

"Excuse me, brothers—" This, coming from behind us, accompanied by the distinct scent of pine. "Brothers, would you like to have a word about our shared interests?"

Ernie and I hit the brakes on our little argument and turn as one, coming face to face with tidy incarnate. This is, without a doubt, the most clean-cut individual I've ever seen east of La Cienega Boulevard. Short, cropped hair, blue worker's shirt, tan khakis, and a sparkle in the eye that tells me we've got nothing short of a full-blown live-wire nut-job standing in our midst.

"Our shared interests?" I say, playing it cool. Ernie and I decided on the hike down here to give ourselves into their little game, but only after a hard sell.

"We're the same, the three of us," says the dino, and though I know it's not possible, it's as if he sends me a little pheromonal wink, an extra burst of that pine and baby-oil scent.

Ernie huffs, "There's lots of us around, pal. We're not tourists, we don't want to buy your toys."

"It's a free service, brother," he says. "No charge whatsoever, and I promise you'll learn more about yourself in thirty minutes than you ever thought possible. There is more to this than trinkets and T-shirts, I assure you, brother. Come inside, we can speak."

"About?"

"About each other. About our common ancestry."

Now we're talking. Rupert's letter to Louise was littered with references to ancestral mumbo-jumbo. "Ernie, you interested?" I ask. We've made a conscious decision to use our real names—our first names at least—because the last time we tried out undercover names we kept slipping left and right. Ernie was supposed to be Patch and I was supposed to be Jimmy and the number of times we referred to each other incorrectly ran into the dozens. Fortunately, it was just a routine roust on a two-bit counterfeit toenail operation, so despite our slips, the bad guys were too small-time to notice.

"What the hell," Ernie replies. "We got time to kill."

The clean-cut dino grins—the lip stretch not too wide, not too thin, and somehow very sane—and says, "Follow me." We do so.

Jules was right—the tourist shop is both incredibly tacky and not much more than a front. The storage room leads to a back office that leads down a flight of stairs and to a rusty metal door set into the wall below.

"Where the hell are we going?" asks Ernie.

"The subway," says the dino, and the door swings open without a creak.

I'm proud of my hometown, if only for its excesses. The Los Angeles subway system is widely recognized as one of the most fraudulent, wasteful, and potentially dangerous uses of public tax money since the good old bacchanalian orgies of the Roman Empire. At least in Nero's time you could get yourself drunk, laid, or both; in the LA subway you can mostly count on getting yourself dead. The genius engineers who came up with this radical mass-transit plan neglected to take into account the fact that the ground out here has a tendency to move without the courtesy of giving two weeks' notice, and that subway tunnels don't take well to being rerouted by shifting tectonic plates. As a result, nearly everyone in the city derides the notion of riding the subway, leaving a select few individuals to adopt it for their own use. It should come as little surprise, then, that the Los Angeles subway system has become a haven for the city's burgeoning dinosaur population. New York has alligators swimming the sewers beneath its streets; we have Stegosaurs.

"I caught *your* name, Ernie," says our guide as he leads us out onto a platform adjacent to the subway tunnel, "but I didn't catch your friend's."

"That's Vincent. And you?"

"You can call me Bob," says the dino. "For now."

I can't let that pass. "Is there something else we should call you?"

"No," he says. "Bob is fine."

We hop down into the subway tunnel—looking left, left, and left again—and climb up onto a walkway that runs parallel to the tracks. Dim overhead lighting illuminates the path for a good twenty feet before it drops off into murky darkness.

"Is this safe?" I ask, peering down at the tracks below.

"We're fine up here," says Bob. "Don't worry about the third rail."

"The rail, hell. What about the trains?"

"There are no trains in Hollywood yet. They're still working on getting the downtown system running straight." Which means we're in the clear for at least the next few decades.

Out of the shadows in the distance a silhouette detaches itself from the wall and angles toward our party. Instinctively, my muscles clench up, as I sense the real possibility of an ambush. No one knows we're down here, and there aren't many who would care to go hunting for us if we didn't show up in the real world for the next few years. Next to me, I feel Ernie tense as well.

"Good afternoon, Sreeaal," says Bob, waving a hand in the shadowy figure's direction. The last word is more of a shriek, a strangled roar, than an actual string of letters, and I take it to be the other gentleman's name.

"Good afternoon, brothers." It's another blue-shirted, tan-Dockered Progressive, I can see now, and he's got that same wholesome aura floating about his perfectly groomed body. There's an urge rising in me to rub my hands through the subway muck coating the walls and transfer some good, honest filth over to these two dinos, but I imagine it would bring a rapid end to the proceedings. "Are your friends interested in their ancestry?"

"I'm interested in getting outta the subway," says Ernie, and the two Progressives laugh as one unit, too loud, too long.

"You have a strong spirit, brother," the newcomer says to Ernie, to which my partner emits an audible grunt. Then, to Bob: "Be well, Baynal," this last name yet again nothing more than a throaty growl. Before our guide has a chance to return the salutation, the dino is past us and lost in the shadows once again.

"He didn't call you Bob."

"No. He didn't."

"You wanna explain that?"

"My true name is Baynal. Bob is my slave name."

"Your slave name." Is my sarcasm poking through?

"The name that I have taken on in my mammal form. We're all just slaves to our guises. Progress shows us that."

"I'm sure it does," I say.

"Don't you ever feel it?" he asks. "That you're a second-class citizen? That you have to hide your natural beauty every day, that by imitating the mammals, we're slowly becoming them? That through their very nature, they're controlling us—how we act, how we dress, how we think?"

"Never gave it the once-over," says Ernie.

"So it's . . . Baynal," I clarify, trying to fit my voice into that terrible shriek of a name.

"Correct. But call me Bob if it makes you feel more comfortable."

"I'll do that."

I decide this might be a good point to go fishing. "I like your outfit," I tell Bob. "I knew someone who dressed just like that. . . . What was his name, Ern?"

"You mean Rupert?"

"That's right," I say. "Rupert Simmons. Swell fella, wore those same clothes as you and your friend."

If there's a reaction from Bob, I can't discern it in the darkness of the tunnel.

We eventually leave the subterranean world through another unmarked metal door, climb a flight of stairs, and arrive in a large, well-lit room separated by row after row of solid gray partitions. It's like any other modern office space, and I fully expect to see Garfield cartoons and family snapshots tacked up on the barren walls. But there's nothing in these cubicles but a contingent of guised-up dinosaurs, each speaking on their own separate phone, jabbering away at a low, easygoing pace. Dino smells flow down the makeshift corridors, mixing and merging with one another into a soupy pine melange.

"Big place," I say. "Who runs the joint?"

"Just some friends." We enter a small, glass-walled room. "Please, take a seat. You'll find some pastries on the table behind you."

Sure enough, there's all manner of tasty dessert treats lining the shaky card table set up in the corner, and I've almost downed a scrumptious-looking fruit tart and a cup full of punch before I remember that even though I'm playing an innocent rube, I can't fall too deeply into character. I know nothing about this place or these people, including whether or not they have a tendency to drug their new recruits. "You know, I had a big lunch," I say. "I'm not very hungry." Ernie echoes my sentiments.

"Fine, then," says Bob, his expression not changing in the least, "let's get started. I'm sure you'll be amazed—I know I was."

Ernie and I sink into cushioned leather seats around a solid wooden desk, pointedly making ourselves as comfortable as possible. As Bob opens up a large wooden cabinet on the far wall with a shiny brass key, Ernie leans over and whispers, "You get a load of this place? There's money here."

"Question is, where'd they get it?" I mumble back. "Not selling snow globes on Hollywood Boulevard, I'll tell you that much."

With a grunt and a heave, Bob lifts a lead box no more than two feet square out of the cabinet and hauls it over to the top of the table. It lands with an audible thunk. "It's small," he says, "but quite heavy." A moment later, the cabinet is locked up tight once again, and Bob seats himself across from us.

"Who's first?" he asks.

Ernie scoots his chair forward. "Whadda we gotta do?"

"I'll need you to remove your gloves, first of all. The tests must be administered to natural dinosaur flesh. Latex is a poor conductor, to say the least."

"I'll do it," I volunteer. My underclaw's been itching to come out for some time now; it's been at least three days since I disrobed completely, and if I don't wash under this guise sometime soon, I'm going to have my own little fungus circus to take care of. Can't have that—I look terrible with a rash.

Feeling for the buttons hidden beneath my fake mammalian flesh, I work the silicon knobs around and out of their holes until the gloves loosen of their own accord. Then it's just a matter of a light pull with the other hand and I've got the freedom to release my claws into the air. My underclaw is sticking slightly, chattering along its tracks like a stuttering, sputtering go-cart, and I should probably have that looked at by a dino doc at some time in the near future.

"You have a beautiful natural skin," says Bob. "It's a shame you have to cover it up all day."

"Not much of a choice there," I say. "Council doesn't look kindly on a Raptor strolling down Wilshire, huh? My tail might knock out some window displays."

"And if you could go without a guise?" asks Bob. "What then?"

"Pointless question," I respond.

"Hypothetically, then. If you could just rip it off and go natural . . . ?"

"What, all day? If I could . . ." It's an intriguing proposition, I must confess—the freedom to open up and expose my skin to the air, to banish all worries about these girdles and straps and buckles that constrict my flesh and impede my natural movement, to use my tail and my legs and my body the way it feels it *should* be used. "If I could, I would," I admit. "But I can't. So I don't."

Bob's grin is infectious; I find myself smirking along. "Good," he says. "Let's begin."

With a flourish, Bob whips off the cover to the metallic box, exposing a ridiculous gadget time-warped out of the space movies of the 1950s. It's the decapitated head of Robby the Robot, only with an array of lights and buttons and switches and knobs and meters set into the side, each currently dormant save for a single pulsating button.

"This is an Ancestrograph," says Bob, extending his arm, palm upright. He turns to me. "Please, give me your hand."

My initial reaction is to refuse, but I've already come through the subway and down into an undisclosed location with the guy; if he wanted to put me out of my misery, I imagine he would have done so by now. I place my hand in his—the grip firm, insistent, but not painful in any way—and he leads my index finger, claw extended, toward a small, dark opening at the top of the box.

"Retract your claw, if you could." I do so. "Good. It's not usually a problem, but claws have been known to jam the machine. Better safe than sorry." More than happy to comply. It would most likely hurt my singles-bar pickup techniques if I had to walk around with an Ancestrograph permanently attached to my hand.

As my finger disappears into the hole, the device emits a perceptible hum; accordingly, a series of green lights flick on and the needles of the meters start to twitch. Meanwhile, the metal surrounding my finger begins a palpable drop in temperature, and within thirty seconds my once-warm digit is well on its way to becoming a fish stick. I look up at Ernie and issue a game little grin. "Piece of cake," I say. Ernie looks dubious.

"This is the first phase," says Bob. "It's testing your pheromones."

"It's smelling me?"

"Not exactly. That slight cooling sensation you feel is starting a process of condensation. Whatever hormones are seeping out of the pores in your finger are being turned into liquid form by the low temperature, which the machine can then test."

"Test for what?" I ask.

"Purity," is the only reply. I do not ask for an elaboration.

A minute of this, and now my finger is starting to turn numb. Is this their little scheme—frostbite me to death, piece by piece? If he asks me to put any other body part inside that hole I'm going to whack him to next Tuesday.

But just as I'm about to complain, a moment before I yank my digit from the hole and go back to good old-fashioned interrogative techniques involving browbeating and bloodshed, I feel a sharp prick at the tip of my finger.

"Hey!" I shout, my arm flexing backward involuntarily. Pain, small and sharp, accompanied by fluid. Bringing my hand up for inspection—sure enough, there's a small stream of blood trickling down toward my palm. "What the hell was that for?"

But Bob just grins that maddening grin and says, "Taking a blood sample, Vincent. We can't do an Ancestrograph without a blood sample."

"Obviously," drawls Ernie, holding back a chuckle.

"You could have told me."

"And then you wouldn't have done it. As it is, I'm going to have a harder time getting your friend here to go along now."

"Damn straight," says Ernie.

But it doesn't take much in the way of persuasion to convince Ernie to do what all the other cool kids are doing. Bob removes my samples from within the guts of the box—I try to peer inside, but can't make out anything other than a few wires and some diodes—and recalibrates the machine. Ernie unwraps his hand and repeats the procedure, but his anticipation of the pinprick allows him to stay stone-faced when the pain comes. Makes my earlier protestations look foolish, but I bet if situations were reversed, he'd have cried like a Compy.

"We done yet?" Ernie asks.

"Nearly." Bob unveils a new machine attached to the wall—a Pheromonitor, I am told, which looks like a cross between a condom dispenser and a blood-pressure gauge—and places the small vial holding my bodily fluid samples into a receptacle in the bottom. "Let's see what we've got here," says Bob, flipping a switch on the side.

Lights flicker, engines whir, and the vial is snatched up in a furious rush of air. I watch the murky liquid inside being sucked up to the tune of a bubbling vacuum, and the needles on the machine's meters begin to convulse.

Bob clicks his tongue and says, "Oh, this is very . . . interesting. . . ."

I find myself actually leaning forward, trying to decipher the seemingly random blips and beeps of the machine, tracking the needle jumps, attempting to interpret this strange mechanical language. "What's it saying about me?"

"It's determining your ancestral purity," explains Bob. "Over time, each of us has gotten further and further away from the pure dinosaur lineage. We've become mongrels."

"I don't see how," I say. "My parents were Raptors. Their parents were Raptors. None of us can produce kids unless it's with another of the same breed, so I'm as pure as they come."

"I don't mean breed purity, Vincent. I mean dinosaur purity. Every day we put on these costumes is another day we lose part of ourselves. Here, see for yourself."

A long sheet of white accountant's paper has scrolled out of the bottom of the machine, black numbers set in bold, even type filling the page. It's all data and figures and mathematical hoo-ha, but at the very bottom of the page there is what amounts to a declaration of my inadequacies as a member of the greatest species on earth: 32% DINOSAUR NATURAL.

"Thirty-two percent 'dinosaur natural'? What the hell's that supposed to mean?"

Bob says, "Many of us are very upset to learn how far we've fallen—"

"Damn right, I'm upset. Stupid machine—"

"But for every problem, there's a solution. I'll let you in on a little secret—when I had my first Ancestrograph, I was only twenty-nine percent natural."

"You don't say." Doesn't make me feel that much better, to be honest. I'd hope I'm at least a good twenty percent higher than Bob here on any standardized test.

"But now, with a little Progress, my last test read at sixty-seven percent." Bob beams with pride.

And I can't help but find myself a little intrigued by the notion of raising what seem to be arbitrary numbers produced by an obviously rigged machine. "How'd you do it?" I ask.

"Oh, it's not an easy journey," Bob assures me. "But it is a possible one, and the most rewarding experience there is. Here, let's see how your friend measures up, and then we can talk some more."

"I'm on the edge of my seat," Ernie deadpans.

Ernie's fluids take a path similar to mine, and when all the sound and the fury is over and done with, he's listed as 27 percent natural. No two ways about it—I gotta gloat a little. "Beating you by five points, buddy."

"So what's all this mean?" I ask, giving Bob the opening to make the sale.

"It means we can help you," he says. "It means that although your impurities are strong, there's still hope."

I make a show of nodding, thinking it over. "You say 'we.' Is this a business?"

"No, no," says Bob, who has begun to put the machines back into their proper places. "Think of it as a club."

"A club."

"A social club. With benefits." Bob opens another drawer and pulls out two leaflets printed on muted green paper. "Here, each of you take one." The top reads *You're Invited to a Special Event* in a strong, flashy font. "It's short notice, I know—tomorrow night—but I think you'll get a lot out of it."

"What kinda event?" asks Ernie.

"We meet every once in a while to discuss dino-related issues, that sort of thing. It's like a cocktail party. Free food, free drink, music, good friends. A lot of fun, really. And tomorrow night, we'll have a special lecture from Circe."

"Circe?" I know that name from the few weeks I spent studying mythology for the botched Therakropolis case—don't ask, don't ask—but the exact nature of the creature involved eludes me.

"Circe is ninety-six percent pure," says Bob.

"You don't say."

"She's become something like a president to the club. A fascinating lady. Perhaps I can arrange an introduction."

"That'd be super."

Bob gives our hands a hearty shake and says, "As you can see from the invitation, the party is up in the Hollywood Hills. There's driving instructions on the bottom."

I peruse the invite. All's in order. "Sounds like a swell shindig."

"So . . ." says Bob, "can I count you two in?"

No need for signals between us this time; Ernie and I know we're at least halfway into where we want to be, and much faster than we had ever imagined. Finding Rupert and the end of this case is but a mere step or two down a well-paved path.

"We'd love to come to your party," Ernie says, and the deal is done.

Later, after Bob's taken us back up to the street via a separate exit and subway tunnel, Ernie and I hop into the car and make our way down Highland. There's dirty work to be done before the party, and though I hate to deceive my partner, sometimes it's necessary. He doesn't always know what's best for him, the old biddy, and I'm often the one who has to drag him into this decade kicking and screaming.

So I wait until we pass Santa Monica Boulevard, then veer the car sharply into the right lane. That's when it hits my partner—rather sooner than I anticipated, actually, and I hope he doesn't try to leap out of the automobile and make a break for it. Ernie knows full well where I'm taking him, and he fixes me with his best why-hast-thou-forsaken-me stare.

"C'mon, kid, you can't do this to me."

"If we're going to a party in the Hills tomorrow night—"

"It's not a party," says Ernie, his voice rising with something approaching panic. "It's a cult meeting. I got lots of stuff to wear, Vincent."

"I can't let you go to a party—I can't even let you go to a cult meeting—looking like something outta the Sears catalog from 1978. Not if you're gonna be standing by me."

We pull onto Melrose.

The place: The Hills of Hollywood, one vertical mile north of the Boulevard. The time: Round about seven in the P.M. The mood: Tense. The clothing: As stylish as it is uncomfortable. I'm driving, Ernie's complaining, and all is right with the undercover world.

"We get in, we listen to their shpiel, we find Rupert, we get out."

"Works for me, Ern."

"And then I get outta these goddamned silk pants."

I shake my head. "It's not silk—it's linen. It's very in."

Ernie doesn't care; he pulls petulantly at his Calvin Klein shirt and Armani slacks like a five-year-old dressed up for Sunday church. I drive on.

In the twenty-four hours between our marathon session down the corridors of Melrose Avenue—during which time Ernie was introduced to the wonders of all sorts of clothing whose designers do not advertise for Kmart, and whose fabrics do not trace their origins to the Poly or Ester families— and our "club meeting" with the Progressives in the Hollywood Hills, we did some more grunt work trying to track down Minsky's babe of the week. It's not rare that we work multiple cases at the same time. A PI's plate is never, ever full; if it's piled too high, we just get another set of dishes.

First step was trying to find a home address, and though this was easy enough with the help of Dan Patterson, a Bronto friend of mine on the LAPD, the rat hole that Star Josephson used to live in has been red-tagged and condemned by the Board of Health. I guess we could have gone in, tried to case the place, but great cracks had made their way down the exterior walls and across the roof of the building, like crevasses in a glacier, and the whole structure looked ready to collapse under its own weight. Unfortunately for us, even the more daredevil mammals and dinos had abandoned the joint, and roaches don't give out forwarding addresses, so we were on our own.

We had a few pictures—Polaroids, mostly, snapped by Minsky in a fit of hormone-fueled lust—and we showed 'em around with all the vigor we could muster, eliciting gasps from old ladies and knowing leers from young gents.

"I know the tramp," one particularly foul-smelling Compy told us. His name was Sweetums, and he was a pimp working the dino hooker trade up on Sunset. I've used Sweetums before, mostly to find missing girls, as he's the kind of pimp who makes them go missing in the first place. Not your midafternoon tea kind of fellow, but he knows what he knows, and he always needs cash. Poor sap's got a furious saffron habit, and that delicious toxin doesn't come cheap. "I seen her cooling her heels out on the Boulevard."

"And you tried to take her in," I said.

"Take her in, break her in, it's all in the game," cooed Sweetums.

"You're a saint. Just tell me where to find her." I emphasized my last point with two folded twenties, and Sweetums snatched them between his teeth, shaking the bills around like a dog with a chew toy.

The pimp licked his lips and pocketed the money. "Last visit I paid her was at the St. Regis Hotel. Sweet piece of tail . . ."

"St. Regis?"

"Up on Franklin," said Sweetums. "Rents by the minute."

The St. Regis manager wasn't too keen to give out info on the hotel's guests, but it only took a sawbuck to affect hotel policy. Yes, she'd been staying in the hotel, and yes, she had a room on the third floor, but no, he hadn't seen her in over a week. But there were no foul smells emanating from under the door, so he didn't feel a need to contact the police, especially since she paid for an entire month up front.

By the time Ernie and I decided to sneak around the back of the St. Regis and break into the tart's hotel room, it was nearing five o'clock and we had to get back to the office and change for the Progressive party.

"Star can wait," Ernie pointed out. "Dames like that, they might move around, but they don't *go* anywhere."

Now, two hours later, Ernie's probably wishing we were still tracking down the mistress, if only because he could do so in a workshirt and chinos. But not here—not now—not faced with the kind of extravagant opulence that would send a Saudi sheik running for his interior decorator.

This is not a house in front of us. I'd even hesitate to call it a mansion. It's a gargantuan affair, white marble on top of white marble, pillars and columns and a whole sampler of Greek architecture thrown together into a single, monstrous parody of the Acropolis.

"You seeing this?" I ask Ernie, but all he can do is stare, slack-jawed, at a home that, even by LA standards, is fantastically ostentatious.

We drive up to a large wrought-iron gate set off to one side of the house, and a uniformed guard emerges from a large white door. The setting sun bounces off the marble, reflecting a steady stream of light into my eyes, throwing the guard into sharp relief.

"Can I see your invitation, please?" he asks, and though I'm dazzled by the sunlight, I'm aware enough to catch the scents of popcorn and model airplane glue coming from his direction.

Ernie produces the flyers and hands them to the guard, who inspects them casually and reaches behind him for a button. "You're cleared. Just go right on into the main house."

The main house. "You mean—this isn't—this thing here—"

"This is the guardhouse," he says. "And sometimes a ballroom. But mostly the guardhouse."

Suffice it to say that the main house is to the guardhouse what the planet Jupiter is to my ass. Contemplating its size is like attempting to get your brain around the concept of infinity—not much point, and it's only going to wind up in a migraine. It's nice to see that they've kept the architectural parody going, and that this Goliath of a domicile would be right at home in ancient Athens, provided, of course, that they hadn't spent all their money fighting off the Spartans.

Ernie and I park the car amid a cornucopia of makes and models—there's two hundred cars here if there's a dozen, and still the lot is barely half full—and trudge our way up a set of stairs set into the side of a hill.

"I wanna know where they get this money," says Ernie, panting a bit from the climb.

"Where'd *they* get it?" I say. "Hell, I wanna know where *I* can get a piece."

Even before we reach the front door—twenty feet high, shining alabaster, brass doorknobs the size of my head—and even before it opens for us of its own accord—swinging wide, no creaks, no rustles, just a smooth, simple glide—and even before we step into a hallway filled with archaeological treasures and works of art I am sure no human has ever seen before— original portraits by Modigliani, Rubens, Pollock, all dino masters—Ernie and I pick up on the array of scents twisting and braiding around one another into an olfactory licorice whip, streaming out of the house, bursting from beneath the doors, the windows, squiggling out from behind the insulation. The smells come at us with force, as if exploding from within, shoved along their way.

"Welcome, brothers," comes a soft voice as Ernie and I step into the hallway, our shoes clacking on the marble floor below. "May I take your belongings?"

A thin female Ornithomimus holds out her hand, beckoning us closer. "We came empty-handed," I apologize. "Shoulda brought a gift, right? I'm lousy at party etiquette."

The Ornitho laughs, her cheeks bouncing fetchingly. "By belongings, I mean your guises. May I take them?" She points to a sign above her head: PLEASE CHECK YOUR COSTUME AT THE DOOR.

I issue a game little laugh, but my partner is not amused.

"Can't believe you made me buy this crap," Ernie grumbles as we undress in a shuttered room next to the guise check. "You set me up with all this silk and leather and fancy shoes, and we ain't even supposed to wear our guises here, let alone this shit. Almost a grand for one outfit, and it's wasted."

"You'll have it for the next time."

"Ain't gonna be a next time, I promise you that. After tonight, I bonfire this garbage."

We disrobe, then begin the real task of removing our costumes. Ernie and I help each other with the G-series, and quickly remove the rest of the trusses and buckles ourselves. My mask is sticking a little, the epoxy I applied yesterday morning a bit too strong for the job, and it takes a thin layer of my own hide with it as I rip the fake face away.

Ernie might be getting up there—though he's never admitted his age to me, he's at least fifteen years my senior, I'd bet—but back in his natural form, you wouldn't sense anything over-the-hill about the guy. His Carnotaur muscles are quite evident beneath his dark brown hide, and I know he's not squeamish about using them when the droppings hit the fan.

We hand our guises over to the Ornithomimus, and she carefully places them on a row of hangers, one for each series in the costume, tagging them all with the same number so as to keep the set together. I'm number 313, and Ernie's number 314.

Carefully, she places the hangers holding our costumes onto what looks like a dry-cleaning rack behind her and presses a blue button set into the wall. Two tall, thin doors swing wide and the rack begins to move, the hangers going with it, disappearing into a room beyond. For a second, I can make out row after row of human skins hanging in orderly fashion like a ghastly war experiment, limbs drooping limply to the ground. Then the doors close, the Ornithomimus sits back down, and we're directed down the hallway and to our right.

It's a ballroom like any other, no big deal, nothing impressive, except this one is inside a house and larger than all the apartments I've ever lived in put together. About three hundred dinosaurs mill about unguised, a veritable slime-fest of pheromones choking the air, staining the walls, the ceiling. Gonna be hell for whatever team of housekeepers has to clean this place out Monday morning.

I see Raptors and Stegosaurs and Brontos and Ankies and Hadrosaurs and pretty much every one of the sixteen species that survived the Great Showers sixty-five million years ago, and though I can't find a Compy in here at the moment, I'm sure I'll come across one when I least expect—or want—to do so.

And standing among it all, fifty feet tall if it's an inch, a center-piece to make all other centerpieces hide their heads in shame: the perfectly preserved, expertly assembled, fossilized body of an ancient ancestor. It's a T-Rex—an original—a party-goer who showed up at the door sixty million years too early and couldn't subsist on cocktail-hour nibbles for that long. The modern dinos in the room mill around the dead giant as if it's not even there, barely giving the skeleton any notice. Odd—I thought these freaks worshiped the ancestors. Shouldn't they be bowing? Chanting? Offering up a virgin or two?

Making my way through the stifling crowd, I notice something missing, though it takes me a second to put my finger on it: no plates. There's always appetizers at these functions, and more often than not I find myself trying to balance delicate cocktail conversation with a goblet of water (or wine, at human events) and a plate full of toast and spread. Here, the dinos have the drinks, but they don't have the food. Across the room, near the dance floor, I see a Hadrosaur carrying a covered silver tray. I approach.

"Care for an appetizer, sir?" he asks, and I nod hungrily.

I expect the waiter to whip off the cover with a flourish, but all he does is open a small slot at the top of the tray and look at me expectantly.

"Perhaps I didn't make myself clear," I say. "I'd like something to eat."

"Yes, sir," he drawls, "and that's why I've opened the slot."

"Isn't it easier to just take off the cover?"

Surprise and confusion on his face, one of those looks I get from witnesses sometimes when they think I've had a few too many blows to the head. "Goodness, no, sir. They would escape."

Escape? I've never seen a cocktail wiener with feet before. Enough with this. I reach out and shove my hand down that hole—

And into a writhing pile of spaghetti.

I yank my hand back with enough force to send the tray smashing to the ground, the cover popping off with a furious clatter. A mess of small black snakes, each no more than a half-dollar around, varying in length from six to twelve inches, slither out of their confines and quickly spread throughout the ballroom in all the cardinal directions, eliciting a cavalcade of carnal shrieks and screams. The waiter fixes me with a hard stare.

"Why did you have to go and do that, sir? Now we'll have a feeding frenzy on our hands."

And indeed we do. While a few of the other dinosaurs in the room are acting much as I did—jumping backward, avoiding the beasts at any cost—the majority of them are snatching up the critters with their bare hands and shoving them into their mouths, past their jaws, swallowing them whole if need be. Laughter and roars of culinary ecstasy fill the air, and I find myself ashamed for having been rattled by what isn't even a rattler. They're garden snakes, nothing more, and despite our tenuous genetic link, none of my brethren have any qualms about digesting the buggers wholesale.

Ernie comes up behind me, mumbling through his lips. "Good party," he says.

I turn to find a small, green tail—still wiggling, mind you— poking out from between my partner's lips. I hold back my strong desire to cringe.

"That a snake?" I ask.

"Newt," he mumbles, and finishes it off with a hearty swallow. "Been a while since I had fresh meat."

As the last remaining appetizers are rounded up and summarily digested, Ernie and I take a spin around the room, scoping out the crowd, sniffing for familiar scents.

"He's not here," Ernie tells me.

"You remember what he smells like?" I'm surprised. As far as I know, the last time Ernie and Rupert saw each other was well over five years ago.

"Coffee, maybe . . . dessert tray . . . Can't say as I definitely remember," says Ernie, "but I know I'd recognize the boy if I smelled him. Hell, he spent half a year living at our place after he got back from that god-awful India trip. Smelled like curry for a few months—I remember that for sure, so I should be able to pick it up."

A trio of dinos scurry out of a pair of swinging double doors and begin setting up audio equipment at the back end of the dance floor. A microphone, some speakers, and a host of electrical cables snake out from beneath eighteen-inch risers, which are quickly bolted together to form a makeshift stage. It's all very Woodstock, and I feel the strong urge to flick a lighter and scream out a song request. Minutes pass, and Ernie wanders off for more food. Meanwhile, I'm watching these Raptor roadies go to town when I feel a tap on the rough hide of my shoulder.

"This turf's covered, Rubio. You're steppin' over the line."

The voice isn't familiar, but the tone certainly is. Ooze on top of grease with a generous helping of smarm. I turn, trying to fix some type of grin to my face. It's the kind of thing he'll expect, and though I don't care whether or not I alienate the guy, I've got too much business to attend to without catering to his whining.

"Sutherland," I say, catching a strong whiff of that burnt-milk-and-spoiled-egg scent with which this rival PI is unfortunately saddled. "What the hell are you doing here?"

"I got cases, see," he says, drawing out his lines in a horrific Cagney impression. "I got a job to do, and to do it right."

"Can the nightclub act," I suggest, "and stick to the day job."

He drops the accent and asks, "Your partner here?"

I nod over toward Ernie, who gives Sutherland a perfunctory nod and raises another newt—this one struggling, kicking, not ready to meet his reptilian maker—in salutation.

"So," I ask, "what's the story? You're on a job . . . ?"

"Undercover work," he whispers. "Real hush-hush. I get a lot of the big jobs now, you know."

Now that he's hot-to-trot with the boss man's sister, sure he gets the big cases, despite the fact that Sutherland is probably one of the least-qualified private investigators I've ever come across. This guy couldn't find Go on a Monopoly board.

"So Mr. Teitelbaum thinks I'm a great detective . . ." he rambles on, ". . . and wants to start talking—get this—*partner.*" He emphasizes this last part with a tight forehead scrunch, a difficult move when the area above your eyes isn't much other than a few bony plates fused into a marginally flexible mass. Ankylosaurs have difficulty expressing emotion visually. Think Al Gore. "So long as I finish off this case right."

"So that's why you're here. For this big case."

"Right. But it's real secret, so keep it under wraps, willya?"

"What am I gonna say?" I ask. "You didn't tell me about it."

"Exactly." He looks relieved.

"I mean, it's not like some kid got mixed up in this Progress thing, went all nutso and broke off ties with the outside world, and the family came to the office and wants someone to break 'em out. . . ."

Suddenly crestfallen, cheeks blanching of color, shoulders drooping into sharp slopes of defeat, Sutherland slams a fist into his open palm. "Goddamnit! God—damn—it! I knew Teitelbaum would send another team in, I goddamned knew it!"

"No, no, he didn't—"

"Now we gotta split the fees, right? You're taking half—your partner gets the other half—damn it all . . ."

"Hey, hey—"

I'm sorry, but Mr. Sutherland can't be reached right now. He's lost in the depths of self-pity. Please leave a message. "Look—you take it, Rubio. I don't need to be here. I'm no good at this—"

"Lower your voice and quit whining."

"I should have been a doctor. That's what my mother wanted me to be."

"Sutherland—Sutherland! Shut up and listen to me." Amazingly, he does so. I've noticed that we're drawing a crowd, so I pull the hack off to one side and lower my voice to a loud whisper. "We're not here for Teitelbaum."

The beginnings of relief. "You're not?"

"No. And we're not on your case. We've got a private matter, probably similar to yours, but not the same thing. You can keep your stupid fees."

"I have a mortgage to pay," he says, a semblance of color— appropriate shades of brown and green—returning to his face.

"I know you do."

"I have kids."

"I know." They are ugly made flesh. "They're adorable."

"Oh. Oh. Oh, good. Thank you."

"No need to thank me. Go get a glass of water and have a seat. Put your head between your legs, take deep breaths." I pat the PI on the back and urge him toward a nearby waiter. "Grab a newt, I hear they're delish." Sutherland trots off, and I can't help but chuckle a bit.

Ernie walks over and I clue him in; he shakes his head in resignation. "See, kid, we ain't so special. I betcha half the dinos in here are dicks on the job. Wherever you got confused kids, you got parents willing to shell out dough to look for 'em."

The roadies in the corner have just about finished setting up and plugging in all the audio equipment they've lugged out onto the dance floor, and it's not long before a tall, muscular Iguanodon strolls onto the stage, long neck spikes glistening in the spotlight, the wooden risers creaking beneath his considerable weight. His hide is a deep emerald green with not a miscolored fleck on it, and though I don't usually feel complexion envy, I can't help but stare in awe at the sheer natural beauty of those scales.

A tap on the microphone, the requisite squeal, and in a resoundingly deep voice, the Iguanodon says, "Welcome, brothers and sisters."

"Welcome!" comes the overwhelming reply, the shouts buffeting me in all directions. I notice that a good quarter of us remain silent, bouncing back and forth on our feet, unsure of what to do. Recent converts and potential inductees, I would imagine.

"If everyone would take a seat . . ." And with this, the majority of dinosaurs in the room plop onto the floor without ceremony, and I'm shocked to find that the marble doesn't crack and buckle beneath the sudden assault.

"Please," says the Iguanodon, speaking directly to those of us who remain on our feet. "Anywhere is fine, no chairs are needed here."

Shrugging, Ernie and I take our positions on the floor. It's relatively cold, but nothing new to me—my desk chair is broken at one armrest, and dumps me onto the office hardwood once every few days. Most of the time I'm too lazy to drag myself back into the seat, so I do the rest of the day's work from that position instead.

"Before we begin," continues the Iguanodon, "I'd like to welcome and congratulate all of you who were at our convocation last week and decided to return and learn more about yourselves and your ancestry. I'd also like to welcome those of you who are joining us for the first time. It's a long journey from where you are now to where you could be, but it's the most rewarding, fulfilling journey you can take." Seems I've heard that somewhere before.

"My name is"—and here he gives one of those elongated, strained growls that has no mammalian equivalent whatsoever—"but until you get the hang of it, feel free to call me Samuel.

"We'll have punch and more to eat after the talk today, so be sure to stick around and get to know your fellow dinos. We're nothing as one million, but everything as one." I consider asking for a clarification on that point, but Ernie bats my hand down even as it rises of its own accord.

And now, as the Iguanodon steps down off the riser, a spotlight illuminates a Velociraptor musical trio set up on the opposite side of the dance floor. They're wielding instruments the likes of which I've never seen before, and, as they begin to play, I realize that I've never heard the likes of it, either. There's a long, stringed instrument that could pass for a bass, but its composite elements are nothing more than a stick and what looks like an elongated tendon or ligament. Some sort of conch shell, easily ten times larger than average, serves as a blaring horn, and a set of flat rocks, expertly banged upon by the largest of the dinosaurs, serves to create a rhythm. They all croon together, a series of growls and whoops coming across as lyrics, and though it's easily the most horrific cacophony I've ever heard, though the crowd is barely even swaying back and forth, I can feel an electric hum of intensity growing within them. They love this stuff. This younger generation has no taste; someone should introduce them to the blues.

Another spot, this one green, swings up the wall and holds on a set of double doors high above the stage. There's no balcony there, just a closed portal set into the wall. I'm surprised I hadn't noticed these before, but my attention had mostly been diverted toward the floor since the snake incident, on the off chance that one of the appetizers had escaped and would be looking to make a home somewhere on me. The band's number picks up in tempo and volume—rocks banging louder, horn honking harsher—and the tense passion in this crowd rises.

A whisper from my left. "She's coming . . ."

And the doors fly open, slamming into the wall behind with tremendous force. The dark corridor beyond is suddenly filled with the green spotlight, and then, a second later, a ravishing female Raptor leaps to the edge of the doorway, balancing precariously thirty feet above the ballroom floor. From here, I can make out the long, delicate lines curving through that supple body, the graceful swan curve of the neck, the tremendous definition in the underclaws, the meaty slab of a tail, and that shining, almost iridescent hide soaking up the rays from the spotlight and blasting it back out at the crowd, blinding us with its brilliance.

Before I have a chance to mumble my amazement, the Raptor raises her snout to the sky and lets loose with a bone-chilling wail, the corners of her mouth turning up, up, and out, teeth snapping at the ceiling, tongue waggling through the air. The crowd, as one, leaps to their feet and begins a furious round of applause as the Raptor flexes those powerful yet delicate leg muscles and leaps away from the wall, falling toward the dance floor below. I can't bear to watch.

But it's a perfect landing as she uses her tail to take the brunt of the force, and a moment later she's standing at the microphone, soaking in the crowd's adulation.

"Welcome," she says, her voice feminine yet oddly deep, a tightly spun web of varying tones. "Welcome, brothers and sisters."

"Good entrance," Ernie mumbles to me.

"For those of you who don't know me," says the Raptor once the crowd has quieted down and returned to their seated positions, "my name is Circe, and I've been on the road to Progress for many years now. It's been a hard path, but a fulfilling one, and I believe I am closer to the ancestors now than I have ever been before. I believe that we can *all* be closer to the ancestors now, if we can only believe in ourselves and in our shared history. We can all learn to Progress from where we are now."

Circe motions toward Samuel, the Iguanodon whom we'd seen earlier, and he wheels over a large television set attached to a familiar-looking machine.

"Ancestrograph," I mutter to Ernie, and he nods.

The crowd had begun to murmur, with either approval or disdain, I can't tell which, as Circe retracts her claw and places the first delicate finger of her right hand into that dark little hole. The Iguanodon presses the appropriate buttons, and the contraption spins to life, working whatever voodoo and hoodoo it needs to do to come up with that nonsensical number. Soon, Circe's fluids are transferred to the vacuum tube, and the lights, meters, and needles start their crazy little dance.

Hush from the crowd. They're holding their breath. If they pass out, maybe I can raid the kitchen and find some real food.

After a burst of static, the thirty-six-inch television screen lights up with the pronouncement on Circe's purity: 96.8% DINOSAUR NATURAL.

A new thunderous round of roars and howls echoes throughout the ballroom, and I can only hope that either the walls are soundproofed or whatever neighbors live within a few miles of this home are under the impression that MGM is filming an *Out of Africa* sequel nearby.

"Please, please," says Circe, clearly basking in the glow of admiration while still maintaining a distinct air of humility, "take your seats, take your seats. I have a story to impart to you. I want to tell you all how we came to be where we are today."

"This oughta be a doozy," says Ernie, and we settle in for a good listen.

t is a story from not so long ago," Circe begins, "though to some of you whose purity has become muddied over the years with human effluvia, it may seem like ancient history. But remember—ancient history to the mammals is nothing more than yesterday to us.

"I first heard this story from our great founder Raal"—this name my best approximation of the grunt she emitted—"and he heard it from his parents, who heard it from their parents, and so on. It has lived through the ages, and now I pass it on to you."

"This Raal must be the vacuum salesman," Ernie mumbles to me, and I'm impressed at how well he pronounces the difficult dino name. "The one who started up the cult and then died off."

"Less than one million years ago," continues Circe, "our ancestors were faced with a problem. A certain branch of the hominid family, a species which they had been watching carefully for some time, had begun to evolve along a different path than that of their close relatives, the great apes. The change had become more significant, more pronounced over the last few hundred thousand years, and the great Councils were concerned that the evolution was somehow speeding up, that these hominids whose braincase was quickly enlarging might soon learn a form of communication, and with it, create a society. This was something never before seen in the course of our shared history: a potential rival.

"But the Council members urged caution. Surely these . . . monkeys could pose no threat to our well-being. They were gangly, they were dumb, they were loners, for the most part. And they were small, much smaller than we were. Even though we were no longer the size of the Great Ancestors, our forefathers of a million years ago still stood taller and broader than the dinosaur of today—ten, twelve feet at the minimum."

"How's she supposed to know this?" Ernie grumbles to me.

"It's a story. You heard of stories, right?"

Circe goes on. "But it soon came to light that one band of humans had indeed organized itself and begun to live in a loosely based nomad society around the area that has now become Ghana. There was concern that the other hominids would do likewise within the next ten or twenty thousand years, and that something ought to be done about it.

"The most vocal of those urging action were three brothers, whose names and races are unfortunately lost to us. But these brothers were widely known to be the strongest, bravest of their kind, to have battled other natural predators with great skill and valor, and so it was decided that they should attempt to make contact with that first group of hominids.

"The first brother was a genial fellow—kind, giving, and always had a knack for putting others at ease. The second was uncommonly large and powerful, and some say he stood higher than the trees in the forest. And the third was particularly cunning, able to wrap his mind around the sharpest of problems. They were a perfect choice.

"The brothers wanted to go together—that had always been their way, and that indeed was how their own forefathers had defeated an attempted coup by a dinosaur faction earlier that eon. But the Council had mandated that each of the brothers would go singly to the valley of the hominids, and, as we know, when it comes to the Council, rules are rules. We may have evolved some in the last million years, but the Councils have not." Laughter here from the audience, and I find myself chuckling along, caught up in the story's flow.

"The first brother set out for the valley and, after a long and arduous journey, found his way to the outskirts of the hominid camp. These prehumans were living out in the open back then, not even bright enough to cover themselves with a simple lean-to or hut. The first brother hid in the forest and watched them for days, trying to figure out how best to communicate with these new creatures. After some time, he decided that the best course of action would be a direct and simple approach, perhaps with some pantomime thrown in for good measure.

"At dawn one morning, he strolled into the valley, head held high, trying to win them over with his best smile. He wanted to welcome them to the race of sentient beings, to glean their intentions toward the valley and toward the dinosaurs, and to see if they would be interested in forging a friendship.

"He was massacred on sight."

An electric shock passes through the crowd, rocking us all backward as one. Circe's voice hit a hard note with that last part, a flick of vitriol hitting hard on the word *massacred,* and it did the job right.

"When a few days had passed, and they had yet to hear from the first brother, the second was sent out to see what had become of him. He reached the valley quickly and proceeded to do the same as his sibling before him—hide in the forest nearby and observe the creatures before making his move. But that night, as he watched from a distance, he saw the whole tribe of hominids feasting on his brother's carcass, shoving gnawed bones and bloody entrails into their disgusting, greedy little mouths.

"Without thought, without any preparation, the enraged dinosaur rushed into the clearing, teeth bared, claws slashing out, and fell upon the unsuspecting hominids, bloodlust erasing all thoughts of danger or consequence.

"He killed twelve of them before he, too, was slaughtered.

"Now quite some time had passed, and neither of the brothers had returned. The Council had no choice but to send out the final one of the trio, and he set out willingly, eager to learn what had become of his siblings. But the third brother was the cunning one, the cautious one, and he took his time coming to the valley. He examined every trail, every path, attempting to get a true feel for how the hominids acted and hunted and ate and lived.

"So by the time he arrived at the valley and, like the others before him, hid in the woods to watch the hominids from afar, his brothers had already been consumed and their bones picked clean. All that remained of them were a pair of partially intact skeletons scattered across the valley floor.

"Perhaps because the remains of his brothers were unrecognizable to him, or perhaps because it was simply his nature, the third brother did not become enraged. He did not set out immediately to destroy the creatures, nor did he step down into the valley in the hope of forging a peace treaty between the species.

"What he did was come up with a plan.

"He tucked his tail between his legs and secured it there with a soft, flexible sapling, tying the edges around his waist. He covered his body in mud, slathering it across his scales, so that his natural hide looked like nothing more than that of any other creature who hadn't bathed in some time. He retracted his claws. He broke off the two teeth that showed even when his mouth was closed, snapping them at the base. He pulled back his ears and touched up his eyes and covered his snout in a homemade mask of twigs and branches. He slathered himself in feces, so as to obscure his natural smell.

"The next morning, costumed up in the first guise ever, he walked out of the forest and into the heart of that hominid camp, sat down in the middle, and grunted along with the best of them. His costume was shabby, of course, and nowadays would seem downright ludicrous, but the humans were slightly dumber then than they are now, and they accepted the dinosaur as one of their own. That night, he even went so far as to partake in the marrow of one of his own brothers' bones, so as not to raise suspicion. He looked like a hominid, he acted like a hominid, and he smelled like a hominid.

"And that night, when all of those upright mammals had gone to sleep, the third brother crept up to each and every one of the creatures, and cleanly, quietly, and efficiently slashed them all to death."

A great cheer goes up from the audience, as if we're personally welcoming the great and conquering dinosaur back from the battle. Circe raises her arms for silence.

"Now—can anyone tell me if this dinosaur, who tricked the humans by guising himself up as one of their ilk, was a hero?"

A few hands pop up instantly—brownnosers, no doubt, who've heard this story before and know the appropriate response. I chuckle at their eagerness to impress the teacher, but my laughter soon dribbles to a stop when I see that long, green finger being pointed in my direction.

"You," says Circe, and there's no doubt that she's turned her attention to the one Raptor PI in the room who isn't interested in playing twenty questions. "Tell me, was he a hero?"

Gotta stammer, a little hemming and hawing. "I don't—I, ah—"

"Gut instinct. Hero or not?"

"Hero," I say. "He killed those who had killed his brothers. Revenge factor right there." I assume this is the correct answer, considering that the whole story seemed to be primarily up-with-dinos intensive.

"True," says Circe, and the class goody-goodies fix me with envious glares. "But in doing so, did he not compromise his identity? Did he not force himself into an unnatural position?"

"Yeah, sure," I say, "but it's nothing different from what we're doing now."

An ooooh from the crowd—including Ernie, the bastard—and I realize quickly that I've just made Circe's point for her. But that smile she shoots my way smoothes over all possible feelings of ill will, and I find myself gravitating toward those beautiful pointy teeth and that shimmering green hide.

"What that one dinosaur started one million years ago as a means to avenge his family's death has become our way of life. Some may say he was a hero, but we believe he was nothing more than the catalyst to our eventual downfall."

Murmurs of agreement as those head-of-the-class shoe polishers turn their noses up in my direction and go back to their business of being superior.

"I don't tell you all of this to make you angry," Circe says to the audience. "In fact, I don't tell you all of this to make you feel *anything*. That's not my job, to tell you how to feel, to give you . . . propaganda . . . despite what others might say. But it is important for each and every one of you to know who we are and where we came from, and why the dinosaurs of today are so much different from our true ancestors."

Sure, I got it, but she didn't have to make me feel like a problem student.

"Pooched that one pretty good, kid," jokes Ernie. I don't respond.

"This is where the issue of purity comes in," Circe continues. "How natural are we as dinosaurs? How far have we strayed from our lineage? Stories tell of the days when our pheromones would carry for miles, when we could sense large packs of one another across entire seas. Now we're lucky if we can sniff each other out across the dinner table."

Around here is when she launches full force into a lecture about purity and naturalism and the torture we dinos put ourselves through every day, both physical and emotional, in order to blend in with the so-called ruling majority. I learn, over approximately one hour's time, how the costumes we put on actually absorb certain chemicals, sapping us of our natural pheromones; how studies have shown that over prolonged exposure in a guise, a dino's brain waves will actually become more similar to that of a mammal's; how our Jekyll-and-Hyde, persona-by-necessity lifestyle has splintered us into thinking of ourselves as sixteen separate races of dinosaur, as opposed to one single species. It all makes a heck of a lot of sense, especially when it's coming from the beautiful, sensuous snout of Circe.

Ernie is not quite as taken by this creature as I am; he uses the claws from one hand to pick at the other, occasionally looking up and nodding in mock enlightenment.

It's another half-hour, perhaps, before the speech is all good and done, and another ten minutes after that before our applause settles down. As the band begins to play again—this time, the music jibing a bit more with my jangled ears—Circe takes leave of the stage, disappearing among a crowd of well-wishers.

"That was a big freaking waste," Ernie says. "I didn't smell him the whole time."

"Smell who?"

"Rupert."

"Rupert who?" I ask, and Ernie slaps me in the back of the head. Now it all comes rushing back—the ex-wife, the brother, the fact that I'm standing in the central room of some sort of cult. Whatever brain-fog I fell into during Circe's speech dissipates, and I shake my head a few times to clear the last cobwebs.

Ernie puts a hand on my shoulder, catches my eyes with his. "You all right?"

"Never better. Let's scram."

But it's not quite that easy. A receiving line has been set up by the door, Circe greeting her visitors and bidding farewell to the departing guests. Three beefy dinos, Samuel the Iguanodon one of them, stand by her side, watching the crowd with what is certainly dubious intent, insisting that anyone who wishes to leave first pay their respects to our esteemed hostess. There's something just short of paranoia in those eyes, and Ernie and I realize that it's best to go with the flow. We take our place in the back of the line and slowly make our way forward.

"You catch that?" Ernie asks me after a few minutes spent shuffling forward six inches at a go.

"Catch what?"

"That scent—the cappuccino-flavored one."

I flare my nostrils as wide as they will go and take in a deep breath of the surrounding air. A rush of pheromones invade the olfactory nerves, and I have to close my eyes, my ears, shut down my other senses, in order to concentrate on separating the wildly varying scents. Yes . . . Somewhere in there, intertwined with the pine nuts and the oranges and the ocean breeze, is a distinct smell of after-dinner coffee drink, flavored lightly with cream, maybe a hint of chocolate.

"That's him?" I ask. "He's a mocha?"

"Can't be certain, but I think so."

We take a quick scan of the room, trying to direct our snouts toward the different dinos standing about us so as to isolate their individual scents. This is not simple—the practice of direct-line smelling is more art than science, and some would claim more hocus than pocus. The line continues to move forward, and we continue to come closer to our brief audience with Circe.

"Quick run past the dame, we shake hands, say our thanks, and then we get ready to track him. Clear your nose, for what it's worth."

It's another twenty minutes before we reach the front of the line, Ernie ahead of me. I'm anxious to get this part over with so that we can find Rupert, take him home, and close the case so that I can get in a good workout tomorrow morning. It's been three weeks since I've played my *Richard Simmons Sweatin' with the Stegosaur* tape, and my hind thighs are feeling a mite paunchy.

I stand back as Ernie approaches Circe and issues what I imagine to be polite thanks and some insincere toadying. I fully expect to repeat the performance.

But when I'm actually standing in front of her, when I'm fully face-to-face with that voluptuous Raptor body and those full Raptor lips, it's hard for me to even stammer out "Thank you."

"I hope I didn't embarrass you," she says. "With my question."

"No, it's—I learned a lot." And then, like the babbling moron I have instantly become, I repeat, "Learned a lot."

There's an intoxicating aroma streaming out of Circe's pores, and it's more than just the strong whiff of a Raptor female that's got me going. At this close distance, my head is spinning from whatever magical smells are dripping out of her body; Circe's essence smells of the natural intoxicants— basil, oregano, cilantro. Never before have I encountered a dino with such pheromones, and I doubt I will again. The room tilts to the left, and I try to adjust my head in order to counterbalance. It doesn't work.

"What's your name?" she asks me.

"Vincent," I say. "My name's Vincent." Then, because I haven't made quite enough a fool of myself this evening, I give it one more go-round. "That's me. Vincent."

I'm being drawn in, somehow. Circe is three feet away, then two, then one. Those eyes, that snout are encompassing the whole of my vision, and the scent grows stronger. Even beyond basil and its brothers now, moving into thyme and rosemary and fennel—all of the most powerful herbs I've ever known—the scents are invading my head via these two wide nostrils, taking long, powerful strokes up my sinuses, spawning upstream toward my brain, and every care and worry in my head liquefies at once, pouring out through my ears . . .

"Vincent, it's wonderful to meet you," she says, and I can feel my lips curling into a goofy smile. Part of me is quite aware of this transformation from a detached private investigator to a drooling, dribbling schoolboy, but the other part is happy to lower the safety bar and hang on for the ride.

A hand on the back of my head—and Circe draws me closer, tighter. Is she going to kiss me? I pucker, waiting for the sweet feeling of flesh on flesh, but my head is pulled past those lips, past that perfect left cheek, and around to the back of the neck. I get it. I get it. I prepare to hold my breath. Can't do this.

No time. Before I even have a chance to ready myself for that delicious smell-taste of Circe's pheromones, I am hit full-on by a tidal wave of condiments cascading over my body, drenching my senses in a herbological assault.

And then I'm no longer in a house in the Hollywood Hills; I'm no longer standing in a receiving line, bent awkwardly and possibly obscenely over our host, my nose pressed to the back of her neck. In fact, I'm no longer in the City of Angels or its environs, and I'm no longer in this millennium.

Instead, I'm running through an endless forest, the trees overhead scraping the sky, leaves the size of Chryslers, my legs blurring as they churn faster and faster across the muddy ground, a warm wind whipping past my hide. A sweet wail fills the night and I find myself calling out in my own Raptor-tones, answering in some language that, although I have never heard it before, trips naturally off my tongue.

Circe is beside me, running strong.

A cliff approaches in the distance, and we increase our speed, some primal need accelerating our run into madness. There's no slowing down now, no stopping as the cliff looms larger, the overhang and infinite drop below coming sharply into view. A turn of my head, a look toward my companion, and she grabs my claw in hers and smiles as we leap high into the air and off the cliff, rising higher and higher before gravity takes its toll and we begin the inevitable plummet . . .

We make love on the way down.

incent! Vincent!" A voice coming from somewhere in the forest. My eyes are closed. I am peaceful. The birds are singing, the lizards are licking, and all is well and good.

"Don't make me knock your block off, kid. Snap to, we got work to do."

It's Ernie. Why is Ernie in the forest? Where did Circe go? Reluctantly, I open my eyes, squinting at the bright light that invades my vision. Has the sun come up already?

Hallway chandelier, glowing bright. Works of art, framed with skill and class. The ballroom is behind me, and Circe continues to receive her guests.

"I smelled him back this way," Ernie says. "We gotta get tracking."

"Ernie," I say, my mouth thick, still stuffed with the meaty air of that prehistoric world, "was I . . . ? I mean . . . did you . . . When you said goodbye to Circe . . ."

"Nice enough gal," he says. "For a cult leader."

"No—I mean, did you smell her?"

"Sure, I smelled her. Kinda herby, right?"

I know it's not possible for a dinosaur to regulate her smells—our gland production is simply a product of our metabolism, chugging away at a steady pace. It can't be flexed like a muscle; at least, that's what I've always been told. But that last burst of Circe's scent, the one that threw me over the edge and out of this space-time continuum—that wasn't normal pheromone production, by any standard. And even if it were, Ernie would have experienced the same thing that I did; and judging by his nonchalant reaction, nothing went on for him in that receiving line except a polite handshake and see-ya-later. But she definitely did something there, something strange and different and unnatural and yet decidedly *right*.

I decide not to bring it up right now. Ernie's correct—we have to get tracking.

We're just about to leave the mansion when a familiar voice calls us back into the hall. "Gentlemen, your guises?"

Of course. We trot back to the Ornithomimus, Ernie mumbling to me, "Let's hurry up. I think I smell him, but the scent's fading."

We toss our tickets at the guise-check girl and wait impatiently as the multitude of costumes slowly rotates around toward the delivery slot. I tap my claws against the marble counter, the clack-clack-clack mimicking that of the dry-cleaning rack. No time, no time.

"Three-thirteen and three-fourteen," she says, and we snatch the costumes without a second thought, throw them on, and hightail it out of the mansion. As soon as we hit the open night, I'm dismayed to find that the LA air is as dry as usual, making pheromone detection difficult. The thicker the air, the more water there is clogging up the surrounding atmosphere, the longer any given smell remains available for tracking. This is why no one ever goes missing on Miami Beach.

Still, there's something of that Starbucks scent wafting toward us from behind the mansion, so we follow the odor as best we can. A beautifully landscaped path leads us around one of the many corners of the house and onto a sloped walkway paved with giant stepping-stones. Small sprigs of grass pop up between the grouting, interspersed with the occasional weed. Probably tasty, but no time to sample.

As we follow the smell of congregated dinos, the path grows more convoluted, twisting about in a knot of missteps and jumbled directions. The woods have sprung up around us as we've walked, and the weeds are thicker here, the ground poorly maintained. Soon the stepping-stones give way to cracked slabs of asphalt, which give way to broken rocks, which give way to nothing but dirt. The smell of pine, though—and inside it, a thimbleful of cappuccino—has intensified.

A hundred yards or so into the forest, I can make out a set of monkey bars, rusted over but still usable, and ten old tires placed in football-training fashion along the ground. There's a rope swing and a twenty-foot hurdling fence, and the ground is covered in natural dino tracks, both three- and four-toe alike.

"Playground?" asks Ernie.

I shrug. "Everyone needs a little release, right?"

"You think they're keeping kids here?"

"Could be. Some of these cults you hear about, it's whole families."

Ernie shakes his head, top lip turning up in a sneer of disgust. "Can't keep kids in a place like this," he mutters.

"What, at a mansion in the Hollywood Hills? You're right, such squalor."

But there it is again, the coffee and the pine, and it's not another hundred feet of walking before Ernie and I catch sight of three large bungalows set between the trees. Like the brothers in Circe's story, we hide behind the oaks and watch the natives go about their routines for a few minutes. Dinosaurs wander about in their natural states, protected by the leafy canopy overhead, and much as it was in the ballroom, all of the species are represented. I even see a few Compies this time, scurrying back and forth across the compound like rats searching after a bite of cheese.

"You see him?" I ask.

Ernie shakes his head. "Don't remember what he looks like unguised. We've gotta go in for a closer smell."

"And they'll pick us out right away."

"Not necessarily," says Ernie. "They've got new converts coming in every day, right? Who's to say we haven't just joined up?"

Can't argue with that. We hop out from behind the tree and strut into the camp, every step announcing that we belong, we belong, we belong.

"Evening, brothers," says a Coelophysis who's busy stripping bark off a nearby tree.

"Evening, brother," I return, and we pass by with a merry wave.

"See," says Ernie. "Easy."

A quick tour around the camp with our nostrils flared wide and it soon becomes evident that the conglomeration of smells, while closer to us now, makes individual detection difficult, if not impossible. At least we've got the species narrowed down, but there are easily ten T-Rexes in sight, and any of these dinosaurs could be Rupert. Unfortunately, they seem to band close together, and it would take close quarters before we could make a positive identification on any one of them.

"We could just walk up and ask for him," suggests Ernie.

"And then he'd see us—see you, at least—and he'd spook. Cut and run is my guess."

We wave to a passing "brother," and Ernie takes another glance at the group of T-Rexes sitting by the third bungalow. "I'm sure it's one of them," he says. "There's gotta be a way."

A moment later, a small Compy whizzes by, humming under her breath. I reach out a claw and snatch her by the shoulder. "Excuse me, sister," I say. "I was wondering if you could do me a favor. Please."

"In a hurry, brother," she replies, and tries to zoom past. But I exert a little more pressure, and the Compy stays put.

"Please," I reiterate. "It would mean so much for your Progress."

That gets her. Although I'm sure I made absolutely no sense, especially in what is bound to be a hyped-up lexicon of jargon and catch phrases, I've caught her attention nevertheless.

"Good," I say. "Could you find . . ." I'm searching for the name, sending my memory back to that meeting with Louise, reading that heartbreaking letter that her kid brother sent her way, skipping past the mumbo and the jumbo and eventually finding the signature. *Your Brother, Granaagh.*

"Could you find Granaagh?" I say, scratching my throat in what I hope is the proper Progressive pronunciation.

"He's right over there," says the Compy, pointing to the crowd of T-Rexes in the distance. "See—"

"Yes, but we're in a hurry. Please, tell him that Circe wants to see him by the monkey bars."

"The monkey bars?"

"The—ah—the play set . . . near the swings—"

"Oh," says the Compy, "the mammal bars." Then, with whatever suspicion that little brain can muster: "You say Circe wants to see him?"

"That's what she told my friend here."

The Compy thinks it over, the minuscule cogs and wheels in that brain turning at 10,000 rpm, threatening to overheat, the tiny face scrunching up even tighter, and she finally says, "Okay. I'll tell him."

"He's gonna recognize us the second he gets here," I say once we reach the playground.

" 'Course he will. Then we reason with him."

"Is reason a quality you'd ascribe to most of these Progressives, Ern?"

My partner shakes his head at me, clucking his tongue loudly. "I never shoulda let you get that Word-a-Day calendar. 'Ascribe.' What kinda word is 'ascribe'?"

Before I have a chance to defend my vocabulary, there's a scuffling from the trees. The leaves part, and a smallish T-Rex—six-two, six-three, still much larger than myself, mind you, but on the puny side for the so-called King of Reptiles—makes his way into the clearing. He squints through the darkness, cupping a hand over each eye. "Miss Circe?" he asks.

Miss Circe. Ain't that cute? "Evening, baby brother," says Ernie, stepping out of the shadows and into the meager rays of moonlight that fight their way through the LA haze.

Rupert doesn't run. He doesn't scream. He doesn't even change his expression much—maybe a little sag at the eyes, perhaps a slump to the stance, but that's about it. "Good evening, brother Ernie," he says. "I suspect my sister sent you." A small smile lights up his face, and there's the Rupert I remember from days of old. The kind of kid who could somehow be good-natured, but serious about it.

"Hey, Rupe. Sorry about the deception."

"No apology needed. I trust you enjoyed the lecture."

"You knew we were there?" I ask.

Rupert nods solemnly, and there's that infectious grin again. "I've known Ernie's scent since the day he first started to court my sister. Yours, too, Vincent, from all the times you came to the house to mooch food at dinner."

"Louise—she's real worried about you." Ernie takes a few steps toward his ex-brother-in-law and the T-Rex stands his ground. "She's crying herself to sleep every night since that letter, doesn't know where the heck you are."

"Then you may tell her I'm in good hands. Tell her I'm being cared for and that I'm learning the truth about myself. If she cares about me, that should stop her crying."

In all honesty, Rupert looks to be in much better shape than I ever remember seeing him before. Once upon a time, he was a gaunt, pale specimen of a dino; but now, despite his lack of height, he's managed to fill out that gangly body into what looks like a strong, muscular frame. His hide, like all of the Progressives, is clear and shiny, his tail long and firm, and his sharp claws glint in the moonlight. He's the picture of T-Rex health.

"It ain't that easy—tell him, Vinnie."

"He's right," I say, also making my approach, keeping a watchful eye on those claws of Rupert's. "I spoke with her for quite some time, and though we understand that you're comfortable here, and though we understand how the Progressives have helped you—really, we do—that doesn't mean that you can't further your learning at home. She's got space for you there, a nice bed, lots of love—"

"I get all the love I need here," says Rupert. "I have a place to sleep. I have space. It's not a question of location, it's a question of my Progress. Here is where I need to be."

Rupert's head cocks to one side, then the other, tick-tocking back and forth, as if he's hearing something in the woods and can't quite make it out. "I have to get back to the camp," he says. "It's been nice to see you two. I hope you'll stay and learn more about your ancestry."

He begins to clomp back through the bushes, and I turn to Ernie. "Great. Like I said, he ain't interested. Now what?"

"No idea."

"We can't leave now. We gotta do something."

Ernie looks to Rupert, who's nearing the edge of the clearing, and calls out, "Wait a second! Please, brother!"

It's the "brother" that does it again—a magic word if ever I've seen one, abracadabra be damned. Rupert stops, turns on his heels, and slowly walks back to us. His tone is even, but masking a growing impatience.

"Yes, *brother*?" Tinged with a hint of sarcasm this time.

"I want to show you something," says Ernie, and I'll be damned if I know what he's up to.

Rupert starts, "I'm not going back with you—"

"No, no—" interrupts Ernie. "You can see it from here. Look." Ernie points into the distance, just beyond the mammal bars and the tire course, into a small copse of oak trees. Rupert dutifully turns around and squints his eyes, peering into the blackness of the night.

"I don't see anyth—"

The next thing I know, Rupert's on the ground, unconscious, Ernie's standing above him holding a large branch, and I'm just about as lost as a platypus in a beauty contest.

"Grab his legs," Ernie tells me. "I'll get the arms."

A chorus of words form in my throat but refuse to breach the barrier of my lips. As a result, I choke for a while, making small gasping sounds while staring at Rupert, who has yet to regain consciousness.

"Quit panting, kid," says Ernie. "Don't need *you* passed out, too. Rupert's gonna wake up soon enough, and we gotta get him to the car."

"You didn't—you can't—" I begin, and finally opt for, "We didn't discuss this!"

"We did discuss this," Ernie says calmly. I believe at this point that he would make an excellent sociopath. "We discussed this very scenario."

"We said there was a chance that he wouldn't go along with us—"

"And he didn't," says Ernie.

"Right, he didn't. And then we said we'd discuss what to do."

"And we did. You said 'Now what?' and I said 'No idea' and you said 'We gotta do something'—that's verbatim, kid—so that was the discussion, and then I came up with my plan."

"And your plan," I say, "was to knock Rupert unconscious with a big tree branch and kidnap him."

"Yes. Well, the tree branch was improvised, but . . . more or less, yes."

The kid's beginning to come around, I see—the eyelids are fluttering, the hands beginning to clench, small mewling sounds emerging from his throat like a lost litter of baby kittens crying out for mama—and I have to make a decision, quick.

Clearly, there will be another time for anger, a choice moment for me to lash out at my partner for violating what I thought was a sacred trust, but one way or another, I'm going to make a concerted effort to remain pissed off at Ernie this go-around. In the past, he's skipped away on an apology and a smile, but this time Ernie ain't getting off the Vincent Rubio blacklist any time soon, no sir.

"*You* take his legs," I say, hoisting Rupert's arms into the air. "You're the one who got us into this, so you're the one who gets to smell his feet on the way down."

8

The small studio apartment located just above our office in West-wood is not, by any means, soundproofed, a fact that has recently come to our attention by way of some very personal experience. For the past two days of Rupert's incarceration up there, we've heard all manner of banging, shouting, and a fair number of expletives, most of which have yet to make much sense. At least I've got some good words to mutter under my breath next time I'm audited by the IRS.

Tell the truth, I can't understand what all the fuss is about. Sure we've got him locked up against his will, sure he was knocked on his head and dragged through a dirty, muddy forest, sure he was put in the trunk of a Lincoln Mark VIII and driven over potholed alleyways, but the guy's got water, a place to sleep, and all the take-out food he could ask for. We even ordered in from Twin Dragon one night, and MSG does not come cheap.

"You gotta eat," Ernie told him.

"You gotta drink," was my refrain.

"Thank you, no," was his only response. He'd shut us out entirely for that first day, begging off all manner of nourishment with a polite refusal and a tight little grimace. The plan was to get him to a state of acceptance, lull him into an easygoing frame of mind, then drill it into his head full-bore that he wasn't a Progressive—he was just a kid who needed help, with a sister who loved him—but all this *no thank you* crap was throwing a monkey wrench in the works.

"Maybe we need professional help on this," I suggested to Ernie that first morning.

"What's a shrink gonna do that we can't?"

"Get him to eat, maybe."

"I can do whatever one of them fellas can, kid. Watch and see."

But such macho answers didn't help Rupert, and Ernie's protestations and hour-long lectures bounced off deaf ears. It was a Tony Robbins moment (an Ankylosaur to be sure, like John Tesh or Rosey Grier—no natural human could possibly be that massive) gone horribly, horribly wrong. Rupert simply sat there and stared at us staring at him.

"This gonna help your Progress?" Ernie asked him. "Eating nothing and drinking nothing and saying nothing's gonna wind you up dead, and you think being dead's gonna help?"

No answer. Sarcasm and rhetoric were either beyond the boy or beneath him, and Rupert simply sat cross-legged on the floor or the fold-out sofa bed, prepared, if need be, to wither away just to spite us.

We didn't tell Louise. She didn't need to see him like this.

By afternoon of the second day, the basic pangs of hunger must have overridden whatever meager philosophical constraints had bound Rupert to his prior convictions, and he was more than willing to eat the copious leftovers from the previous day's meals. He wolfed down two orders of pad thai and a generous helping of spicy fried chicken from KFC before excusing himself to the bathroom, where I believe his stomach revolted at the unnatural combination.

"Will you talk to us now?" Ernie pleaded, but he was asking too much.

"At least we got him eating, Ern," I pointed out. "Talking can come later."

Later on, we attempted another amateur deprogramming session, consisting mainly of us knocking on the door, telling Rupert he was crazy, and being told to go away.

Still, we felt it better not to tell Louise. Yet.

We both slept over that night, worried that Rupert would attempt to break out of the apartment, even though we'd done our best to make sure such a thing was impossible. Boards on the windows, locks on the doors, phone cord taken out of the wall, and any means of communication with the outside world pretty much sealed off from his use. I felt like a criminal, locking him up in that manner—and, sure, technically, we were—but enough of it rang true as something good and right that I forgot about the felony and carried on with the plan.

So Ernie and I were both there the other morning when Rupert decided to abandon the peaceful part of his resistance and get down to the nitty-gritty of making himself a real nuisance. He started banging on the floor, the walls, the doors, shouting our names at the top of his stuffed-up lungs (he's got a cold now, of all things), threatening us with civil action and bodily harm. Clearly, this couldn't last for long, as the other denizens of the office building would be arriving for work shortly, and it would be unseemly to have a T-Rex shouting for all the world to hear that the two dinos on the third floor had kidnaped a twenty-two-year-old and are currently in the process of holding him against his will. That's the kind of thing that attracts attention, even in LA.

This time we called Louise.

She came over twenty minutes later, cheeks flushed from either anticipation or the sudden exertion of guising herself up and rushing down to Westwood.

"He's a little argumentative right now," I warned her. "You may not get anywhere."

But Louise said she had to try, and we respected her decision. So, for the last three hours, she's been up there with Rupert, presumably talking him down, and hopefully talking him out. Ernie and I have been twiddling our claws down here on the third floor, unable to help and unable to research the other cases that badly need our attention.

"Hey," I suggest, "I could run down and check out that lead on Minsky's babe. Won't take a half-hour."

"I need you here," Ernie says to me. "In case he tries to bolt."

So I sit. And I wait. I clean my claws. I read the paper. I clean my claws again. I go downstairs and run them through a patch of mud, just so I have something to do. I clean my claws for a third time.

Eventually, there's a knock at the door, and Louise steps inside. The human makeup she's so expertly applied to the mask of her guise has run in great streaks down her cheeks, staining the latex a deep purple. We both rush to her aid, but I back off and let Ernie bear the brunt of the consolation.

Between weeps, Louise explains that Rupert didn't say a syllable to her, that she didn't even know if he had heard a word she said, and that he'd barely even registered her presence the whole time she was up there. "It's not him," she says to us. "I don't recognize my own brother."

I look to Ernie, and he shrugs. I've yet to chew him out good and proper for starting these shenanigans in the first place, so the lug knows he owes me one. It's time to get this thing settled, once and for all.

"Louise," I say, "how would you feel about bringing in a professional?"

"I've heard about those guys," Sergeant Dan Patterson is saying to me over the phone less than ten minutes later. Dan's my contact at the LAPD, a one-time private detective who took the jump to law enforcement once he tired of the freelance life, and probably the best Brontosaur I know. We take the occasional fishing trip together when both of our schedules mesh and we get some spare moments—that's once in the last two years, mind you—and aside from his prowess as an officer of the law, he's an incredible fisherman to boot. A hundred-and-fifty-pound bass would be nothing more than a laugh and a throwback for Dan Patterson, but he's kind enough not to begrudge me my catches of minnows and guppies. "These Progressives got a place up in Hollywood, right?"

"Right. But what I need from you now," I say, "is a name. You must have worked with cults before, maybe heard about someone who can deprogram a member."

"Risky business."

"You know someone or not?"

Dan says, "Not offhand, but I can ask around. Actually going through with it, though . . . that's a different story. Usually you gotta kidnap the guy first, and that ain't always what you'd call legal."

Silence from my end. I fear it's telltale.

"Vincent, you still there?"

"Hm? Yeah, yeah, kidnaping's illegal, I know. Can we forget about that part right now?"

"Do I wanna forget about it?"

"You do," I say, and to my great relief, my good friend on the LAPD is quick on the uptake. He's got a see-no-evil, hear-no-evil policy when it comes to his friends, an attitude that has saved my green butt from the county poke countless times.

"Done and done. You give me a little bit of time, maybe I can round up someone for you. Any preferences—male, female, that sorta thing?"

"Someone fast," I say, worried for the future of the furnishings in the upstairs apartment. If anything's dented beyond repair, Minsky's gonna take it out of our ever-dwindling security deposit. As it is, he has only the most glancing knowledge of what's going on up there; we told him the weeklong free rental of the empty studio was in lieu of further "research fees" for his case, and he reluctantly agreed to back off.

I hang up with Dan and give Ernie and Louise the good news. "He's going to find us somebody," I tell them. "Just a matter of time."

From upstairs, I hear a sharp crack and believe it might be the legs of the sleeper sofa being snapped in two. "Just a matter of time," I repeat optimistically and sit down to order up some lunch.

Six hours later, the phone wakes me from a light snooze and a dream about licorice whips and bottomless elevators. The infernal device has already rung three times within the last few hours, but each time it's been for a purpose unrelated to the case at hand. Two were wrong numbers, and the third was another lead on the Minsky affair, from Sweetums, the dino pimp. He'd claimed to have seen Star hiking her way back up to the St. Regis, but as I was confined to quarters for the evening, I was unable to follow up on the tip. He whined and pleaded with me to messenger him a bit of informant cash in advance, but the rules are the rules: I don't wire money and I don't write checks. Western Union is dead to me—don't ask, don't ask—so he'll have to wait for the moola.

I answer the phone, still a little groggy from the catnap. "Rubio."

"Y'all lookin' for a little help down there, I hear." The individual words are not quite that clear—running together like a stream of thick molasses, drawn out into a long drawl, as if the speaker has slowed his 45 rpm voice box down to 33⅓—but after some thought I'm able to piece together enough of the syllables to make out an actual sentence.

"This is Vincent Rubio," I repeat. "Can I help you, sir?"

"I said that word is out that y'all are in need of a professional service. I might be able to provide such a service."

The meaning behind the words cuts through my stupor, and I blurt out, "You're the cult guy?"

"If that's what y'all choose to call me, then yes, I'm the cult guy."

I backpedal now, not wanting to foster any ill will. "No, I didn't mean— we can call you whatever you want—"

"Cult Guy is a fine name, son. I've been called much worse, believe you me. But if you'd like to refer to me by my Christian name, it's Dr. Beaumont Beauregard."

I almost prefer Cult Guy better; at the very least, it doesn't make me want to fall headlong into a laughing fit. I steady my lips and repeat the name out loud, trying to stifle the giveaway trill of my voice. "Dr. Beaumont Beauregard, thank you for calling. I'm Vincent Rubio."

"I gathered. And, son—I know my name's amusing to folks, so it's okay to laugh. You don't go through grade school with a name like Beaumont Beauregard without finding out it's funny somewhere along the way. Makes it any easier, you can just call me Bo."

I nod, then realize he can't see me over the phone. "I'll do that, Bo." I feel an instant camaraderie with this deprogrammer, and he hasn't even set foot in my door. "How do you know Dan?" I ask.

" 'Scuse me?"

"Sergeant Patterson," I amend. A lot of people refer to the cops by their rank and last name only; it's a sign of respect, and I make a mental note to do similarly in the future. "He gave you my number, right?"

"Sure did," says Bo. "I'll tell ya—when you've been doing this as long as I have, there's not an official in the country you *don't* know. It's a messy job I do, but ain't nothing more rewarding than returning happy kids to their families. Tell me, what's that situation out there lookin' like?"

When I'm all done running down the basics, Bo asks what group Rupert got himself mixed up in. "Progressives," I say. "They're Hollywood-based, and—"

"Hollywood-based, hell," he says. "Them folks is all over the world."

"You've heard of them, then."

"Son, I am practically an expert."

"I don't know if we're talking about the same Progressives," I say. "I doubt they're national. I mean, I'd never heard of them before—"

"They practice ancestor worship, am I right?"

"Yes . . ." Then again, so do most of the so-called true dino religions. Truth be told, the standard human Bible—Exodus, Numbers, and the rest of 'em—isn't exactly revered in our society as the holiest of books. We've got churchgoing dinos, sure, and a number of them really get into the holy rolling, but it's more of a cultural and ethical consideration than anything else. Our species has been around long enough to know that if Adam and Eve existed, they did so quite some time after my forefathers were long fossilized, so, at the very least, the Bible's missing about six thousand chapters before Genesis even gets going.

"And these Progressives you're talking 'bout," continues Dr. Beauregard, "they've got themselves enough money to choke one of them Arab princes, am I right in that as well?"

I concede that he is.

"Then you and I are talking 'bout the same group, son."

He's sold me. The only remaining questions I have are how much Dr. Beaumont Beauregard charges—a prince's ransom, and up front, but Louise has the bucks to cover it—and how soon he can be in Los Angeles. Quicker the better, because the sounds of splintering wood from upstairs have intensified over the last few hours.

"Next flight outta Memphis is first thing tomorrow morning," he tells me.

"Memphis, huh? You treat Elvis?" I joke.

"Don't poke fun at the King, son. Man with a heart that big, did such good for people . . . Ain't his fault if he needs a little help getting outta where he shouldn't be."

Bo's got me surprised once again. "Elvis is one of your patients?" I ask him.

Dr. Beauregard snorts into the phone, and I can almost feel the wet spittle dripping out of my receiver. "Don't be daft, boy," he says to me. "Elvis is dead."

Somehow I know that two thousand miles away, Dr. B. is shooting me a sly wink.

I'm back up on Franklin Avenue in Hollywood a short while later, ready to make a full frontal assault on the St. Regis Hotel. Ernie's agreed to baby-sit our special package for the evening, freeing me up to do some investigative work on the Minsky case without having to worry whether or not our bird's gonna stick to his cage while I'm gone. Seemed like a generous gesture from my partner at the time, but now that I think about it, I realize that he just wanted a few extra hours with Louise. They've gotten chummy again, and I've got to keep an eye on those two.

Three flights up, I'm winded. Four and I'm panting. Five, and I'm wondering if I should have had an EKG the last time I was at Doc Zalaznick's. Since when did flophouse floors get so tall?

By the time I make it to the sixth-floor landing, I've got to take a second for a breather—and I thought *Ernie* was outta shape. Dragging myself down the hallway, I take a quick listen at the door of room 619. Creaking, mumbled grunts. The music of intercourse. This should be fun.

A well-placed kick at the intersection of doorjamb and knob, and the flimsy wooden door flies inward, slamming into the wall behind. The man on the bed—a mammal, a filthy little human—withdraws from the guised-up hooker beneath him, clutching a mass of the stained, filthy sheets in his trembling grip.

"What the—who—"

I don't bother responding—at least, not with my voice. A quick bounce forward and I'm in the room, knocking whatever I can off the nightstand and dressing table, hoping for a loud, disorienting crash. The sight of this pig violating one of our kind—even as low-down, disgusting, and cheap as this streetwalker might be—is enough to send me into overdrive.

"Five seconds," I say, trying to keep my voice to a dull roar. My teeth are itching to break free, my claws flickering in and out behind their gloves.

The human is confused. His penis has quickly gone limp, dangling between those pasty white legs like a useless little worm. Viagra is no match for a pissed-off Velociraptor. "Wh—what?"

"Okay, *no* seconds." I take a step forward and remove a large gold ring that adorns the third finger on my gloved right hand. This is to indicate that I will be using my fists at some point in the near future.

This john's seen enough mob flicks to get the signal—tell the truth, that's where I picked it up—and he doesn't even bother dressing before grabbing his clothes under one arm, scurrying out of the room, and down the stairway, flabby butt cheeks flopping with each step.

I turn my attention to Star, who has yet to move from the bed. Her naked human costume glistens with whatever she's passing off for sweat nowadays—I tend to use genuine Nakitara Perspiration Bulbs, but I've heard of poorer slobs resorting to water from the Pacific, or, in a pinch, their own urine. Disgusting, what some dinos put themselves through in order to save a few bucks.

"He was a good customer," she drawls. A line of drool stretches from her mouth down to her chest, and it takes all my concentration to focus back on that too-pale, drugged-out face. "He'll be back." Her bubblegum and fresh-sod scent drops in and out, spiking and falling, spiking and falling.

"What is it?" I ask, coming closer, slapping her cheeks to try to convince a bit of color to return. "You on the basil?"

She laughs—it's a typical streetwalker cackle—and pushes me away. "Basil is so over, asshole. Cayenne's where it's at this year. Cay-yaaaaan . . ."

Another slap, this one more for the pleasure than the efficacy. "Where'd you put Minsky's stuff? You fence it?"

No answer. Instead, she leans over the side of the bed, flicks out her un-capped tongue—didn't the human john notice it was a bit too long, a bit too dexterous?—and takes a sloppy wet lick off the top of the nightstand. A rust-colored line of cayenne has been sprinkled there, but it disappears into those taste buds two seconds later.

I open the nightstand drawer and find a pharmacy of plastic baggies filled with cayenne pepper and some other noxious herb I don't immediately recognize. Rosemary, maybe? I open the window—struggle with it, in fact, the damned thing probably having been stuck shut since the Paleolithic— and a warm breeze flows through the room, circulating the stench into new and interesting places. I open the plastic bags and pour the rest of the tramp's drugs into the alleyway below, an herbal cascade drenching the trash and cracked asphalt.

She starts whining again and tries to lift herself off the bed. "That's my stash, you bastard."

"Correction. That *was* your stash." I push her back with a flick—her skin nothing more than brittle tissue, muscles weak and useless—and she falls down hard. "I wanna know what you did with Minsky's stuff."

"Who?"

"You know who I'm talking about. Minsky, the guy you've been seeing."

"I see a lotta guys," she says, and tries to pull me toward the bed. "I could see you, too. We could do it right." She pulls back a corner of her guise at the neck, exposing a hide whose natural color has been obscured by a sickly pallor.

I hold down my gorge, pull away easily, and take a seat in a rickety chair. "Minsky. His ether. The instruments. Talk."

"Oh, the midget!"

"Now we're on the same page."

She gives me a sly once-over. "Lemme get this straight. You think . . . you think he *cares* about all that crap?"

"Lady, thinking ain't part of my job. Just tell me what you did with it and we don't need to get into any unpleasantness." I make a show of unsnapping my gloves, preparing my claws, taking my sweet time in order to make my intentions obvious.

But Star isn't going for my tough-guy act. "The midget don't care about his drugs," she says, hopping off the bed—human breasts drooping lasciviously off that pale chest—"believe me. You wait a second, you can ask him."

The hell is she talking about? "The hell are you talking about?"

With exquisite timing, there's a knock on the partially opened flophouse door, and a familiar stunted arm pops through the doorway, grasping a bouquet of roses. "Sweetie," calls the heliuminflected voice, "did I come too soon?"

I rush the door, grab that arm as tight as I can, and yank hard, dragging Minsky off his feet and into my face. "Give me one reason why I shouldn't give you a rose-bouquet suppository," I growl.

That little body sets to trembling, but I refuse to back off. Minsky, dressed in a fine wool suit and ridiculous tiger-stripe tie, glances back and forth between me and his mistress, as if one or the other of us will somehow disappear and leave him in a good, happy place.

"I—I—she didn't—"

"What the fuck are you doing here?"

"She—I didn't mean to—"

"You sent me to find her and get your stuff back," I say.

"Please," Minsky pleads softly. "Not in front of Star—"

"You know she was making it with a human when I got here?"

Not even a cringe from the dentist. He's probably known about her interspecies dalliances for some time; maybe he even gets off on it. The realm of dino depravity knows no bounds. "Please," he says again. "You don't understand."

"Then explain."

Minsky looks to Star again; I can tell he'd be more forthcoming if she weren't in the room. "Scram," I tell her, tossing a dollar bill at her feet. "Go get yourself a soda."

The tart picks my dollar up off the floor, crumples it into a ball, and tosses it back in my face. I try not to flinch as the rough paper scratches my cheek. Then, still costumed but otherwise buck naked, she strolls out the door—running her hand across Minsky's chest as she goes—and into the hallway, disappearing from sight.

I throw Minsky onto the bed and he goes down hard, the rusty springs creaking beneath the force. "You been wasting my time," I bark. "Ernie's time, too. You think this is the only case we got? You think we do this 'cause we're nice?"

"I didn't—I told you guys the truth—she stole those things from me—"

"And?"

"And . . . and nothing. She stole them, I was mad, I wanted you to get them back."

"So it's okay now. The stealing, the lying."

"No, it's—yes . . ."

"Because you're still fucking her."

Minsky looks away. I grab his fleshy cheeks with one hand and turn him back around. Our eyes meet for a second—embarrassment, pain, desire—but he quickly averts his gaze once more. "I can't help myself," he admits. "I just can't stay away."

With but a flick of my wrist, Minsky goes flying backward again, bouncing off the bed and landing hard on the floor. I've spent enough time on this dog of a case already without throwing more good time after bad. "Tell you what you *can* stay away from," I say. "My office."

I slam the door and don't look back. Two flights down, I pass an open doorway, a familiar cavalcade of shrieks and moans emanating from the room within. It's Star again—I know it without looking in—and in some petty way it makes me a little happy that Minsky has to wait upstairs twiddling his underclaws while his love of the month is three flights down, shtupping a stranger for fifty bucks.

Strike that. It makes me *very* happy.

It's one week later, and, for the most part, things have quieted down around the offices of Watson and Rubio. Louise has ceased her vigil in our offices and returned to her home; we've promised to call her the moment anything breaks. Ernie misses her presence, I can tell, and he finds at least two pretenses every day to dial her number and fill her in on some insignificant detail of the case. I wonder if Louise's new husband knows Ernie's been calling. If so, I wonder if he cares.

The last twenty-four hours have been blissfully silent, but the days before were filled with an unwelcome cacophony of screams, roars, and blasts of anger from the studio apartment above. Rupert Simmons was not taking well to deprogramming.

Dr. Beaumont Beauregard—Bo, as I call him now after a week of fetching fast food and diet peach iced teas for the guy—showed up on our stoop the morning after I got back from the St. Regis Hotel. He's a big 'un, the doctor is, a good ol' boy in the finest plantation-owning tradition, with a shock of white hair and a similarly colored mustache and goatee—Nakitara brand, Colonel Sanders #3. Smelled mainly like a foil-covered chocolate bar, but I thought I may have detected some wheatgrass in there as well.

"You Rubio?" he asked me when I approached and offered a hand with his luggage.

"Dr. Beauregard?"

He grinned and grabbed his own bags, easily hoisting the heavy suckers without so much as a grunt. "No need to waste your time with these, son. Ain't nothing but books, anyway. All my clothes I got on my back."

I got my first smell of the doctor right then, and commented on what I thought to be a pleasant aroma.

"Don't know what you're talking about, son."

"Your smell," I said. "Your scent. I'd guess you were an Ankie, but I'm not too good at this."

Again, no recognition. Had I made a fatal error and somehow contacted a non-dino deprogrammer? Would Dan have been dense enough to give me the name of a mammal?

I tried again. "It's okay. We're all . . . we're all of a kind here. No one eavesdropping. All I'm saying is I like your scent."

Bo threw me an exasperated glare, then softened it to one of mild annoyance. Lowering his voice, though there was no one else within a hundred yards, he whispered, "Listen—if I'm gonna have to convince a patient to come back to the real world, if I'm gonna be telling him that he ain't one of the ancestors, I can't be walking around talking dinosaur the whole day. Long as I am in this guise, I am as human as the next fella. You got that?"

Ernie, Louise, and I camped out in the office below while Bo and Rupert went at it upstairs in what sounded like the world's greatest pro wrestling grudge match. If I thought I knew banging and screaming before . . . Let's just say that it was chamber music compared to the struggle—both physical and emotional—that has been taking place upstairs for the last few days.

Every day at one and at six, Bo would emerge from the apartment, sweaty and slick beneath his guise—though of course we weren't allowed to mention the costume in any way—and put in his fast-food order for the day. Hamburgers, hot dogs, the odd taco or two. Rupert's meals, on the other hand, were carefully prepared banquets concocted by his sister, slaved over for hours in the small kitchenette attached to our office, and more often than not returned untouched come nightfall.

Louise was losing weight. She was losing sleep. And she was losing her sanity. We were relieved when she finally bailed out two nights ago.

So it's just Ernie and me who are around to look up in shock when Rupert appears at the door to our office—well-dressed, a little thin, but seemingly sane—and says, "I feel better now."

Bo, standing just behind him, glows with pride. "It wasn't easy," he says. "No, sir. But we're over the hard part now. It's all level ground from here on in."

"Are you sure?" I ask. "I mean . . . everything's . . . better?"

"I understand what happened to me," says Rupert. "I understand what the Progressives were trying to do to me, and I'm glad that you got me out of it. And that's a step."

"And the other thing?" prompts Bo.

"Right," says Rupert. He approaches Ernie and me, and, in an effort that must stretch his arms to their maximum limit, envelops us in a group hug. My face squishes up against his shoulder, and since it would be bad manners to back off, I deal with the pain. "Thank you for rescuing me."

"Anytime, kid," says Ernie, and I second the emotion while pulling away. Enough with the huggy-huggy.

"Could you maybe call my sister?" asks Rupert. "I don't want her to worry."

"Course we can," I say, but Ernie's already on the phone telling Louise to hurry her little self on over to the office.

That night, we all head out for a celebratory dinner at Trader Vic's, the Polynesian joint near our office, and the tiki torches and huge fruit drinks with uncommonly large parasols serve as a perfect reflection of our elevated mood. Dr. Bo proves to be a fascinating conversationalist, and we learn about his exploits curing cult members all over the world. A few sprigs of basil are passed around the table as a further means of enhancing our good feelings, but Bo forbids Rupert to take any of the weed. Probably a wise choice.

Still, I feel that I can't let the night end without a proper toast. Plucking a sprig of basil from the side of my pu-pu platter, I thrust it into the air and say, "To Rupert, for coming back to us."

"To Rupert," is the chorus that echoes me, my dining companions holding aloft their own herbal buddies.

"And to Bo," I continue, "for leading the way."

"To Bo." We munch up. We feel good. It's a happy day.

And so it is that on March 19th at eight forty-five in the evening, Rupert Simmons was successfully deprogrammed from the dinosaur cult known as the Progressives and returned to his friends and family, a happy, healthy, and well-adjusted Tyrannosaurus Rex.

And so it is that three days later, Rupert Simmons is dead.

The funeral is a lovely affair, done up with all the taste and black velvet the Simmons family could rustle up on such short notice. There's an open coffin—mahogany, with gold inlay— Rupert inside, looking to all the world like he's just getting in a good forty winks. There's a preacher, droning on about the youth of society, about how they take so much for granted, yet are so reluctant to ask for help. There's Louise and her elderly father, a smattering of aunts and uncles, all looking pale and weak and shattered and, more than anything else, confused.

Louise found him. At least, that's what Ernie told me, and I have no reason to doubt either one of them. As it is, Louise has been somewhat incommunicado for the last few days, dealing with the petty tasks that the death of a loved one brings on: phone calls to the mortuary, to the clergy, to caterers. Duties that are best left to someone else—anyone else—are unfortunately the domain of the bereaved, and as a result, I've gotten in barely a word of condolence to my partner's ex-wife.

And then there's the whole issue of guilt. If not a sea of it, a river, perhaps.

Rupert's note read BECAUSE I HAVE NO MEANING, and that was the end of that. Five words, each one a little BB pellet into my heart. The self-blame game goes like this: had he not been deprogrammed, had he not been locked up, had he not been taken from the Progressive compound and thrown into my trunk in the first place, Rupert Simmons would be alive and well today. Worshiping his ancestors and prattling on about the truth behind

Progress, sure, but at least he'd have vital signs and a healthy, active scent. As it is, his smell has disappeared from the corpse in the box before me, and I can barely bring myself to stop sniffing for that cappuccino and cream.

"And so we see," the preacher is saying, "that life is not a gift. It is a privilege granted to us. . . ."

Seconal. One of the few mammal-oriented drugs that has similar effects on our kind, and that's what they found, a big bottle of it clutched in Rupert Simmons's right hand. He hadn't even undressed before downing somewhere around 2,000 milligrams, roughly twenty times the recommended dosage for these sleep inducers, which means he entered the world of the dead still tied up beneath the buckles and the girdles and the zippers and the latex. Maybe it was a message to all of us: *See what you did? See how you made life so unbearable for me?* Maybe it wasn't. No way to know, since a note reading BECAUSE I HAVE NO MEANING leaves a lot open to interpretation. I think I like it better that way.

An elderly gentleman to my left smelling of stale graham crackers and codfish covertly hands me a small stash of basil, like a fan passing a joint at a rock concert. I take a nibble, instantly feeling the slow mellow rush spreading through my veins, warming me up from the inside out, and pass it on to Ernie, who samples and continues the chain. This is how we deal with death: an herb, a gnaw, and let's move on with the whole ugly shebang. The preacher, though—a human, I gather, from the way he won't quit babbling—isn't hip to the scene.

". . . and so it is with young Rupert, who in death cannot tell us why he felt he had no meaning in life. . . ."

It had been going well, or so we thought. Rupert was back in his old apartment, meeting up with his previously estranged group of friends, and had been talking about finding a job with a nonprofit organization. "One of the environmentals," he told us over the phone two days after that dinner at Trader Vic's. "Saving the rain forests." And as I've still got a few relatives back in South America eking out a living beneath the jungle canopy, I thought it a fabulous idea. Bo told us that a job search was one of the first stages of reintroduction to everyday life, that it indicated that the patient—that Rupert—was interested in rejoining society. He'd even expressed interest in volunteering for a cult-awareness group for young at-risk dinos, another idea we all greeted with enthusiasm.

Plus, he was talking to his old high school girlfriend for the first time in a few years, and they'd already made plans to go out on a pre-pre-date at a local Spanish tapas restaurant. Again, Bo was optimistic: "A little nookie don't hurt anyone." What's more, Louise said he'd begun playing the guitar and cooking dinners again, and already a blush of normalcy had returned to his eerily youthful hide. Thumbs-up status on all accounts.

Doesn't sound to me like he had no meaning. Then again, some folks have a talent for putting up a good facade even when their infrastructure is shot through with rotting beams and crumbling struts. Rupert must have been one of them.

On the night of March 21st, Rupert had invited his sister and her husband to come over the next morning for one of his special brunches, a meal the young T-Rex was known by his friends and family to have perfected during his world travels. All manner of ethnic foodstuffs went into these elaborate presentations—quail's eggs, green pancakes, sushi, tandoori shrimp—and he somehow managed to combine the disparate flavors into a meal that would make Wolfgang Puck's naturally brown hide tarnish green with envy.

Terrell—big as a house, dumb as the stucco—wasn't able to make it to brunch that morning, so it was just Louise, alone and unprepared, who found herself confused when the doorbell didn't bring her brother. And it was Louise who found herself pounding on the door after a few minutes had passed with no answer from within. And it was Louise who eventually got the landlord to unlock the door, and it was Louise who found her brother, dead, slumped across an unmade bed with a bottle in his hand and a five-word suicide note by his head.

While Louise wept and held her brother in her arms, the landlord—an Ornithomimus who was drunk off his ass on cilantro but functional enough to use modern appliances—dialed the dino division of the cops and the morgue, and soon enough the place was swarming with badges. They scoped the scene, took samples, and, once a rapid inquest had been processed at Dan Patterson's request—a result, of course, of my own request—declared the death to be what we all knew it was: a suicide.

Dr. Beauregard was beside himself with guilt, calling nearly every day from Memphis to proclaim his sorrow at Rupert's passing.

"I can't believe this happened," he kept saying. "The boy seemed so . . . His behavior pattern never indicated . . . This just ain't right. . . ."

We didn't blame him. At least Ernie and I didn't blame him, and Louise certainly professed to bear no ill will toward the doctor. Still, he sent flower arrangement after flower arrangement, even spicing up a few with the odd medicinal herb here and there, anything to assuage Louise's sorrow and his own feelings of failure.

He even sent back the check for services rendered. Now *that's* a doctor for you.

"Please follow me outside for the interment," the preacher is saying, finishing up his epic tribute to a dino he barely even knew, "where we will return young Rupert to the ground from whence he came." I've never understood this—are we supposed to be made of dirt? I consider raising my hand, but the preacher has already moved past me, down the aisle and into the bright light of day.

"Vincent!" Ernie hisses. I look over—he's cocking his head toward the back of the small funeral crowd. Behind the array of foreign and domestic automobiles is a long stretch limo, five-window style, green as the hide on a Hadrosaur's behind.

"That just pull up?" I whisper back, and Ernie nods.

A chauffeur, duded up to the nines in an emerald tuxedo, hops out of the driver's seat and runs around to the passenger door. It's quite the jog. With a flourish, he pulls open the door, and I only wish I were more surprised at what gets out.

It's Circe, and she's dressed to mourn. Long black overcoat, green velvet dress down to the perfectly sculpted latex ankles, sensible pumps padding through the damp dirt below.

"What the hell's she doing here?" Ernie asks, a bit too loudly. A number of the bereaved turn to shush us, but Ernie does a stupendous job of ignoring them.

"She must have thought of herself as a friend," I say, finding myself defending the leader of the Progressives. "Friends come to these things."

"Friends don't brainwash each other."

"Nothing you can do about it. I'm sure she wants to pay her respects, that's all."

Ernie starts to rise from his seat—"I'll show her respect"—but I'm able to grab his forearm and force him back down before he starts anything unseemly. The progress he's made with Louise over the past few weeks has put him in a much better mood; causing a scene at her brother's funeral might land him back in the mammal house for good.

"Let it go," I counsel. "Let her watch, and let her leave."

And that's all she seems to do. Circe takes her place at the back of the gathering, and as the preacher continues his endless sermon, I can almost feel her stare boring through the back of my head, as if she were trying to crawl into my brain and gaze out through *my* eyes, to place herself in my position. But every time I turn around she's looking somewhere else, seemingly focused entirely on the clergyman and his dubious words of wisdom.

"Ashes to ashes," the preacher is chanting as the gears turn and Rupert's coffin is lowered into the ground, "dust to dust . . ." It's a human ritual but serves us well nevertheless. The days of burning our corpses or letting them sink to a watery grave are all in the past. We're just like the mammals, nothing more than pack rats when it comes to our dead nowadays, secreting them in boxes underground as if we might want to dig them up again should they come in handy at some point in the future.

As the funeral comes to a close and the group disbands, Rupert's friends and family empathizing with one another in a huge cat's cradle of consolation, I feel a familiar presence rise up behind me. It's the smell that gives it away, more than anything else, that wild concoction of herbs accompanied by an intense burst of pine boiling out of her pores—a common dinosaur scent somehow elevated to another level.

"I didn't expect to see you here," I say even before I've finished turning around.

"Nor I you," replies Circe. She's at least three inches taller than me—new ground for a dame—and I find myself unable to look away from that gaze. "Do you have a cold?" she asks.

She's referring to the fact that I'm pinching my nostrils closed with two fingers from my right hand, doing my best to shut out that intoxicating scent. The last thing I need right now is another trip back to the Jurassic. Then again, maybe it's the first thing I need. As it is, the evolutionary process hasn't completely localized all of my scent-sniffing glands in my nose; scents are still partially the domain of my taste buds, and I can smell every inch of this Progressive leader each time my tongue comes in contact with the pheromone-laced air.

"Yes," I reply. "My sinuses are all a mess. Forgive me."

"Did you know him well?"

"On and off," I explain. "Friend of a friend. Last time I saw him was the night that the . . . *club* . . . met up at your place."

Her laugh is high, airy, and if it weren't for the circumstances, she would most likely let it transform into a full-fledged giggle. "Oh, it's not my place," she says. "It belongs to all of us. Tell me, did you enjoy yourself the other evening?"

"It was . . . educational," I say.

"That is what we strive for," replies Circe. "Then again, all work and no play . . ." And for a second, I'm pretty sure I can feel her pinching my rump. But her hands aren't anywhere near my derriere, and a quick 360 spin shows me that I must be hallucinating. I clamp my nostrils tighter, shutting out the last remaining olfactory vestiges of those evil weeds. "Perhaps you might like to come to another session."

I'm about to reply in the negative—the strong negative, the desperation negative—when my fingers fail me. Muscles loosening up, blatantly disregarding my orders to clench, engaging in full-scale mutiny even as my brain screams at them to fall in line. But soon my nostrils are wide open and flaring of their own accord—I'll have to add them to my blacklist of misbehaving body parts—and sucking in Circe's sweet scent.

"I'd love to come back," I find myself saying. Somewhere, Ernie's calling for me to come to the car, to say goodbye and to hurry up, and somewhere else I'm telling him to hold on one second. But right here and right now it's just me, a verdant goddess named Circe, and the tallest, thickest, most fragrant jungle anyone's seen this side of the Triassic. Trees burst from the ground, soaring into the sky; vines surround us, reaching out with their leafy fingers, caressing our bodies as they entangle me and this perfect female Velociraptor in a vortex of lush foliage. We're not running this time, but even standing still I feel that sense of urgency, that raw natural power welling up within, bursting with pure energy. Holding my face—holding hers—tongues whipping out, lashing at one another, teeth clashing in the furious rush for pleasure, growls and roars forming deep within our throats, calling out in a language I don't even know—

And suddenly I'm back in my Lincoln, driving out of the main gates of the funeral home.

". . . which is why I have to suspect her motives," Ernie is saying. "I'm not telling you she's wrong or she's evil or anything, but I want you to watch out."

"Right . . ." I respond, trying to get a bearing on the conversation. Where was I just now? *Who* was I just now? "What was that part about watching out, again?" I ask.

Ernie slaps the dashboard. "Damn it, I knew you weren't listening to me."

"I *was*—I *was*—it . . . You wanted me to watch out . . ."

"For Circe," he supplies.

"Why?"

Ernie doesn't even try to suppress a sigh. It bursts out of his lips, a long, drawn-out wheeze of frustration. " 'Cause every time you talk to her you get all googly-eyed."

We do not discuss it further. The rest of the ride home is uneventful, but when we arrive back at the office and step out of the car, a funny thing happens: I find myself unable to control my lips. This is not your basic Vincent Rubio careless talk—this is a fully undeveloped thought coming to the forefront, blindsiding me even before I have a chance to choke off my throat and cut off the air to my own vocal cords.

"You wanna check out another Progressive meeting?" I hear myself saying.

Ernie takes a step back, ducking as if I've swung a bat at his head. "I don't think you said what I think you said."

"It might be fun. See what they're really all about."

"Kid, you feeling okay?"

And that's all the time it takes to regain control over my rogue brain. I throw the offending part in the stockade and shake my head, attempting to banish all remaining inklings to a nonintrusive nook in my noggin. "Just thinking we could do some more snoop work, see if any other kids are messed up in this," I lie. I wish I could tell Ernie the truth, that I don't know where either the thought or the words came from, but I fear that'd freak him out more than the fib. Certainly gives *me* the willies.

"Forget about it," says Ernie. "And forget about all the Progress crap. It's over. Progress is behind us."

"Progress is behind us," I repeat. I think I will make that my mantra for the week, once an hour, twice before bedtime. And if, after all that time and all those repetitions, I can still smell that powerful, pleasurable, pungent scent—as I can now, on my clothes, in my hair, on my skin, behind every bush and every tree and every passerby—then I will make it my mantra for the next month. And the year. And the decade, if need be. Yes, it's settled.

It's been a quiet few weeks in the office. Minsky hasn't bothered us in quite some time, instead leaving short messages of apology on our machine, which we listen to, laugh at, and erase. Louise, meanwhile, is managing to work through her grief with a little help from Ernie, who sees her and the new husband a few times a week for dinner. It's a little weird if you ask me, the ex hanging out with the new couple all the time, but if Terrell doesn't complain, I certainly won't. I get the feeling that the guy isn't home a lot, and maybe Ernie is providing some comfort for his ex-wife at a time when she desperately needs it. Maybe he just wants to screw her. Don't ask me; I'm no shrink.

Teitelbaum, the T-Rex who owns and runs TruTel Enterprises, a massive PI firm here in the basin, was kind enough—hah, he doesn't even know how to *spell* the word *kind*—to throw a few cases our way. I'd like to say that we reciprocate, that Ernie and I occasionally find ourselves so swamped with work that we have to pass on clients to others, but it's simply not the case. We do okay for ourselves—I've got a home, nice clothes, a car that's nearly paid for, and I get in the occasional special stash from time to time—but it's not like we can afford to be trading cases back and forth with the big boys. As it happens, Teitelbaum doesn't expect us to hand over our clients. He just wants our souls.

"Two thousand in fees, flat deal," he announced, flipping a case file onto the desk in front of me. I'd come down at six in the morning at Teitelbaum's request, and I wasn't in the mood to be lowballed by Jabba the Hutt.

"Missing-persons case, right? That could take months."

"Yeah, and . . . ?"

"And two thousand won't begin to cover it."

"Do what you want," he told me, knowing exactly which body part—well, parts—he had me by. "I can give it to Sutherland."

"He's a hack."

"He's a *cheap* hack. And he doesn't bitch like you do. You want it or not, Rubio?"

I agreed to the fee. Ernie would kill me for doing it, but I had no choice. We're hard up for cash.

So we're running down some missing persons, we're trailing a few deadbeat dads, we're spying on a few salacious spouses. Still, it's a job, and it pays the bills. Even with Teitelbaum skinning us alive.

If the jerk's going to take half of our fees, though, I'm going to make sure to use his facilities as often as possible. As a result, I find myself spending a perfectly lovely Los Angeles spring afternoon—temperature in the low seventies, not a cloud in the sky, smog in remission for the week—holed up inside a darkroom, squinting at blurry negatives and nearly passing out from the overpowering smell of photographic chemicals.

The guy we're trailing is a Raptor, a two-bit con artist who makes a play out of taking old ladies for a run and then splitting town with their cars and their cash. Unfortunately for him, he scammed the grandmother of Tommy Troubadour, a local lounge lizard with reputed ties to the mob—the dino one, I mean—and I can only hope he'll enjoy eating his meals through a straw for the rest of his life.

Here's a nice photo of the slimy Raptor now, coming out of an '89 Oldsmobile with a member of the Social Security set on his arm. His greasy black hair contrasts horribly with her blue coif, and even through the black-and-white of the photo it's a painful sight. The contrast isn't quite right, though, so I dunk the print again, waiting for the images to sharpen. I should be timing the developing process with a stopwatch, but sometimes I like to feel my way around the procedure instead. Photo-developing for snoop work always takes me somewhere between the spiritual intuition of the artistic process and the workaday photoboard cut-and-paste of a third-grade science fair project, and I like to take my time and find a decent midpoint.

I'm almost to where I want to be—there's the image now, coming in nice and clear, the son of a bitch's face center-frame and ready to be identified—when the darkroom curtain pulls open, a blast of fluorescent light nearly blowing me off my feet.

"What the hell—" I shout, trying to protect a string of negatives that have yet to be developed. "Shut the outer door first, you moron."

"Ooh, man, Vincent, I am so sorry." I can't see who it is behind the glare, but it only takes a second to place the voice. Sutherland. "I am so, so sorry."

"I got it, you're sorry. Now shut the fucking door!" I hate to resort to vulgarity, but the cretin isn't reacting to direct commands.

"Right," he says. "Right, right." And finally, the light from outside is extinguished, leaving us in red-tinted darkness. He grins sheepishly, points to the print in my hands. "Photo looks okay."

" 'Course it looks okay, it's developed already. I got three rolls back there strung up you might have just burned out."

"I am so sorry—"

"Enough. Do you need something, Sutherland?"

He doesn't even have the self-respect to look away or seem ashamed when he responds. "Please. I'm not too good at this."

I grab a cartridge of exposed film from Sutherland's hand and help the guy begin the developing process—hell, I'd do it for him if it would get him out of here any quicker.

"So," he says as I pull his film from the canister, "how's tricks?"

"Tricks are fine. If you're gonna stand around, you might as well watch what I'm doing. Maybe you'll learn something."

"Certainly, absolutely." Sutherland makes a play out of taking great note of my movements, humming and yes-ing under his breath, but I know the guy's just putting on a show. None of this is going to stick with him; his brain is Teflon-coated. But meanwhile, he's standing behind me all the while, rancid breath combining with that rotten-egg scent to create a horror show of unequaled proportions for my sensitive snout.

"Listen," I blurt out after an unbearable five minutes have passed, "why don't I just do this for you, huh? I'll leave the photos here, you come back and pick 'em up later."

"Would you?" he asks innocently, and I know that I'm being played for a chump. But it's a small price to pay in order to secure the return of my privacy and a relatively odor-free environment. "That's . . . that's great of you, Rubio. Tell ya what. I'll take you to that herb joint up on Franklin later tonight, my treat."

"Not necessary," I say. "Not my kinda place." I know the establishment of which he speaks; it's a small run-down dive of a basil bar where the waitresses are hooked on the very stuff they're doling out. Vacant eyes and lazy tails are the name of the game at the Pesto Palace, and it just serves to depress me every time I step inside. The Hollywood bars have that effect on me, for some reason, and I make it a point to avoid them as much as possible.

"Hey," he says, "how'd y'all do at that wacked-out Progressive thing?"

I shrug and say, "We made out. Did what we came there to do. You?"

"A whole mess," he says. "Don't get me wrong—I got my info all right, and Mr. Teitelbaum was real happy with me. Real happy." He reaches into his pocket and withdraws a wallet stuffed to bursting with receipts and coupons. From within the depths, he extracts a business card and hands it to me. HORACE "HAPPY" SUTHERLAND, it reads—and I've never known the guy's first name or this moronic nickname until just now—EXECUTIVE SECOND VICE PRESIDENT OF INVESTIGATIONS. "That's almost like partner," he confides.

"How pleasing."

"But a lotta weird shit went down after I got back, I'll tell ya." Sutherland shoves that wallet back into his pants pocket and makes to leave. But something in that last sentence has grabbed me. Maybe it was his tone, his quick delivery, or maybe it's just a buried suspicion of my own snagging a reason to show its ugly face, but I reach out and grab Sutherland by the shoulder.

"What do you mean, 'weird shit'?"

"What do you mean by what do I mean?" He pulls away, eyeing me carefully.

"Don't start with—look, you said weird shit went down, I'm just asking what it was. Idle chitchat."

Sutherland sighs, tries to turn away again and meets up with my body wedged between him and the blackout curtain. "It was a mess," he says. "You don't want to know. Just wasting your time."

"Humor me." With every moment of stalling, I've become more interested.

The Triceratops shrugs and takes a seat on the developing table—his butt spilling over the sides, pants nearly dipping into the pool of chemicals—and opens up. "We had this case come in, some woman whose daughter had disappeared. Only this note left behind said she'd found Progress and all that jazz."

I've heard of such things. "Go on."

"When you saw me at the party, I was there looking for the girl. Picked up on her scent, followed her when she went to the powder room, and had a little confrontation. First she claimed to be someone else, said I was crazy, but I'd smelled her old sheets from her bedroom at home, and this here is one dino who doesn't forget a scent. It was her all right, and so I pressed her and I pressed her and I pressed her and finally she admitted it, but wouldn't come back with me. My orders were not to get physical, so I let her go. Disappeared into the crowd and I couldn't find her the rest of the night. Good appetizers, though.

"So I returned to the office, relayed my information, and they sent in a team to extract her—that was their term, *extract her*—from the compound. A few days later, I hear they've got her at home and she's all better, Mr. Teitelbaum gives me a promotion and a raise, and everything's hunky dory."

"Seems fine to me," I say. "Nothing messy there."

"That's what I thought. Then I get called into the big man's office a few days ago, and he tells me that the girl is dead, and I have to submit all my documents from the trip. I mean, all my notes and everything. Like I keep these things—pain in the ass, right? So I have to go digging through my files—"

"Wait a second," I interrupt, my mouth having taken a few seconds to catch up with my suddenly racing thoughts, "did you say she was dead?"

"Hm? Yeah, ain't that a shame? We get her outta that cult, turn the girl's life around, and then poof, she's gone."

"How'd she die?" I'm up off the stool now, volume raising, voice echoing in the small chamber.

"You're very excitable today, you know that?"

"Sutherland . . ." I snarl.

"Car accident, it was a car accident."

"Oh." I don't know what I expected, but a car accident wasn't on the list.

Sutherland notices my disappointment, and elaborates further. "She hit a pole."

Now we're talking. Next to the overdone overdose, the single-car accident is the bread and butter of the suicidal set. "Was she by herself?"

"Solo accident, that's what they said, out on some deserted road up near Angeles Crest." He's talking the mountains, the Angeles Crest National Forest, a favorite spot of serial killers thanks to the excellent canopy coverage it provides a rotting corpse. Suicides like it up there, too—something about getting away from the smog and the noise and the heat and the traffic and just hanging out with a blue jay and the wind for your last minutes on earth, I suppose.

"I'll see you later," I hear myself saying, even as my legs are moving me past Sutherland, past the safelight and the developing table and the trays of chemicals, and through the inner blackout curtain.

"Wait!" Sutherland cries out. "What about my pictures?"

"Take 'em to the Fotomat," I reply. The outer door opens—bright light poking sharp needles into my eyes, but I pay it no mind—and then closes behind me, and I don't even know if the hack PI can hear me anymore. Tell the truth, I don't really care. I've got something else developing.

rnie said it was all just a coincidence. I said it might be. Ernie said I was wasting my time. I said I might be. Ernie said that the two dead dinosaurs were only that, two dead dinosaurs, and not connected in any way. I said they might be.

But it hasn't stopped me from going to the coroner's.

"All I need is a list of suicides and accidents over the last few years," I'm saying, trying to get past Dr. Kalichman's initial reluctance to let me into her files. "Just the dino ones, won't take long at all."

"No can do."

"You wrote the reports, you can give me the information."

"Of course I *can,*" she tells me. "But I'm not supposed to."

I whip out two twenty-dollar bills and throw them onto the autopsy table between us. They flutter down onto the chest of a well-preserved human corpse, where they sit untouched. Dr. Kalichman raises a single eyebrow in my direction.

"I'm not looking to be bribed, Mr. Rubio."

"Sorry," I respond, plucking the bills off the body and shoving them back in my pocket. "Force of habit. And please, call me Vincent."

"Fine. Vincent, I can't give you the report."

"Look," I say, "we've known each other for how long? Years, right? We're colleagues, in a way. Colleagues do *favors* for each other." I emphasize this last part, particularly to remind Dr. Kalichman that I did some complimentary detective work for her a few years back when she thought her husband was fooling around on her. He'd been working too late down at the Natural

History Museum, cataloging fake fossils, a job that had never previously necessitated anything more than a standard forty-hour work week. Their joint bank account had been gradually depleted of funds, marked by withdrawals of sizable chunks of cash. And he'd recently been reluctant to engage in marital relations, all of which led Dr. K. to her assumption of infidelity. Didn't take more than a few nights of surveillance to find out that he wasn't sneaking out at all hours of the night to meet his mistress but was instead heading down to the track every afternoon and gambling away their mortgage money, then hopping down to Tijuana at nights in order to recoup his losses by riding a mechanical bull for spare dollars thrown at him by the other tourists. At the very least, he was too damned tired to screw his own wife. I think they're in counseling now.

"I know what you're getting at," the coroner replies, a flush coming to her cheeks, "and I thank you for your help in that matter. I do. But it would be breaking some serious rules to give you—"

"Then don't give it to me," I suggest. "Don't give it to me at all."

". . . Okay . . ." She's confused now, and I'm comfortable with that.

"Isn't it about lunchtime?" I suggest. "Don't you have that lunch meeting with the rest of the morgue set? That meeting a few miles away? Take about two hours or so?"

Dr. Kalichman sighs, but it's a sure sign of acceptance, and I know I'm in. "Be careful with the files," she says, "and put everything back the way you found it."

"No problem. And the next time you need snoop work, it's on me."

A few minutes later, she's gone, the door is locked, and I'm digging through the files, flipping past endless names of the deceased, checking a third of the way down the first page for the small green dot in the margin that indicates a corpse of reptilian heritage. After that, I let my eyes drop to the bottom, where Dr. Kalichman or one of her assistants has marked the assumed cause of death. I then cross-reference all the suicides, accidents, and unresolved cases with the date of demise written up at the top and toss out anything more than two years old. I'm sure there's a smorgasbord of interesting information I'll be losing out on by using this method, but I'm not getting paid for my time, and I've got to draw the line somewhere. Even hunches have their limits.

An hour later, I've got twenty-three names in twenty-three folders whose information matches my criteria, all stacked in a teetering pile at my feet. I guess I could use this as my base set, take down the names and numbers and make my phone calls, but I get the feeling that there's something else I'm missing, some way in which I can cull out the slag.

Gender? Nah, the Progressives are quite fair when it comes to their unisex recruiting policies. Just the two cases I know about—Rupert and the girl that Sutherland was after—prove the point right there. Income? It seems to me that a cult would be interested primarily in those members who could drain their families of whatever reserves they had—much in the way that Rupert had consistently funneled cash from Louise into the Progressives' coffers—and there's no doubt in my mind that they didn't come to that fancy mansion and the workstation in the subway by selling miniature "Best Grandfather" Oscar statuettes on the Boulevard, but these autopsy reports don't have a window into the victim's financial status.

What's left? Hair color? Sexual preference? Age?

Well there's a key, right there. Seems to me that most of the Progressives I saw at the meeting were in their younger years, only a very few even approaching middle age. The oldest one I saw, in fact, was Samuel, the Iguanodon who introduced Circe, but I'd consider him one of the cult's organizers; certainly, he was no ordinary member. Youth is my cross-referencing tool, without a doubt—there might be the odd case of the octogenarian seeking spiritual fulfillment, but by that point in life, most of us have had our heads screwed on tight and rusted over for a good many years.

I run a quick hippie check on the list, culling out anyone over thirty, which brings the pile down to a manageable twelve unlucky souls. I hurriedly scribble down the names and phone numbers of the closest relatives, and doing so further cuts the list to nine, as three of the victims left behind no known survivors. I carefully replace the files in their proper order—filing never having been one of my strong suits, I must admit, so I can only hope that whatever mistakes I made in alphabetizing don't gum up the works too badly—take my leave of the coroner's office, and close the door tightly behind me. Wouldn't want folks snooping around where they shouldn't be.

After a bit of arguing and more than a bit of guilt, Ernie's agreed to check out four of the names; I take the remaining five. My first two phone calls are not answered, and I'm reluctant to leave messages for what are most likely still-grieving parents regarding children who are years in the grave. No need to pick at old wounds for no good reason. The third one, however, goes through three rings—I'm getting ready to hang up again—and then abruptly—

" 'Lo?"

"Mr. Levitt?"

"What are you selling?"

"I'm not selling anything," I respond.

"Oh," he says, a bit surprised. "Good. I don't wanna buy anything. I got that waffle maker already, and I don't like it."

"I'm not selling anything, Mr. Levitt. My name is Vincent Rubio, and I'm a private detective."

A grunt. "Don't need detective work. Don't wanna buy it." A pause. "But if you want, you can tell me about it."

"No, no," I explain, "you don't understand. I'm not selling you anything."

"That's what they all say."

"Who?"

"The salesmen. They say they ain't selling, and then they start selling. I'm on the phone six hours a day. Am I happy with my appliances? Do I want a six-pack of abs? What kinda equity do I have in my home? Everybody's selling. You're gonna start selling soon."

"I promise you, I won't." And if he's so sure I am, why is the guy still on the phone with me? "I just want to ask you a few questions."

"What about?"

"About Jay."

A hiccough on the other end. Silence, but in the background, I can hear a television, blaring out some sort of infomercial. Someone is very excited about a cutlery set.

"Mr. Levitt?"

"I hear ya," he says after a few seconds. "You wanna sell me somethin' for my son, I bet. He don't want nothing, either."

Exasperated, I stammer, "I—how do I explain this—I don't want to sell you anything. I am not—I repeat, *not,* a salesman. I just want to know about your son. Before . . . before he died."

More silence, and this time I think he might have hung up on me. I repeat his name a few more times, and now I can't even hear the television anymore. I'm about to chalk it up to a no-go and replace the receiver—

"You wanna come down to the house?" asks Mr. Levitt. "I can make us waffles."

Mr. Levitt's home in the suburban city of Thousand Oaks, a quiet residential town about forty-five minutes outside of Los Angeles with rolling green hills, friendly neighbors, and a surprising lack of smog, is at the same time cluttered and immaculate. Littered with the conquests of a thousand telemarketers, the house is stuffed to the gills with doily-cutters and ribbon-curlers and wall-painters and burger-flippers and chicken-roasters and twist-tie-twisters and a host of inventions over which the fellas down at the Patent Office probably had a good chuckle for a year or two. But every single inch of these semi-useless appliances—and the house in general—shines like the chrome on a schoolboy's new ten-speed.

"You have a lovely home," I say as I enter the door and nearly trip over a defunct appetizer-serving robot.

Mr. Levitt eases himself into an old BarcaLounger in the front living room, and I take a seat on a sofa draped in a blue slipcover, itself coated with a slick substance that makes it quite difficult to remain seated in one place.

"That's Protect-o-Gel," says my host. "Fella came 'round the house last month sold it to me. Keeps the slipcovers from getting stained. Makes 'em waterproof."

"I see. Fascinating." And disgusting. It's like sitting on Vaseline. Most likely, it *is* Vaseline.

Mr. Levitt sets a cup of tea in front of me, served in a gyroscoping mug that I've seen advertised on television. It's supposed to make it easier to drink coffee and drive at the same time, wholly useless in a stationary environment, but as my butt won't stay still on this sofa, it might actually come in handy. "I've got the waffles cooking back in the kitchen. And I'm dehydrating some fruit if you'd like to stick around."

"Thank you, no," I say, and then, seeing the crestfallen look come across his face, amend it to, "We'll see."

Mr. Levitt is a small dino—a Coelophysis or Compy if I had to guess—whose recent lot in life has only served to shrink him even more. The human guise he's wearing over what seems to be a meager infrastructure only accentuates this sense of loss, the face etched with wrinkles deeper than I'm used to seeing on guises of dinosaurs twenty years older. Perhaps he ordered them from Nakitara to suit his grief. I knew a widow once who was so distraught over her husband's untimely demise in a tragic reaping accident that she purchased sixteen sets of Bette Davis Eyebags from the Erickson guise company in Sweden and shoved them all beneath her ocular cavities so that her outer appearance might properly reflect her inner misery.

"I wanted to ask you about your son," I begin.

"About Jay."

"Yes, about Jay. He took his own life, I understand?"

"He was a good boy," says Mr. Levitt, nodding his head as if to agree with his own statement. "Never caused me any grief. Some kids, they're skipping school, doing the basil, speaking back to their elders. Not my Jay."

"Of course not." Mr. Levitt seems to be stuck in nostalgia mode, and I don't want to do anything to shake him out of it, but I don't have unlimited time out here in the 'burbs. I need to return to the Westside at some point and resume making phone calls. "I'm sure he was a great boy."

A sharp *ping!* from the kitchen, and Mr. Levitt pops up from the easy chair. "Waffles are done," he says.

"That's okay, I don't need—" But he's out of the room already.

Now, I'm not here to feel sorry for anyone—at least that wasn't my original intent—but I can't help but commiserate with one of the most definitive descriptions of loneliness I've seen in quite some time. My eyes wander around the room, taking in the multitude of gadgets and devices that have taken the place of Mr. Levitt's only son.

No less than six cuckoo clocks line the walls, four of them different in size, shape, and color, but two exactly the same—he must have accidentally purchased this model a second time without realizing it. Each of the clocks is set to a different time, I notice, and since I left my own watch at home this morning, I'm thoroughly confused as to how long I've been sitting here, trying not to fall off the sofa.

"Those are my favorites," Mr. Levitt says of the clocks as he enters with a plate full of pancakes. "They keep me company. Like a bunch of old friends."

Yep, there's the pity train, arriving at the station right on time.

He places the pancakes down on a small coffee table that doubles as an aquarium—no fish inside, just water, some plastic plants, and a multicolored ceramic castle—and invites me to take one.

"I thought you said you were making waffles."

"I am. The pancakes were done first." He grabs one off the plate and begins to take small nibbles. Never one to be rude, I do likewise. They're rubbery.

"Like I said," Mr. Levitt continues, "Jay was a good boy. Ran with a nice crowd."

"Mm-hm," I mumble through the pancake.

"Very clean-cut, I always felt. Especially today, what with the punk look most of these kids are into."

I don't want to throw the guy more out of time-alignment than he already is, so I decline to tell him that the punk look has been dead for decades. "Did he ever mention a religion?" I ask. "Maybe he was getting into spirituality?"

"No, no, nothing like that. We've always been something of lapsed atheists around this house."

"These friends . . . did they seem odd at all?"

"Odd? No, sir. Very nice boys. Very clean-cut." There's that word again. I center on it.

"Clean-cut, huh? In manner, in style . . . ?"

"Sure. Dressed real nice, too. Guises always looking tip-top, hair not too long. Very respectful of the elders. Always made sure they were respecting the elders."

Now we're getting somewhere. "Is that what they said— respecting their elders? Did they maybe say 'respecting their *ancestors*'?"

A little light blinks on behind Mr. Levitt's eyes. Someone's home after all. "Yes . . . yes, that sounds familiar. In fact, I believe that's exactly what they said, now that you mention it."

On the right path, no doubt about it. "Do you mind if we talk about Jay in detail, Mr. Levitt? About his death?"

"Those waffles will be ready soon," he mumbles.

I want to let myself be distracted, I really do—it's no fun getting information out of someone I have no reason to hurt—but I'm too close to back off. "Was he acting strangely in the days before his death? Had he left home, maybe been taking some of your money?"

"He was a good boy," Mr. Levitt repeats, volume rising, agitation creeping into the tone. "He never stole a thing."

"I understand that. I do, really. But what I'm saying . . ." A breath, collecting my thoughts. "Had he ever talked about Progress? About Progressing?"

Possible recognition from my host, but there's no time to tell. A second *ping!* from the kitchen, this one louder, tinnier, and Mr. Levitt is up again and out of the living room. I sit back on the sofa, trying desperately to maintain some purchase on the slick surface, and close my eyes. This conversation has been a little more strenuous than I expected, and I hope Ernie's having more luck talking with a family he contacted in Newport Beach whose child met with a similar fate. At the very least, he's probably not being fed as well. I take another bite out of my pancake.

Mr. Levitt returns from the kitchen, a heaping plate of waffles stacked like an Aztec pyramid held out before him. Wordlessly, he places the waffles next to the pancakes, then straightens back up and walks out of the room again. Have I pushed him too far? Have I offended the poor guy? This wasn't in the plan at all.

A few minutes later, after the sounds of ruffling and rumbling from a back room, Mr. Levitt returns holding a crumpled sheet of white looseleaf paper. He shuffles across the room in a zombie shuffle, feet dragging through the blindingly clean shag carpet, and wordlessly holds the paper out for me. I take it by one corner, guessing already what this might be, and give it a read.

In a sure, even script made with a crisp felt pen, the note reads simply: THERE IS NO POINT IN GOING ON WITHOUT PROGRESS.

"We were supposed to go bird-watching," Mr. Levitt says as I return the note to his shaking hands. "I'd woken up early, got the cameras and the binoculars all packed and ready to go, and then went to wake the boy. He'd been all excited those last few days, talking about how his life was looking up, how he was feeling better about himself, and so I figured he'd do good with a nice photo safari. Everyone does good with a nice photo safari. . . ."

"And then?" I prompt.

"He—he never woke up," Mr. Levitt chokes out. "I kept trying to wake him, real quiet like, but he didn't move. In his hand . . . in his hand were some of my sleeping pills, I guess—"

The note—the mention of Progress—Jay's "clean-cut" friends—his reverence of the ancestors—all of this tells me exactly what I came here to find out. The rest of it is just a sob story, no doubt quite tragic, but not important enough to the case at hand to keep me here any longer.

"Thank you for your time, Mr. Levitt," I say, trying to rise from the sofa without giving myself a hernia in the process. My guise is tight today— must have been packing down those french fries during Rupert's incarceration in the upstairs studio—and it's difficult enough to move around without having to lift myself off a vat of Jell-O.

But Mr. Levitt is persistent, if nothing else, trotting after me as I walk to the door. He's suddenly become animated, more alive in this last minute than he has been for the whole half-hour I've been at the house. "Please, stay," he implores. "I've got some cookies in the Quick-Bake, won't take more than two and a half minutes at full setting."

"I wish I could," I explain, "but I've got to get going. I'm very sorry to have disturbed you."

"I understand," he says in a low, uninflected monotone. "Everybody leaves." Without another word, he turns away and sulks back into the living room, sits on the slipcovered couch, and slides off onto the floor, where he lies, motionless, in a fetal position.

Ah, Christ. I'm not a statue.

We play Parcheesi for a few hours. I win every game despite a thorough misunderstanding of the rules, but Mr. Levitt beams from ear to ear the entire time. I'm not in this business to make people feel good, and in fact I'm causing distress more often than not, but in those instances when I can work in a good deed—what my Jewish Allosaur friend calls a *mitzvah*—I'm more than happy to add it on, free of charge.

The waffles are terrible.

"Overdose of sleeping pills, probably Seconal," I tell Ernie once I've returned to the office later that evening. "And a suicide note that indicates he'd left the Progressives."

"Do you one better," replies my partner.

"How?"

Ernie whips out a photograph of a young, well-dressed woman, no more than twenty if she's a day, standing in the middle of a speedboat on some unidentifiable lake. There's a small birthmark right near her navel—a trademark of the Nakisoba Corporation, an offshoot of the larger Nakitara guise manufacturer. They're also into high-tech electronics, computers, publishing, the film industry, and personal sexual protection, but that's neither here nor there. The girl in the photo seems happy enough, smiling and waving at the camera, one hand poised on a raised hip.

"And she would be . . . ?"

"Crystal Reeds," says Ernie. "Diplodocus, and heir to the Reeds pencil fortune."

"There's a pencil fortune?"

"Well, not so much anymore," Ernie admits. "Been going downhill since computers hit big, but they still do a nice business with schools. Point is, the family has money."

I say, "And lemme guess—they were losing a big chunk of it to the Progressives."

"Even better. They lost their house, too. They'd put it in Crystal's name for some obscure tax purposes, and in a fit of religious ecstasy, she signed it over to the group. Six months and about two hundred thousand in legal fees later they got it back, but it was the end of the end for her parents.

"They sent in these two dinos up from Nevada who claimed to be specialists in extraction, and sure enough, they got her out and into a safe house for deprogramming."

"They were shrinks?"

"No, they were just the extraction team. The family hired some therapist from back in New York to shake the Progress out of her. Stier, they said his name was. Dr. Frank Stier."

"Wonder if Dr. Beauregard knows him," I say.

"Point is, they had this girl in a safe house because the parents were all worried about rival pencil-makers trying to take advantage of their situation—I didn't mention that they might like to get themselves checked out for paranoid delusions. And then, a few days after she's supposedly cured, she winds up dead."

"Suicide?"

"Nope," says Ernie. "Botched robbery attempt."

"That's a good one."

"Wait, you gotta hear it. They'd put the girl into one of the pencil operation's warehouses down in Long Beach, set her up in the furnished office on the second level overlooking the warehouse floor. That night, cops say, some burglars broke in, she tried to put a stop to it, and they offed her. Shot her up so bad they could barely identify the body."

I grab a pencil off my desk and take a look at it. NUMBER 2, it says. And sure enough, at the bottom, right near the eraser, small green type reads: REEDS PENCIL CO. Ten similar pencils lie scattered in the plastic tray of my organizer. Maybe there is a fortune there, after all. "Nothing so odd about that," I say. "Long Beach has burglaries every day."

"Sure it does," replies Ernie. "And that's the point—the criminals down there aren't greenhorns. They know what they're doing. They know what goods go to what floor, and the pencil warehouse—not exactly a cash cow—was surrounded by sixty others just like it, except they were stocking furniture, consumer electronics, jewelry . . ."

I toss the pencil back onto my desk and stand up. It's late, I need sleep, but there's enough pressing on my mind to force me back into some semblance of action. I lay it out for Ernie. "We've got three deaths—two by overdose, one in a car—that occurred in otherwise healthy, young individuals just a few days after their departure from the Progressives. We've got witnesses who say that the victims were feeling well just before they met the Reaper, that they didn't seem depressed in any way—"

"And, at least in Rupert's case," Ernie chimes in, "one suicide victim who didn't even have a prescription for the drug that supposedly killed him."

"This is new."

"I just found out today," Ernie says. "Did a search at damn near every pharmacy in town. No prescription on record, and the vial they found in his hand was both empty and unmarked."

"Is this enough for you?" I ask my partner. "Are you ready to give up on coincidence and join me in conspiracy?"

"Do I have to dress up again?"

"You can wear whatever the hell you want," I tell him. "Go naked for all I care."

"Shut up and get in the car, kid."

11

By the time we've made our way out to Hollywood and begun the climb up through Laurel Canyon, I've worked up a pretty good head of steam. I'm incensed enough that there might be a cover-up going on here, but even angrier that I may have been taken for a fool. Rupert was under my care when he died—okay, technically he'd been declared officially sane by Dr. B., but that doesn't preclude the fact that it was me who got him into the mess in the first place—and I don't take well to playing the chump.

"I want you to stay away from that . . . that woman," Ernie tells me. "Let me do the talking."

"No problem," I say, though I know that the problem is actually very real and very large. Ignoring Circe when I'm in her presence is like ignoring a polka-dotted elephant doing a samba through the Russian Tea Room. She's been on my mind more and more often since the last burst of pheromones at Rupert's funeral, and I've got to admit that more than a few dreams have been haunted by that ethereal presence and those savory seasonings.

We arrive at the outer gate to find it, predictably, shut, and the guard, predictably, stubborn. It's the same fellow from the last time, but he doesn't recognize us.

"We were here a few weeks ago," I say. "For the meeting. The *meeting*."

His hand doesn't move toward the gate button. "Don't care if you were here for the Pope's birthday party"—and I wouldn't be surprised if this had been the venue for such a shindig—"you still can't come in without a pass."

"Can you make a phone call? This is all I'm asking."

"If you don't have a pass—"

"One lousy phone call!" I yell, then drop my voice back to a lower register. "Tell Circe it's her friend from the funeral, that's all. She'll—"

"Please turn your car around. This is private property, sir, and I don't make the rules."

"I appreciate that—"

"I don't think you do," interrupts the guard. Now he's moving toward us, and instead of the typical dino gesture of threat—baring of the teeth, unsnapping of the gloves—he actually pulls his jacket aside and flashes a gun. A gun, of all things!

"That's disgusting," says Ernie, unable to help himself. I can see distaste well up past his throat, making for his tongue, his lips. There's a great aversion to unnatural weapons, especially among the older generation of dinos, and Ernie's no exception.

But the guard doesn't move an inch, doesn't even try to cover the weapon up. He feels no shame. "You fellas wanna move along now?" The gun glints in the remaining sunlight, the barrel shiny and new. Probably never been fired, but I can't take the chance that his lack of practice guarantees bad aim.

Ernie leans across me and out of the car window. "Now you listen to me, you chickenshit piece of a Compy—you pick up your little phone there and tell the boss that two gentlemen from the other night are asking to see her—"

"No can do," says the guard. "Turn the car around. I'm not going to ask you again." His hand moves slowly toward the weapon on his hip, coming to rest lightly on the butt. With a grunt, I push Ernie off my lap and back into his seat. I get into enough daily trouble thanks to my partner, I don't need to be shot for trespassing by a rent-a-cop who thinks he's the dino answer to Charles Bronson. "Maybe we can go back to Hollywood Boulevard," I suggest to Ernie. "Get our friend Bob to wrangle us another invite."

Too late. Unsnapping his seat belt in a smooth, single movement, Ernie pops the locks on my Lincoln and leaps out of the passenger seat, volume at eleven and rising. "Bullshit! Get on your phone, apefucker, and call up to the house—"

I'm up and out of the car, but not before Ernie and the guard have met face-to-face in front of the hood, human-guised noses no more than a centimeter apart. If they were to take off their masks and facial straps right now, their snouts would certainly bump into each other, causing two ugly nosebleeds.

"Hold up," I say, trotting around to get between these two hotheads. "Hold up."

But simultaneously each puts out an arm to block my way, and the combined force sends me sprawling back across the hood of my car—scraping my leg on the ornament—and onto the asphalt on the other side.

I look up just in time to see Ernie spitting out his bridge—the worn, human dentures clattering to the ground like a prizefighter's mouthpiece, kicking up dirt where they land, the bright, sharp teeth snapping hard against one another—as the guard reaches for his gun, fingers grasping the butt tightly, pulling it up and out of the holster, taking dead aim on my partner and best friend's unprotected chest—

I should probably scream here. *No,* or *Stop,* or something of that sort, which can be so moving when played back in slow motion.

The phone rings.

Ernie's midair bite comes to a halt, leaving his mouth in a confused, half-open grimace. The guard relaxes his grip. The phone rings again. Backing up slowly, keeping a quarter of an eye on me but the rest on Ernie and his rows of sharpened teeth, the guard reaches into his booth and lifts the handset. "Yes? Yes, ma'am. Yes, they . . . No, he was going to . . . Yes. Yes, ma'am. I understand. Thank you."

We get a pass. We get an apology. We get super-detailed instructions on how to drive up to the main house and where to park. We make the guard repeat them three times even though we already know full well how to get there. We spin the wheels and kick dust in his face as we drive off.

The little smattering of daylight that remains before the sun drops over the hills reflects off the marble columns of the main house, throwing the whole thing even further back to its ancient architectural roots. Ernie and I trudge through the parking lot—surprisingly, there are quite a number of autos parked here—up the hillside stairs, and into the main corridor, fully prepared to check our costumes. But the Ornithomimus from the other night's meeting is not at her assigned spot, and the guise-check room is locked up tighter than the waterproof sealant on a Nakitara Gold series Latex Bonding Package #9.

"We're not always so informal," comes a voice from down at the other end of the corridor. "We like to be natural, sure, but it's a hassle if you're running errands in the outside world all day." An Iguanodon—unguised—is walking toward us, familiar in some way. It's the deep voice that gets me, the one two shades lower than that of James Earl Jones—who is, by the way, one of the dinosaur community's most prized actors. I saw him do *Othello* once in an all-dino cast, and to see such a masterpiece performed the way Shakespeare intended it—with an Allosaur in the title role—was nothing short of breathtaking.

Got it now—he's the one who introduced Circe at the party the other night. The memory returns just in time, for as the Iguanodon approaches, I'm able to stick out my hand and say, "Samuel, right?"

"Yes. Circe sent me to come get you. Please, follow."

We trail after Samuel, his tail swishing mesmerizingly back and forth along the ground. Even though I've been told it's not necessary, I feel an urge to rip off my guise and go naked and free, but we don't stop in any one place long enough for me to unfasten any of the buckles. Ernie notices what I'm trying to do and slaps my hand away. "Leave your damn clothes on," he mutters. So old-fashioned.

The house becomes mustier as we make our way through, and whether it's from dust bunnies or something blooming nearby, my sinuses are starting to act up. A few sneezes later, I take a handkerchief from my pocket and wipe down my nose, dismayed to find that nothing's coming out; I must have misaligned the nostril holes again, which means by the end of the day, I'll end up with a lovely trail of mucus gumming up the works beneath my mask. It's times like this—the misalignments, the pinched buckles, the poorly tightened straps—that make me want to throw myself headlong into the Progressive lifestyle, to rip it all away and go running wild, much as the ancestors must have done in the carefree days when the mammals were more interested in swinging from trees and having sex with anything that moved than they were in eradicating other sentient species from the planet.

We wend our way through another series of corridors, passing through countless doors and passageways, everything set off by more of that dino artwork. Many of them are unfamiliar, as I've always been something of a Philistine when it comes to the visual arts, but some of the pieces are nevertheless familiar to me, due to whatever cultural concepts have filtered into my brain by chance over years of osmosis. I know that for every mammalian piece that Modigliani put out, for example, he produced at least one in a more naturalistic state. *Woman with Child* was meant for humans to marvel at; *Bronto Lies Down* was painted strictly for our persuasion. And, lo and behold, there it is on the wall, resplendent in its verdant hues. And it is, no doubt, the original.

I try not to sneeze on it.

A series of winding staircases are next, a double helix of steps curving round and about one another, and after what feels like a climb through the Andes, we arrive at the top floor and a tight, narrow corridor leading to a single door at the end of the hall.

"Vincent," cooes Circe as we enter a room filled with cushioned chairs and throw pillows scattered on the plush carpeting below. It's the 1970s version of a harem, only green instead of pink, and a shade too bright to be accidentally tacky. "It's so good to see you again. Better times, yes?" A flowing green gown covers her otherwise naked, natural Raptor hide, a slit in the back cut out for that sensually curved tail. "And Mr. Watson, a pleasure."

We're each given a hand to shake and a peck on the cheek, and I must admit that my body instinctively dives in for a whiff of that maddening scent. Strangely enough, it's barely present. I expect to be transported to a world of Pterodactyls and Diplodoci, but I find only a hint of cilantro and marjoram, hardly enough to send me back in time even five short minutes. I'll get more accomplished this way, sure, but I can't say I'm not disappointed.

"Lovely room you have here," I tell her. "Very . . . comfy."

A little lip-curl, a bat of the lashes. "It's my lounge. I come here before large events, to . . . prepare, if you will."

"Large events?" I ask.

"Yes. I'm sad to say, but we've had some misfortune of our own," purrs Circe. "A dear friend has passed on—"

"I'm sorry—"

"She was very old, her time had come. She was at peace with the ancestors. But the funeral is downstairs in a few minutes—we do seem to meet at these occasions, don't we?"

"We could come back," Ernie suggests, some vestige of social graces clinging to his investigator's tone.

"Please, stay. I have a few moments. Now, what can I do for you boys?" asks Circe, curling her tail up and around her body. She's got incredible control over that thing—it glides through the air with ease, flicking out at my knee, almost teasing it while she speaks.

"My . . . friend and I have been talking," I begin, "ever since that first night. About Progress, about what you believe in, what you stand for."

"Good, good. We encourage discourse," she says.

"And then the funeral, when we saw you . . ."

Circe nods empathetically. "Yes, quite a shame." That tail of hers still on the move, still making for me. I try to evade, but that thin slab of flesh manages to work its way down to my feet and up into the leg of my pants, seeking out the latex covering beneath. I leap backward, and Ernie shoots me a confused look.

He takes over. "Did it bother you when Rupert left the group?"

"Bother me? No. Was I concerned for him? Of course. We're all free to live our lives however we choose, Mr. Watson, but it saddens me when a dinosaur, so previously entrenched on the road to a meaningful, fulfilling life, strays from the path of truth."

"He seemed happy enough."

"Until he killed himself, you mean?" Point one for Circe.

I step up. "We're interested in your organization. In the next step."

"You wish to join, then? It's not an easy path."

"We understand. But it . . . it *intrigues* us. Though we have some questions."

"Don't we all?" she says. "Please, anything I can do to help is purely my pleasure." Another caress with the tail.

Now a wholly different part of my guise is tightening up, and I have to think about nuns and painful vaccinations and old horses being sent out to pasture in order to relieve the tension. I'm quite glad at this point that I was unable to disrobe earlier; the H-series of buckles wrapped tightly around my groin is keeping me from a world of embarrassment.

"Well, gentlemen," says Circe, "are we going to stand around all night or get to it?"

"Get—get to it?" stammers Ernie. He's flushed, the old dickens! I'm glad to see that it's not just me who's been rising to the occasion.

"You had questions, didn't you?" Circe backs up to a massive beanbag chair on the ground and plops atop it. "I assume some of these questions you have are about your friend."

"And yours, if I'm not mistaken."

She nods and amends her statement. "And mine. Though I must be frank, I did not know your friend very well. We've had a great number of converts in recent years, and though I wish I could get to know them all personally, I am unable to."

"But isn't the goal one of personal communication between dinosaurs?" I say.

"Of unfettered communication, yes. We believe that our costumes—like that guise you're wearing now, manufactured by an impersonal conglomerate somewhere in Japan—"

"Taiwan, actually," I correct. "It's a Nakitara, but from their secondary plant."

"Taiwan, then. These costumes only serve to separate us from ourselves, but perhaps even more importantly, they separate us from our fellow creatures. Did you know that back in the days of our ancestors, we could make positive identification of one another from miles away?"

"I didn't—I mean, I'd *heard,* but it's just an old wives tale, right?"

"Why is it," ponders Circe, "that an old husband is wise, while old wives are full of nonsense? No matter. There are others—old wives, young husbands—who say we were able to communicate with our scents. Not verbally, mind you, but almost in hallucination. In meaning. In spirit." Is she talking directly to me here? Did she feel what I felt back at the party the other night? At the funeral?

"What's the point?" asks Ernie. "We've got phones nowadays."

"And maybe that's a problem, too," says Circe. "We rely on such modern conveniences only because we're following the mammalian construct. We had the ability to create such technology tens of millions of years before the humans climbed down out of the trees, but did we? Certainly not. Because we didn't need to. We had everything we wanted, and none of the problems inherent in this so-called modernized society."

"Sounds romanticized to me," I point out.

"How so?"

"*Everything* was better back in the good old days," I say. "Talk to any geezer, they'll tell ya."

Circe can't help but laugh, a giggle that sends a tingle down to the tip of my tail. "Perhaps you're more advanced than we thought," she says, and leaves it at that.

We chitchat our way through more of the Progressive belief system, most of which revolves around reestablishing closer ties with both the ancestors and their ways, and in doing so, becoming a whole dinosaur. Or something like that; even after a fifteen-minute in-depth discussion on the matter, I'm not quite sure. "Are you saying we're only part dinosaur now?" asks Ernie.

Circe nods. "I'm saying we're but mere fractions of our possible selves."

All of this philosophy has got my head spinning 'round. I stand up from my cushion and stretch my legs. "I must say, it's a fascinating system you've come up with."

"Oh, it's not mine," says Circe. "Any more than the group is mine, or this house is mine. It's all of ours, all of it, but we do owe a lot to our founder."

This must be the one that Jules told us about back at the wax museum—the vacuum-cleaner salesman with the ego complex. "And where is he?" I ask.

"Oh, Raal doesn't come around much anymore," says Circe, and that name strikes a chord with me. Raal. "He's one hundred percent dinosaur natural, and I'm sure you can imagine how difficult it is to maintain such an incredibly high level of Progress living in a mammalian-dominated society."

I assume that "doesn't come around much" is her euphemism for dead, but it's possible that Circe actually believes that instead of moving on to a better place, this Raal simply moved on to a *different* place. "So we can't see him," says Ernie.

"Oh, not until you're further along," is Circe's response. Then she stands up and brushes off the few strands of dust that have clung to her green velvet robe. "I'm afraid the funeral is about to begin. Would you boys like to attend?"

Odds are, there'll be some free grub afterward, so Ernie and I hop after

Circe as she makes her way downstairs. Her movement is effortless, grace-ful, Audrey Hepburn all the way, and I feel like the most awkward of tod-dlers walking next to her.

As we approach the ballroom, there's a murmur similar to the one from the other night, but this time it's lower, more somber, and behind it is a fa-miliar pop and crackle that I'm currently unable to place. Halfway between a giant bowl of Rice Krispies and the white noise of a radio tuned to a miss-ing station, it almost sounds like . . . like . . .

Fire. Flaming licks of heat steam up from a wide hole carved into the ballroom floor, the air above shimmering in a decadent belly dance of car-bon dioxide and ash. The sheer temperature variation pushes me back out of the ballroom for a second, but I steel myself and enter the sweltering area, making myself at home among the horde of other dinos—some in cos-tume, some natural—waiting for the festivities to begin.

I certainly didn't notice anything like this the first time I was inside the ballroom, but as I look closer—shielding my eyes against the glare with the side of my hand—I can see that the floor has been retracted, possibly me-chanically, and that the miniature version of Hades ten feet down is filled with what looks a lot like molten lava, if my Discovery Channel memory serves.

"Nice fire pit," Ernie whispers to me.

"Sure is," I reply. "You bring the marshmallows?"

We are shushed by at least five different dinos. Progressives, as a rule, lack the crucial humor gene on their DNA. Then again, if I had to eat raw newts all the time, I'd be pretty miserable, too.

It doesn't take long for the funeral to get started. Circe takes her place atop a slightly raised dais, and begins a long monologue about the de-ceased, about how she'd found her way in life through Progress, and a bunch of other hoo-ha that has the effect of bringing the crowd to tears.

It is Samuel and another Progressive, a pudgy Triceratops wearing no guise but sporting a pair of Armani spectacles, who wheel out the body of the old Ornithomimus. Yep, she's dead, all right.

"As many of our ancestors met their end in the fires of the Great Show-ers, so we now admit our sister into the heart of our shared heritage. As the ancestors left this earth, so shall we."

"So shall we," echoes the audience, Ernie and I excepted. No one gave us cue cards.

At this signal, Samuel and the Trike place the deceased atop a long, wooden plank with four wheels and begin to push the improvised gurney toward the open, roaring fire pit. The dead Ornitho's arm drapes over one side, but no one seems to notice, even as her claws scrape along the floor, sending up a terrific screeching noise as the plank draws nearer to its incineration.

"Fire to fire," intones Circe, "ancestor to ancestor."

"Fire to fire," repeats the crowd. "Fire to fire."

With a final shove by the pallbearers, the Ornithomimus and her wooden conveyance slide off the ballroom floor and fall into the pit, wheels clattering for an instant against the marble before the rejuvenated flames tear up into the air, rejoicing at a new source of fuel. The congregants sway back and forth in unison, a massive underwater plant drifting with the current, low gurgles trickling off their throats. And Circe stands above it all, arms held high, tail raised to the ceiling, light from the flames flickering, caressing her body.

I can smell burning flesh. Next to me, a T-Rex is crying and salivating all at the same time. Something has grabbed hold of my stomach lining and is proceeding to twist it into all manner of Boy Scout knots, wringing out my belly like a towel thick with water.

"We oughta get outta here," I gurgle to Ernie.

"You feelin' okay?"

"Let's just—" A burp surfaces, and I'm barely able to suppress the accompanying nausea. "Let's just go." Ernie, God bless him, agrees.

But we're not more than halfway to the door when the crowd parts—aha, an easy exit—and Circe appears, standing in our way. I'd usually be more than happy to see her, but at this point there's not much more I'd like to do than make it to the safety of a restroom or, should it be necessary, a copse of bushes.

"I should have warned you about the smell," she says, instantly diagnosing my problem. "It can be rough the first time out."

And just like that—I don't know if it's the words, the sentiment, or some burst of her own magic scent—my nausea is gone. In fact, I'm starting to feel a little hungry. I'm about to thank Circe for her intervention, but she's already on to the next topic, two small envelopes suddenly appearing in her hands.

"Before you go, I wanted to have a word with you."

"We're in a hurry," explains Ernie.

"One moment, please. We're having a get-together this weekend," she says, "sort of a Progressive convention, and I'd be honored if you two would come as my guests. I'm embarrassed to admit that there's a slight fee involved. . . ."

"That's not a problem," I say immediately. Even if the group isn't in need of money from their recruits, we nevertheless want to fit in with their upper-middle-class member profile. Money should not seem like an issue.

"Excellent," she says. "If you need quick travel arrangements, you'll find some numbers here for a few agents we use over in Santa Monica."

"Travel arrangements?"

"For the flight."

"The flight?"

"To Hawaii," says Circe, and I can feel the cash bottoming out of my pocket already. "You can fly into Maui or Kauai, it doesn't make a difference. The hydrofoil will pick you up and bring you over to our private island in the afternoon, so make sure you book a flight that arrives in the morning."

Ernie's managed to get his invitation open, and he's already gaping, slack-jawed, at the finely printed words on the rice-paper backing. ATTAIN A HIGHER LEVEL OF PROGRESS AT OUR NATURALIZATION CONVOCATION, it reads. SPECIAL SPRING PRICE, $4,000, INCLUDES ALL FOOD, DRINK, AND LUXURIOUS ACCOMMODATIONS FOR THE WEEKEND. PREPARE TO PROGRESS!

I take a long swig of self-confidence, follow it down with a jigger of bravado and a dash of foolishness, and wait for the mixture to settle in my belly. "We'll be there."

"We sure as hell *won't* be there," Ernie is saying as we pull up to the office. "I'm not asking Louise for this kind of cash—"

"Do you wanna find out who killed Rupert?"

"If he *was* killed—and I'm still not so sure of that—then, sure, I wanna find the guy. Or gal."

I let that last bit go. If there's one thing I want to believe, it's that Circe is innocent. I don't know where this impulse comes from—though I must say that the notion is tinted in the same colors as those herb-induced fantasies I've been so prone to lately—but at least 83 percent of my intuition tells me it's true, and majority rules in this brain. "And if you wanna find out who killed Rupert, don't you think his own sister would be willing to shell out a few extra bucks?"

No response from Ernie. I park the car too close to the curb, so I back out and try it again. My contacts are drying out in the arid night air, and I'm forced to blink nonstop like a southern belle trying to land a mate.

"Listen," Ernie says after I've slammed into the curb six or seven times, "I could get the money out of my ex-wife with no problem. I can go upstairs and call Louise and tell her that we've been following up on Rupert's death. And I'll tell you what—for that she'll be pleased. I can tell her that we've begun to view it more as a homicide than a suicide. For that, she'll be intrigued. But if I tell her that we've been associating with the Progressives, if I tell her that we've been socializing with their leader, if I tell her that we want almost ten thousand dollars to give to the very same group that had been draining her coffers for the past two years—for that . . . for that, she'll be nothing more than hurt. And I won't hurt her. Period, paragraph, end of story." Ernie gives me a second to let his little soliloquy sink in.

We climb the stairs in silence, and though I want to bring up the Hawaii trip again, and I think it's not only a good idea but a *necessary* one—we are, after all, investigators, and neither rain nor sleet nor lack of available funds should stop us in our appointed task—I keep quiet out of respect for Ernie's respect for his ex-wife. My reticence won't last long, though—I'm giving it five minutes before I bring the matter up for a second review.

The office door is open.

"You don't think . . ." says Ernie.

"I do."

"Little apefucker . . ."

It's Minsky once again, suit and tie rumpled, wrinkled, all a shambles, and this time he's pacing back and forth rather than sitting nonchalantly on my desk, but the sight of the little guy in our private space is enough to throw me into a frenzy registering 4.3 on the hissy-fit scale.

"How many times do I have to tell you this is illegal?" I bellow, drawing as much out of my natural dino self as possible. I hope to work in a good roar or two. "And how many times do I have to tell you that I don't want to see you again? I haven't had to crack heads in a while now, but you're pushing me, Minsky. . . ."

But he's not even listening to me—if he were, he'd be stumbling backward, away from my advancing claws, rather than coming toward me, his own stubby arms raised beseechingly.

"You gotta get her," he whines, that tinny little voice like a champagne glass shattering across my ears. "The bitch went too far this time."

Ernie's not having any of it. He grabs Minsky by the back of his wig—attached with some incredibly strong epoxy, it seems, because the whine turns to a howl in no time—and proceeds to drag the bite-sized Hadrosaur across the floor.

"Waaaait," he whimpers, "it's all different now! It's all different now!"

Against my better judgment, I place a hand on Ernie's shoulder. He's still got Minsky by the hair, but the mousse the midget put on this morning is slicking up my partner's hand. "What is it now?" I ask. "You know we've put a moratorium on doing any business with you."

Ernie loses the battle with Minsky's hair, and the midget falls to the ground. He lifts himself up, doesn't even brush off, and storms back toward me, shaking his finger up at my incredulous expression. "I want you to find her, and I want you to—to—to do whatever it is you do to those people." His face has flushed the guise skin into a deep crimson, and I won't be surprised if I get a chance to use my CPR training in the next few minutes.

" 'Whatever it is we do'?" echoes Ernie. "I don't think you're asking us what I think you're asking us. . . ."

"Are you telling us to hurt Star?" I ask.

Minsky's sneer of revulsion is genuine. "Do what you have to."

"I think you've got us pegged wrong," I begin, though I'm sufficiently intrigued by the little guy's anger to hear him out. "We don't do that sort of thing. Violence. I mean, sure, if it comes at us first, or if there's a *really* good reason. Or if I'm in a pissy mood. Or if—"

"Just find her. You do *that,* don't you?"

I nod and set a pot of coffee on the burner. "Of course. Then again, it seems we've been hired to find this girl before, but you did a pretty damn good job of finding her yourself."

"Why don'tcha just use your dick?" Ernie jokes. "Made a pretty good divining rod last time."

Ooh, that's got him going good. The pacing starts again, rapid little pitter-patter steps that shoot him in small circles around the office, anxious as a racehorse at the gate. "Last time, last time—last time doesn't matter. Never happened. I was a fool for going back to that—that—"

A string of profanities rarely heard by these delicate ears follows, and Ernie and I check our watches as the tirade carries on well past five minutes. When he's done, Minsky is out of breath, but a little of that rancor has slipped away from the muscles lining his heart and into the open air. He's out of coronary danger at least.

The coffee has begun to percolate into the pot, hissing with every drip. "She's dropped out again, I take it."

"She has," Minsky admits.

"And this time, it's more than just ether."

"How'd you know that?"

Ernie fields this one. "Last time you weren't this upset. I think last time you wanted us to find her so you could pork her again."

I turn to Minsky, fold my arms across my chest. "What'd she take? Money? More drugs?"

Ernie chimes in. "Your basketball net? Shoe lifts? Stepladder?"

A mumble from the midget, a susurrated slur, and for a second I think I hear what he's saying. No, that can't be it. "Come again?" I ask.

"She took my . . ." Minsky pauses, sighs, stares at us with his hands on his squat hips. "You're gonna make me say it again, ain't ya?"

Ernie clears his throat. "It—it sounded like you said she took your . . . your dick."

The protest I expected from the dentist does not emerge. He just stands there, defeated, eyes glancing the short distance down to his feet, cheeks flashing crimson.

"She stole your shlong?" I ask, my normal voice rising up a notch in surprise. "She pinched your penis? Detained your—"

For once in his weaselly little life, Minsky's eyes are filling with true shame. Stumbling toward the door, little legs pushing hard against the worn floorboards, he slams into Ernie's legs, bounces, rebounds, and makes for the hallway in a flailing blur, shouting, "Forget it, you two just forget it—"

But Ernie catches him with an easy left-field snatch and hauls the pipsqueak back into the room. "This ain't the kinda thing you can just forget," he explains. "It ain't every day a client comes in tells us his Johnson got jimmied."

Ern and I run through a few more good euphemisms for the old trouser snake, then make a quick U-turn back to business. "We're talking the human kind, I take it."

"Of course," says Minsky. "It was a Mussolini."

Ernie's low, impressed whistle echoes through the room. "Musta set you back a pretty penny."

"I inherited it," explains our client. "It was my father's, and his father's before him."

Unfortunately, I'm not doing too good of a job following the conversation. My standard-issue human phallus has always served me quite well, and since most of my romantic trysts take place out of guise—with a few notable drunken exceptions—I don't find that I need to employ its services all that often. Somewhere in the back of the rotting file cabinet of my memory there's a manila envelope with the name Mussolini on it, but the secretary is out of the office today, and there's no hope of retrieving it myself. "What's a Mussolini?" I ask, expecting a barrage of incredulous stares.

I get them. "Only the finest handcrafted human phallus in existence," Ernie says, shocked at my naivete.

"A mere seventeen left in the entire world," Minsky says proudly. "Three in America. Benito Mussolini's half-brother, Alfredo, handcrafted them during a four-year period just before the Second World War, and to date there is no finer instrument. It's like a glockenspiel, only longer. Precision ball bearings, clockwork timing, dual-thrust motion sensors. We're not just talking pricks—we're talking phallic perfection."

"They're worth millions," Ernie tells me. "But nobody ever sells."

"They're priceless," Minsky clarifies. "Priceless."

I get it—I think. "And Star . . . she took it?"

"We were sleeping after one of our . . . Anyway, we were sleeping—at least, *I* was sleeping—and when I woke up, she was gone. And my Mussolini was gone. I looked down at my guise, and all I saw was this. . . ." He starts to choke up, tears welling in his squinty eyes. "All I saw was a big gaping *hole* . . . where it used to be."

"You think she plans to hock it?" Ernie asks.

"I think she plans to use it. She loves that thing, can't get enough of it. I tried to take it off once, to have sex with . . . you know, with my real . . . Anyway, she wouldn't go for it. She has to have that Mussolini. And now . . . now she does."

Oh, super—my favorite kind of case: retrieve the golden dildo. When I got into the PI business, I expected to have to pay my dues, to spend a lot of time in cars and crappy apartment buildings, eating take-out food and snapping off cheap photos, but it's very possible that Minsky's case will sink me to a new investigative low.

"And you want us to retrieve it?" I ask.

"You have to. You find her, you grab hold of that no-good, rotten . . ." Once again, Minsky's union-truck-driver alternate personality emerges, and the profanities spring forth from his lips like a filthy, frothing fountain.

By the time he's done ranting, the coffee is ready. I dole out the cups, and we all have a nice sip of java to get our nerves jangling good and hard once again. "Partner, can I see you alone for a second?" I ask.

"Sure, kid," he responds. I've asked him not to call me *kid* in front of clients before, but as it's meant as an endearment I let it go. Undermines my authority a little, but you gotta give up something in the name of bonding.

We step out of the office and into the hallway, making sure to ensconce ourselves in an echo-free area. I've had an idea brewing ever since I put that pot of coffee on the fire, and I think it's just about time to serve it up.

"You think he'll go for it?" Ernie asks once I've laid out the basics for him.

"I think he wants his fake dick back so bad he'd sell his own real one to get to the girl."

"Think it'll come to that?"

"Hope not," I say. "But let's not count it out."

We step back into the office, plastic grins plastered across our faces. "We've got some good news for you," Ernie announces, and the grin that springs to Minsky's face is half joyous, half crazed. "We've got a lead on where she might be, and we think we can find her, not to mention your whang."

"Whatever it costs, do it."

"Cost is an issue, yes. We'll most likely have a good deal of expenses . . . at least ten thousand dollars' worth, maybe more."

"Anything," he says. "Find her, bring her back, throw her to the cops, and get my Mussolini back. That's all I care about."

"It may take a little bit," I point out. "A week or so. Longer, perhaps."

"Didn't you guys hear me?" says Minsky. "Whatever—it—takes. I want you to get her and get her good."

"Are you sure about this?" Ernie asks, completing the triumvirate of double-checks.

"Sure as a pile of shit behind a dead-eyed Diplodod," says Minsky, and though I don't exactly know what this means, I'm pretty darn sure that he's pretty darn sure. And when it comes to the amount of cash we're talking about, that's good enough for me.

The next half-hour is spent getting Minsky to sign documents and budget agreements that pretty much let us spend whatever we need wherever we need to in order to get the job done.

The next two hours after that are spent at my condominium as I rifle through my drawers and closets, trying to pick out and pack the proper clothing for our upcoming adventure. For the first time in some time, I'm actually at a fashion crossroads—I haven't got a clue what to wear.

Aloha, native Hawaiian girls. This is one Velociraptor who is ready to get leid.

First things first, work before play. It's a hell of a way to live, but the taskmaster who resides in my brain doesn't put away the whip until I've got things tied up in a neat little package for him. In the few remaining hours before our flight to Hawaii, the land of sugarcane and coconuts—the most potent of aphrodisiacs for any Diplodocus female, for some reason—there's a stop I need to make closer to home. West Hollywood comes before South Pacific.

Jules has come in useful for favors before, down-and-dirty details that a dino in drag—especially one who works in the reconstruction business—has more access to than a straight bum like myself, and I need to hit her up one more time for a little assistance on the case. But she doesn't pick up the phone, even after I let it ring for nigh on three minutes. Doesn't answer the private line at home, either, which can mean only one thing: Jules is helping out her friends.

The Shangri-La is a small nightclub perched on the west end of West Hollywood, barely dangling over the line between undifferentiated LA and highly differentiated Beverly Hills. The owner is an Iguanodon named Patrick who, though not gay or a cross-dresser himself, has a sweet spot in his heart for those whose friends and families don't understand or appreciate their lifestyle. Word on the street is that Patrick gives out more in food, drink, and spending money than he takes in. Must be true, because when I arrive out front, a huge spray-painted banner hanging over the club entrance reads: SHANGRI-LA GRAND CLOSING TONIGHT! EVERYONE MUST GO!

But despite the demise of the only dino drag club in greater Los Ange-

les, the party inside rages as hard as ever. Music blasts from speakers recessed into the walls, green confetti rains from the ceiling in an unending
torrential downpour, and a bevy of beautiful dinosaurs of indeterminate
gender bop and hop on stage, on the dance floor, at the bars, in the bathrooms. This is truly hedonism at its finest.

"Jules around?" I ask the bartender, a passable Audrey Hepburn I
haven't seen around here before.

"Who's asking?" she shouts over the noise, her voice low, gravely, the
kind of thing you hear out of construction workers. Needs some practice if
she's gonna make it as Holly Golightly.

"Rubio," I tell her. "I'm a friend."

Audrey gives me the once-over, and, after deciding that I must not be
that much of a threat, nods her head toward the back door. "You know the
knock?"

"My favorite tune," I drawl, but sarcasm is wasted on the gal.

A quick knuckle-rap of the theme from *Yentl,* and soon I'm granted entrance to the smallish dressing room tucked behind the stage. Jules is here,
done up nice for the event, a short, black skirt showing off a pair of finely
shaped legs I know to be surgically enhanced. In fact, I was there when
Jules was shaving off the final layer of epoxy from them a few months ago,
but the knowledge only increases my admiration of her talents. The matching halter top hides little of the ample chest attached to her guise, and as
she bends over to pick up a dropped bobby pin, I nearly fall into the Grand
Canyon of her cleavage. "Gotta hand it to ya," I say as I enter the dressing
room, "you're making a lot of real human women look bad."

"I'm not here to boost egos, honey," she replies, consciously replacing
her initial smile with a cultivated pout. "I'm here to shine."

After a hug, a peck on the cheek, and a full-body embrace, I am quickly
bombarded by a host of others who want a piece of the Rubio action. Jules's
friends have always been a hoot, every one a dear, and I've done my share of
work for them in various capacities, never charging more than the bottom
line, often throwing in a free snoop shoot or two for good measure. I think
they get off on the fact that I'm a real PI, Bogie-made-flesh, tail notwithstanding.

"Darling!" cries one such friend, a dead-on double for Judy Garland's
raven-haired daughter who, when he's not masquerading as Liza Minnelli

up in WeHo, is actually Hector Ramirez, a Coelophysis and toxic-waste shift worker at a chemical plant in Carson. In her best *Cabaret* strut, Liza sidles up to me and throws a sculpted leg around my waist, squeezing tight. "You've come for the action?"

All around me, male dinosaurs are buckling up more than their fair share of dangling appendages (using an improvised P-clamp, for obvious reasons) and shoving themselves into female human costumes, all in the name of fun and a little bit of soul-searching. It weirds out most of the dinos I know, but to me a guise is a guise is a guise.

"I've come for help," I explain. "I need Jules to help me out with a few things on this dog of a case."

"Jules is busy," coos Liza, to which my plastic surgeon friend—pins stuck between her lips, hands fiddling with a piece of loose flesh—nods her head. "Besides, if you want the dirt on a fellow, who better to ask than me?"

"I'm sure you could crack the Pentagon, doll"—they love it when I talk this way, makes them feel like they're inside the movies they try so hard to emulate—"but I'm gonna need Jules's help on this one."

Jules looks up from her work—trying to stitch up Rita Hayworth's rump, the pinup model's glutes squirming all over the place, refusing to let the master do her job. "Whatever you need, I'll do it," she mumbles, a needle clutched between her thick, red lips. "I've got two mask lifts today and this butt-cheek implant, but as soon as Rita stops fidgeting, I'm here for you."

"The information might be a pain in the ass to get," I warn her.

"Best kind."

"And you might have to cross a few Progressive paths. . . ."

"It's only getting better."

Eventually, Jules finishes up her work and sends the redhead sensation wiggling back out to the dance floor. "Okay," she says, sticking the needles back into an apple-shaped pincushion, "lemme tell you something about your Progressives."

"They're not mine—"

But she's not interested; the gal's already on a roll. "I've got three girls who are all bent out of shape 'cause of those bastards, you know that? Whitney won't go on tonight because she's nursing a black eye, and even though I offered to sew on a new cheekbone, she's too rattled to perform."

"What—what happened?" I ask.

"Progress happened," she drawls. "I was working on some costumes back at the Wax Museum for some of the ladies, and when they left, they headed up Hollywood way. Next thing they knew, they were down some alley, and a herd of blueshirts were on 'em, slamming away, shouting that they were freaks, they were unnatural, they were making it harder on the rest of us . . ."

"I'm—I'm sorry," I stammer, unsure of whether or not to apologize for a group I personally dislike yet in whose company I am about to spend the next three days.

"Forget it. I've got to go stage-manage in five minutes. But for you, I'm around. Any way I can help you bring down these prehistoric pieces of crap?"

I run down the details we've accumulated on the Progressives, omitting the more personal details such as my occasional hallucinations and more than favorable impressions of Circe. Recently I've been trying not to admit them even to myself.

"You think it's smart to go to this thing?" she asks me once I'm all done. "Seems like a hard place to keep your head screwed on straight."

"I'll try," I promise. "But I need some help from you. You know photos, right? You've got scanning equipment and all that?"

"Beyond the beyond, darling."

"Good. I've got photographs—" and here I produce the meager few shots I was able to get a hold of in the past few days: Jay with his waffle-loving dad; Crystal, the gal who met the wrong end of a rifle at the hands of bungling warehouse thieves; a few other Progressive expats who made it to safety before completing the journey to the great beyond. And in every photo, their loyal deprogrammer, those who helped free them from the mental ravages of Progress.

"This one's a nice shot," she murmurs. "Good light work."

"I need you to try and identify everyone in these shots. Get beneath the guise, give me some idea of who's down there."

"Whatcha lookin' for?"

"No idea," I say with all honesty. "I was hoping you'd stumble onto something."

Jules scoops the photos into a bundle, rolls them up tightly, and stuffs them into her blouse, much as she did with the cash Ernie handed her a few weeks ago. I wonder if she's got a safe down there. "I can do some extra snoop work if you want me to," she offers.

"Thanks, Jules, but I can handle that."

"You sure?" she asks me. "I'm itching to get after those sons of bitches, and my friends are always ready and willing to help. Gina's on the force out in Riverdale, you know."

"She's a cop?"

"Shhh, keep it down. They don't take to us all that well, so she keeps it a secret. Twice-decorated lieutenant. I made her a special set of tits with a hollow inside so she could hide her handcuffs. They're fabulous. She could be a real help—"

"Thanks, but—"

"Ain't nobody like a drag queen can move in and out of a place without being noticed."

"Liza's already offered," I explain, "but I'll be okay. See what you can do for me, and I'll call when we get onto the island."

We end with a hug and a promise to each other to be careful. I give her Dan's number at the LAPD in case she should run into trouble, then make my way back through the Shangri-La, snaking through the dwindling crowd. There's dancing and singing and tasting and loving and all sorts of naughtiness going down tonight, but as I'm leaving, it feels more like a wake than a true party. It's all a mask atop the mask—behind the laughter and the smiles is the knowledge that six hours from now, there will be no place left in Southern California for these folks to hang their wigs.

Notwithstanding the myriad articles on the subject produced over the years by the world's greatest academics, I can say with all certainty that right here and right now is truly a Velociraptor's natural habitat: lush, leafy trees, temperatures hovering somewhere in the mid-seventies, water lapping at my feet, subservient creatures scurrying around (though never underfoot), enough fresh herbs to last a lifetime. And a blended virgin daiquiri with extra coconut shavings and a massive multicolored parasol of which even Mary Poppins would be envious.

Jurassic, my ass. The Westin Maui Hotel and Suites is where it's at.

We got to Hawaii a day early—my idea—ostensibly in order to prepare ourselves for what is sure to be a trial by fire, but really just to get out of Los

Angeles before Minsky realized we conned him into bankrolling another client's case. Which is not to say that it's entirely impossible that Star Josephson has fled to the enchanted islands; it's just highly unlikely. Better chance finding her in another flophouse in North Hollywood, but you've gotta start an investigation somewhere, and Maui's as good a place as any.

I'm all by my lonesome out here, soaking up the rays, sipping my drink, and clearing my mind of detective effluvia. It tends to build up after a while, junk information clogging my neurons, and I should really hire a housekeeper before it clogs the entryway with a pile of false leads and red herrings. Ernie was sunning himself here on the pool deck for some time, but he recently picked himself up and waddled away, complaining about the heat building up inside his guise. I suggested to him a long time ago to upgrade his old Americraft guise to a newer Japanese model with PoreRight breathable skin, but the old wanker's resistant to change.

The pool is a remarkable feat of engineering achievement, a series of waterfalls and plastic slides interweaving through one another into a giant Gordian knot of liquid entertainment, and I'm sure I'd be more enthused about it if it didn't attract such a young clientele. A mess of bratty little human children scamper by one by one, strobing out the sunlight on their way to the local splash-fest, their screams piercing an otherwise tranquil afternoon. As one toddler stumbles by, my nostrils inform me that he's already made a mess of whatever diaper is beneath that bathing suit; as he jumps headlong into the pool, I resolve to stay dry for the rest of the day, or at least until the chlorine has had a chance to work its delousing magic.

I brought a book, a nice thick tome by some fellow with an unpronounceable middle name and astounding linguistic skills, but I'm barely into the second page when I catch a whiff of pine. Instinctively, I raise my eyes, shielding the glare from the sun with an outstretched hand. Before I know it, that hand is grabbed, pumped, released, and grabbed again. I've got just enough time to sit up before I'm shaken once more.

"Good to meetcha," says one of the silhouetted figures in front of me. "My name's Buzz."

"I'm Vincent," I mumble.

"Wendell," says the other one, his voice eerily similar to the first.

My eyes take their own sweet time in adjusting to the light; when I was a kid, these peepers went from pitch-black to screaming halogen in milliseconds, but with every passing year my aging pupils lose a bit of their edge. Eventually, I'm treated to a view of a tall, lithe fellow with an elongated face and protruding chin in a shrieking Hawaiian print shirt and baggy shorts—

And another tall, lithe fellow with an elongated face and protruding chin in a shrieking Hawaiian print shirt and baggy shorts. With the same hair. And the same eyes. And the same nose. And the same voice.

"We're twins," they sing in unison. The chorus effect is astounding.

"I see that."

"Smelled ya from over there, I did," says Buzz.

" 'Bout the same time *I* smelled ya," Wendell chimes in. "We're like that."

"Aha." Their scent is practically the same as well—a little acetone, some burning sugarcane—and their movements are similarly synchronized. As Buzz pulls up a chaise lounge to my left, Wendell drags one over to my right. They sit, flanking me, big goofy grins etched into those long faces.

It's not odd for dinosaurs to come out in multiple identical births—I knew a set of Triceratops triplets, in fact, who treated me to a triumvirate of titillation at their aunt's beach house in Ventura—but they tend to artificially distinguish their guises from one another once they're past puberty and tired of the myriad tricks that can be played on others when you've got a look-alike sibling. Yet Buzz and Wendell don't seem to have moved past this stage in their relationship. The closer I look, the more I believe that they've never even bothered to order two separate guises; most likely, they use one or the other's ID number and just ask for two of the same costume to be manufactured each time they have to reorder.

"Is this your first time at the hotel?" Buzz asks me, pulling himself closer. "With . . . us? With our kind?"

"Yes," I say, hoping this will end it, "it's my first time." I pointedly lift my book back to eye level and attempt to get in a few sentences; it's pure show in the hopes that they'll get the hint and excuse themselves, but I don't have much faith in its efficacy.

"We've been here three times," Wendell whispers to me, as if such a thing might be taboo. "We love it."

Buzz grins, ear to mawkish ear. "Absolutely love it."

"Three times . . . wow . . ." I'm trying to muster up interest, but it's just not happening. "You don't say."

"You know how we paid for our plane fare?" Wendell asks me, a childish excitement spinning his words into small, individual chuckles of delight.

"Can't say that I do."

"We saved it up," says Buzz.

"In change—"

"—in a jar—"

"—a big snowman jar—"

"—with pennies and dimes—"

"—and quarters and nickels. And three half-dollars that we got from our Uncle Joe."

It's the verbal equivalent of a tennis match trying to listen to these two, my neck twisting back and forth, trying to keep up with the shifting audiological focus. I opt for staring straight ahead and letting my ears do all the work.

"That's a lot of change," I say.

"We've been collecting since last year's trip."

"We always stay here before the journey," says Buzz.

"The journey?"

Wendell shakes his head. "I like to call it an adventure. Buzz says journey, I say adventure. We're different that way."

"Of course you are." I put on my best grin, beam it out to the twins, and start in on reading my book again. But it's a little hard to concentrate with the brothers sitting to either side of me, snickering over some inside joke, mouthing whispered syllables to each other. Tweedle-Dum and Tweedle-Dumber are starting to irk me, but I'm loathe to adopt an overtly hostile demeanor while ensconced in such a sedate environment.

I put the book back down. "And what journey would this be, then?"

The twins shoot each other a short glance, their slightly protruding eyebrow ridges raising in question to one another. "The great journey," says Buzz.

"The mystical adventure," says Wendell.

"The path to enlightenment."

"The way to salvation."

Oh, good. I was worried that I might not make my loony bin ratio today. "You guys here to preach to me?" I ask.

"Preach to you?" cries Buzz, clearly offended. "No! No, no, no . . ."

And then, as if in the same breath as his brother, Wendell scopes the area, sits back in his chaise lounge, and asks me, "Have you found Progress, brother?"

I sigh and toss my book in the pool. Nice vacation while it lasted, but the shop is open again and ready for business.

"They're on the same flight out tomorrow morning," I tell Ernie as we make our way down the hallway of the Westin Maui, nodding to the other tourists as we pass. There's some type of virus going around the islands— forces complete strangers to smile and nod affably at one another, and I'm afraid I've got a bad case of it. I may need to go to New York for the cure. "Talked my ear off for an hour."

"First-timers?"

"Fourth-timers. From what I gathered, they've already spent about sixty grand on these convocations."

"Sixty grand apiece?"

"There is no 'apiece' with these two."

"That's a lotta spare change."

"You don't know the half of it," I say, and leave it at that. "Point is, I think I might have made some inroads with them; once we're on the island, I'd like to try to get to know them better, see if they can give us some of the inside scoop. Maybe they knew Rupert."

"Good thought," says Ernie. We reach the elevator bank and wait for a lift to arrive. Dinner's already started, and I fear we're going to miss out on the good seats. Buffet-style food is of no use to me if I have to walk more than thirty feet to get it. At that point, I expect a waiter to do the messy work.

"Meanwhile," Ernie continues, "while you were sunning it up with the Bobsy Twins, I had myself a chat with the hotel desk clerks. Showed 'em Rupert's picture—"

"And?"

"And I got nothing. But the valet was listening in and caught up to me in the hall afterward. He knew our boy—not well, but he'd carried his bags once or twice—and said that the last time he came, he'd checked in with a lady friend."

That's a new one; as far as we knew, Rupert hadn't been seeing anyone for quite some time. Most of his relationships had been severed once he joined the Progressives, but it's wholly possible that in the intervening years, he'd shacked up with another truth-seeker. Nothing like the warmth of another body to keep the spiritual fires stoked.

"Something to look into," I say, and Ernie agrees. "Any description?"

"Stock. Asian, pretty, leggy."

"Welcome to Hawaii. Scent?"

"No clue," says Ernie. "Valet was a mammal."

We curtail the conversation on the way down, the rest of the elevator cab filled with humans and their own . . . *special* odors.

The doors can't open soon enough, and we pour out into the lobby, only to be shoved back a second later by a mass of redolent bodies. Dinos, all of them, and each one ruder than the last. They push, they shove, they make their way onto the elevator without letting us step off; we squirm and twist as we try to exit to the lobby.

"Big crowd," I mutter as we spawn our way through to the other side.

"Progressives?" suggests Ernie.

"I don't think so," comes a familiar voice from behind us. I turn to find Buzz and Wendell dressed in their finest Hawaiian livery, decked out head to toe in delicately strung flowers. They look like floats in the Rose Bowl Parade, and I suck up a good amount of air to keep myself from laughing. No doubt I will be burping soon, but it's worth it.

I do the introductions all around, and soon Ernie is inviting Buzz and Wendell to eat dinner with us at the hotel-sponsored luau. My initial instinct is to slap him across the back of the head—he doesn't know what it's like to talk with these two—but once again, my partner's got the right idea. If we can get in good with the twins now, it will be that much easier to get to them once we're on the island together.

"There's a convention in town," Buzz says as we head out of the hotel and down to the beach. "Accessories, mostly. Guise manufacturers, the big boys."

Does he mean the major manufacturers or just those who create plus-size guises? My grandmother, Josephine, who suffered from a glandular problem that, as far as I could tell, forced her to eat everything in sight, was a regular patron of the Lane Bronto catalog, and I spent many a night listening to her prattle on about the difficulties of finding appropriately sized guises that also suited her refined tastes.

From a hundred yards away, the smells of the dinner buffet begin to work their way through the Hawaiian air and up into my nostrils, and for a moment, I catch a whiff of something that's distinctly neither food nor drink. It's herb—fresh, sweet herb—and enough of it to flash me back to Circe, to her own intoxicating aroma, to our brief, unreal romps through an impossible jungle. But there's no seductress here, nothing in the way of yielding flesh and soft tail; there's simply pu-pu platters, coconut rum, and all the foliage I can stand.

I think I'll go get drunk now.

They roast pigs underground here. I don't mean in a little as-seen-on-TV rotisserie or wimpy So-Cal backyard fire pit, either—we're talking six feet down, Egyptian-mummy style, wrapped in foil, covered with sand, slowly cooked atop a pile of smoldering coals, and the resultant flavor sets off firecrackers of delight against my taste buds. And somehow, those bursting M-80s are managing to scurry their way off my tongue, up through my sinuses, and into the backs of my eyeballs, setting off a resplendent display of exploding reds and blues before my astonished eyes. Then again, it might just be the banana leaves talking.

"Good luau," I mumble to Ernie. My speech hasn't been affected quite as much by these leaves—the powers of which I never knew I was susceptible to until about twenty minutes ago—as has my vision, which continues to produce stunning hallucinations, mostly of an abstract variety.

"Good luau," Ernie echoes. He's morosely sipping at a fruit drink and pining away, probably for Louise. We're sitting at a small table set up right on the beach, the plastic legs of my chair sinking into the sand, the water lapping up against the shore no more than thirty feet away. Above, a multitude of stars gather themselves into the predictable patterns: Big Dipper and Orion for the human set, Baobob Tree and Luna the Lizard for my own species' zodiac.

Buzz and Wendell are also half in the bag, clucking their tongues like two farmers surveying their property, long rosemary branches dangling out of their mouths. "Whassa matter, Ernie?" asks Buzz.

"Don'tcha want some?" offers Wendell, plucking the spittle-coated weed from his mouth.

But Ernie just pushes it away, shakes his head, and returns to his drink. Slurp, pout, and slurp again.

"You gotta perk up," I find myself telling him. "Find a dame. Have a go at it."

A hard stare from my partner, almost a slow burn, but he can't bring himself to draw it out to any effective length. I grin right on through. "Have another banana leaf, kid," he mutters.

"Seriously," I continue. "How long's it been since you've got some in the sack?"

Now I'm getting the slow burn. And an impressive one, to boot. "In my day, we didn't go around asking each other how we were feeling and how long it'd been since we'd been with a broad—"

"It's a new age, Ern," I tell him. "You don't have to fess up, but you gotta deal with the rest of us."

I try to get Ernie to open up that Pandora's box of a heart of his, but the majority of my attention is suddenly, violently yanked across the back lawn of the hotel, past the volleyball net, the rent-a-snorkel booth, beyond the pool and the waterfall and the swim-up bar, all the way back to the hotel's veranda—

It's a Velociraptor. It's a female. As Ernie would say, it's a broad.

And what a broad. Her tail is long, curvaceous, enchanting, a Nile River of flesh. The snout strong and powerful, teeth flashing out like a row of diamonds. Eyes that glint with emeralds and the hint of more to come, a torso that holds the package together in just the perfect way, at just the perfect height.

She's naked. And she's coming this way.

"Ernie—" I stammer. "Ah—there's—"

"Knock it off, kid."

Making her way through the throng of humans, none of them paying her a lick of attention as her tail whips across their legs, their backs— raising great red welts on their flesh—her sight set on the luau, and, if I'm not mistaken, on our table. Two hundred feet and closing, Captain.

"Guys . . . ah, Ernie . . ."

"Knock it off, kid."

"No—Ernie, listen—"

"Two years, okay?" my partner barks at me. "It's been two years. You happy now?"

Two years? My god—I think I'd explode after two *months* without a little release. But even his admission of sexual dormancy isn't able to break through my shock at watching an unguised Raptor walk smack-dab through the middle of the Westin Maui Friday Night Luau, past the pu-pu platter and on her way. She's taking a long, serpentine path through the array of tables set up here on the beach, but I can tell from the set of flashing green eyes locked on mine that we are, indeed, her final destination. "Not that, Ern. Check it out."

I nod toward the approaching dino—something odd, now—is that a hint of clothing I see? And where did the tail go?—and Ernie takes a glance. "Nice looking, I guess," he says, and goes back to his drink.

By the time she's arrived at our table, the hallucination has dissipated. What was once a stunningly nude Velociraptor female is now nothing more than a fully guised female dino of undetectable lineage. The guise is impressive from a mammalian standpoint—native Hawaiian, mocha skin, thick lips, long limbs, straight black hair down to her petite mid-back—but I'm disappointed that my mind has chosen this moment to wake up on me.

"Mr. Rubio?" she asks, tapping me on the shoulder. It takes me a moment to wrest control of my body—*hyah, steed, hyah!*—and nod my head in the appropriate gesture.

"There's a phone call for you," she says. "They've been paging you for half an hour."

I blink, hoping to see that nude dino appear before me once again, but the Hawaiian mammal look-alike remains. "On your way back," mumbles Ernie, "grab me another one of these." And he returns to the solitude of his drink.

We walk across the sand, arm in arm, my legs a little wobbly either from the recent surprise or, most likely, the continuing effects of the banana leaves. "You knew who I was."

"Why do you say that?" she asks. Her voice is soft, light, inflected with a slight Hawaiian accent. Perfectly melodic.

"I saw you coming for me back there. Did someone point me out?"

A light blush spreads across the skin. Nice capillary action on that guise. "I smelled you when you registered. I like your scent."

I smile back and say, "I like yours, too." But in all honesty, I'm having a difficult time finding one. The pine is there, certainly, but beyond that I'm a little lost. My olfactory detection skills are always slightly hampered by the usual vices—fenugreek dries my nose up something fierce, clogs my sinuses like I'm drowning—and I assume these banana leaves are having a similar effect.

"I asked the desk clerk for your name," she admits. "I remembered you."

"So when they needed someone to come find me—"

"I volunteered. Yes."

Fair enough. Nothing like a nice little ego boost this late in the evening. I decide to play it out. "Is this what you do? Find guests who've been paged?"

She giggles, shaking her head coyly. "I'm in special sales, but I'm off for the night. This is just a favor to a friend at receiving."

"You like to do favors?"

"Depends on who's asking."

"And what if I asked?"

A hair toss, a light shoulder shrug, nice human moves for a dino. "Then we might need to work out a deal."

We've arrived at the hotel lobby, where I'm directed to a green courtesy phone. "You'll wait for me?" I ask my new Hawaiian friend. "You can teach me to hula."

The phone call is mercifully short. It's from Samuel, and he wants me to know that the hydrofoil will be picking Ernie and me up at the dock at three o'clock the following afternoon.

"Unless you'd prefer to take the ferry," he says. "It's not quite as rough a ride as on the hydrofoil."

"Might be nice," I muse. "Open water, peaceful trip."

"Takes about four hours, leaves from the port of Kauai."

"That's another island," I point out.

"Right."

"And how do we get there?"

"Hydrofoil."

They're not making this easy. "Forget the ferry; we'll go straight from here. Hey—can you give me an idea of what toiletries I should bring? I'd like to leave some stuff here on Maui to lighten the load, but—"

"No toiletries," he says.

"No, no, I'm talking about toothpaste, toothbrush, that sort of thing—"

"Exactly. No toiletries needed."

"Oh." I'm surprised—didn't expect a full-service resort on a tiny private island. "So you'll provide soap and whatnot?"

"Vincent, you're getting back to nature," says Samuel. "Don't concern yourself with such matters. The only things that need to get on that hydrofoil tomorrow afternoon are you and Ernie."

"And our check."

A pause, but certainly not a long one. "Yes. And the check."

When I hang up the phone and stroll back out into the main part of the lobby, I find my Hawaiian girl waiting for me on a plush tapestry-covered papasan chair. She matches the decor perfectly, and I wonder if the hotel ordered her out of some special catalog. I'd like to get myself put on *that* mailing list.

"I don't know your name," I tell her as I approach. "But when I ask a woman out, I always try to do it in a formal style."

"It's Kala," she says coyly.

"Thank you. Would you be so kind as to accompany me for a drink, Kala?"

"You drink?"

"For nourishment only. I do, on the other hand, enjoy a chew. . . ."

She holds aloft a small black clutch purse, bursting with unknown pleasures. "I brought my own," she purrs.

I feel like a teenager again as we huddle in a service nook off the lobby and tuck into the herbal delights Kala produces from her bag. A fair amount of locally grown date leaves—this is what they meant when they called it Maui Wowie—and some other native elements with which I have little prior experience quickly make their way through my digestive tract. There was a short period between the banana leaves and the phone call from Samuel when I had decided to quit the herbs altogether—even on a social level—go cold turkey, but in no time, I'm back off the wagon and rolling around in the mud below.

There's a lot of touching, a little squeezing, a heap of kissing, and a growing desire to rip off my guise right here, right now, and have at it. We're banging noses, bopping heads, uncomfortable enough in our costumes without herb-enraged lust complicating matters even further. My tongue delves into her mouth, seeking and finding the same, now snaking around hers; the caps pop off, allowing us free reign. I can taste the epoxy that holds that damned mask around her lips.

A minute later, laughter sets in. It's always that way—first, the slow, mellow rush of the drug working its way through the system, waving a friendly hello at all the organs as it passes on through; then, with certain herbs, the sexual rise, but by the time it's begun to knock on the brain's front door, the giggling takes over. Speaking is relegated to a second-class activity; what with all the kissing, it's difficult to breathe, much less get a full sentence out, "What—what is—whadda we got here—"

"Sugarcane. Bark."

"Ruff."

This sets off another twenty minutes of laughing and fondling, during which time we're asked by an overly officious member of the hotel staff to take it outside or upstairs. This sobers us up for but a moment.

"Outside?" I ask her.

"Upstairs?"

A little sidelong glance at each other, some unspoken agreement on the delightful future of this delightful evening—and we race through the lobby, hand in hand, barreling through tourists and not giving a good goddamn about it.

We're alone in the elevator, which is fundamentally good and right. Desire leaps up sixteen notches with every floor we pass, and it's amazing that our guises are still on. I hate kissing through this mask, these teeth, but even lust can't get me to violate the daily code of conduct—yet. If this elevator should stall, I'm fully certain that when the mechanic finally opens up the doors, he'll find two overgrown lizards going at it with all the primordial fury they can muster.

But the lift makes it all the way to the top and soon we're stumbling down the hall, our lips locked, mumbled nonsense syllables welling up from our chests, muted groans of craving that don't—and shouldn't— mean anything. My wild, wild hands are roving, trying to dig deep beneath that odd hourglass human guise in search of the true shape beneath, but every time I reach for her buttons or zippers, Kala whispers, "Not yet . . . not yet . . ."

We've reached the hotel room. It better be *yet* already.

As we crash into the room and stumble past an opened suitcase lying on the floor, I trip and go down hard, landing, with exquisite luck, faceup on the bed. Air whooshes out of me for a moment like a balloon with its knot untied, but by the time I've regained my breath I'm already laughing, calling out for Kala, reaching to pull her down with me and continue what is likely to become one of the better evenings in my considerable years of experience. But she's curiously absent from my grasp, and as I sit up, the room not so much spinning as it is line-dancing, I call out, "You still here?"

"In the bathroom," comes the reply, and I sigh and plop back down. Of course—time for the primping and the preening. In that respect, the female of the dino species is no different from that of the humans, except with the dinos there's less makeup and more basic hide care.

"Worked here long?" I call out, knowing that if I don't keep up a steady stream of chatter, I'll pass out good and hard. As if on autopilot, my hands begin unbuttoning my guise, ripping off clamps and girdles, tossing the foul things to the beige carpet below. My natural flesh ripples as it comes in contact with the damp Hawaiian air, and my groin is waiting for similar treatment.

"No," she replies. "You're on vacation?"

"Working vacation," I answer. There's a nice odor invading the room, perhaps some potpourri coming in through the air conditioning, or maybe streaming in from outside. The foliage on these islands is like nothing else we've seen on the mainland, and I've been having a great time sniffing around like a dog looking for the perfect place to poop.

"What do you do?" she asks me.

This always gets 'em. "I'm a private investigator," I say proudly. "I'm working a case for a friend."

"That's interesting."

"It's a job." Part of my humble routine. Works like a charm.

But there's no charm going on in here to match the one this Hawaiian beauty is working on me. There's the unmistakable click of a lightswitch being flicked off—my wooziness intensifying with the sudden lack of light, head sinking into the pillow, arms leaden and motionless—come on, Vincent, this is something you're gonna want to stay up for—and a tail flicks out from the darkness and slowly caresses my chest, the tip working its way down, down, knowing just where to go, just how hard to press, just when to release—waves of desire rising, lifting me off the bed, rising, straining, stretching—my mind fluttering away, letting itself drift, drift, and enjoy . . .

I hope Ernie doesn't wait up.

hangover, I can deal with. A pasty, numb mouth that tastes like I've eaten stale carpet—fine, no problem. Ringing in the ears, in the head, jaw aching, body trembling at the 3.0 Richter mark—okey-dokey by me. A nauseated feeling deep in the pit of my stomach, a family of hamsters scurrying around in my intestines—not fun, but acceptable.

It's the memory loss I could do without.

"You don't even know if you slept with her?" Ernie is chiding me as we trundle our bags through the marina on the way to the hydrofoil that will take us to the Progressives' island. We're a little late—half an hour by my watch—due to my inability to wake up and meet Ernie by noon, and the frantic pace has got me ready to lose what little lunch I was able to shove down on the way out of the Westin Maui's front door.

A tip: Poi is not appropriate hangover food.

"The act itself? No, no, I don't remember that."

"Nice habit you've got there, kid."

"Don't lecture me, I'll throw up on you. Look, I remember the foreplay. I remember the aftermath . . . sort of. It's that middle part that's a bit hazy."

All of it's a bit hazy, actually—the fondling before, the pillow talk afterward—but it's true that the actual act of sexual congress has completely escaped me for the moment. This has happened before, once or twelve times, mostly after a night of frolic and fun and bingeing. I'm sure there's a repository in some alternate dimension bursting with all of the things I've forgotten over the years, but it's probably filled more with algebra equations than sexual relations.

"What was she?"

"In what sense?"

"In the only sense," Ernie says. "Carno, Raptor, what?"

"I . . . I don't remember."

"Of course. You tell her why we're in Hawaii?"

"I'm sure I didn't."

"You're *sure*?" Ernie checks.

"Sure I'm sure. Sure." Not in the least. I could have given her my name, rank, serial number, and favorite breakfast foods for all I know. The only thing I'm positive about is that Kala was gone this morning when I woke up. Probably for the best. "Hell of a gal," I say. "A real firecracker."

"As far as you remember."

We make it to dock seventeen only thirty-nine minutes after our scheduled departure time, and the other passengers on board are not exceptionally thrilled with us. Buzz and Wendell, who haven't changed their clothes since last night—unless, of course, they brought duplicates of those godawful outfits—make a show of tapping their feet, checking their watches, but the twins are too grateful for our friendship to work up any real negative emotion.

"We made 'em wait," Buzz informs me as the dockhands gather up the mooring lines and prepare to cast off. "They wanted to go, but we said our friends were coming."

"That's what we said, all right. That's exactly what we said."

And that's how the next two hours go, Buzz and Wendell regaling us with tales of their heroic adventure of keeping the hydrofoil in dock. The telling of the story lasts at least three times as long as the actual event, I am sure, but Ernie and I use the time to shut off our brains and take a gander around us at the other dinos who have decided to live life the Progressive way.

Their human guises show no outward signs of mental instability; the hair is mostly washed, combed, and few of them are babbling incoherently. The smells aboard the hydrofoil, though mixed and braided through one another, are strong and don't have the pungent after-aroma so often associated with clinical wacko-ness. Once upon a time Ernie and I tailed a cat who was so far gone that his usual cookies-and-cream scent had curdled into a stench strong enough to track from twenty blocks away, unassisted. Good thing he couldn't smell himself, or it would have driven him even farther off the beaten path.

But what in the world—this or the next—could possibly be drawing this seemingly random collection of otherwise healthy dinosaurs into a semi-mystical, full-bunk organization like the Progressives? Is it the camaraderie? The reverence for past generations? Or is it the idea that they may somehow reconnect with their inner selves, that they can become more dino than human once again?

"I can't wait until we get naked," giggles Buzz.

"Me, too," says Wendell. "That's the best."

Indeed, by the time we reach the island, the others have become restless enough to shed their guises, ripping away at the buttons and zippers in a mad nudist frenzy. As I fumble with my own costume, I realize how out of practice I am, and, by extension, how skilled these Progressives are in the fine art of disrobing. As I struggle with the hidden snaps beneath my human pecs—nicely inflated but not too strapping, despite Jules's insistence on pumping them up with a new polymer she ordered from Korea—a G-2 buckle flies out of the crowd, through the air, and beans me on the noggin. A few seconds later, I duck to avoid a tail strap. They're not particularly careful with their guises, throwing the human skin around like a bunch of old rags. Dino mothers are famous for teaching their children to take care of their costumes—*Do you have any idea how much these cost? Do you know how hard your father works so you can buy new legs every year?*—but these superego lessons didn't seem to take with this bunch.

Ernie and I are more sedate in our divestiture of clothing and costume, but in short order we're standing free and clear alongside the others, ready to disembark and begin our Progressive journey. Some small part of me—a part that shrinks with every passing year Ernie and I work together—is reeling off a grocery list of reasons why we shouldn't be here, why our best course of action would be to turn around, reguise, and have the hydrofoil take us back to Maui and a little more of that fresh banana leaf. Daniel into the lion's den, Abel baiting Cain, stepping on a mad dog's tail. But I know the risks, I know the rewards, and I'm here to do whatever's needed in order to get the job done.

"You ready to crash this party?" I mumble to my partner, already knowing from years of experience what his response will be.

"So long as I don't have to dress up."

"Don't worry," I assure him. "We're going casual."

The Hum-Vee ride into the heart of the Progressives' island is uneventful, unless you count the multitude of trees we nearly slam into at speeds approaching NASCAR records. Our convoy of military trucks runs roughshod through the jungle, the wide bodies barely able to negotiate the way. Samuel, unguised and redolent, is at the helm of our six-man open-air assault vehicle, his curved green foot heavy on the accelerator, claws digging into the floorboard. Though I've been around dinos all my life, I've never seen one driving a car in the buff, and I have to force myself to stare at something else; don't want to give the guy the wrong impression.

As we rumble down a barely beaten trail, I notice another path branching off to the left; as we pass, the Progressives don't so much look away as they do expressly *not* look away. It's a weird sign, whatever it is, and I take a gander down there as we shoot by at forty-five miles an hour. The jungle vegetation is thick down that road, I notice, and the path soon disappears into the trees. But something at the end of it catches my eye, my brain, and nags enough to get me to talk to Samuel again. "What's down there?" I ask.

"Nothing. More of the jungle."

"Trees looked sorta . . . odd."

"Trick of the eye," he says, and his silence closes off further conversation.

Soon the Hummer slows, and Samuel reaches over and clicks a small button on what looks like a remote control clipped to the auto's sun visor. Somewhere nearby, a thin creaking sound joins the mix of jungle noises. The bumping slows down as we pass onto a section of well-packed dirt.

"What's that?" I ask.

"What?"

"The creaking."

"Animals."

"Creaking animals?"

"Hawaii is a fascinating land."

After a few more minutes of Mr. Iguanodon's Wild Ride, we pull onto smooth terrain, and the glory—perhaps not the appropriate word—that is the Progressive compound is laid out before us. I don't suppose it would have been fair of me to expect another luxurious Xanadu similar to the complex back in the Hollywood Hills—it's a fair enough chunk of change to buy up an island in the Pacific, so I can't begrudge the Progressives for taking it easy on the accommodations—but bare-bones roughing it has never been my bag. It's hard to make out specifics in the all-but-complete Hawaiian darkness, but as the headlights from the wide-track stream over the camp, I'm a little put off by what masquerades as living conditions around here: simple wooden huts dot an otherwise barren landscape, the occasional weed poking up from beneath a thin layer of brownish crab-grass.

"It's . . . nice," I say as the truck drives into the heart of the camp, kicking up a cloud of dust that stings my eyes and chokes my throat.

"This is a simple life," Samuel responds. "It's closer to the way we were meant to live."

"Ah. Without the huts and the Hummer, you mean."

". . . Yes." I think Samuel is finally learning to dislike me. This would not be atypical.

We hop out of the transport, and Samuel leads Ernie and me to one of the larger huts. The wooden door doesn't so much creak as it complains, and I find myself scanning the walls to check the structural security of this ramshackle domicile. There's a lot of bamboo and dried palm leaves, and though this was more than enough to shelter the castaways of Gilligan's Island, I don't put much stock in its ability to protect us should anything stronger than a light breeze decide to come whistling about.

"Any other accommodations?" I ask.

"How so?"

"Something . . . better?"

Samuel cocks his head. "Like an upgrade package?"

Aha, luxury at last! "Exactly. That's *exactly* what I mean."

"No."

Strewn about the floor of the hut are all manner of branches, leaves, and twigs. "What this for?" I ask, lifting a branch, hefting it to test its weight. "Bringing nature inside for us?"

"That's your bed," explains Samuel, the tone a mite more rational than the words.

I shake my head. "I'm really more of a Posturepedic kinda guy."

"Mattresses and frames are human constructs, made for human bodies," he explains. "You will need to make a nest, much as our ancestors did in the wild."

Now, I am fully aware that the currently popular human theory about our species is that we evolved into birds, that our body types and bone densities are more similar to modern aviators than they are to lizards and the like, but this is pure rubbish. What's more, it isn't even a dinocentric theory. Most of the time, we've got paleontological "plants" doing the dirty work for us, injecting theories here and there, but this whole bird concept is a purely human one, and I can't believe that Samuel would be parroting such nonsense.

"You have two hours," Samuel continues, "and then dinner will be served. Circe has invited the two of you to be her guests at dinner tonight, and then to join her during the Ring."

The Ring? I'd ask Samuel what the heck he's talking about, but Ernie is fixated on the nest situation. "You're joking, right? Tell me there's a cot around that corner."

Samuel shakes his head, a missionary overjoyed to be preaching to the heathens. "We all make our nests every night, and take them apart every day. It is what the ancestors did, and it is part of the natural way."

And, as if on cue, our other hut-mates ooh and aah over this afternoon's chore, eagerly rushing forward, fighting with one another for the best pile of sticks. A pair of Compies rush by, beaks chattering in some language I can't understand; I promise myself that wherever they choose to bed down for the night, I will sleep far, far away.

My nest-building skills are not quite on par with, say, my trumpetplaying skills, which are not quite on par with, say, my juggling or fire-eating. Suffice it to say that once I am done tucking and bending and shoving and mushing, my bed for the evening resembles nothing so much as the chaff left over after a once-mighty redwood has been converted into six hundred reams of InkJet paper. Sticks and branches and bristles and all manner of leafy shards stick out in every possible direction, poking me expertly in all the wrong places.

Ernie's nest is, of course, impeccable, a seamless puff pastry of a bed frame, with perfectly rounded edges, downy-soft leaf interior, and a pillow made out of what looks to be bark shavings held together with twisted vine. If this is all just a giant IQ test thrown at us by the Progressives, I'm sure to end up in the remedial class sometime soon.

"You want help?" he asks.

"Screw off," is my only reply. "I like it this way."

Wendell and Buzz, no surprise, make theirs in identical fashion, forming a series of rounded triangles stacked atop one another until they've got an inverted Aztec pyramid in which to sleep. All the while, as they construct, the twins keep up a furious stream of chatter.

"I love this part," says Wendell.

"The beginning of the journey," says Buzz.

"You do this a lot?" Ernie asks as he puts the finishing touches on his nest, gracing the tips with a little cotton fluff.

"Oh, yes, yes," says Buzz. "We make nests every night, and we've been coming here . . . oh, a long time."

"How long exactly?"

"I don't—I can't remember—"

"Give it an estimate," I suggest. "Give or take."

Buzz and Wendell confer among themselves, whispering back and forth like a Senate witness and his attorney deciding to take the fifth, and eventually come back with, "Five years."

"You've been Progressing for five years?" I say. "Well . . . that *is* a long time. Very impressive." The twins beam with pride, and I'm glad I've got them on the right track.

"It's the only way to live," says Buzz.

"The only way to *be,*" says Wendell.

I nod, close my eyes, pretending to soak in this valuable information. Then, as if it's the most natural segue in the world, I say, "Actually, I did know one other fellow who was around the group these last few years—maybe you guys knew him."

"I doubt it," says Ernie, catching on. "These boys can't know everyone."

Buzz jumps up and down, his tail slapping the ground with a meaty thunk. "Oh, but we do! I'm sure we do! What's his name?"

"Rupert," I tell them. "Rupert Simmons."

No reaction. Buzz and Wendell don't even make their usual aside to deliberate on the issue; they simply shrug their shoulders.

"I think he was called Granaagh," says Ernie, and I'm impressed with his excellent dino pronunciation.

Aha! Now there's talking and crying and sobbing and condolences and a hearty dose of caring all around. They knew Rupert, all right, and knew him well.

"Like a brother," sobs Wendell, great streams of salt water running from his eyes. "I loved him like a brother."

Buzz is similarly upset, though he seems unable to match his twin in sheer tear production. "What a good soul. I can never understand why he did what he did."

"Kill himself, you mean?"

"Abandoning Progress," cries Buzz. "He was so close. Seventy-three percent dinosaur natural. He was almost ready for the Ring."

There it is again; that phrase keeps popping up. "The Ring," I say. "This is a prize, of some sort?"

"No, no, it's—it's the ultimate test. The test of Progression."

Mumbo, mumbo, and more jumbo. Don't know why I expected anything different. "This something everyone goes through?"

"Eventually," Buzz tells me. "But it takes a true natural dinosaur to make it through the Ring."

Ernie puts an arm around Wendell, a golf-buddy hug of camaraderie. "You boys pass this test yet?"

Wendell recoils from Ernie—whether it's the arm or the question, I don't know—and shakes his head rapidly, as if he's watching a tennis match between hummingbirds. "Goodness no!" he yelps. "We're hardly ready for that."

"Hardly ready."

"The Ring is only for those who are ready to move on to the next level. We won't be there for some time."

"A long time."

Interesting. It doesn't come as much surprise that Buzz and Wendell, friendly though they are, haven't quite made it up the Progressive ladder. Nice kids. Brains like squirrels. On the other hand, it *does* come as a surprise that Rupert Simmons, after such a short period of time with the group, had. Our estimates had made Rupert a Progressive for three years, max, which meant he moved along quite quickly. "So Rupert—he was high up, huh?"

"He was very advanced," says Buzz. "In fact, he led many of our seminars."

Wendell's eyes go wide, that eerie Progressive look of half excitement/half insanity flaring to life. "Remember the one about the mammals?" he gushes. "It was soooo wonderful!"

Buzz turns to me to explain. "He showed us how the mammals were rightfully under us in the food chain."

"Under *us!*" shouts Wendell.

"And how dinos are technically the dominant species, even though we're a population minority."

I cluck my teeth—hard to do when your chompers are sharp as knives, but I've got it down to a science after years of practicing disapproval—and say, "No love lost for the humans here, I take it."

"Why should we care about them?" asks Buzz. And now that casual, friendly tone is conspicuously absent from his voice. It's all business. "They keep us down. They keep us from realizing our true selves."

"They're hideous," Wendell chimes in. "They must be stopped."

Buzz fixes his twin with a hard stare, and Wendell immediately drops his eyes. "He takes it too far sometimes," says Buzz. "My brother's very excitable."

I'm about to go on, to press Wendell along this path, when a distinctive scent begins to make its way through the cracks in the walls, the ceiling. My head is already beginning to float a foot above my body, my sinuses filling with a potpourri of herbs and spices, stretching through my nostrils, snaking down into my throat, nearly choking off my ability to breathe.

"What is it?" Ernie asks, hands on my shoulders. "You okay, kid?"

"Yeah," I manage to gurgle. "It's—it's—"

"You're turning purple—"

"It's—"

The door swings wide, blowing open on a breeze as if it's made from the flimsiest of woods, and suddenly the scent drops to nothing, undetectable, a figment of my imagination the entire time. Air comes rushing back into my lungs and my heart resumes its normal pattern, albeit with a slightly faster beat, the adrenaline rush courtesy of this magnificent creature standing in the doorway.

"Good evening," whispers Circe, her breath tickling my ears even from ten feet away. "I want to show you two something."

14

t's a barn, and nothing more. I mean, it's fine, as barns go, but when Circe said she wanted to show us something, I was hoping for something a little more on the . . . erotic side. And a barn, certain human fetishes aside, is not a particularly sexual place. Then again, the Progressives have already surprised me; perhaps there's a full-tilt party going down inside that barn. That might explain the otherwise inexplicable human attraction for Amish country.

But for now we're standing outside this tall wooden structure, and I don't quite get it. I express my displeasure, muttering, "It's a little cold out here to be looking at the side of a dumb barn." Despite the warm Hawaiian clime, the nighttime temperature has been dropping steadily since we began the climb up this hill, and the brisk wind up here whips the air into icy little pins that manage to send my hide into miniature convulsions. With the exception of a few mutant species who flourished during the first Ice Age—a rather dismal period, I am led to understand—we dinos were constructed for more temperate climes. Very few of us live north of Buffalo.

"This 'dumb barn,' as you call it, is what enables us to maintain this property," she says, "as well as the other properties we hold around the world. Come, have a look."

We enter through a solid steel security door that opens only after Circe has inserted her finger into a hole that looks suspiciously like the one on the side of the bogus Ancestrograph back on Hollywood Boulevard. I'd try putting my finger inside, just to see if it's got that Frigidaire feel to it, but

I've already gotten a glimpse of the security in this place, and I'd like to leave the Hawaiian Islands with all of my digits intact.

"Security measures," explains Circe, and I grin stupidly, as if I understand what the hell she's talking about. It's a *barn*, for chrissakes. Since when are horses a classified secret?

Since they've started decking out their stables in gleaming high-tech lab equipment, I guess. A sea of dinosaurs—all unguised, frenzied, sweaty, and reeking—hover over individual workstations and lab tables, furiously applying their skills to whatever the heck it is that they're doing. The interior walls of this simple farm structure have been plastered with metal plates at least three inches thick, the only available light streaming down from six massive overhead halogen fixtures hanging from the ceiling.

And in the middle of it all stands the end product of all this attention, the raison d'être. It takes a moment for my eyes to adjust to the increased luminescence, but once they do, I am compelled to focus on one of the largest dinosaur skeletons I have ever seen, bar none.

Sure, I've seen complete fossils before, and, sure, the Museum of Natural History in LA has a few real gawkers—but they're much smaller, not as well preserved, and of a dinosaur type far more common than this unique creature. It's eighty feet long if it's an inch, double-decker-bus wide, and tall as a California palm. Down on all fours like an ancient Brontosaur, but with a long, spiked tail that twists its way down and around the large, stumpy legs. A jaw full of sabered teeth rounds out the weapon display, sitting firmly in front of a sloped-back head that leads to a long, thin neck and barrel chest.

Bleached-white bones three feet in diameter have been fastened together with large lumps of alabaster putty, support rods jammed into crucial joints and welded to the base beneath, the entirety of the structure further supported by a series of thin cables wrapped around the uppermost limbs and vertebrae and anchored to the ceiling. It's a gigantic marionette of some long-forgotten ancestor, and though I'm a bit taken aback by its presence, I can't think of a more fitting place for such a monstrosity than in the company of these Progressives.

"What . . . what is it?"

"That's Freeangggh," says Circe, roaring with the best of them, "but mostly, we just call him Frank."

"What the hell are you doing with the old guy?" I ask, then correct my-self—"the ancestor?"

"We're making him, that's what. He's not really old, actually. Or really dead."

"Not really dead?" I ask, unsure of the specific mechanisms with which one could be classified as not *really* dead. "Looks like a goner to me."

"And that's the idea. That's the idea precisely. Here, come have a peek."

We follow our host across the barn, taking a serpentine path around and about Progressive dinosaurs crouched over desks, across blueprints. Fifty-gallon vats of a strange white bubbling mixture block our way, and Circe warns us to take care as we step around them.

We arrive at the base of the gargantuan fossil, nothing more than ants invading the dead giant's picnic, and it's only while standing in this Go-liath's shadow that I come to a startling realization: even if I were somehow able to transport myself back in time to the Jurassic, I'd be stepped on or eaten in seconds flat. A few sharp claws and a wiseass attitude don't get you very far when you're outweighed by twenty metric tons.

I don't recognize the bone structure, though I imagine that this is more a function of my point of view—looking straight up into the beast's nostrils—than my lack of ancestral fossil knowledge. Nevertheless, I hazard a guess. "Brontosaur? Triassic period?"

"No and no, but a valiant attempt. Don't try again—you'll be wrong."

"How do you know?"

"Because this is neither one of the species of dinosaurs that died out during the Great Showers nor one of those that survived. This is an entirely new species of dinosaur, Vincent, and I'm proud to say he's of my own de-sign."

"Your design?" asks Ernie, stepping forward and into the conversation.

Circe takes a seat near Frank's phalanges, stroking his three-foot-long toes as she speaks. "We'd been hearing some rumblings from the paleonto-logical community for some time about the lack of new finds, complaints about grant money going to waste, so we've been preparing for a baby like Frank here for quite some time. Gave me a little head start on the blue-prints. But when it comes to the actual construction, we only work under contract, so it wasn't like we were going to go ahead and start the projects on spec. . . ."

"Wait a second," I say, catching the drift as it wafts by. "I get it—you're fossil-makers. You guys make some of the fake fossils they plant out in the desert."

"Some?" Circe huffs. "We're responsible for eighty-seven percent of the West Coast fossil finds, thank you very much. No one has the quality we do."

Ernie gives the dinosaur's shin a little knock. It echoes right on back. "So Frank—this thing here—is a fake?"

"What new fossils aren't? And for that matter, what old fossils aren't? Do you know how hard it is to get a bone—a real bone—fossilized? It's not like all the ancestors took off time to go search out a peat bog they could die in. There are very specific conditions under which fossilization can take place, and if we relied solely on natural fossil finds to stock the world's endless hunger for new discoveries, there'd be quite a number of museums out there without their endowments."

"My uncle was a fossil-maker," I say, trying to inject a little spirit of camaraderie.

"Was . . . ?"

"He got bought out," I shrug. "Fossil Time offered him a lump sum. Now he just sits at home and writes angry letters to *Reader's Digest*."

"That's us."

"What is? *Reader's Digest?*"

"Fossil Time."

I shake my head. "We must be talking about something different. This is a joint back in Chicago out near—"

"Near Evanston," Circe finishes. "I know. It's one of our outlets—we don't have many in the Midwest, actually, but it's profitable, so we keep it up. We're also Fossils-R-Us and Bone Dry Diggin' and Good Tyme Mineral Creations and about sixty other companies I can't keep track of. Samuel's in charge of the group's business affairs."

This certainly explains where the Progressives get the cash to front such an expensive operation, but it cuts the legs out from under my idea that young Progressives—like Rupert, Buzz, and Wendell—are pumped solely for their moola. Compared to an outfit like this, a thousand bucks from Daddy's IRA is chump change.

"You do good business?" Ernie asks, his mind clearly on the same path as my own.

But Circe's been to school on the matter. "We do all right," she says, and leaves it to our imaginations to conjure up the millions of dollars that must be flowing into Progressive coffers.

She leads us to a workstation manned by three dinosaurs of different lineage—there's an Ankie, an Allosaur, and a Procompsognathus all working together in harmony. I'm surprised that a Compy has the cranial capacity to carry out such detailed work, but hold any outward signs of my disdain in check. The trio of dinos are hunched over a mica-topped table, fiddling with a long, slender bone about three feet in length and six inches in diameter.

We're introduced—the three Progressives having completely unpronounceable throat-clearing growls as their names once again—and Circe gives us a rundown on the task at hand. "The thing about fossils," she says, "the truly crucial thing about attempting to duplicate the beautiful structures of the ancestors, is age."

"Age? What age? They're new," I say.

"But they don't look it, and they don't test it."

"And I don't get it," says Ernie.

"Artificial aging is where most fossil producers come up short. It's a difficult task, to say the least, but nothing short of perfection makes the grade with us, whereas precision is not as important in the other factors. For example, I could take you back to the firing room, where we cast the molds and pour the liquid dentin, and you could appreciate how we come up with the initial shape of the bones. It's fascinating, believe me, but a slight imperfection here or there won't break six weeks' worth of work. We could sand down, we could build out, or we could leave the mistake as is and let the mammals theorize over its implications for years to come. Remember when that paleontology team from USC found a baby Camptosaur out near Palmdale?"

"Sure," I lie.

"Started out as a Hadro, but one of our mixers threw in too much dentin. We figured, what the heck, the world needed a new species, anyhow."

"It did . . . ?"

"We could also take a tour and go back to the design center," she continues, "a delightful section of the business, and I could show you how we determine the exact length and tendon pairing for each individual piece, how we plan to 'discover' a certain number of pieces first, that sort of thing. Again, while this is an important part of the puzzle, there is room for leeway. A Diplodocus jawbone might be scattered a few extra centimeters away from the rest of the skull, but it's nothing that would set off alarm bells in the average ape.

"But this station right here—and the ten others on the floor—this is where the magic takes place. This is where the slightest miscalculation could bring down the whole house of cards."

Ernie shakes his head, lips pursed. He hates being confused. "Still lost me."

"You've heard of carbon dating, Mr. Watson?"

"Measures the age of an item. So . . . what? You put carbon in these things?"

There's the laugh again, and though it's at my friend's expense, I can't help but feel a warm glow at her every giggle. "No, no," she says. "Carbon dating is actually very limited in scope, and it certainly wouldn't help date an object from the ancestors' time. In fact, when human scientists locate a dino fossil, they're not even able to date the object itself—instead, they rely on the age of the rock surrounding the object. And that's where the fun starts."

"We weren't having fun already?"

"Let me explain: There are two main ways to date any rock stratum. The easiest method is by determining its relative location. The deeper the layer, the older it is. Fortunately for us, paleontologists have come up with quite the intricate dating system—most of it determined long ago by Council planners and carefully spoon-fed to the human scientific community until they took it on and accepted it as their own. And they follow it to a T, so it makes our job that much easier. If we want some scientists to find a Raptor thigh from eighty million years ago, then we just go out to the site, dig to the proper layer—don't even ask what those tools cost us—plant, and bury it back up again. You'd be surprised how no one seems to care, and if any human starts to make a fuss, there's always a dino higher than him on the academic totem pole to kick the little ape off the dig site and send him home to teach Archaeology 101 to a bunch of stoned hockey players."

Circe's getting all worked up now, and I can smell the herbs beginning to flow, ebbing in and out as her mood elevates. Oregano first, like we're passing an Italian joint, but soon the basil and marjoram's kicking in as well. I grab the edge of the table firmly so as to keep my mind—and body—from wandering off to a distant forest.

"Second method is a little harder, and that's what my fine brothers and sisters here are working on. Scientists can take the layer of rock surrounding any given fossil and subject it to a test for radioisotope decay—similar to carbon dating, only on a much grander time scale. At least, that's what we've got them thinking, and that's all the help we need. What we're doing here is impregnating the rock chips surrounding the fossil with a certain amount of radioisotope and a larger amount of the substance it decays into, in order to give the impression that the mineral's been decaying over time—"

"And therefore creating the impression of age," I finish.

"Exactly. The paleontologists dig it up, note the surrounding rock layers, and test the substance. Their computers decide it's gone through twelve point six half-lives—or however long we want the computers to tell them—and they dance around for a while, announce the discovery to the world, and prop the old boy up in a dusty showcase somewhere."

"And who pays you for this?" asks Ernie.

"The museums, mostly. Everyone needs visitors, Mr. Watson. The fine example you saw back there is going to be the newest and hottest thing on the paleontology circuit over the next six months. You just watch."

"Six months?" I ask.

"It takes time, Vincent, it takes time. The fossil structure is completed, but we've still got to disassemble the creature, break off the necessary bone chips, ship the whole mess out to Los Angeles, prepare the burial, truck it out to Utah, scatter and plant every single piece, wait a few months for the sand to cover up our tracks, and convince some influential foundation to take another crack at the area to see if there's anything they might have missed. Have you ever worked with mammals? It's exhausting."

"What are you calling it?" asks Ernie.

Circe dismisses the question with a wave of her hand. "We try not to prename the fossils here. Oh, we had a division a few years back that would come up with some of the labels—they're the ones that thought of Megalosaur, actually—but it's usually better to let the community pick a name by themselves. Gives them a sense of ownership. I'm sure they'll be extraordinarily creative with this one—Largosaur or Tailosaur or some other braindead flight of fancy."

"It's all very impressive," I say, "and it's good to see that everyone's so . . . productive."

"That's a part of the Progressive way," Circe insists. "There are no free rides on the path to a natural lifestyle. We gladly participate in deceiving the humans in this manner so that we are able to be free in our choice of non-costume."

"Everybody works, then?" asks Ernie.

"Everybody."

"Even you? Seems to me you do a lot of philosophizing and not a lot of hands-on labor."

"Even me," Circe laughs. "I run the planting sites in Utah and Nevada, mostly, and the work couldn't get any *more* hands-on. Most of the time, I'm down in the holes, digging away at the dust with my own eight claws."

Great—now Ernie's got her pissed off at us. "He didn't mean—"

"Please, please," says Circe, "there are no wrong questions. Everything is open here."

"Great," I say, getting back to the matter at hand. "What did Rupert do, by the way?"

"Who?"

"Rupert—our deceased friend. The one who's frolicking with the ancestors now . . . ?"

"Of course," says Circe, not a stammer in sight. "Forgive me, please. I'm not accustomed to addressing Progressives by their slave names." There's that term again, and it gives me the willies.

"That's fine. What did Gran—Granna—what did he do?"

"He was a bonewright, I believe. They shape the molds, sand the fossils into the proper shapes before they're sent here for aging."

"I see . . ." I don't—not exactly—but such an admission is unnecessary at this stage.

"Did he have friends?" Ernie asks. "Coworkers?"

"Of course."

"Can we talk with them?"

"To ask them . . . ?"

"Just to talk," says Ernie. "To see if he'd been depressed. It's tough, when a friend goes like that."

Circe takes Ernie's hand—is she blasting him with pheromones now?—and strokes it gently. "I understand," she whispers. "It's very difficult, and I grieve with you." Then, volume back to normal, dropping the hand back to its place: "But I'm afraid I can't interrupt our brethren right now. We've got to come through on Frank here within the week or we'll run past deadline. The Coalition of Natural History Museums will have my hide for sure if we don't fill this contract."

"We understand," I say, nudging Ernie away from the fossil and his next series of questions. I'm all for pushing to get answers, but I don't want to blow it with a premature interrogation.

Circe takes a cursory glance at her watch. "Brothers, I believe it's time for dinner. Shall we?"

Circe takes us by the arm—first me, then Ernie—and with a simple tug easily leads us from the barn. The other Progressives continue their work, though I can feel the combined weight of their stares as we are ushered from the building and back into the night air.

"So . . . do you have any more questions?" she asks, once we've cleared the barn area and are making our way back down toward the compound.

"Just one," I say, remembering the newt and snake snack we were treated to the last time we attended a formal Progressive affair. "Is dinner dead or alive?"

The evening meal is a casual affair. There are no tuxedos. There are no evening gowns. There are no hors d'oeuvres, ice sculptures, string quartets, wandering waiters with toppling trays, or lectures by pretentious people who are famous mostly for being pretentious in the first place.

There is, however, a lot of raw pork.

"It's not a religious objection," I assure Circe. "I think one of my grandmothers might have been Jewish, and I'm sure I've got some Muslim blood in me, but it's really more of a . . . I mean, it's pork. Rare. Raw. It's a pig."

"It's disgusting," grumbles Ernie. He's ready to fast if need be, and, truth be told, he could do with a few days of food restriction. Seeing him out of his guise for the last twenty-four hours has told me more about my partner's body than I ever wanted to know; the nudist lifestyle does not compliment all somatotypes.

"You are worrying about diseases," begins Circe, who is dressed to the nines—well, to the eights at least. She's the only one in the large dining hall to wear anything other than her natural skin: a small emerald pin, the glimmering jewel cut in a tapered oval—an egg shape—that sticks delicately out of her hide just above her tail. Sex-x-x-y.

A long time ago, a Coelo hooker I was tailing on a case let me in on a little trade secret: the two square inches just above the area where a female dino's tail meets her body is the most erogenous of erogenous zones. Pleasure beyond pleasure can be found in that small patch of hide, and over the years, I've used that knowledge to my great advantage with the ladies. And even as I sit here and calmly talk to Circe, keeping my own erogenous zones safely in check, I find myself hoping that later tonight I might get a chance to try a little cult exploration of a different kind.

"Trichinosis is very rare among our kind, Vincent," Circe continues. "And we've never had an outbreak here on the island. I wouldn't worry about it."

I take another look at the dinner table, at the mostly intact pig lying on its back, sides split open by a sharp claw, the meat and guts spilling out onto a bamboo platter. The other diners at our table—a motley collection made up of Samuel, several unnamed dinos from Circe's cadre, and a few other Progressives whom I don't recognize—don't seem to share my rising gorge; they tear into the thing with their claws and snouts, pecking at it like a pack of vultures on a fresh corpse.

"You're sure?" I ask. "About the trichinosis."

Circe nods, looks me in the eye. I could lose myself in those big green globules, though I'm more worried about losing my lunch. "If you want to journey down the road to Progress, you have to take that first step by yourself."

Trite, no doubt, but it does the job. Circe reaches into the pig—puts her hand right inside the damned thing!—and comes out with an unidentifiable bit of organ meat. Without asking, without warning, she lifts the goo up to my snout and gives me a whiff.

Blood-scent. Strong. A sliver of hunger carving its way up through my stomach. I turn to Circe—to ask her to back off with the meal, to request something different, something cooked, something closer to lunch—but suddenly there's a familiar dagger of herbs heading straight for my nose and all is lost. Cilantro and basil whip themselves into a noose around my brain stem—the scent burst short, instantaneous, there and gone again, but that's all it takes.

The forest. The leaves. The running. The trees. Hunting. The joy of the chase. Finishing it off. The end.

There are pig guts in my mouth. Worse still, I believe there are pig guts in my guts. When I regain my senses in the here and now and manage to open my eyes, I find that I'm bent over the dinner table, my snout buried deep inside the dead hog, tongue grasping, licking up loose bits of flesh. The other dino diners have backed off; they sit back, either impressed or disgusted by my sudden porklust.

Applause, led by Circe. Ernie does not join in. Abashed and, to be honest, quite full, I sit back in my chair, wipe the blood from my lips, and let loose with a long, deep belch. Part of me wants to regurgitate, right here, right now. But there's another part of me, smaller yet somehow more intense, that wants a second helping.

"I'm very proud of you," Circe murmurs to me, and her breath on my ear makes it that much harder to keep my groin in check. The naked form is undesirable for males of any species in certain circumstances; what I wouldn't give right now for a pair of Dockers. "Have some more if you like."

Ernie's on the other ear, whispering his own sweet nothings. "You're making me sick, kid. Pull it back a little."

And whereas I want to follow Circe's advice—to tuck in, to really make an animal of myself, figuratively and otherwise—I know Ernie's right. I'm a professional, and I need to act that way. Undercover only goes so far before you get turned inside out.

"I've had enough for now," I tell Circe. "Quite . . . tasty."

Even if I wanted another bite, I don't think I could get a place at the feast. Now that I've backed off, the others have resumed chomping away, huddled around the platter like a gaggle of bargain-hunters at Filene's sweater table, and soon there's not much more than skin and bones left of the once plump porker.

I do notice that aside from Ernie—who has managed to get someone to rustle up a plate of simple white rice for his more discerning palate—there is one other dino, a Stegosaur with closed eyes and calm demeanor, who isn't partaking of the raw animal flesh. He's not partaking of the conversation, either, and if I didn't notice his chest rising and sinking in a rhythmic pattern I'd guess he wasn't partaking of the available oxygen either. "Who's that?" I ask Circe. "You didn't make *him* eat the pig."

"His name is Thomas," she says, this appellation the closest approximation of the throat-clearing hack that is his "natural" dino name, "and he hasn't eaten since he was chosen. He's preparing himself."

"For . . . ?"

"For the Ring. Tonight is his first."

There it is again—this Ring that keeps coming up in conversation. "You chose him for this thing?"

Circe shakes a finger at me. I stifle an urge to lick it. "*Progress* chose him, Vincent."

And with that, she's standing, rising to her full height. There's no audible signal, nothing that tells the crowd of dinosaurs that it's time to listen up, but as one, they turn in their seats, ligaments and intestines hanging from their snouts, their beaks, between their teeth, hands still full of bloody organ meat, and give their full attention to their beloved leader.

"Today is a blessed day," says Circe, her voice expanding to fill all the available space in the dining hall. This is pure natural amplification, and it beats any sound system I've heard save Mariachi Night last summer at the Hollywood Bowl. *That* was six hours of my life I'd like back, by the way.

"Today is a natural day," the dinos chant back.

"The food of the ancestors is within us."

And, again, the audience takes its turn: "The power of the ancestors is behind us."

Circe's tone drops, and though she's speaking at normal levels now, I'm sure it's still perfectly audible anywhere within the cavernous room. "Welcome to the first night of our glorious convocation," she says. "I'm sure you're all ready for a productive, Progressive day tomorrow, so I won't be long.

"Tonight, one of our fellow soul-searchers will be given the opportunity to attain a new level in his Progress. Tonight, he will know what it is to move beyond mammalian constraints, to understand himself as he was meant to be. Tonight, he will become a natural dinosaur."

Circe walks behind Thomas, and his eyes open for the first time this evening. I can just make out his scent, a leather/lime Jell-O mixture, and it seems to me that it's warbling in and out, somehow vibrating in tandem with Circe's. Impossible.

The Stegosaur stands by Circe's side, his gaze transfixed by hers. "Are you ready to accept the challenge of the ancestors?" she asks. "Are you ready to reclaim your dinosaur heritage?"

"I am ready."

Slowly, calmly, as if this ritual is commonplace, Circe places a hand on the back of the Stegosaur's head and draws him into her body, cradling him with her strong, supple arms. I can see his nose searching out the back of her neck, sucking down that alluring scent, his body filling with the maddening aroma.

Minutes pass, and no one dares to speak. No one dares to breathe.

When it's over, Thomas leans away from Circe, his body automatically righting itself, though that vacant stare in the eyes tells me some part of him is no longer inside this dining hall but running free through the wilds of the Triassic.

"It is time," says Circe. "Let us go to the Ring."

15

Contrary to popular opinion, few, if any, professional wrestlers nowadays are dinosaurs. Sure, there was a time when the leagues were full of Raptors and Rexes wrassling to their fake hearts' content, but in modern times it's mostly been freakishly built humans who have taken up the sport. Still, the occasional dino makes his way into the fabled ring, though it's more common in the Spanish leagues—The Pow-Wow from São Paulo comes to mind, as does a Hadrosaur who goes by the name of Pepito el Carnito—and whereas our Latino brothers don't bother to mask the phoniness with extravagant costumes and pounding entry music, they commonly lavish spectacle on the ring itself. Only in the land of the original corrupt prison guard could they come up with the steel cage death match—along with the razor-wire death cage match, the barbed-wire death cage match, and, my personal favorite, the electrified death cage match—and it's served to gain them quite an audience over the years.

Pepito el Carnito would feel right at home here in Hawaii.

Beneath a makeshift tarpaulin canopy stretching for a hundred yards in every direction, tied taut between the tops of some of the tallest trees I've yet to see on this island, lies a single cylindrical cage that I'd guess measures around fifty feet in diameter. Steel bars six inches thick form the walls and the ceiling of the massive cage, with but a single metallic entry portal granting access on the near side. It's like a giant see-through Campbell's Soup can, and though it wouldn't be too effective at holding soup, if it did, the potatoes would be seaworthy.

Rows and rows of hard metal bleachers surround the Ring, eager Progressives filling each and every seat, the preshow murmur growing with every passing second. A few mill around in back, shuffling their feet in the standing-room section, but they don't seem to mind. The crowd knows what's about to happen—at least they have more of an idea than I do—and I sense an odd mixture of excitement and anxiety in the air. Then again, maybe it's just the aroma from my drink.

Ernie and I are away from the maddening crowd, seated on a long raised dais next to the bleachers, our butts comfortably mushed into thick cushions, our thirst slaked by fruity pineapple and guava slushies, each garnished with a delightfully naughty sprig of fresh mint. This fits my night-out plans to a T. If you're going to a show, you might as well go first-class.

Circe sits between us.

"This is an age-old tradition," she says, taking a sip of her own concoction.

"Like, what?" I ask. "Ten, twenty years?"

Disappointment on her face. "There is tradition beyond Progression, Mr. Rubio. What we codify in ritual now was once nothing more than natural."

I don't understand a lick of what she said, but I nod knowingly, if only so she'll quit it with the condescension. I get enough of that from Ernie.

At precisely the same moment, a contingent of four dinos step out from behind the bleachers and march in lockstep toward the Ring. As they approach the door, one steps forward with a set of keys and ceremoniously unlocks the contraption with a showy flourish.

The crowd is hushed. I stifle a burp. Pig-taste wells up in my throat.

The dinos march back toward the bleachers, disappear for a moment, and then return just as quickly, this time with one more added to their ranks. It's Thomas, the Stegosaur who's about to make his debut, and whatever fate the guy's in for, he certainly seems resigned to it. Odd coming-out party.

"He will be escorted to the gate of the Ring by his chosen compatriots," Circe explains to us, voice a low whisper. "And they are the ones who will give him his final blessings and listen to any words he has to say."

"He chose them?" I ask, pointing to the four dinos who are conferring with Thomas down below.

"If it was up to you," says Circe, "to either choose those who could save your life or have them chosen for you, which option would you prefer?"

I mull it over for a second. "That's a hypothetical question, right?"

Down by the ring, the Stegosaur has said all he needs to say to his co-horts. Turning on his heel, he takes a deep breath, sets his tail high in the air, and walks confidently through the portal and into the Ring itself.

Circe continues to narrate the action for us. "Now that he's inside, his compatriots will lock him in and allow him to prepare himself. Meanwhile, they will return to the holding area to fetch his opponent."

"And that would be . . . ?"

"It is different for everyone. Hush."

Indeed, hushing is what the rest of the crowd seems to be doing. All noises—grunting, talking, or otherwise—have ceased, and an eerie silence reigns under the canopy. I keep expecting to see vendors climbing up and down the bleachers, selling popcorn, pretzels, maybe a raw pig's bladder or two, but all I can make out is snout after snout, tooth after tooth, eye after gleaming eye, all of them rapt on the Stegosaur at center Ring.

As Thomas prepares himself for whatever is to follow, I watch as the four dinos he's chosen as his assistants in this endeavor carefully wheel out another cage, this one much smaller than the Ring itself and covered with a bright red blanket. Suddenly there's a burst of audio emanating from the cage, and its origin is certainly not reptilian. A roar, a scream—this one deeper, angrier, more truly *animal* than anything I've heard come out of a dinosaur since the last time I blew off a date with Brunhilde, a Lufthansa stewardess and T-Rex about twice my size.

It sounds feline.

By the time the cage has been affixed to the Ring's entrance via a series of metal bolts, my guess has been confirmed. With a vicious shriek, the animal inside lashes out a tan-and-yellow paw, ripping aside the red blanket and exposing the ravenous mountain lion within. The hulking creature—broad, rippling shoulders, powerful limbs, teeth beyond teeth beyond teeth—paces back and forth in the cage before wolfing down the blanket in two seconds flat, feathers and all.

It is still very hungry.

"That's the opponent?" Ernie blurts out. "Christ, that's not fair."

"You'd be surprised," Circe says. "Lions can be quite strong."

"I mean it's not fair for the Stego. It's impossible—he'll be killed instantly—"

Circe gives me a look—*He's your friend, isn't he?*—and I try my best to reflect it right back at her, though I suspect it comes across more as gas pain than anything else. "When we reach a certain level of Progress," she informs my partner, "nothing is impossible. Besides, we do take precautions."

"Such as?" I ask.

I will receive no answer. On some unspoken signal, the bars separating the mountain lion's cage from the Ring proper are raised, and the great cat springs out of his confines and onto center stage. It's showtime.

Thomas waits for his opponent, his claws fully extended, but his demeanor calm, composed, as if he's simply waiting for the Number 5 bus to come around the corner. The lion, unsure of what to do with prey that won't run away, paces around the Ring, taking slow, deliberate steps, never taking his eyes off the fresh meat in the center.

Slow, barely perceptible movement from Thomas now, as his back begins to bend, curving ever so slightly, his arms stretching out, reaching for the floor, legs curling inward, bracing. With this new curvature of the spine, the plates lining the Stegosaur's back pop an inch or two farther into the air, and the tail makes its way out from between his legs, straightening into a long, fingerlike appendage, waggling back and forth like a giant spiked metronome.

He's down on all fours, small head parallel to the floor, body low, a sponge for all the surrounding gravity, using his own weight to anchor himself in place. There is nothing familiar about the way in which he's standing now, nothing familiar about the way in which his head cocks back and forth. This is not the same fellow who was meditating during dinner half an hour ago. Thomas is becoming something different, something more animal than the mountain lion. It's almost as if he's becoming something he always should have been.

He's becoming a true Stegosaur.

As if it has noticed the change yet is unaware of what it means, the mountain lion takes a tentative step forward, batting a paw through the air. Kitty wanna play. The lion's claws slide in and out, the beast ready for action. Kitty wanna do damage.

In a sudden blur of action, the lion leaps for the Stego, launching itself up and over the dino, aiming for the back of Thomas's neck. It's blindingly fast, and I've barely got time to register the attack before Thomas's tail swings up and over, the spikes glistening, shining as if already covered in blood, and catches the lion behind the front paw, tumbling the cat upside down in the dust.

A new roar, this one from the Stegosaur, a monstrous screech that would send any nearby Japanese scurrying for their Mothra handbooks. A return bellow from the lion, and the enemies have duly stated their intentions.

"When do you stop this?" I ask Circe, who is wholly rapt by the scene below.

"We don't," she says. "Unless . . ."

I assume there's a signal of some kind, but I don't get a chance to ask what it is. With a new series of yelps, the lion is once again on the attack, leaping atop the Stegosaur, straddling the conical spikes lining his spine, planting its teeth into the tough hide protecting the dinosaur's neck and back.

Not tough enough. Blood bursts out of the Stegosaur's hide, and he rears back in pain, his tail flapping through the air, aiming for the lion, trying to make itself useful. But just as the tail orients itself on the attacker, the lion falls from Thomas's back, leaving an open, unprotected patch of skin as an unfortunate target area, and with a sickening squish the Stegosaur flails himself with his own spikes and cries out in what must be horrendous pain. That's gonna hurt tomorrow morning.

The lion is back to stalking his prey, circling the Stego in an attempt to get back up and cause some more damage. A layer of blood has spread across the floor of the Ring, slicking the surface, making the footing slippery. With a sharp jolt to my eardrums, I realize that the crowd has ceased its silence and now shouts unintelligible phrases of encouragement in any number of human languages, as well as some dino dialect with which I am unfamiliar.

Another blur, another furious attack, and this time the Stegosaur's on his back, fending off a rapid series of bites—snapping jaws tearing at the neck, at the arms, at the soft stomach—as his tail swings powerfully, with control, but to little good effect. The bodies roll around the Ring, slamming into the metal bars, limbs entangled, escape impossible for either one.

What I'm noticing, apart from the blood and the bile and the spectacle, is that Thomas is moving like no creature I have ever seen before. His motions are not those of a rational being, nor quite those of a wild animal, either. There are no parries, no formal lunges, no counterattacks, no sense of a defense of any kind—sort of like watching the Redskins play the Eagles. But there is a method to this instinct, a fight-for-life intelligence, and it's fascinating to watch the process develop, which is distinctly *unlike* watching the Redskins play the Eagles.

Now the crowd noise has grown to a frenzy and I find that I'm standing along with them, pumping my fist into the air, shouting out a string of nonsense syllables, grunting in time with the mob. Ernie's on his feet, too, doing the same thing, similarly caught up in the action; only Circe, still sitting between us, remains stoic, though the intensity of her stare tells me she's more into this scene than the rest of us put together.

The Stegosaur plants his tail on the ground and pushes, flipping himself onto his side, throwing the lion off his stomach and to the floor. But the cat's not down for long—it rears back and launches itself yet again, claws extended on all four limbs, shredding whatever flesh manages to get in their way.

Limbs are intertwined, torsos locked, teeth grinding at hide and skin. If there is a victor when all this is over—something I wouldn't be willing to wager on at this time—he will need extensive recuperation. The Ring has become a slaughterhouse, blood sluicing down backs, fronts, tails, legs, and onto the floor an inch deep. A desperate charge at the Stego's neck is stymied by one of the last layers of protective hide, and the lion backs off for a moment, somehow sure that his next bite will indeed be the final one.

Staring. Pacing. The hunt is the only game in town.

A question of speed, perhaps. The mountain lion is faster. It makes the first leap, preparing to nail down final justice and settle in for a nice Stego snack.

But Thomas is ready for the assault, some instinctual part of the brain working to keep that big body fighting despite the life fluids raining out of it at an amazing rate, and he pitches himself backward at the lion's headlong attack, allowing his back-spikes to cushion the fall. In the same move, his tail flips quickly up between his legs—a puppy waiting to be scratched on his belly. The spikes whistle through the air, screaming toward their target, and I can see it coming a split second before it happens:

The tail-spikes sink into the lion's stomach.

A terrible wail of pain cracks the air, and the feline collapses to the ground, blood pouring from this new, gaping wound. Viscera drag on the floor as the lion's bowels let loose, a steady stream of urine soaking the Ring, and a cry of victory errupts from the crowd.

With a pitiful yelp, the mountain lion slinks to the edge of the Ring, trying to find some method of escape. But the bars are too thick to bend and too close-set to squeeze through, and though the lion bites weakly at his confines—teeth grasping the metal struts, mewling pathetically as he tries to snap through steel—there will be no Great Escape tonight. Perhaps the cat can't see that the ceiling of the Ring, twenty feet above, is caged as well, but he makes a few feckless attempts to leap to safety, each time gaining less and less altitude, like a bouncing rubber ball slowing to a stop.

Pain and terror in the creature's eyes, and, throughout it all, confusion. This isn't the way things were supposed to happen. The prey doesn't fight back. The prey should do what the prey has always done, which is sit back and let itself be eaten. Something has gone terribly, terribly wrong.

Compassion has never been a significant part of the animal kingdom, and it's not coming into play now. Before the lion has a chance to mount even a feeble counterattack, the Stegosaur has blanketed him with a volley of tail-swipes and claw-slashes, and by the time I've blinked twice, the lion's carcass has been ripped into a hundred pieces and scattered across the floor of the Ring. The roar of the crowd is thunderous, and I may need to have my hearing checked when we get back to the mainland.

I have a strong feeling that the Progressives are not endorsed by the AS-PCA.

The four dinos who acted as Thomas's confederates return to the cage, unlock the door, and lead the blood-splattered victor out of the Ring. It's an odd sight, as Thomas still walks on all fours, an ancient Stegosaur direct from the pages of an encyclopedia, while those who flank him tread along human-style, upright and stiff-backed.

"You understand something of Progress now," Circe says to me.

"I understand the Ring now," I reply. "Progress . . . I don't know."

Thomas disappears beneath the bleachers and into the jungle, a contingent of dinos trailing after him. The lion's corpse is dragged from the Ring, and the crowd begins to mill around, preparing to leave. "What now?" I ask.

"He'll be cared for by a team of doctors, his wounds healed, his body given time to mend."

"And then?"

A momentary pause from Circe, as if she's deciding whether or not to continue this conversation. Her lips purse. "What happens then is not something that can be explained. It must be experienced. Perhaps someday you, too, will be ready."

I'm not sure why Circe has fallen into Yoda-speak, but I am pretty damn positive I'll never be at a point in my life where I need to fight a starving mountain lion in order to feel good about my lineage.

As a host of workers bearing mops and buckets descend upon the cage—what level of Progress nets you the janitor job, I wonder—Circe rises from the dais and prepares to make her way down to the crowd below. But as she begins her descent, a new voice calls out from within the mob of Progressives.

"I am ready!" comes the cry. "I am ready for the Ring!"

The rest of the crowd hushes as Circe climbs back to her chair and peers down at the lone Velociraptor who has made his way into a clearing below. He's big for his race—I'm about average for a Raptor, and he's got at least four inches and twenty pounds on me—and his claws, zinging in and out of their slots, look especially sharp. Too bad his brain doesn't.

"Progress has chosen me!" he shouts up at Circe. "I must be allowed my chance."

The susurration rippling through the crowd is more of appreciation than disbelief, and the Progressives retake their seats accordingly, preparing for an encore performance. Can it be this easy to call destruction down upon yourself?

Ernie reads my mind. "Can he do that? Just announce he wants in?"

Circe nods. "Progress chooses when Progress chooses."

"But he didn't prepare," I point out. "None of that fasting, the meditation, all of the rituals . . ."

"If he is ready for the Ring, then the Ring is ready for him."

Circe, Samuel, and a few other Progressives gather for an impromptu meeting to work out the logistics for the next part of the evening's symposium. The cleanup crew is ordered to abandon their work, and they gladly desert the Ring, its crimson floor still slick with fluid. The Raptor, who has spent the several minutes since his pronouncement in a state of mild hyperventilation, sits on a bench by himself, eyes closed, hands working over each other. This must be his form of meditation, his method of releasing the dino within. Hope it works.

Circe leaves the dais and approaches the young Raptor. "Choose your confederates," she says, and I can hear her perfectly despite the distance between us. The dino quickly approaches four friends—two Raptors, a Diplodocus, and, goodness gracious, a Compy—and they fall into line behind him.

"This is insane," Ernie says to me. "If Rupert was up for the Ring next, I'm glad he got out when he did. Better to die at home than in this . . . nonsense."

Circe repeats the ceremony from the dining hall, announcing that the Raptor is ready to move on to the next level, asking if he's prepared, going through the whole shpiel verbatim. By the time she's fed him a healthy dose of her scent and sent him on his way, Circe has made her way back up to the box. This time, there is no gleam in her eyes.

A cough from the leader, a barely spoken phrase, and though it's but a whisper, I think I can hear her sighing.

The Raptor approaches the entrance, barely keeping his balance, a muscle tremor shaking his left leg as if it's standing on a localized earthquake. But his eyes are steady, his arms calmly by his side, and despite the anxiety welling up in my own chest, this Raptor looks just about as ready to battle untamed beasts as the Stego before him.

A new cage, different from the mountain lion's. This one's covered in a patchwork blanket of blues and blacks, and the four dinos wheeling it toward the Ring have a difficult time keeping it in place, the cage rocking back and forth on its wheels. Whatever's inside that thing is unhappy with its current state of confinement.

The Ring is closed. Locked up tight. The second bout begins.

Once the door between the cage and the Ring has been raised, it takes less than a second for the bull inside to come charging out, six hundred pounds of angry top sirloin aimed at the Raptor's vital organs. Now, I've seen rodeo before—forced into it, actually, by a Hadrosaur I was dating who had a raw leather fetish—but I've never seen a beast like this one. Five feet at the shoulder, horns filed to a dagger point, and mad as an alcoholic who's been eighty-sixed from the IHOP.

Oh. Oh. That's not good. That's not good at all.

The crowd isn't cheering anymore.

I would like to defend my Velociraptor brother, to say that he put up a valiant fight, that he lashed out in a frenzy at the beast, that the total blood loss was equal, but the simple truth is this: the bull gores him right at the get-go.

Without even giving the dino a moment in which to mount a proper defense, the bull charges the Velociraptor, digs its horns into his fleshy side, lifts him into the air with those bulging neck muscles, and easily tosses the Raptor into a heap on the far side of the Ring as if he's nothing more than a used tissue.

It doesn't get any prettier.

I am torn between fascination and repulsion as the fight continues. Mere seconds have gone by, but it feels like this is the end of a twelve-rounder, and I wonder when someone's going to throw in the blood-red towel. I know the last bout on the undercard ended up as a fight to the death, but if it goes that far this time, I doubt the outcome will be so favorable to my species.

It can't be more than ten seconds after the initial goring, and already it's quite clear that the Raptor won't be rejoining the battle anytime soon. He's nothing more than a paper doll to this bull, and just as I'm about to make my objections known, Circe stands and claps her hands three times in succession. At this cue, as if they had been waiting for this all their lives, the four comrade dinos standing by the Ring reach into a long wooden box attached to the bottom set of bleachers. Each pulls out a rifle.

Ernie stands—so do I—so does everyone else in the joint—as the dinos quickly load, take aim, and fire their guns. I expect a sharp report, a typical rifle boom, but all I hear is a swish and a thwip, and suddenly four darts are sticking out of the bull's hide, no more than a half-inch away from one another. Big target, sure, but these were the kind of shots that would make Robin Hood gasp.

With rapid precision—the kind of skill that can only be gained by practice, practice, and more practice—the dinos reload, reaim, and reshoot, and by now the bull has slowed to a halt, lazily glancing around the Ring for the source of these annoying mosquito bites.

The Raptor in the corner is moving, but not in any coherent, connected manner. His claws paw at the steel bars of the Ring, his tongue waggling lazily out of the side of his mouth. The bull turns back to his toy, preparing perhaps to finish it off, but whatever drug they're using works quickly on the bovine beast, and as it takes another step toward the downed dino, the bull's eyes roll up, up, and away, and he goes down hard.

The bull is carted away. The Raptor is carted away. The Ring is cleaned up, polished, sparkling, as if nothing ever happened.

"He will live," Circe says, answering my unasked question.

"He was hurt pretty bad."

"And I've seen worse."

The crowd below is looking up at us, and for a moment, I get the feeling that they're staring at me, as if I somehow caused this to happen to their friend. I want to protest, to proclaim my innocence, but my paranoid delusion wanes as Circe steps in front of me and addresses her followers.

"Progress is a right we all share, yet it is also a responsibility. It must be gained through effort and through introspection, but it is not something which we can choose as we see fit. Progress chooses us; what we do here simply allows it into our lives. This evening, as you lie in your nests, as you replay this evening's events in your minds and wonder if you will ever be ready for the Ring, ask yourself if you can understand the ancestors. Ask yourself if you are capable of releasing your learned inhibitions. Ask yourself: Am I acting through Progress, or is Progress acting through me?

"Goodnight, brothers and sisters. I will see you tomorrow."

And with that, the group disbands. Circe falls back into her seat and watches the crowd stream out of the amphitheater; Ernie and I do likewise, waiting for the right moment to excuse ourselves and hoof it back to our hut and the oh-so-comfy confines of the nest.

Time passes, and soon there are few of us left in the vicinity of the Ring. Circe continues to stare out into space, not quite catatonic but not quite *here,* either, unresponsive to the few acolytes who approach to bid her good evening. There won't be a reception line tonight, it seems, so Ernie and I take this opportunity to sneak off—

"Wait." It's Circe, and I have no choice but to stop. Ernie's got his hands on my shoulders, holding me tight, but I can't help but turn around. A single tear has wormed its way out of the corner of her eye and leaves a trail of moisture as it slides down one delicately rounded cheek, across her face, and between those two luscious lips.

"Vincent, would you like to join me for a nightcap?"

It's not appropriate. It's not proper. And I'd bet half my take-home pay that behind my back, Ernie is blasting his disapproval toward me with a stare that would make Medusa envious.

"I'd love to," I say, shaking off my partner's hands and trotting over to the fragile cult leader. "Your hut or mine?"

Did I say hut? The Raptor was mistaken. Whatever funds were not being spent on the overall adornment of the Progressive compound were obviously rerouted to the construction and interior decoration of Circe's pleasure palace here in the center of the island. The walls sparkle with some unidentifiable substance that is not quite diamond and not quite pearl, but I have a feeling that a square foot of it would buy my condo, my car, and all of the basil I could eat for a decade.

Not that there's a shortage of the evil herb. From the moment we make our way into the main house via the twelve-foot double doors, my arm interlocked with Circe's, our mood already jovial from the refreshing half-mile jaunt up the private walkway, we are surrounded by sycophants bearing all manner of earthly delights. Platters piled with parsley, trays towering with thyme—it's available, it's fresh, and, best of all, it's free.

I am not a mooch, but I play one while undercover.

"Help yourself, Vincent," Circe tells me. She's already downed a quarter-pound of marjoram, and she's onto the fenugreek without stopping to take a breath. "The cumin is quite good."

I'd like to have a taste of it all, actually, to romp through this spectacular buffet of mind-benders, but part of my reason for allowing Circe to take me back to her place is to do some serious probing—*questions,* probing *questions*—and I'll need a comparatively clear head if I'm going to pull it off. Still, a lick or two of cumin can't hurt . . .

And some saffron for good luck.

And some fennel, because I haven't tried it in years.

And a few handfuls of basil to take back to Ernie, because that's the kind of guy I am.

Before I realize it, my bloodstream is full to bursting with sprigs and leaves, and Circe and I are out of the foyer and walking down a long, ornate hallway. Through a far door, I can make out row after row of dry-cleaning racks and a host of drooping human guises hanging to the ground. This must be where my costume is being kept; I hope they've got it smelling piney-fresh.

Soon, before my body has had a chance to dart a memo up to my mind, Circe and I are seated in a large leather loveseat, the high back and wide arms encompassing our bodies, cradling us as one. Circe's long legs dangle over mine, her left underclaw scraping lightly against my knee. We're in a study of some sort, the walls lined with old portraits of austere dinosaurs unfamiliar to me.

"I hope you've been enjoying yourself," she says.

I play it coy. "You've got a nice little island. Nice little group. How long has this Progress thing been around, anyway?"

"Has the time come when we ask each other questions?"

Her initial reluctance to answer my offhand remark reminds me why I'm here in the first place. Yet all of this chitchat, the easy access to herbs, and, yes, the close proximity of a perfect dinosaur specimen of my own race and opposite gender has indeed lulled me into forgetting the task at hand. But now you're back on track, Vincent—full speed ahead and no tugging at the brake.

Grunting with the effort—both physical and mental—I remove Circe's legs from my own, stand, and stroll as steadily as possible across the study. "We can play footsie anytime. I'm here to learn, remember?"

"And so you are. And so you shall."

"You get off talking that way?" I ask her.

"It's better than the other way."

"What's that?"

"Grunting."

Strange lady. Strange place. "You've got a nice island."

She nods, smiling. "Thank you. We try."

"Big. Lots of forest. You only seem to be using a small part of it, though."

"The jungle is beautiful," Circe admits, "though we rarely go in. The other side of the island is . . . different."

I nod, pacing slightly. One step forward, one step back, cha cha cha. "Different how?"

"Changed. Mutated. This island was one of the original sites used for early atomic testing."

Instantly, my skin begins to crawl with a thousand radioactive particles, my entire body sending out a furious, massive itch signal to my frantic brain. Isn't this how Godzilla was born?

But Circe can read me well enough to understand my concern, and she's quickly shaking her head, caressing my arm to assuage my fears. "We're fine over here," she insists. "This side of the island is free of radiation; we have bimonthly Geiger counter sweeps."

"So what's over there?" I ask, ever the curious kitten. "On the other side?"

"I don't know. We've declared it off-limits, for everyone's safety."

We stare at each other. She's lovely.

Time to break the silence, if only to hear myself talk, make sure she hasn't pulled an herb trick and charmed me into a mute. "So, *you* go through a test like that?" I ask. "The Ring?"

"At some point, we all have to 'go through' our little tests. Some are different from others."

I scratch my chin, making a big show of it. This is my attentive look. "So you're saying you've never been in the Ring."

"Very perceptive, Mr. Rubio." I think she may be mocking me, but the herbs have made it difficult for me to distinguish sarcasm from sincerity. "Suffice it to say that the Ring would not be a substantial challenge for me, but if I were to test myself in that arena, I would no longer be fit to lead the group down their path to Progress."

"Would you like to elaborate on that?"

"No."

A polished mahogany desk with brass handles has become my new seat; I place my butt on its surface, the cool wood providing a nice counterpoint to the steamy climate. Haven't these people heard of air conditioning? At least the ancestors were bright enough to manufacture a fan or two, I'd imagine.

"Kind of messy back there, that Raptor getting gored by the bull," I say.

"Sadly, it happens."

"Often?"

"No," she says, "but even once is more than I like to see. Our members are eager to reclaim their true identities, and sometimes their enthusiasm gets in the way of good judgment."

"It was a big bull."

"And he was a strong Raptor. When the combatant is ready, I assure you, there are no unfair battles in the Ring. He'll be taken care of by the doctors, and I doubt he will make such an error again. The next time, he will let Progress take its course." Circe slides over on the chair. "Are you ready to take a seat again? There's room."

I ignore the come-on and stay put. "You have Ring competitions every night?"

"Only when they're called for."

"What if some Diplodod wants to go head-to-head with Simba but you're not in Hawaii?"

"We have other Rings," says Circe, "in other locations."

"Where?"

"Some things are better to find out as time passes. Stay with us and you will know in time."

I jump off the desk and start to wander the room, staring up at the oak-framed oil paintings hung on the maroon walls. All manner of dinosaurs have been captured in delicate portraiture, each one a study in wrinkles and creases and worn hides. These dudes are old.

"The ancestors?" I ask.

"Hardly. That one to your left was a university president back in the late nineteenth century; the Coelo next to him is J. Edgar Hoover. Other than that, I don't know who most of them are, to be honest. This was Raal's study."

"*Was.*"

"Yes, was."

"So he's dead?"

A lick of those lips, focusing on the corner of her mouth. "So they say."

Odd how this little duckling keeps changing her story. Earlier, she was quite adamant that he was alive and kicking, just unavailable for comment. "Did you know him?"

"Yes."

"How long did you know him?"

Circe stands and turns away from me, heading to a wet bar jutting out from the far wall. A steady waterfall streams out from a tap there, and Circe reaches out with that long tongue and laps up some of the elixir. Even from here, I can smell the herb infusion. "I invited you up here for a nightcap—"

"—and I'm staying for the company," I finish. "If you want me to stop with the questions . . ."

"Fifteen years. After that, he was gone."

"And you presume he's dead."

"I presume nothing. Raal was nearly one hundred percent dinosaur natural, and he could accomplish quite a great deal more with one flick of his tail than we could do in a lifetime of struggle."

I suggest, "You were his protégée."

"If you want to call it that. He led me into Progress."

"How?"

Seemingly a simple question, I think, but that one syllable sends Circe back to the waterfall to slurp up another gallon of happy juice. Strangely enough, she's not getting drunk off her beautiful behind; if she is, I am unable to notice the least change in her demeanor. I'd be knocking into walls and excusing myself to doorknobs by this point, but maybe she's worked up a tolerance to the stuff.

"Stay here," she says, and then slinks out a side door, leaving me to my lonesome in this boring study; she could have at least left me alone in a game room. A high-backed leather recliner stands behind the desk, a classic power chair if ever I've seen one, brass buttons dotting the extra-thick cowhide, the leather burnished to a high gloss, the fabric nearly as slippery as Mr. Levitt's slipcover formula back in Thousand Oaks. This thing's a lawsuit waiting to happen—I bet if I sit on it right, I can fall off at just the angle to split my head open and let the punitive judgments come pouring in.

But my greed muscle isn't flexing as strong as my snoop muscle today, and so as soon as I take a seat at what must have been Raal's desk, I can't stop my fingers from grabbing a paper clip out of the desk organizer and bending it into a makeshift lock-pick. This is not a matter of choice; it's a reflex that simply takes over at various times, and there is little I can do to halt the action. There are five drawers in this desk—two to either side, one directly in the middle—and all are practically pleading with me to unlock and uncover their hidden treasures. I'm like Geraldo, only without the TV cameras to provide that extra level of embarrassment.

After a few moments of twisting the small bit of metal in the lock, I realize that the damned thing isn't even closed all the way; whoever used it last was negligent in locking it back up tight, and I'm not one to finish others' work. I open it wide.

Accounting sheets. Red ink, black ink, red ink, black ink, it's a mess of gains and losses, income and expenditures, and I can't figure out a lick of it. The last math class I ever took ended with a protractor stuck halfway up my nose—don't ask, don't ask—and since then I've steered clear of the world of numbers.

But there are certain subheadings under which even I can recognize some massive outflows of cash. Something on the order of six and a half million dollars left the coffers of the Progressives no more than a month ago, and though it doesn't say where this money went, there are very few herb dealers who charge more than a few bucks per kilo of basil.

It's not just good old American sawbucks, either. There's lira and deutschmarks and kroner and a number of other types of currency I don't even recognize. Whatever it is they're buying, they're buying it in more countries than just this one; I only wish I knew what the Progressives were paying so much for. But one thing's for sure—no matter the breed, this puppy is global.

I'm about to look further when I hear familiar footsteps making their approach. I quickly shove the papers back into the desk drawer—crumpling them in the process, I am sure—and toss the paper clip in the direction of a nearby trash bin. It misses. My three-point shot needs a lot of work.

When Circe enters the room, she's holding a thin photo album, the cover blank, the spine unwritten upon. Retaking her place on the loveseat, Circe beckons to me. "I haven't shown this to anyone in years," she says softly, "and if you're going to look at it, you might as well sit by me."

Fair enough. Not that it's such a chore, mind you, but I was hoping to keep this professional.

Ah, who am I kidding? No I wasn't.

The scrapbook opens up with a modest three-bedroom house somewhere in the suburbs. Lawn jockey, pink flamingo, station wagon in the driveway, the works. On the front porch, man and wife, smiling at the camera, picture of domestic bliss. "This was my house," says Circe. "These were my parents."

I'm surprised, mainly because the broad in the photos is all made up good and proper, like she's going out for dinner and a show. Dinosaurs are usually frustrated enough with the morning routine of buckling in and strapping on that the females rarely have the time or patience to apply an extra layer of face paint to a face that's not even theirs in the first place. In fact, the more granola a female, the more likely she's a lizard in ape's clothing. We go for simplification as often as possible; it's no coincidence, for example, that the bra burning movement was started by a Bronto who had dealt with one strap too many.

"They look nice."

She smiles wistfully. "I'm sure they were. They died when I was one."

"I'm sorry. You were an orphan?"

"Not until then." She turns the page. A baby, pink and gurgling—well, mid-gurgle, anyhow—lying in a bassinet, reaching up for the photographer, chubby little fists stretching to the air.

"You?"

"Before my parents . . . went away. The guise was a Blaupunkt—it's the one thing I have from my childhood. At least, it's the one thing I want to keep."

The next series of pictures are not quite so rosy. Rows of girls ranging from toddlers to teens lined up in precise formations, smiling robotically at the camera, shabby uniforms and shiny shoes, eyes dead and defeated.

"St. Helena's Home for Wayward Girls," says Circe. "They didn't like me much," she explains. "I got picked on, but that wasn't the worst of it. An orphanage isn't the best place for a young girl—"

"I know," I interrupt, eager to console. "I saw *Annie.*"

Laughter—unexpected, but welcome—as Circe shuts the book and turns toward me. "*Annie* might be the representation of a human orphanage, Vincent—though I doubt it—but the facilities for dinosaurs were even worse than your theatrical version would have you believe."

"That's not—I didn't mean—"

"The sisters who ran the place had decided that since the world was mostly human anyway, they would teach us to be more mammal than mammals. Horrible creatures, every one of them, shrieking at us every time they smelled an iota of scent coming from our bodies. We were forced to wrap our necks in heavy cloths in order to soak up the pheromones, then spray ourselves with Lysol to cover up the remainder. Hot baths were next, steel wool raked against our hides—anything to get rid of the scent.

"All they wanted to do was drill the dino out of us. They wouldn't be satisfied until we were indistinguishable from the apes. I spent every single morning in that place staring at myself in the mirror, at that hideously pointed snout, those terrible claws, that horrendous tail, hating every last vestige of my reptilian heritage.

"My best friend even went so far as to cut off her tail—went into the machine shop one morning, turned on the buzzsaw, and just sliced it right off—and even though she died, even though her desire to be human was stronger than her desire for life, I remember at the time not horror, not revulsion, but thinking *Janine's so cool, why can't I do that?*"

Can't help but swallow, a big throat-clearing gulp. "Why didn't you?" I ask.

"Raal found me before I worked up the nerve. He came to the home, interviewed a few of the girls, and when he found me, he said he was done. He said he'd been searching for ten years for the one who could lead our people out of bondage. He didn't even wait for the adoption papers to come through—he came for me that night, snuck me out of my room, out of the orphanage, and we took off."

"You believed him, then?"

"Not a bit. But he had food, he had herbs, he had freedom, and for a girl about to hit her teens inside an orphanage, he was Moses and Jesus and Keith Partridge all wrapped up in one."

"And then?"

"And then my training began. Years of patience and understanding, of Raal trying to show me who I was—more importantly, *what* I was. Teaching me to use my natural gifts, and teaching me to love myself again."

I can't help myself; maybe it's the story, the late night, or the last remaining herbs in my system, but this thought jumps out of my lips before I can close the drawbridge—"He taught you the scent trick."

"He taught me the scent trick," she repeats, taking my hand in hers, and a fiery tingle shoots up my arm and straight into my chest. "Which is not so much a trick as it is a natural function, like breathing or walking. It's integral."

"How?"

"The scent allows us access to our true selves. Anything is possible—connection, extension, even hibernation. When you are sure of yourself, it fades into the background, becomes part of your system. It's all natural.

"But each dinosaur is different," she tells me. "We all have many things in common, but we're like humans in the sense that we all have varying degrees of talent."

And as she speaks, I can feel her talent beginning to come on strong. Not a quick jab like the other times she knocked me out, but a slow, steady massage, rolling over me in waves of sugar and spice and everything nice. The room begins to waver, the walls shimmying in and out, waving to me as if to say *Goodnight, Vincent, y'all come back real soon* . . .

But I'm continuing with these questions, damn it, and I use whatever strength I've got left to fight past the smells and form the proper words. "And that's why he picked you," I manage to say. "You had it in spades. . . ."

Circe nods, and from my vantage point, it looks like her whole body is nodding along. The walls are losing their opacity, becoming more and more transparent. "I left the world," she is saying, "and learned from Raal. He said I had a gift he hadn't seen before. He said that together we would free our species from their shackles. He said that the only path to understanding ourselves was tooiagh greaarlar, and by doing so, laareeeeach orrarelearghhh in the wrolaaergh—"

A babble of nonsense yelps and groans pours from her mouth, mixing some foreign tongue with the only language I know. But she goes right on speaking—growling, grunting—as if it's the plainest English in the world.

As the last remaining walls give way, I reach out and try to grab hold of the loveseat—something to keep me rooted in place. My hands encounter fabric, a good sign, but it's not long before it changes to bark. I look down to find my fingers grasping tight to an ancient tree stump, and by the time I look up again, the study is gone.

I'm in the forest again.

You'd think by now I'd know my way around this darn jungle, but it's got a different feel to it this time. In the previous experiments with Circe and her magical scent, the forest was almost as translucent as reality, a not-quite-here slice of un-life, but this tree trunk is real enough to be scratching my butt something fierce, and should the Pterodactyl hovering above me—a creature that should be long extinct—decide to do its business over my head, you can bet I'm not going to sit tight and hope it's all a mirage.

I stand, and the leaves beneath my feet crinkle against my toes, tickling them, caressing them. Unfamiliar sounds—songs, calls, the joyous shout of all this nature—bounce from tree to tree and back to my ears, delighting me every bit along the way. A thick layer of air blankets everything in sight, and I find myself laboring to breathe, relearning the very act itself. I touch another tree, and it, too, is solid. Right here. Right now.

A caress across my chest, a light finger tracing down, down, the motion coming from behind. Hot breath on my ear. "Do you like it?"

It's Circe. "How—"

"Shh. Do you like it?"

"Yesss," I sigh, hissing the last in a long, sharp exhale. This is not the way my relationships usually start out—I am the seductor, not the seductee—but as long as I'm already standing in a world that can't possibly exist, I might as well let nature take its course, no matter how twisted it may seem.

"Let go," she whispers. "The end of days."

Arms grasping me tighter, encircling my body, and I turn to face my new lover, our tongues already seeking out each other, snaking in and out and around, licking sweat, saliva, scent. My arms, rising of their own accord, holding Circe tighter, lifting her off the ground, fingers clenched around the base of her tail, stroking her back, placing her where she needs to be— where *I* need her to be—

And we're moving now, our feet stationary but the ground beneath rippling by, churning ahead as we begin to make love, rocking back and forth as I plunge myself into her, rolling over in a bed of air, the trees streaming past, leaves whacking past our naked bodies, her legs tight around my body, mouth open, calling out—

Speed rising, growing faster, Circe's claws snapping into place, raking down my back, the pain exhilarating, my snout pulling wide, teeth biting down hard on her shoulder, pelvis thrusting into hers, hard as I've ever been, sweat pouring off our bodies, dripping down our tails, onto the ground below, disappearing in that brown-and-yellow blur, head spinning, sky overhead cartwheeling around and about our bodies—

My own smells rising, mixing with hers, our pheromones making their own sort of love as a howl rises up from my chest, matching Circe's own scream of craving, both of us slamming against each other, no simple sex but a furious animal assault of carnal lust—every tree disappearing now, the world going with it, the leaves, the dirt, the ground, the sky, circling, cycling, nothing holding us up as we tuck into each other, claws imbedded, teeth imbedded, my entire body wrapped up in hers and hers in mine—

Mind shutting down, body left on autopilot, thrusting, feeling—

Never-ending—always like this—

Pain, pleasure, pain—

Then a light, streaming from above—a shriek, not animal, not living— the sky, burning, a hole torn in the clouds—heat, fiery heat as I begin to blast my seed inside her, as I grunt and let loose, a sizzling stream, burning me, needling me—Circe pulling me down, pulling me in, mouth open wide, a low moan of horror and of ecstasy—we are together—we are one— and still from above, louder now, that terrible noise, that ferocious noise, that apocalyptic noise—growing closer, the burning larger, larger, encompassing the sky, everything on the verge of everything else, and—and—

Darkness.

My pillow tastes like poi, which tastes like nothing so much as . . . nothing. If I've learned anything in Hawaii, it's that both of them—poi and my pillow—are useless gobs of empty nutrition, neither of which should be in my mouth at any point during the day or night. But as the morning light streams onto my face and I awaken lethargically in my nest, Ernie lightly shaking me—then not-so-lightly shaking me as I tell him where to stuff it—I find my arms clutched tight around a roll of twigs and my snout stuffed with leaves and bark shavings.

"Wake up—we're gonna miss breakfast."

"That'd be a shame," I mumble.

It takes another five minutes of poking and prodding before I'm up and halfway willing to face the world. I should have a hangover, but for some reason I've been spared the anguish, and this seems like a good omen for the day. As I climb out of my nest—perfectly formed, by the way, which means that Ernie must have done me a construction favor sometime last evening—my knees popping, my arms automatically stretching, reaching for the sky, I hear Ernie's low whistle behind me.

"Did a number on yourself last night, eh, kid?"

If I did, I certainly don't recall which number that could be. There was a trip to Circe's castle, dining on some herbs, a little Q&A, a little romance, a little dream, and then . . . nothing. "Whatcha talking about?"

"Your back."

"What about it?"

"You can't feel that?"

Still confused, I try to reach an arm up and over my body, hoping to get a feel of whatever Ernie's talking about. No luck. Lucky for me, though, Ernie's got perfect access. He jabs his finger into my spine, and there's a sharp needle of pain, the kind of sting you get when you jump in the ocean and find out exactly where every single tiny cut on your body happens to be located.

"The hell is it?" I ask.

"A scratch. You got a whole crossroads back there. I got a feeling you weren't exactly interrogating the witness, were you?"

Depends on how you look at it. "Sure, I did," I tell him, and then fill him in on the details of Circe's induction into Progress by the ever-elusive and probably dead Raal.

"And the scratches?" he asks.

There's no need to tell him about the forest and the running and the . . . the . . . that last part, with the light and the fury and the explosion. Eventually, perhaps once I figure it out myself, I'll let him in on whatever induced fantasies I've been privy to, but for right now my hallucinations are a private party, and I'm the only one on the guest list. "No clue." Then, to change the subject, I tell him, "I did find a pretty strange ledger, though. Lots of foreign money jumping around this place. Almost as if they're laundering it."

A rising cackle bursts through the walls of the hut and assaults my ears, almost like a trumpet but two degrees more annoying in tone and timbre. And whoever's playing the damn thing doesn't even have the simple dino decency to play "Summertime" or "Take the A Train." No, this is "Louie, Louie." And it's endless. "The hell is that?" I cry, my jaw shaking, my claws zinging out of their slots of their own accord.

No answer from the others, but suddenly the stampede is on. Arms and tails whap me across the face, torsos slam into mine, as I collapse onto my nest, shattering it back into its component parts, a thousand undifferentiated branches and brambles scattering across the ground.

Ernie stands over me, shaking his head back and forth. "Can't go back to bed yet, kid. Breakfast is served."

It takes a good deal of mental effort to stumble naked out of the hut, fighting the urge to guise myself up all the way. Even if I were to give in to the desire to costume my nude body, though, the decision would be moot; our guises have not been returned to the hut. I can only guess that once they're available, Samuel will hang them on the outside doorknob like a hotel dry-cleaner, but there may indeed be some arcane method of guise retrieval in this place.

"Feels strange, huh?" I ask Ernie as we prepare to step outside.

"Been quite a while," he agrees. "Strange doesn't begin to cover it."

Indeed, this weekend may be the first time since my middle school days—rebellious times, wild times—that I have left the confines of a home without my human skin on, the first time I've stepped onto soil without wrapping myself up in interminable buckles and belts and straps and latex and false goodwill for the rival species. At the very least, I'm sure to get a sunburn in some naughty places.

I may like it. I may not. I can't decide yet.

The clearing looks a little better in the bright morning light—now I can see larger structures situated nearby, a few buildings that look like they're made of something more than Lincoln Logs—but it still ain't Fantasy Island. A steady stream of other dinos make their way toward the low, long redwood dining hut set off to one corner of the encampment, and Ernie and I join the herd.

The trumpeter is still bawling for all he's worth, and on the way inside the hut, I lash out with my tail and flick the Hadrosaur making all those god-awful screeching noises across the snout. For a moment, at least, "Louie, Louie" is silenced.

The pheromones are overpowering in the mess hall, but it's nothing compared to how it smelled during last night's dinner. Morning's always a weak time for pheromone production; our glands don't really get moving until the rest of us does, which makes it hard to track malfeasants anytime before nine A.M. But it's still coming strong, the combined fragrance of a hundred "brothers" and "sisters," and it takes all my effort to keep myself from searching out Circe's scent. Time for that later. Eat first, detect next.

Breakfast is served family-style, and Ernie and I take a seat at a long, wooden bench next to a young, strapping Coelo and a not-so-young, not-so-strapping T-Rex. The poor thing's already-shrunken arms have withered away to flappy little stumps, and I wonder how he's going to reach across the table for his food.

Or why he would want to. In the center of the table are a host of large ceramic bowls, each filled to the brim with our breakfast: eggs. Raw eggs. Raw eggs still in their shells.

I look to Ernie, who looks back to me. We stare at each other in quiet desperation. "Maybe there's an omelet line," I suggest.

By way of answer, the other dinos at our table reach for the bowl, grab an egg in each hand, and toss the little boogers into their mouths, shell and all. A furious crunching fills the air, yolk and shell splattering the table, teeth chomping and throats swallowing, my stomach doing topsy-turvies in anticipation of the salmonella to come.

A glance around the room shows me that Ernie and I aren't the only ones who aren't hip to the raw-egg scene. At least two or three dinos at every table are glancing worriedly around the mess hall, looking for someone else—anyone else—who's maintaining a decent level of sanity and hygiene. My eyes meet up with those of a female Triceratops whose frantic mouthings I can read from across the room: *Do we have to?*

Then again, I did eat some version of raw pork last evening, so I shouldn't have any qualms about ingesting something further back along the developmental time line. What's more, I have to play this out like Olivier doing Hamlet if I want to stay in the Progressives' good graces. Sad to say, I live for my job. Look out, lips—watch out, gums—sorry, ol' stomach, 'cause here it comes.

Gooey. Chewy. The shells scratch my throat.

"I like the big ones, myself." A familiar voice, rising behind me.

"I like the little ones."

"We're different that way."

I turn to find Buzz and Wendell hovering over me once again, watching me chew down the excuse for food that has the audacity to call itself breakfast. They're fully unguised, of course, and the twin Carnotaurs let their tails dangle down to the dirt floor below. I've been trying to keep mine aloft since I woke up—I'm not a stickler for cleanliness, but something about a dirty tail has always unnerved me—yet I doubt that the muscular control will last.

"You boys want my share?" asks Ernie, holding out an egg in each hand.

"We couldn't," say Buzz and Wendell in unison. "We shouldn't." Then, after a perfectly timed pause—technically *just* long enough for Ernie to recant—they reach out and snatch the eggs away, much as I imagine my close ancestral cousins, the Oviraptors, might have done millions of years ago. The twins don't even bother munching; they swallow the eggs whole, like giant caplets of Tylenol, and grin all the way.

"Aren't you having a blast?" says Buzz. It is not a question.

"Thrilled," I respond.

"It's the best," says Wendell.

"The best. Are you ready for the training?" Buzz asks eagerly.

I shake my head. "What training?"

"I love the training," Wendell chimes in. "The training is the best part."

A gong sounds at the front of the breakfast room, and before I can turn around to locate the instrument itself, the rush for the doors is on. Brown clouds of dirt rise in the air, and I'm pushed in every direction, battered about by a score of tails and flailing limbs. It's like midnight at Altamont (the rumor, by the way, that all Hell's Angels are Raptors is rude, scandalous, and not without merit), and within seconds, it's just me, Ernie, and a few more dazed souls staring around, wondering what the hell happened to our peaceful little scene.

Guess it's time for training.

"The first thing you need to teach yourselves is how to run," our group leader is saying. She's a beast of a Brontosaurus—firm, stocky legs and a tail with muscular definition rippling the thick hide. With inflections somewhere between a loving mother and a Marine drill sergeant, she's been riding us all morning on the basics of her subject.

For this first part of the morning, we've been split into groups by our Progress level. The eighteen first-timers—"virgins," as they're fond of calling us—have been clumped together and thrown headfirst into the rough waters of dino training. As such, we spend a lot of time looking at one another with mystified glances. This is one of those times.

Fortunately, a hand in the crowd shoots up. "Don't we already know how to run?" asks a fellow Raptor, whose own lower body ripples with power.

The Bronto, whose name is Bleeeach—or Blanche, as she instructed us newbies to call her—gives a shrug of those overbuilt shoulders. "You think you know how?" she asks.

"I ran track in high school," says the young Raptor. "All-State in the hundred-yard dash."

"Impressive. Which state?"

"Utah."

"A lot of good dinos from Utah." No kidding—Joseph Smith was the first to codify the needs of the dino public, but he bathed his group in a spiritual, rather than physical, light so as to avoid detection. The Mormon flight from New York was not at all religious in nature; rather, it was reptilian. "I imagine you believe you could beat me in a footrace."

The Raptor waves his hand through the air, though not in a dismissive gesture. "You're a Bronto," he points out, his tone respectful, embarrassed to remind her that her race isn't capable of achieving the same frightening ground speed as his.

"And? Aren't we all brothers and sisters?"

"Yes, but . . . I'm a Raptor." No response. He elaborates. "We're just . . . faster."

Within a minute, the implied challenge has been accepted and an impromptu racetrack set up. The contestants—Blanche and the young virgin— take their places, our instructor cool and confident, not even bothering to drop into a three-point stance at the line, while the Raptor has tensed himself up, limbs trembling, ready to jump at the sound of the starting shriek. He's a spring coiled and ready to explode, while our trainer is just a loose rubber band dangling on a hook. It appears that the student will eclipse the teacher on this day.

"Down the road, around the far tree, and back," says the Bronto, marking out a trail a good hundred yards long.

"Is that all?" Now he's cocky.

"Still think you can beat me?" she asks.

No time to answer. The designated shrieker, a female Compy whose tea-rose-and-ocean-spray scent is remarkably pleasant for one of her type, marches forward, counts down, "Three—two—" and then issues forth a piercing yelp to signal the start of the race.

By the time the Raptor is clear of the starting line, Blanche is thirty yards down the field, a murky blur kicking up dust. It's hard to tell, but I think she's down on all fours, her legs cycling so fast I can't be certain.

By the time the Raptor has sped a quarter of the way to the tree, Blanche has already made the turn and is heading back.

By the time the Raptor has collapsed in the dust, tripping over a caval- cade of rocks that have managed to fall precisely in his path, Blanche has crossed the finish line, sat herself down on a nearby tree stump, and crossed her arms to wait for his inevitable, groveling finish.

"Now," she says once we've all gathered around and the young Raptor has sucked up all the available oxygen in the air, "is everyone ready to learn how to run?"

At first, there's nothing different about it. It's your basic jog-of-the-mill running, no record-breaking times in my near future—those Hadrosaurs who win the Boston Marathon every year have nothing to worry about. The legs pump, the feet move, the body comes along for the ride. Maybe the tail gets in the way once in a while, but running is running and it's something we've done since we could stand up and take a look around. Don't see how that's going to get us to achieve the supersonic speeds that Blanche dis- played.

"Don't think human," Blanche tells us. "It's so ingrained in us to move like them, to walk like they walk, to run like they run. It's not natural for us to worry about how foolish we look with our tails bouncing up and down, or if we're keeping our butts tucked in tight enough. Let loose. Forget human- ity."

Forget humanity. There's a dream.

Nothing still. An hour, two hours, and my muscles are fatiguing, throw- ing off slow, steady waves of pain, demanding of the other parts of my body that they unionize as soon as possible and insist on regular coffee breaks from management.

I ask to be excused. Permission is denied.

But just as I'm about to give up, once I've informed my legs that their services will no longer be needed today, that they can take off and head out to dinner—following hours spent running under the warm Hawaii sun, my tail no longer held aloft, away from the dirt below, but instead released, al- lowed to dangle to the ground, to push and to thrust and help out if need be—once I'm at that point of complete, dial-911-and-don't-hang-up ex- haustion, some part of my body sends a telegram to my brain to the effect that I may very well be moving faster than before.

Trick of the mind. Can't be.

But there it is, an odd sensation of speed, accompanied by a new muscle memory in my legs. I can't explain it, but I can feel it. A loping move, a lurching leap that is anything but natural in the human-inflected world in which I usually live, but that's what it is. I can't say that the motion is pure dinosaur, and I'm sure as heck not going to say that it means I've Progressed, but for the first time in my life I'm running free, unencumbered by all those straps and buckles, my naked face turned up to the sky, the ground flowing strong beneath me, trees streaming by in a steady brown blur, my legs and arms and tail and whole being churning in some motion that should be impossibly uncomfortable but somehow strikes me as purely and simply . . . natural.

It's time for lunch.

Which is hen. Not cornish, not roasted, but a game hen of some sort, un-plucked, uncooked, and very much un-dead. Inside the mess hall, a wooden stake has been hammered into the ground next to each table, and a flock of these hens tied to each one with a single strand of twine. A fren-zied squawking and flapping fill the air—these poor girls can sense that it's all over for their little birdy selves, and I can't blame them for going out with as much noise as they can muster. I can't imagine the proper proce-dure for lunch, but I have a feeling Martha Stewart would not approve.

As the Progressives enter the mess hall, famished from a hard day swimming with crocodiles or some other inane bloodsport, they coo with delight. Hen Day! What a treat! With careful deliberation, as if they're de-ciding on the purchase of a new luxury automobile, each dino chooses his or her bird from the buffet post, snaps the tether with a single claw, lifts the hen to a wide, gaping mouth, and bites the poor flapping thing's head clean off before spitting it into a nearby bucket. Once the body has stopped mov-ing, it's time to feast on the goo inside.

"You gonna try that?" Ernie asks me tentatively.

"You?"

"You seemed to like breakfast," he points out.

I can't deny that. Maybe it wouldn't hurt to give this a try; I am fam-ished, after all, and nourishment is nourishment. I've eaten cornish game hen before; perhaps not so animated, but what's a little sentience when it comes to nutrition? The more I watch the others eating, the more my own hunger grows.

Before I've even spoken to the rest of my body about the matter, my arms act of their own accord, reaching out and snatching a hen from the closest post, snipping the wire tethering the bird to its only form of protection.

Somewhere, far in the background, Ernie is asking me what the hell I think I'm doing.

It's as if I'm outside myself, watching a completely different Velociraptor stretch his jaw wide open, drool slavering from between his teeth, and lift a squawking, flapping game hen up to his mouth.

My lips close around the bird before I let my teeth crunch down, and in that moment, I can feel the hen's beak pecking furiously, frantically at my gums. It wants out, in a big way. But I have no control over my jaws; they begin to make the final movement that will snap the head off this bird and send that beautiful, tasty fluid deep into my mouth, my throat, my belly. I will be sated. . . .

A hand on my shoulder. "Vincent!"

I turn, game hen body poking out of my mouth, the bird having stopped his pecking for a moment, as if to listen in. Ernie's disapproval is palpable; he shakes his head back and forth, slowly, deliberately. "Put down the bird, kid."

That's all it takes. Reason suddenly floods back into the void of my brain, and I realize that if I bite off this hen's head, it will most likely continue with its Woody Woodpecker imitation inside my mouth long after decapitation, which will, in turn, make me nauseous enough to lose not only lunch, but probably this morning's breakfast as well.

I gingerly withdraw the hen from my mouth, apologize to my fine friend, dry off its feathers with a few quick puffs of air, and tie the creature back to its tether. Of course, it's no sooner back at the post, its stay of execution granted, than another dino snatches it by the legs and tosses it down the hatch.

Circe is not around today, so there will be no safe and sound mammalian lunch for us. Then again, if she were here, I wonder what direction my afternoon meal would have taken—would she find me some cooked, non-flapping comestible, or would she somehow have convinced me, through pheromones, hormones, or rational debate, to partake of the live bird? Better not to know, perhaps.

Buzz and Wendell make their way over, plucking feathers from the corners of their mouths, wiping up stray drips of blood with long, waggling tongues. "Great seminar today, don'tcha think?" says Wendell, slapping me across the back. "One more, and then it's free time. Lounge around, practice what we've learned."

"Walk around the facilities, work up an appetite before dinner," adds Buzz. "It's a nice time of day to relax."

Free time sounds like an excellent concept to me; perhaps something productive might come of it. "Think you boys would be interested in giving us a tour of the place?" I ask. "During this free time of ours? There's some areas of the island I'd love to see."

"We'd be delighted!" gurgles Buzz.

"Thrilled!" says Wendell.

"Any place you want to go, we'll take you."

"Anywhere?"

"Anywhere," Buzz confirms.

"The other side of the island?" I try.

Wendell pulls his brother aside and whispers a few choice words into his ear hole. "That's off-limits," says Buzz, coming up from the huddle. "Anywhere other than that."

"Why?" asks Ernie. "What's wrong with that?"

"Radiation," whispers Wendell.

Buzz nods hard enough to snap his neck and joins in. "It was a testing site—"

"A nuclear testing site—"

"And the radiation is dangerous—"

"It could kill you—"

"Before you even know it!"

"That's what they told you?" asks Ernie.

"That's what we know," replies Wendell.

I make a big show of clucking my tongue and widening my eyes, but inside the gears are starting up, working off the accumulated rust. Sure, they tested atomics in the South Pacific, and it's distinctly possible that Bikini Atoll had a few brothers and sisters, but why would the Progressive leadership go to such lengths to scare their members away from this area?

"It's off-limits," Buzz tells us for the second time. "But there are some lovely waterfalls just down the way. You'll love them."

But Ernie and I know where we want to go now, and no arbitrary rules are going to stop us. We're going to get to the other side of the island, horrible radioactive mutation or no horrible radioactive mutation. Personally, I'm hoping for the no-horrible-radioactive-mutation option, but beggars can't be choosers.

First, though, I've got to take a swim.

Buzz and Wendell have chosen to join Ernie and me for this post-lunch seminar—a swimming class, we've been told—and I think they're becoming attached to us, which is good, in the sense that they'll be easier to manipulate when it comes time to do so, and bad, in the sense that they have a tendency to get severely on my partner's nerves. But despite last evening's festivities with Circe, we're not here for fun; we're on the job.

A quarter-mile away from camp, our group takes a small footpath leading off into a separate part of the jungle. The trees here are different—mangroves instead of palms, for example—and the ground is becoming softer, mushier beneath my bare feet. Soothing, really.

Swampland. That's what it is—a perfect amalgam of the Florida Everglades, the Louisiana bayou, and every nature special I've managed to catch on the Discovery Channel. It's artificial, without a doubt—I can even make out the concrete sides of the large, forboding swimming hole that spreads out before us—but still impressive in its size and scale.

I take a peek into the murky waters below. The surface of the pond is covered in a light blanket of green algae, and I wouldn't be surprised to find out that this is tonight's dinner. "So . . . what? We jump in?" I stand on the edge of the dirt and prepare to showcase my diving skills.

Wendell's hand shoots out to grab me by the shoulder, locking me firmly in place. "Don't," he says sternly, his face not set into a goofy smile for the first time since we met. "If you splash, they'll think you're food."

"*Who'll* think I'm . . . ?" And then I see it, a pair of eyes emerging from the water, two small golf balls floating on the surface, staring out at the swamp, taking in everything with a fierce intelligence and cunning. Next to those, another pair, and behind that, yet another. All around the swamp, the stillness of the water is broken by eyeball after eyeball after eyeball.

Crocodiles.

In a flash, Ernie's turned on his heels, heading back toward dry land. "Tell teacher I ditched class," he calls back.

I catch my partner, haul him back to the edge of the water. If I'm going in, he's going in. If I'm going to become a part of the crocodile's food pyramid, he's going to become part of the crocodile's food pyramid.

After a few strict rules from our group leader—no sudden movements, no taunting the crocs, no putting your head in their mouths like a circus trainer—advice that I would basically consider simple common sense—common sense, that is, *if* you've willingly chosen to swim with these snappers—we slowly enter the swamp, letting the water rise inch by inch over our feet, our legs, our torsos.

Hide, sliding against mine. Is it Wendell's? Is it a crocodile? The feel is quite similar, I notice, as is their method of gliding through the water. The more experienced swimmers among us dive beneath the surface, taking so much air in their lungs they don't come up for minutes at a time. I prefer to stay safely near the shore of the swamp, ducking my head under the water every so often for a glimpse of our cousins swimming merrily beneath my feet.

Ernie dog-paddles up beside me, his spastic swimming confusing the surface of the water with miniature tidal waves. "I'm starting to get the feeling that Progress is regress."

"Not my concern right now," I tell him, my attention on a nearby set of eyes poking out of the water, eyes that are currently looking in this direction with a decidedly *hungry* look to them. "Take your splashing elsewhere, please."

The lesson ends with nary a dino eaten, though one of the Hadrosaurs does get her bum and tail nipped. To her credit, she neither screams nor splashes about, which is more than I could say for myself if some sixteen-foot behemoth decided to engage in a little taste test on my tuchis.

We slowly make our way out of the water. The Brontosaurs among us are raving about the experience—big wonder, as their bloated bodies float better than they walk, which, I'm pretty sure, is why that blowhard Alexandra hasn't moved her fat ass out of Loch Ness in thirty years—while the rest of us are grumbling about the stink of algae now clinging to every crevice in our bodies. That's gonna make for a lovely smell in the mess hall tonight.

But first there's free time, and a little jaunt we need to take. Ernie and I approach Buzz and Wendell—still grinning away, wiping the pond scum from their hides—and ask if they'd like to go on an outing. "You can show us those waterfalls," I suggest. "Wash off some of the algae."

The twins are delighted to get the show on the road, and soon enough we're tromping through the underbrush, shoving aside branches and overgrown palm fronds, tearing them with our claws when the path is too tight. We proceed in silence, climbing over rolling hills, avoiding those plants that look like they might either sting, bite, or cause nasty rashes. "So," I begin, wishing to bring a little light conversation back to the jungle, "bummer of a time in the Ring the other night, huh?"

"It was a shame," says Buzz. "Yanni shouldn't have tried to Progress ahead of schedule."

"A shame."

"Lucky those friends of his were good with the dart guns," Ernie points out. "Pretty good shots."

"Definitely lucky," I say.

As Buzz whips his claws through a dense set of foliage ahead of us, he calls back, "There was no luck to it—that was skill, and nothing less."

"We practice," says Wendell proudly. "I can almost hit the bull's-eye on all five shots."

"You practice what? Shooting?"

"Dart guns, mostly," Buzz explains. "But we hear there's a more advanced class once we Progress a little further. I think around sixty percent dinosaur natural you can opt to take a quick-fire seminar."

Without even looking over at my partner, I can tell that he's incensed beyond incensed. I've had a lifelong dislike and, to some degree, fear of firearms, a bias that's instilled in most dinos from birth. We've got enough natural weapons without having to resort to a hunk of metal and blasting powder, and notwithstanding the Crusades and such, everyone pretty much got along before the mammals decided to mass-produce these things. Then again, Samuel Winchester was a Velociraptor who, I believe, had strayed a little too far from his roots, so I can't blame it all on the humans.

But Ernie . . . for as long as I can remember, despite the infrequent but occasional necessity of firearms as a natural part of a PI's existence, Ernie has had a passionate hatred for guns that rivals his passionate hatred for marzipan—don't ask, don't ask—and that dislike runs deep.

"That's . . . that's disgusting," Ernie spits.

"It—it's only a s-s-seminar," stutters Wendell. He doesn't want to upset his new friend, that's clear, but he's stepped into some pretty hot cooking oil this time.

But Ernie's suddenly laughing, a good old-fashioned chuckle, hands covering his head, shoulders shaking in full-on mirth mode. "This—this is great—" he says. "You—you guys preach natural living, getting back to ourselves, our true side . . . and—and you have *riflery* classes?"

The irony is lost on the twins. "In order for us to understand the enemy," Buzz says soberly, "we must try to think like the enemy."

"Is that what they told you?" I ask. "That you practice shooting in order to understand humans?"

"Yes. You think that's wrong?"

I mull it over. "Not entirely."

We arrive at the waterfall. It's large. It's wet. As Buzz and Wendell promised, there are no crocodiles in it.

"Where to next?" I ask, thoroughly underwhelmed.

Wendell jumps up and down. "Oooh, there's another waterfall just up the way, we could go there. Or there's the one down by the—"

"I'm just about waterfalled out, fellas," Ernie interrupts. "Maybe there's something more interesting to show us." Without even having to take a glance at his eyes, I know Ernie's ready to move on to the next phase. With every year of partnership that we log, our signals are getting easier and easier for the other to read. In the beginning, I practically needed him to hold up huge cue cards, but now all it takes is a stress on a syllable, a certain nuance in his diction.

"Yeah, let's go farther into the island," I suggest. "Somewhere . . . different."

Buzz and Wendell have no clue what we're talking about. They stare at us blankly, a couple of sheep asked to do trig equations.

"The off-limits area," Ernie says flatly. "That should be interesting."

"But it's off-limits," whines Wendell.

I nod along, pretending to agree. "Thus the name. We wouldn't want to go there, Ern."

"No?"

"Nah. I mean, it might be interesting to go *near* there, to go *up to* that point, but we wouldn't actually want to go in."

"Oh, no, not actually *in*," Ernie repeats.

Now I've got Buzz's attention, too, and I think the little bit of bait I've tossed his way has been snatched up nice and tight. "Well, if we weren't going to actually go *into* the off-limits area . . ."

"Right, right," says Wendell, the excitement crawling back into his voice. "Not into, just near, just near . . ."

Within a few moments, Buzz and Wendell have worked themselves back up to a trailblazing frenzy, and we're off through the jungle again, hacking away at leaves and trees on our way to the next destination.

"Hey," Buzz calls back, "you know who showed me this path?"

"No clue," I say honestly.

"Your friend, the one you call Rupert. About two years ago, after Wendell and I grew to fifty percent natural."

"No kidding," says Ernie. "He knew a lot about the island, then?"

"Of course," Wendell says. "He was a guide. He and Rachel and . . . what was that nice Coelo's name, Buzz?"

"Walter."

"Right, Walter. They were all great."

I trip over a low-lying vine, stumble, catch myself on another low-lying vine, and voila, I'm back to walking again. Greystoke, I am not. "You say they *were* all great?"

"They don't come around anymore."

"Did they all . . . die? Like Rupert?"

Buzz shrugs. "We didn't hear much about them. They were here, and then they weren't. We only heard about Rupert through the grapevine. I think Walter may have passed away, too, but I don't know about the others."

Others, eh? "How many dinos do you know who have disappeared?"

"Since when?"

"Last year or two," I say.

"Six?" says Buzz, unsure of his answer.

"Seven, eight, something like that," says Wendell. They're both completely unconcerned with their own answers and go right on hacking through the jungle.

I'm about to point out to them that they might like to hire some personal protection should they ever decide to leave the group when Buzz stops, eyes roving in his head as if he's looking for an answer and might be able to find it somewhere in his field of vision. "You know, come to think of it, last time we came out here, I was pretty sure Rachel was somewhere out here, too, though everyone had heard that she had met the ancestors. . . ."

"You saw her?"

"I smelled her, right here on the island. Very strong scent of lavender and paint thinner, couldn't mistake it." He turns around and starts hiking again. "It was so strange, but . . . then again, I could be wrong."

As we've been hiking, certain small changes in the surrounding foliage have begun to attract my attention. It's nothing much at first—a misshapen leaf here, a strangely twisted twig there—but as we push farther through the forest, I notice that the trees have begun to thin out, the vegetation becoming more scarce. And those few hardy plants that have cared to keep their roots in the area are all different, as if somewhere down the line a twisted gardener traded in his green thumb for an orange one. Examples:

A palm, the fronds thick and wide, stretching out and providing shade for the root system like any good palm tree will do. Unfortunately, it's only two feet tall.

Hedges ten feet high, brambles with thorns like hypodermic needles, vines sporting flowers that are dead before they even get a chance to bloom, petals rotting inside the buds. A jolly old greenhouse as imagined by Dr. Frankenstein himself.

And it's warmer here, the usually pervasive ocean breeze practically nonexistent, as if the air itself is afraid to make an appearance. The forest animals seem to have all gone on permanent coffee break, and the absence of noise is more unsettling than any jungle cat's scream or coyote's howl. Buzz and Wendell grow more anxious with every step, their voices warbling as they try to call an end to the half-day tour.

"Th—this is good," stammers Buzz. "You've seen it."

"Yeah, you've seen it," Wendell joins in. "Let's go back now."

"What's farther in?" Ernie asks. "I think I see some sort of path."

Buzz is already shaking his head, the trembling matching the rest of his body. "No, no, there's no path."

"No path. Let's go back now, guys, okay?"

But there is—if I squint just right, I can make out a beaten dirt road leading into a clearing, and my legs start a-movin' before the rest of the gang is able to stop me. The misshapen plants, the trees reaching out for me, the sand underfoot that somehow feels more like broken shards of glass than anything else, is all forgotten as I make my way toward that odd little path. There's a building down there, a brick building with . . . I can almost make it out . . . a steel door, I think. Set in the middle of an otherwise deserted clearing, the sand around it black, practically onyx, the very essence of this building is, not unlike the women I generally choose to date, sending out two distinct messages: *Stay far away* and *Vincent, I'm yours.* I heed the latter.

Which is precisely when the world explodes. Accompanied by a throaty roar, a tidal wave of dirt rises out of the earth, a tsunami of branches and brambles and soil, and I fall back to avoid the messy onslaught. Something scrapes against the tip of my tail, a tremendous pressure that sends a shard of anguish tearing up my spine, forcing a yelp out of my snout.

"Electric fence," drawls Ernie. "Nice find, kid."

I don't know where it came from, though I imagine I was so set on conquering the building in the distance that I neglected my short-focus vision; but before I have a chance to exact my revenge on this wire monstrosity, there's another voice booming out of the wilderness, familiar but quite unexpected. "What are you four doing out here?"

We all jump as one—I actually keep it down to a mild hop, thank you—and turn to find Samuel and another Iguanodon climbing down out of a camouflaged Hummer. In the back of the vehicle, a wide tarp covers a pile of some bulky substance; it's difficult to make out the exact cargo.

"Where'd you come from?" asks Ernie.

Extract of displeasure streams out of Samuel in waves; he's the God of Stern Disapproval, and is about to dispense a trademark harsh warning. "The two of you," he says, doing his best to stare down Ernie and me, "shouldn't be worrying about things beyond your Progression level yet. And as for you two"—now focusing his attention on a cowering, shaking Buzz and Wendell—"you should know better. I'm going to have a word with Circe about this. Now get in the car, all of you."

In a cloud of petulance, we climb into the back of the Hum-Vee, a bunch of kids caught in a dumb juvenile prank. I half expect Samuel to call our parents and let them know just what it is we did this night, but I think we might get off with just a warning.

During the wordless ride back to the compound, the tarpcovered pile next to me clanks and clinks with every bump, but I resist the temptation to pull the cloth aside and soak in a good look. I'm in enough lukewarm water as it is, and I don't want to get thrown off the island before I've had another shot at Circe. I'm sorry—at interviewing Circe.

When we arrive back at the camp, Ernie and I are sent to our hut and told to prepare for the evening's banquet; Wendell and Buzz head off with Samuel, presumably to get their spanking.

"I'd hate to get the little pissers in trouble," I tell Ernie. "I mean, they were just doing us a favor."

"They'll be fine," my partner says. "Slap on the wrist and off to eat some raw pork. Wait and see, they'll be bothering us again in no time."

It is two hours later, and Circe has just announced to the dinner crowd that Buzz and Wendell have been chosen by Progress. In a scant forty-five minutes, they will enter the Ring.

And Ernie and I get to help them.

Whispering: "I thought you said you weren't ready for this."

"We must be. We were chosen, so we must be. Right?"

I'm leading Buzz and Wendell down a long corridor and between the two sets of bleachers, acting as their guide as we walk as slowly as possible toward the Ring. The stands are filled with Progressives, and the view from down here is very different from what it was up on the dais last night. From this vantage point, it seems like every dinosaur up there is looking down on us to mock our passage, as if on some hidden signal, they will all leap down and tear us into a million pieces.

But they're just cheering, cheering on their friends who have so valiantly chosen to attempt Progress together. Little do they know that the twins themselves aren't exactly enamored of the idea.

"Call it off," I urge them. "Stand up and say you recant. Did Circe tell you that you should do this?"

But Buzz shakes his head, and I believe him. Still, something—some-*body*—has gotten to him since that Hummer pulled away, and though he's clearly petrified of entering the Ring this evening, he refuses to disavow the decision he and Wendell have made. "Progress has chosen us," he says. "We must go."

"How do you know Progress has chosen you?" I ask, hoping to force some logic into a completely illogical situation. "Did Circe tell you that? Samuel?"

"No." Emphatic, truthful.

"Then who did?"

No answer. We approach the Ring.

It was right after the announcement that Buzz and Wendell would be attempting this night's inanities that we were approached by Samuel, taken away from the main dining hall, and informed that the twins had chosen Ernie and me as two of their confederates for the evening.

"The guys who lead them in?" I asked. "The ones with the cage and the—"

"And the dart guns, yes," said Samuel. "It is a great honor to be chosen."

Ernie shook his head. "We don't know how to shoot," he lies. "We can't—"

"To refuse a request like this is to do your friends the greatest dishonor there is." Once Samuel started talking like Bruce Lee, I couldn't back out. I already felt somewhat responsible for getting the twins in trouble earlier on, and now that they'd gone over the edge of sanity, I couldn't stand back and let them leap alone.

"Your job is simple," Samuel explained. "You will walk them out, you will lock them inside. You'll return for a cage, wheel it out. The other two compatriots your friends have chosen are longtime Progressives; they will know what levers to release."

"That's not the part I'm worried about. The dart guns—"

"Should not be needed." Samuel reached into a duffel bag he had brought along and pulled out one of the rifles we saw last night. "Progress has chosen them for this task, and that means they should emerge victorious. On the off chance that something should go wrong, the operation is very simple." He lifted the rifle to his shoulder, locking the stock against his powerful chest. Meanwhile, I was taking mental shorthand at light speed, trying to get all of this information to take root in my brain as quickly and deeply as possible. "Circe will stand, clap her hands twice, and then, simply, you shoot."

Without even taking aim, Samuel's finger depressed the trigger, a shot zinged out of the barrel, and a few seconds later, a light thud on the ground nearby announced the demise of a small red-red robin who would no longer be bob-bob-bobbin' along.

"Great for you," said Ernie, "but we're not skilled at this."

"And it won't be a bird you'll be aiming at. You've seen Ring opponents;

they tend to be a little larger. It works like this: point the barrel at the bad thing and press the trigger. That's all there is to it."

From there on in it was a jumble of confusion, accusation, and apologies, Ernie and I trying to ascertain why on earth Buzz and Wendell would want to do this to themselves when they had explicitly stated to us earlier that they were nowhere near ready for the task.

"Now's the time when we tell you whatever we think is important," gulps Wendell. We're at the entrance to the Ring, and the outdoor amphitheater has taken on a hushed, almost spiritual tone.

"Now's the time when you call a halt to this nonsense," replies Ernie.

But they're beyond that point. "If anything happens, tell my brother I love him," Wendell whispers to me.

A few feet away, I can hear Buzz murmuring in Ernie's ear. "Take care of my brother," he says. "That's all I ever wanted to do."

We lock them inside the Ring.

A hundred different emotions and courses of action flip through my mind as Ernie, the two other confederates—both Carnotaurs—and I make our way back toward the clearing where the second cage will be ready for us to deliver. Do we bolt? Do we refuse to release the animal inside? For the first time in a long time, I find myself mired in a swamp of indecision.

What I will do, it seems, is exactly what others before me have done. The cage is waiting there in the clearing, Samuel standing beside it, checking the security of the brown tarpaulin draped across the top. "Are they ready?"

We nod, and the cage is turned over to our possession. As we wheel it through the jungle, toward the amphitheater, I notice that there are no animal noises emanating from within, and it doesn't shake any more than the bumps and breaks in the path would give it cause to. Could the thing possibly be empty? Could this all be one huge practical joke to play on Ernie and me? It's heavy, no doubt, but the cage *itself* is heavy.

I bet that's it. A joke, nothing more than a high school prank. Buzz and Wendell and the rest of them are just screwing with our minds. It's a fraternity hazing, the last step before official initiation, and I almost got tricked.

Well, if it's a joke they want, they've come to the right place. I can play along with the best of them.

We wheel the cage into the amphitheater and the two Carnotaurs begin to hook it up to the entrance of the Ring. I look up toward the dais, catch Circe's eye, and give her a sly wink. *I know your game,* this wink says. *You almost got me, but I know your game.* Her return gaze is inscrutable, but at least my cards are on the table, and I know that she knows that I know, and that makes me all the more willing to play along.

Inside the Ring, Buzz and Wendell are really laying it on thick, their breathing shallow, their faces flushed. It's a great act, and I have to remember to congratulate them on their skills after we're sucking down some basil and joking about it in a few minutes.

"We're ready," one of the Carnotaurs says to me.

I nod my head like a Roman emperor giving the order to execute. This is my chance to don the thespian mantle; the drama club never wanted me— this'll show 'em. "Raise the gate," I command.

Nothing. No animal roar, no ferocious beast rushing out of the cage to attack the hapless twins. Stillness from the crowd.

Ernie, mouthing to me: *What's going on?*

A joke, I mouth back. *It's all a joke.*

Ernie cocks his head—he doesn't understand. I shuffle closer to him and whisper in his ear, "It's a hazing ritual. They're trying to spook us."

"I don't think so," he replies. "This is a helluva long way to go. . . ."

But there's still no action in the Ring, and the crowd is growing restless. "Here," I say, "I'll prove it to you." I take a few steps closer to the cage, reaching out for the brown tarpaulin covering. "There's no danger to Buzz and Wendell, because there's nothing inside this thing."

Like a magician uncovering his latest and greatest trick, I whip the blanket from the cage and turn to Ernie, showcasing the emptiness inside. "See?" I say. "Nothing."

Nothing plus two grizzly bears, that is.

Furious at my sudden intrusion, the bears leap up from their sleeping positions and launch themselves against the bars of the cage—the crowd roaring as the adrenaline hits—and I'm falling backward, away from the massive paws and heavy claws snaking out from between the bars. Scooting away from the cage on my butt, heart pumping a week's worth of blood in a few seconds—the crowd on its feet now as the bears wisely pass on me and reorient their sights on a more accessible target.

Buzz and Wendell are not prepared for the sudden onslaught. The bears don't even bother dropping onto all fours—they stand straight up for the charge, whipping those long, lethal paws through the air—two seven-foot towers of shaggy brown fur that have just found out it's dino-hunting season, and they've got two more to bag and tag before they reach their limit.

One of the bears squares off against Buzz; the other takes Wendell. I can do nothing but watch, frozen in place, numbed by my incorrect assumption, my moronic bullheadedness, and, yes, by guilt. I'm sure those bears would have attacked the twins sooner or later, but perhaps they wouldn't have been so pissed off about it if I hadn't interrupted what were probably very nice dreams of picnic baskets and honey pots.

Wendell's fighting mostly with his jaws, trying to sink his teeth into the bear's jugular, but every time he gets to snapping near the creature's neck, the bear takes a swat at the Carnotaur's head, sending Wendell scampering backward with long claw marks gashed across his face. Buzz isn't doing much better, but at least he's keeping his opponent at bay, using his tail to carve out a semicircle of protection.

I don't know if there are any rules of combat in the Ring, but even if there are, the bears don't have much use for them. For just as Buzz has advanced on his adversary, almost driving the bear all the way back into his cage, the other one forgets about Wendell and swoops in from behind, biting down hard on Buzz's neck, the teeth sinking deeply into unprotected flesh, and a geyser of blood sprays up and out, soaking the floor.

With a roar of his own that surpasses anything I've heard from the bears, let alone any special-effects wizard in Hollywood, Wendell charges, jaw spread wide, teeth glistening, ready to swallow his brother's attacker whole, if need be.

But a well-placed swat, this one from the other bear, puts a stop to Wendell's charge, and he, too, sinks to the ground. Both dinos are down for the count and barely putting up a fight.

Circe's hands are still. I await the double clap, staring up at Circe, my arms spread wide—*When? When?*—but she deliberately looks away. Samuel is nowhere to be found.

A piercing scream from within the Ring. I can't look.

"Screw it," I say, and reach for a gun.

Ernie's already way ahead of me. I do just like the guy said—point the barrel at the bad thing in front of me and pull the trigger—

Nothing. No click, no whiff, no zing. The bears continue to maul Buzz and Wendell, the twins' battle cries slowly dying to a whimper.

Frantically, I lift the gun again, sight down the barrel—the bear's back directly in front of me, easy shot, point-blank, eighty-year-old woman with cataracts could make this—and squeeze the trigger with all my might.

Zero.

Unable to work this infernal human contraption, I look over to my partner for help, but Ernie's having just as much trouble as I am. I watch as he takes aim and fires, only to have a staggering amount of nothingness take place.

Now the crowd has begun to scream. It is not, I surmise, in joy.

"It's jammed—" shouts Ernie. "The gun, it's jammed—"

One of the Carnotaur confederates rushes over with his own weapon, raising it expertly to the proper level. He lets a dart fly, and it whizzes across the ring, missing the bear by a good three feet. For a moment I think he's missed on purpose, that he swung the barrel around at the last second, but he stares at the gun in awe, like a tennis player checking his racquet for holes after missing an easy shot, and I know he had that thing aimed perfectly.

Inside the Ring, Buzz and Wendell are dying. They've managed to scoot backward, their bodies pressed up against the bars of the massive cage, the brothers holding on to and cradling each other, their blood truly flowing as one. Our chances left to save them are dwindling, but we've not yet exhausted all options.

"Open the gate," I shout to the one Carnotaur who has yet to lift a claw. "Do it, now!"

My tone is insistent enough to frighten the dinosaur beyond his training or common sense, and he leaps to the Ring entrance, fumbling with the keys. I'm right behind him, still trying to force my gun to fire, a task as futile as trying to buy a decent fast-food fish fillet. There's ammo in there, but it won't load, and I don't know how to force it in. But if I can get inside that Ring, I'll pull a Davy Crockett and shove these darts into those bears' chests with my hands, if need be.

"It's stuck—" cries the Carnotaur, and I shove him out of the way. Ernie rushes to my side and we set to pulling on the bars, the Carnotaurs joining in a moment later.

We strain. We pull. We exert every bit of energy left in bodies that have been malnourished and deprived of sleep for two days, the tumultuous blare of the crowd egging us on, goading us to new feats of strength. The bars will twist. The bars will bend. The bars will snap.

But the combined force of four dinosaurs don't mean a hill of beans to an indifferent mass of steel. The door stays firmly in place, absolutely nothing we can do about it. With a final tug, I lose my grip and fall heavily to the dirt, the wind knocked out of me and not coming back for some time. I can't watch, but I can listen, and there's not much mistaking the gruesome sounds that invade my trembling ears. Within seconds, the bears finish off our friends and, after deciding that the overgrown reptiles are inedible, proceed to cross to the far side of the Ring and drift back to sleep.

The crowd continues in its aimless fury, small skirmishes breaking out below the forest canopy, miniature Ring battles of their very own. High above, up on the dais, I can see Circe, head down, shoulders wracked with sobs. Her skin is dry, pale, dull, but her scent—tinged, somehow, with ragweed and pollen, the stuff of sadness—is stronger than ever, pervading the amphitheater, as if trying to draw me away from the anger of the crowd and into her grief. For a moment, I am lost, captive in her melancholia, and I know deep down that Circe knew nothing of this, that whatever has occurred tonight was either a freak accident or rigged without her knowledge. But that moment of clarity and sorrow soon passes, and the tumultuous frenzy of hundreds of my fellow dinosaurs zaps me back into action.

"Vincent! Vincent!" Ernie's calling to me, pulling me through the crowd, away from the guards, away from the dais, away from the amphitheater and into the darkness, and I follow him with a mindless intensity. There is nothing to say to him. There is nothing to say to anyone. This is the only thing I am thinking, and I am thinking it over and over again:

Buzz and Wendell died in each other's arms, and in that, I hope, the pain of their passing was somewhat diminished. But I swear to Raal, the ancestors, or whoever the hell is listening that when I find the creatures responsible for orchestrating this debacle, they will not be so fortunate.

We have spent six hours lost in this jungle, slamming into tree trunks, tree branches, tripping over stumps, over roots, frightening small woodland creatures, and if it takes another six, I'm more than willing to collect whatever bumps and bruises may occur. The other side of the island and the fence blocking access to that off-limits area is around here somewhere.

We've got to break into that building.

Ernie and I snuck away from the amphitheater with little fanfare. Don't even know if they noticed our exit; they'd have a big enough job calming down hundreds of rioting dinosaurs, and two little infidels cannot have been significant enough to worry themselves over. We don't have maps, but no matter. We don't have a compass—no matter. We don't have the vaguest clue as to where we're going or what we'll find when—if—we get there. No matter.

What we do have is a furious anger, a sense that we've been played for chumps, and a burning desire to get to the heart of the beast, ferret out the weasel, or weasels, responsible, and exact justice. The only problem is that we're naked, and we're lost.

"You been dropping those pine cones?" Ernie asks me.

"Fat lot of good that'll do. Look for the freaky trees, that's the key."

We proceed deeper into the jungle, the moon and stars completely obscured by the canopy overhead, and by the time I'm starting to believe that we're irretrievably, irrevocably lost, that they'll find our bodies in three thousand years, clean up our skeletons, and place us in museums so that schoolkids can marvel at the advanced stage of lizards back in our time and write misspelled thank-you notes to the curator, Ernie's picked up on a scent.

"What is it?" I ask.

"It's . . . it's me," he says, a little abashed.

Great, he's smelling himself again. I thought we'd gotten that habit taken care of back in '89. "I don't get it."

Ernie's moving quickly now, his legs moving independently of the rest of his body, torso coming along for the ride. "When we were out by the fence with Buzz and Wendell earlier on—when Samuel found us—I took the liberty of relieving myself on a few bushes. I think I've caught the scent."

A deep breath, soaking up the jungle air. I've got urine smells coming in, all right, and when you work in the city—especially if you're running a job in downtown Santa Monica—you can't be squeamish when it comes to matters of the bladder. Still, I'm unable to distinguish Ernie's urine from a raccoon's from a blue jay's—at least, not at this distance. But I'm sure Ernie's been tracking it for miles. Even though humans have a rough time detecting their own body odor—the ones with *bad* body odor have an especially hard time at it, natch—and dinos are unable to smell their own pheromones, we've each got a keen sense of our own waste products. Sure, call it disgusting, but anything that'll get me oriented in this jungle is worthy of some respect.

I follow my partner, who is now working a beeline through the forest, and it's not another ten minutes before the trees begin to take on that Brothers Grimm look. Knotholes elongate, forming great, gaping maws, branches reaching out like arthritic fingers ready to pluck me up and finish me off. Of course, Ernie's walking through it all like it's downtown Brentwood at high noon, but then the old fart never did have much of an imagination.

"There's the bush," says Ernie, pointing to the small urine-soaked hedge. I applaud, he bows, and we stare up at the fence looming before us, thirty feet high, completely unscalable by anyone older than ten.

"Now what?" I sit on a stump, my chin falling into my hands.

"How about getting that gate open?"

I shake my head. "No good. I think it's remote control. Remember when we got picked up in the Hummer that first night? Samuel clicked some box near the dashboard, and I heard creaking—"

At which point my partner opens his hand, green side up, to reveal the most beautiful six-inch box of plastic I've ever seen. The white push button on the side glistens in the moonlight.

"I snatched it from the truck before we got out," says my partner, his grin stretching across those wide-set teeth.

"But you've got no pockets."

"Correct."

"Do I want to know where you hid it?"

"No, you do not."

A click, a whirr, and the gate squeaks open, the hinges bitching about it all the way. "The path works in from here," I tell Ernie. "Should be just along the way."

My partner agrees, and after a few minutes of searching in the darkness, we stumble onto a four-foot-wide area of jungle that looks to have been cleared out a little more than the rest. The mutation is even more evident here, the ground slick beneath our feet, buckling up and out from the monstrous roots beneath its surface. A pair of tire tracks still set in the mud clinches the deal—this is the way in, no doubt, and our pace turns quicker as we slog through the mud, a stroll giving way to a spirited walk giving way to a jog giving way to a run.

We're eating up the land, mud churning beneath our feet, and over the smells of the jungle, our sweat, our excitement, I get a whiff of something else. Something familiar and yet slightly foreign. Can't place it yet, but as I concentrate on the path ahead, I'm collecting samples and letting the forensic scientist in my brain sort through the evidence.

New sounds, too. High-pitched squeaking, a gerbil in distress. Only I don't think gerbils are native to Hawaii. Animal calls, echoing off the trees, howls dying in the stillness of the night. And like the prior absence of sounds, these new noises are not soothing.

"Do you smell . . . others?" I ask Ernie.

"Other what?"

"Other dinosaurs. The pine, the dew . . ."

Mid-run, Ernie takes a deep whiff of the surrounding air, pivoting his head in all directions, nearly whacking into a koa tree on the way. "They may be following us," he says, and as one, we pick up the pace.

Almost before we get a chance to slam on the brakes, Ernie and I burst into a clearing, the moon showing its mocking little face once again, and wind up in front of our very own Holy Grail: the redbrick building. The tire tracks we've been following lead right up to the front door and then stop, and we slow to a quick walk and circle the structure, hoping that an easy way in will materialize if we stare hard enough at it.

No such luck. The only entrance remains a steel door set into the brick wall, and the only lock is an infernal finger-hole next to it, an exact replica of the one Circe used on the fossil-making barn. "Can't hurt to try," I suggest. "No other way in."

"Be my guest."

"Oh. I thought maybe *you'd* want to. . . ."

"Go ahead," insists Ernie.

Good luck, finger. Closing my eyes, I tuck my claw back into its slot— remembering the lesson from Bob, our first Progressive contact back on Hollywood Boulevard—and shove my pointer into the hole, gritting my teeth in expectation of some type of searing pain. If it matters, I prefer amputation to electrocution, but I doubt the door will take requests.

No pain. No miniature guillotine, no shock pads. The door doesn't open, but at least I've still got all eight digits intact. "Your turn," I cheerfully say to Ernie, removing my finger from the hole. But his grubbies don't do the job either, and so we're stuck out here staring at the door, twiddling our claws and scratching ourselves.

The animal calls have intensified. And that smell—pine, perhaps, though not herb-infused. It's not Circe, and even if it were, I wouldn't be worried about getting caught in off-limits territory; they've already killed our friends for a seemingly minor infraction, and I don't doubt but that our next interaction with the Progressives, whatever the situation, will be decidedly violent. But Circe's working on a different plane from the rest of them, and I wonder how well she knows and trusts her right-hand dinos.

Ernie runs his hand across the door, looking for any flaw to exploit. There is none.

"We're stuck."

"Still not natural enough," I sigh.

"Not by ourselves, at least."

"Not by ourselves."

I don't know who thinks of it first, me or Ernie, but soon we're both scrambling for the aperture, trying to shove both our fingers in at once. "Move—move to the left," Ernie complains. "Further. Further."

The fit is tight, but we're eventually able to force both of our fingers into the slot at the same time. There's the familiar cooling sensation as some hidden device sucks the pheromones out of our pores, and a whirr as a different mechanism checks our scent level against whatever percentage "dinosaur natural" it has been designed to grant access to.

I doubt this will work. The contraption has got to be able to discern Ernie's pheromones from mine; it can't be this easy to fool such delicate machinery.

The door swings wide.

After we get our fingers unstuck, we tentatively step inside the building, being careful not to set off any alarms. But it seems that the one steel door is the only barrier to the place, and soon we find ourselves in a small, round antechamber, stone floor and low ceiling, the walls plastered with old, yellowed maps. The entire world is duly represented, with small red and green pins stuck into various islands and peninsulas in nearly every country. Whatever they're tracking, it's done a great job of spreading itself all over the globe.

Ernie calls me to the far side of the room—he's pointing to a large crimson pin smack-dab in the middle of the ocean just off Hawaii, and I pluck it out of the map. Nearly eradicated by the pinhole itself is the outline of a very small, very isolated island.

"You are here," says Ernie. "But I can't figure out the rest of these. The red ones, the green ones . . ."

"Other Progressive camps, maybe?" I take a quick trip around the room, trying to locate a chart with Southern California on it. Sure enough, there's a red pin stuck into Los Angeles, up in the Hollywood Hills specifically, and I'm willing to make a leap of logic and agree that each pin represents a different stronghold for the group.

"You're right about the maps," I say. "Check it out."

No answer from Ernie. I turn, but the room is empty. "Ern?" I call out. "Ern?"

The reply, coming from down a long hallway, is hard to hear: ". . . might want . . . see this . . ."

"What? I can't hear you," I call back.

Ernie's voice is stronger this time, warbling slightly—fear, anger, or just the echo from the chamber walls?—"I said, you might want to see this."

Leaving the map room, I quickly make my way through the cold, tight corridor. Ernie's silhouette is sharp against the glare of a single uncovered hundred-watt bulb dangling from the ceiling, his shadow harsh against the brick walls. His shoulders are shaking, but I don't think he's laughing.

"What'd ya find—" I begin, and the words stop halfway up my throat.

Guns. Boxes of guns. Racks of boxes of guns. Guns in piles, guns on the wall, guns strewn haphazardly about the floor. Rifles, revolvers, semiautomatics, fully automatics, large caliber, small caliber, every make of every ballistic weapon I've ever seen is stuffed to bursting inside this twenty-by-twenty room, a weapons stash that would warm the cockles of Charlton Heston's cold mammalian heart.

"These don't shoot horse tranquilizers, do they?"

Ernie and I make our way into the room, stumbling over steel, picking our way through the morass of firearms. Ernie hasn't said a word since stepping inside—he simply walks in a circle, eyes downcast, some silent fury building up within him with every passing second.

Beneath me is a large cylindrical weapon with a grip like a video-game joystick. I lift the thing to get a better look at it—heavy little bastard—and stare down the barrel.

"Grenade launcher," Ernie says, his voice even, dead of emotion.

Ah. I carefully place it back atop the pile, just in case I hit the wrong button and become the latest Darwin Award recipient. "The hell do they need this for?"

"The hell do they need any of it for?" My partner lashes out at a pile of the firearms, kicking them with a bare foot. "This is the sickest fucking thing I've seen since we got here. All this talk about Progress and nature and understanding our true ancestors, and meanwhile they've got a weapons stock that would make NATO jealous."

I can't argue with the guy; these Progressives clearly have their heads screwed on backward, and I can't imagine what would make them want to amass this much firepower in one location. "We'll get back to LA," I suggest, "call the Council down on their ass. See how they take to a bunch of dinos hogging mammal weapons."

Ernie's hide has flared into a bright green hue along with his anger, the sudden rush of blood drawing out his best skin tone. He should definitely wear more fall colors. I doubt he'd appreciate the fashion advice right now, though, so I leave it alone. "That's right," he growls. "Confiscate the island, that house, throw 'em all in the clink."

Without realizing it, we've backed our way out of the gun room, as if our bodies knew more than our minds and forced us to retreat from such an unnatural location. By the time we're back in the hallway and heading toward the map antechamber—I'd really love to show Ernie those dates above the maps, maybe figure out what the hell they signify—I catch a whiff of the smell again, this time much stronger than before. Definitely pine, definitely swamp gas, and we are definitely not the only dinosaurs in the vicinity.

"Shhh," I tell Ernie, who's clomping his way noisily toward the exit.

"Why?"

"Sniff." Ernie takes a whiff, and instantly silences his movements.

Rustling, outside the building. The trees, shifting in the still air, leaves crackling under someone's feet. Huddling in the doorway, Ernie and I try to get a bead on the new intruder, but it's hard to localize.

"From the left," whispers Ernie. "I think they followed us."

"No," I whisper back. "This is something else."

And then another sound from the right. And another in front of us. The jungle has come alive, trees rustling in every direction, and the smell has only gotten stronger. It's the scent of a roadkill, of towering ferns, of a newborn baby dino, of steaming swamp pits.

Coming in tandem now—a shake of the trees, a burst of smell—and a new addition to the fun, a distinct howl, an animal call of *This way, boys, I found somethin' to munch on*—and I'm hoping that it's just the Hummer again, I'm hoping that it's Samuel come to lecture us and drive us on out of here—but something in me knows that's not the way it's gonna go down.

"Go," I say, my voice lower than I expected, as if my vocal cords know more than I do about the upcoming events.

"What?"

"Go," I repeat, louder this time, rising on panic. "Go!"

Sprinting from the get-go, we burst out of the building and into the jungle, clambering onto the path and letting loose. It's hard to concentrate on anything other than the road ahead, but I try to keep an ear and a nostril open, just in case.

Now the howls have intensified, deep calls of pain and rage, and it spurs me on to greater speeds. And there's another smell separating itself from the rest of them, riding high on the pine. Leather. New, though a part of me recognizes it. No time to think—time to run. But Ernie's lagging behind, panting hard, and I can't leave my partner in the dust. I fight back against the panic and slow my legs down a notch.

It gives our pursuer all the opportunity he needs. With a sudden piercing screech that nearly bursts my eardrums, a Stegosaur bursts out of the underbrush on all fours and slams into Ernie, a headbutt to the midsection tossing him to the ground. My partner goes down hard—rolling over a foothill of roots and landing against a thick tree trunk—but he's up again in an instant, claws sliding out of his fingers and locking into place.

"Wait a second—" I shout, hoping to stop the Stegosaur with some rational conversation.

But the look in its eye is pure animal; it doesn't even have the common courtesy to try and understand what I'm saying. Lunging forward again, its own claws extended, the Stegosaur stumbles toward Ernie, catching its front foot on an outcropping of rock and going down with a thud.

I take the opportunity to let loose—if we're gonna play this way, let's get it on—and leap feetfirst at the beast, my own sharp underclaw aimed for the throat. But a swinging tail catches me off guard, and it takes a midair pretzel twist to avoid winding up with a back full of spikes. Gotta watch all five limbs when dealing with a creature like this one. Adjusting my position, I slide to the left, narrowly avoiding a one-way trip to eternity.

Ernie's got his jaws set around the Stego's neck, his arms tight around the head, gnawing for all he's worth. I'm jumping around to the other side, sliding onto my back, trying to aim for the beast's soft, unprotected stomach, but it's tough going, as this thing insists on fighting on all fours. The multitude of sparring matches Ernie and I have engaged in, combined with the few real-world skirmishes I've gotten myself into, haven't prepared me a whiff for this kind of down-and-dirty battle.

Coming underneath, I'm just about to make a good stab at the stomach when the scent hits me again, snaking its way out of the back of this creature's neck, down and around its bulging belly, curving up my nose, and slamming directly into the recognition center of my brain: leather and lime Jell-O.

It's Thomas. We're fighting the Progressive who made his bones in the Ring the other night, the one who beat back a mountain lion with nothing other than his claws, his tail, and his wits. I understand the whole post-traumatic stress disorder concept—I ate a Pop-Tart with a cockroach on it once and couldn't look at another breakfast treat for months afterward—but this is beyond modern psychology. What the hell happened to this guy?

But my pause to indulge in conscious thought has given this natural dino a chance to escape my attack, and soon I'm forced to roll to my right as the Stegosaur leaps into the air and comes down hard, attempting to squash me beneath his stubby legs. An unfortunate woodchuck takes my place in rodent heaven. Fair trade.

Tucking into a somersault and popping to my feet at the end—those prepubescent Romanian gymnasts have nothing on a Raptor with his dander up—I spin and prepare to renew my assault on Ernie's attacker. But there's another rustle in the trees behind me, and I turn to investigate the new noise—

Just in time to avoid a claw slashing at my throat. I backpedal, throwing my arms up and out, batting away the matchstick arms reaching for my vital organs. Filling my field of vision now, a gaping jaw, mouth dripping with saliva, two sharpened rows of teeth; Jaws has sprung legs and crawled his way onto land for a jaunt in the jungle.

Close enough. It's a T-Rex—I don't recognize this one on a personal level, but I'm sure he was a busboy or ophthalmologist once upon a more rational time—and, like the Stegosaur, it pays no heed to any of my protestations to cut out the nonsense and start acting like an adult. Fortunately, he's inherited his race's propensity for inefficient forelimbs, so I'm able to keep his claws away from the rest of my body while I defend my snout against those snapping jaws. While guised up as a mammal, of course, this beast would have arm prostheses to help him blend into human society, but unassisted like this, he's at a distinct disadvantage. Then again, he does have quite the set of chompers at his disposal. They crack the air with each vicious bite, and I know from one look in his eyes that wherever the Stegosaur's mind has gone, this T-Rex's brain is riding sidecar on the journey.

Can't even see Ernie—no idea how he's holding up—but the space between my ears is filled with howls and shrieks and wails and bellows, a full cat's-night-out cacophony, and I don't know how much of it is coming from my partner, from the Stegosaur, from the T-Rex, or even from myself.

A tail whips out, tripping me from behind, and I flop to the ground, landing squarely on my back, crushing a pile of twigs and leaves beneath me. For a moment I can't even think about the dinosaur reaching down to finish me off; all I know is that oxygen and I have parted ways, and there's little else that currently matters.

Nearby teeth convince me otherwise. As the T-Rex lowers his head, jaw gaping wide in anticipation of victory, I kick out with my leg—still unable to breathe, mind you, so put *this* on your list of impressive feats—slide my underclaw to its fully extended position, and slam it up and clean through the roof of the Tyrannosaur's mouth.

Now he's flailing backward, a wail of pain curdling the air, flapping his runty arms against my leg, trying to dislodge my claw. I'm going along for the ride; my limb is still stuck inside his mouth, but I don't want to leave it there for long. Soon enough, he's going to get the idea to chomp me off at the knee, and I still have many years of plans left for that appendage. I quickly withdraw the hooked claw back into my body and snatch myself away from the bloody-mouthed dino.

"Little help?" I hear Ernie cry over the din.

"Little busy," I reply, fending off a new, feeble blow from the T-Rex.

He doesn't need my assistance, anyway—Ernie's got this Stego outsmarted and outfought. The larger animal is already beginning to tire, his charging attacks coming slower, coming clumsier. Four large wounds crisscross his back, crimson streaks forming new lines to add to the barely healed scars left there yesterday by the mountain lion.

Working our way into a defensive position, Ernie and I wind up back to back, fending off attacks from either side, keeping ourselves in check and lending a claw when necessary. My T-Rex, though certainly vicious, is on the smallish side, but what he lacks in natural ability he makes up for in pure insanity. Every charge is a kamikaze rush, a lunge for my throat, my belly—there's no defensive strategy in sight.

Which gives me an opportunity to work my own brand of pugilistic magic. I'm ducking and weaving, bobbing and hopping, Muhammad Rubio with a vengeance, and soon the Tyrannosaur is covered with bloody marks of his own, that *gone to lunch, be back at two* look still in his eyes. Ladies and gentlemen, the undercard looks like it's about to come to a close, Watson and Rubio the victors.

Until there's another rustle in the bushes, to my left. And another to my right. And another directly in front.

Until one dinosaur pops into view. And another to my left. And another to my right. And two more directly in front. Raptors. Brontos. Carnotaurs. Hadrosaurs. Ankies. It's the zodiac of dinos, a pantheon of prehistoric pugnacity, and they've come to teach the interlopers a lesson in manners. Taking a quick glance around, I assess the situation and realize that we're completely, hopelessly surrounded. Within a matter of seconds, Ernie and I have gone from Spanish conquistadores to bow-and-arrow targets at Custer's last stand, and I don't like the odds.

The howls drop to low, panting growls as the pack closes in on us. I can almost hear the digestive juices churning. Even the Stegosaur and the T-Rex I was fighting back off and sink into the relative anonymity of the crowd, content to be a small, yet important, part of our upcoming demise. Step by deliberate step, tails wagging in expectation of a kill, the dinos advance, tugging the noose tighter and tighter around me and my partner.

"Suggestions?" I ask Ernie.

He mulls it over for a very quick second. I can almost feel the saliva dripping on my feet, and I take this time to lament the fact that I have to die in so humid a location. I always figured I'd bite the big one in Los Angeles, where at least there aren't any bugs to feed off your corpse. That is, of course, unless you count the agents.

"Run," says Ernie. And we do.

Using my tail as an extra propellant, I leap over the shortest dino in the bunch—a Compy, whose look of genuine confusion as I soar over his head is so comical I nearly break down laughing upon landing—and begin my sprint into the jungle. I hope to hell I'm going the right way.

Ernie's next to me, kicking up leaves as he throws that husky body of his into Carnotaur overdrive. Behind us, I can hear new cries of frustration, drool being slurped back into waiting mouths, and the combined sounds of half a ton of angry dinosaur crashing through the underbrush. It's the kind of incentive that inspires world-record times, and I'm aiming to bring home the gold.

I don't know if that running class did me any good, but I'm hoping some of the lessons sunk into my subconscious enough to keep me zooming along faster than the others. Forget humanity, forget humanity . . . I feel the panting of my partner, his cardiovascular system pushed way beyond the acceptable limits for one of his age, body type, and previous exercise habits (read: none). "You think"—*pant, pant*—"we're going"—*pant, pant*—"the right way?"

"Better be," I shout back. "I'm not turning around."

And it's a good thing, too, because the pack is right on our heels. Taking a cue from our earlier experience with the crocodiles, I flash back to a nature special I caught a few months back on the boob tube. Some Australian fellow who got his kicks out of wrapping cobras around his head and getting his wife to give enemas to rabid gorillas was adamant about one fact: if you're ever being chased by a crocodile, run in a zigzag pattern. Or maybe it was an alligator. No matter; I figure these Progressives have already flipped back to a distant era when alligators, crocodiles, and dinosaurs were just about equal on the great wall chart of evolution, so I resolve to give this evasive tactic a try.

Grabbing Ernie by the arm, I veer sharply to the left, dragging my partner along with me. For a moment, it seems like the trick may have worked, and I resolve to do a lot more televisionwatching should I make it out of this alive. But then there's a sharp pain shooting down and across my back, a trickle of fluid dripping to my feet, and I realize I've just been sliced by a nearby claw.

Time to run straight again.

The fence looms ahead, and with it, the prospect of having to get to the other side. Ernie's frantically slamming his claw into the remote-control button, but we're so far off the beaten trail that the gate might be miles away. There's no time to sit back and pick out the best tree to scurry up; any stalling will give our assailants the chance they need to tear us into tiny bite-sized pieces, and I refuse to be an appetizer. So even as we continue, full speed, directly toward the fence, I'm letting my eyes scan the trees, in hopes that they'll find a means of egress before it's too late.

"Sausage tree," Ernie calls out.

"What?" Has my partner snapped?

"Sausage tree," he repeats, and points to a spot fifty yards ahead, at one of the most bizarre examples of plant life I've ever come across. A good fifty, sixty feet tall, this sizable tree is draped with hundreds of vines dangling down from its wide branches, but that's not the strange part. At the end of each of these vines, hanging there like an embryo from an umbilical cord, is what looks to be a giant kielbasa. Two, three feet long at least. I blink—still in mid-run—and open my eyes again, and the tree remains. This is not a hallucination. I guess I shouldn't be surprised, radiation or not; evolution, after all, has made some weird, seemingly drug-induced decisions along the way. Who would have guessed, for example, that the apes would learn how to use tools or balance their checkbooks? They still can't program VCRs, but they should get that worked out in another million years or so.

Adjusting course slightly, we head straight for the vines, leading the pack over an unbeaten trail. Speed's not as great now—trees in the way, fallen branches to contend with—and the snarling behind us grows closer. We're Frankenstein's monster, they're the mob, and hope for a happy ending is dwindling fast.

Sausage tree in front of us, the vines hanging just above our heads, and I take the mightiest leap these exhausted legs can manage, grabbing on to one of the weiner-shaped fruits and hauling myself heavenward. Ernie's right next to me on a nearby vine, and we shinny up the tree in tandem. My junior-high gym teacher would be proud.

By the time we're twenty feet into the air, Ernie takes a look down. "Hey," he says, a little awestruck and a lot relieved, "they're not following us."

Indeed, the pack of dinos has remained on the ground, staring up at us with famished eyes and slavering lips. They take turns hopping into the air, trying to claw us on a single jump, but they're a good fifteen feet short of the mark every time.

"Why aren't they climbing?" asks Ernie. "Not that I'm complaining . . ."

"Maybe they can't," I say. "Think about it—climbing is ape behavior; we just learned it as kids."

"And they unlearned it as part of Progress."

So they're down there and we're up here, safe for the moment, but it doesn't help the fact that we still don't have any easy way onto the other side of the fence. The only choice is to exercise some more human traits; it doesn't make me happy, but it keeps me alive.

We swing from vine to vine, carefully grasping each thick strand before gingerly building up momentum to get the next one moving again. Tarzan I am not. But after a few minutes of this, we're over the fence and climbing back down to the ground.

Sunlight is beginning to make its way into the jungle, and in the early morning mist, I can make out the gaggle of shadowy figures behind that fence, defeated and shuffling back into their protected compound. Mumbled growls stream into the air and dissipate, and Ernie and I are back on the path to civilization.

"They weren't . . . thinking," Ernie says as we pick our way out of the jungle.

"Agreed. Whatever they've become, Progress has done it to them. And Rupert . . ."

"We got to him just before he went into the Ring," I say. "And probably just before he became one of the pack."

"And they got to him right afterward."

"Exactly."

"But why?" asks Ernie. "What's the point of all the cover-ups, the secrecy? The guns, that building, those maps—"

I can't help but shrug. "I don't know. I've been trying to figure out the whys and hows of this place since we took on the case. But I think I know a way to find out."

It's time to confront Circe.

She's not here. The study, the bedroom, the foyer, all empty, and except for the few guards surrounding the pleasure dome, the whole place seems deserted.

We're sneaking our way through a garden outside Raal's once-upon-a-study, when it hits me. "Wait a minute, Ern—what day is it?"

"Sunday, I think," he says, catching on as soon as it's past his lips. "It took us about six hours to get out of the jungle, a few more sneaking in here. Sunday morning."

"They all left the island. Conference over, everyone scatter."

"Which means that Circe's gone back to Maui," he continues.

"And then probably back to LA."

Time to boogie on home. I turn away from the mansion, back toward the camp, eager to make my way to shore—

"Wait," calls Ernie, reaching out to stop me. "Our guises."

Right. The guises. I look down at myself, at the natural hide sitting so easily, so calmly on my bones, feeling the warm Hawaiian breeze caress my bare skin, my tail flapping open, flapping free, and for a second, I want to say, *Screw it all, screw the guise, screw humanity, I'll go join the others back behind the fence. . . .*

But reason floods past desire a second later, and I stomp past Ernie and back into the mansion, muttering, "I know where they keep 'em. Follow me."

No guards are posted outside the guise-check room I saw earlier, and it's an easy entry. Most of the costumes have been removed from the racks—

certain nudist clubs exempted, bare hide is usually frowned upon in the real world, so the Progressives have reconcealed themselves behind buckles and straps for the hydrofoil trip back to the main island.

There are no dry-cleaning tickets corresponding to our costumes like back at the house in the Hollywood Hills, nor is there a fetching Ornithomimus to help us out; we're on our own and pressed for time. The rack of guises spins as I hold down a black button, sluggishly cycling through costume after costume.

My guise pops up a moment later—I recognize the strong jaw, an aluminum-dentin blend—and I think I get a glimpse of Ernie's next to it. Without wasting the time to double-check, I pull down guises number 151 and 152, and Ernie and I help each other to strap on the buckles and the girdles and the clamps and the trusses, moving like undercranked footage of the Keystone Kops.

But by the time we've gotten ourselves wrapped up good and tight—the confines of this costume feeling more restrictive after days of unlimited personal freedom than they ever have in my adult life—it is quite obvious that something is wrong.

"Um, Vincent . . ."

"Wait a sec," I say, trying like the dickens to align my mask with my actual eyelids, compressed jaw, and nostrils. I don't know why it's so difficult to get this thing into place.

"Vincent," my partner insists, "I think you put on the wrong costume."

With a rubbery snap, the mask clips into place, and the room comes into view once again. "What are you talking about?" I ask, turning to the mirror across the way. "We look great."

And there I am, dapper as can be. And next to me—in the flesh, a product not of my dreams, my herb-induced fantasies, or some knock-on-the-noggin concussion—is a beautiful, high-cheekboned, mocha-skinned angel whose features, guise or not, I will never forget.

It's Kala.

I leap to my left, away from my partner—is this one of his jokes, dressing up like an ex-fling?—and land hard across the room, staring at another familiar character: me. And when the Vincent Rubio I'm looking at speaks, it's Ernie talking. "Like I said," sighs Ernie/Vincent, "I think you're wearing designer duds, kid."

"Me?" I cry. "What about you? You're gonna stretch that thing out!"

Ernie's just as dismayed to find himself in my skin as I am to find myself in Kala's, though my predicament worries me on other levels. Can I move in this thing? Can I fight, if need be? Can I run?

Reaching up, his rough fingers pulsating behind my unsullied costume glove, he touches the cheekbones on my new face. Ernie asks, "Isn't this . . . are you . . . the girl, the one you . . ."

"Slept with, yes," I finish, angry with myself, angry with everything that's brought me to this point. "Or didn't sleep with. Kala, from the Westin Maui."

"She was a Progressive?"

"She didn't say so. In fact, she *said* she worked at the hotel, and *said* she'd never been off Maui itself."

"So she lied."

"Seems that way."

"So who is it? Who's the dino that fits in there?"

"Me, for now." For a brief moment, I consider going on a Cinderella hunt, traveling the land with a swatch of human skin draped across my arm, forcing maidens into the costume and finding out who fits and who bursts the guise at the seams, but it's probably a mite impractical, given our time constraints. All I've got time to do is get out of this costume, find Ernie his own flabby guise, and dress again in record time—

Footsteps, coming down the hallway. Ernie and I glance at each other, his eyes going wide—is that what I look like when I'm nervous?—and we scan the room for an exit. There's only one window, not more than two feet wide, but it might have to do in a pinch.

Forget that—pinch me now, the footsteps are coming closer. And with it, another pair, walking in lockstep. Muted voices, laughter, approaching in tandem, and the only way out of here is through that glass. Ernie crawls out first, wiggling his rear—my rear—as he goes, and I'm taken aback at the sheer expansion forces he's putting my poor costume through; my rump is not usually that big. At least, I don't think it is. I'm next, and though it takes a bit to squeeze my new breasts—a C cup, if I know my human sizes— through the aperture, I do a fine job landing on the other side and hauling my tight little ass across the island.

By the time we make it to the marina, the hydrofoil is long gone; even if it were still around, I doubt it would be safe to take it back to Maui. I might be in a different guise, but I still carry my scent around, and I'm sure by now they're on the lookout for us. Maybe not; perhaps they assume we're dead, lost, or both, and couldn't be happier about the matter. I hope that's the case, as I plan on surprising them with a cameo appearance at some time in the near future, and I always enjoy making a grand entrance.

But a few hundred yards farther down the beach is a dilapidated, deserted marina that we find by following the scent of gasoline and salt water, a surefire trick learned during water-skiing lessons at sleep-away camp. It's a short while before we pick out a rickety boat with accompanying outboard motor.

"Probably here for the benefit of the long-termers," Ernie guesses. "Bring food back and forth for those animals behind the fence."

I don't see the natural dinosaurs as take-out or delivery kinda guys, but there's no reason to argue the point. I hop into the boat, these long, tan legs soaking up the warm Hawaiian rays, and for a split second—less than a split second really, maybe no more than a nanosecond, I swear it—I can understand how Jules could feel . . . comfortable . . . in a woman's guise. But the feeling quickly passes as I force myself to think of football, boxing, and stereo equipment.

The creature who sounds like my partner but looks like me pulls the motor to life, and the air ripples with a loud roar. The boat rocks against the dock, wood scraping wood, and slowly eases out toward open water. Bracing myself against the bow with my new, slimmer, tanner arms, I toss my long, black hair in the breeze and point the way toward Maui.

It is ten-thirty in the morning, and as soon as we can ditch this boat and get on shore, I need to make a few phone calls in preparation for our trip back to the mainland. Our flight back to Southern California leaves this afternoon, and it should take another five hours after that before we touch down at LAX. That will give my contacts enough time to collect the information I need, so that the second we step off that plane, Ernie and I can hit the ground running. There's enough seemingly unconnected conspiracy data bouncing around in my head to make the Warren Commission Report look like a children's book, but something tells me that the link is nearby and drawing closer. No question about it, I want this case wrapped up by midnight.

Unfortunately, the marina where the hydrofoil docks is packed with tourists fresh off their cruise ships and we're forced to take the boat on a roundabout path in order to avoid a possible run-in with any Progressives. We end up making a detour that puts us a few miles away from the main harbor and pull the boat into a small, isolated inlet protected by a semicircle of large, gray rocks that form a natural breakwater.

A few of the local surfers crest by on small waves as we pilot the boat into the cove, whistling at us as we pass. Ernie and I raise a hand in salutation, but they keep coming back around for more, gawking at us like we're some type of new and intriguing sea creature.

One, a blond raggy type who just stepped out of *Pro Surfing Magazine* glides his board directly alongside our craft, grabs hold of the side of our boat, looks deep into my eyes, and says, "Hey, beautiful, wanna learn how to surf?"

I hope the apefucker drowns.

We abandon the boat in shallow water and tread up the beach, Ernie giggling all the way. "Whatsamatter," he asks, "never been hit on before?"

By the time we get to the airport, our flight is almost ready to board. I leave Ernie at the gate and find a pay phone; my first call is a quick one to Dr. Beauregard. If anyone will be able to help me decipher the mysteries of these Progressives, it will be the expert himself. I may have information for him of which he was previously unaware, and it's distinctly possible that my data will combine with his to give us an overall picture we were unable to see separately.

A ring, two rings, three rings, and an answering machine. No time to beat around the bush—I leave a clean, concise message.

Another calling-card charge, another set of rings, and another answering machine. Jules is neither in the office nor at her home, and it's futile leaving a message for her at this stage of the game. I only hope I can track her down once I set foot back in WeHo territory. In the background, I can hear our flight being announced over the PA—*"Flight number 515 to Los Angeles, boarding all rows at gate 16"*—so I hang up, search the change receptacle for any leftovers, and grab Ernie on the way down to the plane.

On the way through the gate and down to the tarmac—the elevated jetway is broken, they tell us, so we have to take stairs down to the runway and another set up into the plane itself—I fill Ernie in on the fruit of my labors.

"We'll check in with Jules as soon as we return," I'm saying. "And once we get Dr. B. to call us back and confirm my suspicions, we should be able to—"

It's just then that I hear a sharp, pinched bang that comes only with the sharp report of a rifle. Another comes, and another, and I'm ducking, running, evading as best I can. But Ernie's not next to me anymore. Ernie's not next to *anyone* anymore.

Twenty feet away, on his knees, grasping his shoulder with one thick hand, Vincent Rubio—Ernie guised as Vincent Rubio— grimaces in pain, blood oozing out from between his fingers, breath coming short and ragged, and the first thing I think is not *My friend is hurt* or *The Progressives have found us* or *I've gotta do something,* but *So this is what it looks like when I get shot.* . . .

"Ern?" I call out, breaking through the throng of other passengers who have gathered around now that the shots have ceased. I drop to my knees beside him. "Where are you hit?"

Ernie moves his hand, and a new river of blood gushes from the shoulder wound. "Fucking . . . guns . . ." he mutters through clenched teeth.

"Rifle?" I ask him.

"Sniper—up on that roof—" Unable to use his left arm, and clutching his shoulder with the right one, Ernie points with my delicate nose to the top of a nearby terminal. "I saw him—running away—tried to call out to you, but—" A grimace of pain cuts him off, and he slumps farther to the ground.

As I understand it from a lifetime of watching fine American films, this is the point where I cradle him in my arms, he tells me some story about how he always had dreams of relocating to Montana, and he passes calmly into oblivion as I gaze furiously up to the heavens and bellow out his name. But it's not gonna go down like that—Ernie's only got a shoulder wound, and while I'm sure it hurts like hell, it's six degrees from fatal.

"You need a hospital," I say. "Can't go on a plane with blood spurting out; they won't let you sit in the main cabin, and then we'll miss the movie."

But Ernie's shaking his head, just as I knew he would be. "I'll be okay. Get—get back to LA and find her. Stop her, whatever it is she's doing."

"It can wait," I say. "They can—"

"It can't. Whatever—whatever they're doing—you have to stop it—"

I'd argue, of course, if I had more time. Play the good partner, stay by his side, forgo the investigation for the sake of sticking by a friend. But he's right; the plane's about to take off.

I stay by his side until the ambulance and police cars arrive and I can locate one of the dino paramedics on board, inform him of Ernie's special circumstances. At least now I know he'll be safely routed to one of the dino wards of Maui's hospital system, taken care of by the best our species has to offer, his guise expertly mended by seamstresses dressed as nurses and candy stripers.

He's up on a stretcher, the crowd beginning to thin out, the passengers being shuttled back on board, rattled but ready for a nonterroristic flight, and I'm right beside Ernie as he's trundled into the back of an ambulance. "When you find Circe," he says, "give her a good swift kick in the ass for me."

"I'll give her two," I promise.

The paramedics strap his stretcher to the floor of the ambulance and prepare to burn rubber down the runway and to the local hospital. Ernie lifts his head, a modified crunch, and stares me dead in the eye. "Take care, kid—and watch your back. That sniper was too far away to smell me, so he had to go on sight. This bullet was meant for you."

The doors swing closed and the ambulance pulls out, carting away someone who looks very much like Vincent Rubio, Private Investigator.

've been shot at before. Never vicariously, mind you, but I have been shot at. So there's nothing new to me in hearing the bang of a gun or feeling a bullet whiz by the ear, barely a millimeter to spare before van Gogh syndrome sets in. Doesn't make it any easier each time it happens, but there's nothing new in the experience itself.

Seeing yourself shot is a different matter entirely—the blood, the wound, the sheer ickiness of it all—and watching Ernie take a bullet that was meant for me has got me unnerved enough to get good and toasted on the flight back to LA. But the stewardesses are out of condiments, and though mustard seeds have in the past sufficed in a pinch, I refuse to suck on one-ounce plastic packets of Gulden's just to get a rush. I'm one of only a few dinos on the plane, too, so such an action would probably net me a lot of discomforting stares.

Then there's the safety factor. I don't know for sure that the shooter was acting alone, and I don't want to do anything to alert any Progressive hit man to my presence inside Kala's costume in case he's also flying the friendly skies this afternoon. Someone in the Progressive organization has decided that my continued existence is no longer required, and it's the direct threat that rankles me more than anything else. If you're going to try to kill me, at least have the balls to do it face-to-face, the old-fashioned way. Then again, I'm the last dino who should talk about having balls right now.

It is with thoughts of Circe, of the Progressives, of the trouble at hand weighing heavily on my mind that I fall into an uneasy slumber. When I wake, the plane is landing in Los Angeles; the pilot announces it's a quarter past eight, and I set my watch accordingly. Westwood is twenty minutes away—*everything* is twenty minutes away if you play it right—but by the time I get my Lincoln out of the U-Park lot, argue with the attendant as to the exact number of days my automobile spent in their substandard facility, and eventually burst through the gate, cracking off a chunk of wooden barrier with my front bumper, it's already nearing nine.

No time to take a quick drive by the office, which is not such a problem since I'm not anxious to meet up with Minsky. It's not that I feel guilty about taking his money and not doing a whiff of work on his missing Mussolini case, but I don't have the time to explain anything to the little tyke just now, let alone why I'm guised up like a geisha. With my luck, he'd kiss first and ask questions later.

Anyway, I'll dissolve into the maddening crowd up in Hollywood, which is just what I need right now. Anonymity with a supermodel figure doesn't come easy in any town, but in LA you've got a fighting chance of being outshone by the next ingenue off the bus.

On the way in, I punch up my voice mail on the car phone and take a listen. Three messages. Number one: Friday, 4:15 P.M. Minsky, calling to check up on our progress a scant half-day after he sent us on the mission to find his floozy, as if he doesn't trust us to get the job done in a timely fashion. The nerve. His high-pitched warble floats through the air—"and when you find her, bring her in to the cops, throw the book at her, but get the Mussolini first, get the Mussolini—" The last thing I need is a Minsky migraine, so I punch number three, erase, and move on with my life.

Number two: Jules, nine o'clock yesterday evening. Worried that I haven't given her a call. I've already taken care of that concern. Skip and erase.

Number three: Dr. Beauregard, today at 10:00 A.M. Aha, now here's a call I've been waiting for. "Vincent, I'm in town helping out another family," he drawls, "a sad case, really, a boy who got himself all mixed up with some humans, believe it or not—and I thought you might be having some more questions for me. I'd be glad to oblige, of course . . ." He goes on in that big, charming, Southern way of his, eventually getting around to giving me the name and number of the hotel he's staying at; it's the Nikko, a Japanese-run establishment just on the other side of Beverly Hills.

A quick return call, and I'm instantly put through to the doctor's room.

No rings, just an answer. "Where were we?"

That doesn't sound like Bo. "I'm sorry," I say hastily. "I must have the wrong room—"

"Vincent?" says Dr. B., and now I can hear the drawl, the syrupy inflections. "Is that you, son?"

"Oh, hey—I didn't—you sounded different—"

"I was talking to my grandkids. We got cut off. Glad y'all are back in town."

It takes five minutes to run through my story, omitting the more graphic details but generally making clear to the doctor that I need some answers, and I need them quickly. "I may need help identifying another deprogrammer, one who may be siphoning information to the Progressives. And there's more. Much more, I think."

"Are you sure?" asks Bo. "That would be highly unethical of any practitioner—"

"We're way beyond ethics, doc. You know a bunch of the others in the field, right, their human guises?"

"Of course, son. If you get me a picture, I'm sure I can identify the man for y'all."

Dr. Beauregard agrees to meet me at a private location, and I suggest a nightclub I know near his hotel. "I need someplace dark," I say. "I think I'm in danger."

"I would not be surprised," says Bo, and this doesn't do anything to assuage my anxiety. "We will be as careful as possible." We set an eleven o'clock meeting time, which gives me an hour or so to get up to Hollywood, squirm out of this costume and into a new one, and soak up whatever information Jules has managed to squeeze out of this town.

"Darling," she cries as I slink my way into the Wax Museum workroom, her eyes roving over my new curves in appreciation and delight, "you've come over to the winning team! I'm so proud of you. . . ."

"Zip it," I tell her, hoping that there's no blush-action veins in Kala's mask. "Last time I came in for work, you made a copy of my guise, right?"

"Down to that cute little navel of yours."

"Could ya get it for me?"

"Why? You look fabulous, darling!"

"Jules—"

"We could use you in the new show. I'm trying to get us booked into Vegas. You could do a hula number. . . ."

Finally, she disappears into a back room and, after a few minutes of rustling around, reemerges with a spare Vincent Rubio draped over her arm.

"How was Hawaii?" she asks as I begin to undress.

"Sticky. And a little bloody, but I don't have time to go into it."

"Where's Ernie?"

"That's the bloody part." I give a quick five-minute rundown of the events, Jules working up a head of steam with every passing detail, and by the time I'm done, she's pacing the workroom, doing Indy 500 laps around the surgical tables. Meanwhile, I've reguised and chosen a nice slacks outfit from the racks of clothing she's got stashed in one of the many workroom closets.

"I knew something was up with them," Jules is saying, voice rising. "I knew it—"

"No time for an ego check. Tell me what you found."

"What *didn't* I find? I've got newspaper reports, I've got eyewitness accounts, I've got spectroscopic photoanalysis—"

"Let's start there. Can you show me?"

Jules's computer system is state of the art, but for me, it's art of the abstract variety. Folks these days go cruising around the Internet, bouncing from information to information; the closest I've ever come to surfing was that blond-haired dude who tried to pick me up back on the beach.

"Watch this window over here," Jules is saying, her long fingers slapping away at the keyboard like Elton John playing "The Bitch Is Back." When he had that charity auction, by the way, and sold off all of his more lavish costumes, a buddy of mine got a great deal on this Turkish guise that Elton— a Hadrosaur, according to my friend—would use to walk the streets in relative anonymity.

"I scanned in the photos you gave me," Jules is saying, continuing to type as she speaks, "and ran them through a few programs I use to show my clients how the plastic surgery I perform on their guises will meld with the substructure below. You wouldn't believe how many clients I have who simply can't understand that no matter how much liposuction I perform, a Brontosaur is never going to have the same waistline as a Coelo. Work with what you have, I tell them. Everyone can be fabulous."

"Very life affirming," I say. "Back to the computer."

"Okay, so I scanned in the photos, one by one, and checked each for an underlying structure." As she speaks, a series of images—the photos I had given her earlier—pop up on the screen. I pull up a wooden crate stamped NOSES, SWEDISH and take a seat.

Happy families, reunited with their loved ones. Mothers, fathers, siblings, an ex-Progressive grinning out at the camera, and next to him or her, in every picture, an extra reveler, often a deprogrammer, smiling along, arm around his newest success story. Jules has already circled the key element in each photo, and I watch as the computer eliminates all the irrelevant information and hones in on the sweet cream filling.

Photographs whirl around the screen, enlarging and shrinking themselves, superimposing one shot of a deprogrammer atop another. Nothing looks different to me, but Jules is *yes*ing and *aha*-ing under her breath, clearly impressed—either with whatever she's finding or with her own investigative skills. I've been known to high-five myself after a good case, but self-gratification only goes so far.

After a scant few minutes, Jules pushes back from her desk, the chair scooting backward on its casters and clunking into a stack of raw guise flesh behind it. With a flourish, she points to the screen, at the same six pictures that have been up there all along, and declares proudly, "There you go."

Should I be impressed? Should I have any idea what's going on?

Jules notices my confusion and relishes the opportunity to explicate her findings in detail. "Diplodoci, all of 'em. See that slight bulge where the neck joins the back? The indentation at the stomach?" No, but I have a feeling if she takes the time to tell me exactly how she can detect dino lineage beneath the human skin, I'll be late for Armageddon, let alone my eleven o'clock meeting with Bo. "Maybe not the third and the fifth," she continues, " 'cause it's tough to tell with that big costume head—but the rest of these characters are definitely from Diplodod stock."

Does this indicate, perhaps, the presence of a race-based cadre within the Progressives? A group of isolated Diplodoci preying on the others, bending them to their will? Premature assumption, perhaps, but it's what I've got to go on.

"Thanks," I begin—

But Jules won't let me go. "That ain't all, honey. Keep your tush right there, and I'll show you what else I dragged out of the pits."

Jules digs into another nearby box, this one purportedly filled with EYE-LASHES, KOREAN but actually empty except for a file folder and some stapled pages. "I cross-referenced every Progressive who left the organization and died soon afterward with the amount of time they'd been in the organization. Did the same with those kids who left the Progressives and didn't die. Any guesses as to what I found?"

"Nothing?"

"Everything. Let's look at Rupert for a sec. How long was he in the group?"

I shrug. "Three, four years, they thought. Give or take."

"Fine. Four years, and he's dead. Same with the girl down in Long Beach—she was in for six."

I must be missing the point, because Jules's eyes are twinkling, and I don't think it's due to one of her special New Year's–themed contact lenses. "We knew that already. If you leave the Progressives, you bite it."

"Wrong. I found a lot of kids who left the group and are hunky-dory to this very day. The difference is they got out early."

Jules flips me the papers, and I scan through her information. The trend continues. Four or more years equals death. Two or less equals life. There's not a lot of data for those in the middle, so it's hard to judge exactly where the line between assassination and live-and-let-live actually is, but it's not necessary to confirm my theory: Rupert knew too much.

During his rise up the Progressive ladder, Rupert became privy to more and more information, and by the time we'd cold-cocked him and dragged him back to Westwood, he was too infused with intimate intelligence, too much of a liability to leave dangling out in the real world. You've got two choices when your fine-knit sweater is snagged on a loose bit of wood: you can delicately sew the string back into the weave or cut it off at the base. The Progressives went the easy route.

It must have been the same for the others, which at least means that the cult isn't indiscriminately killing off their errant members; it's just killing off those who can blab about what they're up to—the guns, the brainwashing, the foreign coin jumping from hand to hand.

"This is great," I tell her as I stand, brush a spare nose off my shirt sleeve, and prepare to head back down to mid-city. "Circumstantial, but great. The Council will be interested, I know that much."

But as I head for the door, papers in hand, ready to meet Bo, get his opinion on the situation, and then hightail it to Council headquarters and bring the roof down on the Progressives' miscreant noggins, Jules reaches out an arm to stop me. "One more thing," she says. "And it might not make much of a difference—"

"Everything makes a difference."

"They're not the only ones who went away. The Progressives, I mean." I'm not following her, and she must be able to tell. "I was checking through the papers," she clarifies, "looking at the days around when Rupert and the others died, and for every twenty-something Progressive that bit it, there was another one, someone not in the group, that disappeared that same day, usually nearby."

"Same age?"

"Right around there. Rupert said bye-bye on a Thursday—previous day, some kid named Blish—a T-Rex, only twenty-eight—vanished. Middle of the night. Not that weird by itself, but it happened over and over again. Strange enough for twenty-somethings to be dropping off like that—"

"And stranger still that they're doing it in pairs." Suicide pacts? Assassination clones? Most information focuses investigations; this is only fragmenting it more.

Jules leads me to the door, her hand reassuringly on my back as she gives me a short little hug, pleads with me to be careful, and opens the double deadbolts. "Any idea what all this means?" she asks me. "The photos, the obits, all of it?"

"Got a hunch," I tell her as I check my watch and notice that I'm running a good fifteen minutes behind schedule, "but there's no time to explain. I'm late for my dinner date." And then, just because I know it will tickle her to the bone, I elaborate: "He's a doctor."

La Brea Avenue, while not mired in gridlock, is still stop-and-go, even at this time of night. It takes a full half-hour to travel three miles, and as I near Wilshire, I can make out the problem: construction. A whole mess of it. And, of course, the city workers, who by all rights should be serving me tea and crumpets as part of their public-servant duties, are instead sitting on their massive mammal behinds, eating doughnuts and sucking down gallons of black coffee. Meanwhile, the rest of us are forced to breathe each others' exhaust due to their inability to get any project done on time and under budget.

The traffic ahead suddenly clears out, and a horn blast from behind spurs my foot toward the gas pedal. I pull away with a lurch, the catcalls and laughter of the construction workers trailing behind. Some part of me is itching for a fight, a full-scale battle to do away with all the human nonsense that gets in the way of our daily lives. *I'll get a freakin' army,* I want to yell out. *I'll go rustle up some of those dinos from the jungle and then we'll see who eats the final doughnut, Mister Homo sapiens, master of the food chain.*

The Tar Pit Club isn't one of your more private locales; it's a rocking joint in the Miracle Mile part of town, just east of Beverly Hills and just west of some areas you don't want to be in too late at night. There's a five-dollar cover charge and a no-drink minimum, so the place is usually packed with dinos and humans of all shapes and sizes flailing away to whatever the music craze of the moment happens to be.

Tonight there's a live ska band jamming out some backbeat rhythms, and the club is filled with Beverly Hills teenagers, desperately hip, whatever the cost. Dancing consists mostly of bouncing up and down, occasionally in couples, but mostly as a group. This isn't how we did it when I was a kid, but I'm sure I looked pretty stupid back then, too.

I told Bo to meet me at a booth in the back-left corner of the club—my usual spot whenever I abandon my solitude for the evening and make the drive out here to mid-city—and sure enough, the doctor is waiting there patiently when I arrive, dressed nattily in a big-shouldered blue suit, the kind plantation owners wore in the wintertime back before the Civil War up and took the market out of cotton. Sliding into the booth, I begin to apologize for my late arrival—

"Y'all aren't that late," he assures me. "I just got here myself. Traffic ain't so bad at eleven at night, but it's still a mite worse than in Nashville."

"Nashville?" I ask. "I thought you said you were from Memphis."

"Memphis is my home now," he explains after a short pause. "Nashville's where I grew up."

"Ah. Got it. You want some basil?" I motion for the waitress, but Bo reaches out and puts my arm down.

"No herbs," he tells me. "I'm driving. Now, let's get down to business—did you bring the photographs?"

I slide the pages across the table into the doctor's eager hands. "I had a spectroscopic analysis done," I say, proud to pronounce the words properly and evincing at least a glancing idea of what they mean, "and I've been told that the dinos beneath those costumes are Diplodoci."

Bo laughs and tosses the pages on the table. "Hell, I coulda told you that, son. You didn't need a fancy analysis."

Sure, tell me *now*. "How can you tell?"

Dr. Beauregard isolates three of the pictures and spreads them out across the desk. Pointing to the deprogrammer in each—one with a mustache, one with a beard, one somewhere in between—he shakes his head and smirks, "I did a fellowship with that one. In these three pictures here, he's wearing his usual guise, just with different accessories. Think he goes clean-shaven normally. . . ."

That's it—Dr. B. has the information I'm looking for. "So you know him."

"I know him well. His name's Carter—Brian Carter, I believe—and the man is a specialist in field paleontology."

"He's a human?" I ask.

"He's a fossil-placer," explains Dr. B.

So that's how he hooked up with Circe—they travel in the same business circles. She must have contacted Carter and convinced him to help out with her plan to keep a tight rein on the Progressive organization.

"Brilliant fellow," Bo muses.

"A brilliant fellow who's also connected to the Progressives," I point out. "Did you tell this Carter fellow anything about your contact with Rupert?"

Bo turns away slightly, avoiding my gaze. "I—I may have mentioned I was coming out to Los Angeles for some fieldwork. . . . May have mentioned Rupert's name, but . . . professional courtesy, a case study, y'all understand—"

I could be harsh on the guy, tell him that his lack of doctor-patient confidentiality may have cost a young T-Rex his life, but there's no point in flogging past indiscretions. If Samuel is at the bottom of Rupert's disappearance, then he'll be the one to pay in the end. "What about these other ones?" I ask, shoving the other photos into his field of view.

"Don't recognize the costumes, but I wouldn't be surprised if it's Carter going with a black-market guise. Boy never had a real fondness for the *rules*."

This Carter, then, is the key to the whole ugly mess. He's the one who's been telling the cult where their lapsed members are located, and he's the one figuring out ways to bump them off in secret. But if I can locate this fellow in human guise and apply the Vincent Rubio interrogation method (read: lots of pain, little mercy), I may very well be able to find out exactly what happened to Rupert and the others, stop whatever insidious plan Circe and her cadre have been cooking up for years now, bring down the Progressive organization, turn them all in to the honchos up at the Southern California Council, and get this case wrapped up by the end of the evening so that I might return home for a solid week of frolicking in the produce section of Ralphs.

"I don't suppose you'd know where to find him?" I ask Bo. He's already been more than helpful in every possible way, but I have a tendency to run favors into the ground. "Carter, I mean."

He's about to shake his head, ready to give me a "no" answer, when I see a little buzzer going off behind those eyes. "Actually," he says, rising higher in the seat, his excitement growing along with mine, "last I heard, he was sponsoring a dig right near here, down in the Tar Pits."

I'm pretty sure he's talking about the Pits themselves, not the nightclub we're presently in, though the sound system would indeed make this a good lecture hall. Ten blocks to the west of us is the George C. Page Museum of Natural Discoveries, a twenty-thousand-square-foot structure dedicated to the La Brea Tar Pits, the large black morass on which it is situated. There isn't a bona-fide dino bone anywhere near the Tar Pit confines, but within this LA landmark, scientists have found a wealth of Ice Age material, everything from saber-toothed tiger bones to woolly mammoths to old, discarded condoms—the nearby park contributes to much of the nonfossil material—and the excavation shelters erected during the halcyon Eisenhower years now serve as stops along many a visitor's tour of the area.

"Can you tell me exactly where he's been leading the digs?" I ask. "Which site?" There are ten or twelve of the shallow basements, and if I can narrow down the information, it will keep me from having to break and enter a dozen times this evening. No chance that Carter is at the park now, but at the very least, I might be able to break into some files or pick up an errant scent.

"I think it's site seven," says Bo. "But I'm not sure. Tell you what: I'm all done up for the night, and this sounds like more fun than watching pay-per-view back at the hotel. I'll come along."

I'm grateful for the company—missing Ernie's presence at my side after only seven hours, like an amputee with nothing but a ghost limb—but I can't put the doctor in what might possibly be harm's way. And even if I find this Carter before the Progressives find me, and even if the only pain incurred is strictly on Carter's side of the equation, Dr. Beauregard doesn't need to know the rumpled details of a PI's life. Better if I run the interrogation solo.

"Thanks, doc," I start out, "but there's . . . there are elements to my job—"

"That ain't a problem—"

"Messy elements," I clarify. "Unsavory elements."

"You think I ain't seen it all?" he interrupts. Leaning forward, pride in his profession, in his status, riding on every word, he confides in me, "I deprogrammed some of the *Manson* kids, son."

The Tar Pits—a mixture of tar and water, actually—run right next to Wilshire Boulevard along the Miracle Mile, separated from the busy street by only a thin chain-link fence that wouldn't keep out even the laziest vandal. Not that anyone's interested in diving in for a swim, of course, but if they choose to, we'll only know about it in twenty thousand years or so when they dredge up the bodies and prop them up for display.

It's an odd mix of entertainment and education here in the Tar Pits, where on a sunny summer day, the temperature can climb to over a hundred degrees and the resultant Glacier Bay stench can carry for miles. For example, the local curator must have thought the Tar Pits were too bland to attract the proper amount of attention—who wants to look at an oil spill all day?—so in order to spruce the place up, the George C. Page Museum has erected life-sized statues of woolly mammoths and mastodons inside the Pits themselves, depicted in a realistic life-and-death struggle with the imprisoning tar. On a small island of granite poking up from the center of the pit, a concrete baby mastodon watches its mother being sucked under the surface. There's even a hidden sound system bleating out the elephant calls of death and pain; it's a morbid little display, really, but the tourists *ooh* and *aah* at it from a raised viewing station just outside the museum walkway.

Not many tourists here 'round midnight, though. A few of the local homeless, pushing their shopping carts and singing their songs and arguing with the manhole covers, a Russian gentleman who swears that our fortunes can be accurately predicted by his cat, nothing out of the ordinary. Bo and I park in an empty lot and trot across a new stretch of sod; they've just finished a refurbishment of the area, and though it's a lot greener now, there's not much else to show for two years' worth of construction.

"So," Dr. B. asks as we walk, "what else y'all been figuring out on these Progressives?"

"A lot. Nothing. Everything. I've seen more than I'm supposed to, I know that much—dinosaurs running wild, reverted back to some primal version of themselves. A storage hut full of weapons—"

"Guns?" he asks incredulously.

"Rifles, pistols, bazookas, you name it." Okay, technically, I didn't see any bazookas, but it's the kind of minor exaggeration that can make a story more interesting, so I go with it. "They have something planned—something international, I believe."

"I've been studying the Progressives for years," he says, "but I never heard anything like this."

"Believe it, doc. I plan on filing about six hundred motions with every Council I can find once this is all over with. Hell or high water, the Progressives are going down."

No response from Bo; I hope I haven't worried him with my John Wayne side. I can be pretty intimidating sometimes.

We arrive at the excavation site, just a hole in the ground surrounded by more wire-link fence; a metal staircase leads down into the viewing area overlooking the pit. It's impossible to tell if the small room is currently occupied—note previous comment on used condoms—but I take the chance of being the *interruptus* in some unlucky couple's *coitus* and descend, Bo right behind me.

A single lightbulb hangs from a wire in the center of this three-walled room, and I flick it on, illuminating the decrepit viewing area with a burst of harsh white light. To my left, right, and behind me are ten-foot-high metal walls, the steel floor beneath littered with soda cans and beer bottles.

Strangely, the smells of the tar aren't as strong down here, perhaps because the constant shade keeps the sun from baking the stench into the air.

Where the fourth wall should be, there's nothing but a guard rail and a plaque, and beneath it, the pit itself. EXCAVATION 7, reads the sign. OPENED JULY 12, 1959. Squinting into the darkness of the pit down below, I can make out a heap of tar, but nothing in the way of fossils or mummified creatures.

"Pretty boring place for a lecture," I say. "I thought it would be more . . . open."

Bo is beside me, also gazing into the pit; he picks up a pebble and drops it down, watching it thunk onto the surface ten feet below. The pebble does not sink; it simply sits on top of the black goop and waits to be sucked under. Death by delay. It's like waiting in line at the DMV, only it smells better down here.

Dr. Beauregard leans back against the far wall. "These places . . . they're very isolated, aren't they?"

"From what I can tell. Hey, you know if that Carter guy lives in the area?"

I've put him off guard—Bo flusters. "I—I don't know—"

My cell phone is out in a heartbeat—I'm the fastest draw in the west when it comes to mobile communications—and I'm dialing Dan's home number. I'm sick and tired of being routed and rerouted every time I call his LAPD office, so, hopefully, I'll get through this time. "I'm calling Dan—Sergeant Patterson," I tell Dr. B. "You wanna talk to him, say hi?"

"No—no, you feel free . . ."

Two rings, and a real, honest-to-goodness voice—"Yello . . . ?"

"Praise the Lord, he's home," I say into the phone. "You are one hard Bronto to get in touch with."

Instantly contrite, Dan is apologizing all over the place for not speaking with me earlier. "I tried over the weekend," he says, "but you weren't answering, and I didn't want to leave a message—"

"Forget about it," I tell him. "Let you off the hook if you do me a favor."

"Anything."

"I need the address, priors, and whatever you got on some guy named Brian Carter. A doctor, I think."

"Sure, no problem. What's up?"

"Just a little investigation," I say, giving a wink to Bo. He does not wink back. I turn, staring into the tar pits as I speak. "I'm out here with the deprogrammer you turned me on to."

"Huh?"

"Dr. B. Bo. Beaumont Beauregard." How many times does he want me to say the name for him?

"I don't know what the hell you're talking about, Vincent."

I sigh loudly, then carefully explain, worried for my friend's failing memory. "When I called you, back about three weeks ago, I asked you to recommend a cult deprogrammer—"

"And I said I'd get back to you, I know, I know. But that's why I'm apologizing—I kept forgetting to tell you, I don't know anyone who can help."

"What? No, no, I got a call from the doctor, and he said that you—"

"This Dr. Beauregard you're talking about . . ." says Dan, "I have no idea who he is. I've never heard of him in my life—"

It's right about then that the pain begins, a bursting pressure starting in my sinuses, traveling through my nose and up into my head—my entire body suddenly stuffed full to bursting with every imaginable scent: carnivals and Cracker Jacks, carburetors and cola, a cavalcade of smells wracking every muscle, every ligament—

I can barely turn around, vision dimming, the viewing area fading, dissolving away, that prehistoric jungle quickly vibrating into place—Dr. Beauregard, standing in front of me, here but not here, carefully taking the cellular phone out of my hands—Dan's voice, calling in the distance, *"Vincent, can you hear me? Vincent, hello, are you still there?"*—an ancient oak blasting up from the ground, plants popping into existence, mosquitoes the size of eagles materializing, laughing, and flapping away—Dr. Beauregard tossing the phone into the tar pits below—a strange, content smile spreading across his wide, kind face—and I'm wondering if the phone is still on, if Dan is still talking, if my cellular company is going to charge me for the extra minutes—

Another sudden burst of scent, and now I can smell the herbs forcing it along, the basil and cilantro spreading into every pore of my body, my nostrils the gateway to this wonderful, horrible experience—and soon there's nothing else except for me, Dr. Beauregard, a single metal rail, and a prehistoric world alive with a billion natural specimens running wild, running free.

A push on my chest, a trip, a stumble, and I'm over the railing and falling backward, floating on a cloud before I come to a landing in something wet, something sticky. Dr. Beauregard is so far away now, high above me, and he's looking down, waving to me, waving *bye-bye, bye-bye.*

"Goodbye, Mr. Rubio," says the good doctor. "Give my regards to the ancestors."

I will, Bo. I will . . .

There is a strong possibility that I am dead.

It's not so bad.

I am myself in here.

Some time later, whenever that might be—*time* has about as much meaning in this place as *restraint* does in Las Vegas—I find that I am unable to move, unable to breathe, unable to do any of the things one normally associates with living, but somehow I know, instinctively, that I am not dead. This is a new step for me. My last will and testament has been written and rewritten in my head a hundred times since Dr. Beauregard, or whoever he is, bade me farewell, and the really sad part is that there isn't much I have to say. Ernie gets most of my stuff; a nephew of mine in Topeka gets some pocket change and a humidifier for his asthma.

I've also been counting—first up to a hundred, then up to a thousand, then ten thousand, and so on. I lost track a while back, but I think I abandoned the plan somewhere around 16,800 or so. It wasn't even making me sleepy, as I had forgotten to associate sheep with every passing digit.

Tar surrounds me on all sides. At least, that's my current belief. It's distinctly possible that I'm dead and just in denial or reincarnated as a lucky boy's pet rock, but the tar explanation suits me better for the moment.

Fortunately for me, I have remembered the one interesting fact I learned during my first visit to the George C. Page Museum ten years ago:

The more you struggle in a tar pit, the faster you will die. Your movements will only help suck you farther beneath the surface, and even if you're able to live without air—a feat I seem somehow to be accomplishing—the lack of food and water will get to you eventually.

Also, fortunately for me, much of the polar ice cap has gone and melted away over the last few millennia, which means I have a distinct advantage over the saber-toothed tigers who found themselves trapped with no means of escape: a high water table. And I'm buoyant, baby.

Allowing myself to sit completely still is a difficult task, especially with an itch on my nose that refuses to go away. But if I reach up to scratch it, I run the risk of aggravating the tar and sinking farther into the pit; better to lie still, deal with the maddening prickling on my proboscis, and let the water help me rise to the surface.

I feel like an errant Monopoly piece when it comes to this dog of a case; every time I start to round Ventnor and Marvin Gardens and prepare to hit the really good part of town, something or someone sends me scurrying back to Baltic Avenue, and I have to start all over again. There's only so much a dino PI can take, and I'm one and two-ninths of the way past my limit, a mixed fraction for God's sake.

A bright speck of light before me—is this the tunnel that will take me to greet the ancestors? Is my Uncle Ferdy going to leap out of the grave and into the spotlight any second and start up the vaudeville act that used to bring down the house in the twenties? The light does, indeed, grow closer, stronger, more intense, but for the moment, at least, my dead relatives stay put.

Suddenly I can feel the cool night air touching parts of my bare hide, and something in me snaps. It feels like a switch has been thrown, like the fuse box has been fixed, and all of my organs turn on at once. My eyes flick open of their own accord—the bulb in the viewing area burning brightly overhead—and I let out a hacking cough, expelling a thick wad of tar from my esophagus. A deep, gasping breath follows, and my lungs expand with the most tar-and-parasite-infested air I've ever come across. It's the sweetest thing I've tasted.

Everything is revving up once again, coming back to normal. It's as if I was simply sleeping that whole time and needed a few moments in the morning to stretch and work out the kinks. Still, I'm not out of the woods yet. I wait until the water table has pushed me well up over the surface of the tar, being careful not to squirm around any more than necessary. My ideal plan would be to stretch my arm over the surface of the pit, grab on to the side wall, and gradually, carefully, roll myself up and out of the tar. But as I slowly reach for the nearest outcropping, I realize that it's not going to work that way—my arms are far too short to make the trek.

The legs and toes are long enough but don't have the proper dexterity required to do the job. Jaw is too far away from the railing to consider biting my way to safety, and I don't relish having to wait for a flabby tourist with ice cream stains on his Sunset Boulevard T-shirt to fetch me out of this quagmire. The tail will have to do.

The only problem is, it means I have to turn on my side in order to free the dexterous slab of meat from its costumed confines. Rolling to my right like a mother hen carefully sitting on her eggs, I slowly expose my side to the tar, being careful not to stick my arm any farther in than necessary.

With my mammal bum exposed to the open air, I reach back and attempt to unsnap the G-3 series of tail buckles with only one hand. I was especially adept at this in my younger days, only it wasn't my own buckles I was undoing at the time. The task is made more difficult by the layers of clothing and fake skin between my digits and the strap, as well as the omnipresent threat of the thick molasses of death waiting to gobble me up whole.

My tail suddenly springs loose, the open buckle flapping around inside my polysuit. If I get out of this pit, it's going to look like I've got a load in my pants, but no matter; I'd rather be embarrassed than dead any day of the epoch. Now all it takes is a few more snaps at the waist skin, a gentle tug to the hips—

And my tail is free, a small part of me natural and Progressive all over again. Working quickly and assuredly, I elongate my tail as far as it will go and wrap the tip around a chunk of rebar poking out of the Pit wall. Rather than try to force myself up all at once, I use my tail like a fishing rod, reeling it around and around the bar, slowly dragging my body out of the tar and onto dry land.

Wasting no time, I get my tail in on more action, using it as a balance as I leap up and out of the tar pit and into the safety of the viewing area. I reguise myself rapidly, tucking the tail back into its confines and loosely fastening the buckle in place before bounding into the park, a tar baby with vengeance on his mind.

It's all starting to come together now—the murders, the rituals, the doctor who really isn't. I may need some assistance on this one—at the very least, I need someone to bear witness to my knowledge—and since Ernie's still laid up in Hawaii, I need to get to Jules, and I need to get to her fast. But as I lurch into the parking lot, my thighs sticking together—now I know how Oprah feels—there's a curious lack of Lincoln where my Lincoln should be, with nothing but a pool of oil to remember her by.

Okay, *now* it's personal.

With my car stolen, there's no way to get up to Hollywood short of public transportation, and I strongly doubt that our friendly neighborhood bus drivers will let the Swamp Thing come on board, even if he has the required eighty-five cents, which I believe I do not. A taxicab is out of the question as well, if only because they're about as frequent in Los Angeles as trust-fund babies driving Pintos, and if I lift the handset of a public telephone in order to call one, I may become stuck to it for good.

Walking it will be, then, squishing along as fast as my crude-oiled legs will take me. If someone were to come along and scrape my shins, they could power Manhattan for weeks. I stick to alleys and shadows, hoping to avoid contact with any other forms of life. On my way into Hollywood, I pass a mongrel sipping God-knows-what out of an old soup can; the pitiful critter looks up, takes in an eyeful, and promptly scurries away, fearful of losing his Most Decrepit status to a shuffling, panting dino.

But the trip is taking me forever, and this is not my only destination of the night. I've managed to make it up near Beverly Boulevard, surprised to find the streets not quite as desolate as they should be this time of evening. A steady stream of streetwalkers prowl the sidewalks, wobbling on three-inch heels, tucking glitter skirts up and in so that the average hemline comes to somewhere just below the neck.

They reek of strong perfume—not the somewhat appealing, somewhat repulsive feminine musk that a lot of human women give off, but a cannonball of potpourri shot directly at the sinuses—and I have to cover up my nose in order to block out the stench.

But it's that smell, the eau de whore, that sets off a series of rapid-fire thoughts in my mind. Soon enough, I've got the semblance of a plan, and my sniffer is released back into the open once more to do its dirty work.

Bringing in the cool night air, I let my schnoz filter through the stronger, bigger bullies of human-made perfumes, searching for the one scent that might be cowering down in the olfactory region as if to blend into the crowd. As I travel up La Brea, I know I should locate it soon enough, if only because this is her usual stomping grounds, and tonight is prime time for eager johns. Unless, of course, she's already retired to the Chateau for the evening. . . .

Every step is another deep breath, another cleansing exhale. Every non-dino smell rejected out of hand, not what I'm looking for tonight. Not what I'm looking for *any* night.

And then, faint but sure, there it is. Pine, autumn air. That's it—that's the basic odor. Quickly then, refining it further, separating the wheat from the chaff, and soon it's a perfect olfactory portrait: bubble gum and sod.

And there she is, strutting her stuff for the clientele who drive by with their windows down and their libidos out, shaking her costumed rump for all to see. Body tightly packed into a red mini-mini, a sleeveless number with a skimpy top and nearly nonexistent bottom. Silver stilettos, makeup caked, fake fingernails as long as her heels and capable of some serious dorsal damage. She's by herself, walking all alone past shadowy side streets and empty storefronts.

I sneak around a back alley and come up right behind this hooker I know so well. "Star," I whisper in her ear, "it's time to pay the piper."

Before she can react, before she gets a chance to alert the other ladies of the evening that anything is amiss, I clap my hand around her mouth and pull her back into the darkness of the alleyway. She tries to bite down on my fingers, but the tar gets stuck in her mouth, and she spends the next two minutes spitting out the foul substance.

"I've been looking for you," I say, keeping my voice low but firm. "You're a hard bird to catch."

"The fuck are you?" she spits.

"My name's Rubio, we met once before. Nice little party at your place."

"Yeah, so, like I said—who the fuck are you?"

"Don't like that answer? Okay, how 'bout this: I'm the guy that's gonna keep you from spending the next year breakin' rocks in the hot sun. Betcha there ain't a lot of johns down at County. A few Janes, I'd imagine . . ." It's this kind of bad-cop, bad-cop confrontation I could really get into; too bad they only come along once a year or so.

"Keep talking," she says, suddenly interested.

"I believe you have my client's penis."

She tries to shake off my grasp—"What? I don't—"

"A very valuable penis, I'm led to understand. A Mussolini."

"You can't prove it—"

"And I don't have to," I tell her. "For that matter, I don't want to. You don't worry about that. All I'm asking of you is a favor. If you do it, I stop looking for you, and I make sure Minsky stops looking for you, too. I know you like that . . . thing, and it's all yours if you do what I ask."

"And you'll protect me from the cops?"

"Just on this," I tell her, making clear my intentions. "Anything else, you're on your own. But maybe I can put a good word in for you down at the station. I know some people."

I give Star a few moments to think it over, but there's no easier decision than this. "Whaddaya want?" she asks, softening up a touch.

She has a pen in her purse, and I grab a pamphlet from the street advertising some new punk band up at one of the Sunset clubs. "Bend over," I say, and Star willingly assumes the position. She begins to lift her dress, allowing me access—

"Keep your goddamn skirt on," I shout, then lower my voice again. Softer: "I'm not interested in—look, I don't want sex, I just want to write a note."

"That's it?" she chirps, and for a split second, I can see the little girl that once held sway over this young mind and body. An innocent relief spreads across her features, softening her eyes, her grin. Then it's all gone, and the streetwalker sneer returns to her ruined face. "So I can keep the dick, right?"

"Right. I write the note, you deliver it, we're even."

A hastily scribbled letter to Jules, detailing all I know and all I think I know and a hasty plan of action for the evening. If I don't come back from this little journey, I want to make sure someone goes to the Council, the cops, to anyone who can bring these bastards down. Folding the letter into fourths, I tuck it deep into Star's purse and make her swear not to peek. I'm guessing that she probably will anyway, but she won't understand half of it. I can only hope that Jules does.

That taken care of, I send Star and her Mussolini on their way and plot a course for my next destination: a certain piece of neoclassical architecture nestled up in the Hollywood Hills. And this time, I hope to be coming back with a few party favors.

It's been hard going, my feet directed, as they are, on the sticky side of the street, but with every passing mile, the tar has worn thinner, the trip grown easier. A digital display outside a bank I passed on the way into the Hills told me it is nearly five o'clock in the morning, which means I must have been lying dormant in the tar pit, not moving, not *breathing,* for just over two hours. Can't think about that now.

On my way through a poorly tended backyard—this must be where the rich white trash of the Hollywood Hills hang out—I snatch a few clothespins off a laundry line and shove them deep down into my tar-filled pockets. There is a serious doubt in my mind as to whether or not they'll ever make it out of these pants again, but if the need arises, I'll pull with all my might. The Hills provide a bit of cover, and I find myself sneaking through more and more backyards in order to remain hidden behind the trees and shrubbery. Along one small stretch of land, it almost feels like I'm back on the Progressives' island, caught in that jungle once again.

Up ahead is the Progressive compound, and inside are the players in tonight's performance; little do they know I am no longer an understudy. But the curtain's going to fall early unless I can figure out a quick, painless way into the theater. There are sure to be sentinels posted somewhere on the grounds, and I only hope that my current state of camouflage—tar black is in this year—will do the job.

A low brick wall is the only perimeter, but I look before I leap, making sure there isn't a pit of snakes or a rabid guard gorilla on the other side. Nothing would surprise me when it comes to this group.

No snakes, no gorilla, no booby trap of spikes and monsters. Sticking to the trees, I make my way across the acreage, marveling once again at the sheer extent of the land. Fifty, sixty, a hundred acres might be a postage-stamp lot out in Iowa, but in the Hollywood Hills it's practically enough to split off from the union.

In time, the main house comes into view, the blazing white columns and archways beginning to wake up to the first light of dawn, preparing to sparkle and blind the hell out of anyone who has the misfortune to look in their direction, a perfect blend of architecture and protection. The parking lot is filled with cars of every make and model, each space filled and those in between squeezed as tight as they can go, double-parked to the limit. Makes the overfill lot at the Hollywood Bowl look like the Serengeti.

Much like our entrance into the palace back on the island, sneaking into the mansion is a heck of a lot easier than, say, crashing Spago's post-Oscar bash, and results in many fewer bruises—don't ask, don't ask. Soon enough I'm slipping down the main hallway, sticking to the shadows, keeping my eyes and nose open and ready. There's a great tumult emanating from within the main ballroom, and a cacophony of smells intertwined with the noise. But that's not where I'm going. Not yet, anyway.

Footsteps behind me, clomping down the hall, and I fall back into a darkened niche, pressing my body up against the marble walls. Cold. I control the shivering with a good, solid tongue bite, and watch as a couple of dinos in guise—two businessmen, it looks like, three-piece suits and all—stroll purposefully toward the ballroom. As they walk, the two begin to undress, first removing their human clothes, quickly followed by their human skin. A mask is lifted, latex straining against the epoxy, then snapping free, the Hadrosaur beneath flipping his flexible beak into place a moment later. Tails are unfurled, horns released, and soon I'm walking behind two natural dinos, pacing them from thirty feet back.

". . . said they'll be ready in Europe," one is saying. "Same time we are here."

"On his signal, though—"

"—of course, of course, not without his signal."

And they duck into the ballroom—filled to capacity, my nose tells me. Barring the one time I was erroneously placed in the dino immigration ward down in San Diego, I've never been in one location so tightly packed with our species before. There's a dino density of massive proportions in that ballroom—they must be packed in snout-to-tail in there—and I hope the walls are strong enough to prevent a leak.

I come upon that familiar hallway, and at the end of it, Circe's room. *This is my lounge,* Circe told Ernie and me less than one week ago. *I come here before large events, to . . . prepare, if you will.* Well, we've got a large event brewing downstairs, and my guess is it won't be just Circe preparing inside this room. Of course, there's only one way to find out.

Embedded in the wall next to the door is a finger-hole of very familiar proportions, and I know what I have to do. There is no doubt in my mind that these locking systems, the Ancestrograph, and the rest of the mockery of mechanics utilized by this group, are a scientific crock of shit, technically speaking. *Dinosaur natural* is a term created by the few in order to scare the many, but that's as far as it goes. Yet there is also no doubt in my mind that they *do* measure increased pheromone production, a magic trick the higher-echelon Progressives have learned to do on command, without smoke, mirrors, or lovely assistants.

Now it's my turn. David Copperfield, outta my way.

With Ernie out of the picture, I've got to do this thing myself. Squeezing my finger inside the hole, I try to free my mind of mammalian thoughts. Mortgage payments are the first out my mental window, followed quickly by the rampant spread of computer viruses, my dry-cleaning bill, and the Lakers' hopes in the postseason. All I want to think about is running, eating, sleeping, sex. Jumping, hopping, roaring, sex. Fighting, winning, prancing, sex.

I close my eyes and take myself back to that fern jungle, that place where the past surges into the present, where the Jurassic bursts through the walls and makes itself known, where my feet sink into the soft earth, and my cry is a death knell for all the lesser creatures. I try not to feel the cold steel around my finger, growing colder with every second, sucking out my juices. I try to keep it warm, moist, a hot summer day seventy million years in the past, every tree and every bush and every leaf a natural part of my body, warming me, keeping me on my toes—open movement, never constricted, never constrained, loose and running free. My eyes opening, taking in the vibrant, natural colors, unblemished by smog and smoke and gas, my ears drooping back, angling upward to hear the calls of the Pterodactyls, my feet curling inward to feel the long, slimy bugs crawling between my toes, thousands of legs working over my bare hide. A herd of Compies—not crude, not crass, but a pack of simple, beautiful creatures— scampering over the lush, verdant landscape.

And I'm on the run, alone and alive, at liberty to move how I want to move, eat how I want to eat, kill how I want to kill, the consummate hunter with a belly full of hunger and the claws to satisfy it—streaming over the open land, head set against the wind, eager like never before to begin the chase, to begin the hunt, to begin—

The hole suddenly spits out my finger like a kid expelling his rutabagas across the kitchen table, and for a moment I'm stuck in both worlds, the prehistoric world and the modern, superimposed on each other, an acetate overlay atop a brilliant Kodachrome print. The hallways are filled with twenty-foot flowers, the door crawling with thirty-pound beetles. A marble Allosaur statue twenty feet away has filled out with flesh and muscles and skin and a roar that echoes out across the hills and down into the basin.

Boom—with a flash, the jungle shatters into a million pieces before my eyes and dissolves into nothingness, and I'm left in front of an open doorway in the heart of a mansion in the Hollywood Hills. For a moment, I almost think I can perceive the remnants of my own scent—if I whiff the air just right, I believe I can get that Cuban stogie coming through. But I know that such a thing's not possible, and it's foolish to even think it at this stage of the game. As it stands, I was able to produce enough pheromones to get the door open on my very first try; it's good to be an overachiever, but let's take this Progress thing one step at a time, Vincent.

As I enter the lounge, I make sure to leave the door open behind me. Those inside are bound to be a mite upset at my presence, and I don't want to foreclose the possibility of a hasty retreat. I've never had a showdown without Ernie by my side.

The 1970s beanbag theme has remained the dominant motif, unfortunately, but a thick mahogany desk and wide-backed leather chair on the far side of the room—the power side of the room, as management consultants would say—belie the design presence of someone other than Circe. A silhouette on the wall doesn't budge an inch as I step into the room, clear my throat, and announce, "I know what you're doing. Ernie knows what you're doing, too, as do a few friends of mine at the LA *Times*." This last part is a bluff, but it's always good to bring up the media at times like these. "I suggest you give it all up now, come with me, and if you help out with the investigation, the Council might be lenient with you."

No answer from the chair, save for a—a giggle? Is that laughter?

"I'm glad you think this is a joking matter," I say, a portion of my confidence draining out through my feet and disappearing into the cracks in the floor. "Because gun smuggling, kidnaping, and murder are all federal offenses, and that's before we bring the Council into it. They'll want to hear about—"

"Who did I murder?" comes a low, even voice, still tinged with a side order of good humor. "Who exactly did I kill?"

"Rupert Simmons for one," I blurt out. "Try that on for starters."

"Did I? Now, that's odd . . ."

And with that, the chair spins around—he must have known I was here, must have been setting up this chair-spin gag for the last ten minutes just to mock me, the crazy son of a bitch—and I'm suddenly face to face with the reason I took on this goddamned case in the first place.

"I'd say I look pretty good for a dead guy," grins Rupert. "Don't you think?"

You—you're dead," I stammer.

"Yes, you keep insisting that," drawls Rupert. He stands up from the chair and walks across the room; unguised and standing tall, the young T-Rex is a good five inches taller than I, his body lean and muscular. Meanwhile, I'm sitting here wrapped in my constricting latex, which is, in itself, wrapped in a continually hardening layer of tar. This is not good.

"We—I saw your body," I tell him, still trying to replay the funeral in my mind. Closed casket, if I remember correctly. Okay, maybe I didn't see his body. But his sister was the one who found him, and siblings don't often make that kind of mistake. "Louise, she—she found you—"

"My sister found me in my room," he finishes. "I'm quite aware. But she found me in costume, didn't she?"

I don't know why it hits me now, and at the same time, I don't know why it didn't hit me before. Damn my intuition to show up at the party ten minutes too late. "The T-Rex who went missing near your house that night," I say. "He's the one—they killed him, then dressed him in your guise. You took a total stranger—"

"Not a stranger," Rupert corrects. "A guy I knew from high school, actually. Dan Blish, an asshole football player who liked tying me to the tackling dummys and giving the offensive line a few whacks at the sled. Trust me, he deserved it."

"No one deserves death," I say. "They—you—the Progressives kidnaped and killed this kid so he could take your place at the funeral."

"Wow," says Rupert mockingly, "you're pretty quick on the uptake—when the whole thing's handed to you. Big deal. I knew my sister was a fool for hiring you in the first place."

"Why?" I ask, going against my better judgment and leaning closer to the boy. "Why would you come back to this?"

"Why would I ever want to leave it? All my life, I've been searching for happiness. I was a miserable little kid, a miserable teenager, and a miserable adult, and now that I've found something that makes me content, everyone wants to take me away from it."

"Because it's wrong," I explain patiently.

"How? How is it wrong to want to be what you are? How is it wrong to be able to come out and sing 'I am dino, hear me roar'?"

"It's—it's not that simple—"

"It *is* that simple," Rupert insists. "It's that simple, and it's nearly complete. You and my ex-brother-in-law took me away before I could compete in the Ring, my final challenge before I was to become truly natural, and for that I can never forgive you. But I can forget. Soon, it all comes down to the final battle. Now we'll know for sure who should dominate the earth: the mammals or the reptiles. Would you like to bet on how it will turn out?"

I shake my head. Haven't placed a wager since I lost twenty grand on the last Foreman fight. Some bum told me he was a Raptor, so I laid it down out of respect for the brotherhood and I'm not going to start up again with a bet on the fate of the world. "I can't let that happen," I say. "I'm sorry, but I'm going to take you back to your sister."

"You are?" he asks, the cheery tone mocking me from all directions at once. Then, dropping to a lower register, taking a step forward and puffing out his chest like a robin searching for a mate, his hard-earned muscles pressing against his hide, claws flashing in and out like the needle on a sewing machine, he asks, "You and who else?"

Good question. Who else?

"Me, for one."

I turn, expecting to find the media, the governor, anyone—but under the circumstances, it's ten times better. With his arm and shoulder wrapped up in a gleaming white cast and his own guise situated comfortably on his body, Ernie is a model of blasé as he enters the room and struts confidently up to his ex-brother-in-law.

"You're a good kid," says my partner, "but you always were a pain in the ass." And with that, he whips that solid cast up and around, cold-cocking Rupert one last time, sending him to the mat for a final ten-count.

The boy goes down hard.

Ernie's all over me before I have a chance to thank him. "You ever heard of the word 'backup'?" he shouts. "Partners don't go in solo, especially not something like this. If Jules hadn't called the office when your note showed up, I'd still be wandering the city looking for you, and you'd be the raw meat at tonight's dinner."

"How the hell did you get here so fast?"

"I flew out on the red-eye."

I shake my head; a loose bit of tar flies out of my hair and lands on Rupert's prone body. "That wouldn't get you here until a few hours from now—that's not possible."

Ernie's good hand reaches up to feel my forehead, as if he's checking my temperature. "You thinkin' straight, kid? I stayed in the hospital for a few hours, got myself released against doctor's orders, and took yesterday's midnight flight back to the mainland. Got in LA around nine A.M. I've been looking for you all day." His eyes scan me up and down, taking in the torn guise and the frazzled hair and, oh yes, the tar, and I can see those Ernie gears engaging and turning, trying to figure out what kind of mess I'd gotten myself into. "Where the hell have you been?" he asks.

If Ernie's telling the truth—and I don't see any reason for him to lie, except for the fact that everyone else seems to have been lying to me for the past few weeks—then I wasn't in the tar pit a mere two hours; I was there for closer to twenty-four. But there is no possible way I could have survived an entombment that long.

Actually, there is one way.

"I was hibernating, Ern." Laughing now, the humor bubbling up from within, the concept so irrational and yet so right that if I don't laugh I'll start screaming instead. "I'm pretty darn sure I was hibernating."

A crash behind us as the door flies inward, slamming into Rupert's leg. Doesn't anybody knock anymore? "That's a Progressive ability, did y'all know that?" says Dr. Beauregard, stepping over the fallen T-Rex's prone body. "Sustained hibernation—animated suspension, basically—is a very primal trait of ours. It might have been that last burst of scent I gave you back in the pits, but I'm pretty sure your body learned that one on its own. I'm proud of you, son."

"And I'm sick of you," I reply. "I'm sick of the whole damn lot of you."

Circe struts in behind Dr. B., tail wagging lasciviously, hands on her hips and a sad, almost disappointed look on that perfectly formed face. She can't meet my eyes, her gaze wandering away every time I try to snag her attention, and her scent is nearly impossible to discern.

Before they can get out another word—or, worse, another smell—I reach into the one pocket that isn't filled with goo and toss Ernie two clothespins. "Snap 'em on," I suggest, whipping off my human mask so that I can affix mine tightly around my natural nostrils. As my snout expands into place, like a sponge growing with water retention, I place a second pin across the first; the double action stings a bit, but it's a small price to pay for protection.

"I don't know what you think you know, Vincent," Circe begins, now shooting small, hit-and-run glances up at me, "but I can assure you, you're making a mistake—"

"Can it, toots," says Ernie, and I think . . . yes, I do believe he's in the zone. "We've heard enough outta you for three natural lifetimes."

"We know quite a lot," I continue, "and none of it's a mistake, not anymore. How you find kids who are scared, who are lonely, and take them in. How you tell them they're a part of a special group, teach them ways to get back to nature."

"And what's wrong with that?" defends Circe. "It's true, it's all true. You've felt it yourself—you can't deny it. Vincent, you're a beautiful, natural Velociraptor, and no social constraints should stand in the way of your natural powers."

Ernie usually takes the closing argument in these cases, but I figure after this ordeal, it's time to make my bones. "May I?" I ask my partner.

"By all means," he says proudly. "Lay it on 'em."

"We knew something was wrong from the moment we saw the second battle in the Ring, the one where the young Raptor lost out to the bull. The dinos he chose as his confederates, by all accounts your average Progressives, were simply too good with a dart gun. Their aim couldn't have been the result of occasional target practice with a tranquilizer rifle—those shots were made with military-style precision, and you only come by that level of skill through a mess of practice. And why should dinosaurs, especially those who are trying to advance beyond human means, be practicing with any firearms whatsoever?"

I walk behind the mahogany desk and take a seat in the chair, facing my audience with a wide grin. I could get used to this. "Now, let's backtrack for a second and look at what happens to those dinosaurs who make it past the challenge of the Ring and join the ranks of mindless carnivores. They're shut up in a paddock, corralled, and drop-shipped live cartons of pigs and livestock they can tear apart to their heart's content. But why deal with a whole island full of naturalized beasts? Is that truly the goal, to populate a bunch of islands with dinosaurs forced to live off whatever a hydrofoil can ship in on a daily basis?"

Circe tries to cut in. "No, but—"

"Ah, ah—everyone will get their turn. No, of course it's not. And this started to dawn on me from the moment we saw that building in the jungle filled with those maps, those weapons—"

"Weapons?" Circe interrupts, head vibrating in a speedy spasm. "We don't have weapons. Now you're talking crazy, Vincent—"

"Don't play dumb. Of course, I didn't know what to make of it for a while, and the tidal wave of reason didn't crash over me until I got into a confrontation with some construction workers back here in LA."

"Isn't it always that way, though?" says Ern, always at the ready to pop in with a line.

"So here's the big question: What is the goal of any organization that creates two classes out of its citizens, one skilled and the other brutish?"

No response. These folks don't play along with *Jeopardy!* from the comfort of their sleeper sofas, I bet.

"The goal," I tell them, "is simply this: to form an army."

"What?" Circe is not happy, to say the least. Her hands clench into tight balls of fury, and I'm no longer sure that she knows what I'm talking about.

"Sure," I continue, "it's obvious. And not just one little battalion on one little island. We're talking worldwide, large-scale outposts on every island in every country in every continent in the world. Brontosaurs, Raptors, Steogsaurs, T-Rexes. Dinos marching side by side, mowing their way across the globe, exterminating any and every human in their path. Mammals, beware—it's time for the blitzkrieg.

"Tell ya what—why don't you ask Raal about it?"

Slowly, deliberately, I turn toward Dr. Beauregard, making my gaze and my intention quite clear to everyone in the room. My eyebrow raises of its own accord, and I'm pretty sure some drums should be kicking in right about now.

"Oh, quit it," grumbles Dr. Beauregard, whipping off his beard and mustache, dropping the Colonel Sanders routine altogether. The rest of the guise quickly follows, and I'm not surprised in the least to find that beneath that costume is, of course, a Diplodocus. "Everyone knows who I am. Don't start pretending you're Sherlock Holmes on us now."

Ernie raises his hand. "I didn't know. Not for sure, at least."

"Thanks," I say.

"No problem."

But Circe's not interested in joining the banter; her anger is genuine, and she spins on Raal, hide flushed, eyes flashing. "What are they talking about? Do you know what's going on?"

"It's the final culmination to our plans," insists the Diplodod. "The core of the idea, intact and made real."

"That's not what you taught me," insists Circe. "All those years, you taught me that the core is Progression. The core is getting back to a state of nature."

"Yes," Raal agrees. "And after it, conquest."

Ernie gives me a nod, and I'm glad to concede the floor to the honorable Carnotaur from the great state of California. "You see, Circe, Dr. Beauregard—Raal—isn't content with an island or two like you are. He's not content with feeling good about himself or understanding what he is and how he fits into the evolutionary picture. I was worried about you at first—I even warned Vincent to stay away from you. I suspected your motives were . . . shall we say disingenuous?—but you proved me wrong. I believe now that you believe in Progress. Unfortunately, you're not in charge, and the real leader has some other ideas up his triple-fake sleeves. Progress isn't enough for him. It's not fair, he'd say, that the dinosaurs should only get an island to themselves—"

"It's not—" interrupts the cult leader.

"See. And it's not fair, he'd say, that the mammals should have all this land to themselves. It's apartheid, it's oppression, it's deserving of a revolution."

"I like your style," says Raal. "You should come work for the team."

"I don't think so," replies Ernie. "Because while I'm no fan of the human race—believe me, I'd rather eat dinner with a blind mole rat than one of their kind—it doesn't make me want to commit genocide. This is what you meant from the very start, isn't it, Raal? You found Circe because she had the gift, the ability to use her powers and draw others to the cause, but the real goal was to return this world to the way things were before the humans showed up. All this talk about worshiping the ancestors—you don't want to revere them, you want to *be* them."

Raal issues a tight little grin. "And what's wrong with that?"

"What's wrong with that?" I echo. "How about gun smuggling and kidnaping and murder?"

But Raal is guilt-free; it slides off him like grease off Teflon. "Those who died did so for the good of their kind." Circe, on the other hand, has begun to tremble uncontrollably, though whether it is with rage or fear, I can't say.

"Buzz and Wendell?" I say. "They needed to go? You *had* to rig those guns to fail and the cage to lock in place?"

"They had been talking to you, too close to the information. It had to be stopped."

"None of this—" Circe starts. "It wasn't planned."

"Wasn't planned by *you*, perhaps," I reply, "but I'd take a look in your organization and find out who's loyal to your orders and who listens to the big cheese over here."

"And what do you think tonight is for?" Ernie says, keeping his attention focused on Circe. "This little shindig in the ballroom?"

"It's—it's a meeting," stutters Circe, already unsure of the words, the meaning. "To discuss the next conference."

"It's a rally," I say. "It's a pep talk before the onslaught."

Ernie puts an arm around Circe's shoulders, waving his hand through the air, spelling out a banner headline. "The day when the dinosaurs shall rise again."

"You really should join up," insists Raal, coming closer to me, his snout within snapping distance of mine. "I'd hate to lose a mind like yours in the cleansing."

Ernie steps between us, a ref breaking two boxers from a clench, and clears his throat. "Enough with the spat. We're done here."

"We are, indeed," I say, turning on Circe. "The love affair is over, babe, the heartache just begun. You used me for the last time."

"Used *you*?" she spits back. "You're a phony. You pretended to be someone who you weren't from the start."

"But it's my job, doll. You're two-faced for fun."

Ernie puts a nice end to the conversation. "Vincent, you wanna cuff 'em or should I?" He dangles four solid rings of metal in the air, offering me the chance to captivate Circe for a change.

"I didn't mean—Raal, you said . . ." Circe's voice trails off, eyes searching for some meaning, some explanation from this Diplodocus she'd revered for so long. "Everything you taught me . . . it was a lie. . . ."

"It was the truth," Raal insists. "All of it. And then an even greater truth lays beyond."

Grabbing a handcuff, I break up the little soap opera. "Enough with the fortune-cookie talk, kids. It's time to go get charged."

"You can't arrest us," Circe mumbles.

"No, but we can haul your ass down to the Council. We're not talking jaywalking, here—your group was planning *the extinction of the human race,* sweetheart, and even though you didn't have intimate knowledge of the plan, you were involved enough to be indicted right alongside your precious leader. You think this is slap-on-the-wrist time? I'd say goodbye to Mr. Sun as soon as we step outside, 'cause it's gonna be a while before you get a glimpse of him again."

A sudden burst of discussion, filtering in from down the hallway, a cascade of casual conversation trickling into the room. I look to Ernie—he looks back—and suddenly I can feel the tide turning again, the undertow starting to drag me back out to sea. "You know what that is?" beams Raal, the corners of his mouth curving up into that pear-shaped head of his.

"Vienna Boys' Choir?"

"That's the cadre coming to get us for the rally," he says. "And there's only one way out of this room. When they see us coming out, I promise you they'll attack."

Enough of this game, the bluffs and counterbluffs. Spinning myself in a wide circle, I grab Raal from behind, whipping out my claw and placing it at his throat. "Let's see how quickly they'll attack now."

Circe steps in. "Vincent, don't—"

But Ernie's right behind her, pressed tight to her back—some guys get all the breaks—and soon we've got the two cult leaders handcuffed, strapped, and ready to transport up to the Valley and the local Council representative. Despite every muscle and tendon in me aching to tell Ernie to let Circe go, my quavering sense of duty says otherwise. Circe may not be responsible for any of the more violent aspects of the group, but it would be patently wrong to allow her to escape unpunished.

From the moment we emerge into the hallway—the five Progressives walking toward us have stopped short at the sight of their leaders being led away in chains—insanity takes control.

"Stay back," warns Ernie, pressing the tip of his claw far enough into Circe's neck that it makes a visible indentation. "I've got an itchy finger."

"Do what they say," Raal says calmly. I'm glad he's cooperating.

Unfortunately, the dinos are not. As one, they begin to advance on us, and Ernie and I find ourselves taking instinctive steps backward. Soon we're trotting back the way we came, through the lounge, and out another doorway. This place is a veritable fun house—hallways, mirrors, more hallways—though I'm not actually having much fun.

The dinos follow us as we lead our captives down a winding staircase and into another, smaller hallway, a single door waiting for us at the end of it. "You don't want to go in there," Circe suggests, but Ernie quiets her with a stern glance.

There's no other choice. The dinos behind us are keeping up the pressure, and this door represents our only hope. With luck, we can exit, get into Ernie's car, and get this all finished up within the hour. Success is climbing up the vine, and already I can feel the comfort of my bed, the gentle hum of a ball game on the radio, the warm caresses of some premium parsley running through my veins.

Then it all breaks down faster than a Yugo.

As the door swings wide, vertigo slams into my brain without hitting the brakes, my body reeling as the ballroom thirty feet below rocks and rolls like a rowboat caught in a tsunami. The assembled Progressives glance up as one, hundreds of dino snouts and beady eyes focusing on the soap opera thirty feet above them, and I realize that we've just stumbled out of the pan and into the deep fryer.

With a piercing cackle that nearly vibrates my eardrums to kingdom come, Raal lashes out with a tremendous kick to my shins before landing a firm blow to my midsection. My arms go limp and the elusive cult leader dances away, knocking off my clothespins in the process. With incredible athletic prowess, Raal steps out onto the very platform where I first saw Circe and executes a flying leap into the crowd—which parts as he hits the ground—and rolls to a three-point landing. "They're trying to kill us," Raal cries, his voice carrying across the ballroom. "They're here to kill us—and they're here to take us away—"

In the few milliseconds I have to scan the room, I notice that the giant fake fossil they were constructing back in Hawaii has been relocated to the ballroom, and I'm impressed that they were able to reconstitute him in so short a period of time. A thin gridwork of scaffolding surrounds Frank's tenuously coupled bones; still, his recent reconstructive surgery seems to have come off better than half of Hollywood's. Even at the height of this platform, I'm only halfway up his long, curving neck, and I marvel once again at the impressive skills of this misguided group.

Behind me, Ernie's maintaining his hold on Circe, but I don't know for how much longer. As the Progressives down in the ballroom go their own ways—those who only showed up for the free food scattering for safety, wanting no part of this melee, others gearing up for what looks to be a cakewalk for their side—the cadre of dinosaurs in the hallway huddle together, and déjà vu returns one more time as I recall the scene back in the jungle. There's a new pack of beasts after us now, and even though these might understand English, it doesn't make them any less deadly.

But here's where things get interesting:

Before I can make a move myself, even before my claws have flashed to their full length, Circe is leaping away from Ernie, the element of surprise clearly to her advantage, a wellspring of unnatural strength throwing my partner up and away by a good three feet. Hands still clasped tightly behind her but no matter, no matter—her entire body is a single speeding bullet streaming onto the platform, out through the ballroom, aimed at the middle of the crowd, legs and sharp underclaws shoved out in front as if she's doing a sit-up while flying through the air. She slams into the pile of dinosaurs with explosive force, and a whole section of Progressives go down in a heap of hide, blood, and saliva. Now *that's* a kind of bowling that might get better Nielsen ratings.

This must be the cue for the rest of the Progressives to start their engines, because soon Ernie and I are engaged in our own skirmishes, ripping off our guises, sliding down curtains like Errol Flynn, beating back paws and jaws and tails from all sides at once. I'm the Raptor version of Chuck Norris, using the tail from an Ornitho in front of me to fend off the chomping attack from a T-Rex to my right. I'm spinning, I'm flailing, and my turn as the last dino action hero is finally upon me.

Statues and busts crash all around the room as we leap atop whatever furnishings might assist us in winning the battle. Marble flies through the air, small bits of bone and rock peppering my hide, but I'm jumping from side to side, lashing out with my tail, with my feet, trying to keep my attackers directly in front of me, preferably out of tooth-and-claw range. It's a defensive battle, a stalling tactic—

"Where the hell are they?" I call out to Ernie, who's busy breaking a bear hold by a Bronto.

"I—don't—know," he yells back, cracking his head against the other dino's with a sickening crunch. The Bronto's grip on my partner slackens, and he slumps to the floor like a drunk being tossed at closing time, just as another takes his place.

I don't know where Circe and Raal have gotten to, and I'm not in a position to find out. Soon enough, I'm surrounded by five snarling dinos who could listen to reason if they wanted to but choose to close themselves off from logic and instead take quick, painful swipes at my head and body. I'm lashing out as well, ripping my underclaws into hides, into flesh, protecting myself as much as I possibly can, but there's only so much a Raptor can do when faced with overwhelming odds.

My back impacts hard on a slab of wood, and for a second I think I've been attacked, that my spine must be severed, and I will be forced to live the rest of my life—if I live—in a wheelchair, my tail up in traction, my legs useless for all eternity. But it's just a piece of scaffolding surrounding Frank's rickety forty-foot skeleton, and I use the same tactic I did in the jungle and climb, climb, climb. I may only be a pseudo-simian, but I can ape monkeys with the best of them.

Unfortunately, so can my attackers, who haven't yet unlearned their more helpful human qualities. As I scramble up the elongated bones, kicking out with my legs at snarling faces and snapping jaws, they zip right up behind me, a swarm of dinosaurs crawling like ants over this brand-spanking-new ancient fossil. The entire structure sways and trembles as we zip across its facade, but there's nowhere to go but up.

A Raptor rears up in front of me, lashing out with a slicing sideswipe, but I leap into the air, catching my tail on a scaffolding bar at the last moment, swinging out and around the open space and landing safely on the other side. I resume my climb, shutting out the commotion around me.

And wind up atop Frank's massive skull, the snout itself longer than my entire body. The head of this fossil perches precariously atop the long, shaky neck, and within moments, two Progressives—a Trike and that Raptor who won't give up—pull themselves up and onto the top of Frank's spine, heading straight in my direction.

I look down for an exit—maybe by hanging off of his nose, swinging down and across the teeth—but scratch that plan when I see a new contingent of dinos swiftly scampering up the scaffolding on that side as well.

To my left, an Ornitho and a smallish Stegosaur await my arrival; to my right is a T-Rex.

They close.

There is truly nowhere for me to go. Spontaneous hibernation will not be my ticket out this time around. Now that my demise is imminent, I wish I were at least outside, in the fresh air, sucking up the sweet smell of nature, but if heaven is anything like I suspect, there will be a jungle and soft earth and a bed of ferns in which I can lie down at night and look up at the stars.

I hope Ernie gets there, too, but not for a long, long time.

A sudden rattle at the closed ballroom door, and everything slows down for a moment. Another rattle, an earthquake shake—the dinos around me staring about in confusion, momentarily halting their advance, the noise engaging my curiosity as well, raising my hopes—and suddenly there's mass confusion as the barrier bursts inward with a mighty crash and a storm of figures stream inside. The cavalry has arrived.

"Sorry we're late, darling," calls Jules, decked out in her finest ball-gown livery, "but Marilyn had to do her hair."

Miss Monroe issues a girlish giggle and turns coyly to the side. "But it's my best feature," she pouts, lips working overtime.

Jules stands tall in the middle of the barn, flanked on either side by a contingent of the best dinosaur cross-dressers LA has ever seen in one venue. Their hair is perfectly coiffed, nails impeccably filed, clothing flawlessly tailored. It's a cavalcade of stars, each one a perfect to-die-for diva, right down to the skin tone and beauty moles. They're good, and they oughta be—the ladies pay big bucks for those costumes.

With a smile of her own that would make the devil blush, Jules raises a stylish, sculptured arm in the air and announces sweetly, "Get 'em, girls."

Bette Midler launches herself into a pack of Progressives, who are too startled at the attack by a superstar to fight back. She's carefully rolled up the left leg of her guise, so the Divine Miss M has access to a muscular leg and the sharp claws within. A perfectly timed turn-turn-kick-turn lands three of the other dinos in a heap atop one another, and soon she's off and running to the next unfortunate group.

I'm quickly assisted by Jayne Mansfield and Greta Garbo, both of whom are stunning, graceful, and a whirlwind of fighting prowess. Taking the Raptor and the Stego for myself, I land my own blows while watching these two bombshells make short work out of the remaining Progressives on the scaffolding. At one point, Jayne's wig falls off, and she issues a tremendous scream of anger, disemboweling the T-Rex responsible for the injury before reaffixing that shock of long, platinum hair.

I've just leaped back atop Frank's neck, ready to tag-team with Greta on a pair of Diplodoci intent on having us over for dinner, when a rolling roar streams across the floor. Thirty feet down, a blurry wheel of dino flesh flows across the marble, blood flying out at all angles. I can just make out the lines of this furious Diplodod as Raal grabs hold of Frank's ankle and begins to climb. His eyes are locked on mine, and I've got a pretty good idea of his final destination.

No help from the ladies—they're tied up in their own battles, whacking the remaining Progressives into submission. I look around, trying to find a way out, but there's no easy exit. If I leap from here, odds are I'll break something on the way down; perhaps if I'd gone to the jumping seminar back on the island, I'd be okay, but unfortunately I was forced to ditch class that day.

"You can't stop it. . . ." pants Raal as he drags himself onto the platform, a thin stream of blood trickling from his mouth. Every breath sounds a concomitant gurgle, a surefire indication of internal injuries, but it doesn't seem to be sapping his strength. "You can't stop Progress."

"That's what they say," I point out. "They also say you shouldn't shit where you eat, but you seem to have made a career out of it."

The momentary pause of confusion is all I need to get in the first swipe. With my torso leaning back and tail set at the proper angle to spring me, I leap forward, legs first, letting my natural blades do all the work. But Raal's got a few tricks of his own, and though the Diplodocus genes don't equip their possessors with nearly as many deadly weapons as Raptor DNA, his training in the lethal arts is quite evident. With surprising speed, Raal evades my attack, tucks his head back into his body like a frightened turtle, and slams headlong into my side. We go down in a rolling heap, grabbing at Frank's delicate vertebrae to stop our fall.

I manage to scramble back up the fossilized neck, leaping across the skull and out toward the elongated snout once again. There I stand, waiting for the attack, wondering what the hell I'm going to do if he comes at me again. Every breath I take comes with a bee sting to my side, and I think I may have ordered up the Broken Rib Special.

Down on the ballroom floor, dinos are rolling in ten directions at once, the walls caked with all manner of bodily fluids, the priceless art now in definitive possession of a new designation: worthless. And somewhere, somehow, some skirmish winds up with one soldier or another slamming into what happens to be a very dangerous button:

Forty feet down, the fire pit slides open.

"Ernie!" I call. "Barbra, Liza, Jules—anyone?" But they're all too wrapped up in their own battles—and doing quite nicely—to help; even if they were free and clear, it would take them too long to climb up Frank and offer assistance.

Raal advances.

His scent is strong, stronger than Circe's ever was, an entire vat of Aramis as compared to her meager Pine-Sol, and my first thought is *Jump, Vincent, jump, and it can all be over, over so easily. . . .*

I look down, the fire pit below beckoning, its cleansing flames awaiting my arrival.

But I've been through enough crap over the past week to realize that if I'm really talking to myself, I'll probably recognize the sarcasm. Fighting back against Raal's voice, taking a mental firehose to the overpowering scent, I try to stand tall, stand firm, bracing myself for what will probably be the final attack and my final seconds on Earth. But if I'm going down, Progress is going down with me.

Sinking into a crouch, drool dribbling from one side of his chin, Raal prepares to end the charade. There is nothing rational left in that melon-ball brain of his; I can tell that he is no longer in control of his actions, that he has suddenly Progressed into a purely natural state, more Iguanodon than I will ever be Raptor. I am so very, very screwed.

The pressure comes first, a wrecking ball blow right to the midsection, followed quickly by a radiating burst of pain and the inevitable loss of breath. I'm propelled backward at a tremendous speed, flying through the air, no trapeze in sight, Raal's head tucked deep into my abdomen, driving me up, up, and back down, slamming my back onto the protruding ridge of the giant skeleton's first vertebra.

Claws are digging at my hide, my own arms employed full-time as a shield for my soft underbelly, but it's not long before my strength will give, and my guts are strewn on the floor below. Raal is tucked deep into that embryonic position, legs tucked up, in, all four limbs working at once, claws fully extended, wordless growls and grunts lurching out his throat as he bites for my ears, my snout, my eyes.

"Ern—Ernie—" I try to call, but with every successive attack, the cry is cut short. He'll never hear me; I hope he gives me a nice funeral and keeps the paparazzi away.

Strength is draining out of every pore in my body, and though I'm trying to whip my tail around—catch an eye, an ear, any soft spot I can manage to hit—I'm just not connecting. With a hungry growl, Raal steps up the attack, and already I can feel blood seeping out from my stomach; he must have ripped away part of my hide, making for the insides—

When another ferocious roar joins the chorus, harmonizing for but a split second before breaking off into its own riff of anger and betrayal. Raal's body stiffens suddenly, giving me enough time to squirm out from beneath him, nearly clearing myself of his limbs. But a second later, he's on the attack again, rushing forward—

And getting slammed from behind, and then a second tremble wracks his torso a moment later and a new dribble of blood trickles from his mouth. A cough, a sharp breath, a final mortal shudder, and Raal is falling forward, forward, a gaping wound across his back, his frame teetering on the brink, falling over the side and off of the mammoth fossil—

And taking Circe with him.

I'm leaping even before I realize it, my leg outstretched, my claws extended as far as they can go, hoping that my aim is right and that the bones on which I'm jumping can withstand the force. As I land, I grab hold of an eye socket, grasping the ocular cavity with all my might.

My leg is heavier than it should be, about four hundred pounds more so, I should think. Looking down, I find Circe clinging to my outstretched underclaw, her fingers, still coated with Raal's blood, wrapped around its sharp, finely serrated edges, the blades digging into her flesh. And grabbing on to *her* legs is Raal, still very much alive, still very much enraged.

Below their feet, the fire pit roars with delight, eager to be fed. Herbs assault me from all directions now, not a calm, soothing mixture enveloping my body, my senses, but sharp blows to the head, the body, the mind. I'm battered left and right by Circe's scent, and I don't know if it's fear, anticipation, or some combination thereof, but it's knocking me silly. My claw cannot hold on much longer.

Raal begins to climb, grabbing at Circe's body, his claws digging into her flesh, using her beautiful body as nothing more than handholds. He's coming for me, and he doesn't care if he destroys his protégée along the way. A steady slobber of drool and blood drips from his mouth, the fire raging hard below him, shadows dancing across that insane face.

But it's Circe I'm concerned with, Circe who I want to pull to safety, Raal or no Raal. If I save her, I save him, but no matter; I'll deal with it when the time comes.

"Hold on," I grunt. "Just—hold on—"

She's oblivious. "It was right," she says to me, her eyes dancing a two-step in their sockets. "Progress was right."

Straining my leg muscles, trying to bring them to bear, but the extra weight is so hard to handle. I pull on Frank's eye—the head jostling with my effort—and manage to scoot up no more than an inch. Raal is farther up Circe's body now, his torso even with her legs, and he's coming quick.

"Don't worry about that," I tell her, scooting myself back another few inches. "Just hang tight—"

But she's shaking her head, not paying attention to a word I'm saying. "Remember," Circe whispers to me, her softly spoken words easily cutting through the clamor of the fire, the shrieks of battle. "Remember how it feels. . . ."

Another hit of herbs, this one a paprika uppercut that slams my head back against my neck, and I'm in for the standing eight-count. Like an alcoholic rescued from his blackout, this little hair o' the pup reaches into the recesses of my memory, grabs hold of a recent evening, and opens it up before the rest of my astonished brain:

I am in the hotel room at the Westin Maui, and Kala is coming into the bedroom. I am tired, so very sleepy, but holding on to consciousness for the promise of great sex. I'm saying something about my job, something about why we're in Hawaii, and by the time Kala is done in the bathroom, I can't decide what's a wall and what's a painting and what's a tree and what's a prehistoric lagoon. And as she emerges from the doorway, steam rising up behind her, I see a familiar Velociraptor coming toward the bed, hushing me with a long, perfect finger, kissing my lips before I have a chance to react in beautiful, beautiful surprise.

"Love me, Vincent." Circe sighs. "Love me tonight."

And back in the Hollywood Hills, Circe, who has known from the very beginning how I was feeling, what I was feeling, why I was feeling it, gives me a nod. What I have seen is true. My little native girl was here with me all along.

"Hold on," I tell her, redoubling my efforts, grinding my teeth with the strain. "Hold on—"

But Raal is coming up, and coming fast, climbing aboard Circe's back, his claws ripping her body into long, bloody strands, ready to leap atop her shoulders and make the final jump back to safety, but for the first time since we met, Circe is in full command of herself and her senses.

This beautiful Raptor shakes her head, looks me in the eyes, in the heart, and says, "It is time for me to meet the ancestors, Vincent. It is time to become natural."

And as Raal prepares to make his final leap, as he steadies himself for the final and fatal attack on yours truly, Circe lets go. Simple as that. The fall is swift, the flames are hot. There is a moment when I think I can smell singed basil, a brief second when I think I hear the cry of a burned songbird, but it's just my imagination, and it is over in a matter of seconds.

Ernie is next to me; I don't know when he got there, but he's gingerly pulling me away from the side of Frank's head, directing my gaze away from the fire pit below. Greta Garbo, a nice baker from Santa Monica who gives me free bear claws whenever I visit, has made it to the top as well, and the two of them begin to help me down. "That's it, darlink," she says to me in that lilting Swedish accent. "It's finished."

Not quite—Garbo suddenly grabs my hand (this is one time when she doesn't want to be alone) and holds on tight as the skeleton begins to collapse. The giant legs go first, buckling from the vibrations, followed quickly by the hips and torso, the attachment pins shaking out, falling to the ground, wires snapping. The three of us leap for the nearest wall, grabbing tight to a piece of loose curtain and riding it down to the ground just as

Frank loses all of his structure and collapses into a giant heap of newly minted bones on the floor of the ballroom, his head cracking apart, the jawbone slipping into the still-roaring fire pit.

The other ladies finish up their shows, propelling themselves in the most graceful manner possible while still managing to inflict a frightening amount of damage. Liza Minnelli has a ferocious uppercut, but her mom is head-and-shoulders above her in the knockout department. Judy takes aim at a T-Rex, judges the distance to that cowardly beast, and knocks him clear past Oz with a sharp blow to the head.

Endgame is over in a matter of minutes, Babs doing most of the cleanup on the few remaining stragglers. There's no doubting the woman's pure power of presence as she dances through the room, collecting bodies wherever she goes. Her skill is so great that there's not an ounce of blood shed, yet she fells every enemy within seconds. And to think I mocked her in *The Prince of Tides*.

Epilogue

The last days of December. I hate this time of year. The holidays have come and gone, good cheer flitting in for a moment and then zipping back out the window with a bing and a bang and a boff, which means that the next few days will consist of nothing but driving to malls and taking photographs of husbands hanging out with the mistresses they missed so much during the more family-intensive Christmas celebrations. *Oh what fun it is to ride in a Lincoln with my camera. . . .*

The last eight months have been a constant struggle to forget what happened to me out there in Hawaii, and remember the more interesting, lascivious parts with as much detail as I can muster. Every once in a while I'll catch myself with my eyes closed, trying to imagine Circe, her smell, that jungle, that fantastic prehistoric scene, and every once in a while I'll let myself go. I'll allow myself to feel the breeze and the air and the moisture and the other creatures. Other times, I snap out of it and eat a candy bar.

The highest-ranking Progressives were remanded to the National Council, Ernie and I gave enough sworn depositions to send ten court reporters' children to Ivy League schools up through their Ph.D.'s, and by the time it was all over, no one wanted to tell us the outcome. We wrote letters, petitions, made enough troublesome phone calls to actually have a restraining order slapped down on us by a judge, but still . . . nothing.

I even got so frustrated with the situation that I up and ran for the Southern California Council a few months back, half on a whim, half on a dare, and ended up getting myself elected as the Raptor representative. Lucky me. Now

I get to spend the third Tuesday of every month holed up in Harold Johnson's furnished basement, though I use the term "furnished" very loosely. Harold, the Bronto rep, has an old sleeper sofa and love seat down there, but by the time I'm able to make it over to his ranch house in Burbank, Mrs. Nissenberg and that Oberst fellow have usually claimed the comfy spots as their own, so it's the floor or the top of the washer/dryer for me. Of course the one time I sat myself down atop said washer, I had to be driven to the hospital less than an hour later, my tail up in traction for two weeks—don't ask, don't ask—so I usually opt for standing around instead. Oh, it's a blast. The kicker is that even after all of the hoopla and my new and supposedly influential position, I am still unable to squeeze any information out of the National Council reps. Maybe I'll just have to run for higher office and show them a thing or two.

The Progressives are still going strong, I understand, though their weapons have been confiscated, the military plans dismantled, and the natural dinos brought back to secret hospital locations, where they're having the human drilled back into them. It's okay with me that the group still exists; most of those kids didn't want war in the first place; they were just there to get a better sense of themselves, which is something I can't complain about.

Rupert is all better, but it took six intense months of deprogramming—with a *real* doctor this time, one we picked out of a phone book—until he was able to accept the fact that he was no longer going to Progress, that his days of free living were over. The Council let him off with a slap on the wrist, two hundred hours of community service working with dinosaurs who have contracted Dressler's syndrome and now think they're actually humans, and he seems to be enjoying the responsibility. He's working with Jules now, actually, helping her out with basic procedures, but it's nice that the little pisser's learning a trade, even if it's one with which Ernie is still a mite uncomfortable. But he's always been a searcher, a seeker, and unsure of his place in the world, and despite the steady employment, I expect to hear about another cult he's joined any day now.

True to my word, I did not turn Star Josephson in to the police, nor did I disappoint Minsky. After doing a little research on the Mussolini and its intricate construction—these are not your average libraries I attended, mind you—I obtained a number of pictures, diagrams, and blueprints of the phony phallus and brought them to the greatest accessories designer I know. Within a week, Jules had a nearly perfect Mussolini replica ready and waiting for me, and it didn't cost me a cent—she was so happy with the result, she's already added the Mussolini to her surgical repertoire. Six hours after the news hit the street, there was a waiting list ten months long for one of her new creations, and now I can barely get through to the gal on the phone.

The day after I got Jules's first Mussolini reproduction, I went to see Minsky at his office, told him that I had indeed found Star in Hawaii, snatched the penis from her pocket, dragged her into an alleyway—it's always best to have a shred of truth in these tales—and then, at that point in the story, my voice trailed off, allowing the midget's mind to go wherever it might take him. Imagination is always better than the real thing. Minsky quickly backed away from the gory details, reattached his Mussolini—no idea it was a fake, though I was sweating it through those first few moments—and thanked me for a job well done. I don't think he'll be coming around much anymore.

Ernie and I have been relatively busy; the word of our investigation into the Progressive affair leaked out, and big stories like that always increase your caseload for a few months afterward. So we've been shuffling in and out and barely seeing each other, almost like a husband and wife in a two-income shift-worker family.

But I'm in the office doing some paperwork on a new case Teitelbaum has thrown at us when Ernie comes marching through the door, high on something. I assume it's life, as he hasn't touched a sprig of herb since we got back from Hawaii. He's been seeing Louise again, but just as friends. She's in love with the new husband, the dolt, and even though Ernie's not crazy about the guy, he tolerates the T-Rex's presence in order to be around his one and only love.

"Got us a case," he says affably.

"Cases we got," I reply. "Workers we don't. Sit down, have a drink, fill out some of this crap." I toss a sheaf of papers onto his desk, and they scatter across the surface.

Ernie shakes his head and heads straight for the closet. "No time, no time." He's not sleeping at the office so much anymore, but he still stores certain items here. I watch as he lugs out a set of soft luggage and a heavy wool jacket.

"You going somewhere?" I ask him. "I've barely seen you in two weeks."

"And you can see me after New Year's. I've got an easy way to make us ten grand, no problem." He proceeds to tell me about the murder of a big-time financier in New York, some guy who got offed a few days ago. "Now the McBride family is offering ten thousand bucks plus expenses—Big Apple, can't miss it—with a bonus if we nab the perp. This is an offer I can't pass up."

"And it can't wait an extra day?"

"Sure it can, but—"

"Look," I tell him, feeling more and more like the unappreciated wife with every passing word, "we haven't had any time to talk, to . . . to hang out. All this work is great, but—"

"But what's the point if it's just work?"

"Exactly," I say. "I'm just looking for a few hours here."

Ernie stops, looks at his suitcase, and pointedly throws it back into the closet, where it lands with a heavy thunk. "What the hell," he says. "A bit of fun can't hurt."

I edge my way out from behind the desk before he can change his mind and grab my coat. Ernie dons his hat, and we take our leave of the office, locking the door with the etched words WATSON AND RUBIO, INVESTIGATIONS behind us.

"Interested in a movie?" asks my partner. "Hear they've got a *Land of the Lost* marathon down at the NuArt."

"Seen 'em all," I say as we hit the stairs. "How about a show at the Shangri-La?"

"Thought they closed it."

"They did. But Jules is doing so well with the Mussolini biz, she's got the money to start it up again. Tonight's the opening, and all the girls are in the show—Barbra, Greta, Jane . . ."

Ernie shakes his head. "I dunno, kid. . . . It's not really my bag."

"You'll have a blast," I promise. "Besides, we can just stay for the first few numbers. And Liz Taylor's got quite the crush on you, I heard."

And believe it or not, my dear old partner is blushing. "Sure, kid," he says, barely suppressing a laugh. "Let's hit the Shangri-La. Then it's a quick bite of dinner, and back to work. That good by you?"

We reach my Lincoln—a new Mark VIII, now that the insurance money for the stolen one came through—and I open his door to let him in. "That's fine by me, Ern. That's fine." He's right—you can't live on work alone, but we shouldn't let this fun and frolic thing get outta hand.

Me and Ernie, we've got a hell of a lot more cases left to solve.

ANONYMOUS REX

For my wife, Sabrina,
who is my basil, my cilantro, and my marjoram,
all wrapped into one

And for my parents, Manny and Judi,
whose faith is unending,
and who made me re-wear my socks

Acknowledgments

Thanks, first and foremost, to Barbara Zitwer Alicea, the greatest literary agent in the known universe (and an all-around wonderful person), without whom this book would be in a very different form and still collecting dust on a shelf in my home. And T-Rex-sized thanks to Jonathan Karp, my editor at Random House/Villard, who saw something bright and glittering buried in the tar pits of my novel and helped me to drag it out and clean it off.

Thanks, also, to those who read the book at its inception and were never anything but constructive with their criticism, and to friends and family who were always ready with help and support: Steven Solomon, Alan Cook, Ben Rosner, Julie Sheinblatt, Brett Oberst, Michele Kuhns, Rob Kurzban, Crystal Wright, Beverly Erickson, and Howard Erickson.

*"I have never been hardboiled, but I'm trying.
I'm trying real hard."*

No doubt about it, I've been hitting the basil hard tonight. Half a sprig at the Tar Pit Club, quarter in the bathroom stall, half heading down the 101 on the drive over, two more waiting here in the car, and only now is the buzz crawling on, a muddled high that's got me jumping at my own tail. Scored it fresh tonight, a whole half-pound from Trader Joe's up on La Brea. Gene, the stock clerk, keeps a hidden stash for his special customers, and though it takes the occasional fin or two to stay firmly entrenched on Gene's good side, you haven't truly done basil until you've done Gene's Special Stash basil. Throws out the kind of buzz where you're wishing the high would come on and you're wishing the high would come on and you're wishing the high would come on and then you're there, and you're wondering how the hell it was possible that you ever *weren't* there.

This camera's hanging heavy about my neck, lens cap off, tugging on me, begging for action. It's a Minolta piece of crap I bought for forty bucks, substandard in all specifications, but I can't do snoop work without a camera, and I didn't pull down enough gigs last month to get my good one out of hock. That's why I need this job. That and the mortgage payment. And the car. And the credit cards.

A pair of headlights breaks the darkness, creeping slowly down the street. Flashers, strictly orange. Rent-a-cops. I slouch in my seat. I'm short. I'm not noticed. The car drives past, taillights drowning the peaceful suburbs in a wash of pale crimson.

Inside that house across the way—that one, there, with the manicured lawn, the faux gas-lamp security lights, the pressed concrete driveway—is this month's potential windfall. In the old days, that'd mean a case capable of bringing in anywhere from twenty to fifty thousand dollars by the time Ernie and I threw in fees, expenses, and whatever the hell else crossed our minds as we wrote up the bill. Nowadays it means I'll be lucky to clear nine hundred. My head hurts. I fix up another pinch of basil and chew, chew, chew.

Third day of a three-day tail-and-stakeout operation. Sleeping in the car, eating in rat-infested diners, eyes sore from the strain of picking out details at a distance. For an hour and a half, I've been sitting in my car, waiting for the bedroom lights to click on. It's useless taking pictures of a darkened window, and firsthand personal skinny doesn't make the grade—distraught wives don't give a damn about what a PI sees or what a PI hears. We are persona non grata, big time. They want pictures, and lots of 'em. Some want video. Some want audio. All want proof. So even though I personally witnessed Mr. Ohmsmeyer giggling, cuddling, and generally making cutesy-face with a female who was neither his wife nor a member of his immediate family, and even though my gut tells me that he and the unnamed floozy have been tearing a sexual cyclone through that house for the last ninety minutes, it means crap to Mrs. Ohmsmeyer, my client, until I'm able to grab the shindig on a negative. It'd be my pleasure if they'd just turn on the damn lights.

A halogen pops to life in the living room, silhouettes shimmying into place behind gauzy curtains—now we're cooking. A grope to find the door handle, a simple tug, and suddenly I'm out of the car and stumbling toward the house, my costumed human legs betraying me with every step. Funny how the ground's twisting into knots like that. I stop, catch my balance, lose it again. A nearby tree arrests my fall.

I'm not worried about being seen or heard, but passing out on the front yard in a basil-induced stupor could look bad come morning. Steeling myself, muscles flexed, legs bent ever so slightly, I flounder across the lawn, hurdle a small hedge, and hit the dirt. Mud splatters my pants; it will have to remain there. I have no money for dry cleaning.

Window's a low one, bottom of the frame just above my line of sight. Thin curtains, probably a cotton blend, lousy for photographs. The silhouettes are dancing now, shadowy figures moving back-two-three, left-two-three, and from the muffled sounds of grunts and growls, I'd say they're out of guise and ready for a full night of action.

Lens cap off, pulling focus, setting the frame to get a nice, clean shot. But not too clean—no divorce court's gonna grant a big settlement on the basis of an adultery pic with Ansel Adams composition. The illicit has to look illicit. Maybe a smudge on the print, a casual blur, and always, always in black and white.

Another light, this one in the hallway. Now I'm noticing features, and it's quite clear that the two lovebirds have shed their skins. Unfurled tails snake through the air; exposed claws draw furrows along the wallpaper. Passion is driving the couple to carelessness—I can even make out the female's mammalian guise tossed across the back of the sofa, knitted blond hair flung across the throw pillows, limp human arms dangling like ticker tape over the side. And moving through the hallway now, toward the bedroom, a pair of lumbering shapes both too concerned with libido to hide their natural postures. Gotta get to that bedroom window.

I'm able to make it to my feet before falling back down again, at which point I decide that crawling around to the side of the house might be the best option. There's dirt and mud and grime down here, but it beats elevating my head above my knees. Along the way, I pass a beautifully landscaped garden, and promptly throw up on the begonias. I'm beginning to feel much better.

Bedroom window, a large bay jobbie that is fortunately hidden behind the overgrown branches of a nearby oak. The curtains, though closed, have parted slightly, and it is through this crack that I may just get my best shots. A quick peek—

Mr. Ohmsmeyer, certified public accountant and father to three beautiful Iguanodon children, is fully out of his human guise, tail extended into proper mating position, claws retracted for safety's sake, a full set of razor-sharp chompers tasting the pheromone-stained air. He stands over his lover, an Ornithomimus of average proportions: nice egg sac, thin forelegs, rounded beak, adequate tail. I don't see anything outstanding there, can't comprehend whatever urges are driving Mr. Ohmsmeyer to break his sacred vows of marriage, but maybe it's hard for a lifelong bachelor to understand the passions that overcome married men. Then again, I don't have to understand it; I simply have to photograph it.

The shutter's not as whisper-quiet as I'd like, but with all the noises they're about to start making, it won't make a difference. I click away, eager to grab as many photos as possible—Mrs. Ohmsmeyer agreed to pay for whatever film and developing costs might be incurred during the process of my investigation, and if I'm lucky, she won't realize that she's also picking up the tab for some prints of last year's fishing trip up at Beaver Creek.

A steady rhythm is set—one, two, thrust, pause pause pause, four, five, retract, pause, pause, repeat. Mr. O.'s got a rough,hit-a-home-run-with-every-swing style to his lovemaking that I'm used to seeing with adulterers. There's an urgency to the process, and maybe even a little anger in that hip action. His scaled brown hide scratches roughly against the green Or-nithomimus, and the fragile four-poster bed rocks and creaks with every in-sistent thrust.

They continue. I continue. Click click click.

This set of pictures will represent what I hope is the end of a two-week investigation that was neither particularly easy nor interesting. When Mrs. Ohmsmeyer came to me two weeks ago and laid out the situation, I figured it'd be your basic cheat job, boring as all hell but in and out in three days and maybe I could hold off the creditors for a week. And since she was the first lady to walk in my door since the Council rectification came through, I took the gig on the spot. What she didn't tell me, and what I soon found out, was that Mr. Ohmsmeyer presented a new wrinkle to get around in that he had somehow obtained access to a multitude of human guises, and had no shame in changing them as often as possible. Spare guises are per-mitted in certain situations, of course, but only when ordered from the proper source and with the proper personal ID number. Identity fraud is easy enough in this day and age without dinosaurs changing their appear-ances willy-nilly. Definite Council violation right there, no question, but I'm the last person who's gonna bring Ohmsmeyer up on charges in front of that goddamned organization.

So, sure—I could just stake out the house, place my rump in the car, and watch like a hawk, but who knew where the randy bugger would be throwing it down next? Tracked a guy once who liked to have sex on the girders underneath bridges, of all places, and another who only did it in the bathrooms of the International House of Pancakes. So though a stakeout was an option—and the family home was indeed where I finally ended up—there remained the problem of keeping a bead on Mr. O. But once I decided to trust my nose, my most base of instincts, it all fell into place.

He's got an antiseptic scent, almost grainy, with a touch of lavender riding the edges. Very accountant. Strong, too—I picked up a whiff at two hundred yards. So the next time he tried to pull the switcheroo, it went like this: Into a restaurant dressed as Mr. Ohmsmeyer, out of the restaurant two hours later guised up as an old Asian lady with a walker, but no matter—he left great clouds of pheromones lingering behind like a trail of bread crumbs, and I followed that olfactory path as he led his floozy back to this street, this house, and this bedroom window. Gutsy move on his part, trysting on the home front, but Mrs. Ohmsmeyer and the kids are at her sister's place in Bakersfield for the weekend, so he's safe from direct marital discovery.

Third roll of film spent, and it's almost time to close up shop. Just in time, too, as Mr. Ohmsmeyer's nearing the end of his fun and games; I can feel it in the grunts emanating from the bedroom, growing deeper, harsher, louder. Bass echoes through the house, vibrating the window, the two intertwined dinos flexing before my eyes, and the beat intensifies as the female Ornithomimus begins to howl, lips stretching, reaching for the ceiling, legs locked tight around her lover's tail, that sandpaper hide blushing with blood, sliding from green to purple to a deep mahogany glazed over with excess sweat, Mr. O. panting hard, tongue licking the air, steam rising from his ridged back as he turns his head to the side, teeth parting wide, and begins the last rise, preparing to fully consummate his lust—

A clang, behind me. Metallic. Scraping.

I know that sound. I know that clang. I know that familiar ring of metal on metal and I don't like it one bit. Forgetting my earlier lack of coordination, I leap to my feet and crash through the nearest set of hedges—screw Ohmsmeyer, screw the job—branches breaking as I push through, a crazed adventurer scything his way through the underbrush. Wheeling around, almost losing my balance as I make the turn toward the front of the house, I come to a stop midway between a lawn gnome and the most terrifying sight these eyes have ever seen:

Someone is towing my car.

"Hey!" I call. "Hey, you! Yeah, you!"

The short, squat tow truck driver looks up rapidly, his head seemingly independent of his neck, and cocks a thick eyebrow. I can smell his scent from thirty feet away—rotting veggies and ethyl alcohol, a potent mixture that almost makes my eyes water. Too small for a Triceratops, so he must be a Compy, which should make this conversation frustrating, if nothing else. "Me? Me?" he squawks, the clipped screech tearing at my ears.

"Yeah, you. That's my car. This—this here—it's mine."

"This car?"

"Yes," I say, "this car. I'm not illegally parked. You can't tow it."

"Illegally parked? No, you ain't illegally parked."

I nod furiously, hoping nonverbal cues will help. "Yes, yes, right. There's no red curb, no signs—please, unhook my car—"

"This car here?"

"Yes, right. Yes. That car. The Lincoln. Unhook me and I'll be going."

"It ain't yours." He resumes clamping the winch onto the front axle.

Swinging around to the passenger-side window, I reach in the glove compartment—gum, maps, shaker of dried oregano—and pull out the wrinkled registration. "See? My name, right there." I place the document directly under his eyes, and he studies it for quite some time. Most Compys have literacy problems.

"It ain't yours," he repeats.

I have neither the time nor the inclination to engage this dimwitted dinosaur in a philosophical debate as to the nature of ownership, so it looks like a little intimidation might be in order. "You don't wanna do this," I tell him, leaning into a conspiratorial whisper. "I've got some pretty powerful friends." A bald bluff, but what does a Procompsognathus know, anyhow?

He laughs, the little apefucker, a chicken-cluck guffaw, and shakes his head back and forth. I consider a bit of controlled assault and battery, but I've had enough trouble with the law in recent months without having to add another run-in to the list.

"I know 'bout you," says the Compy. "Least, I know all I gotta know."

"What? You've been—look here—I need this car to work—"

Suddenly, the front door to the house across the street opens up, and Mr. Ohmsmeyer, who must have reguised himself in record time, strides purposefully down the front walk. An impressive display of speed, considering it takes most of us at least ten, fifteen minutes to apply even the most basic human makeup and polysuit. For what it's worth, the D-9 clamp riding beneath the guise across the left side of his chest is unbuckled—I can see it even through his guise—but it's nothing a mammal would ever notice. His eyes dart back and forth, nervous, paranoid, searching the darkened street for any sign of his loving spouse. Perhaps he heard my hasty exit from the bushes; perhaps I interrupted his climax.

"The hell's going on here?" he grumbles, and I'm about to answer when the Compy tow truck driver hands me a sheet of paper. It reads BYRON COLLECTIONS AND REPOSSESSIONS in bold twenty-point type, and lists their phone number and some sample rates. I look up, a host of indignant responses foaming to my lips—

To find that the Compy's already in the truck, revving it up, winching my car into place. I leap for the open cab, claws almost springing forth on their own—and the door slams in my face. The sonofabitch is sneering at me through the glass, his angular features almost daring me to leap in front of the truck, to give my life for the life of my automobile, which in Los Angeles is not unheard of. "You pay the bank," he crows through the closed window, "you get the car." And with a shove of the Compy's scrawny arms, the tow truck hops into first gear, dragging my beloved Lincoln Continental Mark V behind it.

I stare down the street for quite some time after the tow truck's taillights have disappeared into the night.

Ohmsmeyer breaks my reverie. He's staring at my legs, at the mud splattered across my pants. A slow wave of anger carves a wake across his forehead. I grin, attempting to head off any ill will. "I don't suppose I could use your phone?"

"You were in my bushes—"

"Actually, I—"

"You were at the window—"

"There's a technical point here I'd like to make—"

"What the hell's that camera for?"

"No, you're—you're missing the point—"

I don't get any farther before I'm doubled over from a swift hit to my belly. It's a featherweight slap, nothing more, but the combination of the sucker punch and five sprigs of basil has got me woozy and ready to lose the second half of my lunch. Backing away, I hold my hands above my head in half-surrender. It helps the nausea dissipate. Hell, I could fight back—even fully guised I could take this accountant, and without the straps and girdles and buckles on, I could whip the tar outta two and a half Iguanodons—but the night's events have lost their charm, and I'd like to call an end to the festivities.

"Who the hell do you think you are?" he asks, standing over me, ready to deliver another glancing blow. "I can smell you from here. Raptor, right? I've got a good mind to report you to the Council."

"You wouldn't be the first," I say, straightening up again, able to look the fellow in the eye. What the hell—photos'll be developed tomorrow, I might as well give the poor sap a head start on legal matters.

I put out my hand, and to my surprise, the Iguanodon takes it, shakes it. "My name is Vincent Rubio," I say, "and I'm a private investigator working for your wife. And if I were you, Mr. Ohmsmeyer, I'd start looking for a good divorce lawyer."

Silence, as the dinosaur realizes he's been caught, and caught by the best. I shrug, issue a tight smile. But as his brow furrows, I notice that this is not the proper facial expression to register fear, anger, betrayal, or any of the other emotions I expected. This guy's just . . . confused.

"Ohmsmeyer?" he says, comprehension slow to dawn. "Oh, you want Ohmsmeyer? He lives next door."

It is a lovely night out. I choose to walk home. Perhaps I will be mugged.

The window still says WATSON AND RUBIO, PRIVATE INVESTIGATIONS, even though Ernie's been dead for nine months. I don't care. I'm not changing it. Some jerk from the building came by to scrape off the Watson a few weeks after Ernie bid the world farewell, but I ran him off with a broom and a broken rum bottle. Good thing alcohol doesn't affect me, or I'd have been even more upset—it was expensive rum.

The office has that musty-carpet, old-lady, forgot-to-put-the-laundry-in-the-dryer odor that I'm used to smelling every time I return from a marathon stakeout session, which is surprising, considering they repossessed the carpeting two months ago. Still, no matter how well I disinfect before I leave for a trip, those damn bacteria find a way to congregate, divide, and contaminate every square inch of this place, and someday I'm gonna get those little suckers. It hasn't reached the stage of personal vendetta yet, as it's difficult to bear a grudge against one-celled organisms, but I'm trying hard to take it to that next level.

What's more, I forgot to take out the trash before I left, and the place is as cold as a Mesozoic glacier. Seems I left the air on the entire goddamned time, and what that's gonna do to my electric bills I don't even want to think about. I'm just lucky they didn't cut the power altogether; the last time that happened my refrigerator cut out, and the basil turned sour, though I was already on such a high when I started chewing that I didn't realize it until too late. I still get the willies when I think about the nasty trip that brought on.

Speaking of bills, looks like I've become the lucky winner of at least two dozen, each of which is promptly added to the burgeoning heap on the office floor. There's the odd mailer, the coupon for four-room carpet steam cleaning, but that pile's mostly filled with irate missives printed on bright pink slips of paper, wordy legal documents threatening my financial well-being. I'm well past the range of Please Remit Promptly and in-house collection notices. We're talking attorneys and anger here, and it takes a great deal of concentration to pay them no mind. The only good thing about crappy credit is I've stopped receiving countless offers for preapproved Platinum Cards. Or Gold Cards. Or any cards whatsoever.

A blinking light. The office answering machine, once upon a time a useful, even cherished appliance, now taunting me from across the room. I have eight—no, nine—no, ten!—messages and each flash of red tells me I am screwed—blink—screwed—blink—screwed. I suppose I could yank the plug out of the wall, pull off a nice bit of digital euthanasia, but as Ernie always told me, turning away from your demons doesn't make them go away—it only makes it easier for them to bite you in the back.

Unsnapping the buttons hidden beneath the base of my wrist, I take off my guise gloves and allow my claws to snap into place. My long underclaw has begun to turn downward at a distressing angle, and I suppose I should see a manicurist about this, but their fees have become unreasonable recently, and they refuse to barter with me for free investigative work. I reach out and tentatively press Play.

Beep: "Mr. Rubio, this is Simon Dunstan at First National Mortgage. I've sent you a copy of the foreclosure documents from our legal department—" Erase. A trickle of pain lances out across my temple. Instinctively, I walk to the small kitchen set off in the front corner of the office. The refrigerator seems to open by itself, a nice clump of basil waiting for me on the top shelf. I chew.

Beep: "Hey, Vinnie. Charlie." Charlie? I don't know a Charlie. "Remember me?" Actually, no. "We met at the Fossil Fuels Club in Santa Monica, last New Year's." Some vague memory of lights and music and the purest pine needles at which my taste buds have ever had the pleasure to erupt floats through my head. This Charlie—another Velociraptor, maybe? And his job . . . he was a—a— "I work for the *Sentinel,* 'member?" Oh, right. The reporter. As I recall, he left with my date.

"Anyway," he continues, taking up valuable digital space in my answering machine's memory cache, "I thought maybe since we were old buddies and all, you could give me a little scoop on your ouster from the Council. I mean, now that the rectification came out—old time's sake, right buddy?" Bad enough to be a moron, but worse yet to be a dangerous moron. Mentioning the Council or any dinosaur-related topics in a setting where a human could accidentally hear is a strict no-no. I punch Erase and massage my temples. This migraine is taking its own sweet time showing up on my welcome mat, but it's those slow-setting ones that really pack a wallop once they start pounding on the front door.

Beep: Click. A hang-up. I love those—the best kind of message is none at all. They are perfectly, undeniably unreturnable.

Beep: "Hello. Please call American Express at—" Okay, a recording, that's not so bad. They don't really come after you until long after they've exhausted the one-on-one option. Erase.

Beep: "My name is Julie, I'm calling from American Express, looking for a Mr. Vincent Rubio. Please call me as soon as possible—" Damn. Erase.

It goes on like that for three or four more messages, terse, succinct speeches swarming with undercurrents of intimidation. I'm about to throw myself down on the springless sofa in the corner and wrap a ratty pillow around my head like a giant pair of earmuffs when a familiar voice cuts through the litany of vitriol.

Beep: "Vincent, it's Sally. From TruTel." Sally! One of the very few humans I've ever come to grudgingly like, and though she's hampered by her pitiful genetic structure, she's pretty hip to the whole scene. It's not that she knows about us—none of them have the faintest idea of our existence—but she's still one of the less offensive Neanderthals with whom

I've had to interact. "Been a long time, huh? I've got a message . . . a request, I guess, from Mr. Teitelbaum, and he'd—he'd like to see you in the office. Tomorrow." Her register drops, decibels low, clearly whispering into the phone. "I think it's a job, Vincent. I think he's got a case for you."

There's something to think about there, something inherently good about that last bit of news, but too much of my mind is currently taken up with fighting the pain that's decided to take an extended vacation on my synapses. I save the rest of the messages for a time when I'll have either less of an impending headache or a higher blood basil content and stumble toward the sofa. The pain has just begun to radiate out from within the center of my head, taking big, bouncy steps toward my frontal lobes. There's a swinging party going down in my brain, six rock bands and three dance floors, and I'm the only one who hasn't been invited. Standing room only, kids, and stop pounding on the walls. It is time to lie down. It is time to go to sleep.

I dream of a time when I used to be on the Council, of a time when Raymond McBride was just the name of just another dead industrialist, of a time when Ernie hadn't yet been squashed by a runaway taxicab, of a time before I was hooked on the basil and before I was blacklisted from every PI job in town. I dream of a time of productivity, of meaning, of having a reason to get up and greet each morning. I dream of the Vincent Rubio of old.

And then the scene changes, the honeydew days and butterfly skies giving way to a crimson-coated battle working its way through the entire modern dinosaur population, of Stegosaurs and Brontos slugging it out, of Trike horns sliding into Iguanodon sides, of Compys huddling in dark alleys, whining, petrified, and of a woman—a human—standing in the middle of it all, her hair full and wild, her eyes alight with passion and excitement, her fists clenched in titillation of the glorious, blazing corona of violence and fury surrounding her frail body.

I dream that I approach the woman and ask her if she would like me to take her out of this civil war, to take her away from this scene, and that the woman laughs and kisses me on the nose, as if I am a favorite pet or a teddy bear.

I dream that the woman sharpens her fingernails with an emery board, rears back on her haunches, and joins the fray, launching herself into the pile of writhing dinosaur flesh.

eitelbaum is waiting for me the next morning, just as I knew he would be; I can see his hulking silhouette through the glass bricks that make up his outer office wall. He never leaves that oak desk of his, even in the most dire of emergencies—no matter the crisis, the entire employee base is always compelled to convene in that tacky room, filled with the worst that airport gift shops around the world have to offer: a coconut with the Hawaiian islands painted on it. A hand towel bearing the machine-stitched inscription I GOT CLEANED OUT IN VEGAS. An ice cube tray with molds in the shape of the Australian continent. And since there are only two available guest chairs, most of the office staff is forced to sit on the floors, lean against the walls, or try to stand upright during his legendary epic-length speeches. It's all so perfectly demeaning, and I'm sure that's just the way Teitelbaum wants it.

I also wouldn't be surprised to find out that he's permanently wedged into his high-backed leather chair, the big . . . big . . . fatso. But that's neither here nor there, and it's patently unfair of me to criticize a Tyrannosaurus Rex on his weight problems. I'm sure that there's some muscle fiber buried underneath all that flab, and everyone knows that muscle weighs more than fat. Or is it that water weighs less than muscle? Oh, hell—any way you look at it, Teitelbaum's a big ol' chub, and I don't mind saying it twice. Chub!

I've got half a buzz going on, as I figured it wasn't morally right or mentally sound to show up either stone-cold sober or high off my gourd, and this low-grade high suits me quite nicely. The outside world flows by at three-quarter speed, just the proper rate for me to take in all relevant details, omitting and/or ignoring any feelings of hostility. The secretaries in the outer office look up in astonishment as I pass, and I can hear my name echoing in low whispers about the cubicles. I don't mind. It's all swell.

TruTel is the largest private investigation firm in Los Angeles—second largest in California—and, until I fucked up royally, a regular employer of my services. In the days when Ernie was around, we'd often be called in to help on any case that needed an extra helping of tight, confidential snoop work. We got a few jobs that skirted the boundaries of the law, gigs that the company couldn't put on the books, and it paid out real nice. Of course, if you deal with TruTel, you have to deal with Teitelbaum, and that's another matter entirely. He loves to throw out cases to PIs and watch us claw at one another like gamecocks for the right to earn a minuscule commission, but if you want to make your way in this business, sometimes you've even gotta bend over and smile for a T-Rex.

Time to brave the sanctum sanctorum.

"Morning, Mr. Teitelbaum," I say as I enter his office with a false bound in my step and lilt to my voice. "You're looking . . . good. Lost some weight." My legs are in control, my feet are in control, my body is in control.

"You look like crap," Teitelbaum grunts, and motions for me to sit down. I gladly take him up on the offer.

From some of the gossip I heard out in the lobby, the big cheese here at TruTel, whose human guise is a cross between Oliver Hardy and a sentient mound of sweat, has spent the better part of a week engrossed in a new toy that was delivered more than eight days ago, but that he is unable to operate as of yet: Sitting on a corner of Teitelbaum's desk is one of those devices with four metal balls attached to an overhead beam by four strands of fishing line. By pulling out an outside ball and letting it drop against the others, one can witness the miracle of Newtonian physics as the spheres click and clack back and forth for hours on end. Teitelbaum, though, who has most likely never heard of Newton, and perhaps never even heard of physics, is still hard at work trying to figure out the exact machinations of his new plaything. He grumbles at it. He breathes on it. He bats it around with a rough, clumsy swat, his puny arms barely able to reach across the desk.

"'Scuse me—" I say, interrupting this most scientific of procedures. "May I?" Without waiting for a response, I reach out, grasp one of the silver spheres, and drop it into action. The gadget lets loose with a steady clack-clack-clack, echoing about the stillness of the office.

Teitelbaum stares at the balls in awe, clack-clack-clack, his gargantuan jaw gaping wide open, clack-clack-clack. He had a sheep for breakfast; I can make out the fur on his molars. Eventually, the fool regains his composure, even though it's clear he's dying to ask me what miraculous magic I used to start the machine in motion.

"Brought it in from Beijing Airport," he says, evading the issue of his ignorance altogether. "Cathy had some business up Hunan way." Big ol' lie. Cathy is one of Teitelbaum's secretaries, and the only business she ever has—ever, ever, ever—is traveling the world fetching gift-shop trinkets for Mr. Teitelbaum so that he can feel worldly and accomplished without actually having to leave the safety, comfort, and padding of his office chair. And since Teitelbaum puts all of the plane tickets under his name, the poor girl doesn't even rack up any frequent-flyer miles. Cathy's current annual salary (I know, because I snuck a peek at the finance report some years back) is slightly over thirty thousand dollars, and since she's out of town more than five-sixths of the year, Teitelbaum had to hire an additional secretary—that's where Sally comes in—to do all of the actual paperwork that floats in and out of his grimy hands. As a result, Teitelbaum's secretarial bill comes to more than sixty thousand dollars a year, all charged to the firm, which means that his PI hacks have to work that many more hours to pay for the extra overhead. And all so the former homecoming king of Hamilton High can buy souvenirs that he's too stupid to operate. Lord, I hate Tyrannosaurs.

"It's very nice," I assure him. "Shiny." I am glad he's too dumb to know when I am mocking him.

"Got one question for you, Rubio," Teitelbaum growls, leaning back in his chair, his meaty flanks spreading out, spilling over the sides. "You drunk?"

"That's blunt."

"It is. Are you drunk? Are you still hitting the basil?"

"No."

He grunts, sniffs, tries to look me in the eyes. I avert. "Take out your contacts," he says. "Lemme see your real eyes."

I pull back from the desk, begin to stand. "I don't have to listen to this—"

"Siddown, Rubio, siddown. I don't give a good goddamn if you're drunk or not, but you don't got a choice other than to listen to me. I know people at credit departments. I know people at the bank. You got no money left." He seems to relish this little speech; I am not surprised.

"Is there a point?" I ask.

"Point is, I don't gotta have you in here at all!"

"Tell you the truth," I say, "I was a little surprised—"

"You talk too much. Maybe I've got some money for you. Maybe. Maybe I can throw a job your way, God knows why. If—and this is a big if, Rubio—if you're ready for it. If you're not gonna screw it up and screw me over like last time."

On Teitelbaum's desk, a shudder passes through the balls, a metallic buzz, as they slow and die. Teitelbaum fixes me with a hard stare, and I reach over and start them up again for him, apparently one of my new duties as a potential employee. I just hope that starting and restarting this contraption all day isn't the job he's got in mind. The sad thing is, I might take it.

"I'd be very grateful for the opportunity," I tell Teitelbaum, trying to keep the pushpins out of the syrupy drawl of my obsequiousness.

"Sure you would. Eighty hacks around this city'd be grateful for the opportunity. But I didn't hate that Ernie of yours"—and for Teitelbaum, this is tantamount to a declaration of true love—"so I'm gonna cut you this break. Plus, I got no choice. God help me, I got nineteen idiots who call themselves private investigators in this office, and every one of 'em is tied up in some bullshit case or another, dragging out the clock so they can make a few extra bucks. In comes a case with a time limit, and look where I gotta turn—a drunken has-been with a dead-partner complex."

"Thank you?"

"Look, I need assurances here. The last time you went out on a case, you went over the line—"

"It won't be like last time," I interrupt.

"I gotta have assurances. Assurances that what I say goes. No backing out on orders, no screwing around with the cops. I tell you to drop it, you drop it. Are we on the same page here?"

"It won't be like last time," I repeat.

"I'm sure it won't." Now his tone softens imperceptibly from granite to limestone. "I understand how it was for you. Ernie, killed on the job like that. Work with a guy for ten years—"

"Twelve."

"Twelve years, it gets you. I got that. But it was an accident, nothing more, nothing less. The guy got hit by a taxicab, they're all over New York—"

"But Ernie was careful—"

"Don't start that shit again. He was careful, yeah, but not that time. And running around bothering the cops, flapping your lips about crazy conspiracies, doesn't get you any love." He pauses, waits to see if I will speak. I choose not to. "It's over, done with. Kaput." Teitelbaum purses his lips, face screwing up like he's mainlined a lemon. "So what I need to know is, are *you* over it? All of it—Ernie, McBride . . . ?"

"Over it? I mean, I—I'm not—I'm not—they're dead, right? So . . ." No, I want to scream, I'm not over it! How the hell can I be expected to forget about my partner, to let the death of my only friend go down unsolved? I want to tell him that I snooped before and given the chance, I'd snoop again. I want to tell him to damn the Council rectification and damn whatever blacklist I've been put on, that I'll keep searching for Ernie's killer until my last breath wheezes past my lips.

But that was the Vincent Rubio of the last nine months, and anger and resentment haven't gotten that Vincent anything other than sixteen pounds of collection notices, imminent foreclosure, and a costly basil habit. I've got no money, I've got no time, and I've got nobody left to turn to. So I brighten up my best grin and say, "Sure. Sure, I'm over it."

The Tyrannosaur silences the clack-clack-clack of the metal balls with one withered finger and stares me down. "Good. Fine." Silence hisses through the room. "On a related note, you hear about any Council fines?"

"I'm not on the Council anymore, sir." And when I was, Teitelbaum was always pressing me for information. He took it as a major slight that an employee of his held a seat on the Southern California Council, that I had the ability to form policy that would affect his daily life. It was one of those little tidbits that kept me going. "They . . . they voted me out after the New York incidents."

He nods. "I know you're off, they had me testify at the meetings. But you still got friends—"

"Not really," I say. "Not anymore."

"Goddamn it, Rubio, you must have heard something about the fines."

I shrug, shake my head. "The fines . . ."

"On McBride—"

"He's dead."

"On his estate. 'Cause of the human thing."

"The human thing," I echo. I know exactly what he's talking about, but refuse to let on.

"Come on, Rubio," he says, "you were on the Council, you knew what was going on. McBride, having an affair with that . . . that . . ."—his shoulders, if you could call them that, shivering in disgust—"that *human.*"

He's right as rain, but I can't let him know that. Raymond McBride, a Carnotaurus who had burst onto the dino scene out of midwestern obscurity and then risen to great financial standing in a few short years, had indeed engaged in multiple affairs with a series of human women. This is not conjecture; it is fact. We know this from an array of sworn statements given to Council members at official auxiliary hearings, along with ample physical evidence in the form of clandestine photographs clicked off by J&T Enterprises, the largest PI firm in New York and, coincidentally, TruTel's East Coast sister company.

A consummate playboy, McBride had always been known for wooing the females of our species with incredible success despite his intact and lengthy marriage, and the resultant branches of his family tree have been rumored to spread from coast to coast, possibly into Europe. He owned an apartment on Park Avenue, a house on Long Island, and a "cottage" out here in the Pacific Palisades, not to mention the twin casinos in Vegas and Atlantic City. His features, sharp and classically Carnotaur in nature, were masked daily by a team of professional obscurers who knew how to easily make even the most reptilian of dinosaurs appear perfectly human, a task that takes the rest of us countless hours of pain and frustration. Raymond McBride's life was blessed.

No one knows, then, why he chose to delve into another population pool—perhaps he had grown tired of our kind, weary of the egg-laying and endless waiting for a crack in the shell. It is true that he was childless. Perhaps he wanted to sharpen his carnal skills on a different breed of creature. It is true that he was ambitious. Perhaps, as many are inclined to believe, he had developed Dressler's Syndrome, that he thought of himself as truly human and simply couldn't help but be tempted by the pleasures of mammalian flesh. Or maybe he just thought the chicks were cute. Whatever the case, Raymond McBride had broken cardinal rule number one, established since *Homo habilis* first dragged themselves onto the scene: It is absolutely forbidden to mate with a human.

But now he's dead, murdered in his office almost a full year ago, so what the hell's the use in fining the poor guy?

A knock at the door saves me any more questions about McBride or Council meetings of which I no longer have any knowledge. Teitelbaum coughs out a "What?" and Sally pokes her head into the office. She's a mousy little thing, really. Pointed nose, stringy hair, wan complexion. If I didn't know she was a human—no scent, never seen her at any of the dino haunts throughout the city—I'd peg her as a Compy in two seconds flat.

"London on line three," she squeaks. Sally's a great gal, a real hoot to talk to, but in Teitelbaum's presence she shrinks up like a dry sponge.

"Gatwick Gift Shoppe?" asks Teitelbaum, his hands jittering in childlike anticipation. If he weren't so disgusting, I might find it endearing.

"They found the Tower of London toothpicks you wanted." Sally shoots me a quick smile, turns, hops, and flits out of the room, mission accomplished. A surgical strike into the boss's domain: in—out—six seconds! Good for her. I should be so lucky.

Teitelbaum breathes heavily, a ragged paper-shredding growl that trails off into the wheeze of a deflating balloon, and grabs clumsily at his desk phone. "I want two gross," he says, "and send 'em overnight." End of conversation. I'm sure the Brit on the other end is astounded with American courtesy.

An abrupt change in tone now as Teitelbaum moves into business mode. Extending a teensy costumed arm across the expanse of his desk, grunting with the meager exertion, Teitelbaum grabs at a thin file folder. "Now I ain't saying you're gonna be looking for the Hope Diamond or nothing," he says, and flips the folder into my arms. "Just a little legwork, nothing you can't handle. It ain't much, but it pays."

I scan the pages. "Fire investigation?"

"Nightclub in the Valley, lit up Wednesday morning. One of Burke's places."

"Burke?" I ask.

"Donovan Burke. The club owner. Hell, don't you read the magazines, Rubio?"

I shake my head, unwilling to explain that nowadays the price of a single magazine would surely affix me below poverty level once and for all.

"Burke's a big skiddoo on the nightclub scene," Teitelbaum explains. "Had celebrities in and outta that place every day, mostly dinos, a couple of human clientele. Had the place insured up the wazoo, and now they're gonna have to pay off about two million in fire damages. Insurance company wants us to check it out, make sure Burke didn't blow the place 'cause business was lousy."

"Was it?"

"Was it what?"

"Lousy."

"Christ, Rubio," says Teitelbaum, "how the hell should I know? You're the PI here."

"Anybody in the club at the time?"

"Why don't you read the goddamn folder?" he huffs. "Yeah, yeah, lotta people there. Witnesses galore, party in full swing." He takes another swat at his Newtonian balls, a clear signal that my presence is no longer required. I stand.

"Time table?" I ask, and I know the answer—

"A day shorter than usual." Stock reply. He thinks he's being cute.

I try to make the next question sound casual, though it surely is not. "Pay?"

"Insurance company's willing to fork over five grand and expenses. Company takes three grand, leaves two thousand bucks for you."

I shrug. Seems standard to me, at least when it comes to the poverty-level wages most TruTel employees are forced to live on. "But I've got this problem with the pool in my backyard," Teitelbaum continues, "and I need a little spare cash myself. Let's say we split your commission, fifty-fifty." He attempts to grin, a wide shark-toothed smile that ignites in me the most basic urge to leap across the desk and garrote him with the razor-thin wires of his Newtonian balls.

But what choice do I have? One grand's better than nothing, and now with the Ohmsmeyer job busted like skeet, this might be my only chance to fight off foreclosure and eventual bankruptcy. A semblance of pride is in order. Elongating my neck as far as this guise will let it go, I hold my head aloft, clutch the manila folder to my breast, and strut out of the office.

"Don't screw it up, Rubio," he calls after me. "You wanna work again, you won't do your usual half-assed job."

A hard sprig of basil is between my teeth not twelve steps later, and already I'm putting that tyrant of a T-Rex behind me and feeling better about the assignment. Money in the bank, maybe a little respectability, and it won't be long before the other PI firms are itching to contract some glamorous and expensive work out to Watson and Rubio Investigations. Yeah, I'm coming back. I'm on my way up. The Raptor is on a roll.

On my way out the front door, I shoot a congratulatory wink toward a temp receptionist taking down dictation in the vestibule. She recoils from my friendly gesture like a startled rattler and I halfway expect her to bare fangs and slither into a niche beneath her desk.

Six leaves of basil are busily working their special brand of magic through the hills and valleys of my metabolism, and that herbal chill is the only thing that's keeping me from running off this crowded city bus with my hands waving wildly above my head like a chimpanzee. This is the first time I've ever been forced into any form of mass public transportation, and if the meager car-rental allowance Teitelbaum granted to this case will snag me anything nicer than a '74 Pinto, it will be the last. I don't know what died on this bus, but from the tidal wave of scents streaming toward me from the back three rows, I imagine that it was large, that it was ugly, and that it had eaten a good deal of curry in its waning moments of life.

The woman next to me has a strip of tin foil wrapped around her head like a sweatband, and though I don't ask her what the foil is for—it's a policy of mine never to question anyone who clearly has a constitutional right to insanity—she nevertheless feels the need to shout at me that her protective headgear keeps the "terrestrial insects" away from her "moist bits." I nod vigorously and turn toward the window, hoping to squeeze my frame through any opening leading to the rational, outside world. But the window is closed. Locked up tight. A wad of pink chewing gum has hardened over the clasp, and I can almost make out the bacteria dancing on the surface, daring me to try my luck and pluck the rigid mess from its place.

But the basil is coming on stronger now, mellowing the scene, and I lean back against the hard vinyl bus bench, hoping to drown out the cacophony of coughs, of sneezes, of endless rants against society and those damn terrestrial insects. My arms drop away from their protective cross across my chest and fall easily to my sides; I can feel a slight grin tugging at the corners of my lips. Smooth.

I don't know how he did it, but Ernie was a regular supporter of public transportation. That's right—every week, usually on Thursday, at least once in the morning and once at night, my Carnotaur partner parked himself on a street bench and waited for the number 409 to show up and ferry him to and from our office on the west side.

"Keeps you in touch with the people," Ernie used to say to me. "In touch with the good folk." And whereas there is not one good folk on this bus I'd be interested in touching, I believe that he believed. I always believed that he believed.

Ernie.

The last time I saw Ernest J. Watson, PI, was the morning of January the eighth, nearly ten months ago. He was walking out the door, and I was doing my best to ignore his exit. We'd just finished up a particularly petty argument—typical nonsense, the kind of tiffs we'd get into three, four times a week, like an old couple spatting over the husband's tendency to chew his ice, or how the wife babbles endlessly about nothing—that sort of married, been-around-the-block kind of crap.

"I'll call you when I get back from New York," he said to me just before he stepped past the threshold to our office, and I grunted in response. That was it—a grunt. The last thing Ernie ever heard from me was an "eh," and it's only my daily herbal intake that keeps that nagging thought safely on the edges of my brain.

It was a case, of course, that demanded his attention, and here I should say it was a case like any other, but it wasn't. It was big. T-Rex big. Correction: It was Carnotaur big.

Raymond McBride—Carnotaur, connoisseur of human female companionship, and grand exalted mogul of the McBride Corporation, a financial conglomerate specializing in stocks, bonds, mergers, acquisitions, and pretty much any venture that brought in cash by the boatload—had been murdered in his Wall Street office on Christmas Eve, and the dino community was in more of an uproar than usual.

Due to some slipshod investigation by the crack team of forensic docs sent to the scene, it was still undetermined as to whether McBride had been killed by a human or by a fellow dino, so the National Council—a representative conglomeration of the 118 regional councils—took it upon themselves to send in a team of investigators from across the country to do some preliminary work on the case. Dino-on-dino murder will always bring up a Council investigation, no matter the circumstances, and it was imperative that the Council learn, as quickly as possible, which species had committed the crime and, more important, against whom they could levy some massive fines. The Council is always on the lookout to make a quick buck.

"They're offering ten grand to every private dick that takes the case," Ernie told me one Friday morning just after New Year's Day. "Council wants this one wrapped up fast, bigwig like McBride. Wanna know if it's a human who offed him."

I shrugged and waved the suggestion away. "Dino killed him," I said. "No mammal's got the guts to take out a guy rich as that."

Ernie grinned at me then—that stiff-lipped grimace that widened his face by a good three inches—and said, "No such thing as killing a rich man, Vincent. Everybody's poor when they're under the claw."

So Ernie left, I grunted, and three days later he was dead. A traffic accident, they told me. A runaway taxicab, they told me. A hit-and-run and that was the end of that, they told me. I didn't believe a word of it.

I flew to New York the next morning with a brown suitcase full of clothes and another full of basil. I remember very little of the trip. Here are the images that have seen fit to fight their way through a memory shot through with gaping holes of basil blackouts:

A county coroner, the one who worked on both McBride and Ernie, suddenly missing in action. On vacation somewhere in the South Pacific. An assistant, a human, who was neither helpful nor cooperative. A fistfight. Blood, perhaps. Security guards.

A bar. Cilantro. A female, maybe a Diplodocus. A motel room, dank and foul.

A police officer, one of the many detectives who investigated the supposed hit-and-run that took Ernie's life, refusing to answer my questions. Refusing to allow me into his house at three o'clock in the morning. His children, crying. A fistfight. Blood, perhaps. The back of a patrol car.

Another bar. Oregano. Another female, definitely Iguanodon. A motel room, still dank, still foul.

A bank debit card linked to one of the many accounts held by the Southern California Council, in my possession because I was at that time the Velociraptor representative and a member in good standing of the most bureaucratic and hypocritical board of dinosaurs the world has seen since Oliver Cromwell and his cronies—Brontosaurs, to the last—ran rampant through the coffers of the British Empire. A covert withdrawal in the amount of a thousand dollars. Another in the amount of ten thousand. Bribes, in the hope that someone—anyone—would give me a clue about McBride, about Ernie, about their lives and their deaths. More bribes to cover up the first bribes. Useless answers that brought me nothing. Anger. A fistfight. Blood, perhaps. A swarm of police officers.

A judge and a hearing and a dismissal. A plane ticket back to Los Angeles and an armed escort to ensure my departure from the Tri-State area.

Somehow, the Council learned of my creative accounting regarding their bank account and the sizable withdrawals—it wasn't like I was in any state of mind to properly cover it up—and took a vote to boot me off the board. To *rectify* the situation, as the official term goes, and with a single unanimous "Aye" from the Southern California Council members, I had my social standing stripped away from me in the same week as my sobriety, my spotless criminal record, and my best friend. That was the end of my investigation, and the end of my life as a well-heeled, middle-class private investigator working the streets of suburban LA.

If there's one thing I learned from that first week or so last January, it's simply this: It's a long, slow, grueling climb to the middle, but the ride down comes at nothing short of terminal velocity.

The bus rambles on.

Three hours later, the car I rented from a cut-rate agency sputters to a halt in front of the Evolution Club in Studio City, and I say a silent prayer to the automotive gods that the last two miles have all been downhill. This rusted-out warhorse of a 1983 Toyota Camry conked out on me as I was driving up Laurel Canyon, and it took an hour and a half to find someone who would open the door to a total stranger claiming to need a pair of pliers, a length of yarn, and a wire cutter. Turns out I wasn't the only one who'd ever decided to make some on-the-fly additions to this pitiful automobile—one peek into the Camry's engine is like a look into an alternate reality where

children and mental patients are the only ones permitted to become mechanics. Fraying gift ribbon holds together bundles of wires, one of the
cylinders still bears the markings of a Campbell's-soup wrapper, and I'm
pretty darn sure that paper clips do not make for good spark-plug holders. I
simply can't imagine that any of these improvised improvements will hold
up for much longer. With luck, I can squeeze a little more money out of
Teitelbaum and rent a better car soon, as I can foresee the day in the near
future when this little Japanese import will snap beneath the pressure of
jerry-built engine parts and stopgap gas hoses and commit hari-kari, hap-
pily shuffling off its 'motive coil in favor of a less makeshift existence.

And I refuse to take the bus again.

The Evolution Club—gotta be a dino joint, no two ways about it.
We love shit like that, little in-jokes that make us feel oh-so-superior to the
two-legged mammals with whom we grudgingly share dominance over the
earth. My usual haunt is the Fossil Fuels Club in Santa Monica, but
I've logged in some classically blurry early morning hours at the Dinorama,
the Meteor Nightspot, and mid city's very own Tar Pit Club, just to name a
few. The last Council estimate laid the dinosaur community out at about 5
percent of the American population, but I have a hunch we own a dispro-
portionate amount of nightclubs in this country. But hey—when you spend
the majority of your waking hours walking around in human drag, you're going to need a dino-intensive place to unwind at the end of the day, if only to
snap you back into that terrible lizard state of mind.

The rental car complements the new look of the Evolution Club, its
crumbling chassis blending nicely with the charred structural supports of
the fireswept building. "Maybe I should leave you here, old fella," I say,
playfully slapping the car on its trunk. My hand pops through the rust,
punching out a rough hole in the metal. I head inside.

The Evolution Club, so far as I can tell from my vantage point on what
used to be the main dance floor but is now a twisted mess of splintered
laminate, must have been a pretty groovy place once upon a Wednesday
morning. Three levels, each with its own separate bar, flow organically out
of a pair of sweeping Tara-esque staircases, great marble risers disappearing among the shadows. Glitter balls sparkle like distant, dying stars
against the meager daylight that manages to sneak its way in through the
cracked walls, and I can make out a fancy illumination system that, if the

bulbs were replaced, the lenses mended, and the computer control board cleaned of the omnipresent ash, might rival the best Broadway or Picadilly has to offer. Sprawling graffiti art covers the walls, a fantastic mural celebrating the glamour and the glory of unadulterated hedonism throughout the ages.

A hulking refrigeration system lies in ruin, attached to the remnants of what looks to be a walk-in herbidor—I can almost smell the fresh-cut basil and marjoram now, and can only imagine the convenience of walking into that cold, sweet room and taking my pick of any and all substances. Looks like the kind of joint I would have been magnetically attracted to in my younger days, and all my organs are grateful at this moment that I never knew of the club's existence.

As I climb the staircase to the second level, a pinch lances out from my tucked-away tail. I shake my rump, but the pain persists, small and sharp, as if a minnow with shark's teeth has found himself at an all-you-can-eat brunch on my tail and refuses to leave the buffet line. It's my darned G-3 clamp—somehow it has shifted to the left, the metal buckle digging into my hide, and there's no way to rectify the situation other than to completely readjust the entire G series. It's a quick process, simple enough, but would necessitate releasing my tail out into the great wide open for a few precious minutes. If any humans were to come in . . .

But who wanders into burned-out nightclubs at noon on a weekday? Just to be safe, I shuffle up the stairs in a hunchback gallop—the clamp pinching and poking and prodding me all the way—and hop into the relative security of a nearby shadow.

A twist here, a turn there, and pop! the G-1 and G-2 clamps spring open, buckles spinning into the air. My tail swings free of its confines, and I breathe a sigh of relief as the G-3 releases its hold and clangs to the floor. There's a dull throb coming from my nether region, and I can make out the early stages of a bruise where the clamp had nipped my flesh. Now to buckle up again before—

"Somebody in there?" A voice at the nightclub door.

I freeze up. Sweat springs from my pores, instantly cascading my body with rivulets of saltwater. I curse the evolutionary process that brought sweat glands to my species after so many millennia of blissful aridity.

"Private property, buddy. Police scene."

I can't believe this is happening. My hands, thick and clumsy inside their pseudohuman gloves, fumble with the buckles, forcing them rudely into place.

"Hey you! Yeah, you!" comes the call again, filtered past the roar of alarm rushing like tidewater through my brain.

With skill and dexterity somewhere between that of a world-class Olympic athlete and a moderately fit executive-league softball pitcher, I leap into the air and, in one swift move, tuck my tail between my legs, wrapping it up and around my torso. Clamp G-3 slides into place, followed closely behind by G-2. Working furiously now, dressing myself faster than ever before. Buckles buckling—snaps snapping—buttons, knots, zippers, Velcro—the race is on . . .

"You can't be in here." Halfway up the stairs. "No public. You're gonna have to pack it up, pal."

My G-1 clamp is sticking, refusing to budge. It's an older model, sure, but these things are supposed to last, damn it! The last vestiges of my tail are poking out through my open zipper, and even if the person coming up the stairs doesn't recognize it as the tip of a folded dinosaur tail, it looks darned obscene nevertheless. I've done the public indecency rap before, two days in a Cincinnati lockup—don't ask, don't ask—and have no urge to repeat the incident, thank you very much. I shove and push and mush and tuck and—

"Hey, you—yeah, you, in the corner."

Slowly, reluctantly, I turn, ready to lie, ready to chortle and say *pardon my weasel* or *must be my shirt. A tail? Dear God, no! It is for a laugh! A tail on someone as undeniably human as I? How absurd!*

And then the clamps give way. With the sound of a hundred claws tearing across a hundred chalk-caked blackboards, my tail rips free from its confines, cleanly splitting my new Dockers pants in half. Shreds of the comfortable cotton/polyester blend waft through the air.

Slowly, almost luxuriously, the last remaining years of my life flash before my eyes. They begin with this intruder screaming like a spook-house dummy, running down the stairs, out of the building, making an emergency appointment with his psychiatrist, and spilling his guts about the half-man, half-beast that *practically attacked him, by God,* inside the smoking remains of a Studio City nightclub. He's institutionalized (just desserts, I say), but that's no matter. Word gets out about my indiscretion, and I end up lonely and penniless, selling pocket lint on the street corner, formally excommunicated by the Council and ostracized by the dino community for letting out the most classified Secret of all the classified Secrets: our existence.

"Jesus, Rubio," comes the voice again. "With a tail like that, you must get all the chicks."

My eyes focus away from their exaggerated, morbid fantasies and return to the second floor of the Evolution Club, where they alight upon a grinning Sergeant Dan Patterson, longtime detective for the Los Angeles Police Department and one of the greatest all-around Brontosaurs I've ever known.

We embrace, my heart swinging down off its crazy reggae backbeat, rat-a-tat-tatting away inside my chest cavity. "I scare you?" Dan asks, a sly grin curving the corners of his wide lips. His scent, a mélange of extra virgin olive oil and crankshaft grease, is weak today, which probably explains why I didn't smell him as he approached.

"Scare me? Hell, man, I'm a Raptor."

"So I'll ask again: I scare you?"

We tag-team on my recalcitrant tail, alternately taking turns shoving the bad boy this way and that. Dan's taut muscles, evident beneath his guise as a middle-aged African-American, ripple with power as we eventually manage to tuck the critter back into its hiding spot, tightening up the G clamps and strapping on the buckles without causing further injury. I've got a spare pair of pants in the Camry, and so long as the ones I'm wearing don't choose to spontaneously dissolve any more than they already have, I should remain decently outfitted for a few more minutes. I have never known Dan Patterson to be a fashion hawk, and he doesn't seem all that concerned about my current state of half-dress.

"Good to see you, my man," Dan says. "It's been too long."

"I meant to call you . . ." I begin, and then trail off into a wan smile.

Dan puts a meaty gloved hand on my shoulder, squeezing tight. "I understand, man, trust me. How you holding up? You finding work?"

"I'm great," I lie. "I'm doing great." If I tell Dan about my financial situation, he'll offer me money—practically force it upon me, if I know the guy—but I don't go in for handouts, even from the closest of Brontosaurs.

"Listen, you get that watch I sent you, the one—"

"Yeah, yeah I got that. Thanks." A while back, Dan came across a watch that Ernie had accidentally left at his place a month or so before he was killed. After my ignoble return from New York, Dan had the watch messengered over to my house, which I took as Dan's way of saying he was there for me without actually having to say it. It was the greatest consolation I received during the entire affair.

"You investigating for the insurance company?" he asks.

I nod. "Teitelbaum sent me."

"No kidding—you're working for TruTel again?"

"This job, at least. Who knows, maybe there's more in it down the road."

"The good old days, huh? Mr. Teitelbaum. . . . Man, there's a T-Rex I've been trying hard to forget." Dan spent a miserable year and a half working as an outside contractor with TruTel—that's how we met—before he quit the freelance life and joined up with the LAPD, and his run-ins with Teitelbaum were the stuff of legend around the office.

We talk a little more of old times—the Strum case, the Kuhns trial, the Hollywood Boulevard hooker fiasco—don't ask, don't ask—and a little of plans for the future. He's interested in catching some time at Expression, that dino nudist colony up in Montana—hundreds of us, roaming free, unencumbered, baring our natural hides to the warmth of the sun—and though that sort of ego massage sounds like a great way to spend some lazy days, I don't want to tell him that I can't afford any lazy days, much less the cost of a good suntan lotion. "Sounds great," I say. "Make some plans, give me a call."

Eventually, after the conversation of two old friends runs its course, I come back to the matter at hand. "What are you doing up here?" I ask. "Isn't this a little out of your jurisdiction?" Dan usually works out of Rampart division; the San Fernando Valley's far outside his stomping grounds.

"They called in our arson unit," Dan explains. "We give crossover help like this, do it all the time. I'm just here to finish securing the scene; seems I didn't do a good-enough job."

"So," I ask, "whaddaya got for me on the fire?"

"Tired of doing the actual investigating, Mr. Private Investigator?"

"Figure if I can get you to do it for me, I can go home and sleep. Been a long week."

Dan pulls out a faded yellow notepad, mumbling to himself as he flips through the pages. "Lessee. . . . Wednesday morning, 'round 'bout three in the A.M., Fire House Eighteen gets word that the Evolution Club on Ventura is goin' up, and fast. Anonymous caller says there's a big ol' blaze."

"Where'd the call come in from?" I ask.

"Outside source, pay phone. Across the street. Three engines dispatched, along with a fleet of special-service vehicles—ambulances, paramedics, that sorta thing."

"That standard protocol? The whole fleet, I mean?" I whip out my own pen and paper, scribbling down whatever tidbits—obviously important or otherwise—I come across. Never know what you're gonna find.

"Nightclub fire, yeah. Usually it ain't the smoke or the flames that does the damage—it's the patrons scrambling to get out. Gets so everyone turns into a herd of spooked Compys, don't care who they trample on." He licks his fingers, skims the pad again. "The engines arrive, start work on the fire. Patrons are streaming out, they're evacuating left and right . . ."

"Fifty, a hundred, what?" In other words, how many damn witnesses am I going to have to interview?

Dan laughs and shakes his head. "You ain't been to a Valley party in a long time, have you?"

"I try to stay on the west side," I say. "Health's bad enough without me killing my lungs down here in the smog bowl."

"Place like this could pack in four hundred on a good night. Lucky for you—and them, I guess—Wednesday morning's not exactly a club-hopping kinda time. All told, estimates range around one eighty, two hundred."

"Names and numbers?"

"About twenty of 'em."

"Good enough for me."

"Two dead, though—smoke inhalation, we think," says Dan. "One more in critical got caught in the fire—guy who owns the joint, actually."

"Dino, right?"

Dan fixes me with a raised eyebrow. "With a name like the Evolution Club? Come on . . ."

"Kinda shoots down the insurance company's self-inflicted arson theory," I point out. "I mean, if I was gonna torch my own place, I'd sure as hell step out for a bite to eat a good hour before those flames hit."

"You'd think so, right? But my men said it took four of 'em to pry the guy outta the back room. He's half dead, burned like a turkey, and still he's grabbing onto the door frame, putting up a fight. . . . Said they never seen anything like it."

"Like he was protecting something?" I ask.

"Who knows? We didn't find a thing, 'cept a real nice desk chair."

"Lemme guess—he's a Compy, right?"

"Nope—one of your kind. We know them Raptors ain't too bright."

"Least my brain ain't the size of a Ping-Pong ball."

Dan flips me his pad, the papers crackling through the air. "Check it out," he says, pointing to his handwritten notes. "Got these word for word from the attending officer. Witnesses all confirm a loud noise, then smoke. The place starts to clear, the trampling starts, and then a rush of fire from the back just as the firemen arrive."

"Rush of fire, eh? A bomb?"

Dan shakes his head. "We've had inspectors combing the place for the last day, and they can't find explosive traces. But you're on the right track. . . . Here, walk with me." Dan heads down the stairs, and I dutifully follow. The dull ache in my tail is slowly subsiding, and for this I am grateful.

We wend our way past scorched tables and blackened bar stools, every surface covered in a light gray ash. The individual chair backs, I notice, have been carved into the shape of humans at different points along their twisted evolutionary path, each of them wildly caricatured and none of them particularly flattering. *Australopithecus afarensis'* expression of outright stupidity is counterbalanced perfectly by the smug, I'm-running-the-food-chain-now look on the face of *Homo erectus; H. habilis* squats contentedly in a pile of his own feces while the supposedly evolved *H. sapiens* is depicted as a large blubbery mass permanently attached to a big-screen TV. Someone had a bellyful of fun designing this place.

"Look at the spread," says Dan. "Right along the wall here."

I narrow my eyes, squinting in the relative darkness of the club. We're standing far back from the front entrance now, the only available illumination filtering in through a jagged lightning bolt–shaped skylight in the ceiling. But I can see the streaks, vicious skid marks toasted into the walls, and I've been on enough arson jobs to know what it means.

"Blast pattern," I say, and Dan agrees. The long, dark sear tracks emanating like sunbursts from an open doorway lead back to what should be the flash point of the fire. "That the office?" I ask.

"Storage room. Fuse box, too." Dan runs his rough hands along the wall, the cracked, blistered paint peeling to the ground. "Lotsa boxes in there, most of 'em didn't make it through the fire. I got the boys downtown poking through the stuff as we speak."

A weak scent, a familiar scent, wafts through the air—hits me like rancid roast beef, but I've been on enough of these jobs to know better. "Gasoline," I mumble. "You smell that?"

"Yeah, 'course I do. Our chemical guys found some traces, but that's not surprising. They got a generator one room over in case they lose power, and this place here's where they stored the fuel."

Jotting everything down as quickly as possible, I glance back over my notes. Tight letters, strong loops, tall and thin. "You guys got a scenario mocked up already, don't you?" I ask.

"You betcha. LAPD never sleeps."

"Explains all the sugar intake. Okay, lemme guess at this one." I clear my throat and shoot my cuffs, ready to dazzle, or at least mildly impress. "Fire sparks in storage room, smoldering. Probably electrical, fuse box blowing—that's the first noise the witnesses heard. Catches some boxes on fire, holding maybe skin mags, maybe some of that porn from Taiwan."

"Porn from—you got something you wanna tell me, Rubio?"

"Don't stop me now, I'm rolling. So there go the skin magazines, crackle crackle crackle, and half an hour later, clouds are pouring outta the closed office. We got dinos and humans boogying away, and then someone sees the smoke. Rush, rush, rush, trample, trample, trample, everyone clears out, someone calls the fire department. Still just smoke, but a lot of it now. Firemen arrive, lights flashing, siren blasting, big scene, and just as everyone gets outta the joint, ka-BOOM—fire reaches the spare fuel tanks and the place goes up in flames. Freak accident, end of story, everyone goes home and diddles their spouses, 'cept for the two dead guys and the owner up in the hospital."

Dan applauds, and I bow deeply, feeling my girdle stretch under the pressure. "That's pretty much how we have it," Dan admits. "We checked out Donovan Burke's financial records, by the way—"

"The owner, right?"

"Yeah, some playboy hotshot who flew out west a couple years back, set up shop real quick—he's up in intensive at County. We ran a search on him downtown, 'cause we knew you guys'd be snooping around to make sure it wasn't an inside job, but it came up clean. This place was the hottest spot in the Valley—poor sonofabitch was raking it in night after night. Had to hire an extra girl just to count it all."

I know there's a great mystique, an almost sexual allure, to the lone private eye working his case, sludging through the slime-infested streets, digging past the dirtiest of details to finally find his man—hell, I've gotten dates on that premise alone. And in some respects, I actively enjoy that sort of work. Keeps me sharp, on my claws. But when a job's as seemingly cut-and-dried as this one, I like nothing better than to have all the information handed to me by a good friend in local law enforcement. I mean, they have to do it anyway, so why not share the wealth?

Unfortunately, sometimes they miss things.

"You gonna pack it up?" Dan asks as we walk out of the nightclub, heading to my car and a spare pair of Dockers. "Go back to Teitelbaum, give him the info, and tell him where to stick it?"

"I need to keep this job," I remind him. "And my life. Insulting a T-Rex ain't the way to go about it. Anyway, I'm gonna check out a few more leads."

"Look, I'll give you all the witness reports I got. What's left to check out?"

I need a hat to tip, a trench coat to tug, a cigarette to dangle from my lips. Private investigation without props doesn't make the grade. "You said that the anonymous caller to the fire station reported a big blaze at the Evolution Club, right? Those the exact words—big blaze?"

"So far's I know, yeah."

I tap Dan's shirt pocket, my gloved finger rapping against his notebook. "But none of your witnesses actually saw the flames until *after* the fire engines arrived." I pause a moment . . . waiting . . . waiting . . . and then Dan figures it out.

"We got a time conflict here, don't we?" he says.

"Yep we do," I reply, affecting the widest smile in my repertoire, the one that carves a shining half-moon out of my lips. "And you got a bunch more paperwork to fill out."

Dan shakes his head morosely—forms and filing are not the Brontosaur's forte. But he's a trooper, and I know in my heart of hearts that come morning, he'll be hunched over his typewriter, concentrating on detail like a monk illuminating a precious manuscript. "You wanna come back to the house tonight?" he asks. "I'm gonna grill up a few steaks, maybe go wild and do a little oregano seasoning."

A shake of my head, a shuffle back toward the front of the club. Dinner sounds great—steak sounds better—steak and oregano would just about put me through the roof—but I've got work to do. That, and I need a few more hits of basil, pronto. "Sounds great, but I'll have to take you up another time."

"Hot date, eh?" Dan wriggles his eyebrows lasciviously.

I think of the burned Velociraptor up in the hospital, of his perplexing struggle to remain inside a room blistering with heat, with smoke, with a hundred ways to die. Nobody's *that* attached to a desk chair—even Teitelbaum would manage to wriggle his way up and out of the office with five thousand degrees pressing against his back. It stands to reason, then, that Donovan Burke had a reason to stay in that room—a damned good one—and there's only one dino who can tell me what that reason was.

"The hottest," I tell Dan, and make my way out of the nightclub.

Hospitals are a tough gig for anyone, I'll give you that. The last place the sick and dying need to be is around the sick and dying. But for a dino, it's worse. Much worse.

Even after all these millions of years—all these tens of millions of years—of the laboriously slow evolutionary process, we dinos still receive our best information through our schnozzes. Twenty-twenty vision and pin-drop hearing notwithstanding, our main sense is scent, and when we're deprived of the olfactory, it can be quite the debilitating experience. You're not going to find anything on this earth more pathetic than a dino with a head cold. We whine, we sniffle, we complain at the top of our stuffed-up lungs that nothing seems right, that the world has suddenly lost all color, all meaning. The most courageous of us revert into sniveling infancy, toddlers just out of the shell, and those who are pretty sniveling to begin with become downright unapproachable.

A hospital has no smells. None of use, at least, and therein lies the problem. The gallons and gallons of disinfectant slopped along the floors and onto the walls every day make sure that not a solitary odor molecule makes it out of Dodge alive. Sure, it's all in the name of good health, and I can understand where the elimination of bacteria and similar microscopic evildoers might come in handy in fighting off infection and whatnot, but it's a bitch and a half for any dino trying to keep his sanity.

I'm losing it already, and I've barely gotten through the front door.

"I'm here to see Donovan Burke," I tell the thin-lipped nurse, who is busy brooding over a cup of coffee and this morning's—Tuesday's—cross-word puzzle.

"You gotta speak up," she says, a stick of gum smacking rhythmically be-tween her short, blunt teeth. Instinctively, I lean in closer to her pistoning jaws, my nostrils flaring, my brain craving a whiff of Bubblicious, Juicy Fruit, Trident—anything to combat this pervading sense of nothingness.

"Donovan Burke," I repeat, pulling back before she notices me sniffing away at her mouth. "That's Donovan with a D."

The nurse—Jean Fitzsimmons, unless she swapped name tags with someone else this morning—sighs as if I have asked her to perform some task beneath her station such as steel-toe boot licking. She allows the newspaper to flutter out of her hands, and her narrow, birdlike fingers set to tapping away on a nearby keyboard. A computer screen fills with patients' names, their respective ailments, and prices that simply can't be correct. One hundred and sixty-eight dollars for a single shot of antibiotics? For that kind of cash, there had better be some serious street pharmaceuticals in that syringe. Nurse Fitzsimmons notices my gawk and pointedly turns the monitor away from my Peeping Vincent peepers.

"He's on the fifth floor, Ward F," she says, her eyes warily combing down and across my body. "Are you family?"

"Private investigator," I reply, whipping out my ID. It's a nice picture of me in my human guise, from a time when I had the cash and the inclina-tion to keep up my appearance—tailored suit, power tie, eyes glistening, and a wide, friendly smile that betrays none of my sharper teeth. "My name's Vincent Rubio."

"I'll have to—"

"Announce me. I know." Standard protocol. Ward F is a special wing, set up by dino administrators and doctors who designed it so that our kind might have a sanctuary within the confines of a working hospital. There are dino health clinics all over the country, of course, but most major hospitals contain special wards in case one of us should be brought in for emergency treatment, as Mr. Burke was last Wednesday morning.

The official story on Ward F is that it is reserved for patients with "spe-cial needs," a scope of circumstances ranging from religious preferences to round-the-clock bedside care to standard VIP treatment. This is a broad enough definition that it makes it easy for dino administrators to classify all their nonhumans as "special needs" patients, and thus move them and only them onto the ward. All visitors—doctors included—must be announced to the nurses on staff (dinos in disguise, every one), ostensibly for privacy and security, but in actuality in defense against an accidental sighting. It sounds like a risky system, and every once in a while you'll hear some dino raise the roof about the chances that we take, but the whiners never come up with a better solution than the system we have now. As it is, dinosaurs represent a large proportion of the health care industry; respect for medicine and surgery is something all dino parents try to instill within their children, if only because our ancestors spent so many millions of years dying of insignificant bacterial illnesses and minor infections. And with all these dinos becoming doctors, it's easy for them to fill hospital wards—sometimes entire hospitals—with a primarily dinosaur staff.

"You can go up now," says the nurse, and though I'm glad to scoot away from her scowl, that stale gum sure did smell like the finest ambrosia.

As I ride the elevator to the fifth floor, I can only guess at the commotion taking place up there right now. Nurses are scuttling the patients into safe areas, room doors are being closed and bolted. It's like lockdown at County, but without the convicts and much prettier guards. As an unknown entity, I represent a potential threat, and all signs of dinosaur existence must be hidden as best as possible. Cameras and still shots of my approach are of no use; with costumes as realistic as they are these days, there's only one foolproof way of distinguishing a human from a dino in human garb— our smell.

Dinosaurs spew out pheromones like an out-of-control oil well, gushing out gases 24-7-365. The basic dino scent is a sweet one, at least, a fresh stroke of pine on a crisp autumn morning, with just a hint of sour swamp mist thrown in for good measure. As well, each of us has our own individual scent intertwined with the dino odor, an identifying mark roughly equivalent to human fingerprints. I have been told that mine smells like a fine Cuban stogie, half-chewed, half-smoked. Ernie's was like a ream of carbon paper, fresh off the ditto machine; sometimes I think I can still smell him walking by.

But thanks to the layers of makeup, rubber, and polystyrene with which my species is forced to cover up our natural beauty each and every day, it now often takes close quarters—three, four feet—before a dino can be completely sure with which sentient member of the animal kingdom he is dealing. Thus the precautions on Ward F will continue until I am thoroughly checked out, olfactory and otherwise, by the nursing staff.

The elevator doors slide open. I was right—rooms are locked up tight, silence reigns, and the ward is as empty as the last Bay City Rollers concert I went to. Good show, by the way. A solitary nurse lies in wait behind her station, pretending to read a mass-market paperback. She's in the guise of a well-stacked blonde, and even though I'm not attracted to the human female form, hourglass or otherwise, I can tell through the costume that this dino's got one great infrastructure.

Not wanting to cause any further delay, I glide up to the desk, pirouette, and bare the back of my ears, allowing the nurse to get a good snifferoo of my manly, manly scent. Once, in a drunken stupor, I tried this disco spin on a human woman and got slapped as a result, though to this day I still can't figure out exactly what part of the gesture could be construed as obscene.

"He's clean!" calls the nurse, and the room doors fall open in rapid succession, spreading out like dominoes from the center of the ward. Patients spill into the corridors, grumbling as one about the incessant security checks. Beneath flimsy hospital gowns, I can see tails swishing, spikes glistening, claws scratching, and for a brief moment I fantasize about becoming a patient on Ward F, if only so that I might live for a few days in this milieu of personal freedom.

The nurse notices my wistful look. "You gotta be sick to get in," she says.

"I almost wish I were."

"I could break your arm," she jokes, and I politely decline the offer. It would be wonderful—truly, positively magical—to tear free from my girdles and my clamps and lounge around as the Velociraptor that I am for a few days of blithe self-acceptance, but I have to draw the line somewhere, and that somewhere is physical pain.

"I see it all the time," the nurse continues, reading my thoughts. "Gets so we'll do anything just to be ourselves."

"What would you do?" I ask, flipping on my internal flirtation switch. I have a job to take care of, I know, but Burke's not going anywhere, and he can wait a minute or two while I turn up the charm.

The nurse shrugs and leans into the desk. "What would I do? I don't know," she says, raising her eyebrows suggestively. "Breaking an arm can be pretty painful."

"My thoughts exactly."

She thinks, tosses her faux hair across one shoulder. "I could catch a cold."

"Too easy," I say. "And it won't land you in the hospital."

"A really bad cold?"

"You're on to something."

"My goodness, not a disease!" she yelps in mock terror.

"A minor one, perhaps."

"It would have to be curable."

I nod, draw in closer. "Eminently curable." We're inches apart.

The nurse clears her throat seductively, leans in even farther, and says, "There are some pretty benign social diseases running rampant out there."

After I have secured her home phone number, I head toward Burke's semiprivate suite, fourth door down on my left. All manner of patients, undaunted by my presence, shuffle by wordlessly as I saunter down the hall. There are wounds wrapped in bandages, IV bags attached to arms, tails tied up in traction, and everyone is understandably more preoccupied with their own current state of health than the appearance of yet another stranger on an already crowded hospital ward.

The wipe-off placard on the room door bears the names of Mr. Burke and his temporary roommate, one Felipe Suarez, and I poke my head through the open doorway, making sure to plaster a wide smile onto my face. There are two kinds of witnesses in this world: those who respond to smiles, and those who respond to shakedowns. I'm hoping Burke is the first kind, 'cause I don't like to get physical if I don't have to, and I haven't socked anyone for the last nine months; it'd be nice to keep the streak going. Plus, I'd be violating some pretty serious Emily Post rules by browbeating a hospitalized Velociraptor.

But there's no need to worry about that yet—the beds have been cordoned off by pull-along curtains, my only view into the room blocked by a pair of gauzy white sheets lazily flapping back and forth like flags of surrender in the breeze from an overhead fan. An open closet showcases two empty guises strung up on hangers, a pair of deflated human bodies sagging to the disinfected ground.

"Mr. Burke?" I call.

No answer.

"Mr. Burke?"

"He sleeping," comes a drugged-up, drawn-out voice from the left side of the room.

I quietly tiptoe inside, crawling closer to the covered hospital bed. The small silhouette behind the curtain—Mr. Suarez, I assume—emits a grunt like an old Chevy V-8 straining to turn over as he attempts to prop himself up.

"Any idea when he'll wake?" I ask. There is no sound from Burke's side of the room. Not a peep, not a snore.

"Who wake?"

"Mr. Burke. Any idea when he'll wake up?"

"You got chocolate?"

Of course I don't have chocolate. "Sure I got chocolate."

The shadow coughs, scoots higher in the bed. "C'mere," it says. "You pull back curtain, give me chocolate, we talk."

I can't think of a single dinosaur I know who likes the flavor of chocolate. Our taste buds aren't equipped to handle the rich textures of such rough-and-tumble delicacies, and though we've learned over time to ingest all manner of fatty substances, carob and its cousins have never been high on our acquired taste list. Then again, certain dinos will eat anything. With an inkling of what's in store for me (Lord, I hope I'm wrong), I tentatively pull back the curtain . . .

Suarez is a Compy. I knew it. And now I have to converse with the creature. This should take a good six or seven hours.

"So?" he asks, his withered, frail arms slowly spreading wide. "Where chocolate?"

Suarez is uglier than most Compys I've seen, but it's probably a result of whatever illness he's managed to contract. His hide is a mess of speckled greens and yellows, and I can't decide whether or not it's an improvement over his race's usual feces-pile brown. Multiple pockmarks scar his flexible beak, small rotting blemishes that remind me of the antique, moth-ravaged clothing wasting away in my spare closet. And his voice—that voice!—shades of the tow truck driver, with a side of helium ingestion.

"Hey, where chocolate?" he squawks, and I have to suppress an urge to stifle the bearer of those vocal cords with a pillow. It would be so easy.

"Chocolate comes later," I say, slipping farther away from the bed. "First you tell me about Burke."

"Chocolate first."

"You talk first."

The Compy sulks. I stand my ground. He sulks some more. I whistle. He bangs his feeble fists against the bed railing, and I yawn widely, showcasing my excellent dental hygiene.

"Okay," he says, "what you want to know?"

"What time does Burke wake up?" I ask.

"He not wake up."

"I know he's not awake now. I mean how long does he usually sleep?"

"He always sleep."

Enough of this. I reach into my pocket and pretend to grab something approximately Snickers-sized. Holding my (empty) hand aloft, I shrug at Suarez. "Guess you don't get your chocolate," I say. Man, sometimes you gotta treat these schmucks like babies.

"No no no no no!" he screams, a shrill note climbing higher and louder than the greatest alto castrato of them all could ever hope to achieve. Water glasses should be bursting all around the greater metropolitan area.

Once my eardrums have taken down their storm shutters, I lean over toward Burke's bed and perk up my pinnas. Nothing. Not a twitter. And after that precious bit of cacophony . . . well, maybe he really doesn't wake up.

"Are you saying that Burke is in a coma?" I ask Suarez.

"Yep," he says. "Coma. Coma. Chocolate?"

Ah, hell. . . . Why didn't Dan mention this to me when we were at the club?

"Chocolate?"

With no worries that I'll wake my witness, I step across the room and peek behind Donovan Burke's protective curtain. Bad move. The smell of a human Thanksgiving feast comes on strong, the heady scents of smoked ham and roasted turkey slamming into my sinuses. Then I see the bandages, caked in blood—the flesh, rippled and torn from the flames—the sores, the gashes, pus oozing like custard—my eyes glued to the charred husk that this poor Raptor, so similar to myself in size and shape, has become.

Minutes later I come to, my knees wobbly, my hands trembling. Somehow, I have managed to remain upright, and somehow I have managed to close the curtain. Against the gauze now there is only a still, tired shadow that may or may not be the ravaged, comatose body of Donovan Burke. And though I'm glad to be staring at a blank white canvas once again, I find in myself the perverse desire to rip the sheet aside and soak in another look, as if by burning the effects of such an accident into my brain I could prevent it from ever happening to me. But Suarez's insistent whine pulls me from my reverie.

"Chocolate!"

"Does he . . . does he ever talk?" I ask.

"Oh yeah, he talk sometime," says the Compy. "Real loud. Loud loud."

Then he's not in a coma. I choose not to educate Suarez on the distinction. "What he sa—what *does* he say?" The last thing I want out of this adventure is to fall into Compy-speak.

"He call names," Suarez tells me. "He call out Judith, Judith, and then he moan. Real loud."

"Judith?"

"And he call out J.C.!"

"J.C.? Like the initials?"

"Judith, Judith!" Suarez bursts into laughter, spittle drenching his bedsheets. "J.C.! Judith!"

I run a hand through my faux hair, a gesture I picked up when I was just a kid still learning how to act like the consummate human. It is a nonverbal signal intended to indicate frustration, or so I have been told, and I've been unable to purge it from my body-language lexicon. "What else does he say? Go on."

"He cry for Mama sometime," Suarez says beneath his breath, as if revealing the secrets of the ages, "and other time he just cry Judith! Judith!"

I figure now's as good a time as any to start writing this stuff down. *Cries out for Judith* goes right on top, if only because the Compy won't shut up about it. *J.C.* is second, *Mama* is third. So sorry, Mama.

"Has he had any visitors?" I ask.

"I have visitors!" Suarez screeches, and proceeds to showcase the array of three-by-five photos that are scattered about his night table. Some are legitimate pictures of other Compys, small, wiry creatures clearly related to Mr. Felipe Suarez, while others are a tad more suspect—snapshots of good-looking Stegosaurs and Brontos, most likely photo-frame models whose pictures have yet to be removed from their holders.

"That's lovely," I say. "Very nice." I close my eyes, and . . . yep, there it is again, another migraine working its way down the tracks. I take a deep breath and speak slowly. "I want to know if he—Mr. Burke—the Raptor in the bed over there—has had any visitors."

"Oh," says Suarez, blinking rapidly. "Oh."

"You understand?"

"Oh. Yes. Yes."

"Yes he has had visitors, or yes you understand?"

"Yes visitors. One. One visitor."

Finally. "Was it a relative? A friend?"

Suarez cocks his head to one side, like a dog wondering *when are you going to throw the damn Frisbee already,* and a smile comes to a slow boil across his beak.

"Who was it?" I ask. "Did you hear a name?"

"Judith!" he cries, breaking into peals of laughter. "Judith, Judith, Judith!"

I storm out, Suarez's singsong ringing in my ears. Whole trip's been a goddamned waste of time, pretty much the end product of any endeavor in which a Compy is involved. I consider asking my newfound nursing friend—her name is Rita, and she's an Allosaur, va-voom!—for Burke's visitor records. I know she'd do it for me, despite its questionable legality, but I don't want to get her into trouble. At least not yet, not without me, and certainly not sober.

But I give her a little head bob, a catch-you-later nod, as I walk by, and she winks back. "You may want to restrict all chocolates from Mr. Suarez's diet," I suggest, residual anger stemming from the Compy's uselessness breaking through my usual reluctance to cause distress to the infirm. "He's lookin' pretty hyper." I step backward into the elevator.

Rita bites her lower lip—ah Lord, she knows the moves, and it's driving me crazy just to look at the doll—and says, "Are those doctor's orders?"

"Better," I reply. "They're Vincent's orders." The doors slide closed and I congratulate myself on being one smooooth reptile.

Back at the office, I do a fair job bitching at Dan over the phone for not telling me Burke was in such a sorry state and, as a result, generally wasting my afternoon, but my heart's not in it. Despite my dumb little hunches, the Evolution Club fire, tragic though it may be, has all the signs of a true accident, and I'm ready to issue my report, take my thousand bucks from Teitelbaum, and get some much-needed sleep. .

"If it makes you feel any better," Dan says, "I got some background info on the guy. Just picked it up from records. I could fax it over to you."

"Anything interesting?" I ask.

"Birth date, work history, that sorta thing. Nah, nothing interesting."

"Send it over anyway," I say. "Makes the client happy." For the two minutes it takes me to scan the fax, Teitelbaum can charge ten extra minutes to the insurance company; daily rates work on a prorated basis, and the fees are jacked to the sky.

The documents arrive a few moments later, spilling out of the fax machine on six of the eighteen sheets of paper I have left to my name. Most of the furniture has been repossessed, as have the desks, cabinets, and venetian blinds, but I've still got one phone line and one fax machine, remnants of the days when I paid for things in cold, hard cash.

It's the usual claptrap, useless information from which I can glean little or nothing I didn't already know. Donovan Burke, born back east, blah blah blah, parents deceased, blah blah blah, never married, no children, etc., etc., nightclub manager, yadda yadda, last job before Evolution Club was in New York working for—

Oh, my. Now this is interesting.

Last job before Evolution Club was in New York working for the late Raymond McBride. Seems Mr. Burke ran a club for McBride on the Upper West Side called Pangea, then hopped town two years ago, citing "creative differences" with the playboy owner. Within weeks he had found the backing to set himself up in Studio City, certainly not wasting any time in trying his hand at fame and fortune LA style.

Interesting, yes. Useful? Not really.

What is quite the crotch-grabber is this little tidbit, printed unassumingly at the bottom of the page: McBride's wife was the one who was really involved in the day-to-day affairs of the dino mogul's nightclub investments. McBride's wife was the one who worked so closely with Donovan Burke at Pangea. McBride's wife was the one with whom Burke had had his "creative differences," and McBride's wife was the one who sent him packing over three thousand miles away.

Her name, of course, is Judith.

I give Dan a ring and tell him I got the fax.

"Any help?" he asks.

"Nope," I reply. "None at all. Thanks anyway."

My next call is to TruTel's travel agent, and within three hours I'm winging it across the country on a $499 round-trip red-eye, destination Wall Street. Start spreading the news.

The flight is wholly uneventful, but when we land, the human passengers choose to applaud nevertheless, as if they were expecting a different conclusion to the evening's festivities. I have never understood this; the only cause I have ever had to applaud while aboard an airplane was when the flight attendant mistakenly gave me two packs of roasted peanuts instead of my rationed single pack. In retrospect, I should have remained quiet, as my clapping alerted the stewardess to her error, and she took away my extra helping.

Teitelbaum would have me killed and mounted on his wall if he knew my true intentions in coming to the city. I let him know that some leads were pointing back toward New York, requested a company credit card (with a five-thousand-dollar limit, no joke!), and he proceeded to grill me over the phone.

"You gonna stick to this case?"

"Of course," I reassured him. "That's why I'm going out there. For the insurance company."

"No screwing around with that dead partner of yours?"

"Right," I said. "None of that."

But if the case leads to McBride, then naturally, I may have to ask questions regarding McBride's death, and if I have to ask questions about McBride's death, I may stumble across information about one of the initial private investigators on the case, my "dead partner" Ernie. Of course, I don't have to let Teitelbaum know any of it. All he has to know is that the insurance company is forking over even more money for an inflated expense account that now includes a stay in the second most extravagant city in America. Next time I'll just have to hope someone gets killed in Vegas.

I have chosen not to rent a car in the city, a decision that, according to my cabbie, was a wise move. There is a special art to driving through New York, he tells me through an indistinguishable accent, and I gather that the uninitiated should not attempt an excursion on their own. Although the cab driver is a human, he nevertheless has his own special scent, though it is not the fresh stroke of pine on a crisp autumn morning, to say the least.

"Where you want go?" he asks me, and suddenly I feel like I'm dealing with Suarez again. Can no one other than myself speak the language? But he's just a human—a foreigner, probably—and he speaks my native tongue better than I speak his (unless he's from Holland, as my Dutch is practically fluent).

"McBride Building," I say, and he tears into traffic, instantly accelerating to at least ninety miles an hour before he slams on the brakes half a block later. It's a good thing I haven't eaten in a while. We're in Manhattan before he speaks again.

"You business at McBride?" he asks, glancing at me all too often in the rearview mirror. I'd rather he pay a little more attention to the actual operation of his automobile.

"I have some business at the building," I say. "This afternoon."

"He big man, McBride."

"Big man," I echo lamely.

As the cab stutters and stops along the street, flashbacks of my last visit to New York stream before my eyes, a blur of police stations and witnesses, missing evidence and rude rebuffs. And more than a few shopping market produce aisles. New York, if I remember correctly, has some particularly potent marjoram, but their supply of fenugreek is sorely lacking.

With any hard-core investigation comes the requisite accoutrements of the office, and due to my recent financial troubles, I'm light on the proper attire. I consider instructing my cabbie to pull over at the nearest department store, where I could promptly use the TruTel credit card to purchase the needed items, but I doubt such mass-produced items would lend the proper authenticity.

On the corner of Fifty-first and Lexington, I stop the cab at an honest-to-goodness New York millinery and buy a tan and black porkpie hat.

On Thirty-ninth, I buy a trench coat. I get a good deal because it is eighty-three degrees in Manhattan today.

Just below Canal, I buy a package of unfiltered cigarettes, though I do not buy a lighter or matches. These cigs are for dangling, and dangling only.

All decked out now, I renew my request to go to the McBride Building, and we turn in to the financial heart of the city. Minutes later, my destination appears, poking roughly out of the artificial horizon.

The McBride Building, towering symbol of capitalism for the last ten years, stands eighty stories high and a full city block wide, muscling its way through the skyline like an overeager bodybuilder. Reflective glass lines this architectural masterpiece, bright silvery mirrors that suck in the streets of the city and spit them back out again, only in richer, more vibrant colors.

Yeah, okay, it's pretty enough, in a slick/gaudy sorta fashion, though I can't extinguish the thought that in many ways it resembles a monstrous silver-plated condom. I hope this renegade image does not haunt me throughout my interview with Mrs. McBride—that is, if I'm able to arrange one.

Inside, the reflective motif continues, mirrors helping me to follow myself wherever I go. I get a few glimpses of my new look; the trench coat works for me, despite the tropical temperatures that have enveloped the city, and the hat hangs heavily on my head, as if constantly threatening to topple. Humans and dinos whiz by, a blur of smells swinging across the odor spectrum. I catch snatches of conversation, snippets about buyouts and mergers and the pennant race. A bold granite reception booth takes up much of the lobby; through the throng of business-creatures, I can discern the outline of a harried secretary.

"Good morning," I say, hoisting my burgundy garment bag higher onto my shoulder. "I was wondering if Mrs. McBride was available."

With one short, sassy smile, the McBride Building's lobby receptionist proves herself to be both more pleasant and infinitely more frightening than my previous secretarial nemesis, Nurse Fitzsimmons. "You want to see Judith McBride?" she says, the sarcasm crouching behind her teeth, scratching at the enamel, just waiting to spring and pounce.

"As soon as possible," I say.

"And you would have an appointment?"

She knows that I don't. I have a garment bag slung over my shoulder, for god's sake. "Yes, yes, certainly."

"Your name?"

Oh, what the heck. "My name is Donovan Burke."

Do her eyebrows twitch? Do her ears perk up? Or is that my mind singing those golden oldies of paranoia once again? I want to ask her if she knew Ernie, if she ever saw him around, but I silence my tongue before it can do any damage.

The receptionist lifts the reflective handset of her phone and taps out an extension number. "Shirley?" she says. "Guy down here says he has an appointment with Mrs. McBride. No. No. I don't know. He has a suitcase."

"It's a garment bag. I just flew in from the Coast," I mutter. "The other coast." This thing is getting heavier by the millisecond.

"Right, right," says the receptionist, making sure to keep an eye on me as I struggle with my luggage. "Says his name is Donny Burke."

"Donovan Burke. Donovan."

"Oh," she says. "Sorry."

"I get it all the time."

"Donovan Burke," she clarifies for Shirley, and then we both wait for a moment while Shirley checks the appointment book for a name that all three of us know won't be in there. The receptionist beams a capped-tooth tiger smile at me; if she has a Wacko Alert button behind that desk, her hand's getting closer and closer to it.

"I'm sorry, sir," she tells me a few seconds later, "but we don't show an appointment for you." She pointedly hangs the phone on its cradle.

I open my eyes as wide as they will possibly go, affecting my best look of shock and surprise. Then I nod gravely, as if expecting such a turn of events. "Judi, Judi, Judi . . . Judith and I, we've . . . we've had our rough spots. But if you could have Shirley—is that her name, Shirley?—tell Mrs. McBride that I'm in the building, I can assure you that the good lady will see me. We go back."

Another fake smile, another laser look of death. Reluctantly, she lifts the phone. "Shirley, it's me again . . ."

I am shuttled off to wait in a corner while Shirley and the receptionist chat it out. This time, within minutes—seconds, even!—I am approached by the suddenly respectful secretary and told that Mrs. McBride will see me now, sorry for the inconvenience, I will find her offices on the seventy-eighth floor.

High-speed elevator. Love these things. Good thing I don't have eustachian tubes.

On the forty-sixth floor, two dinos in the guise of beefy human secret service guards—black suits, ear mikes, and all—enter the elevator, coming around to flank me on either side. They radiate physical power, and I would not be surprised if either had brought along some sand for the express purpose of kicking it in my face. I suppress a strong urge to engage in isometrics.

"Morning, fellas," I say, tipping my hat. The move tickles me somewhere deep within my archetypal detective conscious, and I resolve to do a lot more hat-tipping.

They do not respond.

"Looking very spiffy in your costumes. Good choices, all around."

Again, no response. Their pheromones—the dark, heavy scent of fermenting oats, brewing yeasts—have already gained control of the elevator, taking as their hostage my own delightful odor.

"If I had to guess," I continue, turning to the behemoth to my left, "and let me warn you, I'm good at this—I'd say that you're an . . . Allosaur, and this li'l tyke over here is a Camptosaur. Am I right or am I right?"

"Quiet." The command is soft. I obey it instantly.

A good word to describe Judith McBride's office—which encompasses the whole of the building's seventy-eighth floor—is "plush." Word of the day, no doubt about it. Plush carpets, plush fabrics, a plush view of the Hudson and distant Staten Island out the floor-to-ceiling windows that comprise the entirety of the structure's exterior walls. If I go to the bathroom, I am sure to discover that they will have found a way to make tap water plush as well, probably via NutraSweet.

"Nice digs," I say to my muscle-bound friends. "A lot like my office, actually . . . in the sense that mine is square, too."

They are not amused. I am not surprised.

"Mr. Burke?" It is Shirley, the infamous Shirley, calling me toward the main office double doors. "Mrs. McBride is waiting."

The guards move to flank the office doors as I enter the inner sanctum, drawing the wide brim of my hat down and across my eyes. The goal is to start out low-key and slowly whip the interview into a nice cappuccino froth, maybe work in a few questions about Ernie for a topping. Light levels are dim, the slatted vertical window shades casting dark prison bars across the carpet. Fortunately, the mirror theme has not been duplicated in this room, so to those random thoughts of *condom building, condom building* I can say adios. Instead, all manner of paintings, sculptures, and objets d'art fill the available wall space, and if I knew anything about the illustrative humanities, I would probably be astounded at the breadth of Mrs. McBride's collection. Might be some Picassos, maybe a few Modiglianis, but as it is, I'm more impressed by the wet bar set off in the far corner.

"I don't have a wet bar in my office," I say to no one in particular. The doors close softly behind me.

"Donovan?" A shadow detaches itself from behind the desk, stands rigidly behind a chair. "Is that really you?" Her voice carries the affected aristocratic lilt of someone who wishes to give the impression of being money-born, of having come from great status through the accident of birth rather than having achieved it.

"Morning, Mrs. McBride."

"My lord . . . Donovan, you . . . you look well." She hasn't moved.

"You seem surprised."

"Of course I'm surprised. I heard about the fire, and . . ." Mrs. McBride is on the move now, arms outstretched, sunlight strobing across her face, coming in for a hug, mayday, mayday.

We embrace, and the guilt sets in. I stiffen. She pulls back and takes a good look at me, soaking in my frame, my features.

She says, "You changed guises."

"In a manner of speaking."

"Black market?"

"What the Council doesn't know . . ." I mutter with practiced indifference.

"I like the old one better," she says. "This one is too . . . too Bogart."

The grin explodes onto my face; I can't help it. Bogart! Wonderful! Not exactly the look I was going for, but darned close enough. But now she's backing away, shooting me sidelong glances, and I have to let the proverbial cat out of the Ziploc.

Slowly, calmly, I spill it all. "Mrs. McBride, I didn't mean to worry you . . . I'm not Donovan Burke." I steel myself for the impending outrage.

None comes. Instead, Judith McBride nods mutely, anxiety welling in those big brown eyes. "Are you the one?" she says, feet backing her body away in a jittery waltz. "Are you the one who killed Raymond?"

Wonderful. Now she thinks I'm her husband's murderer. If she screams, it's all over—I wouldn't lay odds against the notion that those two slabs of dino meat from the elevator are still waiting just outside the door, eager to burst in, beat me into burger, and toss me seventy-eight stories to the bustling street below. I can only hope that my blood and brain matter splatter into a pattern of enough artistic merit to properly complement the building's architecture. Then again, if we can avoid the situation altogether . . .

I gently open my hands to display their lack of weapons. "I'm not a killer, Mrs. McBride. That's not why I'm here."

Relief slides across her features. "I have jewels," she says. "In a safe. I can open it for you."

"I don't want your jewels," I say.

"Money, then—"

"I don't want your money, either." I reach into my jacket; she stiffens, closes her eyes, ready for the bullet or the knife that will send her to meet her husband in dino Valhalla. Why hasn't she screamed yet? No matter. I pull out my ID and toss it at her feet. "My name's Vincent Rubio. I'm a private investigator from Los Angeles."

Anger, frustration, embarrassment—these are but a sampling of the emotions that flit across Judith McBride's face like so many misshapen masks. "You lied to the receptionist," she says.

I nod. "Accurate."

Her composure coming back now, color returning to that middle-aged face. Wrinkles crease her size-seven crow's-feet. She says, "I know people. I could have your license taken away."

"Probably true."

"I could have you thrown out of here in two seconds."

"Definitely true."

"And what makes you think that I won't?"

I shrug. "You tell me."

"I suppose you think that I would be intrigued by all this. That I want to know why you would come in here pretending to be an old business acquaintance."

"Not necessarily," I reply, bending at the waist to retrieve my ID from the shaggy carpet. "Maybe you just don't get a chance to talk much. Maybe you need a chat buddy."

She smiles, a nice turn of her lips that erases ten years from her features. "Do you enjoy detective work, Mr. Rubio?"

"It has its moments," I say.

"Such as?"

"Such as getting to hug beautiful women who think you're someone else." Banter, banter, banter. I love this stuff. It's a game, a contest, and I never lose.

"You read a lot of Hammett, don't you?" she asks.

"Never heard of the guy."

"Rubio . . . Rubio . . ." Mrs. McBride lowers herself into the desk chair. "Sounds familiar." Her fingers twitch, head cocked to one side, as she tries to drag some recollection of my name through the morass of memories surrounding her husband's murder.

"I tried to question you about nine months back."

"About Raymond?"

"About Raymond, and about my partner."

"And what happened?"

"I think I couldn't get an appointment."

"You think?"

"It was a rough week," I explain.

She nods, eyes aslant, and asks, "Who was your partner?"

"His name was Ernie Watson. He was looking into your husband's death when he was killed. Name ring a bell?"

She shakes her head. "Watson . . . Watson . . . I don't believe so."

"Raptor, about five nine, smelled like ditto paper?" I'm starting off on the wrong foot, Ernie's memory taking over my lips, my tongue, asking the questions by themselves, and it takes a Tyrannosean effort to still my tongue.

"I'm sorry, Mr. Rubio. There's nothing more I can say."

We silently examine each other for a moment, feeling out our respective positions. Her scent is strong. Complex. I smell rose petals drifting through a cornfield, chlorine tablets in an orange grove. And there's something else in there that I cannot place, an almost metallic smell that dissolves in and out of her natural odor, tinting it in some implacable direction.

Judith McBride's human guise is attractive enough, pleasant without being too overwhelmingly gorgeous. As a rule, we dinos try not to draw attention to our faux forms by constructing costumes that might prove too enticing to the average human; the potential pitfalls are numerous. I dated an Ornithomimus once who insisted on wearing a knockout disguise— we're talking a 314 on a 10-point scale, curves like a glassblower's experiment gone wrong—and, as a result, ended up as one of the most sought-after bathing suit models in the world. But when a zipper malfunctioned on a bikini shoot in Fiji, the dino community nearly had a full-scale crisis on its hands. Fortunately, the photographer was one of us, and he cleared the set before anyone not of our ilk could notice. The photo shoot continued as scheduled, the incriminating negatives destroyed before they even made it into a darkroom, and the world never knew that beneath that fetching left ankle, so carefully hidden by rocks, seawater, and kelp, was a green three-toed foot scratching wildly at the sand.

"So," says Judith, "I assume this time you came back to talk about my husband's murder."

"And other matters." No need to bring up Donovan Burke at this point. If she wants to talk about McBride's death, I'm more than happy to listen.

"I've already spoken with the police," she says. "Hundreds of times. And a veritable squadron of private detectives, like you, hired by this company or that company. I've signed on my own private investigators, as well."

"And?"

"And they came up empty-handed. All of them."

"What did you tell them?"

She keeps the game alive. "Don't you read the papers?"

"Can't trust everything you read. Why don't you tell me what you told the cops?"

Mrs. McBride inhales deeply and adjusts herself in the wide-backed chair before beginning. "I told them the same thing I told everyone else. That on Christmas morning, I came up to Raymond's office to wrap packages with him. That I found my husband lying facedown, blood pooling, staining the carpet. That I ran, screaming, out of the building. That I woke up an hour later at the police station, unsure of how I got there or what had happened. That I cried for six months straight and only now can I find the strength to reserve it for when I am alone in my bed at night." Her nose twitches; she stops, takes a breath, and holds my gaze. "Does that just about cover your questions, Mr. Rubio?"

This is certainly a moment for condolences if I've ever seen one. I remove my hat, finding yet another use for my newfound accessory, and say, "I'm very sorry about your husband, ma'am. I know how difficult this can be."

She accepts with a curt nod, and I cover my head back up. "They scoured the office," she continues, "they scoured our house. I gave them full run of our financial records—well, most of them, anyway—and still, nothing."

"The investigation . . . stalled, as it were?"

"Dead," she says. "As it were."

"What about the coroner's report?" I ask.

"What about it?"

"Do you have a copy?"

Judith shakes her head, ruffles her blouse. "I assume they have a copy down at the police station."

"I'd hope so. Do you remember anything from the report?"

"Such as?"

"Such as whether or not they decided your husband was killed by an-other dino." This information was never released to the Council—they were "working on it" last I heard before they ousted me from their ranks—and I'm wondering if the geniuses down in forensics were able to piece the info together sometime within the last nine months.

"I don't know what they decided," she says, "but I don't believe that it was a dino attack."

"You think or you know?"

"No one knows, but I am quite positive."

"What makes you so sure?"

"I was told his death was a result of firearms. Does that satisfy you?"

I shrug. "We've been known to carry guns. Capone and Eliot Ness were just two Diplodoci with a grudge to settle, you know that."

"Then allow me a gut instinct. I imagine that those in your profession work off of hunches quite often, yes?"

"When they're justified," I say, "a hunch is indeed a powerful tool."

"Believe what you will, Mr. Rubio." A glance toward a nearby mirror, a primping of the hair. Judith McBride would like to be done with me. "I have a lunch date at noon, did I mention that?"

"Almost done here," I assure her. "A few more moments, please. Did your husband have any enemies? Dinos or otherwise?" I hate this question. Anyone with that much money is bound to have a few, if only for the fact that deep, deep down, no one likes anyone with that much cash.

"Of course he had enemies," Mrs. McBride says. "He was very successful. In this town, that can be dangerous."

Time to pose. I take out a cigarette, flip it toward my waiting mouth. As it flies, slo-mo, spinning toward my lips like an out-of-control bandleader's baton, I realize that for all my fantasizing, I haven't yet practiced this move. The first shot bonks into my nose, and the cigarette drops to the floor. Decidedly nontheatrical. I grin sheepishly and pick it up.

Mrs. McBride frowns. "We don't allow smoking in the McBride Building, Mr. Rubio. An old rule of my husband's that I have seen fit to carry on."

"I'm not going to smoke," I say. Another flip, and this time I catch the cigarette on the edge of my lip. Perfect. I let it dangle. Perfect still.

Mrs. McBride laughs, and another ten years of wrinkles and blemishes vanish into that grin. If I can keep this woman happy, she'll regress into a past life. But that's not my job.

"Tell me about Donovan Burke," I say, and her smile drops away. I watch as she struggles with it, strains at it, pulls and prods and coerces it, but the grin is gone.

"There's nothing to tell."

"I'm not asking for life history, here. I'm just curious about your relationship." I remove a brand-new notepad from my brand-new trench coat and open up a package of brand-new pens. Cigarette still in place, I am ready for action.

"Our relationship?" says Mrs. McBride.

"You and Mr. Burke."

"Do you mean to imply—"

"I don't mean to imply anything."

Judith sighs, a faint huff of air that ends with a tight gerbil squeak. I get a lot of sighs from my witnesses. "He was an employee of my husband's.

Came over to the house for dinner parties, mainly. Once or twice we attended functions with Donovan and Jaycee, sat with them at dinner, that sort of thing."

"Jaycee?" Here's a new name.

"Donovan's fiancée. You did say you were a private investigator, didn't you?"

"Fiancée . . . yes . . ." This must be the J.C. that Burke called out to from within the depths of his coma. J.C., Jaycee . . . close enough. Dan's background sheet on Burke hadn't mentioned any of this. The more contact I have with my pal on the police force, the more I realize what a font of noninformation he has become.

"Jaycee Holden," says Mrs. McBride. "Lovely girl, just darling. She was a Council member, you know."

"Upstate or Metro?"

"Metro." She fishes around the desk for a photo; finding one, she turns it into my line of sight. "This was taken three or four years ago at a fundraiser. It was for a hospital here in the city. Raymond and I had donated a child care center."

"Of course you had." I draw the picture in closer, then hold it at arm's length to wipe away the fuzzies. My eyes aren't what they used to be, and the sprig of basil I downed on the way over has just begun to take effect, exacerbating the problem.

There's Judith, decked out in a light blue dress that would put the sky itself to shame, pearls dancing like clouds about her neck. Raymond McBride, dutiful hubby, is flanked to her right, looking sharp—black tie, diamond studs and cuff links, cummerbund canted like the *Titanic*. These two are instantly familiar; even if I had never met Judith in person, I have scanned my way through enough supermarket tabloids in my time (only while waiting in line, I swear it!) to recognize the wealthy couple in their human guises.

I have never laid eyes on either of their dining partners before, photo reproduction or otherwise, but it is clear that they are deeply in love, or at least in a physical approximation of it. Intense swells of desire stream out from the picture like radiation waves; the glossy surface of the photo steams up the surrounding air. Donovan, the dapper young Raptor, looks a whole heck of a lot better than he did at the hospital, I can tell you that, and my heart dutifully pounds out "Taps" in mourning for my kindred soul. As for his date on that fine evening somewhere in the unreturnable past, she is quite the healthy filly, with a strong back and wide hips. Of course, this could just be a trademark of the guise she's in—like the way that most Nakitara guises have a birthmark on their butts—but I can sense that beneath the costume, her actual body conforms nicely to the polysuit. Auburn hair, shoulder length, frames a face that is cute enough for a guise, nothing to cry over one way or the other.

"Nice couple," I say. "Marriage is so cute."

Mrs. McBride replaces the picture. "Certainly." Then, as if it were an afterthought, though it clearly is not—"Are you married, Mr. Rubio?"

"Lifelong bachelor."

"Does that mean you've been a bachelor all your life or you plan on being a bachelor for the rest of it?"

"The first one, I hope. I'd like to find me a nice female Raptor one of these days. Like Ms. Holden there."

"If you want a Raptor," says Mrs. McBride, her lips twitching as if she'd just ingested a bit of sour wine, "Jaycee Holden wouldn't be your girl. She's a Coleophysis."

This just keeps getting better. "I thought you said they were engaged."

"They were."

"They didn't want kids, then?"

"They did."

I blink. I have forgotten to write all this down—it's bound to come back to haunt me later—but now I'm intrigued. Casually dating members of other dino-races is common, as is marriage if the couple isn't interested in reproducing and furthering the species. But the simple fact is this: mixed dino marriages cannot successfully produce children, and there's no ten ways about it.

This limitation on our reproductive abilities is not a social constraint as it is in the human world, where people argue about the matter to no end—on national television, no less. We are not, as a species, that insufferably priggish. With us it's a simple matter of physiology: A Velociraptor daddy plus a Velociraptor mommy make a litter of Velociraptor babies, while a Velociraptor male plus a Coleophysis female, while it may make for a fun night, will never, ever make a baby Velociphysis. Except . . . except . . .

"Dr. Emil Vallardo?" I ask.

Mrs. McBride is impressed. "You know of his work?"

"I'm on the Southern California Council," I explain. "That is . . . I used to be—"

"Used to be?"

"Rectification."

"Ah. I see."

"It's not what you think," I explain. "I misused some funds, abused a little power." Actually, I misused about twenty thousand worth of funds and a good deal more than that in power, intimidation, and throwing around the reputation of the Council like it was my own weight. But it was all in the name of Ernie, and I'd do it again in a blink.

"So yes," I continue. "I know Vallardo's work."

"He's a good man," she says, and I shrug. The last thing I want to do is get into a philosophical discussion on the nature of interracial children; this is the kind of topic that kills dinner parties in seconds flat, and I can't imagine what it would do to an interview.

"About Mr. Burke—I gather it didn't work out. With him and his fiancée."

After a time, she answers. "No, it didn't. Donovan and Jaycee were no longer a couple well before he left for California."

"Did they break it off because of Dr. Vallardo?"

"I really don't know—I don't think so," she says. "He was there to help them."

"Did he?"

"Help them? I'm not sure. I don't think so. Donovan and Jaycee were very much in love, but infertility can change a couple in ways you can't imagine."

I spin the subject. "Why did Mr. Burke go to California?"

"Again, I don't know."

"Did he have personal problems? Was he into drugs? Gambling?"

Judith sighs again, and I wonder if she's preparing to end our talk. "You ascribe to me a great deal of knowledge, Mr. Rubio. I am rarely able to catalog the ins and outs of my own life—how am I expected to know the details of Donovan's?"

"You were his boss, as I understand it. Bosses notice things."

"I try not to meddle in the personal affairs of my employees."

I should have her give Teitelbaum a call. "I understand there were some . . . creative differences?"

"If you're referring to my working relationship with Mr. Burke, yes, we had some hard times at the Pangea. I felt it was my duty to guard my husband's interests in the nightclub." She's getting uppity now, and I'm back on solid ground. Self-righteous I know how to deal with.

"So you let him go."

"We came to an agreement."

"An agreement that you would let him go."

Judith McBride purses her lips, and the age comes flooding back, wrinkles spotting her cheeks and forehead like engraved cobwebs. Impressive move—she must have one of those new Erickson guises from Sweden, the ones with specialized capillaries for Super Flush Action. "Yes," she says finally. "I fired him."

"I don't mean to upset you."

"You're not."

"Was it an amicable parting?"

"As amicable as a firing can be," she says. "He understood."

Where to go with this next one . . . ? I buzz my lips, pushing them in, out, making noises like an out-of-control popcorn machine. Better to be direct. "Did you and your husband help to set him up in Los Angeles?"

"Whatever would give you that idea?" she asks, a little perturbed.

"He found funding for the Evolution Club awfully quickly."

"Donovan," says Mrs. McBride, "has always been an excellent salesman. He could find funding for a deep-sea fishing company in Kansas." She waves a dainty hand at the multitude of work littering the desk. "I would love to answer more questions, Mr. Rubio, but it's getting late, and as you can see, I still have much to do before lunch. My husband's death has left me in charge of his little empire, and decisions don't get made by themselves."

That's a cue if ever I heard one. I scoot my chair backward, pulling heavy furrows through the shag piling. I used to have a rug like this in my office, long before I was ever faced with the reality that the bank could actually repossess carpeting.

"I may need to question you again," I point out.

"As long as you make an appointment this time," says Mrs. McBride, and I promise her that I will.

At the door, I spin around, having forgotten one last question. "I was wondering if you could tell me where to find Jaycee Holden. I'd like to talk to her."

Mrs. McBride laughs again, but this one does little to erase the signs of aging. If anything, it adds half a decade. "That's a dead-end road, Mr. Rubio," she says.

"Is that a fact?"

"Yes, it is. Don't waste your time."

I shuffle my feet, turn back toward the door. I don't enjoy being told what to do. "If you don't want to tell me where she is, that's fine." I've had my share of reluctant witnesses, though they rarely remain lockjawed for long. "I'm sure I can locate the information elsewhere."

"It's not that I don't want to tell you where she is," Mrs. McBride says. "It's that I can't tell you where she is. I don't know. Nobody does."

This is where the dramatic music comes in.

"She's missing?" I ask.

"For the last few years. She disappeared a month or so after she and Donovan broke it off." She pauses then, a hiccup in her voice. "Lovely girl. Really lovely."

"Well, maybe I can track her down. I'm supposed to be good at that sort of thing. What was her scent?"

"Her scent?"

"Her smell, her pheromones. You'd be surprised how many missing dinos I've nabbed 'cause of their scent. You can guise yourself up however you like, but the smell stays with you. One guy sprayed a stench so strong I tracked him to within a five-block radius ten seconds after I turned off the freeway."

"I . . . I don't know how to explain it," says Mrs. McBride. "It was difficult to describe. Jasmine, wheat, honey, a bit of everything, really."

Not useful. "Last known whereabouts?" I ask.

"Grand Central Station," says Mrs. McBride.

"That's not a home address, I take it."

"She and Donovan had just finished an unsuccessful reconciliation lunch, and he walked her down to the station. Keep in mind this was a while ago . . . I may not be getting this right. From what I remember, Donovan told me that he watched her step off of the escalator and onto an eastbound train platform. They waved good-bye, and a moment later she disappeared into the crowd. Like sugar dissolving in water, he said. There one second, gone the next."

"And that's the last anyone's ever heard of Jaycee Holden?" I ask.

She nods.

Curiouser and curiouser. I thank Judith McBride for her time, her willingness to divulge information, and she sees me out of the office. Do I shake her hand? Do I touch her at all? My usual routine allows for a handshake, but I'm out of my element in all this opulence. She helps me to make up my mind by extending her hand; I grab it, pump, and scurry into the elevator.

I am not shocked when the two bodyguards join me on the sixty-third floor, but this time I'm too busy thinking about my next move to pay much attention to their hulking forms and pungent aroma. They follow me, tracking my every footstep, until I retrieve my garment bag from the information counter and exit the McBride Building through the lobby's revolving door.

Out on the street, I futilely try to hail a cab. I shout, I wave, I yell, and they zip by. Does a light mean they're on duty or off duty? No matter—they're equal opportunity ignorers, and I continue to wait at the curb. I wave money over my head—a twenty, a fifty. The yellow blurs still zoom past. It takes a Bruce Jenner leap into the air to finally catch one's attention, and after I perilously cross two lanes of traffic to enter the taxi, I'm surprised to find that though I have a different cabbie, he miraculously carries the same smell as my old one. Perhaps they, too, constitute a separate species.

We head for City Hall.

6

Public records are a pain in the ass. I'd much rather skirt the boundaries of the law and sneak a peek at some private files than wait in interminable lines in order to talk to a snotty clerk (do they teach these attitudes in receptionist classes?) who may or may not decide to give me the information I need, depending on whether or not he's eaten lunch yet and what phase the moon is in. Give me a locked door and a credit card over the Freedom of Information Act any day. I enjoy my little chicanery; if I wasn't a detective, I'd probably be a fossil-maker, spending day after day in one of the many laboratories scattered deep beneath the Museum of Natural History, coming up with new ways to fake our "extinction" sixty-five million years ago. My maternal great-great-great-uncle was the creator of the first fossilized Iguanodon shoulder blade, placed carefully in a shallow layer of mud in the wilds of Patagonia, and I couldn't be prouder to have him as a part of my lineage. Deception is fun; human deception is a spectator sport.

So maybe later on today I can get in some real snoop-work, but for the moment, I'm stuck sitting in a hard-backed chair originally constructed for the Inquisition, squinting in the darkness of the Records Room at City Hall, and I couldn't be grumpier about it.

Approximately three years ago, Jaycee Holden, according to the documents I am able to procure after five hours of waiting, waiting, and more waiting, pulled a move Houdini would have been proud of. Her name, previously scattered about on credit reports, lease agreements, power bills, court files, Council rosters, and even a few newspaper articles, ceased to appear on any and all documents mere days after she stepped onto that eastbound platform at Grand Central. No funeral was held for the missing Coleophysis, as there was no body, and no actual proof that she was even dead. There was no family to speak of, no one to yell and scream at the authorities to get off their duffs and do something—both parents were deceased, no siblings. Jaycee Holden was an attractive, vivacious young woman who could nevertheless most easily be defined by her association with the Council and her impending marriage to Donovan; such a lifestyle does not readily provide clues to one's disappearance. According to a one-column newspaper article I found in the back of the *Times,* a small but dedicated effort had been made by Donovan and some friends to search for her as a missing person—flyers, milk cartons, etc.—but it was called off after the private investigators they hired came back with a large bill and nothing to show for it.

People vanish. It happens. But no one vanishes this completely. I've tracked missing dinos and humans all my working life, and the one common thread I've found is that no matter how thoroughly their previous existence has been eradicated, the paper trail that has followed them all their lives still clings like barnacles to their personas. Junk mail, for example, will continue to arrive at their residences, imploring them to take advantage of This Amazing Credit Card Offer. Unrelenting TV telethon volunteers will call their last known phone numbers, begging for money to help the children, it's all for the children. And so on. In today's world, where computers can store your personal statistics until long after the last of your great-great-great-grandchildren have taken up residence in the neighborhood retirement home, no one can just dissolve away anymore. No one.

Jaycee Holden dissolved away. Like Judith said, sugar into water. Her name has been stricken from mailing lists, removed from solicitors' files. If I had any idea how to access the Internet, I'm sure I would find that Jaycee Holden had long ago taken the closest off-ramp from the information superhighway. She became a virtual nonentity after that unseasonably warm February afternoon, almost as if she had somehow taken all vestiges of her life with her on her journey into nowhere.

I've heard of stranger things.

On the other hand, McBride's life is all laid out in public record—newspapers, magazines, the works. At least, the last fifteen years of his life; before then, there is a gaping void, but that's not surprising. Most ar-

ticles about the deceased dino mention that he and his wife were originally from Kansas, but none of them elaborated on his life there other
than to say he was orphaned at an early age and was raised by a family
friend. At some point, he met his lovely wife Judith, they moved to New
York, entered the social and business scene, built up a Fortune 500 company specializing in bonds, acquisitions, and the occasional hotspot nightclub, and Wham! a mogul is born. From there on in it's all society pages
and financial records, both of which have the capacity to bore me to tears
within minutes.

I'm heading out of the Records Room at City Hall, eager to grab a quick
bite of dinner at one of New York's luxurious falafel carts, when I come
across a set of stairs leading down to the county morgue. I know this
place—know it too well, perhaps. Nine months ago, this was the spot of my
first altercation with the denizens of New York. I suppose I made some sort
of habit out of pestering the coroner's assistant for information on Ernie's
death, though all I ever got for my trouble was a rude rebuff and a roughing
up by the security guards. I believe there were some threats involved, and
perhaps a physical altercation of some sort. And though the exact details of
those days are hazy—that was around the time when I began the One True
Binge, and my body was filled with so much basil I was practically a walking greenhouse—I'm straighter now than I was then. Only two sprigs of the
stuff today, and one teaspoon of oregano, and I'm ready to ask pertinent,
probing questions in a nonthreatening manner.

"No, no, no—not you again—" whimpers the coroner's assistant, backing away as I stroll through the swinging double doors of the morgue. "I'll
call the guards, so help me, I'll do it."

"Good to see you," I say, holding my hands out in an open, peaceful gesture that works best with canines and some of your dumber humans. No
significant odors coming my way, which means this kid's no dino—with this
kind of fear, the kind that's turning his frail body into a mini-earthquake,
any one of our kind would be shooting off pheromones like a schnauzer in
heat.

"You've got—I've got a number to call, I can have you thrown out—"

"Am I hurting you?"

"Don't—please—"

I slow down, spell it out for him: "Am—I—hurting—you?"

"No."

"No, I'm not," I say. "Am I threatening you?"

"No. Not yet."

"Correct. And I won't. I'm here on official business this time, up and up." I take out the TruTel identification card that I snatched off a receptionist's desk and toss it to the assistant. He falters backward, as if I've just lobbed a grenade in his direction, but eventually he leans over the desk and stares at the card, fingers hovering just above the surface. He seems mollified. Petulant, but mollified.

"You broke my nose," he says. "They had to reset it."

"It looks better," I lie. I can't remember what the old one looked like.

"My girlfriend likes it. She says it makes me look tough."

"Very tough." I certainly don't recall a skirmish involving enough force to break bones, but anything can happen on a basil bender. "No rough stuff this time. Promise. To be honest, I'm looking for your boss again. He can't still be on a vacation." Last time, he split town after Ernie died and stayed split until well after I was thrown out of New York.

"No . . . but he's very busy."

"As are we all. Please, tell him that a private detective would like a few moments of his time, nothing more." I'm trying to be as polite as possible, and the effort is making my teeth itch.

The assistant mulls it over for a while, then wordlessly turns and disappears into a door behind the counter. I'd like to snoop around, open a few file cabinets, but the door swings open once again, as the coroner—bloodstained smock, formaldehyde scent mixing with what must be a natural odor of polished pine and chili paste—steps into the lobby.

"I got a suicide pact back there, three kids up at City College who decided to off themselves by sucking down a couple gallons of JD. It ain't pretty, and it's a rush job."

"I'll speak to the point, then. My name's Vincent Rubio—"

"I know who you are. You're the guy who roughed up Wally last January." Wally looks on from across the room, cringing when his name is mentioned. "Sometimes the kid needs a pop in the head, but I like to be the one doing the popping, you understand?"

"Understood," I answer. "And I've apologized for that. What I'm looking for now are the reports on Raymond McBride and Ernie Watson, both deceased approximately nine months ago. I understand you performed both autopsies—"

"I thought the case was closed."

"It was."

"It *was*?"

"It is. This is unrelated."

The coroner takes a glance at Wally, at the ceiling, at the floor. Decision time. Finally, he motions for me to follow him. We head through the cadaver room and back to his office, a utilitarian space sporting only a small desk, a chair, and three large file cabinets. I stand at the doorway as he unlocks one of the cabinets, blocking its contents from my view. "Close the door, would ya?" he asks, and I dutifully do so. "Don't want the kid to listen in. Like a son to me, but a mammal's still a mammal, if you get my drift."

Two file folders sit on the desk, and the coroner—Dr. Kevin Nadel, from the nameplate on the door—flips through them rapidly. "McBride. Right, it's the same thing I gave everyone else. I counted twenty-eight gunshot wounds to the body, in a number of different places." Small blue spots mark the surface of a smooth human outline, random polka dots spread across the head, the torso, the legs, seemingly without pattern.

I point to a series of numbers scribbled on the autopsy report. "What do those marks mean?"

"Ammunition caliber. Four of the shots were approximately twenty-two-caliber-sized, eight were from a forty-five, three buckshot wounds from a shotgun, two were from a nine-millimeter, and eleven are similar to wounds consistent with an automatic machine gun of some sort."

"Wait a second," I say. "You mean to tell me that McBride was shot twenty-eight different times with five different weapons? That's insane."

"What's insane is not my business. They bring me dead guys, I open 'em up and take a peek and tell 'em what I find." He removes a photograph from the folder and hands it over.

It's McBride, all right, but much less alive than he usually seems in the tabloids. There he is, lying on the floor of his office, splayed out in a spread eagle, and though it's a black-and-white picture, I can make out the individual bloodstains on the floor, on the seat, on the walls. Wounds dot McBride's body, and much like Nadel is saying, they are of varying shapes and sizes, though all look to be projectile-based. A gunshot wound is a gunshot wound, and despite the different ammo sizes, they tend to look alike in these types of pics. I've seen more than my share of similar ones, believe me.

I hand the photo back. "Go on."

"As for your second body . . . I don't recall the case personally, but my notes here say I came to a conclusion that Mr. Watson's death was of an accidental nature, caused by massive head trauma consistent with an auto collision."

"And you have no reason to doubt that?" I ask.

"Should I? As I understand it, there were witnesses on the street who saw the collision. Hit-and-run, I believe."

I say, "I knew Ernie. Mr. Watson. He wasn't the type to—it didn't make any sense, him getting it like that—"

"That's why they call them accidents, Mr. Rubio."

No argument to that, though even after nine long months of investigation, perspiration, and exasperation, Ernie's death still sits strange in my belly. "This is important to me," I tell the coroner. "It's not just business. This man—he was my partner. He was my friend."

"I understand . . ."

"If you're worried about talking to me—"

"I'm not—"

"But if you are, if you're worried for your safety, I can protect you. I can put you in a safe place." This isn't complete crap on my part—TruTel has been known to foot the bill for safe houses if a witness is willing to come forth with information that might bust a case wide open.

And for a moment, it seems like Dr. Nadel is about to say something else. His lips part, he leans forward, and a shine comes to his eyes, the gleam that's always there just before a witness decides to lay it all out for me—and then . . . nothing. "I can't help you any more," he says, eyes downcast. The folders are summarily replaced in the file cabinets and locked up tight. "I'm sorry."

I show myself out.

On those occasions when my brain ceases to function properly—whether I'm daydreaming, sleep-deprived, or, as more recently is the case, drunk off some noxious herb, the rest of my body is more than glad to assume command and direct me wherever it thinks I need to go. Which, I imagine, is how I wind up in Alphabet City, an area of Manhattan near Greenwich Village that is neither quite as trendy nor beneficial to one's health. After I leave the morgue I find myself thinking about McBride, thinking about Burke—thinking about Ernie—and suddenly I'm on autopilot, my feet landing me just outside a dark building with crumbling plaster and a paint-chipped façade. Ah, a familiar locale.

The Worm Hole is a bar-cum-nightclub on Avenue D, owned by Gino and Alan Conti, a couple of Allosaurs who have been known to do some work for the dino Mafia. The front room of the bar is run primarily for mammals, as far as I know, and there's always a steady stream of pitiful clientele, professional drinkers who start tossing it back at noon and don't pass out until nine the next morning.

But past the seedy rest rooms with the DON'T PISS ON THE SEAT signs, behind a false wall covered in graffiti, through a metal door barred with two dead bolts, a chain latch, and a Brontosaur named Skeech, is one of the finest dino bars this side of the Hudson, a joint where a chap can score any sort of vice, herbal or otherwise. I believe I spent a good deal of foggy time here toward the end of my last New York trip, though as I walk inside and take a seat, I realize that I don't recognize a soul in the place. Most are guised up, indistinguishable from mammals on the face of it, but a few brave souls have bared their natural heads and teeth, possibly as a warning to others to stay away and leave them alone.

"Basil, two leaves," I tell the waitress, a Diplodocus who's cut herself a slit down the back of her guise so that her tail sticks out, waving lazily behind her on the floor, sweeping aside the dirt like a broom. The combination of human guise and dino tail is both alluring and forbidden, and, as such, enticing to most of the drugged-out patrons who frequent the bar this time of night. As she passes a group of Raptors, they cackle and reach out to stroke her bare hide, but a slight flick of the tail, a warning whap! with the tip, sends the boys skittering back to their best behavior.

"Vincent? Holy fucking shit, is that Vincent Rubio?" A female, clearly surprised and pleased to see me. Footsteps, and a shadow falls over the table. I convince my head to look up.

"Jesus Christ, it is!" she crows, and even if it weren't for the constant cursing, I would have recognized Glenda Wetzel by her scent, a pleasant mixture of carnations and old baseball gloves. Glenda's a great gal, and it's not that I don't want to see her; it's that right now, I'm not all that interested in seeing anybody.

"Hey Glen," I reply, standing up for the embrace, falling right back into the seat. I motion for her to do likewise.

She pulls out a chair and sits before I get a chance to offer. "Shit, it's been, what . . . a year?"

"Nine months."

"Nine months . . . goddamn. You look good."

"I don't." I'm not in the mood to play make-believe.

"Okay, you don't. But you smell really friggin' good, I'll tell you that much."

We play with idle chitchat until the basil arrives—Glenda giving me worried, sidelong glances as I munch both leaves at once, ingesting the compound in wholesale amounts—and Glenda orders up a half teaspoon of crushed thyme.

"Thyme never did much for me," I say.

"Me neither," she admits. "But everybody's gotta cultivate some habit."

Glenda's a fellow private investigator, a working stiff shelling out her time for J&T Enterprises, TruTel's sister office here in Manhattan. Her boss, Jorgenson, is Teitelbaum's direct analogue, right down to the high blood pressure and subpar social skills. The folks at J&T were the ones who initially investigated the McBride matter for the New York Metropolitan Council, snapping off those infamous photos that were passed around our own Southern California Council meeting like centerfolds in a junior-high locker room. I can still see them now—McBride, in guise, actively mating with a human female, and, from the look on his costumed face, enjoying it immensely. The woman's face had been obscured by a technical photographic process known as Blacking It Out with a Permanent Marker, but body language served to display her emotions quite clearly.

"Shit," says Glenda, easily the most foul-mouthed Hadrosaur I've ever met, "I can't believe this . . . I mean with the last time . . ."

"I know."

". . . after the cops had you thrown on that plane back to LA—"

"Let's not relive it, okay, Glen?"

She nods, abashed. "Right. Right." And her eyes light up again. "Goddamn, it's good to see you! What shitbag you staying in?"

"The Plaza," I tell her, giving my eyebrows a raise. I have yet to check in or make an actual reservation, but I'm sure I can swing a room.

"Look at this guy, he got an expense account, eh?"

"For as long as it lasts." The basil is starting to hit me now, and my nostrils flare out of their own accord. Mood elevating, spirits rising. Glenda's pheromones invade my senses, and I wonder why I never before asked the lady out. She's a Hadrosaur, true, and they're not usually my type, but . . . "Gosh," I gush, "you really smell good. Healthy. Real . . . real healthy."

Laughing, Glenda moves the small ceramic bowl peppered with basil crumbs away from my seat. "That's enough of that shit," she says. "What case you working on?"

"Fire. Out in LA." My words are coming slower now, syllables showing up late at the station though my thought process is right on schedule.

"And some leads brought you back here?"

"McBride. Again."

Her eyes open in surprise. "Oh yeah? Good fucking luck, buddy. Tough nut to crack, right there."

It takes a special concentration of effort to fight past the vines that are growing, spreading, thickening my mouth, but I'm able to stammer out, "You know . . . you know the . . . McBride case?"

"Do I know McBride?" she drawls. "I worked on that goddamn friggin' bastard shitpile of a case for a friggin' month."

"Must have been . . . fascinating."

"Fuck no. Boring as all hell. You ever run surveillance on a goddamn sixth-floor walk-up before?"

"A . . . walk-up?" I don't think these things exist in LA.

"Over a business, no friggin' elevators," she explains. Now I know these things don't exist in LA. Even the poor would faint at the thought. Any distance over twenty feet, vertical or otherwise, must be driven. Preferably with air conditioning. If we want our exercise, we'll use a Stairmaster, thank you very much.

"I mean, the work's okay," she continues. "But lemme tell you—you get pretty goddamned sick of stale air and friggin' take-out food after about the fifth day. And the friggin' goddamned bugs, crawlin' on the floor, on my friggin' food . . ."

"McBride was . . . having affairs . . . in a tenement?" I ask. Can't be—the man had millions, maybe billions.

She shakes her head, picks her nose. This is one classy lady. "Wouldn't call it a tenement, just a shitbag building. Just across the way, in the East Village—it ain't on skid row or anything, just not kept up so nice. Anyway, we was across the street, snapping photos all friggin' day—the building they were screwing in was a little better. The bimbo's place, I think. I bet they had a friggin' exterminator. Goddamn roaches . . ."

Eventually, I work my mouth around enough syllables to steer the conversation toward the human with whom McBride had been photographed in flagrante delicto. I ask for a name. "I give it to you, you can't let it out," she says. "It's my ass on the line. So I didn't tell you this, right?"

"Cross my heart and hope to fossilize."

"We know the little pervert slept all over the city—musta had a frigid wife or something—but that bimbo we caught him with is a real wang-doozer." Is this a curse word with which I am unfamiliar? "Human bombshell, tits out to here, legs like stilts." Why is it that I'm more embarrassed hearing this language than she is using it?

"Her name's Sarah," she continues. "How many friggin' times did I have to hear that on the bug? Oh, Sarah, you're beautiful, Sarah. You're amazing, Sarah. Do it, Sarah, do it. Makes me friggin' ill, something that unnatural. I almost puked once, I tell you."

"Sarah . . . ?" I'm searching for a last name.

"Acton . . . Archton . . . something like that." The Hadrosaur with the muddy mouth shrugs it off and tosses back the last of her thyme. It goes down rough; a few hearty coughs, and she comes up for air. "Screw it. I don't remember exactly, but she sings at a joint up near Times Square. Real friggin' songbird, that one."

In an instant, I'm alert, all traces of basil temporarily banished to some forgotten part of my brain that doesn't deal with speech or decision. "Is she singing tonight?"

"Whadda I look like, her freaking manager?"

"Do you *think* she's singing tonight?"

"Yeah, sure, I guess. It's been a few months since I seen the file, but I think it's a pretty steady gig. What, you wanna go see the human? What the hell for?"

The basil floods back, a mellow rush that melds with my excitement at finding a new witness, a way around the roadblock of missing evidence and cagey answers, a path to McBride, and a path to Ernie.

I lick the bowl of all its remaining morsels and tell Glenda simply, "I wanna hear a song."

7

Two-legged mammals are bad enough by themselves—rude, egocentric, generally sporting bad hygiene—but an entire pack of the filthy apes gives me the willies. It's a visceral reaction, a subconscious tug at my gut that I'm sure is somehow representative of my shared genetic dislike and discomfort. My forefathers watched these creatures evolve from nothing more than hairy toads, and it must have pained them to no end to realize that at some time in the future, they would be forced to recognize the existence of this separate but sentient species. Sure, my ancestors could have killed them off, stomped the little Neanderthals into pâté with a few good whacks of a tail, but by that point they'd already decided to try and live in peace with the humans, even to mimic them if the need arose. Bad move.

Because now I find myself sitting in a human nightclub, surrounded by humans, listening to human caterwauls, smelling human perspiration, *touching* bare human flesh, and if another one rubs up against me, I think I may become ill. Smoke wafts through the air in huge spiraling waves, and though I don't mind the occasional whiff of cigarette, I am almost overcome with the odors emanating from an impressive variety of brands, tars, and filters. A primitive lighting system brightens an otherwise dull stage, set off by a small floor riser and maroon velvet curtain.

"When's it start?" I ask Glenda, who's sipping a gin and tonic. Alcohol slips right through our metabolism like a kid on a water slide, but Glenda's always been one for the When in Rome theory. I ordered a glass of ice water as part of my two-drink minimum, for which I paid enough to cover a day and a half of a good basil binge.

"Bartender said she goes on around ten."

"Good," I say. I can't take much more of this. My garment bag, which is holding up nicely despite the marathon I'm putting it through today, sits on the floor by my feet, wallowing in the filth of a floor stained with the residue of alcohol and vomit.

After a few more minutes enduring the close presence of these slow-witted baboons, I cool down as the lights dim and a single spot strikes the stage. A line of bass notes pumps out of a nearby loudspeaker, a jazzy riff that repeats itself over again with a slightly different beat. Then a rat-a-tat high hat joins in with the buzz of a ride cymbal as the curtains swing wide and a soothing male voice announces, "Ladies and gentlemen, we are proud to present the vocal stylings of Miss Sarah Archer." The show has begun.

A gloved hand, emerald to the elbow, emerges from behind the curtain and snakes its way into the spotlight. Behind it, a long, lithe arm attached to a single bare shoulder waves seductively through the air. A shoe is next, three-inch heels on glittering green pumps, and a leg that, by any human standard, is on the close side of perfect. The crowd leans forward as one, and I can feel a collective breath being held, waiting for the eventual exhale. Now, as if she were there all along, a woman has appeared on the stage, a cascade of fiery red hair falling about her shoulders, across her back, framing a delicate body with ample curves in the proper mammalian positions. Hoots and catcalls momentarily muscle their way through the music, but are silenced almost instantly as soon as Sarah Archer opens her mouth to sing.

It's one of those slow jazzy numbers with a name I can never remember, but her voice is a cascade of molasses that falls all over my body, trickling down into my ears, forcing my eyes closed until I can no longer see the human standing on stage and can instead imagine a gorgeous reptilian beauty to match that contralto. The dino flesh beneath my guise rises into anthills of delight as the warm thrill of the song envelops me. She wants a man to touch her like no man has touched her, I am led to understand by the lyrics, and I have no trouble believing that the songbird means it. A moment later, I force my eyes to snap to attention, and the illusion is gone. It's just another human up there.

A step or two off the stage, a stroll out into the nightclub as she sings, and soon Sarah Archer is sitting at our table, staring past Glenda, trying to catch my eye. I look away. She takes my chin, turning my face toward those pouting lips. I mask my revulsion with the best boredom I can muster and take a sip of my ice water. A playful tug on my shirt sleeve, a wink that's more for the audience than for me, and she's off, back to the stage once again to finish it up.

Applause, whistles, the works. Another number follows, more up-- tempo, and then another, and soon forty-five minutes have passed before Sarah Archer thanks the audience and departs the stage. There are calls for an encore, lighters held aloft, but the stage lights dim, the houselights come back up, and it's all over for the night. Drunks stagger out, forgetting to tip their waitresses.

"There you go," says Glenda. "I told ya. Don't it make you friggin' sick?"

I push my chair back, catching it an instant before it accidentally tips over. My balance is almost too good now that I'm a few hours off my buzz, and I feel the pressing need to pollute my brain chemistry, and quick. "I need to question the singer."

"Now? I was hoping we'd hit Cilantro, this place I know uptown— leaves like you wouldn't believe—"

"No, I need—I'd like to question her now."

Glenda sighs. No one wears down a stubborn Raptor, and she knows it. "Okay. Maybe I can talk to the manager here, get us backstage—"

"You go on, Glen," I say. "I can take this one alone."

She shakes her head. "Forget about it—I'll join you—"

"I can take this one *alone,*" I repeat, and this time the gal swings with my drift.

"I'll see what I can do."

Forty dollars later, after Glenda has arranged a backstage rendezvous for me and then retired to that uptown cilantro bar for the evening, I stand at the entrance to Sarah Archer's dressing room, a frail wooden door upon which someone has spray-painted a ragged gold star. A crate full of old beer bottles sits against the nearby wall, the stench overpowering in the con- fined area. I knock on the door.

"Come in." Her spoken voice is distinctly higher than when she sings; she must take great pains to cultivate the inflections of a smoky chanteuse.

I try the door. It sticks. I try again. Still not working, so I bang at the lock with a closed fist. From within the room, I hear a scuffle, a chair falling over. "Sorry," calls Sarah from the other side. "Sorry about that. I'm trying to get them to fix it—"

The door pops open, and just like that we're staring at one another. She's out of her green dress and into a yellow terry-cloth robe, sash pulled tight across her waist. "You were in the audience," she says.

"Second table in. You sang to me."

"I sing to everyone." She shifts her balance, weight resting heavily on one leg. "Do I know you?"

"I doubt it. I'm from Los Angeles."

She laughs. "Is that supposed to impress me?"

"Does it?"

"No."

"Then . . . no." I pull out my best Jack Webb face and hold out my ID card. "Vincent Rubio. I'm a private detective."

Sarah blows a strong gust of air up and through her hair; she's been down this road before. "Sarah Archer. You don't look like a detective, Detective."

"What do I look like?"

She mulls it over. "A house cat." And with that, she turns and slinks into her dressing room, leaving the door ajar. As per the script, I follow.

Closing the door behind me, I ask, "You knew Raymond McBride?"

"You get right down to business."

"Why mince words? How long did you know him?"

"I didn't say I did."

"Did you?"

"Yes," she says. "But I like to do things in order." Sarah walks to the wet bar set into a niche in the far wall—why does everyone in this town have a wet bar?—and pours herself half a tumbler of Johnnie Walker Black. "Drink?"

I decline, as Sarah kicks off her slippers—lime green, no more than size four—and curls up on a plush green sofa. There are small tears in the cushions, minor eruptions of foam stuffing, but, as a whole, the furniture is in decent condition. A single dressing mirror with three broken lights teeters above a simple wooden makeup table. Polaroids of the singer wearing an array of different hairstyles are tacked to the wall. "Did you enjoy the show?" she asks me.

"Entertaining. You have a beautiful voice."

A smirk, a sip of her drink. She tosses her hair, presumably in a human attempt to be seductive. "And the rest of me?"

"The rest of you has a beautiful voice, too."

"That's cute."

Now it's my turn to smirk. "McBride. How long did you know him?"

A pout from Ms. Archer; I can tell she wants to carry on the banter, and though I'm not usually one to shirk away from a good game of verbal volleyball, I'd like to expedite matters. Already I can feel my allergies acting up from all the mammal sweat dampening the nightclub air. "About two, three years, I guess."

"How did you meet?"

"At a fund-raiser."

"For . . . ?"

"I have no idea. Cancer, leukemia, the arts, I really don't know."

I mutter noncommittally. "And you were his . . . mistress?"

The shock I expected at my blunt question does not materialize. "I prefer the term *lover*."

"You know he was married."

Sarah flinches, eyes narrowing. She crunches on a piece of ice, lips pursing tight. "Yes, I knew he was married."

"Then you were McBride's mistress. When did you two start screwing?"

"That's a charming phrase, Mr. Rubio."

"I'm a detective, not a poet."

"And you could use a course in manners. This is my dressing room at my place of business. I am more than glad to invite you in for a drink and a chat, but if the conversation is going to take on overtones of . . . of vulgarity, then I may have to ask you to leave."

Pushed it too far—I have a tendency to do this. Come to think of it, this is precisely what got me thrown out of New York and the rest of society nine months ago. I back off, and, as a show of my willingness to exercise social graces, I remove my hat and place it on a nearby table.

Sarah smiles, and all is right once again. Her drink has fallen to dangerously low levels, and she licks the rim of the glass with a long, strong tongue snaking out between a set of blazingly white teeth. Patting the sofa cushion next to her, she says, "Come, sit. I can't stand talking to a man unless I can look into his eyes."

A knot has formed in my throat, and I'm hoping she'll offer me another drink so that I may wash it down. "I can see you fine from here," I say.

"But I can't see you. Nearsighted."

Reluctantly, I place myself on the couch as far away from the witness as possible, but Sarah Archer clearly has other ideas. She swings her legs up and around, depositing them in my lap. Her pedicure is recent, her toenails a bright purple hue. "Now, you must understand, this is difficult for me, talking about Raymond. I may not have been his . . . wife . . ."—and once again, that quinine sneer of the lips—"but we were quite close. Even for a 'mistress.'"

"I understand. I don't mean to upset you—"

"Hasn't the case been closed already?"

"So everyone tells me."

"But?"

"But I don't take my cues from everyone."

Pointing her toes at my chest like a ballerina, Sarah says, "Can you imagine what it's like to stand onstage in three-inch heels for an hour? It's hell on the feet, Mr. Rubio."

"I imagine." Time to press on. "Did you ever meet a man named Donovan Burke?"

"This is the point in our relationship where you're supposed to ask me if I want a foot massage."

"Our relationship?"

"Come on. Ask me."

"I'd like to ask you some more pertinent questions," I say.

"And I'll be more than happy to answer them." She stretches her toes, her legs, and her toned calf muscles catch my eye. Not enticing. "Once you agree to massage my feet."

Clearly, I have no choice in the matter. She could, indeed, throw me out at any moment, and extra questions notwithstanding, I would be lying if I said that I was not enjoying the banter of this interview on some level. A vigorous foot rub begins. The dainty feet I hold between my hands are firm, yet smooth, and though my sense of touch is dampened by the gloves I am forced to wear in order to cover my claws, I am unable to detect a single callused inch. "Back to the question at hand—did you ever meet a man named Dono-van Burke?"

"I don't believe so. That's good—right there, on the heel—yes, that's it—"

"Did you ever go to the Pangea nightclub?"

"Sure I did—that was Raymond's place." She sits up slightly, bemused grin, as if remembering a long-forgotten fact. "Actually, I sang there once. New Year's Eve, I think. I did a holiday medley."

"Donovan Burke was the manager of the Pangea."

Sarah spits a chunk of ice back into the tumbler, eyes suddenly averted from my gaze. "Right."

"So I'll ask you again—did you ever meet a man named Donovan Burke?"

"I guess . . . I guess I must have."

"You must have."

"If he was the manager, then I must have. But I don't remember. Ray-mond had a lot of people on payroll. Managers, trainers, bodyguards—even detectives, like you."

I shake my head. "There are no detectives like me."

"I wouldn't be so sure about that. There was another private detective from LA a few months back who was more than happy to give me the time of day—"

Up in half a heartbeat, I'm standing over Sarah Archer, pulse racing, blood running wild laps through my veins. I think I've scared the poor girl, as she sinks down into the sofa like a woman caught in quicksand. "What was his name? Where did you see him? When did you see him?"

"I—I—I don't remember," she stammers.

"Was his name Ernie? Ernie Watson?"

"Maybe—"

"Maybe . . . or yes?"

"It might have been," she says. I've got her backpedaling, nervous, and though I've got no reason to browbeat this witness, at least she's not coming on to me now. "He was about your height. . . . Older, nice-looking."

"How long ago did you see him?"

"It was after Raymond died . . . January?"

Time scale's right—Ernie was killed in early January, only a few days into the McBride case. "What did he ask you about?"

"Not much," says Sarah. "We'd only talked briefly, and he told me he'd call later. He gave me a card, a local number to call him . . ." She leans toward a nearby nightstand—robe falling open slightly, exposing a flash of pale, naked skin—and searches through a small handbag. A moment later, she produces a small business card, and sits upright. The robe closes. I wasn't looking, anyway.

It's a standard business card from J&T, Glenda's firm. Sometimes Tru-Tel employees use J&T as a home base of operations during their stays in New York; Ernie must have done the same. This may mean that his notes, previously unfound, might be discovered with a diligent search. I make a note on my cerebral yellow pad to call Glenda as soon as possible and have her check it out. "Did you ever try the number?" I ask.

"I didn't get the chance," says Sarah. "And I think he was planning on coming back to see me—to ask me more questions, I guess. But I never saw him again."

I am unable to keep a hitch out of my voice, but valiantly attempt to cover it with a cough. "He died," I say simply.

Only concern and surprise on her face. "I'm sorry."

"He was hit by a taxi."

"I'm sorry," she repeats. "At least it was quick."

Our conversation is interrupted by a rapid series of knocks at the door. Sarah looks at me—"Must be the stage manager," she says—I look back—and before either of us can respond, a letter slides under the door, skittering across the wooden floor like an albino spider, bonking into my penny loafers before slowing to a halt. Sarah's name has been scrawled across the top in a shaky, palsied script, as if scribbled there by a third-grader unsure of how to compose his cursive letters.

I reach down to retrieve it, and—

"Don't!" Something in her voice I haven't heard before, something on the other edge of fear. If she were a dino, I'd know immediately—the scent would give it away.

"I was just going to get it for—"

"I've got it," she says. "I'd rather choose when a man bends over for me, thank you." But despite the quip, Sarah's demeanor has taken on a darker tone. Her feet drag behind her as if manacled, and I can see her teeth working over and around her lips, biting down, leaving marks, almost drawing blood. Knees bending slowly, body reluctantly following, she crouches to the floor and gingerly lifts the envelope, running her fingers over the dark black scribbles that spell out her name.

"Something's wrong," I say, half question, half statement.

She shakes her head, grits her teeth. "No . . . no. Everything's okay." Her temples pulse. "I'm very tired, Mr. Rubio. Perhaps we could continue this at some other time."

I offer to make her a drink, to fetch a bottle of wine from the bar out in the nightclub, but she declines. Sarah hasn't moved from her spot near the couch; she's rooted into the parquet, tendrils of apprehension having burrowed deep into the flooring.

"Maybe . . . maybe you should go," she says, and I expect this. I snatch my garment bag from the living room and hoist it over my shoulder, preparing to re-create my role as Vincent the Wandering Raptor, his worldly possessions bundled up and dragging around behind him as he traverses the streets of New York.

"You're right, I should get moving," I say. "Perhaps we can talk again later."

"Perhaps that's best."

"I'm at the Plaza if you need to find me. Late arrival at the hotel was three hours ago. Maybe if I hang out on the streets for a while, I can stay out until early check-in. Won't have to pay for the extra night."

But she's too far gone to trade quips, and I mourn the loss, even if only a temporary one, of a great small-talker.

"I'll see you out," she says, and then makes no effort to move.

"Don't worry, I can do it myself." I open the door—no one in sight. Whoever delivered the letter, most likely a bike messenger flunky who knew nothing of its contents, has disappeared.

"Goodnight," she says, some part of her brain returning to its owner to operate the politeness functions.

"Night. Maybe I'll drop by tomorrow."

"Yes," she says, her mouth back on autopilot. "Tomorrow." The door closes, and I'm back in the dank hallway, rancid beer odors and all.

I need to call Glenda, and I need a strong hit of basil. But there's a tickle in my belly that's growing into a hunch, and if there's one thing Ernie taught me, it's to treat all tickles like hunches and all hunches like fact.

Whatever that letter meant, whatever was inside, deserved a reaction. It got one. Now that reaction deserves some action of its own.

If my instincts are correct—a pretty big gamble nowadays, but instinct's all I've got left—it won't be more than five minutes before Ms. Sarah Archer skedaddles her way out of that dressing room, down the hallway, through the stage door, and into the night.

And I'll be right behind her.

If I can get a cab to pull over.

8

Ernie was like this: a Swiss watch with six gears slightly out of whack. You couldn't stop the guy; he always had an answer. You'd tell him, "We can't go run surveillance, the car's dead," and he'd say, "We'll get a jump start." And you'd say, "The spare battery's dead too," and he'd say, "We'll buy a new one." Now you know you're stuck in the game with him, and this isn't the banter game—it's the Q&A game, and the stakes are always higher. Once you get it started, the only thing left to do is play it out, even though you know you're going to lose. "We don't have the money for a spare battery," you'd say to him, and he'd come back with, "We'll borrow one from a store." And by the time you were done, you'd stolen a car, run your surveillance for the night, outrun local law enforcement, and replaced the car back in its original spot, usually with a full tank of gas. At the very least, Ernie was polite.

We were a great team, Ernie and me, and though our styles might have been different, we complemented each other perfectly as partners. Whereas Ernie could run a tail on the slipperiest of ghosts but had a habit of infuriating witnesses to the point where they'd clam up like a . . . well, like a clam, I preferred the more genteel side of investigation, calmly herding suspects just where I wanted them, convincing them to confess hours before they even realized they'd slipped up. Ernie wore whatever the heck fell out of his overstuffed closet first; I was a Brooks Brothers man. I wore no cologne; Ernie practically showered in the stuff, as he was a Carnotaur and felt some shame about his own scent. An excellent guiser, Ernie could go from dino to human in minutes flat and back again, and more than once he startled himself in the bathroom mirror. Ernie was fat, I was thin, Ernie was a smiler, I was a frowner, Ernie was an optimist, I was a pessimist, Ernie was Ernie, and he could be a real shit sometimes. But he was my Ernie, and he was my partner, and now it's all for naught.

But the big guy's still watching over my shoulder, every day, every case, and no matter how ingrained the PI practices have become within me, they still bear that indelible stamp marked ERNIE WAS HERE. It's a shame that he can't be beside me, especially now, as I'm quickly losing sight of Sarah Archer's taxi.

"Make a right up here," I urge my cabbie. This one smells heavily of curry.

"Here?" He's about to turn down a main road, whereas Sarah's cab had swung into a dark alley.

"No, no—up a little farther."

"Where other taxi go?"

"Yes, yes, where that other taxi went."

"You want follow taxi?"

"Please." I hadn't wanted to hop in the car and tell the driver to *follow that cab!* due to my usual cliché restraint, so I have been forced, for the last five miles, to give up-to-the-second directions like a talking Thomas Bros. map. Fortunately, my cabbie is an excellent listener, almost to a fault. Twice now I've accidentally directed him the wrong way down one-way streets, and he's been too intent on following my instructions like an automaton to pay attention to little things like traffic rules. Hey, this isn't my city, I'm doing the best I can.

"Where are we?" I ask.

"Hmm?"

"Where are we?"

"Yes, yes. Excellent food!"

Even if the cabbie's English ain't so hot, at least he's now figured out that I want the other taxi followed, and at a distance. For a little while, at least, I can sit back, relax, and—

The cab stops.

"Thirty-three fifty," he says.

I peek out the windshield, making sure to keep my head down. A hundred feet away, Sarah climbs out of her taxi and jogs hurriedly across the street. I toss a fifty to the surprised driver—one of the only two I have left, and I don't have time to get change—and, impressed with my tip, he proposes to take me to a place he knows downtown where I can spend my money and find fine female companionship in return. I politely decline the offer and take off down the road.

Sarah is swift, slipping through the shadows of the street with surprising delicacy. I feel like a donkey in comparison, every misstep braying and betraying my presence. I try to remain at least fifty yards behind her at all times, occasionally dropping below garbage bins or scooting behind corners to remain unseen.

Looking around, I can't find a single street name or number; it's as if a confused Pied Piper had strolled through the neighborhood, his sheet music all mixed up, his new tune convincing not rats but street signs to pluck themselves out of their concrete beds and follow him to a happier, less graffiti-intensive land. I do know one thing: Sarah and I are not the only ones on the street. We may, though, be the only nonfelons.

After a few more twists and turns through downtown Crazyville, we arrive in front of what I would assume to be an old warehouse, but for a faded sign that reads CHILD CARE CLINIC in bold, crooked letters. Two shuttered docking bays stand on either side of a covered entrance, and it is this poorly lit door to which Sarah heads. Ducking down behind a mailbox littered with graffiti tags and gang slogans, I am pleased to find out that Reina is Julio's girl, at least as of 9/18/94. I hope all is still well for the couple.

The prospect of dealing with the denizens of yet another hospital is as unappetizing as the Tar Pit Club's infamous Fish and Peppermint Soufflé, but my job necessitates that I suck it up and deal. The clinic door opens for Sarah—I can't tell whether she has a key or someone within the building has emerged to unlock it for her—and she slips inside. After counting ten-Mississippi, I hop across the street and sidle up to the entrance, my eyes pulling Felix the Cat tick-tocks across their sockets, checking out the clinic, checking out the road, checking out the shadows and the darkness beyond.

The door is closed, bolted up tight, and a quick perusal of the clinic's safety precautions tells me that a credit card jiggle isn't going to be my ticket in this time. The direct approach is out as well, though in some respects it would be better for all concerned if I could simply rap away on the clinic door, announce my presence to whomever might answer, and ask if they wouldn't mind terribly if I sat in on their private get-together, maybe take a few notes, record a few conversations, just for posterity's sake. Unfortunately, I doubt I'd get the real skinny on the action using this tack.

The rolling sheets of aluminum that serve as bay doors are padlocked in place, and though I could probably pick them in less time than it takes a hummingbird to sneeze, opening those metallic monstrosities would all but announce my presence over the PA system. Time to look for a back entrance. I slip around the side of the building.

But now, on the hunt, things change:

It is midnight, and something is amiss. Everything has intensified—the smell of decay, the rough gristle of the clinic's concrete walls. The night has grown darker, the graffiti more obscene, and I can taste the sharp sting of metal in the back of my throat. Ernie always taught me to use my instincts, the primal base of my knowledge, to guide my actions in any and all situations. That primal base is telling me to run. To get out.

I press on.

There are noises in any city—the catcalls of the homeless, the cries of lost animals, the moans of a breeze whipping through concrete canyons. But now I am hearing clicks and swishes, the buzzing of lips, the tongue-tooth pop of a guttural stop. I am hearing whispers and I am hearing voices, and I do not know how much of it is real and how much of it is imagined, and I do not know why I have become so apprehensive in a matter of minutes, whipping around at every faint breath of wind on the back of my neck.

Then it comes to me—

Somewhere nearby, there is a backyard barbecue burning away. Odd neighborhood for a family cookout. Odd time of night, too. But I can smell it, smell it strong—the coal, the lighter fluid, the fatty juices stoking the fire, flaming it out, egging it to new heights. And something else in there. Something . . . wrong. Something on the edges of my perception, coming into play, revving up, making a move, jockeying for the pole position . . .

Plastic. Burning, sickly sweet.

I duck.

A spiked tail slams into the wall above my head. Concrete flecks shoot out like shrapnel, and I stumble backward into darkness. What the—

Left arm—fire—a streak of pain, lancing down my shoulder—a ragged intake of breath, not mine, drawing near—I spin and leap away, shoulder screaming, instincts humming.

Sugar-water scent mixed with that burning plastic, sugar in the air, and it is blood that I smell—mine, mine, all mine—streaming down my arm as I back into the wall. There is something back here with me, something on the prowl. My guise is ripped, latex torn to shreds.

A snort—a roar—I brace for the attack—and in the black pit of this alley I can make out the tail, lined with glistening spikes—the claws, filed to razor-edges—the teeth, hundreds of them filling a mouth impossibly wide, impossibly deep. Eight feet, nine feet, ten feet high—taller than any dino has grown in the last million years. This is not a Stegosaur. This is not a Raptor. This is not a T-Rex, and this is not a Diplodocus. This is not any of the sixteen species of dinosaur whose ancestors survived through the Great Showers and evolved into our kind sometime during the last sixty-five million years.

But it is kicking my ass.

With the shriek of a railroad train lying hard on the brakes, it lunges, firm flesh and sharp spikes hurtling toward my body. Shadows—outlines—shift in the darkness, and I take a gamble, leaping right. It pays off. The . . . *thing* I am fighting—evading—bangs against the clinic wall, a satisfying crunch of bone on concrete.

Have to fight back, defend myself. Free up my weapons, let it loose. Let it all hang out.

Shoulder throbbing, I tear away at my guise, girdles belted down tight to prevent mishaps like the one at the Evolution Club. I struggle with the G series, ripping off buttons, destroying zippers. No time to save the wrapping paper. My tail flops out, a wide slab of muscle covered in a thick layer of green leather hide—no spikes, but excellent for hopping, tripping, parrying, countering all attacks.

That scent, that *wrongness*—the smell of burning plastic, of industrial waste, of creation gone awry—intensifies. Anger, frustration pour from my opponent's pores as he/she/it rises to full height and roars out a challenge.

Fight or flight, fight or flight. Adrenaline is the drug of choice.

G series gone. Tail out, legs uncovered.

E series off. My retractable claws, once aching to be clipped, zing out of their slots and curve ever so slightly down and across my hands, obsidian knives glinting in the moonlight.

P-1 and P-2 discarded. With a wail of my own that would send small villages into paroxysms of panic, I tear away at my mask, ripping the rubber from my head. Bones, softened, set into place, as my snout, tucked for so long beneath its polystyrene confines, flips into position.

M series remaining. With a violent spit, I disgorge my bridge, my caps, my mouthpiece, and they clatter to the filthy ground. It has been three months since I have uncovered my real teeth, those fifty-eight sharp syringes, and it feels so good to snap at the air, to break it in half with a vicious chomp.

The thing pauses. I roar in delight. Bring it on, big boy! Bring it on!

Thinking is muddled, primal instinct all I have.

Plastic, burning still, growing, growing, drafts of rage and confusion—

A staredown, a smelldown—

Growling. Watching. Grumbling. Waiting.

To move is to lose. To move is to die.

A flinch—left—screaming, roaring—my claws whip out, reaching for flesh, grasping for muscle, for tendons, for bones—legs pounding the pavement, grappling for purchase—streams of crimson flowing, gushing, can't feel a thing—mouth working, jaws slamming, snapping down on open air, inching, inching toward a throat—

Blood smell, sugar smell—my own, not my own—flying through the air, but there is no pain, there is no fear, there is just the *thing,* this mélange, with a tail and claws and teeth that do not—cannot—go together.

I lash out with my tail, whipping it up and under my feet, leaping into the air, hoping to bring the beast to the ground, and it feels so good, so right to be locked in mortal combat. Through the part of me that is in every other dino, our shared, archetypal memory, I am momentarily flung to the shores of an ancient river, the air thick with moisture and the wings of Pteros, buzzing with insects long since fossilized, the soil littered with the bones of a thousand conquests. And I know that this creature I am fighting, whatever its genetic makeup, can feel it too. Clinics and taxicabs and warehouses are a hundred million years in the future as we grunt and grab, muscles straining.

A break—I retreat, backpedaling hard, blood loss coming under control. Waves of black gauze shimmer across my field of vision, the world rippling with speedboat wake. Shoulder wound, leg wound, tail wound, neck wound—some deep, some glancing, all stinging.

It slinks into the shadows—to recuperate, perhaps, or to rethink its attack. I will not have much time before it reaquires the taste for my blood. I can only hope that its strength, like mine, is running low, approaching the E mark on its internal gauge.

"Enough," I pant, breath coming in ragged heaves. "Tired."

A rabid-dog bark in return, drool trilling the growl into a sizzling roll. Could it be trying to respond?

"English?" I have no idea what this thing speaks, and I don't want to assume anything.

No response. At least, not an understandable one. Breathing, growling, lateral movement in the shadows.

Cautiously—even as I fight against the urge—I raise my arms, claws half-retracted, baring my breast, a nonverbal question, can we call a truce?—traces of my settle-out-of-court upbringing in this human world.

I am vulnerable.

I am wide open to attack.

I am a fool.

The creature leaps high into the air—it is laughing behind that roar, chuckling as it shrieks—and I shrink back—my arms moving into a protective cross, claws outstretched—and the beast falls, teeth glistening, tail aiming, saliva dripping, burning holes in the pavement. My eyes closing, squinting, the end coming near—our eyes locking, our gazes meeting—

And my upthrust claws tear into its belly.

Blood drenches my arm and the howl of a thousand dying wolves shreds the night. My fingers grasp viscera, my claws snip through cavities, and the thing I am fighting wriggles its body like an eel impaled on a slow-roasting skewer.

It flings itself backward, down into a gutter, and my arm, still attached—claws digging farther, digging up, aiming, target-locked—drags me along for the ride. We tumble through the alley, blood streaming in rivulets across the pavement and into storm drains, heading out to sea. Our faces are inches apart, and even as my body is fighting, tearing away, I am looking into those muddy yellow eyes, eyes shocked with lightning-bolt streaks of crimson, searching for an essence, a clue as to its origin. But all I can see is pain, anger, frustration, and confusion. It was not supposed to lose. It was not supposed to end like this.

Blood gurgling up its throat, choking out all sounds, the creature plants its legs and tail against the curb and pushes—jumping—falling—flinging its ravaged body up, up, and away from my arm. I can hear the ripping of tissue as my claws come away grasping an indistinguishable organ.

I am bleeding, no doubt, but the creature that now stands a few yards away has cornered the market on blood loss. My claws and teeth have torn gaping holes in its hide, and I can see its entrails leaking out of that belly wound, flopping like pasta to the pavement. It stumbles backward, not out of fear or caution, but weakness, its legs trembling, barely able to hold its improbably massive body upright.

Flashing in its eyes, then, what I could not see before, hiding behind those distorted, contorted features—beyond the pain, the anger, and the confusion. There is a sadness there, a cry to be let free. To end it all. To not exist any longer. *Thank you,* this gaze says to me. *Thank you for my ticket out.*

With one final wheeze, the beast pitches over and lands on the ground with an unappetizing squish. The plastic is no longer burning.

It is ten past midnight, and I cannot help but cry out, in my Raptor tones, a song of conquest, the howls welling up within me, filling me like so much carbonation, exploding, foaming, bursting out. There is a rational section returning to my mind that is telling my body to move on and get out, to pick up my belongings and hightail it into the darkness as fast as possible before someone comes to take a look at the prehistoric battle site in this New York City alleyway. But it is a ninety-eight-pound weakling, that rational part, and it is overpowered by the stronger need to croon out my victory and feast on the flesh of the vanquished.

Mouth creaking wide, tongue prepping teeth, I instinctively lower my snout, aiming for the throat, the meaty muscles around the neck unprotected, easy access, a victor's supper—

Police sirens. Distant, but coming closer. No time to hesitate. My jaws, still operating under last standing orders, chomp closer to the fallen creature's body, and I have to muster my willpower to give it up and back away. That sugar-water smell, the scent of blood, is pulling my desire into knots, lashing away at my primal need. But there will be no taste of flesh for my raging dino-instincts, not tonight. In the morning, I know I will be happy about this. I rarely eat red meat even when I'm not killing my own dinner, and I can't imagine what this creature's raw flesh would do to my stomach. Shades of my life as a relative pacifist are returning to my mind, embarrassed at the carnage, the gore littering the streets.

The sirens grow louder, coming closer. We were not seen; I am sure of that. But I am amazed that someone in this seedy part of town cared enough about their fellow man—or so they thought—to dial up 911 and report the sounds of a *Wild Kingdom* episode emanating from a nearby alley.

So much to do, so little time. Story of my day so far. There is no way to eradicate all traces of the scene; that would take at least twenty minutes, and by my most conservative estimates, I have about four. I'll have to go the quick route, then, a precautionary measure at best. I hope it will do.

I hobble over to my garment bag, the initial burst of adrenaline wearing off, the 12:12 pain train finally arriving at the station. Inside a compartment, hidden beneath a flap, concealed within a pocket obscured by a strip of cloth, I find the small pouch I am searching for. Grasping it as daintily as possible between my teeth, I limp back to the fallen dinosaur and wrap my arms around its torso. I pull.

And nearly give myself a hernia. This thing is heavy, heavier even than its incredible size should allow. The sirens dopple closer, accompanied by the quack of an approaching ambulance. I tug at the creature again, this time throwing my weight into it, and the carcass budges an inch or two. Straining against dead weight, I work my way over to a nearby Dumpster, every foot a Herculean struggle.

There's no way I'll be able to get this thing inside the Dumpster, though it may be the right thing to do. Even if I were somehow able to clean and jerk it over my head—impossible for my frame, even when out of guise—odds are it would come crashing down on me, flattening me into a Wile E. Coyote pancake. Perhaps if I had an hour—or a winch—but I have neither time nor equipment on my side. I can hear brakes screeching, cruiser doors slamming.

My civic duty as a member of our hidden society requires that I move all deceased unguised dinosaurs out of sight, into a safe area where they can be collected by the proper authorities. It does not require that I kill myself trying to carry it out. Into the Dumpster, then, is simply not going to happen. But behind the Dumpster . . . aha! I drag away.

It's a provisional measure at best, as tomorrow's daylight will illuminate the dinosaur's remains for anyone who cares to take a peek around the alley, but the cleanup crew should have arrived by then, erasing any evidence of its existence. I snatch the pouch from between my teeth and tear off its outer layer.

An incredible foulness—rotting carcasses, long-dead citrus fruits—hits me point-blank like a frying pan, slamming my head back into the warm night air. No wonder the cleanup crews have been known to smell this stuff from over twenty miles away—untrained, I could probably pick it up at ten. Holding my breath as best I can, shielding my sensitive snout, I sprinkle the granules inside the pouch onto the dinosaur's carcass.

Its flesh begins to dissolve away.

I would like to stick around and watch my opponent slowly disappear over the next hour or so, muscle and tissue evaporating, steaming into the air, until only a skeletal frame—suitable for display in any of your finer museums—is left. Maybe I'd be able to figure out what the hell it was that had attacked me in the first place, and why a nightclub songbird named Sarah Archer had business inside a dilapidated health clinic that is clearly anything but. But I can hear police-band squawkers and the conversation of officers, and it has come time to take my leave of the scene. I cover the dinosaur's body with a nearby heap of trash, making sure to spread it around, fixing it to look like the rest of the refuse that naturally occurs in the wilds of the city.

Remembering to grab my clamps and girdles, not to mention my garment bag—poor luggage, ripped and torn, used and abused as it has been—I flex my powerful legs and leap atop the Dumpster, tottering on the edge as I regain my balance. Another hop, this time getting my bruised tail in on the action, and I make it to the roof of a low building. With no idea where I am, and no knowledge of NYC landmarks, I take off across the rooftops of the city, not caring where I end up so long as it is far away from the battle scene.

Sometime within the next two minutes, the police will stumble into the alleyway. Perhaps they will not see the remnants of the fight, considerable though they are. Perhaps the shadows will obscure the evidence we have left behind. But the odds are good that they will find the blood, the bits of organ meat, and the odds are good that they will investigate further.

But they will not find anyone or anything to match up with that blood and that organ meat. They'll chat it out, they'll argue theories—cops and their theories, oh my—and then, once they exhaust their verbal energies, they'll run a spot check of the area. It will turn up nothing. Even if an officer should be bright enough to peek behind the Dumpster, he will find only a pile of refuse, a pack of litter that didn't hit the mark. The odor beneath it, so powerful that I can still smell it eighteen rooftops away, will not affect his worn-out snout; humans are unable to detect those tiny microorganisms that so love our decaying flesh.

And maybe there is a dinosaur among those police officers. If this is the case, he'll be unable to escape the smell of that pouch, will understand immediately what it means, and will attempt to wrap things up in the area in as timely a fashion as possible. His job as an officer of the law is important, yes, but all must come in second in the face of duty to the species. Later, once he's alone, he'll call it in to the proper authorities, and they'll go to work.

And if there is no dino cop working this beat tonight? Then we'll just have to hope that a roving cleanup crew, one of the three-dino bands that prowl the streets of the city—twenty-four hours a day, three shifts of eight hours each, no breaks, no holidays, crappy job but somebody's gotta do it—comes across the beast's skeletal remains before a human accidentally stumbles upon them and goes running to the paleontology department at NYU. We cannot afford any more modern fossil finds.

I leap, and I leap, and I leap, giving a workout to whatever frog DNA might have seeped into my genetic code way back when in the primordial ooze. Soon enough, the rooftop quality changes from rotting wood to merely disgusting, yet structurally sound, wood, and I know I'm well on my way to safety. Eventually, I find myself hopping around without having to worry whether or not my landing pad is going to crumble beneath me, and I figure I'm far enough away from that alley to take a break. There's a large road, possibly a highway, maybe ten blocks away. Time to change.

My last jump lands me on a rooftop that is bordered on all sides by a small support wall. Perfect. First job is to dress these wounds. Tossing my garment bag to the ground, I rifle through my clothing and pick out those outfits for which I care the least. I am full on Claiborne for Men, short on Armani—just two shirts, sigh—so Claiborne it is. Wiping the bloodstains from my claws onto the cement underfoot, I tear a few of my cotton button-downs into long, thin bandages and carefully dress my wounds. I leave my linen Henley unmolested, for it is my favorite shirt, and I can't bear parting with it despite the fact that I am in need of an extra tourniquet for my tail. It is the only piece of linen I own, and I refuse to destroy it. Linen breathes, I have been told, and I find this an alluring aspect to any fabric.

Wrapped up like a sarcophagus, the bleeding having slowed to a light dribble, I unzip the inner lining to my garment bag and pull out my spare guise, laying the polysuit on the ground before stepping inside. As has been the rule since our species first decided to permanently camouflage ourselves over three million years ago, no one dino is permitted to change his or her human appearance without express consent from the local and national councils. Everyone is allowed a spare guise or two, emergency pairs for when the first line of visual defense is ruptured, but they must be ordered through one of the major guise corporations using an ID number specific to each dino and kept on file in classified record books. Mine is 41392268561, and you can bet I've had it tattooed on my brain since day one.

Still, small changes are permitted, individual quirks that the end user can decide to add or subtract from the guise depending on his or her mood. The guise I am now pulling over my torn, bruised body, for example, is an exact replica of my day-to-day costume in every way but one: This one sports a mustache.

It's a charming bit of facial hair, really, a thin wisp of fur that proclaims my machismo without overstating the point. I purchased it from the Nan-jutsu Corporation—Guise Attachment 408, David Niven Mustache #3, $26.95—and attached it permanently to my spare guise as soon as the UPS truck drove away. I was like a kid on Christmas morning, and I wanted to try out my new toy as soon as possible. Slap it on and watch those dates pour in. At least, that's what the advertisement said.

Unfortunately, as Ernie had a habit of erupting into laughter as if he'd spent the day sucking ether whenever he looked at it, I stopped wearing the entire costume after two days of continual embarrassment. But I've kept the guise around as a spare, a you-never-know pair, and I'm sure glad I've got it now. I toss on one of my few remaining shirts, throw on a pair of pants, and mourn the loss of my hat and trench coat, items I carelessly left behind during my frenzied escape.

I climb off the roof and shimmy down a fire-escape ladder, and as I have no urge to waste another hour trying to hail a cab, it takes me little time to seek out the closest pay phone. It's broken. I walk a block, find another one, also broken. We're gonna play it this way, are we, New York? Eventually I locate a working pay phone, call in my location—street signs, finally, and it seems I've wound up in the Bronx—to the first cab company I can find in the decimated Yellow Pages attached to the booth and wait for my ride. It is nearly one o'clock in the morning now, almost an hour since that spiked tail nearly decapitated me, and I can only hope that the taxi will arrive soon. I am tired.

I stagger into the Plaza Hotel thirty minutes later, my casualty-of-war garment bag draped across my body, and stumble to the reservations desk. All thoughts of the case—of Sarah Archer, of Mrs. McBride, of Donovan Burke and his Evolution Club, and even of Ernie have compressed themselves into the subbasement of my consciousness. There is nothing left of me; I am a husk, a shell, my faculties having long since taken the A train.

"My name is Vincent Rubio," I whisper to the desk clerk, a kid so young he could be here on a work-study program from grade school, "and I want a room."

The clerk, surprised perhaps at my luggage, my weary eyes, my brusque manner, begins a stuttering reply. "Do—do—do you have—"

I know what's coming, head it off. "If you say you don't have a room," I tell him, my brain already sleeping, dreaming, letting the body do all the work, "if you say I need a reservation, if you even think about uttering the words *I am sorry, sir*—I will leap behind that counter and bite your ears off. I will tear out your eyes and feed them to you. I will rip out your nostrils and plug them up your anus, and what's more—what is more—I will make sure you will never, ever, father a child, and I will do so in the most horrible, evil, mind-numbing way that your little mind can imagine. So unless you enjoy hearing yourself shriek in agonizing, blood-curdling, down-on-your-knees pain, I suggest you take my credit card, give me a key, and tell me which elevator to take."

My accommodations in the presidential suite are just lovely.

9

I
f the New York Plaza Hotel is not currently considered one of the finest lodging establishments in the world, I hereby nominate it as such. If it is already on that exclusive list, I suggest that a new category be created called Most Comfortable Berth, and that the king-sized bed—the emperor-sized bed—the dictator-for-life-sized bed—in which I had the great fortune to sleep last night take its rightful place at the very top.

Despite numerous wounds to various parts of my body, I tossed not an inch. Despite a full-tail bruise, the night-sky blues contrasting horribly with my natural green, I turned not a smidgen. Despite a host of images overcrowding my brain like passengers on a stuffed subway train, mental pictures that will provide fodder for years of psychoanalysis, I experienced not one nightmare. There were no unsettling dreams of any kind, let alone of mutant dinosaurs on the prowl, and I ascribe it all to that bed, that wonderful bed, not too firm, not too soft, accepting the contours of my wracked body and mind, cushioning in all the right places. Now I know why mammals are so keen to get back into the womb.

I order room service because I feel I am owed it after last night's fiasco. Vincent's Rules clearly state that once you have been attacked in an alleyway by a creature that cannot exist according to the laws of nature, the case you are working on triples its budget automatically.

Breakfast—three fried eggs; two strips of bacon; two sausage patties; side of hash browns; side of grits; six buttermilk pancakes; four waffles; a loaf of French toast; three Southern-style biscuits; one chicken-fried steak;

bowl of Honey Nut Cheerios; low-fat, nonfat, whole milk; and orange juice—is placed on my nightstand by a room service steward named Miguel, and though I consider asking him to bring up a few garnishes from the kitchen, something in me curdles at the thought of sucking on a sprig of basil this early in the morning. Odd. This, too, shall pass.

A quick check of my voice mail back in LA finds, among the threats and pleadings from various loan departments, two terse messages from Dan Patterson, asking me to call him back when I get a chance. I am reluctant to tell Dan I'm in New York, as I know he'll be hurt that I didn't let him in on my hunch, so I put off the return call until later in the day when I can assuage my guilt with a mouthful of herbs.

I've just hung up and returned to sopping up a hunk of melted butter with a stack of flapjacks when the phone gives a ring.

"Hello?" I mumble through a mouthful of pancakes.

"Is this the . . . detective?" A familiar voice, muffled. Not real familiar, but I know it.

"Sure is. And you are . . . ?"

Silence. I tap the phone to see if it's gone dead. It hasn't.

"I think I might . . ." and the voice trails off.

"You're gonna have to speak up," I say. "Hard to hear." Suddenly I realize that the alignment of my guise is off; the left "ear" and its requisite counterparts are not situated directly over my earhole, leaving the cheekbone of my human face to block the path of any sounds. Must have shifted during sleep. Damn, I was hoping to get moving and on the street without having to reapply the mask epoxy this morning. With a little shifting here and there, I am able to realign my guise for the moment, at least long enough to carry on a conversation.

A whisper now, though audible: "I think I might have something to give you. Some information."

"Now we're getting somewhere. Do I know you?"

"Yes. No—we—we met. Yesterday. At my office."

Dr. Nadel, the coroner. "You remember something?" I ask. Witnesses have this tendency to recollect crucial events well after I've left the scene. It's rather annoying.

He says, "Not on the phone. Not now. Meet me at noon, under the bridge near the south entrance to the Central Park Zoo." It's nearing ten now.

"Listen," I say. "I don't know what you've seen in the flicks, but witnesses can just tell PIs information over the phone—we don't have to meet under a bridge or in an alley, if that's what you're thinking."

"I can't be seen with you. It's not safe."

"Whoa, whoa—on the phone's a lot safer than meeting each other. You worried about people seeing you with me? You think only the good guys go to Central Park?"

"I'll be wearing a different guise. You will, too."

Like hell I will. "I don't have a different—"

"Get one." This cat's scared out of his wits. Gotta play him tight. "You'll want this information, Detective. But I can't afford to be seen with you, so if you want it, you'll find a way."

"Maybe I don't want it that much."

"And maybe you don't want to know how your partner died."

Guy knows the buttons to push, I'll give him that. "All right, all right," I agree. "We'll do it your way. How'm I gonna know who you are—"

But he's gone. Ten minutes later, so am I.

There are a thousand ways to obtain black market guises in any major city, and in New York there are at least twenty times that. The textile district alone has been busted by Council operatives umpteen times for running in illegal polysuits, and mixed in with all the electronic wholesalers and porn stores around Times Square is a thriving illicit attachments industry. Any time of day or night, if you know the right dinos, you can walk into the back room of a knife store or Laundromat and pick up new hair, new thighs, a new pot belly if it strikes your fancy. Unfortunately, I do not know the right dinos. But I have a feeling that Glenda may.

"You know what friggin' time it is?" she asks me after I show up on her doormat.

"It's ten-thirty."

"A.M.?"

"A.M."

"No shit," she says. "Long night, I guess. I hit a few more bars after we split. Lemme tell ya, I had a whole goddamn pot of this herbal tea, outta this friggin' world—"

"I need your help," I interrupt. Great gal, but you gotta staunch that word flow early if you want to get anywhere fast. Quickly, I lay out the situation for her: Need a new guise, need it now, need it quiet.

"Jeez, I ain't the gal to come to with this, Vincent."

"You're it, babe. Everyone else in New York either wants me dead or out of the city. Or both."

Tongue roving through her mouth, poking the insides of her cheeks as she ponders my request. "I know one guy . . ."

"Perfect! Take me there—"

"But he's an Ankie," she warns me. "And I know how you feel about them friggin' Ankies."

"Hey, right now I'd buy a guise from a Compy."

Glenda barks out a sardonic laugh. "His partner's a Compy."

"You're funny."

"I'm serious."

We're coming up on eleven o'clock. I have no choice. "I'll hold my breath. Take me there."

Ankylosaurs are the used-car dealers of the dinosaur world. In fact, they're the used-car dealers of the mammal world, too—most every pre-owned auto broker in California is descended from the small number of Ankies that survived the Great Showers, which gives you some kind of idea of the perils of inbreeding. They also fool around with real estate, theatrical management, large-scale arms manufacturing, and the odd brokering of the Brooklyn Bridge. The key to dealing with Ankies is to keep the nostrils open at all times; they might be glib, but they still leak lies through their pores.

"His name's Manny," Glenda tells me as we round a corner. We're up near Park and Fifty-sixth, and I'm surprised that she's taken me into such an opulent district.

"We in the right area for this?" I ask.

"See that art gallery across the street?"

"That's the place?"

"You got it. Met Manny during a routine surveillance of the leather shop next door. Let us use the back room to run a few wires, so long as we bought some merchandise." It's always a trade-off with Ankies; they don't know the meaning of the word *favor*.

"You bought art?"

Glenda laughs. "Nah, I bought a new set of lips. Thicker—knockoff of the Nanjutsu Rita Hayworth #242. Nobody buys art—all these joints are fronts. Shit, you ever see anybody buy anything in a gallery?"

"Never been in one."

"Well, me neither—not till then. It ain't about the friggin' art—maybe a few mammals pick up some lithographs for the living room now and then, but . . ." We reach the front door of Manny's, a tastefully decorated store-front with floor-to-ceiling windows out front. Through a jumble of colorful sculptures, I can make out a salesman speaking with two customers. Glenda holds open the door for me. "You'll see what I mean."

A horrible accident with a tanker truck carrying a payload of primary colors—that's all I can imagine happened to the inside of this store. Posters, canvasses, sculptures, mosaics, all in blazing reds, yellows, and blues, with an occasional dash of neon green thrown in for good measure. It's positively blinding.

Glenda issues a short wave toward the salesman—I assume this is Manny—and he politely excuses himself from the two customers near the cash register. As he walks toward us, arms outstretched, crocodile smile stretching his lips into two tight caterpillars, I can already feel the ooze seeping out of his pores. What's more, I can smell him, and beneath the typical aluminum Ankie scent is the unmistakable odor of petroleum jelly.

"Miss Glenda!" he cries in mock delight. "What a wonderful pleasure it is to see you today." I have a feeling that he's laying the accent on thicker than it really comes—the last bit came out as *wat a waaanderfool pleeass-soore eet ees to see yoo toodai*—but I'll refrain from insulting the guy until I know him a little better.

"We were in the neighborhood, thought I'd drop by and show my friend Vincent your beautiful gallery."

"Vincent?" He envelops my right hand in both of his, clutching it tight. "Is that right? *Veeencent?*"

"Right enough." I force myself to grin.

Glenda lowers her voice a notch and says, "We'd like to talk to you about some of those reproductions you sell."

A notched eyebrow, a wink of the inner eyelid, and Manny turns back to the other customers. "Perhaps I will have what you are looking for next week, no? Manny will give you a call." The couple—human—who know a brush-off when they hear one, exit the gallery. Manny locks the door behind them and turns around an OUT FOR LUNCH sign. When he returns, the accent is softer.

"Mammals. They wanted a Kandinsky. What do I know from Kandinsky?"

Are we supposed to answer? Glenda and I opt to shake our heads in sympathy. I steal a glance at my watch, and Manny steals a glance at me.

"You are in a hurry, yes? Come, come, we go to the back."

And to the back we go, passing crate after crate of paintings and lithographs, boxes of abstract sculptures. An EMPLOYEES ONLY sign hangs on a nearby rest room, and it's through this door that Manny leads us, keeping up a furious stream of chatter along the way. ". . . and when there is a new shipment of latex, I say to my workers, we must install it in the costumes right away, as Manny makes the finest guises around, better than the companies, much better than Nakitara, for example, who don't even use mammal polymers—did you know that?—but instead use some type of cattle product. And I suppose cattle is a mammal but at Manny's we use real mammal products, if you understand me, for only the finest merchandise comes from Manny . . ." He drones on.

The rest room door leads to another, and another, and soon we're hopping through a maze of doorways, each bearing its own innocuous sign: STOCK ROOM, RECENT RETURNS, BLANK CANVASSES. DANGER, DO NOT OPEN: ACID.

Instinctively, I step back as Manny opens this last door, expecting to be doused with a spray of chemicals; instead, Manny steps into a small warehouse full to bursting with empty human disguises of every shape, color, and texture. Specialized hangers—Styrofoam shapes cut to the appropriate mammalian dimensions—line the walls, each one covered in a limp mockery of the human form. An electric hum fills the air.

On the warehouse floor, a dozen workers sweat it out around sewing machines and pressing irons, carefully hand-stitching the buttons, zippers, and seams that are so integral to a perfect guise. The heat is sweltering, and I find myself pitying the dinosaurs forced to work under these conditions. I can still remember the stories of days long ago when we used to embrace the heat and humidity—to thrive in it, no less—to wake each morning and lick the sweet, steamy air, each particle dripping with succulent moisture—but now, all these easy, breezy, well-ventilated years later, I would wager that any one of us would sooner live in Antarctica than, say, Miami Beach. Then again, I do quite enjoy the taste of emperor penguins, so I am admittedly biased.

"Pay them no mind," Manny says, clearly reading my thoughts. "They are very happy to be working here." Then, to prove his point, he calls out, "My workers, are you not happy to be working for Manny?"

And as one, they call back, "Yes, Manny," in a spaced-out, drugged-up monotone. I imagine that this Ankie buys cheap basil by the ton.

"Now, Mr. Vincent, what are you requiring today?" We step down to the warehouse floor, Manny leading Glenda and me toward a row of guises at the back. "We specialize in handcrafted torso attachments. Perhaps some new biceps—"

"I need a full guise."

"A full guise, yes? This is a very expensive thing. Here at Manny's, we have only the most excellent craftsmen—"

"Cut the line, Manny. Price doesn't matter." I've got TruTel's credit card on me. "So long's you can charge it up as a piece of art."

Manny's smile is genuine this time; he clearly enjoys when others dispense with the precursors and jump headlong into his little pit of chicanery. "Of course, Mr. Vincent. Right this way."

The next twenty minutes are spent leafing through a series of guises, each of which has its pros and cons in terms of functionality and aesthetics. Glenda serves as my personal shopper and fashion critic, dispensing with shoddy designs and faulty tailoring. To be fair, Manny's guises are indeed incredibly well made, and I express my surprise that he never went into legitimate guise work.

"Wait until you see the bill," he tells me through that grin of his.

We eventually settle on the guise of a stout, middle-aged man with a protruding belly and slightly bowed legs, a knockoff of the Nakitara Company's Mr. Johannsen #419 model. Maybe five eight, 180, darned close to average for the age and gender, which is precisely what we are looking for. But at this stage, the costume, drooped across the Styrofoam mannequin like an ill-fitting bedsheet, is nothing but a featureless shell, devoid of hair, color, or distinguishing marks. I have forty-five minutes to make this thing look like a real human before I can don the costume and hoof it into Central Park.

"Maria is a genius at the hair," says Manny. We are standing next to an old, withered Allosaur, her guise skin loose, wrinkled, falling off of her like it does with the Styrofoam cutouts. Manny must not include a free costume as part of his workers' benefits package. "She has been doing the hair for . . . how many years now?"

Maria mumbles something we cannot understand. I am convinced Manny cannot understand it, either. "You hear that?" he says to us. "That is many, many years."

We settle on a light auburn style, with a touch of gray at the temples— "for that distinguished look, yes?"—and a minimum of body hair in order to save precious minutes. I don't plan on using the guise more than this one time, and I doubt I'll be disrobing in Central Park during my rendezvous with the coroner.

Trevor is the "genius" at distinguishing marks, and from him we pick up a facial blemish and a military tattoo on the forearm, faded and blue. Frank, the human skin-tone "genius," gives the guise a once-over with an olive spray brush, coating it somewhere between tanned and swarthy. Maria, who it seems is not only a "genius" at hair but also at prescription eyewear, picks out a set of blue contact lenses to cover my natural verdant irises.

As Glenda and Manny help me disrobe from my usual costume and place it in a fine leather carrying case—"a gift for my good friend Mr. Vincent"—the rest of the experts in the warehouse apply the finishing touches to my custom guise. Birthmark here, wrinkle there. It's a rush job, but it's done, and it should hold up for the next hour or so.

I dress, slipping into the guise like a comfortable pair of pajamas. The inner lining is made from a silk polymer, I am told, and it facilitates the process quite nicely. Before I stepped into the empty skin, I imagined that it would be odd seeing out from new eyeholes, feeling through new gloves. But I find that the experience is comparable to that in the old guise; a human is a human is a human. A mirror is wheeled over to me, and now when I wave, a chubby middle-aged fellow waves back. When I grin, a chubby middle-aged fellow's second chin puffs out. When I dance, I stumble over my own two feet. Perfect.

"You like?" Manny asks me when we're all through.

"You do good work." I produce the TruTel charge card with little more than a glance at the bill—by God, more than a glance would probably kill me—and Manny eagerly runs it through.

"Mr. Vincent, you are a good customer. You come back whenever you want."

Manny kisses our hands, our cheeks, and leads us back out of the warehouse, through the maze of doors, and into the art gallery. The entire process has taken no longer than thirty minutes.

"You want me to come along?" Glenda asks as we prepare to leave.

"Solo deal. I don't wanna spook the guy—he's shaky as it is."

"Maybe if I hang back—"

"Glen, it's okay. Go to work."

On the way out of Manny's, I detect a familiar scent wafting through the air and spin around like a top trying to locate the source. But with all of these pedestrians streaming by, many with their own particular smells, it's impossible to localize. A young man walks confidently into Manny's; it's possible that the odor is coming from him, but I don't recognize the face and I don't have the time to worry about it.

I need quick directions. "Central Park is . . . ?"

"North," says Glenda. "The zoo's about halfway up on the east side. Stick to the right and you can't miss it."

"Damn, I almost forgot—" I turn back to Glenda. "Can you do a little checking up for me?"

"Checking up how?"

"At J&T, on the computer."

Glenda's face falls into a frown. "You gonna get me into some shit, Vincent?"

"Possibly."

"Finally." She claps her hands together, rubbing them in anticipation. "Whaddaya need?"

"Got a lead that said Ernie mighta been keeping his stuff over at J&T when he was here last time. Notes, files, whatever you can find."

"Ernie's a part of this now?"

"He might be. And even if he's not—"

"This is the kind of thing that got you in trouble the last time, you know that?" A mild rebuke, a featherweight slap.

"I know it. Please, a favor. For me. For Meester Veencent."

As soon as I pressure Glenda into agreeing to snoop around her offices and phone me with the information, we bid farewell. I have fifteen minutes to walk into the heart of Central Park thirty blocks away, and I set myself toward the tall trees in the distance. North, I think.

Noon. The sun is harsh today, and even through the new costume I can feel its rays heating up my delicate hide. One thing I've already noticed about Manny's guise is that the pore structure is weak, trapping a good deal of my natural moisture inside the skin, rather than allowing it to leach into the air. I pray this does not wear out the epoxy.

No Dr. Nadel in sight, though as he's wearing a different costume and I'm wearing a different costume, sight isn't going to be of much help. Fortunately, the guise I chose has extra-wide nostrils, so I'll be able to catch his scent whenever he should show. I believe it was woodsy, maybe . . . oak? I'll know it when I smell it.

On the way to the zoo, I passed an impressive herbilogical exhibit planted in the middle of Central Park, a series of trees and shrubs from different locales, each bearing a small name plaque describing type, flowering habits, and country of origin. Discreetly, I plucked a few leaves here and there for a little experimental ingestion should I need it later in the day; I may never make it to French Guyana, for example, but if I find that their trees pack a wallop, a trip would be in order. I sit on a park bench and catalog the leaves, tucking them inside the breast pocket of a particularly noxious sweater vest Glenda picked out.

Scent of polished pine, riding on a gust of wind—that's Nadel. I glance around, attempting to localize. Punk with mohawk, strutting this way? Nah, human. Father, angry, storming toward me, holding a squirming child by the wrist? He wouldn't bring along a kid, would he? They pass—both human, I realize now—and the scent remains. Weak, but growing stronger. I look farther afield, into the green pastures of the park.

There—the black woman with short hair approximately a hundred feet away. Brightly colored running shorts, a pink tank top. Thin. And a small folder in her hands. As she comes closer, the smell grows stronger, and as I catch her eyes, there's a moment of unspoken understanding. It's Dr. Nadel.

Not a bad idea for clandestine work, the male/female swap, though I turned down such an offer at Manny's a half-hour ago. Dinos risk enough identity crises without having to worry about transgender mix-ups. Nadel comes closer, not hurrying, not lagging, moving at a steady pace toward the bridge. I expect there will be little in the way of discussion; he will most likely walk by, leave the folder on the bench, where I will retrieve it moments later before walking back into the park. I take a few steps backward, retreating to safety beneath a small bridge.

Another smell, suddenly, overpowering Nadel's pine, and this one is unfamiliar to me. But it's enough to stop me in my tracks, force my eyes to scan the park once again. Nothing has changed—pedestrians walk, children run, jugglers drop their clubs. There it is again—deodorant and chewing gum. It does not belong.

A tandem bicycle enters the scene, two obese blond women somehow remaining upright on the contraption despite an incredibly high center of gravity. They wear identical T-shirts stretched across their bodies that read TOO HOT FOR YOU, and giggle incessantly at some silent joke. They are pedaling quickly, though—almost too quickly even for experienced cyclists—zipping the two-seated bicycle through the park with impressive speed.

The smells intensify and collide with one another, mixing into a soupy mélange that my olfactory organs are unable to separate. Rooted into the spot beneath the bridge, I find myself glancing back and forth between the black woman I know to be Dr. Kevin Nadel and the two heavy girls on the bike, who I don't know to be anything but two heavy girls on a bike.

But I have a hunch.

Before I can convince my legs to leap from their spot, before the thought has even made its way down my spinal cord, the tandem bikers pull up before Dr. Nadel, and, giggling all the way, stop the bike in the middle of the path, blocking his progress. Now I'm starting to get my legs in gear, just coming off the blocks—but even past the din of the zoo, the children, the sounds of Central Park, I can hear buttons snapping and claws sliding into place. The two women have turned around on the bicycle seats, riding sidesaddle, shielding Nadel from my view with their solid bodies. I run.

There's not much commotion—I don't hear raised voices, shouts of protestations. No struggle—isn't that how these things are supposed to go down? There's a zing, a slice, a squish, and a groan, and in less time than it took for the ladies to stop the bike, they've started it up again, reaching cruising speed in seconds. Nadel is on the ground.

As I approach Nadel and kneel over the body, I look up to find that the bike has already slipped down one of the many shaded paths crossing the park, disappearing into the shadows and the crowds. A small river of blood oozes out from a long, thin slice to the black woman's neck, fluid gushing rhythmically with the faltering heartbeat. Scent disappearing, the doctor dying.

One quick slice with one sharp claw; that was all it took. I don't even know which of the "ladies" did it. The guise is holding up well beneath the strain of an injury—I can barely make out the fake skin from the shredded hide below, though perhaps the blood helps to obscure the bond. There's no time left for Nadel to croak out a last confession; the eyes have already glazed over, the mouth opening and closing like a codfish.

The folder is gone.

A crowd has begun to form, more from curiosity than altruism, I am sure, but it remains my duty to ensure the security and eventual removal of the body. I poke my head up and say, "She's all right, little accident. Passed out. Happens all the time."

This mollifies some of the onlookers, and they walk away. Others, perhaps sensing a little more than a fainted jogger, stick around to watch. I catch the eye of a dino in the crowd—young girl, jasmine scent, probably a Diplodocus—and wink slowly.

"Think you can call us somebody to help, young lady?" I ask her pointedly, and she seems to get the idea. The girl runs off at top speed toward a nearby pay phone where I hope she will ring the proper dino authorities.

Meanwhile, I search Nadel's new—and now unused—body, frisking the corpse for any clues or information the two cyclists didn't grab. The search turns up nothing in terms of information, but a full key chain comes out of the running shorts, and I quickly transfer the metallic mass to my own pocket.

I wait around for the ambulance to show up, shielding Nadel from passersby, pretending to speak to the African-American woman lying on the ground as if she were still alive. "You'll feel better with some food in you," I say to the body. "Right as rain in a minute or so."

"Clear out, clear out," instructs the paramedic. He's got two partners, and from the smell of it, they're all Carnotaurs. They huddle around Nadel's prone body, muttering to one another. The protocol here is simple: Get the dino out of sight and into a secured location, away from human eyes. They load Nadel's body onto a stretcher and wheel him/her/it into the back of the ambulance. The crowd, displeased at the lack of gore, disperses.

After we're alone, the lead paramedic turns to me—"You see it?"

"I didn't see it, but I was here."

"You wanna explain that?"

"I don't have time to explain," I say, "but you can call me at my hotel later tonight." I give him my contact information, run down my PI credentials, and discreetly warn him that on the off chance that the guise is registered (mine isn't), it might not match up with the dino inside. Grudgingly, he accepts my word and prepares to leave.

"Oh, and by the way," I say, "you may want to find another coroner to do the autopsy."

"Why?" he asks. "Guy downtown's always done a good job on our kind."

"Yeah, but he's on vacation. Be gone for a while."

No time to change guises; I don't know who sent the two assassins after Nadel, and I don't know if they're after me. Better to remain hidden for the moment. I'm sneaking through the underground service passages at City Hall, trying to find some back entrance into the morgue. If I can get into Nadel's office without being seen . . .

No such luck. I have to brave the front door. Wally, the coroner's assistant, stands behind the desk, and I half-expect him to freak out and call security as soon as I walk in. But I don't look like the guy who assaulted him nine months ago; I'm just another bereaved man with middle-age spread, and his lousy human nose isn't up to the task of uncovering my deception.

"Is . . . is my Myrtle . . . in here?" I choke out.

"I'm sorry?" Wally's already confused—good.

"My Myrtle, she . . . it was a stroke, they said, a . . . a stroke . . ."

"I—I don't know, sir, ah . . . Let me check the books. The last name?"

"Little."

"Myrtle Little?" He doesn't sound the least bit skeptical, and it hurts not to laugh. I hide it in a barking cough, a sob into my hands. Wally looks through the morgue log.

"I don't see anything," he says. "How long ago—"

"A few hours, I don't know. Please—you've got to find her—please—" I'm grabbing onto Wally's white physician's coat now, tugging in a desperate plea for help.

"Maybe you could go back to the hospital—"

"They told me to come down here—"

"They did?"

"Just a moment ago. Please, my Myrtle—"

Wally grabs a phone, dials, and has a short conversation with the person on the other end, a conversation that quickly turns heated. After nearly deafening me with his shouts, Wally slams the receiver on the hook and storms out from behind the desk, face set in a mask of righteous indignation. "I don't know what the hell's going on in this place," he huffs, "but Mr. Little, I'm going to find your wife."

"Thank you, young man," I cry. "Thank you." I keep up a steady flow of tears until Wally's out the door, down the hall, and up the stairs. Then I'm dry as a bone and it's back to business.

The outer door is unlocked, making the first part of this nice and easy. Nadel's office is a different matter, and it's not until I try the very last key on the chain that I find the right one. The place looks the same as when I left it—neat, precise, boring. I put all my faith in the file cabinet, a four-drawer job with a separate key for each compartment; with such precautions, perhaps excitement lies within.

These keys are easy to locate, and the cabinet doors slide open without a sound. In each compartment, hundreds of manila folders are pressed between two aluminum binders, each file labeled with a date of death and organized by last name. I scan through the M and W sections, attempting to locate what I know won't be there: the autopsies for McBride and Ernie. I also know where the folders are—pressed between the sweaty palms of two chubby, giggling cyclists.

I'm about to pack it up, the lack of evidence and wasted time already making me regret this side trip, when I notice a small subcompartment in the back of the bottom drawer, a metallic box covered by a locked lid. It takes another key off the key ring, a small one I almost overlooked, to un-lock and open the box, and inside I find not another file, but a red spiral leather-bound notebook, perfect for writing down names and addresses and the like. I eagerly flip through, ready to be astounded, but all I come across are seemingly random numbers and letters. For example: 6800 DREV. 3200 DREV. Not exactly a case breaker.

But beneath this is a passbook to First National Bank, and it seems that Dr. Nadel has been making deposits as of late. To be more precise, he's been making deposits as of December 28, three days after Raymond McBride was found dead in his office, and then sporadically throughout the past year, and it is these numbers that match up with those in the note-book. The 6800, for example, represents $6,800 that was deposited in this account last December, the $3,200 coming a few months afterward. Now the only thing is to figure out the letters. DREV. I don't see any deposit dates directly around the time of Ernie's death—the closest is thirty-nine days after I got the news—though with diligent study, I'm sure a pattern will emerge.

But I'm sure as hell not gonna do my studying here. I pack up my new belongings, lock the file cabinets, and head back into the lobby, up the stairs, and down the hallway just in time to slip into a niche and watch a frazzled Wally entering the morgue to explain to Mr. Little that his dear Myrtle has, in the last ten hours, stepped down off her gurney and walked away, that she has somehow defected from death.

An unexpected and sudden lack of basil has left my body herb-free for over three hours, and despite the occasional stab of withdrawal pains radiating from deep within my chest, I am pleased to find the cobwebs in the corners of my mind clearing themselves away. I have no particular desire to remain this level-headed for any longer than necessary, but while it lasts I might as well get in some good and heavy thinking:

Without a doubt, there's Judith and Raymond and Sarah Archer and that thing from the alley—all of this deserves more than a moment's thought—but if I want to get back to the heart of the matter, I've got to begin at the beginning, if only to justify the expense account. I've got to start back at the Evolution Club.

Nightclub owner Donovan Burke was dating Metropolitan Council representative and all-around American gal Jaycee Holden, who then disappeared without a trace on a crowded subway platform, leaving her distraught lover to search fruitlessly for her throughout the northeastern United States. Fact. Donovan Burke then fled New York City and his failed romance for the quiet, simple, small-town values of Los Angeles, where he set up shop in a nightclub that burned to the ground despite a team of trained firefighters and eight thousand gallons of water. Fact. During this fire, Donovan Burke risked life and limb by staying inside the nightclub even as the flames were licking his body. Fact. And now a bit of conjecture: Donovan Burke, beset by troubles of the heart, was not particularly attached to this world.

A flashback to the conversation with Judith McBride, and her assessment of Donovan and Jaycee's relationship: "Donovan and Jaycee were very much in love," she told me yesterday, "but infertility can change a couple in ways you can't imagine." Perhaps Donovan had given up on the whole she-bang. Perhaps he set the fire as a grand suicidal gesture. Perhaps he'd had enough of the guising and the lying and the pain from knowing that he'd never be with the one he loved. Two different worlds and all that jazz.

And here's where the aforementioned clearheadedness comes in handy. Judith McBride told me that the doctor who was treating Donovan and Jaycee, the one who allowed Donovan to hold out hope that they could beat the system that had served us so well for three hundred million years, the geneticist whose experiments might someday indeed make possible a Raptor-Coleo mix, was none other than Dr. Emil Vallardo.

Dr. E. Vallardo.

Dr. E. V.

DREV.

And so it is that an hour later, after a horrendous traffic jam on Park Avenue that made rush hour in Los Angeles look like the open plains of Montana, I find myself in Dr. Emil Vallardo's private office, awaiting the arrival of the doctor himself. Even if my amateur cryptography of Nadel's notes about DREV are way off, this is as good a place to start as any. Vallardo—the Spin Doctor, as they called him back in Council meetings because of the rumor that he used centrifuges in his race-mixing experiments—may have no pertinent information to bring to the case, but Ernie always taught me that nothing is coincidence. If a name pops up more than once, it's a name that begs to be checked.

Dr. Vallardo is out of the facility right now, or so the receptionist told me, but he'll be back any minute. After a stylish wash and blow-dry of charm by yours truly, the secretary was kind enough to offer me a seat in the doctor's private office, and though I have a strong feeling that Dr. Vallardo won't approve of her decision, I'm much happier planting my rear in this cushioned leather recliner than sweating it out on those hard vinyl benches in the waiting room. At the very least, I can take this time to peruse the multitude of diplomas and certificates lining the wood-paneled walls. Unfortunately, all it serves to do is make me feel intellectually inferior.

Undergraduate work at Cornell. Big deal. I knew a Stegosaur who went to Cornell and now he's working on cars for a living. Okay, he's designing them, but still . . . Medical degree, specializing in obstetrics, from Johns Hopkins. Overrated. Oh, and a Ph.D. from Columbia in genetics. See, the problem is, this guy's got too many letters after his name—Emil Vallardo, M.D., Ph.D., OB-GYN. Doesn't ring half as nice as Vincent Rubio, PI. Mine sounds infinitely cooler, and would certainly make a hipper TV show.

"I so rarely entertain visitors," comes a voice from behind me, tinged with an accent, no doubt, though I can't figure out exactly which one. It's a European bouillabaisse. "The scientific life is a lonely one, yes?"

"Know all about it," I reply.

Dr. Vallardo, a big, beefy beast with a big, beefy grin, envelops my proffered hand in his and pumps my arm like an auto jack. His left hand is not as strong; it trembles madly, a victim perhaps of spot palsy. "Good to meet you," he says, and maybe there's some Dutch in there? His scent, a stew of anisette, pesticides, and cleansing creams, doesn't give me any clues as to his origin. "Would you like a coffee? Soda? Mineral water? Yes, yes?"

I beg off the drinks, though my throat is a little parched. "I'm a private investigator from LA," I tell him, and he nods rapidly, his shoulders hunching into peaked hills. "I have a few questions, won't take long."

"Yes, yes, so Barbara said. I'm more than happy to help out with . . . official matters, as always." The grin spreads wider, and—Lord have mercy—I do believe it is genuine. "Where should we begin?"

"Your work here . . . fascinating. Perhaps we should start with your experiments."

"My experiments." *Which of the millions?* his tone implies.

"Yes. Your *experiments.*" Hard accent on the last word.

"Ah, yes. My *experiments.* Yes, yes."

I love speaking in vague generalities. It's much better exercise for the brain than simple, direct conversation. Dr. Vallardo squinches his nose—perhaps taking in a whiff of my old Cuban stogie scent—and plops into the seat behind his desk.

"There is no need to couch our terms. You may speak freely in here, Mr. . . ."

"Rubio. Vincent Rubio."

"As I was saying, Mr. Rubio, we may be open in this office. Soundproofed, for various reasons. Yes, yes. Even if we were out in the hallway, we might speak freely. All of my support staff are . . . of our kind, and though I will see the occasional human obstetrics patient, most of my clients are dinos as well."

"Your receptionist—"

"Barbara."

"An Ornithomimus?"

He applauds, his cheeks rippling in genuine delight. "Yes! Yes! Very good! How did you know?"

"Part smell, part hunch. Get 'em all the time."

"Aha! Very nice. Very nice. Allow me to venture a guess . . ." He sizes me up, eyes roving, and if he says I'm a Compy, case be damned, I'll have to kill him. "You are no Sauropod, that is evident. Perhaps . . . a Chilantaisaur?"

He's flattering me, while at the same time acknowledging that I am not the grandest thing he's ever seen. Chilantaisaurs were the largest of the large, massive sentient mountains with decidedly little brain matter. One of the few species of dinosaurs to survive the Great Showers but die out before the Age of Man, the last Chilantaisaur passed into the great beyond nearly two million years ago. His name was Walter; at least, Walter is the closest English pronunciation to the series of whoops and roars he would have been known by in days of yore. Walter's remains, preserved these eons by sharp dino archivists, can be found on display in the anteroom of World Council headquarters in Greenland. I was there only two years ago, and let me tell you, that Walter is one fortunate Chilantaisaur to have died out when he did. He would have had a hell of a time outfitting himself in the modern era, let alone finding anything to slim down those hips.

Dr. Vallardo amends his guess, correctly assuming that I am a Raptor. Then, getting back to the subject, he says, "So you want to know about my experiments. You don't happen to be a Council member, do you?"

"I was."

"Yes?" Distrust now, and a whiff of dislike.

"Stress the past tense," I say. "This is unrelated, I assure you. Nothing we discuss will be forwarded to them."

"I see," says Dr. Vallardo, and for the first time, I notice a crack in that cheery façade. Then it's back up again, all smiles and chuckles. "No problem whatsoever. Always happy to oblige. Yes, yes."

I stand, move behind my chair. It's time to check out the laboratory. "Shall we?"

He didn't expect this so soon in the interview. Flustered, he clambers to his feet. Triceratops, as a rule, are not the swiftest of our kind, but Dr. Vallardo is moving more lethargically than his race would indicate. "Is there a problem?" I ask.

"No problem," says Vallardo, his body alternately moving toward the door and toward his intercom. "I am unprepared to leave the office, that is all."

"Unprepared?"

"I have . . . men. Dinos. They follow me."

Oh no. "Are you saying that you're being followed?" The last thing I need is another case with a paranoid schizophrenic for a witness—don't ask, don't ask.

Vallardo chuckles, shakes his head. "I want them to follow me, Mr. Rubio. For lack of a better term, they are my bodyguards."

Since when does a doctor need bodyguards? "Since when does a doctor need bodyguards?"

"Since the Council leaked the first report on my genetics work," he says, more than a hint of condemnation snaking between each word. "Some members of the dino population were not pleased with my results."

Quickly, then, almost as if he doesn't mean to do it, Dr. Vallardo pulls aside the collar of his shirt and bares a long, wide scar, still healing, an obvious claw mark to those who know how to spot these things. "This is the most recent attack," he says. "A female Raptor who screamed that I was a sinner even as she was reaching for the death blow. A sinner, she called me. In this day and age. Yes . . ."

Releasing any Council-gathered information before an official decision has been made, and before the subject of the investigation can be notified, is a strict no-no, and though I had heard that someone on the NYMC was guilty of lip-flapping, I'd had no idea it had come to this. Once again, I assure the Nobel shortlist geneticist that there is no way that the Council will ever release any information he sees fit to give me this day. I do not tell him that this is because I would sooner live the rest of my life as an outcast than rejoin that group of hypocrites.

A few moments after Vallardo buzzes his receptionist, we are joined by two Brontosaurs in human guise, introduced to me as Frank and Peter. Their costumes designate them as twins, and so far as I can tell from their comparable enormity, they may very well have been actual littermates as well. The evolutionary process that shrank the rest of us dinosaurs into somewhat manageable heights—some of us too manageable—didn't have as much an effect on Brontosaurs, resulting in their current status as the largest dinosaurs on earth. It is no wonder that so many of them play for the National Football League.

Our quartet ready, we set out for the laboratory.

Dr. Vallardo's assigned area inside the Cook Medical Center is deceptive in its size, a tricky optical illusion. At first glance, it is nothing more than a pedestrian suite, comprised mainly of the waiting room, a few examining rooms, and his private office. But through a sliding door behind Barbara's counter, down a claustrophobic hallway, and beyond a series of key-coded metallic portals, lies a budget-busting research center that renders obsolete anything I have ever seen on *Star Trek*.

I am appreciably awed, and Dr. Vallardo does not seem surprised. "Yes, yes, I can see you like it," he says. Pulling at my arm now, his own excitement feeding off mine in a synergy of anticipation, Dr. Vallardo draws me farther into the heart of the operation. Frank and Peter, unmoved, follow right behind.

Aside from the buzzing and the beeping and the whooshing, aside from the spinning and the shooting and the swirling, aside from the beakers and the test tubes and the flasks, I am most taken aback by the scientists. Dozens of them, over a hundred, lined up in rows, bent at the waist like plastic straws, eyes attached to microscopes, to petri dishes, to seed samples. Chalk up one work-intensive environment. It's Manny's, only higher-tech and with better air-conditioning.

"This is my laboratory," Dr. Vallardo says expansively, relishing the opportunity to show off his work space. I, for one, am most willing to be awed by any office sixteen thousand times the size of my own. Where does he get the bread to support this kind of an operation?

"It's beautiful," I say.

He leads me down a row of white-coated scientists scurrying like lab rats between their contraptions, experimenting away, taking off but a second to greet their patron, and then back to work, cracking that self-imposed whip. We approach a bespectacled young man, the duck's-ass hairdo on his guise a humorous attempt to evoke nostalgia for the days of James Dean and early Brando. Must be a Fanjutsu model, like the Jayne Mansfield look-alike they rolled out a few years back. Retro is the hip guise look these days; I've been thinking about adding chest hair—Attachment 513, Connery Style #2—and gold chains to mine. It might complement my mustache, which, I might add, I haven't gotten one negative comment on the entire day.

Introductions are made all around, and it takes two minutes to assure Dr. Gordon—the young scientist—that I am not going to leak information to the Council. Obviously, they've all been under a bit of stress as of late.

"Dr. Gordon is working on the protein transfer for the second receptor site," Dr. Vallardo explains, the scientific gibberish twisting my mind like an old dishcloth. "He's figured out a way to use the cytosine from one strand, and—"

"Whoa, whoa, Doc, wait up." My head hurts already, and I've only been down here for a minute.

"Am I going too quickly?" asks the doctor.

"You could say that." The fact that he's going at all is too much for me to handle. "Can I get this in layman's terms?"

"Have you not read my work before?" he says.

"Sorry to say I haven't. I pretty much got the basics down and that's all."

Dr. Vallardo mulls this over, his bushy eyebrows working like squirming larvae atop his brow. "Come, come," he says, some decision clearly made, and we take our leave of the scientist, who is more than happy to get back to work.

Vallardo leads me through the laboratory and down a set of stairs, saying, "I have been known to . . . how do you say it . . . talk over people." He unlocks another sliding door, and it swishes open. "All these years of schooling and seclusion amongst scientists will do that, yes, yes."

"It's not that," I say, though it partially is. "I was looking for an overview of your work, mainly. Broad strokes."

"Yes, yes. Then perhaps this will be more suitable."

The corridor we enter is paneled wall-to-wall, floor-to-ceiling, in rows of fluorescent tubing, each pulsing with a pale purple glow. Dr. Vallardo steps into the middle of the hallway and raises his arms, pirouetting like a ballerina. Frank and Peter join in, and the sight of these two behemoths dancing *The Nutcracker* nearly breaks me down into hysteria.

"Low-level ultraviolet," Dr. Vallardo explains, urging me to follow the leader. "Kills off surface bacteria. We tried stronger doses, but it made everyone rather ill, yes, yes."

How reassuring. I reluctantly raise my arms and sync up with Vallardo, Frank, and Peter in their surreal dance.

After the curtain call, we emerge from the other end of the corridor disinfected and ready for action. "In a moment I will close the door behind us," Dr. Vallardo tells me—I get the idea Frank and Peter have heard it all before—"and the lights will go out. You will be able to see nothing, but do not worry, this is normal, yes. Another door will open, and I will lead you through it. That one, too, will close, and for some time, it will be quite dark, yes? So stay absolutely still and you won't run into anything. Light levels are low, and for a reason."

I nod. "Ready when you are."

With an electric pop, the lights blow out. I hear the swish of yet another sliding door, and feel a strong hand at my elbow. I am led forward a few feet, and can sense a breeze as the door slips closed behind us. We wait.

"You're right, Doc. I can't see a thing." We have stepped out of the Cook Medical Center and into the Black Hole of Calcutta.

"Give it time," Dr. Vallardo says. "You'll see soon enough, yes, yes."

Still nothing. Nothing. Nothing. Oh . . . maybe . . . a grapefruit glow, balancing between yellow and pink, waist level, but far away . . . and there's another one, more of a homestyle orange juice radiance . . . and another, and another. Slowly, hundreds of small, glowing boxes shimmer into existence, eventually making enough of an impression on my optic nerves for me to finally figure out exactly what I'm standing in: an incubation chamber.

"The different lights you see—the varying colors, hues, shades—are all by-products of the chemical and heating factors of each incubator." Dr. Vallardo leads me around the room, showing off his creations. "The blue ones, for example, are for the most recently fertilized eggs. We won't push them up to the yellow and orange lights for another three weeks. Then, of course, after we've ascertained that we have achieved fertilization, we can move them into a warmer environment, yes . . ."

As Dr. Vallardo prattles on, I find myself searching for evidence of a hoax, looking for the strings on the flying magician's back. Despite all I have read about Dr. Vallardo and his work, my first inclination tends toward disbelief. It was all easy enough to accept while sitting in a Council meeting in a basement clear across the country—okay, there's a doctor in New York who says he can mix the different genes of dino races and produce mixed offspring, and what are we going to do about it if it comes to Los Angeles? But back then it was a policy decision, to be based solely on what would be the best course of action to protect the public interest in such a hypothetical situation, but now, inside this chamber, I feel a more visceral reaction, the consequences slamming home deep within my own reproductive organs.

Every incubator contains an egg, no two alike, their size and shape varying from baseball to football to basketball, but each clearly a dino egg nevertheless. A complex series of clamps and rubber padding sporadically spins each egg in its bed, lifting it up, turning it over, and gently placing it down again. A small monitor attached to the top of each incubator reads off what I assume to be vital signs, though I can't imagine that a just-fertilized specimen would have many vital signs from which to take a measurement.

The entire scene is reminiscent of a singularly ridiculous movie that came out in the theaters a few years back and did tremendous business at the box office; the humans went to see it to confirm their worst fears about our kind, and we dinos went to see it to confirm our worst fears that we are indeed the humans' worst fears and that we would be wiped off the face of the planet the minute we should choose to announce our presence, so it's not surprising that the movie sucked up a lot of money all around. The basic concept of the film, as far as I can remember, involved a human scientist using fossilized DNA—ha!—to create a whole mess of dinosaurs and keep us captive on an island somewhere in the South Pacific, ostensibly to create an amusement park, only we manage to get loose and kill all the humans in sight without forethought as to why or what they would taste like.

Rubbish, the whole thing, especially the way we poor Raptors were portrayed. We can be dangerous, yes, but we do not kill indiscriminately, and I've never known a one of us to kill a human for no good reason. Then again, dragging us up from the depths of a test tube and locking us in cages like wild beasts might be good reason at that.

I realize it's all just fun and games, celluloid fantasies for a mindless human population who could never in their wildest dreams imagine seeing a real live dinosaur, let alone believe that one could run a criminal investigation, process film, serve drinks at the Dine-O-Mat, or head up the world's leading generic drug corporation, but it doesn't make the whole matter any less offensive.

But there I go again, getting worked up, when my whole point is that the one thing—the only thing—the film got right was the incredible financial burden one would have to work under in order to run about splicing DNA, messing with the whole genetic code, all to bring even a single dinosaur egg through incubation. Since the guy in the movie had business contacts up the wazoo, and as the setup Dr. Vallardo has down here is a heck of a lot more incredible in its scope and depth, I find myself wondering once again where he finds the money for his research. This time, I ask him.

"Private donors, mostly," he says. "I cannot use hospital funds, of course, as many of the trustees are human, yes, but I have been able to secure the work space from a few friends of mine on the board."

"Private donors such as . . . ?"

Dr. Vallardo shakes his finger at me. "Then they would not be so private, yes?"

"May I conjecture?"

"Another hunch?"

"Educated guess."

He shrugs, turns to inspect an egg. "I cannot stop you from guessing, can I?"

Nope. "Was Donovan Burke a contributor?"

"Who?"

"Donovan—Burke." I am sure to enunciate.

He shrugs. "The name does not sound familiar. I have many contributors, most in small donations, too many to remember by name."

"He was also a patient of yours about two years ago," I say. "A male Raptor."

Dr. Vallardo makes a good show of trying to recall a name from his past, eyes glancing up, fingers scratching chin, but I don't buy it for a second. "No," he says, shaking his head, "I do not recall a patient by that name."

"His fiancée was a Coleophysis, name of Jaycee Holden."

Again, the head shake, and again, I don't believe him. "They came in for treatments, you say?"

"I didn't say, but yes, they did."

"Yes, yes . . . I have no recollection. There are so many."

"Probably not big contributors, then."

"Probably not."

"What about Dr. Nadel?"

"Kevin Nadel?"

Ring out the bells—the doctor's admitting to something. "Yes, the county coroner. Was he a contributor?"

"I don't believe so."

"But you know him."

"We went to medical school together, yes? An old friend. But he works for the government—there is little money to be made."

"So maybe you gave him some cash."

"I do not loan money to friends."

"Maybe it wasn't a loan."

"Are you trying to make a point?" he asks, and I decide to let the matter slide before he gets the two Brontos to shove me into a glass box and toss me from the building.

"Let's move on," I say. Time for the big show, everybody take your places. "Was Raymond McBride a contributor?"

Fortunately, Dr. Vallardo had removed his hands from the bowlingball—sized egg he had been handling, or that particular experiment might have ended with a crush of shell and a splatter of yolk. He calls over to his bodyguards, busy inspecting the smaller eggs—"Frank, Peter, could you wait outside?"

The twin Brontosaurs oblige, slipping out through the double-lock doors. Dr. Vallardo waits until they leave, and then turns back, his face straining to hold its good cheer. "You have spoken with him?" he asks, and from across the room I can hear his teeth grinding. "Before he passed on, that is?"

I expected a reaction, but not one this juicy. I'll have to squeeze it, work out the pulp. "I've spoken with his wife," I say, mustering all the insinuation I can. "We had a long talk. She told me a lot."

He's not falling for it.

"Mr. McBride, rest his soul, was a contributor, yes. A rather public one, in fact. He supported my work fully, yes, yes."

"Fully . . . So are we talking thousands? Hundreds of thousands? Millions?"

"I'm afraid I can't release that."

"Even if I ask real nice?"

"Even if you beg."

Face-off. Don't flinch. Contest of the wills. This is the way I prefer my battles. Staring contest—first one to blink loses.

Darn. Not fair—I have congenital eye dryness. Okay, so at least I've confirmed that McBride was a contributor, even if I don't have the exact amounts.

"Why would Raymond McBride fund the efforts of a scientist whose work holds nothing for him?" I ask. "Both he and Mrs. McBride are Carnotaurs. They had no need of your treatments."

"How can I comment on a dead man's thoughts?" he says. "Perhaps he wanted to help dinosaur society as a whole, yes, yes."

"Do you think Raymond McBride was murdered by someone who didn't approve of his funding your projects?"

"I have no idea why Mr. McBride was murdered. If I did, I would have gone to the police, yes."

"But is it *possible*," I say, too many recent nights of late night television due to daytime unemployment forcing this Court TV blather out of my mouth, "that Mr. McBride was murdered because of his involvement with your work?"

A deep sigh—I find that I am getting more and more of these from witnesses recently—and he says, "Anything is possible, Mr. Rubio. Anything." This whole time, Vallardo's smile hasn't slipped. It's a costume grin that's getting to me, and I wouldn't be surprised to find out that it's a new guise attachment from the Nanjutsu Corporation—Attachment 418, Perpetual Cheer. There's a wall somewhere in this doctor's brain, strong and thick, and it's going to be a bitch to sledgehammer that baby down. But maybe, just maybe, I can go around it.

I move across the room, forcing my steps into a carefree saunter, casually inspecting the incubators as I go. *No problems here,* this walk is supposed to announce, *everyone relax.* As I delve deeper into the chamber, I find a section of eggs clearly more developed than the rest. They are the senior class of Dr. Vallardo's incubation room, the ones who drive the cool cars and get all the chicks, light pods in their boxes suffusing them with a deep red glow, bordering on brown. Crayola would call it Burnt Umber and be done with it.

"What's this one?" I ask, pointing to an oblong shell. "It's bigger than the others."

With a beam of fatherly pride, Dr. Vallardo snaps on a set of rubber gloves and gently strokes the egg's delicate casing. "This is Philip," he says, his voice a soft coo. "Philip has come farther along than any of our others."

"But he hasn't even hatched yet."

"Of course not," says Dr. Vallardo, still massaging Philip's shell. "We're nowhere near that stage."

"But I heard—"

"—an incorrect report," he finishes for me. "You must be referring to the rumor that I brought an egg to term, yes? As of yet, I have not been quite that fortunate. Innuendo goes a long way."

Sure does. At the Council meeting, they had reported it as fact: Dr. Emil Vallardo had created a live mixed child, though its component parts were unknown. I usually have little cause to doubt Council reports, but if Dr. Vallardo had indeed brought a mixed child to term, why wouldn't he take the credit for something he's been trying for decades to accomplish?

"How long before Philip here comes out of his shell?" I ask.

"If he comes out at all," Vallardo says, "the struggle won't begin for another three weeks or so. He's almost fully formed, but now he needs his strength, yes." Then, turning on a secondary light, a regular twenty-five-watt bulb recessed into the incubator's side, he asks me, "Would you like to see him?"

All in the name of science. "Please."

Dr. Vallardo delicately maneuvers the delicate egg toward the bulb—that left hand of his still trembling—handling it like a young child given permission to hold his mother's favorite porcelain doll. The shell is thinner than I had assumed, and as it comes to rest against the light, a shadowy silhouette appears, floating comfortably in the center of the egg, surrounded by a chalky milkshake plasma.

"If you look closely over here"—he points to the larger, more rounded side of the egg—"you can see the ridged frill around Philip's head, yes."

"Looks like a Trike top."

"Yes, yes, Philip is the product of a Triceratops father and a Diplodocus mother."

Trike father—could this be his child? Physician, help thyself conceive? "Are you married?" I ask.

"I know what you're thinking, Mr. Rubio, and no, the egg is not mine. But it is my brother's. Philip will be my nephew, yes, yes."

Whatever his lineage, Philip is going to be one big boy if he ever breaks out of that shell. Trikes are large enough already without Diplodocus genes amplifying things. Or maybe it doesn't work that way. I have no idea, and to be honest, I don't want to get embroiled in a two-day conference on the matter, either.

But I can see those Diplodod lines in young (very young) Philip, the soft curves of the back, the rounded head, melding and merging with the Triceratopical bony plates that are already beginning to form on Philip's not-yet-infant hide. The tail, too short for a Diplodocus, too long for a Triceratops, is coiled like a Slinky beneath the fetal body, ready to unfurl sometime within the next three weeks. The legs, too, are both long and stocky, a perfect blend of the two creatures, and I find myself wondering what kind of life Philip will lead if he makes it into the world alive: Will he be heralded as a wonder or as a freak?

Which reminds me—"Dr. Vallardo," I say, drawing him closer, making my tone as conversational and nonconfrontational as possible, "are you the only one engaged in this type of research?"

Now he's truly confused; this is no put-on. "As far as I know. Yes, yes, I would say I am the only one."

"No rumors, no reports of renegade scientists, working outside the boundaries of accepted science?" I'm sounding kooky, looney-tunes, and I know it. There is, though, a point in the near future.

Dr. Vallardo shakes his head vehemently, spittle grenades launching themselves around the lab. "I assure you, I would know of any such research."

"What about random mutation? Could it produce . . . well, something like Philip here?"

A chuckle. "Impossible. Mutations are indeed what drive evolution, Mr. Rubio, but they may not circumvent nature."

"That's your job, right?" Dr. Vallardo says nothing, and now it's time to go fishing. "What if I told you," I begin, stepping out onto the thin ice, ready to test the waters, "that some friends on the New York Council told me of some reports of mixed . . . creatures . . . on the streets of New York. Sightings—"

"What kinds of sightings?" he asks, the quick query betraying his interest.

"We've had a few different reports," I lie. "One woman claimed to have seen an Allosaur with a Hadro bill."

No response from the doctor. I move on.

"Another Council member was told—get this—of a fully grown Bronto with Ankylosaur spikes. Silly, isn't it?"

"Yes, yes, quite."

"Then the last one—really, I shouldn't even waste your time with this—"

"No, no," he says, and I'm thrilled I finally got him to say something other than yes, yes. "Go on."

"It's a bit muddled, actually. I spoke with the poor guy myself, and lemme tell you, I've never seen a Raptor this pale before. Frightened right outta his guise. Seems he'd been in a fight, attacked, no less, by a dino— and let me point out that this is how he put it, not my terms, mind you—a dino straight from the depths of hell."

"Oh my," says Dr. Vallardo.

"Oh my, indeed. Most likely a fruitcake, but lemme give you the whole bit. He said this thing had the tail of a Stegosaur—big ol' spikes and all— the claws of a Raptor—I'd take off my gloves for a visual demonstration, but you get the idea—the teeth of a Tyrannosaur—many, and large—and the length of a Diplodocus. That would be long, of course. Now have you ever heard anything so insane? My guess is he'd been tossing back a few at the local basil bar."

I am laughing. Dr. Vallardo is not. "Where was it?" he asks.

"The attack?"

"The attack, the creature."

"Does that make a difference?"

"No—no—of course not," he stammers, and I can feel myself slipping around that mental wall already. "Curiosity."

"Said there was an alley, lots of graffiti there. One of the poorer areas of town, I guess."

"The Bronx?" says Dr. Vallardo, a mixture of hope and denial creasing the wrinkles around his eyes. Aha—maybe now I have a borough in which to search for that health clinic.

"The Bronx," I say, "Brooklyn, Queens, I don't even think the guy knew where he was. You've seen one blurry alleyway . . ."

"Yes, yes. You are probably right. He must have been drunk."

"Wasted outta his mind, that's my guess. He sounded pretty convincing, though, describing the ugly thing. Wooo, Creature from the Black Lagoon." Interesting note here: The more often I poke fun at that thing from the alley, the more upset Dr. Vallardo seems to become. There's a definite causal relationship between my jabs and his blood pressure. I try a new one: "Betcha if we ever found the thing we could get a lotta money for it from the traveling circus."

I may be pushing it now; Dr. Vallardo's guise skin is turning blue, which means the geneticist is practically purple beneath that costume. Neat trick, but I'd better calm him down before a stroke pops him out of the world and out of my case. "Hey, what the heck, you say it can't be, it can't be. You say there's no mutant dino-creatures roaming New York City, then there ain't any mutant dino-creatures roaming New York City. You're the doctor in the know, right? The man with the genetic plan."

He blinks, slowly getting himself under control. The blue tint leaves the guise, which eventually returns to a medically acceptable shade of beige. "Um . . . yes. Yes." He's winded from the effort.

Now I remember why I used to love this job.

Dr. Vallardo suggests we take our leave of the incubation chamber— ". . . the eggs need their rest, yes . . ."—and I am more than willing to follow him back upstairs. My fishing expedition has paid off well; I've got a few more minnows in my boat than I did at the start, and though I don't know how Dr. Vallardo fits onto the fisherman's platter, at least now I'm pretty sure he's one of the side dishes.

As I prepare to take my leave, I toss out a few more questions about Dr.

Vallardo's work, scientific points he can clarify with a host of technical mumbo jumbo that will leave him in a good mood once I have departed. I may wish to return to the geneticist's laboratory in the near future, and if I expect to be allowed easy access once again, I can't have him calling Council headquarters to complain about my visit as soon as I take off.

"It has truly been an honor," I fawn, "a big honor. Big."

"Please, it was nothing, yes."

"No, really, quite the experience. I understand much more now." I tap my notebook, making a big show of waving it around the office. Little does he know it contains nothing but a few notes on the Evolution Club fire, the words *Judith, J. C.,* and *Mama,* and a couple of partially erased erotic sketches I made of the stewardess on the flight over.

We say good-bye and part ways. But I am no more than three steps down the hall when I hear him jogging up to me—the sound as ugly as the sight must be—and feel a rough hand upon my shoulder.

"What happened to your friend?" he asks me, and for a moment I have absolutely no idea what he's talking about.

"The one who was attacked?" I say.

"Yes, what happened to him?"

"As far as I know, he's seeing a therapist."

"Ah. Yes, yes . . ." We stand in the hallway, both of us silent. He's gearing up for something, but I refuse to speak until he does. Then, preceded by a throat-clearing grunt, comes the question Dr. Vallardo truly wanted to ask—"And the . . . creature? The dino mix?"

"Yes . . . ?" I know what he wants.

"What . . . what happened to it?"

I could lie and say it limped into the night, bleeding but otherwise healthy, or claim to have no knowledge of the situation whatsoever, but I am so darned curious to finally see a true emotion on Dr. Vallardo's face that I can't help but tell him the truth.

"You'd have to ask the cleanup crews," I say. "They usually handle the skeletons."

I tell you, it was a Kodak moment.

t's nearing rush hour as I leave the Cook Medical Center, and the cabs shoot by, unconcerned with my outstretched arm. What the hell— everyone else in this town is a willing pedestrian, and as I'm feeling paunchy around the midsection, I figure I could stand to do a little bit of walking. I secure directions from a candy striper in the lobby and set out on the road. The journey back to the Plaza will take a little longer this way, sure, but maybe I'll get some time to think about the case, go over it in my head, see if I can spot any inconsistencies. At the very least, I'll save a fin on cab fare.

I have just returned to the beginning, ready to mentally replay the scene at the Evolution Club on the Betamax of my brain, when a sleek Lincoln Town Car pulls up beside me. I would think nothing of this, except for the fact that it continues to stay by my side, puttering along at five miles an hour. It's going to get horrible mileage that way.

There's no way to get a good look at the driver; the windows have been tinted mine-shaft black, far beyond the boundaries of the law and good taste, making identification impossible. I'm getting a bad feeling about this, but I get bad feelings about everything. Maybe his car is breaking down. Maybe he's lost. Maybe the driver simply needs directions, and assumes that since I'm walking, I must be a native. Maybe I'm just paranoid.

I'm not. A moment later, I am flanked by two dinos gussied up in their best Sunday guises. Neither is much larger than I, but the message I'm re- ceiving from their less-than-gentle way of grasping my elbows tells me I should probably listen up.

"You wanna get in the car?" asks the one on my left, reeking of Old Spice and stale helium. Something familiar there.

"Thanks for the offer," I say, "but I was just getting the hang of walking around."

I'm trying to catch the eyes of the other pedestrians on the street in order to send out a warning, a danger signal. But though we're surrounded on all sides by the civic-minded citizens of New York City, not a one looks me in the face; every nose is pointed down, every speed control set to full throttle.

"I think you'll enjoy a nice car ride." This comes from the dino on my right—bigger than his partner, but his scent is nothing more than a weak dose of children's cough medicine. Hardly threatening, kinda fruity.

I glance over again at the Town Car, its tinted windows, its gleaming hubcaps, its brand-new paint job—Intimidation Black, Color 008—and reaffirm my decision to keep walking. A little faster, maybe . . .

Still keeping pace with me, Old Spice places an arm around my shoulder. Were I watching this from a distance, I'd take it as a friendly gesture, a frat-boy hug of camaraderie and good cheer. But that arm is not so benign—he's pulled back one of the latex fingertips on his costume glove, and I can feel the claw beneath poking earnestly at my tender neck. That's why the smell is so familiar—deodorant and chewing gum—these are the goons from the park, the ones who killed Nadel.

"Do a lotta bicycling?" I say.

"I'm gonna ask you one more time real nice," mumbles the assassin, his breath pounding into my ear, "and then I'll have to drop you. Get in the car."

Okay, okay, I get in the car. Ernie's Rule #5: Dead dicks can't investigate.

We drive along for some time in complete silence. The driver, who I cannot see very well due to a gauze partition between the front and rear of the automobile, refuses to turn on the radio. At the very least, they could entertain me with some tunes. The two thugs who muscled me into the Town Car sit to either side of me, and despite the roomy backseat, our shoulders are pressed tightly together.

"My legs are falling asleep," I say.

My dinonappers don't seem to care. We drive on. "You know," I say, "this just struck me—we haven't been formally introduced. Maybe you've got the wrong guy."

"Nah, we got the right guy," says Cough Medicine. "Ain't two dinos named Vincent Rubio who smell like a Cuban cigar."

I squint in confusion, furrowing my brow until the muscles are ready to pop. "Vincent Rubio? See, I knew you had it all mixed up. I'm Vladimir Rubio. From Minsk."

The dumber one appears to mull it over for a moment before Old Spice craps on my party. "Don't listen to the little shit. He's Rubio, all right."

"You got me," I confess, "you got me. So . . . now you boys know my name, but I don't know yours."

"Oh yeah," says Cough Medicine. "I'm Englebert, and this is Harry—"

Old Spice whacks us both in the back of our heads, bringing a burp out of me and a whimper out of Cough Medicine. "The both of you, shut up," he says, and we promptly follow orders.

It is some time before the hard lines of the city give way to the flowing curves of nature, trees and flowers and shrubbery replacing lampposts, traffic lights, and street vendors. The scents change as well, and I am amazed at how empty the air smells, like a one-thousand-piece jigsaw puzzle with six crucial pieces missing. It's been a while since I've been out of a city— LA, New York, or otherwise—and I'm always rendered a little disoriented by the loss of the piquant odor of smog. In some ways, it's a homing beacon, a signal to the land that I love.

As we move into the countryside, Old Spice reaches beneath the seat in front of him and pulls out a paper shopping bag. "Put this over your head," he says, and hands it over, handles first.

"You must be joking."

"I sound like I'm joking?"

"I don't know," I say. "I've only known you about thirty minutes."

"And you ain't gonna know me much longer 'less you put the bag over your head." Obviously, he never learned the maxim that you can catch more flies with honey. My legs are still asleep.

I reluctantly don my improvised headgear, and all those pretty trees disappear. At least I still have my sense of smell.

"Almost forgot," grunts Old Spice. I hear him rummaging through his pockets, change jingling, keys jangling, and a moment later he slaps something in my left hand. I run my fingers over it, trying to make out the shape—long and thin, two sides, both wood, connected to each other by a twisted metal wire, shaped like an alligator's mouth, only without the teeth. One side opens when you squeeze the other side closed . . .

"Clip it on him," Old Spice tells his partner. "Clip it on tight."

With a Medium Brown Bag from Bloomingdale's over my head and a clothespin clamped shut on my nose, we continue to streak through the countryside. Or so I assume. With my two best senses temporarily on injured reserve, we could have doubled back around toward the city for all I know. My sense of time is beginning to fade, as well—the rest of the drive could be an hour or a day, and I'd have no idea. I only hope that once this bag comes off my head, I don't find myself in Georgia, where there may or may not be a warrant out for my arrest—don't ask, don't ask.

My ears have escaped unmolested, though, and after some time, I can hear a buzz-saw snore coming from my left, low but gaining volume. Old Spice is asleep, and about to broadcast it to the world. A little while later, the car slows, and there's the unmistakable clink of three coins sliding into an automatic counter. The car speeds up again.

Ten minutes later, I hear a cow.

Five minutes after that, the pungent aroma of a landfill makes its way past the clothespin barrier, works its way through my nostrils, and slams hard into the olfactory recognition center of my brain. I gasp involuntarily at the eye-watering whiff, and Old Spice wakes from his slumber—his snores transforming into snorts, sneezes, a cavalcade of novelty-store sounds— and languidly reaffixes the clothespin, shutting out the last vestiges of stench.

We're in New Jersey.

Some time later we pull to a stop. This has happened once or twice before, but this time I'm told to get out of the car. More than happy to oblige, I practically leap out of the backseat, my cramped, tingling legs eager to get in some good stretching.

"Should I take the bag off my head?"

"That would not be wise." Harry grabs my left arm, Englebert my right, as they lead me across a bumpy terrain. My feet send back covert signals— we are walking on a dirt road, littered with loose gravel.

A few minutes later, we break into a clearing. Already I am formulating a plan of attack and escape, should it become necessary. I refuse to die with a Bloomingdale's bag over my head.

"Close your eyes," Harry tells me, and for once I decide not to follow his instructions.

Ouch! Light—bright light—stabbing—eyes on fire, eyes on fire! I slam my lids back down, drawing the shades on my damaged peepers. Harry laughs at me, and Englebert halfheartedly joins in.

"My eyes! What'd you do to my eyes?"

Whap! Another slap on the back of my head. "Quit whining," says Harry. "I took the bag off your head, that's all. It's bright out here, you moron."

Eyes adjusting now, red streaks fading from my corneas. The clearing slowly comes into view, and it's mostly how I pictured it: a rough circle of emptiness hewn out of the surrounding vegetation, the canopy overhead filtering out much of the sunlight, but not enough to give my weary eyes a rest. The one feature I hadn't guessed at is most prominent, though, sitting as it is in the dead center of the clearing: a log cabin, small but sturdy, just like good ol' Abe Lincoln would have made. For all I know, he did.

Harry gives me a little shove, a football pat on my rump. "Go on," he says.

"In there?"

"Yeah, in there."

"Can I take the clothespin off my nose?"

"No."

As I walk toward the cabin, breathing heavily through my mouth, I notice that neither Harry nor Englebert is following me. I'm a good thirty yards ahead of them now, and in theory I could make a break for it—burst across the clearing like a gazelle and crawl madly to safety through the underbrush. Call the cops, alert them to the situation, and live to tell the tale on the talk show of my choosing.

Unfortunately, while I am quite the feisty badger when it comes to burrowing, my speed has always been closer to that of a chubby dachshund than that of a gazelle. Even if I were able to outrun the two lugs behind me, there stands a good chance that they'd be carrying long-range weapons that could drop me in a second no matter how finely tuned my burrowing skills might be. I decide to enter the cabin.

Just my luck, there are no lights inside. Between Vallardo's incubation chamber and the Bloomie's bag, my visual spectrum today has gone from bright to dark to brighter to darker, and my peepers are getting a real workout trying to keep up. I stand in the doorway for a moment, allowing the outside light to stream in, before a female voice—low, insistent—says, "Close the door."

I comply, and find myself in darkness yet again. "Your eyes will adjust," says the voice. "Until that point, I have a few things to say. I ask you to remain quiet until I am done. Is that understood?"

I know a trick question when I hear one. Following orders, I keep my trap shut. "Very good," she says. "This may not be so difficult after all."

Shadows coming into view now—a stove, a chair, a fireplace perhaps, and a long, lithe form standing among it all. "I understand you are here on business," says the shadow, a thick tail slowly distinguishing itself amid the other silhouettes. "And I can respect that. We all have jobs to do, and we all do them to the best of our abilities. You would be remiss in your duties were you to give your work anything other than the full attention you have bestowed upon it thus far."

And now there's a neck, a long, graceful swan curve—arms, small but toned—almond-shaped eyes riding high above two ripe-plum cheeks. "I also understand that you are from Los Angeles," she says, "and though you may be under the impression that you are used to life in a megalopolis, though you may think you know how to conduct yourself and your business in the big city, I want you to get it through your mind that LA is a playpen compared to the Big Apple. What is acceptable at the mother's breast is not acceptable in the nursery.

"I've brought you out here for your own good, not for mine. In fact, I've already saved your life on two occasions. Disbelieve this if you choose to, but it is the truth."

A Coleophysis, no doubt about it, and a stunner at that. Each of her six toes is the perfect length, the perfect circumference, the webbing between bearing not a blemish. And her tail—that tail! oh!—twice again as thick as mine and forty times as dear. I only wish this damned clothespin were off so that I could breathe deeply of her scent.

She says, "I would be lying if I said that I didn't . . . understand your work.

But if you persist with all of these questions, this investigation . . . There is only so much I can do to protect you. Do you understand?"

"I understand your points," I say, my eyes finally finished with their lethargic adjustments, "though I don't necessarily agree with them."

"I didn't think you would."

"I also don't understand why you're dragging me into a cabin in Jersey. You coulda sent a telegram."

"None of this concerns you," says the Coleophysis. "But unlike some others, I don't believe you should get hurt."

"Aside from a scrape with Harry and Englebert back there, I haven't had much danger at all. You know that thug of yours threatened to rip my throat out?"

"They told you their names, did they?" Lips puckered, clearly unhappy.

I shrug. "You don't just pick Englebert outta the air."

"Tell me something," she says, coming closer, hot breath on my throat. "Why do you find it necessary to stir up trouble?"

"Am I stirring? I thought it was more of a shake."

A pause. Will she kiss me or spit at me? Neither—the Coleophysis backs away. "You went to see Dr. Emil Vallardo, is that correct?"

"Considering your goons picked me up outside the medical center, I'd say you know it's correct." Without asking permission—enough with the permission—I squat up and down, up and down, trying to get feeling back in my legs. The Coleo pays my impromptu workout no mind.

"They're not my goons." Then, a moment later: "Dr. Vallardo is a twisted man, Vincent. Brilliant, but twisted. It would be better if you left him to work on his bastardization of nature by himself."

"I gather you don't approve," I say.

"I've seen his work. Firsthand." She pulls up a chair and lowers herself onto the seat. "You've also been bothering Judith McBride."

How does she know all this? Have I been followed since I stepped off the plane? It's distressing to learn that I've been so disoriented by the city that I haven't even been able to spot a tail despite my paranoia. Quick 360s are a regular routine anytime I move through the city; it's an ingrained action for me, like checking the rearview mirror of a car. Heck, I usually check for tails even when I'm in the shower.

"I haven't been bothering," I reply. "I've been interviewing."

A hard stare, and she pulls out a chair for me. "Please, sit." I give up my squats and plop down across the way. I notice that she hasn't mentioned my run-in with the dino-amalgamation in the alley behind the health clinic, but I figure she's either working up to that, or her spies were slacking off on the job that night.

The Coleo takes my hand in hers, and a tingle runs through my guise, up my arm, and stops my heart. Strangely enough, it feels nice. A moment later, it pounds back into action. "The fire at the Evolution Club was a horrible thing," she says to me, and from the glow in her eyes and the soft tones padding each word in cotton, I can tell she really means it. "Dinos died, and that was wrong. Donovan was hurt, and that was horrible. Horrible. And I understand your concern over your partner's death, as well. But it was all an accident. Can you understand that?"

I ask, "Were you there that night? When Ernie died?"

"No."

"What about in LA—at the club?"

"No." And even without my nose to send me clues, I can sense she's telling the truth on both counts. "But I know that what happened was not supposed to happen. Not in the ways it did."

"Fine. What was supposed to happen?"

A head shake, a hand toss—"This is my whole point, Vincent. You have to stop asking questions. You have to leave New York tonight and forget about it."

"I can't do that."

"You have to."

"I understand. I won't."

I can't tell if she's chuckling or crying—her head has fallen into her arms, her body racked with shoulder shudders and full-scale convulsions, easily a sobbing fit or laughing jag—but I take the break in the conversation to stretch again. All this sitting is wearing me out, and my hide is growing clammy beneath my guise.

She arises, her eyes glistening with tears—still no decision on that laughing or crying thing—and shakes her head, forfeiting the conversation. I wouldn't be surprised if there was a sigh in there, too. "I've done all I can," she says. "I can't protect you any more."

"I know," I say, even as part of me wonders why I'm not giving in, going home, and saving my skinny hide. Protection is usually a good thing, and it's only because I feel so close to something so big that I'm still in it at this stage of the game.

The Coleo says, "Is this job more important than your life, Mr. Rubio?"

I think it over, and she lets me take my time. My answer, slow in coming, is out of my mouth before I realize how true it is. "Right now, this job is my life."

She understands, and doesn't press the matter. I am glad. I look at my watch—it's getting late, and now that I'm pretty sure I'm not going to be whacked out in the middle of New Jersey, fatigue has begun to set in. My muscles ache to be released from their confines, already anticipating a nice hot soak back in the hotel bath.

"Are we almost done?" I ask, pointing to my watch. "I hate to be rude, but . . ."

"One more question," says the Coleo. "And then I'll have Harry and Englebert take you back to your hotel."

"Shoot."

"It's a personal question."

"No kisses on the first kidnapping."

"I know you went to the hospital to see Donovan," she says, and the way she says the burned Raptor's name—the tidal swell on the first syllable, the lilt on the next two—tells me she knew him once upon a time.

"I did."

"Tell me . . ." And then a hitch, a snap in her voice. She doesn't want to ask the question, perhaps because she doesn't want to know the answer. "Tell me, how is he doing?"

That pleading look in her eyes, the one that says *tell me everything's okay, tell me he's in no pain,* sets in motion a train of thought I never knew I had on the tracks: She's a Coleophysis—she's been watching me from the shadows—she has experience with Dr. Vallardo—she had her goons clip my nose so that I couldn't imprint her scent on my mind and thus find her again—she has remained out of sight, and wants to continue that way—but most of all, most important, she is still very much in love with Donovan Burke.

Even after all these years.

"He's looking swell," I lie, and the elusive Jaycee Holden smiles. "He's doing just great."

The bag is over my head again, though I've spent the last ten minutes protesting the decision, on the basis that since I already know where we are, there's no use in keeping me blinded in this fashion.

"Orders is orders," grumbles Harry.

"The lady told you to drive me back to the hotel. I was there, I heard her, she said nothing about the bag." Indeed, Jaycee had instructed the two dinos to return me to the Plaza safe and sound, and as quickly as possible. She emphasized this last part, as if she had some reason to feel they would act otherwise, and the dinos grudgingly acquiesced.

There is a grunt from the driver, whom I have yet to see, and Harry leans forward, mumbling something I cannot understand. Englebert has been closed-lipped the entire time, and his earlier willingness to play along with me has disappeared. I consider piping up again, perhaps asking that the air-conditioning be turned higher, but decide to sit back and play it cool for a while, to use the extra time to sort things out in my head.

I'm running over the connections one by one—Vallardo knew McBride, Nadel, Donovan, Jaycee—Judith McBride knew them all plus Sarah— Sarah slept with McBride and had a short interview with Ernie—Nadel ran autopsies on both McBride and Ernie—Nadel was killed by these two dinos sitting next to me—

And I notice that the surface of the road has changed. We're off the highway, off any form of pavement whatsoever, and onto a soft shoulder. Dirt kicking up behind the tires, car moving slowly now as it digs for purchase.

I put a hand on the bag—"Where are we?"

And my hand is roughly batted away. "None of your freaking business."

Brambles and branches scrape against the side of the car, and despite my lack of knowledge regarding the Tri-State area, I'm quite sure this isn't the way back to Manhattan.

"You fellas made a wrong turn," I say.

"No we didn't—did we, Harry?"

"No."

"I'm pretty sure you did. Ms. Holden told you to take me back to the Plaza, and this isn't Park Ave."

Harry leans close, pressing his forehead up against the bag, my ear and his lips separated only by a thin sheet of brown paper. "We don't take our orders from that bitch."

I know what this means even before I hear the snap of buttons, the zing of claws extending, locking into place. I know that I will never be brought back to my hotel room. They are planning to kill me, right here and right now.

With a mighty heave from my legs, I launch myself backward, into Englebert, my hands ripping away the bag over my eyes even as they tear away at the buttons that hold my gloves in place—

"Hold him!" Harry screams. "Get the—"

But I'm a slippery little eel, sliding behind the confused Englebert, pushing him in front of me like a shield. My gloves are sticking too well— no time to unsnap them properly—so I let my claws fly free, the sharp edges tearing through the soft latex fingertips, my weapons slicing up and through these useless human hands.

A tail slams into the seat next to me, nearly ripping the cushion in half, and I scoot back against the Town Car door, propping my feet against the window—it's come down to kill or be killed again, and I'm ready to play. Mustering all my strength, I hurl myself into the warm bodies of my attackers. The driver looks back, worried, slowing the car. The scent of battle is overwhelming, a rich blend of fear and anger.

We're balled in a heap of claws and growls, none of us able to free up our limbs, no time or chance to remove our masks, spit out our bridges. Harry's tail is free, but flails about wildly—if he tries to strike me, he'll hit himself as well, so I hold on to his body, scratching away at the eyes, the ears, any soft tissue I can find. Blood and sweat coat the inside of the car— Englebert's tangled up with us as well, and I think his claws might actually be digging into Harry's side—

"Give—give it up"—pants Harry—"you—ain't—gonna win—"

And the rest falls into a roar as I find some hidden reserve of energy, flipping the Brontosaur up and over, slamming him face first into the passenger seat. I reach back with my right claw, muscles taking control, ready to end it here and now—and an electric burst of pain, four sharp syringes of agony, shoots through my rib cage. Behind me, Englebert's claws come away coated with my blood.

I spin, arms outstretched, momentum carrying them in a wide circle—
not knowing where the blow will land, not really caring as long as my claws
hit something, anything.

They tear through the driver's neck.

The car shoots down the unpaved road as the driver slumps against the
steering wheel, his foot a dead weight against the gas pedal. The sound is
ferocious now, and I cannot distinguish the growling from the screaming
from the roaring from the rumble of the engine as the claws continue to fly
and the blood continues to pour and the flesh continues to vanish beneath
the furious assault and as I come up for air I get a glimpse out of the windshield of the giant tree ahead of us looming closer with every second and as
I fall back into the tangle of shredded human guises and dino flesh—

We crash.

It is a dream of sorts, though I am well aware that I'm lying on the floor of
the Town Car, blood covering my body, claw still extended, one arm buried
in the ripped passenger seat in front of me. In this . . . hallucination, let's
call it, a young human woman approaches the car—the same young woman
from the last few dreams, in fact—and stares down at my prone body. I try
to wave, try to blink, try to signal that I need help of some sort, but it is of
no use. She opens the car door and my head falls out, banging roughly
against the door frame. I am unable to move. Apprehension increases.

I am powerless to do anything but watch as this woman, whose features
are clear but whose overall face is still obscured by that glowing light that
comprises her hair, leans over me like a mother tucking in her child at night.
Our eyes meet, and I can see my reflection within them. She smiles, and my
nerves subside. Wordlessly, her mouth opens, heading toward mine. A kiss in
the making, and I am unable to pucker. Lips parting, tongue snaking out—

And she licks up the blood covering my face, slurping it down with a
smirk upon her lips. I scream and, once again, pass out.

The driver is dead. Harry is also dead. Englebert is not, though he is unconscious, and will probably remain that way for a few more hours. All
three of them were thrown through the windshield of the car when we hit
that big old oak, and I can't thank the Lincoln people enough that they
made their front seats sufficiently sturdy to withstand the force of a Veloci-

raptor propelled forward at sixty miles an hour. My guess is that this is not a standard safety test.

I awoke on the rear floor of the Town Car, just as in my dream, covered in blood, some mine, some not, and stumbled out onto the soft ground. It has taken me some time since to regain my bearings. The highway is nearby; I can faintly make out engine noise and horns in the distance. As usual, my first order of business is to clear the scene, and though it takes me some time, I manage to reguise Harry and Englebert, taking great pains to manually retract their claws and replace their gloves. If for some reason Englebert is unable to deal with the situation once he awakens, or should he croak from his considerable injuries, I can't take the risk of a human coming across a bunch of half-guised dead dinosaurs in the middle of New Jersey.

I'm hoping that a quick search of the Town Car will give me some clue as to who ordered the hit on me. But the trunk is empty, the glove compartment similarly so, except for the standard pink slips. Even the registration doesn't help; the owner is listed as Sam Donavano, an unfamiliar name. A quick search of the dead driver produces a wallet and a smattering of identification cards—sure enough, it's Mr. Donavano himself.

My own costume, though ripped, is certainly salvageable and, as long as I can clean off some of the bodily fluids, should suffice on the trip back into the city. I'm able to hold off the more insistent geysers of blood with a tourniquet made from Harry's shirt, and I'm glad that this time I don't have to waste any of my own clothing for medical supplies. It's going to take some time to pick up a ride back to the city—even if I weren't a little bloody, I'm limping and dragging my poor abused body along like a consummate drifter—and the sun is beginning its plunge toward the horizon. Darkness will only help obscure me, though, and obscuration is what I need right now, in spades. I sit down near the oak tree and try to remain awake.

The plan is simple: I will wait for nightfall, and I will return to the city and to the relative safety of my hotel room. Then I will get undressed, lie down on that cloud of a bed, and complete my trifecta of slumber for the day by passing out for a third and final time.

That is, if no one else tries to kill me.

o rest for the wicked. I have no sooner arrived back at the hotel room, removed my guise, taken a much-needed shower, sewn up more gaping holes in the pseudoflesh, reguised, and begun to dress for bed before there is a knock at the door. I waddle over, penguinlike, pulling a pair of pants up and around my hips, and peek through the peephole. Can't be too careful, what with folks trying to kill me and all.

It's the concierge, a pleasant fellow named Alfonse whom I had the pleasure of meeting this morning on my way out of the hotel. I open the door.

"Good evening, Mr. Rubio," he says, bowing slightly at the waist. "I'm sorry to trouble you."

"No trouble." I pause. "Unless you're here to tell me there's trouble."

"Oh no, sir. You have a message, sir."

I glance toward the phone; the message indicator is not lit. Alfonse must understand, as he says, "I chose to deliver it by hand, Mr. Rubio, at the request of the lady who delivered it to me."

A lady, eh? Alfonse places a small pink envelope in my outstretched palm, and I trade him for a five-dollar bill. Pleased, the concierge thanks me, bids me a good evening, and departs. I close the door and sit on the bed.

The envelope is scented with a strong perfume, which tells me right away it's a human that sent it. Sarah.

Dear Mr. Rubio, the letter reads, *I would be grateful if you would accom-*

pany me to the theater and dinner this evening. They always give me Hal-
loween off, and rather than play dress-up, I would prefer to spend my night off
with someone as interesting as you may prove to be. If you are able to join me,
please arrive at the Prince Edward Theater no later than 7:30 P.M. I hope to
see you there, and remain Yours Truly, Sarah Archer.

In my rule book, it's illegal to turn down a dinner offer from a dame, especially when she's also a suspect. But Sarah Archer . . . she's interesting—
intriguing even—and I can't help feeling drawn to her in some way, even
though the rest of her kind give me the shakes. As it is, logic's been out the
window since I got to New York, and though I'm treading in thick water, I
choose to go with my instinct.

Downstairs, Alfonse gives me directions to the Prince Edward, which—
surprise—consists of him hailing a taxicab to take me there. I'm decked out
in the one suit I brought with me, a well-made ensemble of black and gray
pinstripes, and while it might not have come from the rafters of Rodeo, I
think it looks darned nice over my guise. I hand another fiver to Alfonse, he
shuts the door, and the cab shoots off toward the heart of the theater district. I haven't had any time to stock up on basil, and I find that though I'm
fresh out, the lack of herbs doesn't inspire in me the panic it once did. I'm
sure I'll find a hit somewhere, sometime.

"Prince Edward?" the taxi driver asks me. His accent is pure New York,
not a trace of foreign inflection.

"Meeting someone there," I explain.

"You seeing that show?"

"That show? The show at the Prince Edward, yes."

"Weird fucking show," says the cabbie, shaking his head back and forth.
"That's what they tell me—weird fucking show."

I arrive alive and intact at the Prince Edward ten minutes ahead of
schedule, giving me ample time to peruse the crowd. A surprising number
of dinos here—at least half the audience is of our kind, I estimate, and
that's much higher than the national average of 10 to 12 percent. Odd, but
I imagine it's either a fluke of statistics or that the show has been produced
by one of our kind.

I wait on the curb like a nervous teenager waiting for his prom date,
growing more apprehensive with every passing minute that Sarah will not
show. Has she stood me up? The other patrons have filed inside, and I'm

sure the show is about to begin. I look around, peer into the darkness for a car, a limousine, any sign of Sarah. Nothing.

"Mr. Rubio?" It's not Sarah's voice, but it's calling my name, and that's a start. I turn to find the ticket taker, the poor thing so hypoglycemic she's almost see-through. "Are you Vincent Rubio?" I tell her that I am, and she says, "Your ladyfriend called, said she's running a little late. Your ticket was at will-call, so . . . here." I am handed a ticket, ushered through the doors, and into my seat—third row, center, between a group of Asian businessmen and an elderly couple who already look bored.

The theater is decked out in jungle paraphernalia, leafy trees and papier-mâché caves plastered onto the walls. Tiger-striped and leopard-spotted fabric drape the stage, ambient roars and elephant trumpets fill the air, and whereas the motif might work in the dinner theaters of rural Santa Barbara, it's downright pathetic here on the Great White Way. The curtains are closed, the audience buzzing, and an illuminated sign, thirty feet long and fifteen feet tall, hangs proudly from the rafters.

It reads: MANIMAL, THE MUSICAL! And I know I'm in for a long, long night.

I have to admit, I was a big fan of *Manimal*, the TV show, back in '83. I got a kick out of watching Dr. Jonathan Chase battle crime, getting all heated up and turning into jungle animals at the drop of a hat, but I must have been the only one, as the show lasted about three months before it was canceled and left in the dumping grounds of low-budget, high-concept television. But even the most die-hard of *Manimal* fans couldn't sit through two and a half hours of a half man/half leopard crime solver singing and dancing his way through a drug-smuggling investigation.

The first song is called "Incredible Leopard Man, I Love You," with lyrics such as *Yes I knew you were part feline / so for you I made a beeline*, and it's at this point of the evening that I decide to turn off my brain, as its services are no longer needed.

Twenty minutes pass, during which time I am treated to two more musical numbers and a four-legged tap dance, when I feel a tap on my shoulder.

"Is this seat taken?" comes a whisper, and I turn, ready to defend the empty seat with all the valor I can muster while wedged into these cushions.

"Actually, it—" And then I see the reams of red hair cascading over bare shoulders, a bright yellow cocktail dress that announces its presence from clear across town, and a familiar figure packed into it all. My heart pounds against the muscles of my chest like King Kong beating his cage. "It's saved for a friend," I say.

Sarah casually lowers herself into the cushioned seat and leans over, whispering into my ear. It tickles. "Would your friend mind if I took her seat?"

"I don't think so," I respond, keeping my voice even as I try to bring my heart rate back to normal. "I really only met her yesterday."

"And she's already a friend?"

I shrug. "She must be. She asked me to the theater."

"She has house seats." She crosses her legs, adjusts the skirt. "What'd I miss?"

Forcing myself into a library whisper, I attempt to catch Sarah up on the main plot points of *Manimal: The Musical*. Trouble is, there aren't many. "Let's see . . . we've got this guy running around, he's human, but he's also a cat. And there are some smugglers."

We silently endure a series of songs about leopards, lions, badgers, drug smuggling (*Buy an ounce or buy a pound / cocaine makes the world go round*), and more leopards, and eventually it all winds up before intermission with a particularly morose Dr. Chase lamenting his woeful state as a creature of two worlds. The audience applauds—Sarah and I mindlessly follow along—and the houselights flick on. Fifteen minutes to get in a good stretch before the second act.

"Would you like a drink?" I ask. "I can bring you something from the bar."

Sarah shakes her head. "They won't let you drink in the theater. I'll come with."

By the time we make our way out of the lower orchestra—human men are leering, soaking in Sarah all the way and though she's not my species I'm still walking tall—the few bars in the Prince Edward are packed with throngs of theatergoers already half in the bag, anxious to get a different perspective on the second half of this opus. Sarah and I step to the end of the line, behind a dino couple guised up as an elderly husband and wife. Their smells—a fireplace, redwood logs burning steadily—are nearly indistinguishable from one another, and though I know it's just an old dino's tale that the scents of a husband and wife become more and more similar over the years, every day I find empirical evidence leading me to believe it.

The elderly couple turn around—they must have picked up on my scent—and nod their heads at me, a friendly how-do-you-do that we dinos occasionally give to others of our kind like a classic car owner honking at a fellow enthusiast who's also driving by in a 1973 Mustang Fastback. But then they see Sarah—and then they smell Sarah, or, more correctly, then they *don't* smell Sarah—and the smiles fade, replaced instantly by grimaces of revulsion.

She's a witness! I want to scream, *Maybe a friend, but nothing more!* Then again, I don't want to protest too much.

"The line is long," I say, searching for something, anything to break the silence.

"Sure is," says Sarah. "If we wait for our drinks, we probably won't make it back to the theater in time to catch the beginning of the second act."

"Yeah. Yeah. Wouldn't want to miss that."

"So you like it?" she asks, seductively twisting her skirt with a petite fist.

"The show? Of course. He's a man, he's an animal . . . he's a Manimal. How can you miss?"

"Ah." She seems disappointed.

"You?"

"Oh, sure. Sure. I mean, what's not to like, right? You've got leopards, and . . ."

"And tigers," I chime in.

"Right. And tigers."

We're lying. Both of us. And we both know it.

Giggling, we run hand in hand across the lobby, down the stairs, and out of the Prince Edward like two schoolchildren playing hooky for the very first time.

An hour later we're still chuckling away, the most infectious part of the laughter having died out fifteen minutes ago. For a while there we were in trouble, one giggling jag setting off the fuse of another, neither of us able to control ourselves long enough to order from the menu at a small Greek tavern we found near the theater. Eventually, I was forced to bite my tongue, cutting off the laughter but nearly replacing it with tears and a trip to the hospital—one of my caps had come loose, and my naturally spiked tooth jammed into my tongue with a force I wasn't expecting. Fortunately, I was able to fake a bathroom emergency, fix my tooth, ensure that my tongue wasn't going to flop out of my mouth and onto Sarah's lap during the course of dinner, and make it back to the table in time for a second run at the menu. Now we wait, we talk, and we drink.

"No, no—" Sarah takes a sip of her wine, her lips leaving a precious red imprint on the glass, "it's not that. I can see where *someone* would like it."

"But not you."

"Not me. Anthropomorphism is nice and all—"

"Big word, ma'am—"

"—but it's hard for me to accept a whole society populated by humanoid felines, operating under some obscure self-imposed rules, running around undetected by the rest of us."

"Not realistic?"

"No, not entertaining."

Our appetizers arrive, and we nibble on hummus, *tzatziki,* and *tarama,* lapping up the dip with wide slabs of pita. Our waiter is as Greek as they come—for this Halloween eve, he has dressed as Zorba in an open-backed vest—and he reads off the day's specials with gusto, each word a meal unto itself. Sarah asks for help with her selection, and I suggest the Greek Platter, figuring I can always pick at whatever she isn't able to eat.

I even go so far as to gingerly pick as much basil and dill from my portions as possible, the action almost automatic, fork dipping and removing before I have a chance to regulate the movement. Whatever we're doing now—Sarah and me—somehow feels right, and this is the first time in a long time that I don't feel the need to chew an herb. For her part, Sarah asks for my helpings of basil to be added to her plate, and since it won't affect her like it would me, I'm glad to oblige.

Squinting into the dim light of the restaurant, Sarah carefully scrutinizes my face, her forehead rumpling into precious little foothills. Her eyes roam my features, dropping around my nose, my lips, my chin.

"Do I have food on my face?" I say, suddenly self-conscious. I rapidly wipe my chin and lips with my napkin, flicking the cloth around and around, hoping to soak up whatever Greek delicacy has managed to moonlight as a facial.

"It's not that," she giggles. "It's . . . I mean . . . the mustache."

"You don't like it?"

Sarah must see my injured look, as she comes back quickly with, "No, no, I like it! I do! It's just that when I saw you . . . what, last night . . . you were clean shaven."

I have no response to this. Costume additions are usually meant to be attached step-by-step in order to give the impression of a natural process—the Nanjutsu Pectoral series, which I considered buying during my vainglorious years, for example, must be slowly built up over a series of months—but mustaches, as far as I know, have always been a one-day journey into machismo.

"It's fake, right?"

"Of course not!" I reply indignantly. "It's just as real as the rest of my body."

Sarah, giggling again, impulsively leans forward and tugs hard on my facial hair. This wouldn't usually hurt, but the light layer of epoxy beneath my mask transfers her yank to my hide beneath, and my "Ouch!" is genuine.

Embarrassed, abashed, Sarah turns away, melting into a sanguine flush. "I'm so sorry," she says. "I really thought . . ."

"We grow hair fast in my family," I say, trying to bring our previous light soufflé tone back into the conversation. "My mother was a terrier."

Sarah laughs at this, and I am pleased to see her chagrin get up and excuse itself from the table. "If you don't like it," I continue, "I can shave it off."

"Really, I like it. Promise." She crosses her heart with a slim finger.

We eat some more. We drink some more. We chat.

"How is the case going?" she asks, refilling her wine glass as she talks.

"Is this a business dinner?"

"Not if you don't want it to be."

Is this a come-on? I play it safe. "No, no, it's fine. Case still wide open. Leads, leads, leads, that's the PI's life. Put it together, hit frappe, and see what spins out."

Sarah finishes off the bottle of wine—good god, can she drink—and orders up another. "You still haven't interviewed me yet," she points out. "Not really."

"It's not polite to grill your date."

"Is this a date?" she asks.

"Not if you don't want it to be."

We smile at the same time, and Sarah leans across the table and pecks me on the forehead. She leans back, dress clinging tightly to her bosom. Soft swells of flesh rise up from the neckline, nipples standing at attention, and I find a strange desire to . . . to touch them? Impossible. I think of the pile of bills waiting for me back in Los Angeles, and the illicit thoughts burst apart and vanish.

"I'd rather we get down to it now," she continues. "Ask me what you need to ask me. I don't want you thinking things about me that aren't true or not thinking things about me that are true."

"You know my case is about Mr. McBride. Raymond. It's not—not really—but close enough."

"I know."

"And you feel comfortable talking about him?" Usually I could give a shit over how witnesses feel—I think of that annoying Compy, Suarez, and my stomach turns in knots—but I allow myself a few special dispensations now and again.

"Ask away," says Sarah. The waiter pops over with a second bottle of wine, and Sarah doesn't bother inspecting the label, sniffing the cork, or tasting the sample before bolting it down by the glassful.

With no notebook handy, I'll have to make do with memory. "How long had you known Mr. McBride? Before . . ."

She appears to think it over. Then—"A few years. Two, maybe three."

"And you met . . . how?"

A wistful look clouds her eyes and her fingers crawl aimlessly about her neckline, drawing my attention down, down, down . . . "At that charity event," she says. "In the country."

"Which country?"

"The country. As in the countryside. Long Island, I think, maybe Connecticut."

Doesn't matter. "And Raymond was hosting?"

"He and his . . . wife"—again, some serious animosity there, the words scorching the surrounding air—"were throwing it at their second home."

The questions come quicker, easier, fluttering off my slightly damaged tongue. "Why were you there?"

"My agent took me. It was a charity event. I was being charitable."

"But you don't remember the charity."

"Correct." She clumsily places a finger on her nose with one hand and points at me with the other. Drunkard move, but cute.

"Fine. So there you are hobnobbing with the rich and famous—"

"Mostly rich. I don't think I saw anyone all that famous."

"Just a phrase. So you meet Raymond that night . . ."

"Daytime," she corrects, and now I'm oh for two. "It was a long affair, if I remember correctly. I arrived in the early afternoon, and didn't leave until the next day. Everyone stayed over at the house."

"You hit it off right away?"

"I wouldn't say right away, but it was obvious something was there. The wife and I got along well that day, actually. By the next morning, we hated each other."

File that. "Did you sleep with Raymond that night?"

I can almost hear the SLAP! and see the welts forming as my offhand question smacks into Sarah's stunned face. I didn't mean it that way. I wasn't thinking. It was stupid, it was dumb, but I'm too aghast at my own words to voice any regret. This is not the first time my runaway mouth has shattered fragile circumstances—once the PI part of me gets turned in a certain direction, the gas gets floored and the power steering goes out, which is great if I'm on a straightaway—but if there's a cliff in front of me, so long Vincent.

Sarah's response is low, pained, the voice of a young girl huddling in a corner who doesn't understand why she's being punished. "Is that how you see me?" she asks.

"No, no, I—"

"Talk to a man once and then sleep with him?"

"That's not what I—"

"Because if you do see me that way, I don't want to disappoint you. You wanna leave the restaurant, go home and lay me, okay, let's go." Anger flooding her eyes now, spilling over onto the table, washing out the restaurant. She leaps to her feet unsteadily and pulls at my arm. "Get on up, boy, and let's go home and see how you can put it to me." Patrons turning, listening, eager to get an earful and enrich their workaday lives. I can almost smell the rancor on her.

I place my hand over hers, trying to restore tranquillity to our once-idyllic table for two. "Please," I say, "I didn't mean it like that." Slow subsidence of the anger waves now, flowing away, back out to sea, look out for the undertow. "Please. I get ahead of myself sometimes. It comes with the job."

Two glasses of wine and a few more dips of *tzatziki* later, Sarah accepts my apologies. "No," she says pointedly, returning to the conversation. "I did not sleep with him that night."

"I gathered that."

"I won't say I didn't find him attractive, though. That strong, weathered face, creased with those deep lines—wrinkles that let you know he'd *been* somewhere. Long, tight muscles, broad shoulders . . . On the outside, Raymond was a very durable man. Not physically, mind you, but mentally. Emotionally."

"And on the inside?"

"You wouldn't see the inside unless you knew him well, and then you learned what made Raymond . . . Raymond. He had some interesting peculiarities, some more endearing than others. I doubt anyone other than myself and maybe his wife knew Raymond as he really, truly was."

Should I tell her that her beloved Raymond was widely known as a philanderer? That he'd seen more mattresses than Inspector Number 7? That while she might have been the last of his lovers, she was surely not his only one? But what would be the point in that, other than to hurt the girl—I've already gotten in my quota of stinging remarks today. Perhaps I am jealous of McBride, of his willingness to flaunt societal constraints, of his desires for the forbidden, which were obviously so much stronger than mine. But this kind of thinking is both destructive and completely moronic, and so I snip it off at the source.

". . . but even if he had been interested at the time," Sarah is saying, "I was in a relationship."

"With whom?"

"With my agent."

"Your agent? Is that wise, mixing business and pleasure?"

"Sometimes it's best," says Sarah, and I'm both glad and troubled to see she's moved away from anger, back toward seduction. Anger wasn't fun, but easier to handle. "In this case, no, it wasn't wise. We broke up soon after the party, in fact. Which left me out of a relationship and Raymond still in one."

"Judith."

Sarah waves off the name with an annoyed flick of her hand, as if swatting away a bothersome fly. "We didn't call her that. We called her missus, plain and simple. Missus. It was better for me, it was better for Raymond."

"Was he still in love with her?"

In the time it takes Sarah to begin her answer, the waiter arrives with our entrées. My Lemon Chicken is well prepared, but Sarah's Greek Platter looks positively scrumptious. Fortunately, I'm sure she won't finish it all, and then I can peck away.

The waiter trots off, and we hunker down, tearing into our dinners like Compys come upon a fresh kill. I am not surprised at my appetite—it's been over twelve hours since I've had anything substantial, and although my breakfast this morning was a feast fit for the roundest of royals, I'm famished.

What I am surprised at is Sarah's ability to make food disappear off her plate in what has got to be Guinness time. Moussaka, Chicken Olympia, Pastisio, some eggplant dish I've never heard of before—I watch in growing amazement as each forkful enters that darling mouth, only to emerge empty a moment later and return to the plate for more. My word, where does it all go? Under the table? Into a roving dog? But I can see the long lines of her throat swallowing, so I know she's ingesting every bite. How does that platter of food, which probably weighs more than the model herself, vanish into that body? There is some twisted perversion of the laws of nature going down in this Greek tavern, a clash of food and antifood, but I'll be damned if I can figure out how it's working. If I hadn't had the disappearance of Jaycee Holden solved for me today, I'd think that maybe Sarah had eaten her.

I am unable to talk. I can only watch. Wow. Wow.

Ten minutes later, Sarah is finished with dinner and my jaw is agape.

"Hungry?" I ask.

"Not anymore."

I should hope not. Sarah pushes her plate away, and despite the prodigious amounts she's recently ingested, I can't make out a bulge anywhere on that tummy. People like Sarah evoke a lot of hatred from the body-conscious all around the world, but I'm too astounded to feel jealous over metabolic rates. "Where were we?" I ask, honestly forgetting. That display of concentrated consumption put me off my track.

"You asked if Raymond was still in love with the missus," says Sarah, using the title to refer to Judith McBride, "and I hadn't yet answered."

"Well then . . . was he?"

Again, she pauses, though I would think that she'd had enough time to ponder her answer while digesting the whole of Greece. Of course, it probably takes a good portion of one's brain power to shovel it down like that. "Have you ever had an affair, Vincent?"

"With a married woman?"

"Yes, with a married woman."

"I have not." I came close, though. I'd been tailing a Bronto's wife, trying to get the usual incriminating photos, and found that although she was not currently engaged in an extramarital affair, she was most interested to get one started. She'd caught me snapping pictures outside her bedroom window, and the next thing I knew, I was sipping champagne in the Jacuzzi to the strains of vintage Tom Jones. I had to wait until she'd gone back in the house to slip out of her guise and "into some skin more comfortable" before I could make my getaway.

"Married people are just that," Sarah tells me. "Married. You can't ask if a married man who is having an affair is still in love with his wife, because it's a question without a point. It is immaterial whether or not he loves her, because she is his wife, plain and simple."

I pick at my dinner, mulling over her viewpoint and my next question. "How often did you see him?"

"Often."

"Two, three times a week?"

"By the end? More like five or six. He'd try to spend Sundays with the missus, but by that point she wasn't very interested."

"So she knew?"

Sarah snickers derisively as she leans over and plucks a lemon potato off my plate. "Oh, she knew. She's not a dumb lady, I'll give her that much.

You'd have to be a real piece of granite not to notice something like that. Working late, every weeknight? Sure, Raymond was a driven man, but no one puts in eighteen-hour days at the office for nine months straight.

"I think the missus got the picture after the first month or so, because Raymond started to loosen up on the telephone. Calling me by my name, not screwing around with code words. Before that it was all cloak-and-dagger, and I could tell when she walked into the room because he'd start calling me Bernie and talking about the great round of golf we'd played the other day. And I hate golf. All my life I've been surrounded by golfers. Please tell me you've never played golf."

"Twice."

"You poor soul."

"Raymond loved that damn game. We'd be in Paris, taking in the spring air, walking through the Arab Quarter, stopping in the shops, talking to the people, and he'd be practicing his swing, wondering what kind of club he'd use if he had to hit a ball over that storefront and into the window of that church. Fourth-tier Eiffel Tower was a nine wood, by the way."

"He took you to Paris, then?"

"Paris, Milan, Tokyo, all the hot spots around the globe. Oh, we were quite the jet-setting couple. Surprised you didn't see us in some social column."

"I don't read much. *TV Guide* sometimes."

"Pictures in all the international magazines, Raymond McBride and his traveling companion. They never mentioned his wife, and they never made a deal over it. That's the one good thing about Europeans—to them, adultery is like cheese. Options are plentiful and varied, only occasionally accompanied by a stench."

The rumors, then, were true: McBride had lost his mind. This well-known Carnotaur had obviously flipped out, flaunting his human girlfriend to the world, even going so far as to let magazines link them romantically. And while the International Councils are not quite as stringent about sexual mores as are the American Councils, cross-mating is still verboten across the globe. All it takes is one slipup from any of us, from the smallest Compy in the smallest district of Liechtenstein, and the last hundred and thirty million years of a persecution-free environment could all be over. Not including the Middle Ages, of course. Dragons, my ass . . .

"Did he offer to marry you?"

"Like I said, he was married to the missus and that's that. I assume they had some sort of arrangement."

"Arrangement?"

"He slept with me, she slept with whomever she slept with." Sarah is glancing about the other tables, looking for more alcohol.

"So you think Jud—Mrs. McBride—was having an affair as well?"

"Think?" Sarah tosses her head, clears some cobwebs, and I have to stop her from motioning toward our waiter-turned-sommelier. " 'Course she was having an affair. She was having an affair before I ever came along, that's for sure."

I should be shocked, I know, but I can't dredge up the proper emotion. "Did you know the guy she was sleeping with?"

A head shake, a nod, and I can't tell if Sarah's answering me or about to drop off into sleep. "Yeah . . ." she murmurs. "That damn . . . nightclub manager."

Score one up for Vincent Rubio. My initial queries into the nature of Donovan and Judith's relationship, questions that clearly had put Judith on edge, will have to be brought up again the next time I see Mrs. McBride. Obliquely, of course, and with all tact, and if that doesn't work, directly and rudely.

"Sarah," I ask, "did you know Donovan Burke?"

"Hm . . . ?"

"Donovan Burke—did you know him? Did you know Jaycee Holden, his girlfriend?"

But Sarah's head is drooping now, tottering in all the cardinal directions, balancing precariously atop that long neck, and no recognizable answer is forthcoming. The wine is finally wielding its power, taking its toll despite the six tons of Greek food mopping it up in her stomach. "He wanted to see his children so badly," Sarah whimpers, on the verge of tears.

"Who wanted to see his children?"

"Raymond. He wanted children more than any other man I've known."

She's rambling now, muttering words I can't make out, but I have to pursue this a little longer. I lift Sarah's head, force her to watch my lips. "Why didn't he have children?" I ask her, making sure to enunciate clearly. "Was it Mrs. McBride? She didn't want kids?"

Sarah flails her arms, tossing my hand from her face. "Not her!" she yells, drawing attention from the general public for the third time this evening. "He wanted to have them with *me*. With me . . ." She trails off, sobs wracking her body.

No wonder she's such a wreck—this poor girl lived the last few years of her life under the delusion that she would eventually carry Raymond McBride's child, never knowing that such a thing was a physical impossibility. Who knows what other lies he told her? And the fact that McBride was so involved in it as well leads me to believe that perhaps he did indeed have Dressler's Syndrome, as many have surmised, that he had truly begun to think of himself as human, unable to distinguish his daily deception from the reality within.

The combination of wine and painful memories has made an emotional invalid out of Sarah Archer, and I feel honor-bound to make sure she returns back home safely. "Let's go," I say, tossing a hundred dollars on the table to cover the cost of dinner, wine, and a sizable tip. With the exception of two twenties tucked into my sock, it's the last bit of cash I have in the world—I should pay with the TruTel credit card, but at this point it's better that we exit, stage left, as soon as possible.

Dragging Sarah up and away from the table isn't as easy as I'd expected; she's not as heavy as the dino-mix I towed behind the Dumpster, but her drunken body machinations give her a lot more heft than her small form should allow. We stumble backward, Sarah slumped atop my lap like an oversized ventriloquist's dummy, and I grunt with exertion.

"Are we having fun yet?" Sarah asks, throwing her arms around my neck and hugging me close. This is easier, at the very least, though her proximity is causing some involuntary reactions that are inappropriate for both the location and the species. The other restaurant patrons are wholly involved in our struggle, having as they do box seats for the main event. I can see their faces grimace along with mine as I half-drag, half-support Sarah as we make our way toward the door. Ten feet away, no more, but it might as well be a mile.

The waiters are approaching, offering their help, holding open doors for us, anxious, I assume, to conclude this evening's entertainment, and I'm more than happy to accept their aid. We emerge from the tavern into the torpid Indian-summer air, the humidity wreaking havoc on my makeup, and I glance about the street for the nearest bench. We wobble over to a bus stop covered in advertisements (which have themselves been covered with graffiti), and I let Sarah plop onto the hard wooden slats. Her skirt hikes up even higher than before, betraying a hint of sun-drenched yellow panties.

"Stay here," I say, pulling her skirt down into a more modest position. "Don't go anywhere."

Sarah grabs my wrist, holds it tight. "Don't leave," she says. "Everyone leaves."

"I need to find us a cab," I tell her.

"Don't leave," she repeats.

Straddling the bus stop, one foot on the bench, one foot in the street, my wrist still enveloped in Sarah's hands, I wave my free arm like an SOS flag, hoping that a taxi will emerge from the darkness and rescue us. Sarah has begun to sing, a muddied conglomeration of words, word fragments, and scatting, her song carrying across the busy city street and into the night. That rich contralto, layered with evident training, is strong through the haze of drink, and I'm surprised at the clarity of the melody despite the fractured lyrics.

Five minutes later, we are still taxi-free, and Sarah's song dribbles to a halt. She releases my wrist and falls silent. The hubbub of traffic drifts away as well, the rest of the world dropping out, vanishing, leaving only a single streetlight illuminating a bus bench, a gorgeous woman, and the Velociraptor standing guard over her.

"Your voice . . ." I whisper. "It's incredible."

Her only response is to look up at me—a feat, considering how that head must be spinning—and smile tightly. The streetlight makes golden droplets from the tears in her eyes, and all I can think to do is kiss them away. I kneel down, my lips nearing her eyes, nearing her cheeks, and suddenly I can taste the saltwater, I can taste the pain, and I can't stop it, I'm no longer in control as my mouth slides across her skin, slipping through the tears, slowly, gaining speed, searching out her lips, the soft flesh sizzling between us, moving, tongues roving, muted moans of need rumbling through our chests, a deep kiss that draws me in and blacks me out—

A taxi pulls up, honking.

"You wanna ride? You—lovebirds! You shaking your hand around before, you wanna ride?"

I may have to kill this man. Sarah and I break apart, the stars slowly clearing from my vision. Sarah's eyes are still closed, though I suspect it's more from drowsiness than enduring pleasure.

"I don't got all night," calls the cabbie.

"One second!" I shout back.

"You don't gotta yell about it!"

Sarah is too far gone to help along as I lift her off the bench and onto my shoulder like a Neanderthal carrying his devoted wife across the plains. Already, I feel disgusted with my actions. My mouth and a human mouth . . . the possibilities for disease are tremendous.

"You got your hands full there," says the cabbie as I lower Sarah into the backseat. "Quite a hot little number."

I choose not to dignify his crude comment with a response and wriggle in next to Sarah, who has chosen this moment to completely pass out. Not good—I don't know the fair lady's address. A light slap on the face does no good, nor does a rough shake of the shoulders.

As I close the door of the cab, sealing us tight within its restric-tive confines, the smell hits me—soft leather and canned dog food, a dino scent if I've ever smelled one. The cabbie turns in his seat, my Robusto-tinted odor hitting him at the same time.

"Hey," he says, "always good to have a fellow dino"—he pronounces it "diner"—"in my cab. Welcome aboard." He thrusts out a meaty paw.

"Shhhhh!" I caution, nodding toward Sarah. I needn't worry—she's kilometers from conscious—but you can never be too sure around humans.

"You mean she . . . No wonder I didn't smell—"

"Yes. Yes."

The cabbie wiggles his eyebrows at me, a lewd leer that says *I know what you're up to, you sly dog, you.* He confirms my suspicions by saying, a moment later, "Well, well. If you're gonna do it, go all the way, that's what I say."

"That's not it. We're friends."

"Not what it looked like on that bench back there."

"Really, we—"

"Don't worry about me, pal, I won't say a thing. Damn Council fucks think they can run our lives, hell, I can't vote for all but one of 'em, and my guy's always getting pushed around." This moron is under the impression that the Council actually accomplishes things during their interminable weeklong meetings. Must be a Compy.

"No," I say, possibly more for my benefit than for his, "there's nothing going on."

He leans farther over the seat, nearly planting himself in my lap, and drops his voice to a whisper. "I know a buncha guys like you, and I tell you, I wish I had the guts. I see these broads walking around, and I got urges, too, right? Hey, I live dressed up like this most of my life, I get horny to feel the real thing, you know? But I was brought up real strict, I guess. Can't get past it in my head."

He's implying that my moral fiber is not up to snuff. I consider hitting him, taking Sarah out of the cab, calling the Council down on him for some minor infraction that I'll make up if I have to, but the truth is he's right. That one kiss—moment of weakness or not—proves it.

"But if I could get my hands on one of them real human asses . . . every dino's forbidden gamble, right?" He looks over at Sarah, practically slurping her in through his eyes. "And ooh, boy, have you hit the jackpot."

"Look," I say, gathering all the indignation I can from my withered supply, "there is nothing between us. Nothing. Sorry to ruin your wet dream. Can we go now?"

The cabbie narrows his lids, grits his teeth, temples pulsing—is he going to pop me one?—then shrugs, turns back around, and slams the gearshift into drive with a karate chop. "Whatever you say, pal. I don't give a damn what you do. Where to?"

No point in pressing the matter; as long as he doesn't make a further issue out of it, I certainly won't. "The Plaza," I tell him. By the time we reach my hotel, Sarah will be sober enough to give me her address, and I can pay the driver to take her home.

A grunt of derision from the front seat as we leave the curb and merge with traffic. On our way to the Plaza, we pass by the back entrance to the Prince Edward Theater. Tonight's performance must have just ended, for as the theatergoers stream out, they congregate by the stage door where the cast, still guised up in their costumes and makeup, sign autographs for people who have never heard of them before. But as we drive by, I watch children and adults, men and women alike, singing, dancing, laughing, acting out the musical numbers, and I'm pleased to see that someone was obviously enriched by the *Manimal* experience.

I roll down the passenger window and toss my Playbill into the crowd.

am fortunate in that Sarah decided to throw up inside the cab rather than inside my hotel room, as the cabbie had then been forced to clean up the resultant mess instead of me. I am also fortunate that Sarah's regurgitation, a hearty concoction of eggplant, tahini, and voluminous amounts of white wine, has served to partially sober up my little human model, moving her out of falling-down-disintegration mode into a stumbling stupor.

The upshot of all this is that Sarah is able to help support herself as I guide her through the Plaza lobby and toward the elevators. A little rest in the room, that's all, and then it's back to her apartment. She's wobbly, but walking, and that's more than I had expected. There we wait, as the two supposedly express lifts make their way down from the highest floors. An Oriental carpet lies underfoot, a detailed rug that, if destroyed, would clean out my savings account and then some, so I make a silent wish to the nausea gods to spare Sarah from any more mishaps. If they want an offering, I'll gladly shatter a bottle of Maalox next time I'm in a drugstore.

An older couple enters the elevator lobby arm in arm. How cute. Familiar, in some way, though I can't place it. I have seen them before. Hm . . . The piercing looks they launch at me bring it home—this is the snooty dino couple from the bar line at *Manimal: The Musical*, the ones who had practically given themselves nosebleeds climbing up to the moral high ground.

Sarah slips in my arms, and I do my best to tighten my grip around her waist. She flops against my body like a worn rag doll, draping herself across my frame. Struggling to keep her upright, I smile at the couple, chuckling as if to show my good humor over the situation. *Ha ha,* this chuckle is intended to convey. *What a silly misunderstanding. I'll be telling my purebred Raptor kids all about this one some day.* No response from the couple. The ensuing silence is painful, so I break out with, "Enjoy the show?"

It's hard to discern their reactions with those upturned noses.

For some reason, Sarah chooses this moment to speak in complete, coherent sentences. "You have a good time tonight?" she slurs, each word cresting and crashing on syncopated beats. "'Cause I had a great time."

"Yes, yes, good time. Ha ha, yes, yes."

She tweaks my nose with her thumb and index finger, twisting it harder than I'm sure she means to. The playful gesture brings tears to my eyes. "I mean, I had a *really* great time."

"Great time," I echo, rubbing my nose. I turn toward the couple again, to explain, to shrug, to indicate in some way that this scene, no matter how lascivious it might seem, is not what they think, but the elderly dinos have disappeared.

Sarah grabs at my nose again, and I gently take her hand away, saying, "You need to get some sleep."

"What I need," whispers Sarah, bonking her forehead into mine, "is you."

I pretend not to hear that.

"You you you," repeats Sarah, and this time it's hard to shut out the voice. "I need you." My best response is no response, so I keep my tongue glued to the roof of my mouth while we wait for the elevator, which has obviously entered some type of space-time warp.

The lift finally arrives, and the brass doors slide open. I step back to allow the passengers—a young couple, very much in love, hanging all over each other—out into the lobby. But when I move left, they move left. I move right, and they move right.

It's a mirror. I choose not to think about this. We enter.

The elevator's acceleration nearly throws both Sarah and me to the ground—oh sure, *now* it's express—and once again we clutch each other tightly as we ascend to the top floor.

"Speedy," giggles Sarah, digging into my shoulder for support.

The presidential suite is situated all by itself at the end of a long corridor, set off from the more pedestrian suites in the vicinity. It's a long walk when sober, and I can't begin to imagine what it will be like trying to drag Sarah down there in her condition. Like a weary sailor who knows he has one final leg of his journey before he can return to family, friends, and a home-cooked meal, I wrap Sarah's arm around my neck and set my sails to the wind.

We manage to make it down the hallway with only a few minor slips and spills, Sarah flicking in and out of consciousness like a TV on the fritz. I open the door.

Curse this suite for being so large. I hustle Sarah into the bedroom, using short, quick hops to move across the marble foyer. At this point, my tail would come in darn handy, and I consider loosening it for the short trip. But that would require taking off my pants, and the last thing I need is for a bellboy to walk into my bedroom and see Sarah Archer passed out on the bed and my lower half au naturel. I'll make it just fine with my legs.

Sarah buzzes to life again as I lean her over the bed and attempt to adjust her body into what should be a natural pose. "Wheereermmmm-meyee?"

I take this elongated syllable as an interrogative attempting to ascertain her location. "My bed," I say, and Sarah titters with delight. Her hands crawl up my arms like giant spiders, fingers grasping my shirt, tugging at my collar, trying to draw me down, down, into those sheets, into those pillows.

"Sarah, no." My tone is as firm as tofu. She tugs harder. "No." A little better, but not enough to deter her from pouting those lips, puckering them into two soft taffy mounds.

It would be so easy, so delicious, to say *what the hell it's just sex, who cares about species and nature and right and wrong,* to not just give in to temptation but throw myself bodily upon it, but whereas morality has taken a leave of absence, whatever superego I have left has stepped in to take up the slack. So though my heart and my loins are still pulling me down into the comfort of those arms, those lips, that wonderful mattress, my head knows enough to put down the comforter and back away with my hands up.

"I can't," I tell her. "I want to, but—I can't."

"Are you . . . married?" she asks.

"No—it's not—"

"Do you . . . do you have a girlfriend?"

"No, I don't. Listen—" The phone rings. I ignore it. "Listen," I repeat, and the phone rings again. The message indicator light is on, and has been since I came into the bedroom. Another ring. "Hold the thought," I say, and lift the handset.

"Holy shit, he's home! Rubio, where the hell you been?" It's Glenda.

"Glen, can this wait? I'm . . . busy."

"So you ask my help, then you're too friggin' busy for the answers, right? I can take a hint—"

"Wait! Wait—you found something?"

"Not with that attitude, I didn't." She's pouting now.

Sarah squirms across the bed, reaching for my arms, trying to pull me down. "Hang up the phone," she coos seductively. "Call them back."

Great, two dames to mollify. I hold up a finger to Sarah—one second, please, one second—and step into a darkened corner of the room. "Glen, I'm sorry, I'm just—there's a lot going on. But whatever you got, I'd love to hear."

"Not on the phone, you won't. We gotta meet up, Vincent."

"Last guy said that ended up dead."

"What?"

"Tell you later. We gotta meet now? You can't give me the basics?"

Glenda mulls it over, but her answer is firm. "I'd rather not. Can you get to the Worm Hole?"

"Now?"

"Now. You'll wanna see this."

"Yeah, yeah, sure. Gimme twenty minutes. And Glen—keep your guard up."

"Always."

I turn back to Sarah, already trying to formulate an excuse in my mind, a reason that I would have to leave her at so crucial a point in our . . . relationship, I guess. But as I turn around I can already hear the patterned breathing, the light snore, and I know I can put excuses off for another time. Sarah Archer is drifting off, one hand still clutched around the leg of my pants. "I'm sorry," I whisper. "I'm so sorry."

Her skin shines in the small glow cast from the living-room chandelier, creating a pale ivory surface so pure that it deserves a goodnight peck. As I lean down to kiss her cheek, Sarah's eyes creak open, and she looks up at me with growing wonder. A hand comes up to caress my face, warmth spreading throughout each feature she touches, and Sarah says, "You . . . you look like someone I knew once. A long time ago."

"Who was that?" I whisper.

But Sarah is finally asleep.

On this All Hallow's Eve, the dino bar in the back of the Worm Hole is probably much like it always is: herbs, noise, and drunken louts. But the mammal joint up front is rocking like I've never seen it rock before, packed to the brim with the filthy apes, each dressed in some moronic costume or another. I press my way through bumblebees and ninjas, cartoon characters and French maids, making my way toward the secret entrance behind the rest rooms.

Glenda's waiting for me at a back table, and as I casually stroll over, I run an olfactory scan of the room, checking for familiar scents. It's clean—at least it's clean as far as past assassins go. If someone's sent out new dinos to do me in, there's very little I can do about it at this stage of the game. I pull up a chair and order an iced tea. "No mint," I tell the waitress.

A puzzled look from Glenda. "No mint?" she asks. "You love mint."

I point to the three-ring binder tucked beneath her arm. "Whaddaya got for me?"

"This shit was hidden, and good."

"Deleted?"

"I think so. But whoever wiped the stuff out either did it in a hurry, or didn't think about the temp files. I used a file restorer to bring 'em up again, and most of the crap came through okay." Glenda's a whiz on the computer; at the very least, she's more of a whiz than I am. Ernie's dusty PC sits in my house, currently waiting to be reclaimed by the bank, but as it hasn't been used since he died except as another place to put my used dishes, the repo man might as well haul it away.

"Show me what we got."

The first few sheets are Ernie's handwritten interview notes, pages of them printed out in bold, dark ink. "He scanned them in as is," Glenda explains. "That's what we do at J&T—we got this crappy program that converts our handwriting into text, but it hadn't learned his writing yet, so it left it like this."

A lump forms in my throat as I stare at the loops, twists, and scrawls of Ernie's fractured script. His penmanship was horrendous, and it wasn't infrequent that he had to enlist my help in deciphering some indistinguishable part of his notes. It's almost as if he's sitting next to me now, passing me a pad he's just scribbled on, asking, "Vinnie—does that say *witness claims to have hugged victim* or *witness claims to have stabbed victim?*"

"From what I could figure out from his shitty handwriting, he'd talked to a bunch of the same folks you did—Mrs. McBride, that mammal nightclub singer, a few employees, even that coroner. You can check through it, see if you note any inconsistencies."

"I'll do that. What else?"

"Some of the usual stuff, filed expense accounts, time sheets, a few more scrawls I couldn't make out, appointment calendar—"

"Gimme that—the calendar."

Glenda searches through the printouts and hands over three pages that look to have been copied out of a personal organizer of some sort. Dates are preprinted at the top of the pages (in this case, January 9, 10, and 11), the section below divided into half-hour increments with space to write. The pages are mostly empty, but a number of appointments have been scribbled in.

On January 9, for example, he met with Judith McBride and four of the McBride Corporation's top executives. On the tenth, he saw Vallardo and Sarah, as well as a few others whose names don't ring a bell. But on the eleventh, on the day he was killed by a hit-and-run taxicab in some godforsaken back alley, at ten o'clock in the morning, just a few short hours before his head would crack wide open on a hard city street, Ernie had an appointment with Dr. Kevin Nadel. And only three days after that, when I flew out to New York in a drunken rage and burst into the morgue demanding to see my partner and best friend and the coroner who had so obviously pooched a simple homicide autopsy, Nadel was on a two-month vacation in the Bahamas, incommunicado.

A small, tight note is wedged in the corner of the ten o'clock appointment date, too tiny and smushed to read with the naked eye. "You have a magnifying glass on you?" I ask Glenda.

"I have bifocals."

"Good enough." Glenda passes them over, and I hold the small lens at the bottom of the glasses above the handwriting. Now it's larger, still messy, but if I hold my eyes in just the right position and strain my ocular muscles to the point where they're about to snap and go whipping about the room, I can make out the note: Pickupphotos.

Pick Up Photos.

I look up at Glenda, and she holds out a black-and-white printout of a photo set sheet. "He must have meant these."

The McBride crime scene photos. The *real* McBride crime scene photos. No sanitary gunshot wounds, blood splattered in manageable portions along the floor—a nice, clean, wholesome death as multiple gunshot deaths go.

No, this is something else entirely. Blood fills each frame, covering the walls, the furniture, the carpeting, like an acetate tarp; beneath the crimson pools I can make out the vague shape of McBride, nearly torn beyond recognition, lying in a heap against a sofa set off to one corner, his aristocratic bearing shredded beneath what must have been a furious assault. I see bite marks, claw marks, tail lashings, and more, and I realize that what Judith McBride told me and what Dr. Nadel showed me earlier were the most bald-faced of lies.

Now I have proof: Raymond McBride was killed by a dinosaur.

"These were doctored," I tell Glenda.

"You've seen the other ones?"

"At the coroner's. He showed me one of these pictures, but most of the blood was gone, and the wounds had been . . . cleaned up, I guess. Made to look like gunshots, which is what Judith told me her husband died from. And the doc claimed that McBride had been hit with five different caliber weapons—"

"—which would explain the different sizes of the attack wounds," finishes Glenda.

"Goddamn."

"Goddamn."

"Somebody went through a lot of trouble to make it look like a human pulled this off," I say. "And I bet you Ernie was on to it just before he got iced."

The waitress arrives with my iced tea, and I suck it down in one gulp. Glenda pulls her chair closer to mine, glancing nervously about the room. "I can burn these. You know that, don't you? We can go out back, pour some lighter fluid on these puppies, and torch up. If you're in, I'm in, but I want you to know we can walk away, and that'll be the end of it."

My answer is slow in coming. I want to be precise. "I watched Nadel get killed by a two-dino hit squad," I say. "I almost got killed by them myself. Before that, I was attacked by some freak of nature in a back alley and barely made it away with my hide, and way before *that* my partner was killed in an accident that couldn't have been an accident. I've been misled, laughed at, cheated—I've had my job, my life, my friends stripped away from me. I've been pushed around, and I've been lied to.

"And to be honest, you're right—I should get out now. We should go out to the alley and have ourselves a bonfire with marshmallows, and I should take the next flight to the Galápagos, find a few good trees, and chew myself into a stupor.

"I've got every reason to leave, and it's the smart money that runs through the open door and doesn't look back. But it's like Ernie used to say—it's always the dumbest sonofabitch who finds himself sitting on top of the food chain when the meteors come crashing through.

"This time around that dumb sonofabitch is gonna be me."

During my little speech, a grin has crept its way onto Glenda's face. "Vincent Rubio," she says, "it's nice to see you again."

Tips from doormen come cheap, especially if they're not particularly fond of the building residents. Chet, the fellow who works the late shift at Judith McBride's Upper East Side home, gladly tells me where to find the missus after a fin has managed to work its way into his pocket.

"She's at a Halloween charity ball at the Four Seasons," he informs me, masking whatever dislike he feels for McBride with a smile. And then, still with that maddening grin, "The bitch wouldn't know charity if it rammed itself down her throat." I back away from Chet, into the taxi, and ask the driver to screech away as quickly as possible.

The Four Seasons Hotel is nice—if you like that sort of thing. Me, I'm a Plaza man. Glenda and I wander the opulent hallways, underdressed both for the hotel and the holiday, searching for the correct ballroom. We eventually break down and ask the concierge for directions, and he is neither as friendly nor as courteous as Alfonse, though he does lead us to the right place.

MASQUERADE FOR THE CHILDREN, reads a great flowing banner hanging proudly over the entrance. Behind a great set of double doors, fourteen feet high and gilded to the hilt, I can hear some band swinging it loud and clear—drums, trumpets, trombones, all in a steady 3/4 upbeat. A muted voice resonates through the hallway, crooning about ninety-nine women whom he'd loved in a lifetime.

"Hang back once we get inside," I say. "I'll get to Judith. You . . ."

"I'll steal some food."

I grab one door, Glenda grabs the other. We pull.

And the sound hits us like a shock wave, a blast of unadulterated music spilling past our bodies, pressing us back into the open doorway. The band, the crowd, the incredible noise shuts down my thoughts for a moment, and all I can do is stare. Three hundred, four hundred, five, a thousand? How many creatures are mingling? However many it is, a goodly number of them are dinos, as once the wave of sound has subsided, the second wave of smells hit me, and past the odor of sweat and alcohol, I can make out the pine and the morning and the unmistakable drench of herbs.

Glenda manages to shake off the daze and wander into the ballroom in search of hors d'oeuvres. I set off in another direction, glancing around at the revelers, trying to locate any familiar sight, sound, or smell.

The costumes here are more elaborate than they were at the Worm Hole—these folks have the moola to spend on nonsense like that—and I'm amazed at the intricacy and craftsmanship on some of these outfits. A woman whose breath is so laced with rum I can smell it thirty yards away wobbles up to me and burps daintily in my face. She's wearing what looks to be a large desk, with two drawers where her stomach would be and a table just below her chin upon which she props her arms. A Bible has been glued to the bottom of one of the drawers, as have a pair of reading glasses to the tabletop.

"Guess what I am!" she screams in my ear.

"I don't know."

"What?" she yells.

I'm forced to join in the shouting. "I said I don't know!"

"I'm a one-night stand! Get it? One nightstand. One—night—stand!"

If I push her, she will fall down and cause a ruckus, so I simply excuse myself and squeeze through an opening between two doughnuts in the crowd. Rhinoceroses surround me, horns sticking rudely into my side, and I spin, looking for a way out. But now there's a contingent of aliens, black eyes wide set and menacing, reaching for me with their spindly arms and tumblers of gin and tonics. The other direction—Abbott and Costello, arguing, tumbling, pratfalling—Nixon, claiming over and over again to Abe Lincoln in a pitiful, high-pitched impression that he is not a crook—a piggy bank, replete with dollar bills pouring out of the top—

And a Carnotaur. A real, no-fooling-around, honest-to-goodness in-the-flesh Carnotaur. The rest of the ballroom drops away, falling into some visual abyss as every light swivels and fixates on the dino in the distance chatting it up with Marilyn Monroe. My first thought is that in the rush of Halloween, someone has forgotten to don their guise, much in the way that dino children, once costumed in human skin, will forget that they also need to wear clothing and walk out of the house buck naked, human naughty bits flapping in the breeze.

Without conscious effort, my feet have taken me across the room, and when I get within three yards of the dino, I can smell it—smell the oranges, smell the chlorine—smell *her*—smell Judith McBride. Unguised and chatting it up like it was the most natural thing in the world. I can understand the compulsion, the incredible *need* to be free of the girdles and the clamps and the belts, but not here, not now, not in front of mammals. Without thought as to consequences or social graces, I storm up to Judith and grab her by the crook of a well-muscled Carnotaur arm.

"She'll be right back," I explain to a startled Marilyn, who, I can see up close, is actually more like a Marvin, and pull Judith into one of the more nonpopulated areas of the ballroom, letting her have it all the way.

"What the hell are you doing, going out like that? Have you lost your mind?"

Judith, nonplussed, says, "This time, Mr. Rubio, I believe I will have you thrown out." She raises her hand—her forepaw—toward some unseen protector in the distance, but I grab it before the ascent is complete, holding the fingers in my kung fu grip.

"You can't do this—this is—this is violation number one, the big one—going out unguised—"

"It's Halloween."

"Screw the holiday, you can't risk security because some mammals want to make fools of themselves."

"I'm risking nothing, I assure you."

"You know what I'm talking about—"

"And you're not listening. It's Halloween. This—is—a—costume. A dinosaur costume. Nothing less."

My fingers unclench; the clawed forepaw drops back to her side. "That's not possible," I say. "The mouth—it moves when you talk. It's just like—the teeth—the tongue—"

Judith laughs, and the Carnotaur costume jiggles up and down. "I spent more on this costume than you probably did on your house, Mr. Rubio. I should hope it is realistic. As for its possibility . . . well, you should know better."

"This is . . . a guise?"

"I can promise you—I swear to you—that what I am wearing is the guise of a dinosaur."

Keeping my voice low, though on this night and in this place, no one would think twice if they overheard: "So you're a dino dressed as a human dressed as a dino."

"Something like that," she says, and to prove it to me, she carefully peels back a bit of skin just below her midsection, retracting from a seam I hadn't seen before. Beneath is a wash of pale human flesh, Mrs. McBride's "natural" guised-up skin tone.

"Good costume," I say lamely.

But I've got her laughing, and laughing is better than screaming at her bodyguards to throw me into the punch bowl. "Dance?" she asks, already stepping out toward the floor.

The song's a fox-trot, and I believe I remember the steps. "If you can forgive me," I say, "I would be honored." Casual dance-floor chatter might prove to be the perfect lead-in to my follow-up questions.

It does indeed begin that way, Judith and I talking about the weather, the city, the madness of the holiday as we slow-slow-quick-quick around the dance floor, my lead becoming stronger with every turn and promenade. She's an excellent dancer in her own right, following my moves with the slightest pull, the most delicate of touches. Soon I'm able to talk without counting the beats out in my head, and we fall into an easy patter.

"Are you done with whatever you came to find?" she asks.

"Yes and no."

"I assume you came tonight as you found something that couldn't wait. Isn't that what you people say? It couldn't wait?"

"Us people do say that sometimes, yes."

"And you'd like to ask me now."

"At some point in the evening."

"As we seem to have exhausted our stores of small talk," she suggests, "why don't we dispense with the rest of it and get down to business. I assume you've spoken with the Archer woman by now."

"I have."

"And the rest of Raymond's harem?"

"His harem?"

"Shocked? Don't be."

I was aware that Judith had known about her husband's affair with Sarah—I'd learned that tonight at dinner—but how many more of Raymond's dalliances was she privy to? "You knew about the affairs, then?" We spin around a slower couple, leaving them in our dust.

"Not at first, no. It took me a little bit to catch on, but not long. Raymond was a brilliant man, but in matters of the heart, my husband had long ago outlived his warranty.

"He started out low-key enough," Judith continues, "a girl from the office, I think, and for a while I thought it was cute. You know, he was taking this young thing under his wing, guiding her through the labyrinth of corporate existence."

"And then?" There's always a then.

"And then he started fucking her." The number picks up, the band climbing into a faster rhythm, and we escalate our steps to match.

"What did you do?" I ask.

"The only thing I could do: Deal with it. It happens all the time."

"What does?"

"Infidelity. There's not a friend of mine whose husband hasn't screwed around on her." Now *there's* a sewing circle to stay away from. "But it's not like us to get angry. Not openly, that is."

"Hit 'em when they're not looking?" I ask.

"Hit 'em *where* they're not looking. When you stake your life in the upper crust, the best revenge is always financial. So, in retaliation, we buy things. Furs, jewels, brownstones . . .

"I had one friend whose husband was such a recidivist that she was forced to purchase a small charter airline company and run it into the ground—often literally, mind you—just to get his attention."

"Did it work?"

"For a year. Then he was back at it, and she moved on to passenger trains."

I say, "But you didn't do anything like that, right? You were the good little girl of the group."

"Believe it or not, I was. For a while, at least. I took it all on the chin, accepted Raymond for what he was. Of course, those first few flings of his were . . . normal. Natural. He hadn't yet . . . switched species."

"And when did he jump ship?" I ask.

"Three years ago, maybe four, I don't remember."

"Was Sarah Archer the first one?"

Judith's laugh is humorless, a short bark of derision. "If you mean was she his first cross-species fling, no. Five, ten, twenty girls before her, all the same, all of them leggy and shaggy-haired and beautiful and dumb. Would you believe that some of them would call the house—*my* house—and leave messages for him?

"But if you mean to ask if Sarah Archer was the first one to possess my husband, to claim him as property, to latch on to him as if he were the dock and she were a boat in heavy chop, then yes, I would say she was."

"And that was when it started to grate on you."

"No," says Judith, "it troubled me long before that. There was a period of time when he spent perhaps two nights out of the entire month in my bed. And whereas Raymond and I hadn't . . . had relations in a while"—choice of words definitely less intense now—"there was still a void at night. When you are used to sleeping next to someone all your life, it becomes difficult to adjust to the empty space on the mattress. I believe it was then that I'd finally had enough.

"Money was out—he didn't care. And I couldn't reach him in the bedroom, not directly. So I got back at him the only way I could think of: I had an affair."

"With Donovan Burke," I say.

This does not discompose Judith as much as I would like, but it's a start. At the very least, her assured feet falter a bit, and I have to swing around to her side, shifting the move into an underarm turn, to accommodate the false step. "You know about it."

"I had my hunches from the start." Sarah's comments during dinner tonight only served to corroborate my earlier guess, but I choose not to let Judith in on this. "An affair to punish an affair. Very eye-for-an-eye of you."

"Are you judging me, Mr. Rubio?"

"I don't judge what I don't understand."

Judith accepts this with a wry smile and says, "It wasn't how it sounds."

"It never is."

"My affair with Donovan was not begun solely for revenge, you understand. If anything, it was for companionship. Raymond couldn't be there for me, and I was getting tired of shopping. Donovan was what I needed."

"In your bed?"

"In my bed, in my house, at the park, at the theater, wherever and whenever he could go. Companionship is more than sex, Mr. Rubio."

"And this affair with Donovan Burke—this was after Jaycee's disappearance, I take it?"

Silence from my dance partner, a telling pause. "You were having an affair with Donovan while he was still engaged to Jaycee Holden?"

The reply is meek, a mouse twitter, the first soft-spoken word I have heard out of Judith McBride's mouth: "Yes."

I don't want to be part of the Great Spiritual Oneness when the McBride family karma is finally added up; it's going to take a good portion of eternity to get all of their shit sorted out. "Back in your office the other day you claimed to like Jaycee Holden."

"I did."

"You called her a lovely girl, if I recall."

"I did."

"Then why would you choose to stab her in the back like that?" I hate to sound uppity, but all of this marital malfeasance is making me ill. Can't these people keep it in their guises? Of course, two hours ago I was ready to play amateur magician, rip the tablecloth out from under our Greek food, and throw Sarah onto the bare wood in a fit of passion, but that was two hours ago, and I have since found the control I almost lost.

"Jaycee was no saint," says Judith. "She had her faults."

Aside from a penchant for well-orchestrated disappearances and poorly orchestrated kidnappings, she'd seemed pleasant enough to me. "They had problems before you started seeing him, then?"

"Not that I know of," says Judith.

"Who started the affair?"

"It was mutual."

"Who started the affair?" I repeat. I feel like a father trying to discover which of his children broke the vase in the living room.

"I did," Judith finally admits.

"Did you seduce him?"

"If you want to call it that."

"Why Donovan? Why not someone who wasn't already involved in a relationship?"

Judith is unable to meet my gaze now. She stares off toward the bandleader, elongated Carnotaur snout propped against my shoulder. "Donovan and Raymond . . . they were very close."

"That's why you chose him—his friendship with your husband?"

"Yes. My intention was not to hurt Raymond, let me make that clear. But if he were to ever find out about the affair . . . a little pain might be in order. I chose a confidante of his so that he might feel betrayed as I had felt betrayed. It was a business decision, in many ways."

"I was under the impression that Donovan worked under you at the Pangea. That he had little contact with your husband."

"Professionally, he didn't. Donovan was an entertainment manager, nothing Raymond would have troubled himself with. But they'd been personal friends for a while. Golfing buddies. This was way back when we initially moved to New York."

"About fifteen years ago?"

"That's right."

"Where were you before that?"

"Kansas. Oh please, it was dreary, I don't want to talk about it."

Fair enough. I don't want to talk about Kansas, either. "Did Jaycee find out?"

"You know," Judith muses, "at the time I thought we'd done a pretty good job of keeping her in the dark."

"But you didn't."

She shakes her head. "No. We didn't. I know that now."

"Oh, yeah? And how's that?"

"I simply do. She disappeared two weeks later."

"And a few months after that . . ."

"I fired Donovan," she admits.

"Kind of you. Donovan must have been ecstatic. No woman, no job, no reason to go on."

"You don't understand," says Judith. "Without Jaycee, he was morose. The club was neglected, the books were a shambles. He—he was—"

"Useless?"

I don't get a response. The fox-trot ends, but the band gives us no respite. A sharp tango begins, and my body snaps to attention—the back going ramrod straight, knees flexing, arm curling around Judith's Carnotaur waist. "Can you tango?" I ask, and she answers by spinning into my arms for a perfectly timed dip. A number of other couples join the dance floor, and though it's getting crowded up here, Mrs. McBride and I are Fred and Ginger, swirling and stomping in all the right spots at all the right times.

"You move well," Judith says.

"Why did you tell me your husband was killed by gunshots?"

"Because he was." Two three dip!

"I'll ask you again—"

Her hands disengage from mine, pushing against my chest as she struggles to move away. But I've got her tight around the waist; she's not going anywhere. I force her to continue the dance. "You think you understand everything," she sneers, "but you don't. You don't have clue one."

"Maybe you can help me. You can start by telling me why you lied."

"I didn't. I will show you the crime scene photos, Mr. Rubio, and you will see the bullet holes, you will see—"

"I've seen the crime scene photos," I say, and this shuts her up. "I've seen the real ones."

"I don't know what you mean."

"The undoctored ones. The originals." I'm right next to her ear hole now, whispering harshly into the costume upon costume. "The ones with your husband almost torn in half by the claw marks, the bites running down his side—"

She stops dancing. Her arms drop away, begin to tremble. "Can we talk about this outside?"

"It'd be my pleasure."

I lead Mrs. McBride off the dance floor, and we receive polite applause for our efforts. It takes me a minute to locate a door to the outside, but we soon enter a small courtyard sporting a fountain, a few trees, and a bench. The sounds of the tango disappear behind another soundproof door. With a huff of air, Judith begins to remove the Carnotaur costume, exposing her head and torso to the cool autumn air. Now she's a human with fat green legs and a tail, looking like a drunken dino who's started to pull her guise on from the wrong end.

"Do you have any of those cigarettes?" she asks me. I toss her the entire pack, and she lights up. The smoke coalesces about her head, and she sucks it in deeply.

"Why did you doctor the photos? Why did you get Nadel to lie?"

"I didn't," she says. "I asked someone to do it."

"Who?"

She mumbles a name—"Who?" I say, standing over her. "Speak up."

"Vallardo. I asked Dr. Vallardo to take care of it."

Filling in all the blank spaces now—that's what the money was for, the deposits into Nadel's account. I can't believe it's come together this quickly. "Now, I can't arrest you," I say. "Not officially. But I can hear your confession, and I can make sure the cops treat you okay."

She's up again, pacing the courtyard. "Confession? What on earth would I confess to?"

"Murdering your husband is still a crime, Mrs. McBride."

"I did no such thing!" Indignation streams out of Judith like sunbursts, and I'm nearly singed by the blast.

"Fine, then—do you have an alibi?"

"Some investigator you are—did you even check with the police? I was the first person they came after, of course I have an alibi. I was running a charity event that night in front of two hundred people. Most of them are here this evening—would you like me to have someone fetch them so that you may accuse them of murder, too?"

Confused now. Not the way this was supposed to go. "But why would you cover it all up . . . ?"

Judith sighs and sits heavily on the bench. "Money. It's always money."

"You'll have to do better than that."

"I came back from my charity event, and there he was. On the floor, dead, just like I told you before. And I saw the wounds, I saw the bites, the slashes. And I knew that if word got out about it, the Council would be all over us."

I think I'm getting it now. "Dino on dino murder."

"Always brings up a Council investigation. They'd been looking for an excuse to bleed us dry for years—you know how the fines work. I don't know who killed my husband, Mr. Rubio, but I did know that there was a chance that whoever it was had . . . illicit dealings with my husband. Dealings his estate could be held accountable for. So, in order to forestall any official Council inquiry . . ."

"You had Vallardo and Nadel conspire to fix the photos and the autopsies to be consistent with a human cause of death. No dino murderer, no investigation, no fines."

"And now you know. Is that so horrible, wanting to protect my finances?"

I shake my head. "But what about Ernie? Why lie about him?"

"Who?"

"My partner. The one who came to see you—"

She brushes me off with a casual hand-flip. "That again. This time, I really don't know what you're talking about. Have you found some other imagined evidence to convict me?" Judith holds out her hands as if to be handcuffed, and I slap them away angrily, more because she's right than anything else. I don't have any proof that she was involved in Ernie's death, and the dearth of information is needling me.

"Nadel's dead," I tell her roughly.

"I know that."

"How?"

"Emil—Dr. Vallardo—found out earlier this evening, and he called me soon after. From what I gather, Nadel was found as a black woman in Central Park. Odd duck."

"I was there. He was killed—it was a hit."

"Are you accusing me again?"

"I'm not accusing anyone—"

"I'm sorry you seem to feel that I'm responsible for all deaths in Manhattan, but I'm just as nervous about this as you are. If you look on the other side of that door, you'll see two of my bodyguards ready to burst out here at a moment's notice." I glance at the closed door, but choose not to press the issue. "I'm prepared, Mr. Rubio. Are you?"

With theatrical timing, the door slams open, and I see Glenda pressed between the two beefy bodyguards who had greeted me in Judith's office yesterday morning. She's flailing, kicking, screaming: "—the fuck off me— I'll rip out your goddamned throats—" and inflicting as much damage as her legs and voice can muster.

"Friend of yours?" Judith asks, and I nod bashfully. "Let her go," she tells the bodyguards, and they roughly bodycheck Glenda into the courtyard. I have to restrain her from following them back inside the ballroom, and it's not easy to hold back a hundred and fifty pounds of squirming Hadrosaur. She eases up, and I let go.

"Brought you some cocktail wieners," Glenda says, and dumps a heap of the appetizers into my hands. "Can we get outta here? I think the caterer's pissed at me."

"I think we're about done here," I say, and turn to Judith. "Unless there's anything else you'd like to tell me."

"Not unless there's anything else you'd like to accuse me of."

"Not right now, thanks. But I wouldn't leave the city if I were you."

Judith looks amused. "I'm not accustomed to taking orders."

"And I don't give suggestions." I shove a weenie in my mouth and masticate, the hot meat scalding the insides of my mouth. I had planned a few more parting volleys in Mrs. McBride's direction, but if I speak now, I just may spit up the wiener, and that wouldn't be good for anybody.

Grabbing Glenda firmly by the hand, I lead her out of the courtyard, through the ballroom, past the throng of drunken revelers, and toward the nearest subway stop. I give the token booth operator the last three dollars in my wallet, and we head for the southbound train.

Glenda has gone back to her apartment, and I have gone back to the lion's den. I stand outside the presidential suite, key card in hand, holding it just above the lock. Sarah is inside, maybe asleep, maybe not, and the stockpile of willpower I might have built up on the train ride over is ebbing out through some undiscovered leak. I've got people trying to kill me right and left, no money in my pocket, and no discernible future on the horizon, but it's the next five minutes that could prove to be my true salvation or my downfall. I swipe the card.

No snoring, I notice as I enter the suite, and the bedroom light is on. Sarah is no longer asleep. I make a snap deal with myself: If Sarah is reading, watching television, or just hanging out, I will order her up a pot of coffee from room service, beg a few bucks from the check-in staff, and send her back home in a cab, no funny business. If, on the other hand, I enter the bedroom to find her long, lithe body tucked beneath the covers—above the covers—around the covers—nude and waiting for me to return, I will close the shutters on whatever strands of rectitude remain in me and allow whatever primal instincts are left to guide my body as I leap headfirst into that luscious den of sin.

A note on the pillow. And no Sarah.

The note reads: *Dearest Vincent, I'm sorry for making you say you were sorry. Please think of me fondly. Sarah.*

I drop into the bed, note clutched tightly to my chest, and count the tiles in the ceiling. There will be no sleep tonight.

As expected, I did not reach dreamland even once. My evening was spent in the bathtub, alternately splashing freezing and scalding water onto my guiseless body. After each half hour of this, I would lurch back into the bedroom, toss on my guise in case the maids should break and enter, and attempt to drift off into slumber, which never came. The sandman is a lazy shift-about. I hate him.

At eight o'clock this morning, the phone rings. It's Sally at TruTel back in LA, and she says that Teitelbaum would like to have a word with me.

"Put him through," I tell Sally, and he's there in an instant. I have a feeling he was there all along.

"You're off the case!" is the first thing he yells in my ear, and I have this sinking feeling it won't be the last.

"I'm—what the hell are you talking about?"

"Did we not have a discussion about Watson? Did we not have this god-damned discussion?"

"What discussion—you said don't mess around with Ernie's death, that's all—"

"And that's what you've been doing!" The tumbler in my hand vibrates with the shout, ripples spreading across the water's surface. "You screwed me over, Rubio, and now I'm gonna screw you back."

"Calm down," I say, lowering my own voice so as to demonstrate. "I asked a few questions, just to get perspective on the McBride thing—"

"I ain't one of your suspects, Rubio. You can't pull this on me. I know all about your little friend at J&T—we know what she's been up to."

"Glenda?" Oh, crap—he knows about the computer files.

"And we know you put her up to it. That's industrial espionage, that's breaking and entering, that's theft, that's—that's way over the line. And that's it, it's over." I can hear Teitelbaum pacing the room, trinkets falling, crashing off the desk, and though it's amazing that he's finally made it out of that chair, he's winded, panting from the effort. "You're off the case, I'm cutting off your credit card, you're done. Finished."

"So . . . what?" I sulk. "You want me to come back to LA?"

"I don't give a fuck what you do any more, Rubio. I canceled your return flight back here, so stay in New York if you wanna, they got a nice homeless community under them subway tunnels. 'Cause I've got phone calls out to every firm in town, and the only PI job you're gonna get back here is tracking down where you left your last welfare check."

"I'm onto something here, Mr. Teitelbaum," I try to explain. "It's not bullshit this time, it's big, and I'm not gonna give it up just 'cause—"

But he's hung up. I call back and casually ask Sally to reconnect me to her boss.

A short pause, but Sally's soon back on the line. "He won't come to the phone," she explains. "I'm sorry, Vincent. Is there anything I can do?"

I consider using Sally as my agent provocateur, asking her to sneak into the files, reinstate my credit card, messenger me a new ticket to LA, but I've already gotten Glenda in trouble, and I don't need to add another creature to my list of suffering friends. "Nothing," I tell her. "I fucked up, that's all."

"It's gonna be okay," she says.

"Sure. Sure it is." With no credit card and no cash of my own, I can't possibly afford to spend another day in the city. The room darkens perceptibly.

"You want me to mail your messages back home?"

"What messages?" I ask.

"You got a bunch, sitting right here. Mr. Teitelbaum didn't tell you?"

"Not exactly. Hell, I don't care. Are they important?"

"I don't know," she says. "They're all from some police sergeant, a Dan Patterson. Just wants you to call him. Says it's urgent, and there's four or five of them."

I'm off with Sally in half a heartbeat and connected to the Rampart division of LAPD. A quick, "Vincent Rubio for Dan Patterson, please," and he's soon on the other end.

"Dan Patterson."

"Dan, me. What's going on?"

"Are you home?" he asks.

"I'm in New York."

A pause, slightly stunned. "You're not—not again—"

"I am. In a way. Don't ask."

"Fine," he says, willing to drop the issue. Now that's a friend. "There's something we found in the back room of that nightclub—"

"The Evolution Club?"

"Yeah. Remember I told you I had some guys going through the place? And that one box wasn't torched? Well, they found some mighty weird shit I thought you should know about, and it wasn't illegal skin mags."

"I assume this is something you can't tell me about over the phone," I say. A pattern has begun to emerge in my life, and it's getting tiring following it around the globe.

"It's more like a show-and-tell, and believe me, you wouldn't believe it or understand it unless you saw the damn things in person. I had to turn it all over to the Council, and they're having an emergency meeting right about now, but I made a photocopy of the paper goods for you."

"What if I told you I was off the Evolution Club case?" I ask.

"Easy—I'd still have a photocopy for you."

"And what if I told you that I had no money for a plane flight back to LA, that I'd just been officially banned from every firm in the city, that I don't give a good goddamn about Teitelbaum or his cases, that I'm about four-fifths of the way to getting myself killed out here, and that I'd probably need a heap of extra cash to come back here to New York after I saw you?"

He takes longer to think this one over, but not as long as I'd expected. "Then I'd walk down the street and send you some cash Western Union."

"It's that big?" I ask.

"It's that big," he says, and two hours later I'm standing in line at the airport with my trusty garment bag in tow.

* * *

Dateline: Los Angeles, five hours later. I was not upgraded to first class on my flight. The counter agent told me to talk to the desk agent, the desk agent told me to talk to the flight staff, the flight staff told me to walk back across the terminal and take it up with the counter agent again, and by the time I finally learned that yes, they would love to upgrade me, there were no more first-class seats available because everyone else had already gotten themselves bumped up an hour earlier. So I spent the bulk of the flight crushed between a dyspeptic software designer whose laptop and accompanying accessories encompassed all the available space on my tray table as well as his, and a six-year-old boy whose parents, the lucky shits, had landed seats in first class. Every two hours, his mother would walk back to us untouchables in economy and tell the child not to bother the nice man—me—next to him, and Timmy (or Tommy, or Jimmy, I can't remember) would solemnly swear upon all the cartoon characters he held holy to follow orders. Yet not ten seconds after his mother disappeared through the dividing curtain would he resume banging away on every surface possible, my body parts not excepted. He was a budding Buddy Rich, no doubt, but despite his talent, I was wholly prepared to risk life, limb, and the loss of a future jazz great by throwing him bodily out the nearest emergency exit.

When I could sleep, I dreamt about Sarah.

It takes some time to hail a cab in Los Angeles, even at the airport, but I eventually locate one willing to take me to Pasadena. The money Dan sent me is already going quickly, as the plane ticket cost over two thousand dollars due to the last-second purchase. I resolve to pay him back as soon as I get back on my feet again, whenever that may be. Right now, I'm just about on my chin and going down quickly.

A short swing up the 110 takes us to the Arroyo Vista Parkway and Dan's suburban house, where he was planning on spending most of his day off. Soon enough, we pull up in front of the blue-and-white ranch home, nearly slamming into the Ford pickup parked sideways in the driveway. I pay the cabbie and hop on out.

Spread across the front stoop of Dan's town house is today's *Los Angeles Times,* the open pages blowing in the warm Santa Anas coming up from the south. I gingerly step over this morning's headlines, being careful not to trod upon today's Sunday comics, and rap on the door. It's in dire need of fresh paint, the wood stain having long since been stripped by the om-nipresent air pollutants, but it's still a nice chunk of oak that echoes my knock back to me.

I wait. Odds are, Dan's hanging out in the living room, plopped down in his La-Z-Boy imitation recliner, hooked into a virtual IV tube of Cheetos and Chunky Soups, squinting hard at his twenty-inch television because he's too darned stubborn to be fitted for contact lenses. "It's sad enough I've gotta wear makeup every day," he told me once. "Ain't no way I'm gonna mess around with contacts." Better not to even bring up the subject of glasses.

A minute passes with no response. I try again, pounding a little harder this time. "Danny boy!" I call out, mushing my lips as close to the door as possible without causing actual skin-wood contact. *"Abre la puerta!"* Dan knows the meaning of my words—he can say "Open the door!" in over six-teen different languages and four Asian dialects. Such are the spoils that come from being a police detective in Los Angeles.

Again, nothing. I notice that Dan's still got that door knocker up that I gave him last Christmas on a goof—an oversized, overpriced, overly gaudy gargoyle that would look out of place anywhere other than the Munsters' home—so I grab hold of the brass beast's nose and slam its feet onto the solid plate beneath. Now *this* is a Knock, Knock, Knock, and the heavy thumps nearly throw me off the front stoop. The brass vibrates rapidly in my hand like an overcharged joy buzzer, and I quickly let go of the gargoyle before it has a chance to vibrate into animation.

A minute. Two. Silence. I listen in at the door, straining, pressing my false ear against the wood grain. Music, perhaps, a steady beat droning on and on. It's possible that he's asleep—deeply so, I would imagine, not to hear that gargoyle racket—but more likely he's out back in his small herb garden and has the music from his living room pumped up so he can hear it outside. I head around back.

Brambles and bushes try to stop me, extending their long, thorny claws to rip at my guise. Carefully avoiding the nastier barbs, I pick my way through the brush and eventually come to the tall wooden fence that de-fines Dan's modest yard. No space between these slats, but a knot in the wood provides an excellent peephole, and like a trained pervert, I set to peeping.

Oregano, basil, sage, and their culinary cohorts rise from the earth, making their way toward the sun, straining for its energy. Many a tipsy afternoon was spent sampling the delights of this well-kept piece of land. I see flowers to the left, what might be a carrot patch to the right, but there's no LAPD sergeant in sight. Balling my hand into a tight fist, I pound the fence and yell for Dan again.

Had I not seen his car in the driveway, had he not known that I was coming in today, on this very flight, at this precise time, I might think that Dan had taken a short hop out of the house or out of town, a quick getaway-from-it-all jaunt.

A quick whiff off a passing breeze . . .

Scents flowing in, piggybacking on the air, swirling through my nostrils, and I can pick up everything in the area, from the herbs to the flowers to the car down the street, the chemicals from a nearby one-hour photo, the messy diaper of a newborn four houses down, and the acrid vinegar odor of that bitter, bitter Stego widow who lives next door and always comes on to Dan after she's had a few too many.

But no Dan. Now I'm worried. Time to break and enter.

As I make my way toward the front door, I realize that there's no way I'm getting through that slab of oak short of a battle-ax; aside from the relative impossibility of knocking it in with my meager weight, Dan's job has taught him nothing if not to secure a house with multiple locks. Back to the garden.

Stepping off the porch, I nearly slip as my eye catches a small, dark stain on the ground and my body instinctively pirouettes to get a better look. It's blood. Three, four drops maximum, but definitely blood. Dried, but only recently. I would whip out my dissolution packet and run a quick chemical test to see if it's dino fluid, but I fear that I already know the answer. I downshift and leap for the fence.

The adrenaline rush bypasses my fatigue and I scale the wooden slats with as much skill and grace as my drained muscles will allow, my premiere fence-climbing days well behind me. As I reach the top and attempt to swing myself up and over, my left leg catches against an outcropping and down I go, end over end, toppling heavily into Dan's basil patch. The smell is overpowering, and I stumble to my feet and backpedal away as quickly as possible even as my mouth begins to work by itself, chomping at the air where the basil should be.

The back door is closed as well, bolted tight from the inside. I pound, I knock, I shake the door with all my might, but the only sounds I can hear from within are the swinging guitars and ruffled backbeat of Creedence Clearwater Revival, John Fogerty's tortured voice calling out to his Susie Q. Fogerty, I recently learned, is an Ornithomimus, as are Joe Cocker and Tom Waits, so you can see from whence that vocal trait arises. Paul Simon, on the other hand, is a true-blue Velociraptor, and I don't think I've ever heard a better drug song than "Scarborough Fair," even though rosemary and thyme have never done much for me personally.

"Dan!" I scream, my voice cracking, register climbing into the stratosphere. "Open the goddamned door!"

John Fogerty answers. ". . . say that you'll be true . . ."

A window entrance, then, is my only option. Despite my growing paranoia, I'm still pushing myself to optimism: Dan cut himself while cooking dinner, didn't have bandages, ran to Rite Aid to grab a small first-aid kit, maybe took a trip over to the hospital for stitches, dripped some blood on the way out. Better yet, he was coming back from grocery shopping, dropped a container of lamb chops, the blood splattered a bit, and now he's at a friend's house barbecuing those babies up right this very minute. If I pretend hard enough, I can almost smell the charcoal . . .

The screen pops out in a flash with the help of my Swiss Army blade, and I'm soon faced with a solid, yet thin, window pane, easily breakable. I'm usually above such pedestrian entry techniques, but time is short so I smash away, using my elbow to splinter the glass. I'm not worried about Dan's security alarm—I know the code is 092474 from the time I house-sat for him last October, and if I remember correctly, I've got a generous forty-five seconds to turn it off.

But the alarm doesn't activate. I cannot hear the telltale BEEP BEEP BEEP that usually drives me so insane. I wish I could.

I pull up the window and slide inside, wriggling clear of the broken glass on the floor. Creedence is rocking louder now, the way Creedence should, emanating from the den, good old John still pining for his gal. "Anybody home?" I call out over the din. "Dan? Dan, you here?"

Dan's never been the tidiest of Brontosaurs, so I'm not surprised to see his clothing scattered about the living room in postapocalyptic fashion. A girdle here, a buckle there, a pair of guised-up underwear flopped atop the ottoman.

Though my earlier whiff on the front porch didn't pick it up, there is indeed a lingering trace of Dan's olive oil and motor engine scent, drifting in and out like a fading memory. I suspect it arises from the scattered clothing. Through the open wall in the living room I can see into the kitchen, over the low counter, across the breakfast table, past the Mount Olympus of dishes piled in the sink. No Dan.

His bedroom is located upstairs, and habit pulls in that direction. But Creedence beckons to me from the small den on the first floor, Fogerty having given up on Susie, now concentrating his efforts on doo, doo, doo, looking out his back door. Another rough circle of blood stains the carpet, stretching out into a long, tortured oval, leading beneath the den's door, trailing inside . . .

I open and enter.

Stereo speakers, canted, lying on the floor, blasting away, shoving the music into me, pressing me backward. Pictures, ripped to ribbons, frames smashed, glass shattered. A television tube lying five feet away from its cabinet, a bookcase torn and toppled. Drapes pulled down, lightbulbs popped, Lava lamps cracked and flowing slowly, slowly onto the carpet, their phosphorescence drooping like caterpillars through the light gray fibers.

And Dan, plopped in his favorite easy chair, guise half-shredded, hair half-matted, smidgen of tuna sandwich and overturned bowl of soup on the TV tray by his side, stab wounds covering his body, pocking his flesh, blood having long since seeped through his clothing and dried into carmine stains against his rough, brittle hide. Smiling, staring through the ceiling, to the sky . . .

"Dan, Dan, Dan . . . come on . . . don't . . . Dan . . ."

I'm muttering, I'm mumbling, I'm talking to myself without knowing what I'm saying as I run my hands over Dan's body, searching for any signs of life. I press my nose into his hide, I want to find a scent, I want to find some smell, anything! Working the snaps behind my neck, buttons popping off, carelessly pulling the guise mask up and off my head to get a better whiff, I try again, unencumbered this time, sniffing, snorting, locating his scent glands and drawing them as far in as I can . . .

Emptiness. No scent.

Sergeant Dan Patterson is dead.

I close his eyes, inner lids first, but I am loathe to adjust the rest of his body. The police will have to be called in due time, and they're going to be upset enough that I broke in here, damaging their crime scene. Better to leave his body . . . better to leave everything unmolested.

Dan didn't go without a fight—the demolished state of the den says that much—but I don't know whether it's pride at Dan's courage, the sorrow at his passing, or both that spins a tight knot in my chest, pressing hard against my throat.

"There goes the fishing trip, huh?" I ask Dan's slumped body. "You sonofabitch, there goes the fishing trip."

The wounds are straight-on incisions, knife stabs, the occasional slash. I don't see the telltale markings of a dino attack like those I thought I picked up in the Raymond McBride photo—curved stabs resulting from claw jabs, parallel slashes from slices, conical depressions as a result of a biting attack, or the deep indentations of a tail spike.

According to the LED display on the front of the CD player, it's been playing the same disk over and over for the better part of four hours, which enables me to place Dan's demise within that time, unless the killer threw on Creedence after the murder in some sort of postslaughter uber-'60s ritual.

Dan's thick brown tail, I notice, has been freed from the G series of belts, but from its confined position beneath the overlapping torso girdle, I doubt he got a chance to utilize it during his defense. All indications—the defensive wounds on Dan's palms, the blood trail splattered across the room, evenly distributed, the lack of forced entry into the house other than my own recent intrusion, the undisturbed items everywhere but this den in particular—point to a surprise attack by someone Dan knew or thought he knew, someone he invited into his den, maybe to have a bite to eat, to catch a few tunes. And then—a stab, a slice, a quick filet, Dan stumbling backward, trying to defend himself, trying to rip off his guise, to free up his claws and his tail, but all of it too slow and too late. Then it was simply, quietly over.

On the air, a new odor drifting around, looking for some nose hairs to tickle. For a brief moment I delude myself into thinking that Dan has pulled a Lazarus on me, sprung back to life, and wants to grab a pizza, but though I soon realize it is not Dan's scent, it is somehow familiar. Nose leading the way, body following obediently behind, I search on the floor beneath Dan's easy chair, running my fingers across the carpet, the exposed tacks biting into my polyskin fingers.

There, within my grasp now, a square of what feels like cheesecloth, double-layered. I pull it out. It's a pouch, much like the disintegration packets I carry on me at all times. But this one doesn't radiate that terrible stench of decay, and there's no way the smell could have diminished over time; even empty disintegration pouches have to be burned, buried, and forgotten in some godforsaken landfill in order to conceal that rank odor.

Chlorine. That's it. I can't find any granules left in the pouch, but I've no doubt that it once held that very element. A few other scents are trying to make it into my sinuses, fighting with their stronger counterpart, but it's of no use; that first whiff has taken hold and won't relinquish control. I drop the pouch in the exact spot where I found it, scooting the cloth back beneath the chair in case the police should find some more meaning behind the evidence than I did.

The chaos and rampant destruction are even more evident from this lower vantage point; splintered wood and ripped wallpaper towering overhead, possessions crushed like empty soda cans. Nothing in this room was spared from the rampage, and I can only hope that Dan's eyes had glazed and darkened before he got a chance to see the destruction that had befallen his photos, paintings, and bowling trophies.

Consolation will be long and hard in coming, but at least I have this: Dan Patterson died in his favorite easy chair. He died in the heat of battle. He died while eating a hearty lunch. He died in his home, surrounded by pictures of those he loved. And he died while listening to Creedence Clearwater Revival, to Ornithomimus John Fogerty, which means that he passed into that great beyond borne on the kindred voice of a brother dinosaur. We should all be so lucky.

I want to keep on with my search, to comb the carpet for fiber samples. I want to grab a spare bag of flour from Dan's kitchen and pat down the walls for fingerprints. I want to isolate those bloodstains on the front porch and scan through the DNA evidence. I want a clue, any clue, but there's no time. No time.

What I need is to find this all-important information that drew me back to Los Angeles in the first place, but an exhaustive search of the house turns up nothing interesting except for a drawer full of porn magazines like *Stegolicious* and *Double Diplodod Dames,* strictly soft-core all the way. Didn't know Dan went in for anything other than other Brontosaurs, but I'm the last dino in the world who should be moralizing right now.

Still, I can't find the photocopies Dan told me about, and there's no doubt in my mind that they are of the utmost importance, both to the Evolution Club case and everything else that's been going down the last few days. He did mention something about another set, though—the originals—and though I don't relish the thought of what I'll have to do in order to get my hands on those, I don't have much of a choice.

I return to the living room to place my call to the dino emergency line, a special branch of 911 manned solely by our kind for situations such as these. It's different from the ambulance line and cleanup crew line, but serves a similar function: bringing the proper authorities along at the proper time.

"What's your emergency?" asks the apathetic operator.

"There's an officer down," I say. "Very down." I give Dan's address, decline to tell the operator my name, and hang up quickly.

Back to the den, where I say my good-byes to my friend. They are short, succinct, and a moment after they leave my mouth I've forgotten what they were. It's better that way. If I hang out any longer, wait for the cops to show up, they'll haul me downtown and stick me in some cell with an overblown, overfed T-Rex who'll try to question me until my ears bleed. I don't have time for that. I've got a Council meeting to crash.

arold Johnson is the current Brontosaur representative of the Council, and I know from the official Council calendar they forgot to take back when they kicked me off the board that any emergency meetings held during the autumn months are supposed to be held in his spacious wood-paneled basement. I cringe at the thought of another session with those bombastic buffoons, but it's my only chance if I want to get a look at those papers. That's assuming I can even get in to the meeting. I do have one plan in mind, and it might work as long as Harold hasn't changed from his usual anal, beastly self in the last nine months.

Traffic is light, and I make my way up the 405 with considerable speed. There are two velocities in Los Angeles: Rush Hour Halt and Warp Factor Nine. Due to the constant gridlock on our highways between the hours of seven and ten in the mornings and three to seven in the evenings, any chance we Angelenos have to duplicate Chuck Yeager's sound-barrier experiments during the less crowded moments are duly taken. Fifty-five is a joke, sixty a gas, sixty-five the actual minimum, seventy gaining respectability, and seventy-five the reality. Currently, I'm running about ninety. I've been trucking along these highways well over eighty-five miles an hour for all my automotive life—at least, when my car can handle it—and I've never once gotten a ticket.

Until now. Those lights flashing in my rearview mirror are not Christmas decorations, and that siren is not an air-raid drill. I pull over to the side of the road, stopping as quickly as possible.

What is the proper procedure here? I don't want to reach into my glove compartment to extract my registration—scurrying around and grabbing things is bound to make the officer nervous, and a nervous man with a gun in his hand is someone I'm not interested in meeting. Opening the door is probably a no-no as well, so I raise my arms above my head and spread my fingers wide. I probably look like a moose.

I watch in my side-view mirror as the officer, a portly gentleman in his midforties with a handlebar mustache—straight out of Central Casting— strolls cautiously up to my vehicle. He uses the butt of his nightstick to rap on my window, and I hurriedly roll it down, returning my hand to the air a moment later.

"You can put your hands down," he drawls. I follow orders. Saliva stretches between the officer's lips, a silvery strand glistening in the sunlight. It takes considerable effort to force my gaze away.

"Speeding, wasn't I?" No point in denying it.

"Ayup."

"And you're giving me a ticket, aren't you?"

"Ayup."

Naturally, I should argue it. Stick up for myself, for my reckless driving habits. Almost too late, I realize that this isn't even my automobile—I've taken the liberty of stealing Dan's Ford Explorer, as he no longer has a use for it, and I no longer have any personal transportation—and I'm gonna have my hands full trying to explain why I'm driving a car that belongs to a recently murdered police officer.

Things would be easier if this cop were a dino—his lack of scent tells me he's human through and through—as I could explain about the urgent, urgent Council meeting and be done with it.

But as it is, he's looking at me strangely, head cocked to one side, the movement reminiscent of Suarez and the tow truck driver. "You're a Raptor, ain't ya? Don't meet many of you fellas on the job."

Without thought, without wondering how this human could have possibly learned of our existence, my instinct kicks in—saliva floods my mouth as I prepare to rip out his throat. One of the very first things a young dino learns is that security leaks must be patched up, and quickly. Any human who in any way suspects our presence must be dealt with accordingly, which usually means a death sentence, swift and sure.

I glance up and down the freeway—the cars are coming nonstop, and there is no visual protection along the shoulder. Even if I were able to take him down, I'd be spotted in a moment. Need to find a safe place, a hidden location where I can take care of business and—

"Raptor saved my life over in 'Nam," the cop says proudly. "Best damn sonofabitch I ever did meet." He extends his hand through the car window. "Don Tuttle, Triceratop. Good to meetcha." Stunned, I shake it.

"You . . . you're a dino?" I ask. My spit dries up as my salivary glands go on a coffee break.

"Sure am," says the cop. Then, noting my surprise, he slaps himself on the forehead and says, "Man—you thought . . . the scent, right?" I nod. "That happens all the time. I know I should make a habit of pointing it out, but . . ."

Officer Tuttle turns his back to me, crouches down to window level, and pulls aside the wisps of hair adorning his guise. Working the camouflaged buttons with practiced dexterity, he flips the skin off his shoulders and displays for me the ranger green hide that covers the back of his head. A long, deep scar runs the length of his neck, stretching from ear to ear like a fleshy necklace, with two jagged triangles heading up either end.

"Bullet," he says. "Only time I ever been shot at, but I guess once is all it takes. Went in one side, straight out the other."

"Ouch."

"Nah, I didn't feel a thing. Took out a bundle of nerves on its way through." He covers his natural hide with the polysuit and snaps the covering back in place. "Also wrecked the hell outta my scent glands. Couple of dino docs over at County figured it was better to remove 'em than screw around tryin' to put 'em back in place.

"For a while I got these scent cushions, attached to a battery. Worked like potpourri simmer pots, you know them things? My wife has them all over. Doctors had some Diplodod pharmacist brew 'em up for me, says he does it pretty regular, but my wife said they smelled like old nickels. I didn't know what the hell she was talking about—old nickels? But I knew what she meant. They just didn't smell . . . right, you know? Better to go on without 'em, deal with it as it comes."

"I'm sorry," I tell him, not knowing the proper condolences for loss of pheromone production. I wonder if there's a Hallmark card.

"No big deal," he says nonchalantly. "Only thing is, I gotta watch myself for dinos thinking I ain't what I ain't, you know?"

"Sure, sure." And now that we're on a more familiar basis . . . "Officer—Don—Officer Don, about my speed, I'm very sorry that—"

"Forget about it," he says, ripping the ticket into shreds. The newly formed confetti sinks into the ground, but I doubt he'll slap himself with a littering fine any time soon.

"Thank you," I say, grasping his paw and pumping it gratefully. "I was in such a hurry for the Council meeting that I—"

"You say Council meeting?"

"In the Valley. I'm late."

"How late?"

"'Bout a day. Give or take a minute."

"Well, hell!" he hollers. "We got to get you an escort!"

So it is that fifteen minutes later I arrive at Harold Johnson's rambling ranch house in Burbank, accompanied by three squad cars and two motorcycle units. It's a powerful feeling taking the streets by storm, sirens blaring, lights blazing, and I can understand how that adrenaline rush might lead to unsavory circumstances. I'm ready to crack heads right now, and there isn't a bona fide criminal in sight.

I thank the officers, dinos all, and bid them farewell as I maneuver my way across the cobblestone path leading to the Johnsons' front door. The welcome mat must have a pressure-sensitive plate beneath it, for long before my hand makes it to the doorbell I find myself standing across from the jittery Mrs. Johnson, all five foot four and 250 pounds squished down deep inside a guise constructed to handle no more than one eighty, tops. She needs a new guise, and soon—one more banana split, and the current one will burst under the strain. Her hands tremble in alarm, and she shoots worried glances about the yard, the street, her foyer.

"Go away," she pleads. "Harold won't like this one bit."

I say, "He doesn't have to like it. Just tell him I'm here."

She looks behind her, toward the door leading down to the basement. Even from here, I can make out the shouting and the incessant rumble of roars. "Please," she begs. "He gets so mad at me."

I put a hand on Mrs. Johnson's shoulder, the flesh beneath the fragile polysuit crying to be let out. "There's no reason for him to get mad at you—"

"But he does. He does. You know his temper—"

"Oh, I know it. But I want you to go down there and have him come up for me."

Another glance at the door, as if it's the wood itself she's frightened of. "Why don't you just go down? I'm sure they'd all like to see you."

"If I go down there unannounced, I'll be attacked faster than you can say trauma center, and then you'll have a dead Raptor on your hands. Now is that what you want, Mrs. Johnson?"

Slowly, gingerly, she turns and walks toward the basement door like an inmate walking that final mile. Mrs. Johnson disappears into the basement. I wait in the open doorway.

A crash, a scream, a contingent of bone-chilling growls. The plains of the Serengeti have been transported into the Johnsons' basement. As I stare about the foyer, soaking in the suburban lack of charm, the wooden door flies open, slams into the wall, and cracks into two pieces, falling off its hinges and onto the linoleum.

"Harold, I know what you're thinking—" I start, even before I see his hulking frame huddled in the open doorway, "and you have to give me a chance." He's out of guise, tail poised to strike, his massive body pulsating with anger, with hatred.

No human words that I have ever heard are coming out of this Brontosaur as he prepares to charge at me, head tucked into those powerful shoulders, arms clenched tightly by his sides. Steam should be pouring out of his nostrils. Behind him, I can see Mrs. Johnson scurry out of the basement and into the kitchen like a cockroach when the lights are turned on.

"Wait—wait—I have full right to be here," I announce.

"You—have—no—right."

"I'm a Council member."

"You—were—rectified." I don't like the way he's enunciating each word—he's never been one for stunning verbal intercourse, but the menace in his voice is palpable.

"Yes, yes, I was rectified, I saw the papers, we all know that. You kicked me off the Council, fine."

"Then leave—before I shove your tail down—your—throat."

Here's where I bring out my hidden ace. "But I never signed the papers."

"So what if you didn't?" he asks, and now I've got him speaking without pauses.

"Check the rules," I say. "If I didn't sign the papers in the presence of at least one other Council member, then it's not official."

"Bullcrap it's not official. We kicked Gingrich out three years ago—you were there—and he didn't sign squat."

"Then technically he's still in. No one enforces it anymore, but it's there since time immemorial. Go ahead, I'll wait."

And I do just that as Harold, a stickler for the rules if I've ever known one, retreats back into the basement to scrutinize some arcane rule I hope I didn't pull out of my ass. Ten minutes later, I hear his heavy footsteps clomping up the stairs. Heavy, slow—defeated.

"Come on down," he mutters, barely even sticking his head out of the stairway.

I am greeted by a chorus of catcalls and groans as the fourteen Southern California representatives from the remaining dinosaur species welcome me back with closed arms. They are fully unguised, and wander around the basement in a state of naked autonomy. Tails bat against one another as they swish freely about the floor, and I'm glad to see that there are no blood marks on the walls—yet. Harold has made a smart move and hung large plastic tarps across the sofas, the chairs, the coffee tables, in order to protect his furniture from stains once the stuff starts flying. And at Council meetings, it will always start flying, sooner or later.

There's Parsons, the Stegosaur, an accountant for a small firm downtown, and Seligman, the Allosaur rep, a big-shot attorney up in Century City. Oberst, the Iguanodon dentist, gives me a sidelong leer, and the T-Rex, Kurzban, some sort of evolutionary psych professor up at UCLA, chooses to ignore my presence altogether. But not everyone's a professional—Mrs. Nissenberg, our Coleo rep whose first name I can never remember, is a homemaker and quilter extraordinaire, and Rafael Colon—Hadrosaur—is a hopeless shiftabout who fancies himself an actor because he got a few bit parts back when *Miami Vice* needed scruffy criminals. And of course, there's Handleman, the representative for the Procompsognathus population, and a Council meeting wouldn't be complete without a Compy there to make it all the more excruciating.

"Why you here?" he chirps. "Huh, we kick you out!"

"It really isn't wise," mutters Seligman.

The new Raptor representative—Glasser, according to a name tag rudely affixed to his scaled chest, a tallish fellow with a nice tan hide—strolls up and sticks out his hand. "Thanks for screwing up, mate," he says with a hint of an Australian accent. "No ill will, eh?"

"No worries," I respond.

But the rest of them are mighty worried, screaming about how I abused their finances, abused their trust, abused the power of the Council for my own selfish motives, and I can't disagree with any of them. "You're right," I say. "All of you, one hundred percent correct."

But none of them are even willing to listen until Harold brings the full weight of his body and his power to the floor. His tail flops heavily behind him as he walks, and it clips Mrs. Nissenberg across the cheek. She yelps in pain, but nobody seems to notice or care.

"It's the rules, ladies and gentlemen. The Rules. We live by them here, and even though as individuals some of us choose to ignore them"—sharp glance in my direction—"this group as a whole cannot. If the rules say that the Raptor can stay, then the Raptor can stay."

Renewed arguments, heated debate, and I put up my hand for silence. I get none, so I shout over them. "Wait! Wait! I don't want to stay."

This quiets them down enough for me to issue my ultimatum. "I'll make you a deal. There's some information you now have in your possession, and I would like to be here when that information is presented."

A sharp glance from Harold—he knows what I'm talking about. "When were you going to go over that . . . stuff?" I ask.

"It's listed as new business, so . . . tomorrow sometime." And this is what they consider an *emergency* meeting.

"How's this: Get to it now—right now—let me stay here until it's over—and then I'll sign the papers, and you never have to see me again."

"Ever again?" they ask as one.

"Gone like I was a bad dream."

An electric murmur from the group. Harold asks, "Can we have a minute to think this over?"

"Thirty seconds," I respond. "I'm in a bit of a hurry."

This group couldn't figure out whether or not to breathe in only thirty seconds let alone process my request, but after a short series of motions and calls to order, my ultimatum is answered. Harold walks to the bottom of the basement stairs and yells up at his loving partner.

"Maria!" And, after a few moments have passed with no response, "MARIA!"

"Yes, Harold?" comes the frightened reply.

"Send down Dr. Solomon." Harold turns back to the group, addressing us as one.

"Yesterday morning, I got some information I thought the Council might find interesting. Brings up some new questions about an old topic, adds in a twist I'm not quite sure whether or not to believe. I don't even know all the specifics yet, but we'll learn them together soon enough."

"What is it?" squawks Handleman, and we all tell him to shush.

"Before I share this with you, let me say that despite the potential implications this may have, everyone should remain calm, and perhaps we can come to a solution in an appropriate amount of time." Hah! I'll be long gone before they've even decided the order in which they'll try to kill one another.

Harold Johnson heads over toward Oberst and Seligman, waddling like an oversized mallard. The two dinos flinch as he approaches, arranging themselves back to back, circling their wagons so as to defend their territory. Shooting the Allosaur and Iguanodon representatives a look of disgust, Johnson pushes past them, making for a file cabinet set beneath a rotted writing desk. I cannot see what he is doing, but I can hear a number of locks clicking open, granting him access to the treasures beyond.

He strides back into the middle of the room, a thick sheaf of papers bound by masses of colored rubber bands tucked beneath his arm. The edges of the individual pages have been singed, some to the point of ash. Black snowflakes flutter to the ground.

"This is only about one percent of the original stash," says Johnson, holding the bundle aloft for all to see. "The other ninety-nine percent has been lost to us. It burned in a nightclub fire sometime last week. Owner of the club died in the blast."

"He died?" I blurt out, unable to stop myself.

"This morning," says Johnson. "I got the call a few hours ago." I feel an odd sense of loss; though I never knew Burke personally, I have grown to understand the Raptor over these past few days. I have been privy to his likes, his dislikes, his relationships both moral and otherwise. I can only hope that Jaycee Holden has a strong shoulder nearby when she hears the news.

"But these papers"—and Johnson pretentiously waves the packet around like McCarthy holding his blacklist, crisped edges crackling in the air—"these are something altogether more important than any single dinosaur life. They were found in the bottom of a cardboard box that had been tucked away in the nightclub's storeroom.

"They appear to belong to Dr. Emil Vallardo, the dino geneticist working out of New York. They contain information regarding his . . . mixing experiments."

Eureka! I want to shout. That's why Judith McBride denied ever funding Donovan's nightclub—it was Vallardo who fronted the money all along! Still, funding a nightclub clear across the country just so you could hide some papers there seems like an awful length to go to in order to protect an experiment that has already been heavily documented by the Councils.

"And this," Johnson says, holding aloft a small glass vial, his pudgy fingers spreading across the surface, "is what they found in a hidden safe tucked beneath the floorboards."

Mrs. Nissenberg lifts her head. "What is it?"

Johnson's voice drops three notches. "This is one of his experiments. This is a mixed embryo."

Chaos.

"We must disbar him!" screams Oberst.

"You can't disbar doctors," says Seligman. "That's lawyers."

"We could have his license taken away—"

"The children, what about the children?"

As I lean back in my chair, using my tail as a balancing mechanism, I tune out all of the commotion around me—the harangues against Vallardo and his corruption of nature, the cries of *what shall become of us, we will all become mongrels,* the gasping and the wheezing and the whimpers over the destruction of our species. And despite my congenital aversion to any type of whining whatsoever, I can't say that I blame them. The Council members, like all other dinos, are worried. They are worried about unity, they are worried about the conflict of science and nature, and they are worried about what is right and what is wrong in a world in which we must hide ourselves away, in which morals are topsy-turvy and positions can flip-flop from day to day.

Most of all, they are worried that they will lose their identity. But it is pointless to fret in this manner; we lost it a long time ago.

From the staircase, then: A clomp. Two thumps. Pause. A clomp. Two thumps. The sounds of a tired three-legged horse, of a body being dragged down a flight of stairs by reluctant murderers. A clomp. Two thumps.

The pounding is soon accompanied by a voice, insistent, crotchety: "Well? Are you helping or are you not helping?"

Harold bolts up the stairs—Brontos can haul when they need to—and, a minute later, reemerges holding an elderly man in one arm and a walker in the other. "Put me down," the old man grunts. "I can walk, I can walk. Stairs, no. Floor, yes."

"This is Dr. Otto Solomon," Johnson says, "a partner of Vallardo's from many, many years ago, and I think he may be able to shed a little light on the issue." The doctor—a Hadrosaur, if the scent hits me right—is still guised up in his human costume, and he's a curious little thing. Accent like an SS commandant, five feet high, face like a shar-pei, hair follicles clutching at the scalp, scrabbling for purchase but fighting a losing battle. It's a wonderful approximation of human deterioration, and I can't help but marvel at his choice of costume; I can only hope that when I reach his age I have the guts to so accurately depict my own physical decrepitude.

"What are you staring at?" he asks, and I chuckle, sorry for whomever he has caught in midgaze. "I said what are you staring at, Raptor?"

"Me?" Whoops.

"Are you done staring?"

"Yes."

"Yes, what?"

"Yes . . . Doctor?"

"That is more like it." Dr. Solomon snatches his walker from Johnson and gallops into the center of our circle—clop thump thump clop thump

thump—zipping along with surprising speed for a dino of his age and infirmities.

"Before I give you my analysis of the situation," he says, each word a clipped command of Teutonic control, "is there anyone who has something important to say? Something that cannot wait?"

No hands are raised.

"Good," says Solomon. "Then you will kindly remember to shut up while I am speaking. I do not answer questions until I am done, and I do not entertain speculation at any time."

Again, we agree to his demand. Dr. Solomon pulls himself erect, stares each of us in the eye one by one, working the room. He begins with a short discussion of creation, of the primordial ooze and the single-celled organisms that had nothing better to do with their time than swim around, mutate, and divide. We work our way into early forms of multicellular life before the doctor starts babbling on about DNA, genetic codes, and long-strand proteins.

After nearly thirty minutes have gone by, during which time Mrs. Nissenberg has to poke me with her knitting needle just to keep me from falling asleep, I raise my hand high and ask, "Is there a layman's explanation for this?"

The doctor doesn't even glance over; he ignores me and continues with his speech. ". . . and so, with the ribosomes taking up the available material . . ."

But I'm determined to get to the bottom of this before dinner. "Excuse me, Dr. Solomon, but what does any of this have to do with Vallardo's papers?"

The doctor thunks over toward me, eyes blazing. "You want it so easy," he says. "All your generation, you want it now, you want it on a platter. You don't want to have to think about the answer—you want others to do the work for you. Is that it? Is that what you're looking for?"

"That's the situation in a nutshell, Doc." I look around the room, and the feeling, it seems, is mutual. "Now can you fork it over, please?"

Solomon sighs, shaking his head in pity for us poor unlearned masses. "Dr. Vallardo's papers, along with the once-frozen embryo inside that vial, indicate an experiment in cross-species mating," he says plainly.

"We already knew that!" cries Johnson. "We've known that for six months now."

"Six months!" yelps Handleman, anxious to exercise his vocal cords. "Six months!"

The others join in the harangue, blasting Solomon for wasting a half hour of our time on scientific fiddle-faddle, but the doctor claps his hands three times—smack smack smack—and comfortably commands silence in the basement once more.

"If you would stop your yapping," he says, each word tinged with ice, "maybe you would be able to listen to me as well as hear me. Listen. Dr. Vallardo has long been engaged in cross-*race* mating. But this is not what I just told you."

Handleman again—"Six months!"

"What I said," Solomon continues, "is that all of this evidence, if I am reading it correctly, show that he has begun experiments in cross-*species* mating."

"Cross-species?" Colon repeats, unsure of the term's definition.

"Like what?" Oberst asks.

Colon steps up. "Like a . . . like a dog and a cat?"

"Or a mouse and a chicken?" asks Mrs. Nissenberg.

"A donkey and a fish!" yells Kurzban.

But I understand it all now, the whole thing, the big picture, the kit, the kaboodle, and motives to boot. Well, most of it, anyway. I step up.

"How about the mating of a dinosaur and a human?" I ask, already knowing I've got this one dead to rights. "Is that what Dr. Vallardo's been working on?"

Solomon smiles, a slow, wry grin he casually tosses in my direction. "See," he says, "some of you do know how to listen."

was out of there just after the flesh started flying, but I managed to get nicked by a few stray claws and tails during my retreat. Chaos erupted the moment Solomon laid it out for us, made it clear that Vallardo was attempting to facilitate an interspecies birth, and it wasn't seconds later that scattered skirmishes broke out all throughout the basement, miniature battles of rage and confusion. Dr. Solomon, who certainly wasn't expecting the violent reaction in which the Council specializes, took a nasty club wound to the head before he was able to gather enough strength to pull himself up the basement stairs; Johnson, engaged in a no-holds-barred grudge match with Kurzban, sure wasn't going to help the elderly doctor this time.

So as blood, sweat, and bile splattered the basement walls, I grabbed Mrs. Nissenberg and dragged her into the far corner.

"You have to watch me sign this," I said, and pulled out a copy of the rectification papers. All the while, I was ducking tails, parrying claws, trying anything to remain unharmed and unmolested.

We went through the short motions of signing and notarizing, and then it was all over—I'd officially been kicked out of the Council for good. Mrs. Nissenberg wished me good luck, and I braved a few more swats and close calls on my way up the stairs.

Now, in the rush back to my apartment, no less than eight moving violations are committed by yours truly, including the running of a light that was a good ten seconds into its red cycle. Somebody up there likes me, or at least enjoys watching my shenanigans enough to let me live another day.

But how can I be blamed for breaking a few little traffic rules when my brain is occupied with so many other matters? I need to get back to the apartment, round up whatever valuables I can find, hock them for as much as I can get out of Pedro, the guy who runs the Cash 4 Crap store on Vermont, and get myself another plane ticket to New York. I need to confront Vallardo—I need to confront Judith—I need to find Sarah again, if only to take her out to dinner, squash any notions of this nonsensical relationship, and put an end to what was so unwittingly and unwisely begun.

Solomon's explanation of Vallardo's papers seals it—McBride's mind had indeed taken a long walk off a short pier, but the crazy apefucker had enough cash and enough similarly insane friends to pull off his delusion.

But what amazes me—what sickens me—is that his love for a human— his love for Sarah—was so great that he actually felt the need to father her children. If Sarah ever knew of the bestiality she'd been engaged in, I'm sure it would mortify her to death, but this new information—it might make that mortification literal.

A foreclosure notice has been tacked to the front door of my ground-level apartment, and I angrily rip it off, tear it into little bits, and scatter it along the dirt. The locks have been changed as well, but an overdrawn, otherwise useless credit card gains me quick entrance to my—*my*, damn it— home.

The power's off—I knew it would happen eventually—which means that the funky smell comes from the spoiled leftovers in my refrigerator. I stumble through the house, banging my shins in the darkness. The only good thing about the power outage is that the answering machine light is not blinking at me.

Microwave, blender—hey, the TV's still there. The appliances scattered around the apartment should be enough to score me a coach seat back to New York; even if I have to sit on the wing, I'll take it.

But there's no chance of me going back tonight. The sun's about to set, and even if I could somehow haul all of this crap into the car, I wouldn't make it to Pedro's before closing time.

I am in dire need of a nap. The last time I slept long enough to actually drop into a REM cycle was . . . let's see . . . two nights ago at the Plaza. Counting on my fingers—which are blurring, separating—makes it nearly forty hours I've gone without more than the occasional doze, and I'm amazed that I'm functioning at all. They haven't taken away my bed yet, so I decide to close the shades, lie down, and get in a few minutes of shut-eye.

The doorbell rings. I don't know how much later it is, but the sun has set and the streetlights have popped to life. The usually pleasant electronic chimes that I hooked up to my buzzer last Christmas tear away at my nerves, jangling my eardrums, as the battery-powered bell goes off again. I take a quick peek outside my window, toward the small parking lot in front of my apartment complex, but I don't see any cars other than those belonging to the humans and dinos who live nearby. Off to one side I can make out the hood of what might be a Lincoln parked just behind our Dumpster, but I can't be sure. Dragging my sluggish frame as quickly as I can, I move to the door and take a gander through the peephole, ready to whip off my gloves and bare my claws if need be. My tail twitches in involuntary antici-pation, pulse revving at the starting gate.

It's Sarah. White silk blouse, short black skirt, legs, legs, legs.

The only thing I am thinking is that there is nothing that I am thinking. I've collared a few bad apples in my day who've stood stock solid as I dragged them downtown, and I always wondered why they had that deer-in-the-headlights look. Now I know—the brain shuts down when and where it wants to. It does not follow a schedule.

Sarah smiles at the door, at the peephole, expecting me to be watching her, and the walleye lens distorts her features, spreads her lips into a gold-fish pucker, extends her teeth into great white monoliths, narrows her eyes. Horrifying. I throw open the door.

Without a word, we embrace, my arms encircling her body, pulling her close. If I could envelop her, I would. If I could make her a part of my body, suck her in, incorporate her, I would. She grasps my waist tightly, holding on as if to secure herself against a steady wind, her head pressed against my chest, her hair flung up, over, surrounding my nose, her artificial perfume beautiful to me despite its synthetic components.

We kiss. We've done it before, we'll do it again, and I can't help it so we kiss. It lingers. It sends flares shooting through my head. My hands move all about her body, outlining her curves, her exquisite lines, and I would like nothing more than to rip this guise off my skin so that I might feel her with my true hands, understand her with my real person.

I want to ask her why she's here, when she got in, where she's staying, but I know there will be time for that. Later. Later. Still silent, Sarah takes my hand, squeezes it, and I understand the question implicit in that grasp. I squeeze back and lead my human lover toward the bedroom.

Body is in full control, eyes and brain watching from the bleachers, cheering me on. Sarah undresses me—the outer me—slowly unbuttoning my shirt, pulling it off, tossing it carelessly on the floor. Hands rubbing against my chest, transferring the warm, firm touch to the real skin deep inside. I grab her breasts firmly, my first feel of a human, and she moans softly in response. Whatever I'm doing, it must be right. Sarah leans down and licks the hair on my chest, running her tongue past my nipples, down to my stomach. My guised-up torso is fair enough under human terms—not enough to land me in any of your finer ladies' magazines, mind you, but I've been told by those in the know that I have a passable chest and above-average abs. Still, with Sarah's gaze tickling every inch of my body, I do wish I had shelled out the cash for those pectoral attachments.

Sarah, smiling sweetly as we move to kiss each other yet again, doesn't seem to mind my "natural" body in the slightest, and she moves her attention below my waist, her hands gaining speed, moving from sensual to frantic as she works off my belt, cracking it through the air. Zippers sliding along now, buttons popping off, pants flying into the established heap on the ground, I go to town, being careful not to wrinkle, to crush, as I fumble with buttons and straps and hooks. Women's clothing, though a pain in the tail, is infinitely more delicate than our rough-and-tumble wear, and I have to force myself not to tear the fabric off her body in frustration and anticipation.

I am unaware of just how or when we made it to the bed itself, but as my eyes open in the aftermath of the deepest, most satisfying kiss these lips have ever had the honor of experiencing, I find myself cuddled up with Sarah atop my green and blue patchwork quilt, naked as the day I donned my first guise.

Sarah, too, is nude. And breathtaking. Literally—after a few moments of watching her lithe body squirm in anticipation of things to come, I am forced to slap myself in order to bring about a gasp of oxygen. Once again, Sarah brings my face to hers, cupping my cheeks in her two delicate hands, fingernails caressing my outer skin but still oh so delicious, and we roll together, moving as one as I prepare to betray my species in the most beautiful way I can possibly imagine.

A dino female—and most males, I should imagine—approaches sex in a very rational, practical fashion. The act itself is treated almost as an obligation, not to her mate, her partner, or her own intrinsic femininity, but to the species itself. It is as if we have been unable to work our way out from under the thumb of raw animalistic urges despite a good hundred million years of evolution. When the time comes to procreate (or at least go through the motions), the time comes to procreate, and woe betide the creature who tries to stop a dino female from having her way.

But there is a world beyond, I know now, a level deeper than any Tantric manual can provide. How could I have gone so long without this?

Of course, in the past, I had no experience outside of my own species, no clue that anything was absent from the equation. But now, as I move my body with Sarah's, my costumed skin all but invisible to my hyperextended senses, I realize that there is so much more to this act, an element of sensuality that I have been missing all along. With dinos, flesh grinds and gyrates, hide rubbing roughly into a hot layer of friction. With humans—with Sarah—flesh swells, billows, condenses, an undulation of one. As I stroke myself in and out of her warmth, my engorged member tight against the confines of the polysuit extension, tight within the confines of my new lover, she moves with me, our energies coalescing into one great wave of movement and heat. With dinos, the sounds are shrieks and moans, howls to the religion of pleasure. With Sarah, there are soft murmurs and syncopated heartbeats, delicate gasps and whispers to the night.

I do not feel guilty in the least.

When it is over, when we are spent, when our arms fall to our sides, exhausted from holding one another so close, so tightly, I draw from the last remaining reserves of my energy and place my forearm beneath Sarah's fragile body, nestling her against my chest. It is not macho to cuddle, but my usually ubiquitous sense of self-consciousness has left the building, having been put out for the night like a naughty cat.

Staring at each other, words still unspoken, eyes focusing on eyes, pupils still dilating in the darkened bedroom, her green irises set off beautifully against the shock of red hair cascading across her cheek, I am unable to stop my hands from roaming, searching out her body in their own journey across the uncharted. I fondle her breast, teasing the nipple with my fingertips. I have never touched a human breast before this night, and I find it oddly firm, sensually so.

We make love again. I do not know where I find the energy, but if I ever locate that source, I might be ready to set up shop with a perpetual-motion patent.

One of us must speak first. I suppose it's possible for her to silently dress herself, kiss me, and walk out of my town house without so much as a word the entire time; I suppose it would be romantic, fantastically so perhaps, but someone as garrulous as myself couldn't let that happen. And though I cringe as the PI who rents out space in my mind steps up and asks for a word with the landlord, I do indeed have a few questions to ask.

"How was the flight?" I begin. Sarah is still naked, splayed across the bed; I have covered my costumed body with the quilt. I am cold, my circulation poor. I really ought to see a physician.

She laughs, a high giggle that makes me want to leap up and start all over again despite the strange tingle emanating from my tail and lower extremities. I hope that those repetitive thrusting motions didn't damage my girdle; at the first possible moment I should run to the bathroom and check the apparatus out. A snapped girdle can cause serious circulation problems, which can, in turn, cause temporary and, in some cases, permanent loss of feeling in the affected areas.

"How was the flight?" Sarah repeats, tossing her hair away from her face. "That's what you want to ask me?"

"Figured I'd be asking you at some point, might as well make it now. Good a time as any." I give her nose a peck.

"The flight was fine," she said. "Would you like to know what movie we saw?"

"I'd be delighted to know."

"We saw *Spartacus*."

"Isn't that sort of an old movie?"

"It was an old plane. Besides, it took up most of the flight." She yawns, stretches, and I watch her muscles strain with the effort. "So now you get to ask me what you really want to ask me, which is why I'm in Los Angeles."

"Well . . . now that you mention it . . ."

"A singing gig."

"A singing gig." I am skeptical.

Sarah lowers her eyes, runs a finger across my chest. "You don't believe me?"

"It's not that I don't believe you," I say. "It's that I figured, maybe . . ." Maybe she came all this way just to see me. I can't finish the sentence; it reeks of femininity.

"I found a message on my machine after I got back from your hotel. My agent got me a studio gig singing background on a B. B. King album. We've been recording all day."

"And then you decided to come in and see me? So I'm secondary?"

Sarah tickles me, a vicious blitzkrieg that sends me rolling across the bed before I'm able to mount my own counterattack. Soon enough, we're kissing once again like teenagers going at it on the living-room sofa before the parents get home.

We lie in silence for some time, holding each other, reveling in the perfect fit of our bodies. We are tailor-made for one another. "When do you go back to New York?" I ask.

"I've got an open-ended ticket," she says, "but the gig's supposed to be over the day after tomorrow." I feel a hand pressing against my costumed knee. It is moving up, toward that polyfiber mix that represents my thigh. My tail is really starting to tingle now, and I don't know if it's only from lack of circulation. "Of course, I could be persuaded to stay."

That's all the invitation I need to get me flowing yet again. I am a dynamo today! Someone should bottle my sexual energy and use it to power India.

Nearly four hours and countless lovemaking sessions after Sarah first arrived at my apartment this afternoon, I invite her to stay the night. She accepts.

"Let me go back to the hotel, grab my stuff," she says.

"I'll drive you," I offer.

"I've got a rental."

"You don't know your way."

"I've got a map," she says, laughing. "Honey, I'm coming back this time, okay?" Sarah, now fully dressed, leans over the bed and plants a full kiss on my lips, her tongue searching out mine. I try to pull her back down onto the bed for another episode of playtime, but she backs away, shaking her finger. "Naughty boy," she snickers. "You'll just have to wait for it."

I nod; it will indeed be best if we separate for an hour or so. It will give Sarah time to pack, and give me time to adjust my costume and to the reality of what has just occurred. Now that my brain has been freed from the constant ecstasy of orgasmic highs, it has a chance to be concerned with the ongoing loss of sensation in my tail. Adjustments are in order.

Hopping out of the bed—yep, there's the tingle—I walk Sarah into the living room, toward the foyer. We embrace again, and I hide myself behind the front door as I let her out. I am not an exhibitionist, costume or no.

"An hour or so?" I say.

She laughs, obviously amused at my lack of pretense. I want her, she knows it, end of story. "As soon as possible, Vincent." She blows me a kiss and heads for her car. I shut the door and ensure that the blinds are drawn.

That tingle, that itch, has intensified, spread all across my body. Something major must have quit functioning down in the nitty-gritty of my costume, and I can only hope that I caught it in time to prevent a major injury. I don't bother removing my mask or torso guise, as it's a pain in the rear to properly apply the epoxy in order to get that good, tight grip that will hold up under even the most intense bout of smooching, but I do remove the lower half of my outer layer. The polysuit slowly peels away from my hide, its already gummy backside positively slimy thanks to the buildup of sweat and other natural juices expelled during the last few hours.

Standing in my living room, across from the full-length decorative mirror hung on the far wall, I inspect my supportive trusses and girdles for any breaches in their superstructure. So far, I can see no flaws. Could this sensation, so near to my groin, be a purely psychosomatic one? A result of re-pressed guilt over what is sure to be the most unnatural act in which I have ever engaged? I certainly hope not, because if I have any say in the matter, I plan on being this unnatural again.

Wait, wait—there it is. Right beneath my G series, the clamp that always gives me the most trouble, a fabric strap has somehow managed to double over and work its way into a tight noose atop my tail. I can't imagine how it happened, but what with all of the interesting new postures Sarah and I got ourselves into, I'm not surprised at the result.

Grasping my tail with one still-costumed hand, I work the strap down and away, pulling it into a less offensive position; almost instantly, I can feel sensation, glorious sensation, rush back into my body like a river breaking free of its dam. It doesn't feel as nice as making love with Sarah, but it runs a close second.

Perhaps I should remove my entire guise and make whatever readjust-ments are necessary to keep this from happening again. I'm hoping Sarah and I will have an encore of our earlier performance once she returns to my town house, and I don't want any technical malfunctions to get in the way. The next time, that fabric strap could wrap around something a lot more vi-tal than my tail.

I locate the hidden reverse buttons beneath my nipples and work them away from their confines, struggling to work my torso polysuit away from the hide below. Torsos always give me the most problems, perhaps because there are so few places to squirrel away the requisite attach-ments. Masks have countless hiding places—under the hair, inside the ear, the nose, etc. The lower half of the body allows for zipper and button placement in other, less socially acceptable areas, though it works out well in the end.

I've almost got that last Velcro strip unattached, reaching for it, reaching for it—

And Sarah walks in the front door.

"Vincent, I forgot to ask what street I—"

She freezes. I freeze. Only her eyes move, darting around my half-costumed body, taking in the spectacle before her. And I can project myself into Sarah's head, see myself as I must look through her eyes: a lizard draped with disembodied human skin, a beast who crawled up from the depths of prehistory to terrify and devour young, petite human women. A monster. A freak. Lust and passion and eroticism and, yes, love, are forgotten as my instinct, my damned instinct, orders martial law in my body and takes over all functions.

"Vincent—" she says, but I cut her off with my leap across the room, slamming the door closed with one exposed claw as I bounce off the far wall and pounce atop her chest. Sarah falls roughly to the floor, landing on her back with a surprised whoosh of air. My claws grab for her throat as my roar shatters the nearby mirror, glass spilling onto the carpet.

I know my duty. I have to kill her.

"I'm sorry, Sarah," I manage to say, even as I ready my claw for the final plunge into her beautiful, quivering neck. She's gasping in gulps of air, trying to say something, her breath still not coming—

"Vin . . . Vin . . ."

"I'm sorry," I repeat, and strike the death blow.

It is blocked. Her arm catches mine, holds it in place, the peaked edges of my claws inches from her throat. How is this possible? Perhaps in her fear she has gained strength. I strike out with the other hand, natural knives glinting—

Caught and captured yet again. Sarah struggles with my arms, holding her death at bay, face contorted in pain. "Vincent," she manages to say, her voice two octaves deeper than I have ever heard it before. "Wait."

But there's still that inborn sense of danger, of responsibility, telling me to *push it home, finish the job, kill the human before she lets it all out!* and I contract my muscles yet again, eager to get it all over with and start what is sure to be a prolonged mourning process.

"Wait," Sarah says again, and this time her word cuts through the din of instinct-driven insanity, halting the downward thrust of my arms. Is this foolishness on my part? Is this that human-bred habit of trying to *understand* everything rearing up again, costing me valuable time? In the dino world we do not overanalyze. We see, we react, and we conquer. With my interspecies coupling a mere half hour behind me, I find myself disgusted at whatever bits of humanity I have incorporated into my persona over the years. I should kill her now! But I find myself waiting to hear her out.

I sit back on my haunches, muscles still quivering, ready to pounce if she should try to run, to make a dash to the outside world. I love Sarah with whatever soul I have left in this body, but I cannot take the chance of trusting her. Not with this.

I expect her to try and beg for mercy, to explain that she will never ever tell a single living being about what she has seen in my apartment today, to plead clemency as others have done before her. But she doesn't even open her mouth, doesn't try to speak.

Instead, Sarah simply tosses her hair over her shoulders and reaches her hands up as if to bunch those long locks into a single ponytail. I hear a click, a familiar *zzzip*, and Sarah brings those beautiful arms forward again. I shall be sad to see them gone.

A shift of her features, an impossible slide to the left. Noses don't move like that. Chins don't move like that. At least, not without some major reconstructive surgery. Eyebrows are falling, rosy cheeks following, and what the hell is going on—

Sarah's mask falls off, skin drooping and sagging away from her face. A rich brown hide, a smooth sandpaper texture, peeks out from beneath. Contact lenses pop out of her eyes, green globules fluttering to the carpet. Stumbling backward, my body is no longer under my control as that false layer of flesh falls away, off her hide, onto the floor. I stare in disbelief as she stands and unfastens the rest of her guise.

Polysuit follows polysuit as Sarah Archer slowly and deliberately removes each flap of faux skin, every ounce of makeup, every inch of belt and girdle and truss from the real body beneath. I do not know how much time has passed. A minute, an hour, a day, it doesn't matter as I witness the gradual disappearance of Sarah Archer and the equally gradual unveiling of a very familiar Coleophysis.

"Vincent," she says softly, "I wanted to tell you."

I should have seen it coming, should have known it from the start. I'm a trained professional, for Chrissakes. It was there all along, of course, easy enough to detect if only I hadn't been blinded by my own lust for forbidden treasures:

Sarah Archer is Jaycee Holden. Jaycee Holden is Sarah Archer. Put it however you like it, the two women are one and the same, and I feel the increasingly unstable buttresses that support my world collapsing beneath me as the rest of my muscles give way. Someone, it seems, is dimming the lights . . .

17

We sit on the couch, three feet apart, miles away from each other. Every few minutes, she attempts to speak, but I hold up my hand, refusing to listen. Immature, perhaps, but I need some time to think. It has been almost an hour since I came to, and only now am I regaining enough control of my emotions to allow for rational conversation.

"Vincent, listen . . ." she pleads, tears welling in those soft brown eyes. Her green contact lenses soak in a spare case carried in her purse.

"I can't . . . How could . . ." I am not getting very far with speech, so I opt for a pained expression. It conveys the message properly.

"You don't think I didn't want to tell you? Right there in that Greek restaurant, I wanted to let it all out. Right in front of everyone if I had to, just let it fly, let you know that you and I . . . that we were the same."

I laugh sardonically, shaking my head. "We're not the same," I say.

"We're both dinos."

"Or so you say. Maybe this is a costume, too."

"Don't be childish, Vincent, of course it isn't."

"How the hell am I supposed to know?" I explode, and some part of me is glad to see her cringe. "I mean, Christ, Sarah . . . or is it Jaycee?"

"It's Jaycee."

"You sure? I could go for just about anything now. You want me to call you Bertha, I'll call you Bertha."

"It's Jaycee," she repeats meekly.

"Fine. You got anything left to hide, Jaycee? 'Cause I'm just about done playing around. You're missing, you're not missing, you're a human, you're a dino—"

"There's a reason," she interrupts.

"I would hope so. If you did this just for kicks I'd really be worried. So, you gonna tell me?"

"If you let me."

"I'm letting you."

"Good."

"Good. Now talk."

She begins slowly, shifting about the couch, unable to look me in the eyes. It was so damned easy before, wasn't it? "I don't know where to start," she says, and I suggest the beginning. "There isn't much of a beginning. It sort of . . . sprang up."

"Like a weed?"

"Five years ago," Jaycee continues, "I met Donovan on the streets of New York. Well, not on the streets—we were both at a deli counter down in Greenwich Village. And we were both single and we were both attractive and we were both ready for a relationship, though we didn't know it at the time. I smelled him the second he walked in, the strongest dino odor that's ever hit me. Do you remember his smell, Vincent? From your visit to the hospital?"

I remember the odors of barbecued meat, of roasted Raptor, and though I feel Jaycee Holden deserves some pain for what she's put me through, I don't think divulging this information would represent a fair retaliation. "It was a hospital," I say. "You know how tough it is with those disinfectants."

She senses my tactful avoidance of the subject and nods gratefully. "He could light up a room with his odor. Like a wave of roses, a sea breeze. I used to call him my little sea dragon.

"I had corned beef on white with mayo, and he made fun of it. Said I didn't know how to eat properly. Those were the first words I ever heard him say—'Ma'am, I hate to intrude, but you don't know how to eat right.'"

How cute. "Is this nonsense going somewhere?" This is good old-fashioned jealousy talking, but I really don't care.

"You said to start from the beginning, I'm starting from the beginning. He was a great guy, Vincent, a lot like you. Not just because he was a Raptor, either. Your sense of humor, your style, the way you carry yourself—very similar. You would have liked him, I'm sure."

Flattery will get her everywhere; this helps to soften me up. "I'm sure I would have. Go on."

"It took some time to get Donovan over the concept of marriage, but once he warmed to the subject he really went at it with gusto. You know, planning our lives together, our futures . . . We had a place in the West Eighties, Donovan was still working for Raymond, I was occupied with the Council seat I'd won with his help, and we were what half the world would consider the perfect couple and the other half would consider the perfect Yuppie scum. Either way, we were happy. There was just the one little problem . . ."

"Kids."

"Yeah. Kids." Jaycee tucks her long, brown legs beneath her body and slumps against a pillow, propping her tail along the side of the sofa. I remain rigid against the far armrest. "I wanted them, Donovan wanted them, but with our two different races . . . We could have adopted, I guess. I know there are enough egg donors in this world, but we wanted something we could call our own. Is that selfish? Donovan mentioned it once at work, I think, and Raymond put us in touch with Dr. Vallardo.

"We were an early case for him, actually. He'd been messing around with birds, some monitor lizards, frogs, snakes, but he'd only had a few dino patients before us. Things were still clandestine in his lab, and he had us come to the medical center at all hours of the night for tests and treatments. I still remember this one horrendous stew of chalk and zinc I had to suck down; even today, I can feel it rubbing against my tonsils."

"So you were guinea pigs," I say.

"We knew it going in. But if it was going to give us the chance to be parents, we would have gladly been boll weevils if that's what it took.

"A month went by, six months, a year, no luck. I kept donating my eggs, Donovan kept donating his seed, Dr. Vallardo kept mixing them together, toggling whatever genetic switches he had to toggle to get tab A to fit into slot B, but nothing ever came of it."

I shrug. "It happens all the time."

"Sure, but it doesn't make it any easier. It hit Donovan worse than it did me. He became despondent. Donovan was good at that, switching his happiness on and off. Most of his down times weren't long, and I'd gotten used to trudging through the doldrums along with him, the long days spent asleep, the somber mood music . . . but this one dragged on and on for weeks. He was sluggish, at home, at work, in bed. . . . The weeks turned into months, and soon enough I started noticing that he was avoiding things. Avoiding me."

"How?"

"Take the wedding. Half a year away, and Donovan, who'd been planning this event like it was the invasion at Normandy, didn't seem as . . . intense as he once was. It was like he was questioning things. Not me, not my motives, but himself.

"It was only a few weeks later that I realized he'd been sleeping with Judith McBride."

"Detective service?" I ask.

"Common sense," she replies. "It had been there all along, but I just hadn't bothered to see it." Sounds familiar. "In fact, I'd had my so-called friends—a wolf pack of society bitches who spent their time crooning over their fake human nails and new knitted hairdos—just about dropping it in my lap for over a month.

"'Saw Judith and Donovan over lunch today,' one would tell me. 'Had a marvelous time.' And I would smile and nod and go through the motions of conversation, assuming that she'd seen them as employer and employee, negotiating perhaps a business deal.

"Well, I figured it out eventually, and can you blame me for being crushed? Five years of my life down the tubes, and all because of some withered old bag who didn't have anything better to do with her time than take advantage of an emotionally distraught Raptor."

I ask her if she said anything to Donovan, confronted him with her suspicions, and she shakes her head. "I meant to. Time and time again, I'd approach him, ask him to talk, but I couldn't bring myself to do it. It was like, if I didn't say it . . ."

"Maybe it wasn't true," I finish.

"Exactly. So I sat in the house, sat in Council meetings, sat in restaurants, kept my mouth shut, and moped around just about as much as Donovan."

"And then?" I'm getting wrapped up in the story, despite that high level of resentment I'm trying to maintain, the narration weakening my resolve.

Jaycee glances around my darkened apartment. "Do you have any herbs?" she asks, moistening her lips with a flick of that luscious tongue.

"Fresh out. And if I'm not chewing, nobody is. What I wanna know is where does your little costume act come in?"

"I'm getting there," says Jaycee. "I was ready to break it off with Donovan, move out of the apartment, go on with my life. If not forgive, at least forget. And then we had an emergency Council meeting."

"I'm familiar with them."

"This one was about Raymond and his increasingly open relationships with human women. There was some concern among the group, and, I admit, I was one of the most vocal. Raymond had been playing it up around town with a few of his secretaries, some acquaintances, even a professional or two from a popular human escort service, and the whole thing was just . . . wrong. Meanwhile, the Council was looking for a way to catch him in the act so they could levy some fines—and we're talking heavy. Forty, fifty million bucks in what amounted to extortion. I didn't know who to be more disgusted with—Raymond or the Council.

"Only question was how to catch him in the act. It was decided that we needed someone on the inside. Someone who could make him slip up and let us be there to get the physical evidence."

"Entrapment," I say.

She's about to correct me, then stops, nods. "Yes, entrapment."

"So that's when Jaycee Holden became Sarah Archer," I say, beginning to piece it all together.

"Very good, detective. And now you move into our bonus round."

Now that I think about it, certain elements of my investigation are coming together, making a little more sense. It's amazing I didn't see it all before, but it's like working a maze from finish to start—the twists and turns are there, but you can't see 'em until they've already passed you by.

"That's how you disappeared so easily," I say. "You had Council help."

"I had minimal Council help," Jaycee amends, "but they did manage to pull a few strings. Only two of the other Council members knew that I was the one . . . switching over, as it were. They thought I had disappeared, just like everyone else."

"But a simple costume switch wasn't enough, was it?" I say, thinking back to Officer Tuttle, the nice policeman who let me out of that nasty speeding ticket on the 405 that I so richly deserved. "You had to get rid of your scent glands, too."

Jaycee fingers the small scar on the side of her neck. A light, ragged river of skin tissue, it is barely visible on her ridged hide. "That was the hardest part for me," she admits. "I had a really kick-ass smell." She tries to grin, a wan, melancholy smile, and for the first time in more than an hour I find myself being drawn toward her again rather than repulsed by what I had considered her betrayal.

"Honey and gumdrops," I guess. "Light, airy."

"Jasmine," she says. "Sharp. I could walk into a florist's and you'd never find me. At least, not with your nose. But my desire for revenge was stronger than my desire to retain my scent, so we had our Diplodod representative extract my glands for the undercover work. He was a physician, and we had a little midnight rendezvous in his office, just him, me, a scalpel, and a lot of laughing gas."

"Can they be replaced?" I ask. "I might like to smell you sometime."

She shakes her head. "He kept them suffused with blood and whatever other vitamins they needed for as long as he could, but the tissues died out a few months into it. We didn't know how long my . . . seduction of Raymond would take. No one thought the whole affair would go on this long. He suggested mixing me up a chemical patch that could replicate the dino odor nicely, but I've . . . I've smelled them before. They say you can't tell the difference. What they say is wrong. It's metallic. Synthetic. And I don't like it in the least.

"So I was worried about my scent glands, yes, but the thought of bringing down Raymond, who I guess was pretty much the pawn in all this, was too tempting. Because if it brought down Raymond, it brought down Judith, too, and I couldn't wait to see her suffer like I had suffered. Was that wrong of me, Vincent, to want Judith McBride to suffer? Are those feelings wrong? I like to think I did the moral thing. Eye for an eye, man for a man."

I shake, I nod, I shrug—I've felt those pangs before, given birth to my own revenge fantasies, so I can't deny her those emotions. "And the singing? The gig out here?"

"True, every word of it. Here I am, my scent removed, my guise firmly in place, my past life a fabrication. We faked a place of birth, a few jobs, everything clean and neat, but when you can't come through with the qualifications . . . I couldn't type, couldn't take dictation, couldn't even use a computer." She holds up her fingers, wiggles them around. "Still can't. Pretty useless, I guess. Most of my professional life has been spent messing around in the swamp pits of dino politics, so there certainly wasn't a place for me in the human world."

"But you had your voice," I point out.

"That I did. I had my voice, and, more important, I had that fake body, and I had that fake face. And I gotta admit, it was damn good. We'd done a check of Raymond McBride's likes and dislikes before we guised me up— the goal was to present him with a willing partner who was his ideal human female. It just so happened that it worked in a nightclub setting, too.

"So there I am at this charity event that I've gotten my agent to take me to, and just before I'm about to be introduced to Raymond as Sarah Archer, I get cold feet. Nerves, tension, I don't know what came over me, but I suddenly decided I couldn't do it.

"I was all ready to tell my agent that I wanted to get the hell out of there when I heard a commotion from the kitchen. Bored with the conversation—I think we were babbling on about some opera or another—I wandered in to see what the fuss was about, and found Judith McBride and my Donovan spread out across the preparation counter, thigh-deep in salmon platters, kissing, groping, fondling each other." Sarah—damn it, Jaycee!— leans her head back and stares at the ceiling. I think she's chuckling.

"You okay?" I ask. "We can take a break."

"Please," says Jaycee. "I've had a long time to get over it. Where was I? Right, they're slobbering all over the kitchen counter and each other, and I let out a little gasp.

"Judith looks up and says, 'Do you mind?' No remorse, no guilt, no sense of chagrin at being caught. And that cold, eight-ball blackness in her eyes, that glare the bitch gave me . . . For a moment I thought I caught a glimpse of recognition in her eyes, but then I realized that this was how Judith acted to everyone. If only for that reason, she needed to be punished—if not for me, then for the countless others whose lives she'd made miserable. Well, my resolve was strengthened then and there, and I stared Judith down, then shot my own glance back at Donovan. At least he looked a tad embarrassed at the situation.

"'You should be ashamed of yourselves,' I said to them. 'This is hardly sanitary.' And then I took my leave. Walked out of the kitchen, into the living room, had my agent introduce me to Raymond, and the rest is history."

"He fell for you quickly," I say.

"And hard. Natural charm, of course, but the guise didn't hurt, either."

"And then?"

"Then what?" she says, shrugging. "You know the rest—Donovan came out to the left coast a few weeks later, Raymond and I had our affair, I let the Council members in on when and where to instruct the detective agency to take pictures. You should have seen the trouble I went through to get Raymond to leave the blinds open when we had sex—I had to convince him that I was an exhibitionist, that it added something special with the windows uncovered. That got him moving . . ."

I say, "So the Council got their pictures, you got your revenge. Why didn't you break it off?"

"I was going to," says Jaycee, and once again I can sense her lachrymal glands preparing to spray their saltwater jets. "And then . . . then he died."

"He was killed," I clarify.

She nods, begins to tear up, and I find myself pulling her closer, into me, against my body, soothing her with long, full strokes across her back. I need to ask her about the murder, to ask her what she knows, what she thinks, what she suspects, but for now my foolish emotions are running things once again. "You loved him?" I ask.

"No," she sniffles. "I loved Donovan. But Raymond was a kind man, he was charming, he was intelligent. He didn't deserve . . . what I did."

"Setting him up?"

After a moment, Sarah nods, off and running on her crying fit once more. "And that's all," she says once she's regained control. "Since then, I've been too tired to make the change back to Jaycee. For that matter, there's no reason I should. With Donovan dead, I don't have anyone left for me in the dino world. I figured maybe I'd stay on as Sarah, see what I could make of myself as a human. I sure as heck screwed up as a dinosaur . . ."

"And that's everything?" I ask, curious why she left out what I consider to be a crucial piece to this puzzle.

"Everything."

"What about Vallardo?"

"What about him? I told you, Donovan and I stopped going after a few years." But Jaycee, who's managed a great deal of eye contact throughout her story, doesn't turn those baby browns to look at me when she says this, and I know it's a point I can press.

"But you've seen him since," I say. "Come on, Jaycee, no more hiding."

"Maybe at parties or something, but I don't know why you'd think I've seen—"

"The letter," I say plainly, and this quiets her up. "The letter that came to your apartment the night we met, the one that sent you into catatonia. It was from Vallardo, wasn't it?"

She doesn't try to deny it, nor to stall any longer. "How'd you know?" she asks me.

"Same way you knew without even having to pick the thing up," I say. "The handwriting. Your name was scrawled all over the envelope. When I went to see Vallardo the next day, I noticed that he had a palsy in his left hand, yet he still used it for his daily functions. Didn't put the two together until a little bit ago. So you want to tell me why you wanted to have a kid with Raymond McBride?"

"Because I wanted a child, any child," she spits out. "And Raymond was a lech, but he would have been a hell of a dad. Not a *let's go in the yard and toss around the football* kind of dad, but a strong genetic type. I didn't care about the cross-race mixing. When I told Raymond I wanted a child he said 'wonderful!' and took me to Dr. Vallardo right away. Introduced him to me as the best obstetrician in New York."

"But Raymond thought you were human," I point out. "That's why he'd been funding the interspecies mix experiments."

"You know about those, too, eh?" she says, more than a hint of distaste curling the corners of her lips. "Well, Raymond had gone a little overboard with the . . . human element by this point."

"Dressler's Syndrome," I suggest.

Jaycee's guffaw is a violent bray that knocks me down a peg or two. "Let me assure you," she chuckles, "Raymond McBride did not have Dressler's Syndrome." She does not elaborate.

"But he wanted to mix with your 'human' eggs."

"He was interested in my species, you're right. And, to be frank about it, I wanted his Carnotaur seed. Only problem was Vallardo—once he started harvesting me, there wouldn't be much doubt that it wasn't a human egg he was dealing with."

"All those subtle differences," I say. "Hard shell, exterior gestation—"

"A thousand times bigger," she adds. "So you can see the difficulty. So I did what I had to do; I approached Vallardo, revealed myself as Jaycee, and told him to go ahead with our child but not to tell Raymond that I was a dino. I threatened him with every Council punishment I could think up, including complete excommunication from the community, which I think has only been approved once or twice. Napoleon got kicked out, I'm pretty sure."

"Camptosaur?" I ask, forgetting my fifth-grade history lessons.

"Raptor," she says, and shoots me a smile. "I had always planned to take my child and disappear back into the dino population once he or she was born, so Raymond need never find out that I wasn't what he thought I was. So I went through the process again, though by this time Vallardo had improved it somewhat. At the very least, I didn't have to ingest anything that would make my stomach do cartwheels, so for that I was happy.

"But before anything could come of it, Raymond was killed, and I was left alone. The experiment was over. Since then, I've been pretty much . . . treading water. When I saw that note from Vallardo, I was more worried about having to lie again, about delving back into the whole mess. And all this time I was thinking about calling Donovan, giving it a second try, but now with the fire . . . I knew what was in the Evolution Club, and I'm sure I wasn't the only one. Someone wanted those notes, that seed sample—Vallardo's, all of it—and I guess Donovan just got in the way."

Jaycee lapses into silence, and I'm not yet ready to take up the slack of conversation. There's too much to mentally digest. I choose, instead, to deal with more pressing, personal issues. "I understand why you did what you did," I tell her finally. "And I can accept it. But I'm still hurt that you would do . . . what you did . . . with me . . ." I can't come out and say it, say that she slept with me in order to keep me quiet, or to gain inside information.

But she can say it easily enough. "You think I made love with you as part of all this, don't you?" I turn away, and she lifts my face to hers.

Have we fallen into the gender reversal zone somewhere along the way?

"It's okay," I mutter, shuffling away from her touch. "You do what you have to do."

"Vincent," she says. I do not look up. "Vincent, look at me," she calls firmly, and I cannot disobey. "What I said before holds true—I care for you. Like I said, in some ways, you remind me of Donovan—"

"So I'm a substitute."

"No, you're not a substitute. You're not a replacement. But when I'm attracted to a type, I'm attracted to a type." She leers playfully, caresses my chest. "And lucky you, you're that type."

"That's handy," I say, regaining my balance in the conversation. "You're my type, too."

"I'm glad," she says. "And no matter what happens, I want you to always remember that, okay?"

"Sure."

"No matter what happens?"

"No matter what happens."

We make love again, this time as dinos, as nature intended it to be. Our hides rub against one another, rough skin scratching with a sandpaper sizzle as we move back and forth across the sofa, the floor, the bed, and the floor again. There is nothing naughty about it, nothing forbidden, nothing adventurous or on the sly. And whereas that sharpness, that just-below-the-surface buzz of danger, is no longer with us, the act is somehow more beautiful, more real, than it was before.

At some point, after the sun has sunk below the horizon, we make our way to the bedroom and continue to discover one another well into the night. At some point, Jaycee tells me that she needs me, and I find myself saying it back. At some point, I drift off into sleep, hypnagogic images of lizards and jasmine dancing through my head.

At some point, I awaken into pitch black. A voice is whispering nearby, saying something like *catch the next flight* and *be there for the first crack*. In the meager light that has managed to make its way through my bedroom window, I can make out a silhouette of Jaycee on the phone by my nightstand. In my bleary-eyed stupor, the only thing I can think is that I'm amazed that they haven't shut off my phone line yet.

"Jaycee?" I mumble. "Sarah? Come to bed."

But even as I try to prop myself up on one arm, Jaycee has placed the receiver of the phone back on the hook and knelt down by my head. She caresses me gently, and plants two kisses upon my closed eyelids.

"I'm sorry," she says. "I think I could have loved you."

And before I can either respond in kind or ask her what the hell she means by I'm sorry, there's the glint of a syringe, a sharp poke in my arm, and everything fades into a beautiful, numb shade of black.

lenda Wetzel's apartment in Hell's Kitchen is a lot like my old rental car in the sense that it is small, run-down, and probably infested with vermin. But she's been nice enough to let me crash on her living-room sofa—a pullout, with only six springs busted!—even though I managed to get her fired by J&T and somehow involved her in a no-longer-official case that has gotten no fewer than four dinos killed and a number of others, including myself, terrorized or harassed. My plan, carefully worked out over this morning's plane flight, is as follows: I will solve the case, I will find Jaycee, I will lift her into my arms much as Richard Gere did to Debra Winger at the end of *An Officer and a Gentleman,* and I will take her to Los Angeles. We will not go to the backseat of my car, due to the aforementioned vermin problem.

I woke up with a headache that could bring down Godzilla—whatever was in that syringe packed a wallop, and I wouldn't be surprised to find out it was some sort of concentrated herb. This reminds me of the hangovers I used to get back in my binge and binge days—my God, was it just a week ago?

Pedro turned my remaining furniture and appliances into nineteen hundred dollars in cash, and I thanked him profusely for bilking me out of the last of my worldly possessions. Twenty-dollar taxi to LAX, fifteen-hundred-dollar plane ticket, forty-dollar trip into Manhattan. I am currently as close to penniless as I've ever been in my life, and it's the furthest worry from my mind.

"I can't believe you're looking to bed down with the human," Glenda says as we prepare to hit the town. She's been fired from her job at J&T, but claims to enjoy the freedom of working freelance. I think it's bullshit concocted to keep me from feeling low at a time when I'm already only millimeters in height, but that's her story, and she's sticking to it. "I mean . . . a human, for Chrissakes."

"She's not a human," I explain for the tenth time. "She just looks and smells like a human."

"If it smells like a human . . ." Glenda mumbles, the age-old dino truism escaping her lips. "Okay, maybe she ain't a human, but she's a friggin' hussy."

"And she's not a hussy. She was doing it for the Council."

"I got the pictures, Rubio. Kodachrome and everything. The hussy was friggin' enjoying it."

" 'Course she was," I said. "They were both dinos. Now don't tell me two dinos can't enjoy being together . . . ?"

"Yeah, but—" This stops her, throwing her lower lip into a thoughtful pout. "Okay, you got me."

"Are you going to stop calling her the hussy?"

"Ooh, look at you," she teases. "You've really got the hots for this bimbo, don't you?"

Once we get that cleared up, I set about formulating a plan of attack on the city. There is much to do and, if my hackles, slowly but steadily rising since I stepped off the plane, are any indication, little time in which to do it.

"First stop, McBride's apartment on the Upper East Side," I tell Glenda. "Can you stay here, make a few calls?"

"Shoot."

"Shoot as in *darn,* or shoot as in *fire away*?"

"Just tell me what to do," she says.

"Easy job—check with Pacific Bell and find out what calls were made from my house between six o'clock last night and eight o'clock this morning. Might have been collect, might have been calling card, but they should have the call sheet. Jaycee phoned someone from my house, I'm sure of it."

"And you think when you find that person, you'll find your little huss . . . Jaycee."

I smile at Glenda's attempt, however belated, to be respectful of my wishes. "She has to be somewhere," I say. "No one just disappears."

"Remember who you're talking about."

Grabbing my keys, my wallet, a few disintegration pouches on the off chance I should run into trouble, I say, "You'll get on it?"

"Right away, boss."

"Thanks." I peck Glenda on the cheek and she giggles. It's the first sign of femininity I've seen out of my new, temporary partner, but I think I liked her better when she cursed. This is too off-putting.

"Now get the fuck out of here," she commands, and all is right with the world.

"Lock the door," I suggest as I leave. "Lock it up tight."

Bolts slam into place behind me.

There is no comparison between, say, the Plaza and Mrs. McBride's apartment building overlooking Central Park; placing the hotel, however elegant it may seem, next to this place would be like lining up Carmen Miranda next to Queen Elizabeth for a group photo. What seemed so lush at the Plaza now seems downright ostentatious compared to the reserved elegance of this unnamed structure.

Talk about your exclusivity—the doorman, who is not the same gentleman who gladly offered information on Judith the other day—won't even tell me *his* name, let alone the name of the co-op complex. And there's no chance he's letting me in that door. I explain to him that I have business at the building, then switch it to a personal meeting with Mrs. McBride. He doesn't bite. I try the intimidation tactics that work so beautifully on most I encounter. No luck.

"Is there anything I can do for you to let me inside that building?" I've run out of options.

"I don't think there is, sir." The doorman has remained eminently polite, but considering he's not letting me do anything I want to, it makes everything all the more frustrating.

"What if I ran past you? Ignored you and walked inside?"

His smile is chilling. Beneath his ridiculous doorman's costume I can make out the shape of considerable muscles dancing in powerful rhythm. "You don't want to do that, sir."

Money. Money always works. I pull a twenty out of my wallet and hand it to the man.

"What is this?" he says, looking at the bill in genuine confusion.

"What's it look like?"

"It looks like twenty dollars," he replies.

"You win a Kewpie doll," I say, knowing that there's little need for tact in a situation that turned tactless long ago. "I didn't need it anymore. Cluttering up my wallet."

"But twenty dollars . . ."

I throw my hands into the damp night sky—what is with this humidity? Has someone dumped an entire ocean into the air?—and say, "Fine, fine, fine! You don't want the money, you don't want the money!" I grab for my twenty back, but the doorman holds on tight.

"Whaddaya want from me?" I ask. "You don't want my money—"

"I didn't say that, sir."

"What?"

"I didn't say that I didn't want your money."

It hits me. "You . . . oh my Lord . . . you want more, don't you?" The laughter comes easily, rushing up from my diaphragm and spilling out of my mouth, covering the poor doorman in mirth. "This whole time I'm figuring I've got to have some magic word, and all I had to do from the beginning was bribe you!" I amend my earlier critiques of New York; I love this town!

The doorman does not flinch; to his credit, he remains straight-faced as a wooden nutcracker as he sidesteps me and issues a polite good evening to an elderly gentleman leaving the building. Afterward, he resumes his post and stares out into space, hand casually outstretched toward my wallet.

I gladly hold up a hundred for inspection and slip it into his pocket. There's more in my wallet if I have to lay it on him—if this guy wants a cash shower, I'll turn on the spigot. The $120 does the trick, though; the doorman nods once, grabs hold of the brass pull, and swings open the portal, granting me access to the vaulted hallways beyond.

"Welcome to Fifty-eight Park, sir."

I bow in gratitude. "Thank you ever so much . . . what did you say your name was?"

"That's another twenty," he says, poker face glued on tight.

Judith McBride isn't home. I suspect that such information would have been easier, and probably cheaper, to obtain, but the doorman, like everyone else, is in his racket for the bucks. Can't blame him. I would have scammed me over, too. I ring the doorbell over and over, knock a few times, whistle loudly, call out Judith's name, but there is no response.

I could break and enter, I guess—a credit card won't work on a door this solid, but I've got other tricks up my sleeve—but time is short, and I don't imagine that Judith will have left any wildly incriminating evidence lying around her apartment. I am about to take my leave, to return across town to Glenda's apartment and try to pick up the search for Jaycee where we left off, when I notice the corner of a yellow slip of paper sticking out from beneath Judith McBride's doorway. Actually, I'm only able to notice it after I've prostrated myself on the floor, shuttered up one eye, shoved a cheek against the plush carpet, and peeked through the crack, but the end results are the same, so what do the means matter?

There is no question as to whether or not it is moral of me to reach in and pick up the note—it is my civic duty to prevent littering, even in others' domiciles. Especially in others' domiciles. My costumed fingers, though, are too pudgy to fit beneath the door, so I am forced to bare a claw in order to get the job done.

Package notification. It means that the building manager or reception staff accepted a package for the tenant and is now holding it wherever such items are usually stored. I've heard of services like this, but never before witnessed it firsthand. When I was a renter, the closest my building managers ever came to accepting packages for me were angry notes shoved into my mailbox that read *If I gotta hear that UPS guy complain that you're not home one more time, I'm gonna rip down your front door and let him take a crap on your rug.* I've purchased stain-resistant carpets ever since.

I suppose I could locate Receiving, make a big fuss, try to claim the package as my own, but odds are whatever scam I pulled would either land me no useful evidence or a night in the county lockup.

But here's all the dirt I need, right on this slip of paper. Two separate packages are waiting downstairs, both addressed to Judith McBride. Package number one was sent from Martin & Company Copper Wiring Service and Supply in Kansas City and arrived early this morning according to the time stamped on the note.

Now what on earth could Judith McBride need copper wiring for? Science project? Too old. A bomb? Too rational. Do-it-yourself home improve-ments? Too prissy. I have a theory, but even as it springs to mind, I dismiss it as nonsense.

Package number two is equally curious, coming as it does from a pool supply company in Connecticut. There's nothing on the note to indicate what's actually in the box, but I can't imagine that Judith McBride has vol-unteered to spend her time cleaning out the facilities at the local YWCA.

I check it out. After another twenty dollars leaps from my wallet into the doorman's pocket, he tells me where to find Receiving, and I wend my way to the back of the building. There, another snob extraordinaire waits to re-buff me, but this time I don't have to worry about dealing with him. I just need to get close to the storage room.

"Can I . . . help you?" asks the clerk.

"No, no, just taking in the sights." I lean farther across his desk, and he backs away, startled at my proximity. "They keep the packages in there?" I ask, pointing toward the open space behind him, boxes neatly arranged in rows.

"Yes. . . . Are you a guest in the building?" he asks, knowing full well I am not.

I don't answer. I've got sniffing to do. I exhale quickly, expelling all my used, useless air into the clerk's ruffled face, and then begin a long, slow drag, my nostrils fluttering, my sinuses rumbling with the effort. Smells drift in from all over New York, my brain working on full power in an at-tempt to isolate and sort them out. I orient my nose toward the closed storage-room door and increase my suction. My chest expanding, my lungs filling, I wouldn't be surprised if I sucked all the available oxygen from the air, causing the clerk to faint dead away. That would make things easier.

And just as I think I can't inhale any more, just as the clerk, who has recovered from his confusion, is about to call Security down upon my sorry behind, I catch the slightest scintilla of the scent for which I am searching:

Chlorine. No doubt about it, the nose knows. A few cubes of chlorine tablets, wrapped within tissue paper, shrouded in Styrofoam, enclosed in cardboard, packed in a brown paper wrapper. Yes, I'm that good.

* * *

"Glenda, we gotta go." I have just paid a cabbie three times his fare in order to rush me back to Glenda's apartment and wait downstairs while I grab a few necessary items. He was more than happy to take my money, but I have serious doubts as to whether or not he was able to understand my instructions and actually remain in place. "Got a cab idling on the curb. Hopefully."

"You might wanna take a look at this," she says, and hands me a light, waxy sheet of fax paper three feet long, minuscule numbers and letters scrolling down and across every inch.

"What is it?"

"All the telephone calls from your house for the last month." She peeks over my shoulder, points to a singular 1-900 line. "Goddamn, Vincent, you got yourself a psychic friend?"

"Only once," I say absentmindedly, too concerned with this new evidence to defend myself.

There it is, the call I'm looking for—early this morning, four in the A.M. Collect, but still registered on this sheet, and it's to the 718 area code. "That's the one," I say, pointing it out to Glenda. "Right there."

"That's what I figured," she says. "So I checked it out already. You got three guesses where it goes."

"A child care clinic in the Bronx?"

"Hey . . ." she pouts. "You're not supposed to get it on the first try."

"I have some insider information," I tell her. "You get an address?"

"Sure did. Shit part of town and everything."

"Great. Come on, maybe we can get there before the floor show begins."

The cabbie has indeed waited downstairs, and fortunately for us, he doesn't want to practice his English with his customers tonight. I ask him to turn the radio up, and he puts on a charming Indian song that, by all indications, is being sung by cats in heat. Perfect—I can tell Glenda my story without worrying about having to whisper the whole way to the clinic.

"Here goes," I say, and launch into the tale.

T hat's gotta be the strangest shit I ever heard," says Glenda after
I've laid it all out for her, piece by piece, theory by theory. I must
admit, it's quite the doozy. We've pulled up just beyond that familiar alleyway in the Bronx, the child care clinic looming across
the street. It waits for us, beckoning. I empty my wallet to pay the
cabbie. "Bar none, weird city," she continues. "So that's it, right?
No more surprises?"

"Well . . ." I hedge. "There's this one little thing I haven't exactly let you
in on. But hey, a guy's gotta be sure before he goes blabbing to his friends.
I'm not the kind of PI to investigate and tell. Hey, maybe I'm wrong."

"Yeah, well I hope you got your head up your ass on this one, 'cause if
you're right about what's going down, I don't wanna think about what it's
gonna do to us."

We step out of the cab, onto the street, and stare up at the clinic.
Boards cover the windows like wooden eye-patches, the aluminum sliding
bay doors clamped down tight. The crazies are out in full force this
evening, and the occasional vagrant pinches Glenda's rump as we walk by.
I have to restrain her from attacking anyone.

"Keep your nose open for danger," I say. "Last time I was here I ran into
a little problem." A big, snarling, toothy problem is more like it. "You catch
a whiff of barbecue, you let me know."

Casually, we move across the street, trying to look for all the world like
two nonfelonious humans out for a nice stroll in the back alleyways of the

Bronx at ten o'clock at night with no visible weapons or means of defense. "Move quickly," I caution, "but real natural-like."

The few lights on the outside of the clinic had been knocked out by vandals long ago, so we are able to take our first leg of the journey in darkness. We reach the front door. Closed. Locked. And once again, those sliding metal monstrosities off to each side would make too much noise in the stillness of the evening.

Glenda glances about the building, gauging its size. She says, "There's gotta be a back entrance around here. There's always a friggin' back entrance."

"I don't know. Last time I tried to find one, I got . . . sidetracked."

Glenda heads around the side of the building, and I follow, heart already thrashing away against my chest in anticipation of another attack. Great snorts of the surrounding air don't deliver any of that burning plastic scent to my olfactory nerves, but one can never be too careful. I continue my constant vigilance, glancing behind every corner and outcropping before stepping past.

There is no trace of my battle from last week, though the Dumpster has been moved, either by the cleanup crew once they arrived to take the skeleton away or by sanitation engineers whose truck was slightly out of alignment. We shuffle past the scene of my near demise.

A small metal fence bars our way to the back of the clinic, and Glenda prepares to climb it. Her hand reaches out—

"Wait!" I call, dropping my voice back to a whisper. "Test it."

Glenda turns, confused. "Test what?"

"The fence. They're not kidding around here; a stupid little wire fence like this one isn't going to do much good keeping out anyone who wants in. And I've seen the guard dogs they keep at this place." Tentatively, I reach out with an extended finger, nearing the metal diamonds . . .

Pressure, pulling finger down, trying to make me grasp the wire, drawing in my arm—I'm yanking it back, grimacing, fighting for my own appendage—

I win the battle and fly backward, slamming into Glenda's chest, both of us falling into a heap on the ground. Rolling off the Hadrosaur, I help her to her feet.

"What the hell . . ."

"Wired," I say, rubbing my arm, which is growing more sore by the second. "Electric fence, and from the way it grabbed hold I'd say we're dealing with some pretty lethal current."

No fuse box in sight, no way to short-circuit the fence, no breaches or holes in the structure itself. "Back around front?" Glenda suggests.

"No point. It's not going to open magically by itself." Unless . . . I look up, squinting through the darkness, and notice a small window ledge just above the top of the fence. "Glenda, can you hoist me up to that drainpipe?"

"I can hoist six of you up to that drainpipe. But how's that gonna get me in?"

"I'll work my way in through the back and open the front door. Come on, give me a lift."

After the requisite warnings to each other to play it safe, be careful, watch our backs, etc., Glenda lifts me onto her shoulders like a mother hoisting up her son to watch a parade, and I'm able to grab hold of the drainpipe. It's attached to the side of the clinic by some flimsy L-brackets that quiver as I let my full weight sink against the piping. Good thing I haven't had much time to eat recently; one burger in my belly might send the whole kaboodle crashing down. The brackets shake, shimmy, and shiver, but they hold.

A short climb—the pipe threatening to break away from the wall with every inch I gain—puts me in reach of the window ledge, and it is only after I have pulled myself up and onto it that I realize that much like the other windows in the clinic, this one, too, has been boarded up. Great wooden beams bar my way. And me without my buzz saw.

Glenda has already turned the corner, out of earshot, heading toward the front entrance to wait for me to open the door, so I won't be getting any help from that end. My only option at this point is to jump, but it's a good twenty-five feet down. If I could just unfurl my tail, the added muscular support might be enough to cushion the blow somewhat, but . . .

Well, heck, why can't I unfurl my tail? Rules are made to be broken, and if ever there's a time for rule-breaking, it's now. Grasping a knot in the wooden boards to steady myself, I quickly pull off my pants and my underwear, scrunch down the back of my polysuit, and release the upper portion of my G series.

Lord, it feels good to have my tail out in the open again! The cool night air caresses my hide, bringing me back to last night with Jaycee, the way she rubbed me all over, using her body to . . . Okay, work, Vincent, there's work to be done. But this freedom does feel particularly nice, I have to admit, and I can only hope that I have the chance to frolic in the open air like this in some place other than the Eighteenth Street Child Health Care Clinic.

The specter of that long jump to the hard ground below is certainly helping to stall my efforts, but I have to get moving. Making a quick prayer to the gods above just in case I've been wrong my whole life about their nonexistence, I steel myself, take a baby step onto the edge, and hop.

As planned, my tail helps to soften the jolt, and I tuck into a roll, spinning along the ground, bringing myself to a halt only a few inches from the other side of the electric fence. Popping up as quickly as possible, I stand and brush myself off. "Piece of cake," I say to no one in particular, and my voice scrapes against the stillness of the night. I resolve to remain quiet if there's no one else around.

There's a scent of death, of decay, coming from a nearby corner, odors that should send me back into fighting mode, but it doesn't carry that tinge of danger, so I step closer to investigate, delving into a small niche. I peer around, my eyes taking time to adjust to even less light than before. From the long scrapes covering the roughly rounded walls, I'd say it looks almost scratched out, as if a feral beast had decided to carve out its den right here, concrete be damned.

Animal bones, cleared of their gristle, their surfaces cracked open and marrow sucked dry, lay in a two-foot-high pile around a bed made of tattered mattresses, newspapers, and old clothing. Blood cakes the walls in finger-painted murals, childish pictures of humans, of dogs, of dinosaurs . . .

I think I know who—what—lived in this den once upon a time. Before it attacked me. Before I killed it.

There's an entrance to the clinic within another small niche, and the locks on this one are easy enough to pick with the right tools. The credit card and soda can tricks are useful for the everyday door, but a job like this one requires a locksmith's set, which I was wise enough to bring along this time. Luckily for me, Ernie had a friend who had a nephew who had a pal whose mother worked at a manufacturing plant for such equipment, and he passed a kit on to me at cost. At least, he *told* me it was at cost.

I expect an alarm of some sort—and am relieved to find that none blares out at my arrival. The hallway I enter is dark and dismal, more so than outside due to the lack of ambient moonlight, and has the extra added attractions of mold spores and cobwebs dotting the walls. The corridors meet and converge in a haphazard, almost random pattern. The clinic didn't look nearly this large from the outside, and I wonder if there is some type of optical illusion involved.

I locate the front entrance quickly enough, and unlock the five dead bolts set in place on the inside.

"It's freaking cold out there," Glenda says, and I shush her with a finger.

Together, we move through the corridors, utilizing hand signals to suggest directions and courses of action. A continuous hum echoes through the building, and I imagine we'll find the power source sooner or later. And when we do, we'll see how right or how wrong I am about this whole mess.

"Psst!" I turn to find Glenda standing in front of a partially opened door. "I hear something—through here."

We make our way down a wide, darkened corridor, the walls lined with a metallic substance that picks up whatever electrical charge is running through this place; I can feel the tingle if I place my palm up against the wall. Small blue streaks of light shoot across the length of the walls at random intervals, and I can't help but wonder if we're approaching the center of the hub.

Another door, and behind it a low murmur, like a river pressing on a rusty water wheel, the mumble of an audience after a particularly bad film. "I think it's through here," Glenda says, and opens the door without caution. It's pitch black inside, and she slaps the inside wall in her search for a light switch.

"Wait a second," I whisper. "Take it easy—"

With a crash! a bank of fluorescent bulbs slam into life above our heads, illuminating a long rectangular room, a hundred feet long by at least forty feet wide, cage after cage after cage lining the walls and stacked three high.

The curious babbling intensifies, and as we step inside the room, our mouths falling open involuntarily, we get a perfect view of what is making all the noise.

Each cage contains a . . . creature, for lack of a better term, a miniature version of the beast that attacked me three days ago, but that's not precisely correct. There are Stego genes and Diplodod genes and Raptor genes and Allosaur genes, and I can see the genetic traits of all the sixteen species of dinosaur in every single one of these things. Small, misshapen horns poke at odd angles out of large, misshapen heads atop twisted misshapen necks and disabled misshapen bodies. The sounds we hear are so odd to our ears precisely because no two mouths are alike—for those creatures who have been blessed with mouths. Some of these things have nothing but gaping holes in the sides of their heads, and the tiny, tortured whimpers that emanate from within are amplified by the horrible, empty cavity.

They're small. Two feet at the most. They're nothing but babies. But that's not all. Not by a long shot.

There are fingers. Honest-to-God fingers. And legs, real legs. And ears, and earlobes and noses and torsos, and the kicker about all these body parts is: they're human.

"He did it," Glenda says in a perfect blend of awe and revulsion. "Vallardo actually did it."

"It . . . it seems so . . ." I stutter.

"But what—what's wrong with them—"

"I think—I think they're the misfits," I explain.

"Misfits."

"Nothing gets accomplished without a few failures first. That's them."

As if on cue, they begin to cry out in small wailing tones. Kittens, puppies, babies in need of help and care. "But he's got them locked up, like . . . like animals."

I nod. "In a way, they are—"

"How can you say that?" Glenda nearly shouts, turning on me in anger. Great—Glenda Wetzel's mothering instincts have to make their debut at a time like this. "They're *babies,* Vincent."

In a daze, Glenda walks into the middle of the room, staring slack-jawed at the multitude of misfit monsters surrounding her. Before I can stop her, she reaches into one of the cages and scratches what looks to be a Hadrosaur/human mix behind a grotesque ear. It coos in delight.

"Look, Vincent," she says. "It needs to be loved, that's all." Her face darkens, her tone growing angrier once again. "And that sonofabitch Vallardo locked them up like this."

"I agree, he's wrong and needs to be punished," I say, "but we don't have time for this. C'mon, Glen, step back."

Glenda doesn't seem to agree. She heads toward a console set into the far wall, running her fingers over the buttons, ire rising with each passing second. And a funny thing's happening—as Glenda gets angrier, the noise in the cages begins to increase.

"Apefucker thinks he can screw with nature and then lock babies up behind bars? Is this science? Does this amuse him?"

"Glen, I really think you should stop." The bars are rattling now, all of the creatures awake, alert, and banging at their confines. The whimpering has turned into hooting, and screaming's not far around the corner.

But Glenda doesn't hear my protestations or the rising racket. She's flipping switches left and right, and the console, once dead and quiet, lights up with a burst of energy. I trot over toward her, eager to stop whatever she thinks she's going to do.

"I'll show that sonofabitch what it is to screw with the gene pool," she's yelling. "I'll show him!" And now the menagerie of misfits is really letting loose, jumping up and down in their cages like a pack of monkeys, slamming their bodies against the bars, as if they know that escape is imminent, that a messiah has come to release them from their bondage.

"Glenda, don't—" I shout, just as she slams her palm into the button that pops open every cage at once.

With a wild group shriek that puts to shame Tarzan and all of his jungle friends, a hundred horrible creatures fall out of the sky, leaping into the room, onto Glenda, and onto my back. The attack is on.

My first thought is that I misjudged these things, that they're no more harmful than a flea, but that's over with as soon as the first one takes a nip out of my ear, ripping away a section of guise as well as a nice hunk of flesh. Without thinking, I reach behind me, grab it by the scruff of the neck—a ridged neck?—and toss it through the air, football style. It thwacks against a far wall and falls to the ground. Undaunted, it picks itself up and leaps back into the pile of writhing creatures.

But more are coming my way, jumping at me, using coiled, stunted tails to launch themselves into the air, crooked mouths wide open, razor-sharp teeth deadlocked at my eyes, my face, any soft tissue on my body. It's a deadly combination—those human fingers help some to grip on to my hide while their dino teeth do the dirty work. Through the clamor, I can see Glenda go down beneath a heap of the beasts, and I struggle to fight off as many as I can and make my way across the room.

My claws, poking through my guise like thorns on a rose, rake through any flesh they come in contact with as I use my hands to ward off attacks from the front. My tail, already freed up earlier, comes in handy taking out enemies that take a shot at me from behind, and though I've been bitten and clawed a hundred times in two minutes, I'm dishing out more than I'm taking. The majority of blood on the floor of the cage room is not mine.

"Glenda!" I call over the caterwaul of shrieks, and I hear a "Vincent!" in return.

"Are you okay?" I yell through another lance of pain, this time at my wrist, and I look down to find a set of teeth attached to a misshapen hunk of flesh planted firmly in my arm. I shake the arm up and down, curling the creature as I lift, but the teeth are caught tight, buried in my muscle. With the underclaw on my other hand, I reach out and spear the creature through the head; it issues a slight whimper of pain, then releases its grip and falls to the ground, dead.

And now Glenda's beside me, bloodied worse than I am, but we're both alive, and we're both standing up.

In a corner.

The creatures back off for a moment, at least seventy of the vicious little goblins, each no more than two feet high, horns included. They still cackle and shriek like a pack of mutated pigeons, but it's taken on a conversational tone, as if they are somehow communicating, deciding their next plan of attack.

"Okay, so I was wrong," Glenda admits. "They're not sweet little things."

I take a quick look around. The wall behind us is perfectly smooth, no room for hand- or footholds. "What now? They've got us cornered."

And they seem to know it. Glenda and I try a quick move to the left, and in unison, they shuffle over to block our escape. A quick move to the right produces similar results. "We're trapped."

The sounds are growing louder again, the creatures regaining their blood lust. In the back of the pack, two of them are going at it, little human fingers and little dino claws, fighting to the death, powerful jaws with stunted human teeth snapping instinctively toward unprotected necks and major arteries.

"Go," says Glenda.

"What?"

"You go, lock the door behind you. I'll take care of—of this."

"You'll be killed."

"Maybe not. Look, what you found is too fucked up not to stop. You started this investigation, and you have to be the one to finish it. I screwed this part up, I'll deal with the consequences."

"But I can't leave you—"

"Jesus fucking Christ, Rubio—go!" And then: "Find what's her name. Take her back to LA. Name a kid after me."

I don't have time to argue. Glenda calls out, "Hey, you ugly fucking leprechauns! Take a bite outta this!" and jumps to her left, kicking out with her legs as she flies through the air, claws raking at the tens of bodies already leaping toward her. Instantly, she disappears beneath a mass of improper flesh and disparate body parts.

A path opens in the chaos, and without looking back I take it, running at full speed down the corridor. One of the baby dino/man mixes breaks off from the pack and hops after me, making it out of the room as I slam the door closed and bolt it from the outside. The thing issues a feeble warning cry—cut off from its littermates, the sound is more pathetic than powerful—and makes a futile attempt to chomp down on my shin. I thrust my leg up and out, and the creature goes flying into the ceiling, landing on the floor below with a thud and a squish.

Good-bye, Glenda. Go quickly to wherever it is we go.

I stick to the right wall of the complex, utilizing an old maze-solving maneuver, and soon that hum grows in volume. Opening doors indiscriminately, I wander the clinic, keeping myself on high alert. The run-down sections of the building eventually give way to newer, decorated, *cleaner* areas, and I feel it's safe enough to remove my bloodied mask, free up my true nostrils, and take a good sniff around.

That chlorine scent again, this time mixed with the roses and oranges I had been expecting. Vallardo's scent of anisette, of pesticides, is present as well, and I assume emanating from the same location. Like a cartoon Country Mouse drawn by the aroma of a scrumptious city feast, I follow my nose up, up, and away.

I saunter into the "health clinic's" main laboratory five minutes later, tossing out smiles like so many free-trial magazine subscriptions. Technically one per customer, but I serve up a dozen each to Vallardo and Judith McBride. The two of them pale at the sight of me, Vallardo's naturally green Triceratops hide unable to hide the shock. He blanches into a yeti-white pallor; if I had my camera I could score ten thousand dollars from a national tabloid for offering proof of the creature.

Each of them—Vallardo, Judith, Jaycee (emerging from behind the good doctor)—sizes me up. I can feel the weight of their stares, of their unspoken questions. *How good is he with that stubby body? Can I take him solo? Can we take him together?*

I quench it all with a snap of my tail and a roar that manages to pierce even my own eardrums. They back away.

"You didn't even lock the laboratory door," I chastise, dropping from my growl into a conversational tone. "I'm disappointed in the lot of you."

Jaycee comes galloping up to me then, unsure of what to do with her body. Does she hug me? Does she push me out of the room? She opts for the safety of stopping a few yards outside my striking range and saying, "Vincent . . . you have to go."

"No," I respond. "I think I'm sticking around for this one."

I motion across the lab, toward the largest indoor water tank I've ever laid eyes on, bar none. Sea World has nothing on Dr. Emil Vallardo, M.D., Ph.D., OB-GYN. Glass-walled, over thirty feet high, its length and breadth encompassing a full half of this massive corporate-funded laboratory, they could dump the Indian Ocean into this thing and still have room for Lolita, the Killer Whale. But there is no Lolita in this tank.

There are no fish lollygagging around in there, either, nothing to amuse the kiddies while the parents are getting toasted over at Busch Gardens.

There is only an egg in this artificial womb, a single, solitary egg, maybe a twenty-pounder, floating a few feet below the surface, suspended in the water by a mesh hammock. Brown and gray speckles dot its otherwise albino shell, each one leading to an electrode, a wire, terminating at a computer set up just outside the splash zone. Life signs flit across an enlarged CRT attached to the side of the tank, heart and brain functions beeping steadily.

There are cracks in the shell. Three of them, from my vantage point. I suspect there are more on the other side. Something wants out.

"When were you gonna tell me this part?" I ask Jaycee, knowing the answer is never.

"I . . . I couldn't," she admits, turning to Vallardo and Judith for support. "We . . . the three of us . . . we made the decision not to say anything."

"*We* didn't decide anything," Judith says caustically. "You decided, Jaycee."

"I did what I had to do," counters the Coleo, her claws snapping out, flicking into place.

"Before we start the floor show and you two go at it," I announce, "I'd like to get us all out in the open, okay? Anyone who needs to take off their guise, let's do so now." There's no reaction; they all stare at me as if I am speaking in tongues. Vallardo and Jaycee have shed their costumes a while ago; only Judith McBride remains in human form. I am not surprised.

"Here," I say, "I'll start you off, how's that?" Whipping off the rest of my remaining clothing with a stripper's panache, I casually unsnap my girdles and loosen my trusses, exposing the full length of my natural body. My claws click through the air, my tail swishes with contentment, and I roar my terrible roar and gnash my terrible teeth all for the fun of it.

"Now," I say, "hands up everyone who's a dino." I raise my own arm, just to get the tide moving. Soon, the three others have tentatively put their hands in the air.

I approach Judith McBride, her left cheek having taken on a delightfully humorous muscle spasm, and place my arm over hers, weighting it back down. "Come now, Mrs. McBride. Are you that confused as to your own identity?"

"I—I don't know what you mean," she stammers. "I'm a Carnotaur, you know that. You've heard the stories, you've seen the pictures."

"That's true, that's true," I say, making a big show of nodding, pacing around her body in an ever-tightening spiral. Ah, if I only had my hat, my trench coat. I spy a white lab coat hanging on a nearby hook, and ask Vallardo if I could borrow it for a minute. He's too confused to argue, so I slip into the long overcoat, feeling the comfortable weight upon my shoulders.

"I have seen the pictures, Mrs. McBride, of both you and your deceased husband. And you did make a fine Carnotaur couple. And yes, I've heard the stories. The rumors. The tales of Carnotaur Raymond McBride and his illustrious circle of dino friends. Entertainers, businessmen, heads of state. Very posh."

Jaycee's turn to interrupt. "Vincent, really, I don't think this is the time—"

"But I gotta tell you, I've had some injuries over the years, and I can't trust all my senses like I used to. I don't place too much stock in my ears, for example, ever since this little hunting trip I took with a band of humans 'round 'bout ten years ago. Gun-happy bastards were using heavy-gauge ammo on ten-point bucks, discharging those puppies right by my head. Three days and god knows how many shots later, boom, I've all but lost the high end of my hearing register. So you say I've heard the stories, yeah, I've heard 'em, but it doesn't mean I can *trust* what I've heard.

"My eyes? Forget about it. I was driving around with uncorrected vision for a while before I got wise and had my peepers checked, and lemme tell you that half the time I didn't know whether I was sitting at a red light or watching a really boring laser show. I've got Coke-bottle contact lenses, my vision is so bad. So those pictures I saw of you and Raymond all dressed up nice like the Carnotaurs you claim to be, hey, maybe I didn't see 'em like I should have seen 'em. I can't *trust* what I've seen.

"Taste? Don't get me started. I love spicy foods, it's a habit, but it knocks out my buds. After ten years of Aunt Marge's jambalaya, well . . . can't trust it any more. Touch? Well, you and I haven't gotten that close. But even so, there's saline in this world, there's silicone, there's this polyfiber we all know and love, so I can't trust my touch either, can I? So there's really only the one sense left to me, and as a result I've got to trust it above all else. I'm sure you understand that.

"My nose is my livelihood, Mrs. McBride, and a true dino never, ever forgets a scent. You can't fake it, though as you know, you sure can try. You can try real hard. But in the end . . ."

Ignoring her protests and pleas, her arms slapping me in the throat, in the face, I grab Judith McBride in a rough headlock and, with my free hand, reach behind her head, into the thick nest of hair just above the back of her neck. I quickly and easily find the device I'm looking for, secured to her scalp with a familiar epoxy glue, and rip it free. She shrieks in pain.

The pouch is filled with chlorine powder, with dried rose petals, with orange peels, the mixture emitting jets of manufactured dino odor via a steady electric current supplied by thin copper wires leading from a small lighter battery into the pouch itself.

Waving the odiferous cushion beneath her nose, holding it as if it contained a ripe, steaming turd, I growl, "This is your scent, the chemicals inside this pouch, and this is the only thing that ever made you remotely resemble one of us. I got a feeling that your husband was the same way, right, Mrs. McBride?

"You're no dino," I say, distaste swelling, puckering my mouth. "You're . . . you're nothing but a common human."

Enter the dramatic music, reprise.

My domination is total; Judith is unable to answer me, her mouth opening and closing, opening and closing. Her eyelids flutter uncontrollably. Goddamn human, I should kill her right now, out of not only duty but sheer principle alone. Lying to me like that, sending me back and forth across the country.

But Vallardo cuts us all off with a sharp gasp that commands attention from dinos and dino-fakers alike. "The egg," he whispers reverently. "It's time."

As one, our gazes pan across the laboratory, stopping on the lone inhabitant of that wide-open tank. The few cracks I could make out before have spiderwebbed, fanning the full surface of the egg, new splinters forming every second. As Vallardo taps a few commands into the tank's computer, an external speaker buzzes on, amplifying those sounds bouncing around within the watery confines. A creaking, a crackling, and . . . could that be a wail?

"Come on, baby," murmurs Jaycee. "You can do it. Break out for Mama."

ushing awkwardly to the side of the tank, Vallardo grabs hold of a series of pulleys, twisting the ropes down and around an anchor set into the floor. The left side of the egg's hammock lifts a little in the water, but now needs to be counterbalanced by a lift to the right. "The other side!" Vallardo yells across the room, and I do believe he's talking to me! I didn't come here to assist in a birth, but I guess if I have to do a little midwifery in the middle of my crime-solving, it wouldn't be the worst thing in the world.

"Now what?" I ask upon reaching the ropes. My angle into the tank is sharper, more acute, the water blurring the egg into a long ovoid blob. But I can still hear those splinters over the PA, so I know there's activity going on inside that shell.

"On the count of three," Vallardo yells to me, "pull down to the yellow markings on the rope!" I glance up—the band color shifts to a tawny tone ten feet away—and shout back that I'm ready. Vallardo gives the count, and we hoist.

It comes up easier than I expected, my muscles having primed themselves for heavier exertion. My extra effort forces the right end of the hammock higher than the left, and the egg begins to slide—

"No!" screams Jaycee, launching herself at the ropes, at Vallardo.

Jaycee's added weight quickly hoists her end higher, which forces me to compensate in turn, and for a moment we are the Three Stooges meeting the Mad Scientist, wildly tugging on our ropes in an effort to stabilize the as-yet-unborn creature rolling around on that hammock.

"Careful," Vallardo warns, as if we didn't already know. "Don't let it slip!"

Jaycee anchors her rope and storms up to me, landing a good slap across my cheek. "You did that on purpose," she says. "You want it dead."

I say, "I want no such thing. The only thing I want is to bring Mrs. McBride in front of the National Council, let them decide how they want to handle her. I'm amazed you didn't kill her already."

"She almost did," says Judith. "But we came to a little arrangement, instead."

We turn to face the human interloper, and find that Judith has a gun. I knew she would; the bad ones always do. But I didn't expect a gun so . . . large. The monstrous revolver sags in her hand, her frail human wrist trembling with the effort to keep it upright. Judith uses the barrel to motion me away from the tank, and Jaycee and Vallardo reluctantly follow.

"The egg . . ." says the doctor. "We have to keep watch on it."

"I'll watch the egg," spits Judith. "It's my child, I can take care of it."

Jaycee snaps, a sudden burst of hatred propelling her across the room, tail whipping through the air, teeth bared; as the blur streaks by so fast, all I can see is a brown streak of anger rushing by my face. Everything sinks into slow-motion replay, though without the color commentary: Judith's own reflexes burst into action, bringing up that revolver, the barrel the size of a Hula-Hoop, round, clearly chambered and ready to sear into flesh—my lungs paralyzed, refusing to deliver a breath so I can scream out the perfunctory No!—Vallardo throwing himself in front of the tank, ready to take a bullet, an arrow, a warhead, anything to protect the integrity of its structure—Judith's finger squeezing hard on the trigger, her lips tightening into a satisfied grimace—

And another blur, this one quite unexpected, as a vaguely Hadrosaur-shaped creature crashes through the laboratory door and into the easy target of Judith McBride. The gun reports, blasting its echo through my already-damaged ears.

Concrete chips fly out of the wall behind me, spraying sharp white shrapnel through the air. A shard imbeds itself in my tail. It is excruciating. I pay it no mind.

Glenda lifts herself off the ground, kicking Judith's gun into a far corner of the lab, her leg slamming into Mrs. McBride's rib cage. The human expels a gush of air and curls into a fetal ball.

"The hell's she got a gun for?" a bloodied Glenda says, turning to me. I shrug. Glenda whips back around to Judith, bends down, and grabs her cheeks, pulling the widow close. "The hell you got a gun for?"

Judith's best response is nothing more than a groan of pain.

"Glenda, you—you're okay."

"I'm hurtin', but I'm alive, yeah. Mean little apefuckers you got in them cages, Doc."

Vallardo's expression is constant; he's hard to read. "How's the egg, Doc?"

"It's stable," he says. "There is some time left."

"Then I'm gonna pick up where we left off. Anybody stop me if you get confused."

Ensuring that my lab/trench coat is buckled tight around my waist, I strut over to Jaycee and place an arm around her shoulder. "It must get tiring making things up all the time," I say. "Lying takes a lot out of you."

She tries to cut in with a "Vincent, I—" but as promised, I pay her no mind, running roughshod over her words. "Don't bother," I say. "I'm gonna tell it like it is, and even if you've heard it all before, don't stop me.

"Most of what you told me was true," I begin, keeping my comments directed toward my onetime (but five sessions!) lover. "You just left out a few key elements. Yes, Judith McBride had an affair with Donovan, and yes, you offered to impersonate a human in order to entrap Raymond for the Council. You probably even fell in lust with him, just like you said, and that's all fine and good.

"I'll tell you, I got into this case purely by accident, you know that? I was hired by the insurance company that was supposed to reimburse Donovan Burke for the fire at his Evolution Club. I had no idea it would lead to this, honestly, I didn't. And things were fishy there right from the start—fire trucks that were called before any of the witnesses actually saw the flames. Almost as if it was supposed to be a controlled fire, wiping out a section of the building without torching the entire place." I pause here, waiting for input from the accomplices.

"We didn't want to hurt anybody," Jaycee says eventually. "Especially Donovan."

"But you needed those papers gone, didn't you? And that frozen embryo—now that you had this baby, you had to get rid of the extra evidence. Why couldn't you just ask Donovan for them back?"

"Yes, yes, well . . . He wouldn't give them to me," Vallardo says, stepping away from his computer and into the conversation. In the background, I can see the fragile eggshell continuing to disappear beneath the constant assault from the creature inside. It won't be long now. "Simple as that, yes? He thought I was being controlled," Vallardo continues, "and he wanted to protect me. Donovan was . . . very loyal."

"Ha!" snorts Jaycee, and says nothing more on the matter.

I turn back to Vallardo and say, "Loyal, sure. Especially after you funded his club in Los Angeles. You needed a place to keep a separate copy of your work, a safe haven, and he needed a new job. Who would ever think to look in an LA nightclub for such controversial work? Worst thing that goes on there would be a little hanky-panky in the rest-room stalls.

"But the real question is why were you doing that work in the first place? And for this, we have to go back a little further." Stretching my fingers as if to crack my knuckles—I can't actually crack them, as my tight Raptor joints don't leak enough air—I walk up to Judith, still on the ground, and easily hoist her to her feet. She sags in my arms, but I know she can hear me, and I think she can talk.

"How long ago did you and your husband start pretending you were dinos?" I ask Judith, and Glenda nearly passes out.

"Pretending?" Glenda says. "You lost me."

"Like it sounds. We guise ourselves up as humans every day, she guised herself up as a dino when the need arose. Got away with it for at least fifteen years now, everyone thinking she's a Carnotaur costumed up as a matronly widow when she's really a cold piece of dirt costumed up as a Carnotaur." I grab a loose fold of flesh beneath Judith's arm and tug; it doesn't give, and the woman whimpers. Glenda, beginning to comprehend, takes a tug too, manhandling the flesh presented to her.

"So let me get this straight . . . this one here is a human pretending to be a dino pretending to be a human?"

"You got it," I say, and Glenda drops any pretenses of civility and charges toward Judith's throat, ripping off her guise mask with a practiced ease I have never witnessed before. This has got to be a Guinness record for disrobing. But I swing Judith around, away from the Hadrosaur's suddenly exposed elongated duckbill, pulling the human to safety alongside the far wall.

"Outta the way, Vincent!" snarls Glenda. "We gotta kill her, those are the rules. She's a human, she knows, she's gotta go."

"I know the rules, Glen, trust me. But this is a special situation. We're going to bring her up in front of the Council," I say. "They'll decide what to do with her." I catch Glenda's eyes with mine, pleading for temporary clemency. There are still gaps in my information sheet I need to have filled in. Reluctantly, Glenda backs off, wiping her drooling beak with a short brown arm. I'll have to watch her—she's still anxious to taste Judith's blood. "What I don't know is how she found out about us in the first place. Who let it slip." I spin Mrs. McBride around once again, stare into those vacant eyes. "You wanna enlighten me?"

"It was his Ba-Ba," says Jaycee, taking over the storytelling for a moment. "Raymond's Ba-Ba."

"What the hell is a Ba-Ba?"

"It's what he called his adopted mother. Kid talk for Barbara. Raymond's parents died when he was just a toddler, and he was sent to live with his mom's best friend, who happened to be a Carnotaur. He didn't talk about her much, but I know that she raised him as a dino, taught him how to make the scent pouches, how to act, how to guise up, how to present himself in the dino world.

"He found Judith here working as a waitress in Kansas, introduced her to the only life he really knew—that of a dino—and allowed her to make the choice as to how they would live their lives, as humans or as pseudohumans. They chose to act as dinos, and moved to New York City in order to find a greater population of their—of our—kind. The rest is pretty well documented if you look for it. Raymond's rise up the business ladder, Judith's rise up the social one, all because of their dino contacts. Jumping species can be very lucrative."

Thanking Jaycee for her additions to the evening's symposium, I take over once again, eager to display my crime-solving skills for all involved. "I knew there was something wrong from the moment I stepped into your office," I tell Judith, "but I couldn't figure out what it was. Your scent was odd, sure, but not odd enough to capture my immediate attention.

"I gave Donovan's name to your secretary, solely as a method to gain access to your inner sanctum, and I didn't expect it to last any longer than your first sniff of me. But we spent a good minute together—we even embraced!—and you *still* thought I was Donovan, guised up in a different human costume. And right there was the problem, my first inkling of suspicion, even though I didn't realize it until later—you couldn't smell me! Later in that same conversation, I asked you for Jaycee's scent, a clue to help me track her down, and once again you hemmed and hawed. You couldn't tell me what she smelled like because you didn't know. Human noses, simply put, stink.

"I got another clue when I found a scent pouch at Dan Patterson's house. You remember Dan Patterson, right? The LAPD sergeant you had killed? Nice try, telling your hit men to use a knife to try and simulate dino marks, but even a rank forensics amateur like myself can tell a knife wound from a claw slash from ten feet away."

"She wasn't supposed to hurt him," Jaycee interjects. "She was just supposed to get the papers."

"And Nadel?"

"He was going to give you the photos. The real photos."

"And Ernie?" I ask. "Was she supposed to hurt Ernie?"

Jaycee's head turns away. "I didn't know about that 'til after."

"After she'd killed him?"

"Yes."

"How'd you do it?" I ask, and now I'm getting ready to take a bite out of Judith McBride. My grip on her neck grows stronger, and if I just press a little to the left, I could snap it in one easy blow. "How'd—you—do—it?"

Jaycee pipes up again. "She told me—"

"I'll deal with you in a second," I say plainly, keeping my growing anger below the high-water mark. "I'm dealing with the human now." Back to Judith—"Tell me, or you die right here, Council be damned."

"It was easy," Judith sighs. "A few hits on the head, a false witness report."

"Because?"

"Because he was getting too close. You got lucky with those two morons in the car, or you'd be in the same place."

I throw Judith to the ground, pacing back and forth around her supine body. I need to return to the matter at hand. "So I found the pouch in Dan's den, the traces of chlorine, and matched it up with the pool supplies you received today at your apartment." I saunter over to my pants, lying in a crushed pile on the floor, and search through the pockets, emerging with a yellow note. I hand it to Judith, who mindlessly grips it, staring past the words on the page. "Two packages, down at Receiving," I tell her. "Open till nine.

"So what does all this mean?" I say rhetorically, addressing my rapt audience. "It means that Judith is a human, that Raymond was a human, and that the both of you were indeed fooling around with the other species, but that the other species were us dinos." Then, whipping around—"Judith here had her fling with Donovan, and she's really the one who funded your experiments, right, Doc? It was Judith, not her husband, who'd come down with Dressler's Syndrome. She was the one who wanted the dino/human mixed child."

Vallardo, defeated for once, nods. He says, "She's been looking for a way to have a child with the Raptor, yes? But it was not working."

"Why not?"

"Dinosaur seed, human egg. The fetal process was incorrect, it . . . The mixes are in need of the opposite situation if they are to grow properly during the dino ten-month gestation period, yes? Human sperm and dino egg, a hard exterior shell. Otherwise . . ."

"Otherwise they come out deformed. Like those things you keep in the cages. And the thing that attacked me outside the clinic."

A nod from Vallardo. "My earlier experiments. I did not have the heart to eliminate them."

"Oh yeah," says Glenda, "you're all heart, Doc."

"So when Judith realized she couldn't have a dino/human child of her own, she decided to have the good doctor here use Jaycee's eggs—which he'd already harvested and frozen from their earlier experiments with her and Donovan—and her husband's fertile sperm. It wouldn't be her genetic child, but it would be damned close enough. Vallardo would have made the kid, Judith would have raised it as her own, and no one would have been the wiser. And then—well, I can surmise and surmise all day, won't get us any closer to the truth. Why don't you tell it, Jaycee?"

"If you know it so well . . ." she says bitterly.

"I'd rather you fill us in. Firsthand accounts are always more enjoyable."

We all fix our gazes upon Jaycee, and I suppose that the pressure of silence overwhelms her desire to remain quiet. She begins. "I went to see Raymond to wish him happy holidays, that's all. The office was deserted—the whole building—because it was Christmas Eve, but Raymond was working as usual, finishing up some last-minute jobs here and there. I'd been bugging Raymond for a while, trying to get him to commit to some New Year's plans I had set up. He'd been having some troubles getting out of his party with the missus"—Judith and Jaycee's intense stares of hatred clash in the middle of the room and explode harmlessly—"and I was helping him come up with . . . excuses.

"I don't know what made me do it, but as we sat at his desk, me perched on his lap, laughing about the holidays and our baby and what a wonderful life we were going to have, I felt such . . . I don't want to say love, but closeness . . . Whatever it was, I had to tell him. The truth.

"'I have to show you something,' I said to him, and he laughed and asked me if I was going to undress. 'In a way,' I said. So I stepped out into the middle of the room, took off all my clothes, and removed my guise. I stood there, a naked Coleo, and waited for his reaction.

"Raymond was quiet. Very quiet. I assumed he was furious with me for deceiving him, and was ready to throw me out, call Security . . . But I know now he was weighing his own options. Then he had me come back to the desk, he sat me down, and he told me his story. How he was raised. Where he came from. What he came from. And who he really was.

"He wanted to effect a settlement between the humans and the dinos, to introduce his kind to our kind in as peaceful a way as possible. He was so excited, he told me, that he could be the one to bring the dinosaur community out into the open. To bring us 'out of the closet,' as he put it, was his fondest dream, and he wanted me to be the figure under whom it could all take place.

"I don't know if he expected me to be happy, shocked, dismayed, and to be honest, I didn't know how I felt at the time. There was no time for me to think; you know how it is. I know you know how it is. All of us have been prey to instinct before, it's our species' cross to bear—Vincent, you tried to kill me when you thought I was a human and I had seen you in guise; we saw your partner's reaction to Judith just now. It's inbred, and what's more, it's what we're taught from day one: If a human knows, a human must die.

"I don't remember much about the attack. Honestly, I don't. I do remember coming to in a pool of blood that was not my own and seeing Raymond, who I had grown to care for, dead in the middle of it all. But that drive was still humming in me, and I cleaned myself up, sat down in Raymond's desk chair, and waited for Judith, who I knew would be arriving shortly.

"My plan was to kill her, leave the office, and disappear to another country: Jamaica, Barbados, the Philippines. I hear Costa Rica is fairly dino-intensive. The plan was to live anywhere that I didn't have to be around humans; they'd caused quite enough distress in my life."

Judith stirs to life then, dragging herself up from the floor, keeping a wary gaze on Glenda and me. "She attacked me when I came in. Threw herself at my throat."

"You're lucky I didn't kill you then and there," Jaycee says, then turns back to me. "But she got me to hold off for just a second, and she told me about the baby." Turning back to Judith now—"*My* baby. She said that she would continue to fund the experiment, that after we gave birth, I could raise him on my own.

"If I killed her, the experiment would die out. If I told the Council, they would surely destroy the egg and any of Dr. Vallardo's papers. So we had a deal."

Jaycee pauses, takes a long breath, glances around the room at the audience she has so competently held in the palm of her tanned fleshy hand. "And that's all there is to it. That first night, when you came to the nightclub and I got the letter from Dr. Vallardo—that was a false alarm."

"The egg was showing stresses on its lateral equator," says the doctor defensively. "I thought it best I should summon you."

"Whatever the case," Jaycee says, "it was a false alarm. But I kept in contact with Dr. Vallardo, and last night . . . well, last night was wonderful, Vincent. I wouldn't have traded it for the world. But when I called the doctor and he told me to come back to New York, that it was beginning . . . Can you blame me for not wanting to miss it?"

"Of course not," I say honestly. "But you didn't have to drug me."

"Necessary precautions," she explains.

I begin to pace the floor again. "Doctor, Jaycee, expect to be called up in front of the National Council within the next few weeks. I think they're gonna want to hear this one. And don't either of you make any sudden vacation plans.

"Mrs. McBride, I'm going to take you back to LA with me, and we'll see what the department wants to do with a cop killer. Glenda, a little help?" Glenda and I flank Judith McBride, each taking a firm grasp on her limp arms. She does not resist.

"It's happening!" Vallardo cries suddenly, his call echoing across the lab, accompanied by a gurgling squeal blasting out from the nearby speakers. The crackling has amplified as well, filling the air with hot white noise, drowning out Jaycee's subsequent shriek. Motherly delight? Phantom birthing pains?

"We must get it higher!" yells Vallardo, yanking the pulley attached to the egg's hammock. "It must break the surface of the water!" A strong tug— I run to the other rope, pulling with all my might—something's wrong, something's . . . creaking?

The rope snaps. The pulleys sink. The hammock collapses.

Jaycee screams, this time clearly not in happiness, and speeds toward the far end of the tank just as Vallardo regains his balance. The two of them launch themselves onto a ladder attached to the tank's glass wall and attempt to climb up and over; Jaycee, with her long Coleo legs, has more success than Vallardo, with his stout, stubby body, and she dives into the mini-ocean below. Vallardo struggles to the top a few seconds later and cannonballs in. Warm water splashes out of the tank and splatters against my feet, and the silky sensation reminds me of how much I like to swim.

Glenda, Judith, and I are awestruck as we watch Vallardo and Jaycee through the glass, witnessing their fantastic feats of water ballet. Vallardo dives beneath the surface, unhooking the hammock that has only managed to get in the way, and proceeds to hold the egg above his head, treading water as fast as he can, using his short, stubby tail to whip the water into a frenzy.

Grunts and moans mix with the sounds of splintering shell as the underwater microphones pick up the dinos' struggles. Jaycee helps Vallardo, clutching the egg with her long, brown fingers, doing all she can to keep her child afloat, and that wailing continues to grow and grow, a high-pitched warble somewhere between a human cry of pain and the mating call of a common canary.

And as we watch through that glass, as we listen through those speakers, Glenda Wetzel, Judith McBride, and I find ourselves as three speechless witnesses to the first successful interspecies birth this planet has ever seen.

With a final smack! the egg gives way, its proteins spilling out into the tank, clouding the water with their juices, the shell fragmenting into thousands of little pieces, drifting down through the water like ashes off a campfire.

"Can you see it?" I ask Glenda, not moving my eyes from the increasing obscurity of the tank.

"No," she replies, and I can only assume that she, too, is unable to look away. "Can you?"

"Uh-uh. Judith?" No response. "Judith, can you see the baby?" Again, nothing. I turn to look at our captive, whose arm I find I have released some time within the last few minutes. She's gone.

"Glen, we lost—"

I am cut off by a piercing roar, a shrill banshee shriek the likes of which sends invisible spiders crawling all about my body. It is coming from the speakers, amplified tenfold, which means it is coming from the tank, which means—

It is coming from the baby. Water, splashing around, overcast with clouds of sandy afterbirth, obscures my vision, but through the waves I can make out Jaycee's lithe figure, still treading water, and as she lifts herself to the surface, I get a momentary glimpse of her newborn child. A moment is all I need.

Slight gray claws lance out from a pair of spindly arms, the webbing between dotted with tan lumps of flesh that wriggle and clutch at the unfamiliar air. They are fingers, stubby digits that have formed only as far as the claws jutting out from their sides have allowed them. Rough scaly patches meet with smooth, hairless pink, comprising an outer covering that is not quite skin, not quite hide. Its spine juts out, pressing against this thin covering, a Braille pattern of deformity, and I can make out individual vertebrae dropping up and down like a row of player-piano keys belting out a Dixieland tune. A single tail droops down and away at the end of that spine, no more than a thin strand of bones that effectively doubles the length of the child.

The torso is curved, a long, midnight-black stretch of burnt rubber, and the bloated potbelly, cresting, crashing, jiggling, carves a wake of flesh down the baby's side. Another set of claws, longer, darker, stick rudely out from stumps that might be five-toed feet, rapidly extending and withdrawing, extending and withdrawing.

And the head, that head, a frantic lottery of all conceivable features, nostrils indented, eyes wide yet yellow, ears practically nonexistent save for a single lobe dangling roughly off the left cheek, snout canted downward at an orthopedically undesirable angle, a few teeth already in and threatening to pop through the jawbone itself.

It is an amalgam of all I have ever seen, but somehow it is completely unlike the misfits we saw earlier. It is beautiful. I am horrified. I cannot look away.

And Jaycee Holden is happier than she has ever been; the haunted look in her eyes, the one that said *I don't want to be here anymore,* is gone, replaced with a mien of fulfillment, of purpose. Triumphantly, even as she continues to tread water, Jaycee holds her baby aloft, over her head, in what I can only assume to be a gesture of conquest.

A shot rings out—bangs out—overpowering the amplified sounds of postbirth exuberance—and a crack appears, webbing out from a rough hole on the very top of the tank, just above the water level. We spin toward the far side of the laboratory, toward the sound of the gunshot.

It's Judith. And she's got her gun back. She's aiming for the baby. Or Jaycee. It doesn't matter, because she's preparing to fire once more.

Now Glenda's got all the reason she needs to attack the human she was pulled away from before, and this time I'm sure not going to be the one to stop her. She leaps across the laboratory, her edged bill ready to sink into giving flesh. But Judith is lifting the revolver again—Jaycee, terrified for two lives, no other choice at hand, is ducking beneath the water, clutching the baby to her chest—Vallardo, too, engages his dive mechanism—and me? Ah, hell, I'm frozen in place.

· I'm able to convince my throat to scream, "Watch her revolv—" before the second gunshot rocks the lab. A millisecond later, Glenda is on Judith like a crash-dieter given a one-hour reprieve at a Vegas buffet, sinking her teeth into the human's fleshy neck, searching out the precious arteries that will bring blood and end life.

I'd rush to help, I really would, but as I turn to make sure Jaycee and Vallardo haven't been hit, I find myself staring at the long cracks snaking all across the giant water tank, picking up speed, growing, growing, splintering out like fractal branches. Water is leaking, water is pushing, glass is bending beneath the pressure, and before I am able to convince my feet to *run you fools, save yourselves!* the walls shatter, releasing the floodgates.

I wanted to swim; now here's my chance. Glenda, Judith, Vallardo, Jaycee, the newborn, the lab—all of it disappears under the tidal cascade, as the tables bolted to the lab floor become artificial reefs in this brand-new ocean. I am buffeted against the breakers, thrown beneath the surface, breath bursting in my lungs, screaming to get out. I swim up—and hit my head on the floor. Wrong direction. I swim in the other up, and soon break into the open air, gasping for oxygen.

A second wave rolls by, tossing itself into my open mouth. I gag and fall beneath the surface again, struggling for purchase against the silken water around me. What do they say—three times and you're under? Then I'd better not plan on going down again. With a gargantuan effort, I flex my tail and launch myself out of the water yet again, barely avoiding the onslaught of another wave. Pieces of shell float by me like driftwood after a storm, and I struggle to keep my head above water as each new rush threatens to draw me to my death.

The door to the lab is open, and whatever water is able to escape through it quickly does so, making for a whirlpool of energy around the area. The swells pull me closer to this danger zone, the undertow threatening to overpower my meager swimming abilities, but I fight like a salmon and spawn upstream, grabbing on to whatever looks like it will help me in my struggle. I think I can see a limb flailing away on the other side of the lab, a wriggling similar to mine executed in an effort to stay afloat, but the sting of water in my eyes makes it difficult to make out an exact shape or color.

"Glenda!" I call, the water bubbling my words into "Blenbla!" but I receive no reply. It doesn't work for Blaybee, Bablarbo, or Bludibth, either. Locating a handhold beneath an installed Bunsen burner, I anchor myself in one area and wait for the storm to die down, using my energy to keep my head above water.

In time, the heaviest rush of water filters out of the laboratory, leaving me alone amid broken glass, broken eggshell, and calf-high tide pools. "Anybody here?" I try and call out, and am surprised to find that I don't make any noise. There's water stuck in my throat. It seems that I haven't been breathing for over a minute.

Upset that I should have realized this sort of thing sooner, I lean myself over a shattered desk chair and apply a self-Heimlich. Dino Heimlichs are administered much higher than their human counterparts, but I learned this a long time ago, the hard way—don't ask, don't ask. A spray of water shoots out, landing a good four feet away, adding a few more milliliters to the puddles, and I can breathe good, stale air once again.

"Anybody here?" I try again, my voice weaker than I would like but at least functioning. There is no response except for the sizzle of the PA speakers shorting out. It's a good thing they're mounted high on the wall, their sparks unable to contact this newly formed aquatic center, or I'd be lighting up like the Rockefeller Center Christmas tree.

Making sure to steer clear of any additional danger areas, I tromp out of the laboratory, back into the damp clinic halls, which have been given a thorough cleansing via flood, the walls scraped of their debris by the rushing waters. I call out names as I go, and by the time I've searched a few empty rooms and have begun to worry that I was the only one who made it out alive, I hear a "Vincent?" calling to me from down a parallel hallway. I rush into action . . .

To find Glenda, lying on the floor in her own pool of water, smiling up at me, panting, her Hadro bill covered in a mixture of water and blood droplets.

Judith McBride is in this room as well, limp and lifeless atop a worn oak desk. Her arms are splayed to either side, her legs bent at an impossible angle, her head turned away from me. "Did the flood get her?" I ask Glenda.

"I got her," Glenda says, walking over to Judith and turning the widow's head in my direction. Three great bites mar the flesh across her neck, the gashes clearly visible to me, what with most of the blood having been washed away during the last few minutes. I'm sure there was little pain, and that it was over in a flash. "She knew, Vincent. The bitch had to go."

"You did good," I say, not wanting to cause Glenda any pangs of remorse. Killing someone, even a human, can be tough on the heart and the mind. Despite her easygoing attitude about it now, sleep won't come easy for Glenda anytime soon. "Come on," I say, patting her across the back. "Help me look for the others."

We search the building well into the night, leaving no room, no table, no desk, no beaker unturned. The clinic is tremendous, an ant colony of passages and cloistered rooms, water bearing the dead bodies of a hundred floating misfits—even those that Glenda left alive were washed clean in the tide.

At one in the morning, we find Dr. Vallardo, his hide purple, his body thick and bloated with water weight. Somehow, he had wound up inside a storage closet, unable to free himself from the rushing water. Perhaps his girth kept him down, or perhaps it was his ineffectual tail. Whatever the case, he's dead, and there's not much use in discussing it.

His mouth was stuffed with debris from the flood—yolk, eggshells, afterbirth—and we remove it all in order to simplify matters for outsiders. No need to get them confused, searching into matters at the clinic. There's been enough of that for some time, and the Council investigation that is sure to follow is going to dredge up enough sludge to fill ten of those tanks. We drag Vallardo's body into the room with Judith McBride's, laying them down side by side. This is a purely altruistic move; it's easier for the cleanup crews if all of the corpses are in the same location.

Two o'clock rolls by, then three, then four. Glenda and I have searched the entire building, top to bottom, left to right. "Let's split up and try it again," I suggest, and Glenda knows better than to argue with me.

Jaycee and her child are nowhere to be found. I am not frantic. I am not worried. I'm just an average Joe, doing his job. My throat hurts.

By the time dawn rolls around, we have made our run three times, and I have effectively shut myself down. This is the way I want to be. This is the only way that doesn't hurt.

After we drop a disintegration pouch on Vallardo's corpse, then do the same to Judith's despite the fact that she was never really a dino, Glenda convinces me that if we haven't found Jaycee inside the clinic yet, we will never find her. I'm sure she expects me to argue, to press the matter, to send her back out into the field, but I don't. I accept her decision, if only because it is the same one that the more rational parts of my mind have come up with on their own. If Jaycee is not here, Jaycee is not here. I can't think about what this could mean right now; I don't want to think about what it could mean.

"She must have made it out," Glenda suggests, her tones soft, rational, protective. Miraculously, she's not cursing—the flood must have washed her mouth out—but I'm barely able to register this victory for etiquette.

"Yeah," I answer. I hope she's right.

"She probably escaped, went back to her apartment. You can probably find her there."

"Yeah," I answer. I know she's wrong. Jaycee has skipped town, skipped the country, skipped the world for all I know. I will never see Jaycee Holden again.

"Let's go," says Glenda, and I allow her to dress me in my guise, then take me by the arm and lead me out of the room, out of the clinic, into the bright Bronx streets that are just beginning to wake up to a busy autumn morning. The sun sparkles off abandoned cars and broken traffic lights, making everything shine with its brilliance.

"See, Vincent," Glenda says as she leads me down the road, trying to inject a bounce into every step, a happy slide into every shuffle, "on a morning like today, even the Bronx is full of hope."

Epilogue

A year has passed, and the private investigation firm of Watson and Rubio has become the private investigation firm of Rubio and Wetzel. It took a few months, but I finally allowed the sign painters to take Ernie's name down from the outside window, though I made them leave it on the door to what was once his office. I look at it every day. Glenda and I are running at the top of our games, working overtime to get to all the cases that are thrown our way. We actually have to turn assignments away now, but each one we say *no thanks* to hits me sharp, like a hunger pang, as if reminding me that there was once a time when I had nothing in the fridge but a cherry tomato and a stack of basil.

Speaking of basil and its wicked cousins, I'm attending regular Herba-holic Anonymous meetings, and my sponsor, an Allosaur who used to be addicted to celery salt, of all things, is the shortstop for the Dodgers, so I'm always getting free seats behind home plate. It's been 213 days since my last herb, and I'm due to get my next gold star within the week. Little goals, little steps, but that's the way to rebuild a life.

The so-called Council investigation into the McBride/Vallardo/Burke/Holden affair was squelched by an order from invisible higher-ups who were anxious to avoid a full-scale catastrophe, and I wasn't about to go sticking my skinny hide on the line for this crap yet again. The worry was that the dino population wouldn't be able to handle the implications of what had occurred—the idea that someone so powerful had infiltrated their society at such an elevated level—and might riot, commit suicide, or drive the stock market down. Whatever the case, my dealings in the affair before the National Council were brief, and I only had to go to Cleveland twice to deliver my depositions.

Dan's funeral, held only a few days after I returned from New York, was a lovely affair, with all of his buddies from the force showing up to wish him farewell. We had ice cream and Cheetos at the wake. I spent much of the time drowning in my own sorrow, for any number of related reasons, so I guess I wasn't able to provide much comfort to the other guests, but it was sure nice to have them around to comfort me.

Privately, Teitelbaum eased up on the blacklisting once he got the full story of my time in New York, and now grudgingly contracts out some of his work to the firm. He continues to bust my balls, and, if anything, has only increased the size of his nutcracker. Probably had his secretary Cathy pick one up in Frankfurt. His public reaction to my involvement with the McBride affair was to dock me two weeks' pay for going outside the boundaries of my job and then give me two weeks' worth of bonus money for bringing recognition to TruTel. Let's hear it for treading water.

I've got a new car and my town house is out of foreclosure, and there's enough money in the bank to last me through any rough spots I might hit, but still I come home every night, sit in front of the television set, eat a warmed-up piece of left-left-leftovers, and read my mail.

Bill—DWP. Bill—cable. Bill—spring water. Letter from a friend of mine in Oregon, asking me if I got the last letter he sent. Offer from MasterCard, a huge credit limit, all I have to do is sign on the dotted line. Another letter, this one from an old client, complaining that she can't get me on the phone at the office anymore, I'm so darn busy, and would I just call her already, she's got a case for me. Something about a reservoir and water rights for the LA basin. And a picture postcard, the vibrant colors poking out from the stack of mail, grabbing my attention. The photo is a long shot of a quiet, peaceful beach with soft, silken sand, an ocean of pure blue, and a sky to match. A GREETING FROM COSTA RICA, reads the flouncy yellow lettering printed in bas-relief across the top. I flip the card over.

There is nothing written on the back, save for my name and address, a heart over the *i*'s in Vincent and Rubio. Instead, in the box where the body of the letter should go, are some strange ink markings—three long vertical stripes, curving slowly, carefully up and around five smaller streaks, these dotted with what look to be half-formed fingerprints. I sniff the card, pressing it tightly against my nose, and believe that I can smell the sand, that I can smell the surf, that I can smell that fresh stroke of pine on a crisp autumn morning.

My gaze falls toward a full-length mirror situated at the end of the hallway. I am unguised, and I soak in a long look at my teeth, my hide, my ears. At my nose, my tail, my snout, my legs. At what makes me different from almost every other creature walking the face of this planet.

I let loose with my claws, flashing them out into the open. Long, curved, retractable.

Those are claw prints on the postcard, claw prints mixed with the early formation of some stubby human fingers. I can see it all so clearly now, these marks made by dipping a set of claws in ink and pressing them hard against the heavy stock paper. One set of adult prints, one set of baby prints. There is nothing else to clue me in, nothing else inscribed on the entire card, but this is all the message I need.

I throw the rest of my dinner in the garbage disposal, turn off the television, and head to the bedroom, unable to wipe away the smile that has crept, unannounced, onto my face.